"FROM THE FIRST PAGE,

Korelitz's spellbinding second novel is totally engrossing...
Korelitz gives the reader everything: characters you love to
hate, cultural clashes, mystery, and courtroom drama
at its best." —*Library Journal*

"POWERFUL"
—*Kirkus Reviews*

"SUSPENSEFUL"
—*USA Today*

"GRIPPING"
—*The Newark Star-Ledger*

"ENGROSSING"
—*Salon.com*

"RIVETING"
—*The Boston Sunday Globe*

"COMPELLING"
—*Glamour*

"INTENSE"
—*Booklist* (starred review)

"ABSORBING"
—*The Wall Street Journal*

"SURPRISING"
—*Elle*

"RIVETING."   *—Library Journal*

"Readers who want a courtroom drama will find *The Sabbathday River* most entertaining, but to call this rich, mesmerizing story a legal thriller is as overly simplistic as calling *Moby Dick* a whale hunt."

—New York Daily News

"GRIPPING, ENTERTAINING . . . Ms. Korelitz has delivered a page-turner here—absorbing weekend or vacation reading for those in the mood for a suspenseful morality tale."   *—The Wall Street Journal*

"*THE SABBATHDAY RIVER* IS WONDERFUL—wonderfully written, wonderfully plotted, wonderfully compelling, with its vivid characters and intense sense of place. This story of a murder investigation and the resulting trial in a small New England town is gripping and rewarding reading."   —Scott Turow, author of *Presumed Innocent* and *The Laws of Our Fathers*

"BEAUTIFULLY WRITTEN . . . wholly gripping."

—Newark Star-Ledger

"The book jumps points of view, with success, between Naomi, the transplanted New Yorker and mail-order entrepreneur who finds the body in the stream by the woods, and Heather, who may or may not have put it there. Korelitz builds to her surprising ending with a deliberate prose and a provocative eye for moral issues that have no clean answers."   *—Elle*

continued on next page . . .

"POWERFUL . . . it all works together brilliantly as a combination suspense thriller, courtroom drama, and cautionary morality tale . . . this intense novel adds depth and texture to the courtroom formula and is sure to attract Scott Turow fans." —*Booklist* (starred review)

"What a rich and satisfying novel this is! It's a sophisticated look at the casually deployed but deep-seated assumptions by which women are judged, and not only in small towns like the one Jean Hanff Korelitz knows so well. [A] compelling story of loss and longing, written with great sympathy and intelligence." —Rosellen Brown

"Scarily well-written." —*Interview*

"[*The Sabbathday River*] has the riveting components of a good courtroom drama, enhanced by some finely etched characters." —*The Boston Sunday Globe*

"A powerful tale." —*Kirkus Reviews*

"Engrossing . . . Both the trial and the novel come to satisfying ends . . . a splendid read." —*Salon.com*

"A very well-written book . . . it keeps the reader interested, pulling one along to its surprising and morally complex denouement." —*Book*

The
Sabbathday River

Jean Hanff Korelitz

JOVE BOOKS, NEW YORK

Lines from "Spilt Milk" by Sarah Maguire (from *Spilt Milk*, Secker & Warburg, 1991) and "Sheol" by Craig Raine (from *Clay, Whereabouts Unknown*, Penguin, 1996) are quoted with the permission of the authors.

Lines from "The Language Issue" by Nuala Ni Dhomhnaill, translated by Paul Muldoon (from *Pharoah's Daughter*, Wake Forest University Press, 1993) and "If Luck Were Corn" by Peter Fallon (from *News of the World*, Wake Forest University Press, 1993) and "Terezin" by Michael Longley (from *Gorse Fires*, Wake Forest University Press, 1991) are quoted with permission of the authors and Wake Forest University Press.

Lines from "White" by Paul Muldoon (from *Hay*, Farrar, Straus and Giroux, 1998) are quoted with the permission of the author.

I thank these friends and relations for having generously allowed me to quote from their poetry.

Lyrics from "Glad to be a Woman" are quoted with the permission of Betsy Rose. Copyright © 1975 by Betsy Rose. All rights reserved.

THE SABBATHDAY RIVER

A Jove Book / published by arrangement with
Farrar, Straus and Giroux

PRINTING HISTORY
Farrar, Straus and Giroux edition / April 1999
Jove advance reading edition / August 2000
Jove edition / February 2000

The Penguin Putnam Inc. World Wide Web site address is
http://www.penguinputnam.com

ISBN: 0-515-13011-7

A JOVE BOOK®
Jove Books are published by The Berkley Publishing Group,
a division of Penguin Putnam Inc.,
375 Hudson Street, New York, New York 10014.
JOVE and the "J" design
are trademarks belonging to Penguin Putnam Inc.

PRINTED IN THE UNITED STATES OF AMERICA

10 9 8 7 6 5 4 3 2 1

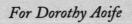
For Dorothy Aoife

Part 1
The First Baby

I place my hope on the water
in this little boat
of the language, the way a body might put
an infant

in a basket of intertwined
iris leaves,
its underside proofed
with bitumen and pitch,

then set the whole thing down amidst
the sedge
and bulrushes by the edge
of a river

only to have it borne hither and thither,
not knowing where it might end up;
in the lap, perhaps,
of some Pharaoh's daughter.

—Nuala Ní Dhomhnaill, "The Language
   Issue" (translated from the Irish by
   Paul Muldoon)

Chapter 1

Eye Contact

THE FIRST BABY WAS FOUND EARLY ON A WEEK-end morning in September, 1985, as the whole broad length of the Upper Valley braced for its annual riptide of strangers, and as the first maples on the banks of the Sabbathday River prepared to burst, obligingly, into flame. Naomi Roth found the baby. It rocked in an eddy, bordered by stones, and lay so white and, facedown, so still, that she first registered the object as a child's doll, seamless and albino plastic and tragically—to that child, at least—left behind here. Eyeing it, she could conjure that child's keening over its loss, over the uniqueness of this particular doll—set so decisively apart from its hundreds of thousands of sexless twins, born from the maternity of their Chinese or Thai assembly line. But then again, this was not the place for children, precisely. Children played downstream at Nate's Landing, where the Sabbathday widened slightly and merged with the Goddard River in its headlong careen south and west toward Vermont. There was a picnic area there, and the Rotary had put in swings a few years back, and a perennially overgrown sandbox where the mothers clustered and their kids occupied themselves. The water, kept safely away by a low picket fence, made its rumble downstream.

But the riverbank where Naomi found the baby was a good mile upstream from that place. Here, its curve through maples and leaning birches was fairly undistinguished, and though the path Naomi sometimes used for jogging did pass here, there was nothing remarkable about this particular stretch. The nearest landmark—and it was a pitifully local landmark at that—was the protrusion of boulders around the bend she had just passed, known familiarly as the Drumlins for the little hills of glassy water they made. Pretty, but lethal, since under that glassy water were rocks sharp as real glass. Who would let a child young enough to cherish that doll climb and wade around here?

Naomi stopped then. Grasping her knees, she put her head down and felt the blood rush to her forehead. She was not a very devoted runner. The temptation to stop was always with her, like a blackfly worrying the flank of a horse. The rasp of her breath overwhelmed the rustle of leaves. She felt the heat in her face begin to throb. Naomi glared at the doll, holding it responsible.

Or not this doll, exactly, but the one it was prodding her to fixate on—a specific childhood trauma, happily undisturbed in its thirty-year slumber but now assailing her with disconcerting immediacy. *Stop this*, she thought, but she had already slipped away from herself and the doll was upon her, and how much she had desired it, and how much, for how brief a time, she had adored it. She saw, freshly, the two blond little girls in smocked dresses on the television commercial; she could hear the happy jingle extolling the doll's mind-bending ability to wet. And her name: *Sallie Smiles!* (The exclamation mark thoughtfully provided by the manufacturer.) Naomi Roth's parents—they of the Little Red School House and Pete Seeger persuasion—had been horrified, naturally enough, but she must have had her fill of ant farms and nonsexist creative discovery objects. The small blond pixies on the television were the company she kept in her fantasy of the parallel childhood she was not leading. She coveted the doll.

When it disappeared, less than a week after her birthday, she had waited before panicking. Then she approached her parents, whose unmistakable relief over her carelessness—the carelessness they assumed, despite her denials—was clear. Naomi's older brother declined to shed light on the situation, but months afterward it was from his window that she saw her doll again, grimy in city filth on the roof of the apartment building next door. It lay on its stomach against the asphalt, its bright face obscured, its fleshy pink hue bleached to stark white, and the legs between which it had wet so endearingly splayed to the extent of its somewhat limited hip sockets. At that moment, long before mortality and years before sex would enter her ken, she experienced a primitive understanding of the terrifying and the obscene. This tiny, blanched, and helpless body: a distilled drop of pure horror, fallen from the sky to splatter within view of her childhood home as a warning of what adulthood held in store.

Naomi Roth shook her head. The thing in the river was some child's missing toy, after all, not a Proustian moment dropped from the clouds. It had probably been lost hold of upstream and then drifted down here, she thought, taking a tentative first step onto one of the boulders: an accident and a force of nature working in hardly malevolent partnership, and not an invitation to moan about unresolved childhood trauma. At some point, a banana just had to be a banana again, and a doll just a doll, otherwise what's the point?

Farther out, the rocks were slippery with moss. She picked her way on all fours, inching ahead as in a game of Twister, with the silvery and frigid water hissing and sputtering at her heels. Drawing nearer to the white gleam of the doll, caught in its eddy between dark stones, she touched the green sludge of the rock near its smooth white leg and felt a preemptive chill. Cold, Naomi thought. She felt her lips move and realized she'd spoken aloud. But why? "Cold," she said again, this time making a joke of it. But it was, wasn't it? Suddenly cold? She should look up, really, see if clouds had gathered, if it looked like rain, here, in the middle of her morning run, with only her shorts and a thin T-shirt on and a good two miles to go before the path gave out onto the road where she had left her car. But looking up would mean taking her eyes off the doll, and Naomi could not seem to take her eyes off the doll.

The leg of the doll. A strand of vegetation wedged into the crease behind its knee and fluttering in the glassy water. That joint was stiff, perhaps, but not unyielding, ultimately, since she could see that it gave just slightly in the current, and at its side the brief fingers seemed to feather the water. *Realistic*, Naomi thought, by now aware of the hysteria edging nearer, the strain of pushing it back. And in the barely perceptible sway of the doll's lower back, where its spindly midsection suddenly widened into a cherubic bottom, a vortex of three dark hairs fluttered below the surface. The doll's shoulder blades uneven, one ridge more sharp than the other, as if the mold had been made deliberately lopsided, the doll's wisps of unglamorous dark hair riding the surface of the water, the doll's eyes . . .

Open, Naomi knew, though she could not see its face,

wedged against its crown of river stones. Open eyes, baffled at whatever great force would summon it here only to show it this frigid and unchanging vision. Only this! She touched its shoulder and felt its newness, even in death. She was gripped now. Something had her about the lungs; some cold thing had infested her, making her grope for the tiny, splayed, and forsaken body in the river. Naomi reached for one alabaster limb and, touching it, felt the burn of a frozen thing. She turned it over then, setting her jaw against its flash of white. The word "bloodless" was forming in her throat. The flesh was smoothly pristine but for a single puckered interruption where something had bored, leaving the same kind of queer, unembellished wound you saw in medieval paintings of Christ—one dainty drop of precious blood spilled from a Roman gash. A girl. Naomi's cheek scratched a granite boulder as she lost her balance. Her own hand finding her belly, her belly heaving onto the surface. Her eyes closing now, then opening, but underwater, too, as if she had only wanted to see what the baby had seen in its long ebb here, with its granite-gray eyes that hadn't had a chance to turn, and she wondered, vaguely, what color they might have become, had they always looked out with such hope as they did now, fixing the awful affront of this radiant sky with a stare Naomi could not bring herself to meet.

Chapter 2

The Famine Child

OH, OF COURSE SHE KNEW — SHE *KNEW*, SOME-where back there in the part of her brain where she kept all rational thought, all sense, everything but this inscrutable fact of the baby in the river—that she was not supposed to touch the body. Every mystery she had ever read, every bad Holly-wood thriller she had endured, had featured some gruff po-liceman who growled at you not to disturb a single blade of grass or shred of clothing, but Naomi hadn't been able to help herself. Her arms had followed a command so deeply etched as to feel nearly genetic, the ingrained rhythm of scooping an infant into the crook of the elbow, and once she held the child a rush of pity—of almost love—had come over her, weakening her and obliterating everything else. The infant was grotesque, but even with her wound bled out and the unreal whiteness that remained, there was a gut-clenching sweetness to her un-marked face. Naomi crouched in the icy water for what seemed a long time, cradling the tiny body as if the child were hers, the toes and fingers hers to count and the slate-gray eyes hers to speculate about. She held the child so long that, in the end, it was not the child at all that brought her back but the aware-ness that she could no longer quite feel her own calves and feet. You can't step in the same river twice, she thought then, recalling and perhaps mangling the meaning of some shard of philosophic wisdom. But couldn't you step in it once and never get out again? It was time to get out now.

Shifting the body to her shoulder, where it barely registered weight, Naomi picked a path back across the boulders to the riverbank, made her way out to the road and her car in a kind of blank daze, and drove into Goddard. There, everything was the same—an immaculate town, suspended in the not-knowing of what she knew, and this suddenly enraged her. She despised the nonchalance of those women on the Laundromat stoop, waiting as their loads churned inside, those lingering summer

people or early leaf-peepers perched on the steps at Tom and
Whit's with takeout coffee and *The Boston Globe*, the trio of
classically solemn Greek Revival buildings: Meeting House,
First Methodist Church, town office. The bank was closing up
its Saturday hours, and there was a half-full parking lot at the
sports center. The normality of it seemed to hover before her
car with its load of tragedy, then part around her as she drove
by, then close behind her again: everything would change now.
Goddard, intent on hoisting itself out of the forest to hail the
tourists up from the lake region and west from the Old Man
of the Mountains, would hardly be pleased by this jolt of
change, but it was in Naomi's arms and out of her hands. She
shook her head and swung into the parking lot of the cement-
bunker police station, then looked again at her tiny, ruined
passenger. Shock and repulsion assaulted her with a devastat-
ing clarity, and the nausea that had sent her reeling into the
river when she had first turned the baby's body gripped her
again. She could not bring her in this way, Naomi thought.
She had a compulsion to swaddle the infant, but there was
nothing to wrap her in, no receiving blanket to receive a
corpse, only one stiff and blackened chamois cloth for wiping
the windshield. She scanned the backseat and saw only
Heather's most recent order there: an alphabet sampler stitched
on old linen. Naomi had picked it up midweek, but for some
reason it was still there, not yet processed and sent on. Uncharacteristically inefficient, she thought, pausing even in crisis
to scold herself. She snatched the cloth from the backseat and
wrapped the baby, besting her instinct to frame its face and
instead enfolding it completely. Like the children of the Ethi-
opian famine, she thought, flashed around the world to the
accompaniment of that summer's global rock concert—
wrapped for burial in gauze, tumbling into the mass graves as
if they were little chrysalises. The cloth was pale yellow and
covered with spidery thread in lush crimson, and the lettering
was more ornate than Heather was wont to favor, a wildly
swirling mesh of letters that covered half the baby's chest and
disappeared behind its shoulder—the client must have provided a picture of what she wanted. She could not send it now,
Naomi thought, letting this bit of irrelevance lead her again
away from the horror, however briefly. She could not send her
customer a sampler that had been used to wrap a dead baby,

and wasn't it a shame that Heather, who'd obviously given the assignment her customary attention and extravagant skill, would only have to do it again, and soon, before the customer had a fit. *As you know,* she imagined writing to the aggrieved party, *"Handmade in New England" is not only our slogan but a commitment to a traditional way of life. By eschewing machinery to provide the quality work we offer our customers, we must rely instead upon far less reliable human beings. In this particular case, the arrival of a new baby resulted in the delay of your order.*

A new baby. Naomi felt herself shake. The car began to fill with sound, something really strange that she couldn't exactly place, but terribly insistent, and so awful that her only thought was to aid the person or animal in such agony. Either rain had come down from the bright clear midday sky to blur the windshield or Naomi was crying. She clawed for the door and ran for the station, moving only to the staccato of her own noises.

"Where's Nelson?" she choked out to the deputy behind the receptionist's desk. In response, he frowned at her. Naomi swiped the back of her hand across her face. *"Where's Nelson?"* she tried again, feeling the edge of hysteria in her throat, pushing her. *"Nelson, I need . . ."*

"You need help?" he said, somewhat bafflingly.

"Please." She thought she might faint. She thought the cloth in her arms might suddenly unfurl like a carpet at the deputy's feet, tumbling the infant onto his scuffed black shoes. She didn't know the deputy. Suddenly that seemed terribly significant.

"Ma'am"—he cleared his throat—"now . . ."

"Oh fuck *this,*" Naomi cried, hearing the intonation of her childhood—her mother on Central Park West, every other mother of every other child in the Ethical Culture school system. The deputy winced.

"Ma'am."

She plunged past him. She had never been inside the police station before, but the geography wasn't hard to figure out. Along the narrow corridor were arrayed a small room with an unwieldy Xerox, a conference area, and a supply closet. The walls were charmless cement block painted beige, plastered with posters. The dropped ceiling muffled the slap of Naomi's feet so that she could barely make out the sound of her own motion. Nelson's office was at the end of the hall, its door ajar, its occupant on the phone.

She stopped in the doorway, feet apart, her bundle before her. In the small mirror behind his desk she caught sight of herself: wild woman, her hair in damp waves about her face, her face with its central ridge: a nose her mother had termed "strong" and everyone else merely "large." She noted the desperation in her own face with extraordinary detachment, even letting the image of a long-remembered painting flash before her, dredged from freshman art history like a fistful of mud from the water: Victorian, unfinished, the portrait of a crazed woman extending a swaddled infant to its reluctant sire, its title a sneer—*Take Your Son, Sir*.

Nelson Erroll was in his seat, leaning forward, each muscled forearm planted atop a stack of papers. His hair had a glint of gold thin over the glint of skin, downgrading to silver with age. The clench of her lungs was noted and promptly, responsibly, ignored. He looked up and frowned.

"Naomi? Can you give me a minute?"

She could hear her own breath. She thought she might breathe fire.

Nelson harrumphed into the phone. He hung up.

"Naomi? What can I do—"

She placed the baby on the table before him. She hated to let it out of her arms. She couldn't take it back now, undiscover it, or silence whatever din its existence was going to unleash. It would never be only hers again either, which at that particular moment seemed almost the worst thing of all.

"I found her," Naomi said calmly. "I was jogging, up above Nate's Landing. On the path. I found her in the river." Nelson was blankly still; his face and body, even the papery softness around his eyes, gave no pulse of movement. He merely, sluggishly, turned one wrist, so that a single blue vein was etched against the white. His vacancy made her smile, ridiculously, but then she felt her body break into sobs. The white doll in the icy currents, the weightless infant over her shoulder, the famine child in its dark communal grave. For the first time, Naomi conjured the hand that had lifted the weapon and brought it down, tearing flesh from flesh and death from life, and so, for the first time, she wept with bitterness and rage.

Chapter 3

What We Don't Know We Know

"YOU MOVED THE BODY."

"It wasn't a body," Naomi said stiffly. "It was a baby."

"It *was* a baby. By the time you got to it, it was a body. And you moved the body."

Naomi let out a ragged sigh. She barely knew what time it was anymore. The Indian summer on the other side of the small window and the long hours in the cinder-block bunker had wrenched her internal clock out of whack. The man was called Robert Charter, and despite the charged and frenetic talk that had swirled about them all afternoon, these were the first words he'd directed to her in private.

"Look, I'm very tired. It's been a rough day and I'd like to go home, if you don't mind."

"But I do mind." Charter took the seat on the other side of the institutionally nondescript table. "That is, I'd prefer your hanging on a little bit longer. We haven't had much of a chance to talk."

She focused on him. He was angular and lean, with gray hair trained in a kind of arched wave over the top of his head from one ear to another, and his cheeks were ruddy. She had only known him a few hours, Naomi thought, but their interlocked glares already had the creak and drone of ingrained adversity. "I don't see what I can add to what I've already said," she told him carefully. "I mean I don't *know* anything. I only found her, you know."

He remained silent. He held his palms together atop the legal pad in a position of vaguely contortionist prayer. Naomi blinked. It occurred to her to wonder where Nelson had got to. He'd been right behind her when they'd returned from the river, where the little knot of men had huddled, murmuring officially as she stood forlornly on the bank. He'd been behind her in the reception area a few moments before, taking her elbow and offering coffee. But now there was no coffee and she was alone with this Charter, the district attorney up from Peytonville, and the room was small—barely big enough for the two of them and the table and the extra chairs, empty and left at odd angles. The interrogation room, she understood, somewhat belatedly. She was being interrogated.

"Am I being interrogated?" Naomi sat up in her chair. "I mean, what the hell's going on here? I can't just hang out here forever. I have a . . ." What? Naomi thought. A child? A life? A limited capacity for horror? Something more important to do? She hated the fact that he was waiting for her to go on. Then, when she couldn't, he began again.

"You aren't from Goddard, is that right?"

"Only for the past nine years," she said stiffly.

"And your home therefore is . . ." He lifted his pen.

Like the punch line it was, she gave it a pause: "I grew up in New York City." This meant, in New Hampshire dialect, *I am a Jew.* "My husband and I came as VISTA workers in '76."

"VISTA workers," he pondered, writing.

"Domestic Peace Corps."

He glared, briefly. "Digging wells? Schools for the little children? Something like that?"

Yes, Naomi wanted to say.

"Of course not," she said.

"I wasn't aware that we were considered quite that backward."

But you were, she thought.

"My husband ran a maple sugar co-op," Naomi said pleasantly. "I worked with women who were quilting and making crafts. After our term was up we decided to stay on."

He nodded. "Do the . . . homesteading-in-the-wilderness routine, yes?"

"Yes," she said, not giving him the satisfaction.

"And your work is . . ."

Satisfying, thank you, she wanted to say, but she also wanted to get out of here. "I helped found a collective business in Goddard, called Flourish. We sell handmade goods, by catalogue mostly. Quilts and samplers. Also hooked rugs."

Charter smiled a disingenuous smile. "And your husband is still teaching the natives how to make maple sugar."

"My husband lives in upstate New York. Woodstock. You

know," she said affably, "like the concert? I'm not sure what he's doing, but I doubt it involves maple sugar."

"Ah," Charter said, "You are divorced."

"We were divorced several months ago." He was writing again. Naomi eyed the brassy wedding ring, thick around his thin finger, the dark cracked leather of a watchband.

"Children?"

She said no. "Mr. . . . Charter?"

"Hm?" He finished his note and looked up.

"Do you have the time?"

"Why?" he said, his voice even. "Are you late?"

"I might be. That's why I want to know what time it is."

"Mrs. Roth," he said heavily, "why don't we move ahead. If we finish everything in the next little while, I see no reason why you can't be home in time for dinner."

"*Dinner?* Mr. Charter, I understand that you've got a big problem here, but I don't *know* anything. I just went out jogging this morning, and that's all. I brought the baby here, I went back and showed you where I found her, and this ends my entire possible contribution to solving your problem. Now please, I'm very upset about all this and I'd like to get out of here."

"Why are you so upset?" Charter said. "I mean, if you are, as you seem to suggest, merely in the role of the good and responsible citizen, then why are you so upset?"

She stopped, abruptly dumb, and noted with scientific detachment the heat climbing steadily to her face. "I am upset," she said with care, "because it is upsetting. That's all. Stabbed infants might be commonplace in your line of work, but I've never seen one before. It's . . ." She groped. "It's upsetting. All right?" To his silence she added, "After all, she was somebody's child, right?"

Slowly, he leaned forward, resting weight on his forearms. "Was she *your* child?"

Breath failed her. She shook her head wildly.

"You see why I must at least wonder."

"I . . . absolutely not. I'm . . ."

Incapable. Unthinkable. "How could you even suggest that I—"

"I did not suggest." He shrugged. "I merely inquired. If the answer is no, then it is no," he said. "You don't have to take it so personally. Unless," he added, "it *is* personal." Naomi shook her head again. "Now, you found the body. This is what you tell us and I happen to believe you."

"Fine," she sputtered. "Thanks for that."

"But look at it from my perspective for a minute. And ask yourself why it should be you who found this body, and not someone else."

"Well"—she said carefully—"because I was there. It *might* have been someone else."

"But it *wasn't* someone else, Mrs. Roth. It was you. Now, by your own account, you moved the body, which—if I may say so—was an extraordinarily stupid thing for such an obviously intelligent woman to have done. And once the body is moved, its relation to the place where you say it was found must necessarily be subjected to some doubt. So what do we have in the end? We have the fact of the body and we have your account of its discovery. Now," he mused, taking in Naomi's horror-struck expression without comment, "Sheriff Erroll knows you, Mrs. Roth, but what if Sheriff Erroll hadn't been at the desk down the hall"—he gestured with his thin wrist—"when you brought that baby in this morning? What if it had been some person you don't know, and who didn't know you?"

Amazed, she felt herself nod. "Yes?"

"Well, like me, for example. What if you'd come scurrying in this morning with that body in your arms, and it was me, for example. I wouldn't have seen my neighbor Naomi coming through the door, would I?"

"I . . . I guess . . ."

"Can I tell you what I'd have seen?" He didn't pause. "I'd have seen a woman of obviously fertile years bringing in the body of a murdered newborn infant. A body, I should add, that's wrapped up in the very kind of product that this woman's company offers for sale. And the woman's upset, too. 'Hysterical,' somebody called her. Took a good half hour to get her to calm down and make sense." He frowned, then flipped back a few pages on his legal pad and appeared to study the writing. "Yes, half an hour." Charter looked up at Naomi and shrugged. "That's what my notes say, anyway."

"Mr. Charter." Naomi's voice was steely. "I don't think I should have to defend my response. Yes, I was upset. I'm *still* upset. But the rest of this is bullshit. Christ, do I look to you like I've just given birth?"

"Mrs. Roth"—Charter grinned—"I'm hardly qualified to answer that on medical grounds, and I wouldn't think of offending you with inappropriate comments about your appearance."

In her fury, she flushed. At thirty-five, Naomi was not a slender woman.

"Let me understand this, please," Naomi said, pulling herself together somewhat. "Am I being asked to prove that I am not the mother of that baby out there?" She pointed vaguely at the door to the interrogation room, though she knew that the baby's body was gone, taken to Peytonville by the medical examiner.

His white brows raised, as if he had just heard a compelling suggestion, one to be given weighty consideration. "It seems to me that it would be helpful to establish that, yes."

"Well then," Naomi said caustically, "I suggest you call my gynecologist. He saw me three weeks ago, for a Pap smear. If I was pregnant at the time, neither one of us noticed." She gave him the name and he wrote it down.

"Fine," Charter said, nodding. "Thank you."

"And this concludes our conversation?"

The man sat back in his chair, studying her. There was the smallest ridge of a scar, she noticed now, tracing a faint half circle from the corner of his left eye, the size of a dime. Fingernail? Front tooth?

"It's a small town," Charter observed.

"Excuse me?"

"It's a small town, Goddard."

"Yes." She was snide. "And yet there are those who love it."

"A dead baby turns up in a small town, somebody knows whose baby it is."

"And hence who murdered it, you mean. You naturally suspect the mother."

"I would like to know who the mother is," he corrected her, his voice tight.

"So that you can charge her with murder," Naomi said. "I understand."

"So that I can be very much closer than I am now to knowing who *should* be charged with murder. Surely you see that."

He sat up a little, then sighed. "Mrs. Roth, someone who lives here was pregnant and gave birth, but has no baby. Do you know that person?"

"Oh, I *see*," Naomi sneered. "If it wasn't me, then I must know who did it."

"You *might* know." He was intent.

"Well, I don't," she said, getting to her feet. He didn't move to stop her and she made for the door.

"Mrs. Roth," Charter said. He was still in his seat. "May I tell you one thing before you leave?"

Naomi paused, her hand on the doorknob. At least he had said she was leaving. She nodded.

"I had a murder once. At a mall down near Winnipesaukee. The victim left her job at Sears and got hacked to death in the parking lot, the week before Christmas. One of the busiest shopping days of the year, and nobody saw a damned thing. Isn't that crazy?"

Perplexed, Naomi nodded.

"We went to an automatic teller machine in the middle of the parking lot and we got the name of a lady who made a transaction at the time of the murder, but when we contacted her she said she hadn't seen a thing. Knew about the murder, of course. Everyone did, it was all over the papers. And this lady even knew that she'd been in the parking lot at the time of the crime. Felt terrible about it, but couldn't give us any information." He paused, Naomi shifted. "Still, this lady knew we had nothing, and she wanted to help. So she agreed to be hypnotized, though naturally she didn't believe in such hooey. And do you know what, Mrs. Roth?"

Irresistibly engaged, Naomi spoke: "What?"

"This lady, she saw the whole thing. It was all back there, in her head somewhere: a man got out of his car, pushed the victim into her car, assaulted her, stabbed her. We got a description: clothes, height, features. Even got two digits off the guy's license plate. We arrested him within a week."

Despite herself, Naomi shook her head. "That's incredible."

"Sure it is. But you see my point, Mrs. Roth. This lady, she thought she knew nothing, but she saw it all. She *knew*, Mrs. Roth." He paused, fixing her with his disconcerting gaze. "I think you know, too. Think about it for me, will you? Somebody in this small town was pregnant and had a child, Mrs. Roth, but now she has no child." Then he smiled, getting to his feet and actually extending his hand. "I'll just bet you know her."

Chapter 4

The Sabbathday Affair

NAOMI'S HUSBAND, DANIEL, HAD BUILT THEIR house in a frenzy of late-summer machismo one year after their arrival in Goddard. The land was cheap, a gift really, from a dairy farmer whose sister—sweet and voiceless, probably retarded—attended Naomi's quilting afternoons at the First Methodist Church in Goddard. There wasn't much to the lot. It consisted of a grove of maples that sank in a triangular wedge to terminate in a brook strewn with stones, and the nominal sale price of one hundred dollars included a verbal right of way for the farmer's herd. But Daniel was living his dream of loving the land, and he simply refused to accept the possibility that the land would not love him back. The house he built was designed—so he told the bemused native farmers and an optimistic Naomi—not by the dictates of fashion, or even of architectural history and precedent, but by the demands of its natural surroundings. Hence its high peaked roof—less an A-line than an inverted V-line, she had always thought, with skylights near the apex that ended up impacted by leaves each November—and the steep driveway down from Goddard Falls Road; this ran alongside a creek which iced it over in winter and bogged it down in muck during mud season each spring. A lone wire that ferried down electricity from the wider world got snagged and interfered with by branches when the wind blew through the White Mountains. In the White Mountains, the wind blew a lot.

They had not been particularly savvy about local demographics at that time—it all looked poor to them, after all—but it was soon clear to Naomi that they had both saved and condemned themselves by settling where they had, halfway between two communities. Aspiring Goddard, which boasted no industry apart from that of selling its most glorious homes to people who lived in them two months out of the year, had an ingrained arrogance on the subject of Goddard Falls. And

Goddard Falls was easily vilified, after all. Poor Goddard Falls, with no town center to speak of, but a dilapidated general store, and no school of its own (the town ferried its kids down the road to the Goddard schools, where they formed a de facto underclass), where the farmhouses were left to rot, the roofs to sway in, the unused barns to crumble. And so, halfway between them— almost exactly halfway on the odometer between the Goddard municipal center and the Goddard Falls general store—she and Daniel had unwittingly established their postures of noncommittal and declared their roles as border guards, negotiators, ambassadors of each community to the other.

By the time she began to think of expanding her women's craft circle into a real business, Naomi was far better versed in the lay of the land. Most of Flourish's workers came from Goddard Falls, where generations of thrift had determined the absolute necessity of reusing textiles and few of the women had to be taught. Their homes, on the rare occasions when Naomi was invited inside, were cushioned by rugs braided from their former skirts or hooked from husbands' worn-out jackets. On their beds were slung quilts made from blocks of old blankets, or pieced together from their children's long-ago dresses, and in their closets and attics plastic bags bulged with fabric awaiting reincarnation into something useful. On the kitchen wall of the sisters Ina and Janelle Hodge, Naomi had long ago seen a rug, hooked out of frayed wool, which seemed to declare the creed: *Use it up, Wear it out, Make it do, Do without*.

From this—who would have thought?—had come a real business. Even she, raised to revere the almost spiritual integrity of "native" crafts, had been mildly stunned. Because, she now saw, it had begun with that same mindless gesture of support for the women that she had been primed to make in her VISTA training sessions. Find out what the women are doing, the brief went, and instill the belief that the work has value. The work of women—the sewing bees and quilting circles and nights hooking rugs before winter fires—has value. They hadn't really believed it any more than she, Naomi thought now, but they had come anyway—out of curiosity about her, and to relieve their individual isolation. They had met in the church in Goddard, in the basement with its fake wood paneling and temperamental coffee machine, for afternoons that stretched on into darkness, well past the point dictated by arthritic wrists and knuckles, until they were disbanded by somebody's husband's suspicious phone call or the acrid honk of a car sent to pick up a wife or mother and take her back home, where she belonged. They had taught one another, passing on the patterns nobody used anymore, their melodic names—Sugarloaf and Drunkard's Path—spoken like passwords to a secret society. They had brought their daughters and sisters, and the circle grew and pulled apart: two days a week, then three, then a separate group for quilters and one for hookers. And over time the older ones assumed more and more a posture of respected supervision and sat with their gnarled hands in their lap, lending weight to a decision about thread or passing comment on the twist a younger hand made as it hooked wool through a length of burlap. And so Naomi had done what everyone—her education and her values, her family and even her husband—had asked her to do. She had made from nothing a community of women. She had infused with pride the activities which had only before been busy-work—*women's* work. She had driven the breath of her will into those moribund crafts, even as they had been set to accompany an older generation to the grave, and from her breath a living tradition grew. And so she watched with some degree of bafflement as the thing seemed to slip beyond her aegis. A meeting time was changed, and no one told her. Everyone had somebody's new phone number except Naomi. Between her and them there was a prism of formality, even as she sat among them, ardently hooking or sewing, her hands hopelessly flustered, her role as catalyst dormant.

She did not quite admit to herself the pain of this, or how great a role that pain would play in the formation of her subsequent move. But that move had been years in the making, she saw now, the years she sat at the periphery of what she had made, watching the women comfort one another and take in one another's children and quarrel and feud and reconcile. For years, too, she imagined the inventory of their products, as if in a brightly lit room, grow and grow, the quilts and rugs and samplers stacked to the ceilings. She saw how they continued past the point when every bed and floor of their own had been covered, every wall adorned, every grandchild gifted. She saw the beginnings of their restlessness.

They themselves, it was clear, lacked the next necessary thing—the next infusion of magic. They were no more capable of offering their products to the market for money than they were of suddenly donning business suits and presenting themselves for job interviews. Here, finally, was her second opportunity to interject her worldliness into their midst, and Naomi took it.

Surreptitiously, over time, she had clipped magazine articles which seemed to track the new values ascribed to the handmade, the traditional, the nostalgic. She had traced the tastemakers' return to an unpolished and comfortably cluttered aesthetic. She saw that the homes of the wealthiest no longer made a display of their wealth by flaunting precious objects but instead favored old things and used things, battered objects left alone to show their wear. She noted the speed with which manufacturers observed and reacted to the trend, offering rugs braided by machine and importing quilts mass-produced in China, and she took note of the stratospheric heights to which the prices of antique textiles soared. She saw the path that was open to them.

Flourish began poorly. Two of her best quilters' husbands refused to let their wives participate—a hobby was one thing, sewing for rich folks quite something else—and there was confusion over the cooperative scheme Naomi proposed, a perhaps unnecessarily complex model involving shares and dues and unwaged hours on such grunt work as inventory and advertising. They began with craft fairs in New Hampshire and Vermont, but it was soon clear that these potential customers were too much like the women themselves to value art forms redolent of deprivation and thrift. What enthusiasm there was for Naomi's idea flagged quickly. But then, with the last of her seed money, she took an ad in a decorating magazine, informing the citizens of city and suburb alike that, in one corner of New England, old ladies were still gathering to make quilts in a church basement and still hooking rugs in their rocking chairs—and the stuff was for sale. Within two weeks, it was all gone. Within six months, the names of disappointed latecomers comprised a formidable mailing list.

She had drilled into a good vein, all right. Live rug hookers, unlike dead ones, could insinuate the image of an adored pet into a design using only a photograph, or custom work a house's year of construction into a hooked welcome mat. Live quilters could endow a wedding quilt with dates or etch a crib covering with names, lengths, and hefts. As many as the requests for "authentic" items were, the special orders far outweighed them. Naomi began looking for more artisans. *New Hampshire Profiles* came to call. *Good Morning New England* snaked its lines down the steep church basement steps and turned its lights on the withered hands of the Hodge sisters. Inside a year, Flourish was flourishing.

And Naomi, to her own surprise, was ready. Though "business," in the glossary of her youth, was somewhat synonymous with capitalist oppression, she had found herself keenly following the wave of catalogues that had risen to command the retail arena of the early 1980s. Indeed, she had even, willingly, offered her name to each, to be shared among them all, until every delivery of mail seemed to bulge with their glossy stock and gleaming photographs of merchandise, their stage decorations of a successful American life: woolen nightgowns, china, dollhouses, strawberry jam, clothing to chop wood in or make an entrance at the ball, furniture, picture frames, and a hundred other unsuspected but, evidently, utterly necessary items. It drove Daniel wild, that tilting stack of then unrecyclable paper, blaring materialism from one corner of their great room. The tchotchkes on those pages incensed him, the edible delicacies sent him into rages as he invoked the human deprivation of the moment—Ethiopia, India, the slums of Rio, the hollow-eyed deprivation of Soweto. He charged her with self-importance. She replied she was merely trying to give the women an income of their own. He charged her with covetousness. And that was true.

There were other accusations, inappropriate to herself, she thought, but somehow less baffling. Because Daniel *was* right: all around them, their fellow soldiers were sounding personal retreats, and each renunciation struck him with both distinct and cumulative vehemence. They knew one Harlem schoolteacher who had quit to publish a newsletter for independent investors. Former political agitators were suddenly Washington insiders. Naomi had a woman friend who abandoned her planned master's thesis on H.D. to accept a scholarship endowed by Cecil Rhodes—she did, however, have the good grace to refer to her benefactor as a "fascist." And after four years in West Virginia, a fellow VISTA worker was back home on the West Side writing ad copy for what he blushingly described as a "feminine deodorant."

In Goddard, Daniel's maple sugar co-op was failing, and he wasn't doing much except reading *Mother Jones* and brooding. For her part, she considered herself fully evolved beyond the dungeon of gender roles in homemaking, but Naomi could not help but notice that her husband seldom reached for a cleaning or cooking implement while she tended to the business that was growing around her. The situation grew even clearer when Flourish moved out of the church basement and into a once-derelict flour mill at the edge of Goddard, which Naomi had bought in '81. He might have helped her, she often thought now. He might have helped her with the company, shaped it, had vision for it. There was no reason why he should have considered benefiting the women of their community somehow beyond his protocol. Organizing and elevating women, after all, was part and parcel of the vision they had professed to share, back in their student days of yore, back in the life they had lived together—that vision of the world beckoning at the end of their inherited and chosen trajectory: the unions, the socialist ideal, the campaign for Mississippi, the free-speech effort, the Peace Corps, the women's movement, the generous dignity of the land, and ultimately VISTA's battle for the home front.

Sometimes she wished so fervently that her time had come a little earlier, that she had been on those buses down South, turning her cheek to the white rage along their route, letting some small dark child braid her hair while she taught it the words to "This Little Light of Mine." She wished she had been there to hear King, and in the Delta for that dangerous summer of '64, and on the boardwalk in Atlantic City that fall for the convention, with the relics of the war—the charred hull of a car, the bell still warm from the ashes of a fire-bombed church—and in Berkeley only weeks later, and again in Washington for the Vietnam marches—all those last great moments of unity. But by the time she and Daniel had come along, there had been so much refraction that their lights were little indeed—so little she wondered why they bothered *not* hiding them under a bushel. By the time she and Daniel had come along, people were so busy splitting apart it was no wonder they hadn't achieved their aims: black civil rights workers who suddenly couldn't share their movement with whites, free-speech advocates incapable of listening to anyone else, anarchists too busy leading the way to let women have a turn, women who wouldn't share the podium with lesbians. Communes and cults, drugs and suicide and business school—truly common ground seemed so truly rare that it was some kind of miracle when kindred souls managed to collide at all. Especially here, she thought with resignation. And yet here she was, the last freedom fighter, waving her flag of quilts and rugs as the Reaganite troops swarmed victoriously over the ruined battlefield. Sometimes she wished they'd just hurry up and shoot her already.

But that was later, Naomi thought, feeling her car tip down the steep drive to the A-frame, the rocks spattering beneath her wheels. In the beginning, the house had been Daniel's manifesto of the New Family, a theoretical entity that did not subdivide into individual rooms for individual people but lived *together* in the truest sense. Thus, their house had boasted one great amorphous room with "areas" rather than walls, mattresses on the floor, cinder-block bookshelves, Mexican rugs in odd places and at odd angles. The smells of the stove invaded the bed linen in a cozy, denlike manner, the bare bulb of Daniel's late-night-reading corner bored into Naomi's sleep like a miner's light descending a cavern, and the woodstove in the center of it all gamely chugged away in a doomed effort to heat the whole thing. Eventually, the privy Daniel had originally built was replaced, but only by an Indian batik cloth strung up on clothesline around a compost toilet he had imported from Maine. The cloth was a pseudo-barrier that did nothing to muffle sounds or interfere with smells, but even this illusion of a barrier Naomi had had to fight for.

It stood to reason, then, that when Daniel left some nine months ago, Naomi had immediately embarked on a frenzy of Sheetrock, carving out areas not much larger than area rugs and moving from room to newly demarcated room in a swoon of defined habitation. The batik cloth and compost toilet were swiftly replaced with actual walls and plumbing. The new three-sided closet was dubbed an entryway or, less grandly, a

mudroom. In the new dining room, the long table sat perennially laden with tasks abandoned and pending, and there was
now an actual guest room, in case she ever had an actual guest.
Then, once this was accomplished, she had declared the con-
ceptual termination of her marriage by hiring Ashley Deacon
to build *out*, indulgently tacking a den (with television! with
stereo!) and a home office onto the original structure. Rooms
upon rooms, Naomi thought. Rooms for sleeping and peeing
and eating. A room for eating more formally than in the other
room for eating, even a room expressly for looking at television, that most shameful of solitary acts. A room for Flourish,
filled with electronic objects not even imagined when Daniel
had first hauled her down into this damp and wooded hollow
and waved the bill of sale in her face. Subdivided so ruthlessly,
the house had imploded into virtual nonexistence: a maze
through which to weave, the dark wood in the middle of her
life.

    She let herself in through the new annex now and climbed
the half flight of blond steps to the main A-frame. In the
kitchen, Naomi dug out a teabag of Constant Comment and lit
the gas beneath her kettle. She eyed the oven clock, immobilized at 3:24 a.m. since some unnoted morning in some year
of the previous decade. Then, somewhat inappropriately, she
felt herself smile. Given the queer circularity of fate—all fate,
perhaps, though clearly Naomi's—this wasn't even her first
macabre brush with the river. The event which she and Daniel
had taken to calling—with prescient self-importance—the
"Sabbathday Affair," or in more sardonic moments, their genuine *Deliverance* experience, had taken place the first autumn
of their VISTA year. They were still living at Bailey's Motel
then, their damp wooded plot and the extension of their tenure
not even vaguely formed intentions. Bailey's, long since der-
elict, was mouse-ridden, and its crumbling cinder blocks gave
shelter to a breathtaking array of insect life, but bad conditions
were a badge of honor back then, mindful as one was of one's
fellow VISTA volunteers in Appalachia, in the Deep South,
and on the blighted reservations. For this reason Naomi and
Daniel seldom did their laundry, preferring to recycle worn
clothes or, if absolutely necessary, to run especially offensive
articles under the cold-water tap (they both ran cold, really)
and lay them over the towel bar for a week's dank drying. So

perhaps it was with a sense of adventure in the making that they had gone into town one Saturday evening that fall, their army surplus duffels crammed to bursting. The Laundromat was empty and they filled every washer.

This left an hour to kill, and something of a dearth of possibilities with which to kill it. There was the tavern, of course—a dubious establishment called Woodstock's—but Naomi wasn't a drinker and even Daniel understood that, in the tavern at least, the town's suspicion of them bubbled over into plain dislike. And there was the porch at Tom and Whit's, which afforded a decent observational post for the teenagers cruising their parents' cars along Elm, the main street through town. But hey—there was the river, tantalizingly close through the patch of woods behind the Laundromat, close enough to hear when you stepped outside and beyond the range of the chugging washers. And it was hot, too, one of those September weeks when Indian summer threatens to sink back to the steamy weather no one in New England ever quite admits to. And they were young, after all, and had taken the precaution of marrying before they came here to live, and they were outsiders without a decent reputation to sully, and in any case, it was hardly anyone else's business, was it, and even if it *were*, it was hardly likely that anybody would see them, would even know that they had gone to swim on this nearly moonless night.

And so they gathered at the river and shed their clothes on a boulder, and the Sabbathday was frigid and pure with its meager sliver of lunar light, and they went in slowly at first—an ankle, a knee—and then yelping at the cold and hurling palmfuls of water at each other so that each would be as chilled and as sodden as the other. The current wasn't strong in that part of the river, but it tugged at them, and after the first moment of resisting, it felt easier to let it push them downstream a bit, so they moved, crouched in the water, feeling with their feet and never quite losing their balance, and in the low light they rounded the river's sharp corner to a stretch where they could not have looked back and seen their abandoned jeans and flannel shirts and sneakers laid across the boulder even if there had been light to see them by, and there—memory differed on this point: Daniel insisting; Naomi, who didn't remember much later anyway, resolutely disbelieving, attributing the claim to Daniel's need to dramatize, or to Daniel's being a man and thus needing to add sex to any scenario which challenged his manhood—they either kissed or actually had sex, half-squatting in an eddy. And afterward they clasped hands and led each other upstream again to their point of entry. It had been, maybe, twenty minutes in all. Maybe even less.

They were nearly on top of their boulder before they saw him: thin, his dark face outlined by darkness, and as naked as they were. They crouched, gaping, as he pulled their clothes out of the water. In his voice, a trill of hysteria. "She threw your clothes in," he said.

"Who's *she*?" Naomi heard herself ask.

"What the fuck—" It was Daniel, more perplexed than outraged.

The man straightened. His penis, at Naomi's eye level, flashed white. She looked away instinctively and saw the girl, slight in shorts and a T-shirt. Naomi didn't see her face. She never saw her face.

"Don't nobody move or I'll shoot," the girl squeaked, and Naomi almost smiled, since the line was so trite, since she herself might have thought of something so much better were she the one holding the gun, her arms straight, glaring at three naked people in a river.

For a long moment they all peered through dimness at each other. This is what a holdup must be like if you're blind, she thought. She had lost the use of her body anyway and could not have moved even if so inclined. Suddenly she was furious at Daniel for bringing her here, though she could not have said whether "here" was the river or Goddard itself.

"Oh *shit*," the man said, though on instant replay the "oh" sounded more like "ow." Naomi heard the actual shot at the same moment, and then somebody else's voice—Daniel's, on further reflection—yelping the phrase "Oh please God. Oh please God . . ." as he grabbed her hand and hauled her up on the bank. Behind them the man fell, cursing, but she herself was running, thinking only of broken bottles, of poison ivy, of roots twisting up out of the ground to trip her. There was another shot and then, curiously louder than that, an outraged voice: "You *cunt*."

The tavern was lit like a beacon through the trees. Daniel let go of her hand and plunged into the back door, disappearing inside. Naomi went behind a tree. She had been deafened by the wind tunnel of her own breath. The tavern seemed unchanged by the naked man who had run inside. She looked down and saw her own nakedness and was abruptly consumed by that, as if there weren't a wounded man somewhere on the riverbank behind her or a girl with a problem and a gun, perhaps, in the forest. Off to one side, in the next lot, a trailer with—oh, fortune—a laden clothesline. Naomi lunged for it, flinging her shaking arms into the arms of a pink housecoat which would not close over her chest. Amid panic, humiliation. She threw it off and jerked a man's shirt off its clothespins. It came to her waist only, leaving her naked from there down. A towel then—thin and faded but large enough, and just in time: men swarmed out the tavern door, the sickly white of Daniel's white chest in their midst, the unmistakable rumble of laughter in their wake.

The man had been shot in the hip. His girlfriend, fourteen and pregnant, went to live with cousins in Maine. And all of that had long been forgotten when, years later, they were still telling how Daniel Roth had streaked into Woodstock's one Saturday night, leaving his wife stark naked in the woods. See what you can expect of people like that?

As for Naomi, the one thing she failed to grasp was why Daniel—with whom she had groped through rebellious agnosticism into the comfortable and eminently mature atheism of their respective parents—should, at his moment of crisis, suddenly have invoked a God he otherwise utterly disavowed. But Daniel would never admit that he'd called to God in the first place.

Taking her tea to the bathroom, Naomi ran scalding water into the tub, stripped off the clothes she'd so carelessly thrown on in the prehistory of that very morning, and stepped cautiously to the mirror. The arc of her day, from guilty exercise dilettante to bearer of death, from murder suspect to, at the very least, unintentional obstructor of justice, wore itself in the indigo smudges beneath her widely spaced eyes, and this, unbidden, brought the image of the infant back to her. She felt herself move forward to the image and could not pull away, until it seemed to hover before her—a ghost image transparency separating her from the world.

Steam gradually claimed the mirror, but she knew what she

looked like; the decrepitude of age apart, indeed, she had always looked precisely the same and—truth in advertising, she thought ruefully—precisely as she *was*. The convex ark of her nose, for example, or the set to her jaw, the thick waves of hair practically hollered *direct from the steppes of Russia!* to anyone who cared to know. For years she had felt older than her age, with whatever beauty she had begun with utterly worn away, like a clock run so far ahead of itself that it had forgotten its own time. It always surprised Naomi when she caught some man's look, because some men did look, and so the looking, in the end, she attributed not to herself, but to what she represented, at least to them. After all, having grown up in a community of people exactly like herself, it had taken her years to catch on to the fact that she was an exotic to most people, that—tethered to history by tribal umbilicus, as it were—she walked among the pale and civilized people of Goddard like something earthy and sensual, a swoon of seductive otherness.

She felt herself grimace; then, light-headed, she braced her forearms against the white porcelain of the sink. All of it, her life and marriage, the child who might have been born by now, her work, the friends who had receded from her and the ones who did not approach to take their places as a circle widened around her, leaving her abandoned: the center who could not hold, the woman left holding the bag, the bag left holding the baby, the baby thrown out with the bathwater.

The baby in the river, Naomi thought.

The emptiness in her belly heaved again, and again she felt herself double over. This time she wept not for the child but for herself, and for the injustice of it having to be herself after all. That it should have been she, and not even a summer person. That it should have been she and not Sarah Copley or Ann Chase or any of the other town stalwarts—from the Harvest Festival committee, and the school board, and the granite stock sunk generations into this rigid New Hampshire soil. That it should have been she, the encroacher, entrenched in her foreignness, her otherness, her Communism-by-any-other-name ideas about business, her glorification of women's work, her hatred of men! How small this was, Naomi thought, to feel sorry for herself this way, when someone was dead. And yet there was a sweetness to it, too.

Surprised, she looked up, wiped the mirror to find her own eyes, and saw it there, unmistakable. In one motion the force that had turned her head, drawing her gaze to the still, white object in the Sabbathday River, had also rent the cloth that bound Naomi Roth—who was also immobilized, who was similarly dead. She could not mend it now, any more than she could return to set the baby back into the river. The same river twice, so the saying went, and nothing—she saw this now—would be left unaltered in its wake.

Chapter 5

Part of the Evidence

TO A NEW ENGLANDER, THE NORTHERN HARD-
woods' annual shedding of their chlorophyll was not precisely
the inauguration of beauty, the ecstatic cacophony of
landscape-induced endorphins, that it was to the gaping outsider; rather, this predictable explosion of wild reds and
speckled oranges, staunch evergreens and punctuations of yellow running the hillsides in their stripes and patches, was a
starting pistol for the brief season in which substantial money
might just possibly get made. Goddard, like any other town
within striking distance of Boston and New York, assumed a
communal and rictus-tight happy face, beginning now and lasting until the last leaf fell, after which anyone wandering into
town would have the same chances as a local of finding a
neighbor in a good mood. The Unitarian church at the north
end of Elm, a dingy building adorned with the steeple of its
predecessor on the site —the one element salvaged from a fire
in 1968—always attained an illusory sheen at this time of year,
a hit of bone-white against the hillside of leaves rising behind
it, as if newly skimmed with paint for an annual show. Downtown homeowners engaged in genially competitive decoration,
lashing cornstalks and spent sunflowers to the doorposts and
loading up their front steps with pumpkins and mums, as if
each resident were intent on advertising his own personal harvest. The flatlanders loved it. Tom and Whit's alone looked
like the cover of a getaway guide to New England, with its
cleverly peeling rockers, each endowed with a cleverly rocking
urbanite in a red down vest or a rag sweater purchased in
Harvard Square, each balancing a steaming coffee on the armrest and a fat Sunday *Globe* in his or her blue-jeaned lap. For
this seasonal blink, the motels were full, even in midweek, and
the most unlikely of stores was crowded with the most unlikely
of customers. Naomi herself was inundated with drop-ins at
the mill, not a few of whom clutched their catalogues,

which made her very happy. People walked straighter, conscious of being observed and thought typical of themselves. There was an inhalation of collective pretension. It wouldn't last, but it wasn't supposed to last. And naturally it all had to happen right now.

Only three days after she had found the dead baby in the Sabbathday River, the drive into Goddard was slow, the road dense with creeping cars. Naomi, whose mood was foul anyway, could practically hear the "oohs" from inside the Connecticut Taurus she followed. She drove with one dull eye on the plate (RT 2 LIF) and another on the summit of Moosilauke, or a portion of its humpbacked summit, which loomed, by increments, into view, lurking like some bald and homely uncle at a family party. Moosilauke, so unlike those furry green mountains across the river, she thought now—incredibly, for the first time—those smooth Vermont mountains, like warm undulations in the landscape. Why couldn't *their* mountains be like that? Here were only jags and bare patches of rock, unapologetic and uncivil. Green Mountain versus White Mountain, she mused. Marble versus granite. Well, what did you expect? In New Hampshire the mountains had nothing to hide; like their appointed spokesman, the Old Man himself, they showed their plain faces to the wind. She supposed it was time for her to show her face, too.

She pulled into the mill's driveway, the right wheels of her station wagon dipping violently into a ditch—a remembrance of mud seasons past—as she rolled toward the front door, and the motion made her bite her tongue. Cursing softly, if gingerly, she stamped up the steps and across the porch, then went inside.

"Let's call Ashley," Naomi said. "We've got to get that ditch filled. And the banister to the attic is jiggling again."

Mary Sully at the front desk was nearly obscured by mail, but not quite enough to hide her stare. "Uhkay. But . . . Miss Roth?"

Naomi, she almost said. But she had given up. "Yup?" She set down her bag and automatically began turning over the order forms: Hawaii, Arizona, Connecticut. South Dakota—a first. There was a message from Heather, still down with stomach flu, who would need an extra week with her orders.

"Is it true? About you and that baby?"

Naomi's face fell. "Yeah. My luck, eh?" Mary looked horrified. Naomi, in defeat, could practically hear her remark ricochet around the town. "I mean, it was terrible. God, I was sick about it yesterday. Couldn't eat a thing."

"I couldn't imagine." Mary shook her head, the faintest ripple in her full, pale cheeks.

Naomi couldn't either, despite the fact that it had happened to her.

"Was it . . . I mean, the paper didn't say. Was it a boy?" Mary asked, her voice thick with dread. She had two herself—one in school, the other still in diapers.

"No," Naomi said with a thin smile, happy, at least, to deliver this wisp of good news. "A little girl."

There was the briefest instant of relief on the woman's face. Then she summoned her horror again. "What's going to happen?" Mary said. "What are they going to do?"

Naomi fell into the nearest chair and grimly eyed the dust beneath Mary's desk. Behind her, the murmurings of women had given way to blaring silence. Whatever she said next, she knew, would have to be loud enough for everyone to hear.

"I don't know any more than anyone else, Mary," Naomi said. "You know, it was only chance that I was there. It doesn't give me any special insight into what it means or what's going to happen." In the stillness, they waited for her to go on. "I do know," Naomi said firmly, "that the police are taking it very seriously, as they should. The D.A. I met, well, he's very determined. He came down from Peytonville to run the whole thing, and I don't doubt that he'll do whatever he feels is necessary. I'm sure he'll find the . . ." She glanced at Mary's face, tight with keen, if guilty, interest. "The one, you know, who put her there."

"The murderer, you mean."

Naomi looked up. Ann Chase was in the doorway. A half-completed rug featuring a dopey spaniel hung limp from her wrist, rendering her own harsh expression vaguely comical by association. Ann, once lithe and blond, had let age both thicken her and darken her hair and was now, blandly, "of certain years" and an indeterminate hair color. She wore pants the hue of river mud and a white sweater. She was glaring at Naomi.

"I suppose."

"Suppose, hell. She murdered that baby."

"She," Naomi managed. "Meaning?"

"What are you, dense? That baby wasn't just *put* in the river. What I heard, she was cut up like a pumpkin. The mother—"

"Now you don't know that!" Naomi's voice rose in alarm. "You have no way of knowing it was the baby's mother!"

"Not the mother?" Ann Chase said shrilly. "Okay, then, where *is* the mother? Why don't we hear her yelling and screaming about her baby's gone missing and who took it? Somebody takes your brand-new baby out of its cradle and you're on the horn to Nelson Erroll before the door slams, you know as well as me. Now where's the mother if it wasn't her?"

"Ann," Naomi said, "it might have been the baby's father, did you think of that? Maybe he was mad about it. Maybe he didn't want to be a father." Even saying the words made her numb.

"Fine," Ann said, her voice suspended between airy and arch. "You want to pretend it isn't true? You go ahead. But that doesn't *make* it not true."

Naomi sighed heavily. She eyed the stack of orders on Mary's desk with something like longing, imagining herself flicking on her computer, setting down her coffee mug. Mary sat stiffly, her eyes averted. In the mill room, the shuffling of feet, but no voices. Ann, with a huff, turned and went back in, and Naomi—almost against her will—felt herself rise and follow. She laid a palm on Ann's white sweater and the woman stopped, rooted. Behind her an arc of six or seven, rugs spread over their laps, faces rapt. They had abandoned the pretense of not listening. "What?" Ann said.

Naomi swallowed. "Do you know something? I mean, you seem . . ." She glanced at the ring of heads. "If you know something, you should go to Nelson, or this D.A. from Peytonville. If you know—"

"If I *know?*" Ann said, smiling unaccountably. "I was born here, Naomi. You think I don't know my neighbors? You think I don't know who lives here?"

Baffled, Naomi simply stared.

"You think we're in some big city and you can get away with thinking it's a stranger?"

This, Naomi thought, was somehow meant to refer to herself, but what it actually meant she found she ardently wished not to pursue.

Ann smiled, showing an equal display of ivory denture, canary tooth, and coral gum. Then she stalked to her seat, smoothed the burlap across her lap, and, with the murmured assent of her company, yanked a vicious length of wool through her unfortunate spaniel's paw. Naomi, for once relieved at the way the circle had closed, shutting her out, swung shut the door to the office and, beneath the fretful looks of Mary Sully, addressed her own work. That she knew fully well the unspoken lines of the conversation just past did not give her any comfort, but having spent the previous days pushing from her thoughts the dead baby in the river, Naomi found that little more effort was required to push this from her thoughts as well.

The mood in the mill did not improve. Indeed, when Ann Chase headed home around lunchtime, and Naomi might reasonably have expected a dissipation of the tension, it seemed to grow even worse, as if, without their self-selected spokesperson, no one quite knew what to say to her and, not knowing, said absolutely nothing. A few times she had ventured into the back room, flashing a newly poured and steaming cup of coffee as if to advertise her willingness to talk—even to talk about *that*. But the heads stayed bowed over their work and nobody would look at her.

Not, in itself, a very unusual state of play. What Naomi missed most about being married to Daniel—possibly, apart from sex, the only thing she *did* miss—was a level of conversational intimacy that dipped below the strictly ephemeral. Over the years she had felt the ties between herself and her women friends elongate into intangibility. There were such recognizable trajectories to their lives, she thought from her distant berth in the north country; they had entered professions, found mates, produced and nurtured children. Their heads were full of play groups and dissertations and organized protests and endless gatherings to talk and talk and talk. They did not talk much to Naomi these days. It had been two years since the last one had ventured upcountry to camp—with her two adopted Vietnamese children—in the amorphous "space" of the A-frame. Naomi's friends were naturally happy to hear from her when she called; they were happy to learn that her business was doing well, that she was adjusting to living alone. But they had new friends now—from work, or seminars, or the playground. Naomi understood that they found it difficult to consider her own circumstances when they neither knew nor could begin to conjure the personalities involved. There seemed less and less to say about any of it.

Meanwhile, there were no rap sessions in Goddard, shockingly enough. Few consciousnesses had ever been raised in the church basements or around the kitchen tables of Flourish's knitters and hookers. Naomi, for her part, would gladly have been open with them—she had never been a secretive person, especially—but here there was no one to talk to. These women showed each other little enough of their lives, and yet they seemed to find ways of revealing even less to Naomi. It was barely possible to worm from them the names of their husbands, the ages of their children, let alone the nature of their various distresses. Now and then she might be able to glean some crumb of coded information, a morose reference to the Woodstock Tavern (which was the local dialect for My-husband-is-drinking-again) or a chilly reference to a sibling, signifying a lifetime of pained acrimony. When they spoke, it was to deflect attention from themselves or to condemn one another outright. When they laughed, it was at someone else's failing. They did not view their own lives as mysteries to be unfurled, perplexities to be distilled, imbibed, and benefited from—the word "feeling" came from a foreign dialect; it simply had no meaning. The notion of emotional exploration, let alone directed counseling or—God forbid—psychiatry, was infinitely suspect. Even Heather, with whom Naomi engaged in a sort of pantomime of friendship, kept so much back that Naomi inevitably felt the scrim of distance between them.

At five o'clock she put together another kit for Heather, scribbled a grocery list for herself, and locked the mill door behind her. The light over the Sabbathday was pink and the leaning birches rosy over the water. Robert Frost—celebrated swinger of birches that he was—would have had little use for these sorry specimens, she thought, revving the wagon's tired engine. The thin trunks here had no spring—unlike the birches in the Frost poem, those catapults into the universe, unlike the graceful birches that had bowed to kiss their own reflections in the Sabbathday near the eddy where she had found the baby. These looked as if no amount of optimism could wring from them any momentum at all. They drooped their sorry lengths at an awkward angle near the mill's back door, near the skeleton of a jungle gym so rusted as to reiterate that no child dwelt here who might inspire them to stand up straight and make themselves useful. They were depleted things, bowed by their own gravity and rooted to the spot. She sighed and tried to ease the car ahead, avoid the sinkholes as best she could in the dimming light.

Naomi dreaded having to tell Heather about the sampler. It had been an alphabet sampler, one of Heather's best, with an outsized A of deepest red in the upper left corner of its vintage linen and the subsequent letters flowing from it with a momentum of inevitability until the honest *H. Pratt—1985* following the final Z. Such an order would have taken her a good week, Naomi knew, since Heather would not part with a piece until she was happy with it, even as orders lengthened in their queue, waiting for her. She had been in the Flourish collective for only a year and a half, but she was by far the most skilled embroiderer Naomi had found thus far, not to mention the only one under sixty. Heather's work, perhaps more than anyone else's, appeared to be benefiting from customers' word of mouth, and it seemed to Naomi that an entire generation of Scarsdale and Shaker Heights babies were currently occupying nurseries adorned with her name samplers and needlepoint birth announcements. How many times, Naomi sometimes mused, had Heather rendered the exotic names of her contemporaries' offspring in florid or classically restrained letters, informing the world that Alyssa or Chloë or Brittany had arrived? Heather—who, as far as Naomi knew, had never left New Hampshire—had been asked for by name from as far afield as Palm Springs. But maybe, she thought ruefully, that was the whole point.

Heather was Goddard Falls–born, to a mother who had gone off to Boston and come back pregnant. That in itself was the sum total of what Naomi knew about the mother, since she had either died or otherwise departed long since, and Heather had been in the care of her grandmother from a young age. Now, except for Polly, a child so lovely she made Naomi's heart clutch, Heather was alone.

Stephen Trask had brought Heather to her or, more accurately, had brought her work, two pieces she had made as gifts for his children. He said that the girl had been some kind of

a manager at the sports center but was needed at home now.
He had seemed anxious to recommend Heather, offering tes-
timonials to her sweet nature, her conscientious habits, but
Naomi, gazing at the exquisite work Trask had brought her,
was already so amazed that she would have taken Heather on
if she had been Medea herself. There were two pieces, silk
thread etched on linen, one an interlocked ABC that moved
with the subtlest alchemy from deepest red to palest yellow,
the other a row of demure but sweetly plump apples with the
prim text beneath them: A *is for Apple*. Naomi was charmed.
The grandmother, Stephen said, had been gifted in this way;
probably she had taught Heather a long time ago. Heather was
always pulling out something during her breaks at the sports
center, crouching over her lap with it. It hadn't worked out at
the sports center, he said, but not for anything the girl had
done—Stephen wanted Naomi to know this, though Naomi
couldn't have cared less—she was a good girl, he said. He
said it again.

Winter after crushing winter the tilting gray house on Sabbath Creek Road remained impossibly upright. There was no
land to speak of, just a back field already returning to forest
from lack of attention. She doubted the grandmother had left
much behind in the way of an estate, and what Heather made
from her samplers wasn't Naomi's idea of a sufficient income
for a very young mother alone in the world, but then again
she had finally—and after considerable effort—gotten out of
the habit of wondering how most of the citizens of Goddard
Falls supported themselves. It seemed a nonissue for the people in question, after all. They themselves were too busy just
getting on with things, and taking the long view was the useless activity of folks with too much time on their hands to
begin with.

In front of the house, a row of humble sunflowers bent low,
as if—Naomi thought, shifting her station wagon into park—
she were some kind of royalty, pulling up to a stately home
with its line of servants in attendance. This fairly absurd association afforded her an unanticipated moment of levity, because her errand, after all, nudged at the core of Naomi's
lingering depression. The alphabet sampler she had picked up
only last week and placed gently on the backseat of her station
wagon—the first stop on its journey to the comfortable home

of an appreciative new owner—was bloodstained now, at least
symbolically. It was in a box probably, Naomi thought, in the
terribly organized possession of that awful man Charter. Exhibit A, she thought bitterly. A is not for apple.

She climbed down from the car and fished out the order
slip: Michel, Menlo Park, California—one alphabet sampler,
traditional colors, no figurative designs. Then she set her jaw
and followed the fraying clapboards of the farmhouse to the
front door, steeling herself. But the front door was open, and
it was Naomi whose eyes widened in baffled concern. "Oh
no," she heard herself say. "What happened to you?"

Heather stepped back, opening the door. She seemed to lean
back against it for an instant, before straightening and pulling
off the briefest of smiles.

"Stomach bug. I caught it from Polly, I guess. I feel terrible."

She looked terrible, too, Naomi observed. Her normally pale
cheeks were a stark white, and her thick brown hair, loose to
her shoulders, gave off an unmistakable and almost animal
odor. She wore a large and limp green sweater over gray sweat
pants, and looked hot. Her forehead, in fact, was shining.

"You have a fever," Naomi observed.

"No, not anymore, I think." The girl's voice was thin. "I
did, till last night." She shrugged, embarrassed. "Sorry, I'm
sure you're not interested."

Of course I am, Naomi almost said, but did not say. The
truth was that she was never entirely certain where she stood
with Heather, whether they were in fact friends, and if so, what
it was that bound them in friendship, beyond the obvious fact
of Naomi's willingness to *be* Heather's friend—something that
plainly set her apart from the rest of Goddard. There were
times, oddly enough, when Naomi found herself actually en-
vying the women who so shunned this girl, for their certainty
about Heather's character, for the solidity of their opinions. In
her own defense, Heather said nothing, and in her autonomy,
she was unknowable: a girl without friends who refused to
experience or, at any rate, to manifest, loneliness, a girl without beauty (and even Naomi—who had, over the years,
worked hard to expand her definition of female beauty beyond
the socially endorsed limitations of white, slender, and blond—
had never considered Heather Pratt to be beautiful) who none-

theless had some irreducible quality that could not be gained at a makeup counter or shaped in a gym. Heather's sensuality—*never* flaunted, never even consciously *displayed*—was nonetheless palpable. She could see why the women hated her. Naomi, in her celibacy, sometimes nearly hated her, too.

She smiled to cover her silence. "Of course I'm interested, Heather. You should be in bed."

"I feel better moving around, actually," Heather said. "I've got Polly in the kitchen. You want some tea?" She turned, walking stiffly, Naomi following.

The baby was in her high chair, doing fairly stomach-churning things to a fistful of hamburger. Even this, however, could not do much more than briefly obscure her beauty. For all that she was a child of sin, Naomi thought, Polly was also a child so radiant that there seemed some alchemy of rightness in her making. Naomi walked to the kitchen table and bent down to stare into her bottomless blue eyes. She was just over one year old, plump and avid, with a brushed thatch of white blond hair and a single, demure extra chin. She looked at Naomi, utterly focused and utterly serene. Then, happily, she extended her mashed and masticated dinner in an open hand.

"You said on the phone there was some problem about the last order," Heather said. She was filling a stainless-steel kettle at the tap and placing it on one of the stove's electric coils, where it hissed. She gave the stockpot beside it a stir, and a drift of apple and cinnamon reached across the room to Naomi. The kitchen was softly bright, painted white, the floorboards rosy peach. Heather had not turned around, and now reached into a cabinet for teabags, her sweater riding up to show, briefly, a band of skin, pale around a shapeless middle. She'd never managed to get her figure back after Polly, Naomi thought. Too young to be plump for the rest of her life, she clucked to herself. What was Heather, anyway? Twenty? Twenty-one?

"Just sugar, please," Naomi said. "That smells great. Is it applesauce?"

"Pick's recipe," Heather said, giving the pot a stir. "Every year I kept after her to make it less sweet, but every year she came up with some reason to add more sugar. Last year she said the baby wouldn't eat it if it wasn't sweet, but it's just cause she liked it that way herself." She shook her head at the syrupy apples. "I don't know why I'm bothering. I've still got some of last year's batch down in the cellar." She turned and smiled weakly at Naomi. "Just couldn't stand seeing the apples out back. She always made a point of getting them in on time."

"Well," Naomi said uncomfortably, "I'm sure she'd be happy you're keeping up the tradition." She took a breath. "Listen, Heather, I'm sorry to have to tell you this, but I— Your sampler was damaged. I'm sorry. You'll be paid, of course, but . . ."

"Oh." The girl turned. "Well, no harm. Accidents happen. Don't apologize, Naomi." She ladled applesauce into a white bowl, blew on it, and brought it to the baby, who laughed in unqualified delight. Heather put the sugar bowl on the table, and the cups with their teabag tails. The hot water turned orange, then amber.

"You know about the baby," Naomi heard herself say.

She looked into Heather's face.

"The baby," Heather said. Her voice was flat.

Back on the stove, the puckering of applesauce at its slow boil. Its wafting sweetness made the air suddenly thick. Naomi had just assumed.

"I'm sorry, I just assumed," she said.

"Assumed?" said Heather. "I don't understand what you're talking about."

"I found a dead baby. Saturday morning, in the river." The girl's eyes widened. Naomi saw abruptly that she hadn't known. Heather was stunned silent. Her short fingers held her teacup at the rim, gracelessly, as the liquid steamed.

"Where?" she finally said. The word came out a kind of sputter.

"Down by Nate's Landing. I was jogging on the path."

"Nate's Landing?" This appeared to shock her even more. "But that's almost into Goddard."

Naomi frowned at the non sequitur. Heather bent forward over her teacup and sipped. She swallowed. Then she took a gulp of air and straightened. "It's terrible, but what does that have to do with me?"

Naomi frowned. "Well, nothing. But your sampler, you see. It was in the backseat. I wrapped her up in it." She paused to shake the baby's face from her thoughts. "I had to. It was the only thing I had to cover her with. She was so . . . She had

been cut, too. Somebody cut her, or stabbed her or something."
She closed her eyes. That curiously bloodless puncture, the
Roman wound in the medieval painting. "I've never seen anything like that." She was speaking less evenly now, the tinge
of panic returning to her voice. She looked at Heather—for
comfort, she realized—and then was suddenly ashamed of her
need.

The girl's eyes were wide. She was not looking at Naomi
at all but at Polly, who pushed the remains of her dinner across
the tray of her high chair with a solemnity the activity hardly
deserved. Heather reached out and touched her daughter's
cheek. Just touched it, as if to make sure it was still there. She
frowned. "I don't understand. You mean, somebody actually
killed the baby? It wasn't just, you know, the baby was born
and it was dead or something?"

Naomi shook her head. "I guess the coroner will decide
about that," she said, suddenly very tired. "I'm really just trying not to think about it right now, actually." Out of courtesy,
she took a long drink of her cooling tea. "Anyway, that's what
happened. I wrapped her up in your sampler. I'm sorry,
Heather. And then it was part of the evidence, you understand?
So the police had to take it away with them, for their investigation. There was nothing I could do about it. I couldn't ask
for it back."

Heather was staring at the tabletop. "Part of the evidence,"
she intoned. She looked up and met Naomi's eyes. "I don't
want my sampler to be part of the evidence."

Naomi looked surprised. "Well, we don't exactly have a
choice about it. This man running the investigation, he's very
much in charge, and frankly I didn't think it was important
enough to argue about. The truth is that even if I'd managed
to keep it . . . I couldn't, you know, I could never just send it
to the customer. Not after that. So we're just going to have to
make another one." She looked at Heather's face. The girl
might be on the mend, Naomi thought, but she still looked
unwell. Shit, Naomi hoped she wouldn't catch whatever flu
this was. The last thing she needed now was a bug that wiped
you out with such evident efficiency.

"Heather," she heard herself say, "you take a few days and
rest up. I'm going to write to the customer anyway, tell her
there was an accident or something, all right? You just get

better, then you can have another whack at it, okay?"

Heather nodded. "Okay. You bring me another kit?"

Naomi fished it out of her bag and handed it over.

"Want some more tea?"

It was a formality, easily deflected.

"No, thanks. I've got shopping to do. Another time." She shrugged on her coat. "Take care of yourself, Heather. I'll give you a call next week, see how you're getting on." She paused. "Look, I'm sorry I told you if you didn't know already." Naomi smiled weakly. "The whole town seems to know about it. I figured you would, too."

"We don't see too much of people," Heather said plainly, without sadness. "I guess I would have heard sometime."

Naomi showed herself out and rounded the muddy yard with its hunchback sunflowers, back to her station wagon. It was getting dark now, though it wasn't yet six. The weekend past she had thought of as Indian summer, she remembered. A T-shirt and shorts to jog in, not even a sweatshirt on the morning she had found the baby. Only two days had passed, but already, in the early evenings, there was the preemptive chill of winter. She reached for the heating lever on her dashboard and gave it its first nudge of the season as she started the station wagon down the drive. She was nearly at the road when a flash of light drew her eyes to the rearview mirror, then made her turn in her seat and peer into the gloom. She shook her head. Heather, in her green sweater, was walking across the field behind the house, weaving through big stones and jumping ruts, a flashlight slapping at her hip. She shouldn't be outside, Naomi thought crossly. How did she expect to get well again if she refused to take care of herself?

Chapter 6

Lilith in the Garden

THE GODDARD STOP & SHOP WAS LOCATED IN A strip mall just north of the town center, wedged on the unimaginative concrete between a Hallmark card shop and a video rental place that did a brisk business in Schwarzenegger but was, Naomi had discovered early on, decidedly unlikely to carry the latest Woody Allen. The supermarket gave the word "monopoly" a whole new meaning, comprising, as it did, the sole large food outlet within fifteen miles of Goddard, and more or less determining, as a result, what Goddard and Goddard Falls inhabitants were going to eat—a diet primarily manufactured by Hostess, Wonder, Coca-Cola, and Procter and Gamble, as near as she could tell. Years earlier she had attempted to interest the management in the nutritional benefits of whole foods, the advantage of developing relationships with local farmers and start-up specialty providers, but these efforts, amazingly, had been resisted. She did still give in to an emergency expedition into Hanover now and then, making a run on the gourmet store on College Street to buy up everything in sight (including pounds and pounds of the bagels they swore were flown in from H & H on the Upper West Side of Manhattan). Mostly, however, she had buckled under years ago. She had to eat. She had that in common with her neighbors.

She even ate meat now. Back in college, Naomi had embraced Daniel's vegetarianism like a dowry, which it was in a way. Daniel considered the consumption of meat to be the primary distorting force in the web of ecological balances, and the primary pollution of the human body. Daniel favored grains cooked to the texture of sawdust, casseroles of parboiled vegetables baked with grated cheese, a rainbow of teas that stretched from malt brown to celadon. Chicken was permissible on special occasions, but only organically grown chicken, which—given where they lived—neatly cut down on the consumption of chicken. He liked beans and always had a pot of them soaking. He collected bottles of condiments whose labels were in Sanskrit or Chinese and whose contents she was secretly afraid would poison them. He went through two copies of the *Moosewood Cookbook* and had just bought a third when they separated. He replenished his supplies from the bins at Tom and Whit's and the garden plot he rented from the dairy farmer next door. As far as Naomi knew, he had never entered the Stop & Shop.

She took her cart from the rack near the automatic door and began her rounds: hormone-laden milk, nominally whole-wheat sliced bread. Recycled paper goods? *Please.* She needed toilet paper and couldn't last the week it would take Seventh Generation to ship some over from Vermont, so it was time to squeeze some Charmin like the rest of the world. A man in a hunting cap was staring at her, down by the aluminum foil at the end of the aisle. She knew him, not by name—somebody's husband—and smiled and waved. Sarah Copley came by her, almost passed, then turned around.

"Naomi."

"Sarah," Naomi said, stopping her cart. She was waiting to see which way the wind would blow.

"This is a mess. There was an article in *The Boston Globe.* My sister telephoned from Dedham."

Naomi looked up and nodded. "I guess that makes sense."

Sarah Copley placed a proprietary hand on Naomi's shopping cart. She had graying hair suspended in blondness, part natural, part bottled. The shade had grown increasingly discordant as she approached sixty, and now was beginning to seem downright silly. Sarah was a quilter, retired from her job in the town clerk's office a year or two earlier. She and Naomi had a bond of civilized mutual tolerance.

"Nelson Erroll called me yesterday. Asked if I had any ideas."

"Ideas," Naomi said flatly.

"The mother," Sarah said. "You'd think somebody's walking around pregnant, we'd be bound to notice."

"You'd think," Naomi agreed. "Well, don't look at me."

"I wasn't." Sarah sounded surprised. She set her jaw. "Janelle Hodge said there were some kids camping in their upper pasture last week. Through hikers, she said. She thought she'd give them twenty-four hours before she called the police, and they were gone the next day. They had a girl with them, she said."

Naomi was listening to this, but she couldn't engage. She wanted to be left out of the gossip chain, but she couldn't cut Sarah. Cutting Sarah might rank, if possible, even higher on the hierarchy of Goddard crimes than slaughtering a newborn.

"Was the girl pregnant?" she said instead.

"Who the hell can tell, stuff they wear. Big baggy sweater can hide just about anything. They'd be off along the Trail now, anyway. I said to Nelson, I said if I was him I'd set up a checkpoint on Mount Washington. Be just as easy as punch to drop a baby in the river and then disappear. That kind of person would do it, too."

Which kind of person was that? she wanted to ask. Instead, she said, "Nelson have any other ideas?"

Sarah Copley nodded. "Said he was talking to everybody. 'Covering all the bases' is the way he put it. Couple of women in Goddard Falls living with men they're not married to. Went and talked to them, of course."

But of course, Naomi thought.

"DHSS gave him a list of women on welfare, everyone within thirty miles. Going to talk to them, too."

"*That'll* take a bit of time," Naomi said, disgusted.

"Oh, they have time." Sarah had missed her tone. "They're gonna find whoever did it, no mistake." She shook her head. "Makes me sick, throwing away a life like that. Just tossing her out in the river like so much garbage. A perfect little baby like that, and so many people can't have children and want to adopt!"

"Yes, that's true," she agreed. Her hands were on the bar of her shopping cart. She rolled it back and forth experimentally.

Sarah Copley took her own hand away, releasing the metal. "Well, I won't keep you," she said stiffly. "I'm sure you've got things to do."

Naomi looked up. At the end of the aisle, Ashley Deacon was reaching for a can of coffee. Saved by Ashley. It wouldn't be the first time.

"Well, I need to grab Ashley. You know he never returns calls, and the banister at the mill is going to get somebody killed." She smiled her most winning smile. "See you soon, Sarah."

Naomi pushed ahead, circumventing Sarah's half-full cart. Ashley began to turn, and she called his name.

"Naomi," he said. His voice was soft. "I've been thinking about you."

She gave this the look it deserved. "How's Sue?"

Sue Deacon had had a baby boy a few days earlier.

"Tired," he said. When he smiled, which he did now, two bottomless dimples appeared in his cheeks. He had thick hair pulled tightly back in a ponytail, a clever face that seemed to suggest a degree of intelligence he really didn't possess, or at any rate didn't use. It was also a face, it had sometimes occurred to her, that failed to retain a record of either his years or his deeds. They appeared to be accumulating somewhere else, as in the story of Dorian Gray, because Ashley was a good thirty years old with the skin of a man ten years younger. Angelic, too—he who is without sin, as the saying went, though Naomi knew perfectly well he had sinned. She liked him, though. She had always liked him.

"What'd you name him?"

"Benjamin. Benjy." He grinned. "Tough little guy. Think we'll keep him."

Under the circumstances, it was a fairly sick quip, Naomi thought, but Ashley's face was untroubled. Then again, with a brand-new baby, it was just possible he hadn't heard yet. She didn't want to be the one to tell him.

"Listen, I don't know when you want to start working again, but—"

"Oh, I'm working all right. I did a job this morning, on Sabbathday Ridge. I put in a French door for these people who just moved in. They want a new kitchen, too. They're ordering up stuff from Boston for it."

"Well." She stopped him. "So you might not have time for any little jobs, then."

"I have time," Ashley said amiably. "What do you need?"

The attic banister, she told him. And the parking lot leveled somehow, if it wasn't too expensive. And maybe it was time to look at her own roof again, since the one Daniel had so lovingly installed was beginning to assume the consistency of oatmeal. When Ashley had time.

"I'll make time," he said warmly.

Naomi shook her head, gave him the benefit of her goodwill, and left.

Well, that was how it went in Stop & Shop, she reasoned, turning the final aisle. Come in for a few marginally palatable foodstuffs, leave with an update on the current police investigation and a semiformal commitment from your contractor. A veritable agora on the Greek model, she thought, flinging a bag of rice cakes into her cart with happy abandon and heading for produce, such as it was.

Where, sharp enough to make the cans in her cart rattle against the mesh, she stopped short.

The woman was standing before a case filled with pale green iceberg lettuces, each wrapped in shiny plastic, each looking less appetizing than the next. Wedged on one side of the lettuces was a box of orange tomatoes, the kind that looked bad and tasted bad (as opposed to the kind that looked good and tasted bad), and on the other a neatly arranged waterfall of waxed cucumbers—as if some brilliant grocery clerk had taken it upon himself to relieve the shopper of the necessity for creativity in salad composition: iceberg, tomato, cucumber, *voilà!*

The woman was poised before this vision, legs slightly apart, hands on hips. The shopping cart beside her held precisely one item: a large bottle of generic seltzer. She wore heavy boots, a big sweater jacket with a dark brown pattern, and overalls of magenta cloth with long shoulder straps that knotted through the front bib. The sweater came from Mexico, and the overalls, Naomi knew, had been bought in a shop called Reminiscence, on a side street in Greenwich Village. She herself had two pairs just like them at home, one black, one pea green—very useful for days you felt fat or had your period. The woman was tall—taller than Naomi—and wide-hipped, and her black hair hit her shoulders with the kind of dense, tight curls some people who weren't Jewish tried to achieve through chemicals.

My kind, it came to her.

She remembered something she had read long before, in an anthropology class, about the lone survivor of a Native American tribe, adopted by whites, studied by whites. He had lived his whole life among whites, with nobody to talk to. Sharp as a knife, she felt her own longing.

The woman was probably a summer person. But then again it was late in the year for that.

The woman was probably a leaf-peeper. But leaf-peepers ate at country inns, they didn't visit the Stop & Shop, and if they did, it was for maple syrup, maple sugar, Cheddar cheese.

She looked like about twenty women Naomi had known in her life, but Naomi was reasonably certain she wasn't any of them. She looked like the person who would probably be her closest friend by now, if she'd never come to New Hampshire.

Naomi and her kind, she thought. The sight was riveting: Lilith in the garden. *So this is what I must look like to them,* she thought.

The woman shook her black hair in disgust. She reached for her cart and began to push it away. Naomi stepped forward. "Can I help you with something?" she heard herself say.

The woman turned to look at her for a long moment. Then, slowly, she smiled broadly and shook her head. "I should have known." Her voice was deep, underpinned by jubilant sarcasm. "Only I never thought it would be *this* bad. I told my husband, let's move to Putney, at least. In Putney they've got a co-op. I *know* people in Putney. But no. Because he fell in love with the house. A house without a kitchen, I might add." She swung her head around and coolly surveyed the produce department. "Not that we'll have any use for a kitchen."

"You're moving here?" Naomi said, refusing to make the inferential leap without confirmation.

"Moved already." She grinned. "No turning back now. Hey"—she put her hand out, three chunky silver rings glinting in the supermarket light—"I'm Judith Friedman."

Of course you are, Naomi wanted to say, but it wouldn't come out. She reached her own hand forward across the carts between them: the outstretched fingers of the Bering Strait, the clutch and unclench of the relay race. "Oh, thank you for coming," said a voice; as it happened, her own.

Chapter 7

Our Bodies, Ourselves

"A MOMENT OF YOUR TIME, MRS. ROTH."

Naomi looked up and, despite herself, groaned. She'd been sitting in her office at the mill, entering addresses at her IBM and being progressively deafened by the grader Ashley was running in the parking lot. She hadn't heard them, naturally.

He came in, followed closely by Nelson, who ducked his head. Charter, she realized, had loomed larger in her memory than perhaps he deserved: a tall and gaunt inquisitor in a black cape, beak-nosed, with lines etched deep across his forehead. She allowed herself a small, private smile. He must have really freaked her out to leave such a distortion of himself behind, Naomi thought, since—before her now—he was by comparison so ordinary. Just a man in his fifties or so, with that faintly comical comb-over and iron set jaw. It was no feature, after all, but the cumulative pinch of his expression and the tractor beam of his gaze, the acrid odor of his ambient distrust.

"I'm not interrupting," he observed, rejecting the courtesy of phrasing it as a question.

"Not now, you're not." Naomi watched them find seats in the small room. Beyond, in the main work area, the women hadn't noticed the police were here; they continued to speak together, loudly, over the grader. "Mary," she said to Mary Sully, who had stopped filing and was staring at the D.A., "would you give us a few minutes?"

"Uhkay," Mary said. She looked happy to leave them. She wedged her way out from between the desk and the cabinet, and moved heavily into the workroom.

Charter watched her go, pursing his lips. He turned to Naomi and offered his facsimile of a smile. "It must be nice not to have to dress for work."

She crossed her legs to show off the hole in the knee of her jeans. "I hope I don't look undressed, Mr. Charter."

"I only meant that most women are required to dress formally when they work."

"Most of the women I know work all the time," Naomi observed. "Women's work has never been limited to men's business hours, unfortunately."

The D.A. sat forward in his chair. "I beg your pardon, Mrs. Roth. I'm not here to malign your lifestyle or your livelihood, and I certainly apologize if I gave that impression. I only have a few questions."

Automatically, she began to protest, but Nelson cut her off. "Place looks good, Naomi." He hadn't been out since the winter, when they'd had a break-in—broken glass all over the workroom floor and a pair of grubby underpants in the attic. "You get that window fixed?"

"Ashley did it." She nodded toward the workroom. "Did a nice job."

"Any more problems?"

Not unless you count fishing dead babies out of the Sabbathday, she thought. "Nope. Nothing here to steal but ratty old rugs."

"I understand you sell your ratty old rugs all over the country," Charter said. She wasn't sure, but she thought he meant it as a compliment.

"That's true. Outside of Goddard they're known as unique living examples of an original American folk art."

"My grandmother hooked rugs," he said. "I still have a few myself."

Naomi looked at him, then at Nelson for help. His silvery hair fell forward over his eyes. She found, suddenly, that she could not remember the color of his eyes and almost asked him what they were. Thankfully, the moment passed. "How goes your investigation?" she said instead.

"It is continuing," Charter said, his voice even. "It is narrowing."

"Well, I hope you haven't come to accuse *me*." She was arch.

"I have not," he concurred.

"You had a word with my doctor, then."

"I did."

"Patient-doctor confidentiality be damned!"

Charter smiled. "Within the context of a murder investigation, yes, I think that's appropriate."

"Of course, women shouldn't patronize male doctors at all," Naomi said, a little wantonly. "That's my view. Women's health in the hands of women, don't you think? Our bodies, ourselves, that's the ticket." She really detested him. "I suppose I should be grateful that you talked to my doctor, under the circumstances. It's inconvenient being considered a suspect. One's neighbors tend to react badly."

He sighed. "I apologize for the inconvenience, but I had my reasons. I should tell you that over the years I have consistently lost faith in the power of chance. Sometimes, when I finish with a case, I lay it out on paper. Easier than keeping it all up here." He tapped his temple with a long finger. "Like a family tree: the victim, the perpetrator, the person who called the police, the witness. Not necessarily an actual family, but all connected nonetheless. Just like a family tree, Mrs. Roth. Everyone who touches the crime advances it in some way, or advances its solution. Believe me, there is very little in the way of random influence. Everyone has a role. Just now, I believe I understand a part of your role in this crime. Perhaps, when it's all behind us, I'll understand the rest."

She was staring at him. She shook her head slowly. "I don't have any idea what you're talking about. I hope you know that."

To her surprise, Charter smiled. "I do know that." He reached into his coat pocket and retrieved a small spiral notebook, its coil of metal clogged with strips of paper left behind when the sheets were torn away. "And now, I wonder if you might help us with a small problem."

Dimly, she noted that the grader had stopped. They were speaking more softly now. In the next room, the women, too, had stopped speaking.

"You may have heard about some of the directions our investigation has taken," Charter said.

"Sure," Naomi said. "Through-hikers, impoverished women, women who're living in sin with men they're not married to. I naturally assume you've hauled in every prostitute in the state of New Hampshire." She leaned forward and whispered, "Do you think there *are* any?"

"I know there are many," he said grimly. "But no, I don't

think a prostitute is responsible for this baby. I think the person responsible is an ordinary woman, in extraordinary circumstances."

Naomi shook her head. "Can you just explain to me why you're not even considering 49 percent of the population—the 49 percent that's responsible for almost 100 percent of the crime? It could have been a man, you know."

"It wasn't a man." His gaze drifted to the window. "But a man might have known, or might have helped. Mrs. Roth," he sighed. "I am not here to justify my deductions to you. I am very good at what I do. I will be making an arrest very shortly."

She stared at him, then at Nelson. His face gave nothing away. It took her a moment to catch her breath.

"Perhaps you would like to close the door, Mrs. Roth," Charter said, nodding at it. Naomi found her feet.

"I didn't want to disturb you in your office," he said when she returned to her seat, "but frankly time is short now. People talk in this town." He smiled. "That's been made abundantly clear to me this past week. And I don't want our suspect disappearing. I'm sure you understand."

Dumbly, she nodded.

"Well then"—he held his pen poised—"why don't you tell me what you know— or perhaps I should say what you *think* you know—about Heather Pratt?"

The gasp knocked what remained of her smugness away. Naomi opened her mouth in shock. First breath she got, she took the opportunity to laugh at them. "You have to be kidding."

They were both silent. Charter watched her carefully.

"Oh, absolutely not. Heather *Pratt*." She shook her head. "No way."

He was still waiting.

"You couldn't be more wrong. It's just totally out of the question."

And she found herself remembering how, when Heather had first joined the collective, she had brought her work to the mill like the other women, and poured herself coffee, and taken a seat, but how quickly the poison had seemed to spread out from her, like Cecil B. DeMille's version of blood in the Nile, that bitter silence and those bent heads, intent on ignoring the

girl. Naomi had not known much about Heather then, except
what Stephen Trask had told her—she was leaving her job at
the sports center, her grandmother was ill and needed her at
home—and one other rather critical thing: that Heather possessed that trace element of desire which seemed to operate
on the sensually alert like catnip on felines. Even her plump-
ness, which Naomi had not, at first sight, recognized for the
pregnancy it was, was somehow not unappealing. But she also
remembered the unnatural quiet of those first days, the brittle
collective mood in the workroom, and how, at last, comments
were made within her hearing—*for* her hearing—and some of
the regulars began to say that they would prefer to work at
home now, it was so much less pleasant here, and how she
was determined not to understand them, not to take their outrageous part, no matter what they thought the girl had done.

Now, somewhat belatedly, she thought, Heather would
never murder a child.

"Heather would never murder a child," she told them.
"She's completely devoted to her daughter, which I'm sure
nobody's bothered to tell you. Polly is a lovely, enchanting
little girl, who is absolutely adored by her mother. Heather
would never be capable of doing any harm to an infant." She
shook her head vehemently. "You just couldn't be further from
the truth. Hey, I'm the one who even *told* Heather about the
baby I found. She hadn't even heard about it till I went by her
house on Tuesday."

Charter made a note. The sight of his moving hand inflamed
Naomi.

"She was just stunned when I told her. She thought it was
horrible."

"Of course she did," Charter said, writing. "How else would
she react?"

"No, you don't understand. She's a *great* mother. And
somebody would have to be sick to do that to a baby."

"Perhaps she *was* sick." Charter's voice was even.

"Oh yes, the crazy new mother." Naomi shook her head.
"Christ, you guys just love this stuff, don't you? Anything that
smacks of respectable science telling you what you've always
known: women are *nuts*."

He didn't react. He was merely watching her.

"And may I ask how you came to be such an expert on the insanity of new mothers?"

He said placidly, "I am not an expert on the insanity of new mothers."

Beyond the door to the workroom, the hum of intense communal silence.

"Let us not get sidetracked," the D.A. said finally "I am here with specific questions about Heather Pratt. Your evidently very strong feelings aside, I hope that you will give my questions the benefit of your serious attention."

Struck by his gravity, Naomi felt herself nod. "I will, of course."

"Thank you," Charter said affably. "Now, you first met Miss Pratt when?"

Naomi thought. "A year and a half ago. Stephen Trask brought me some of her embroidery. She'd been working for him over at the sports center."

"You'd never seen her before."

"Never seen her, never heard of her. Of course, she was in high school before, so I really wouldn't have heard of her. Then she went to work for Stephen. As a receptionist, I'm pretty sure."

"And she was living with her grandmother up on Sabbath Creek Road at that time?"

"Yes. Her grandmother passed away last winter. But you probably know that." Naomi paused. "I remember Stephen Trask told me she did pretty well in school. She could have gone to college, I think he said." She looked squarely at Charter and said, deliberately, "Perhaps she still can."

He sighed and met her gaze. "I would consider that increasingly unlikely, Mrs. Roth." He waited for her to take this in. "Can you tell me anything else about her life?"

Naomi, weary, shrugged. "I didn't, you know, I don't really know Heather that well," she said.

"Few seem to," Charter said helpfully. He was writing again.

"I mean, I go out to the house sometimes, to collect her work, and sometimes we chat a bit. I was out there earlier this week, as I said. But she doesn't really put herself forward. She doesn't talk much about her life, you know. She's just quiet,

I guess. She's a *wonderful* mother," Naomi said again, sounding rather lame in her insistence.

Charter pursed his lips, reading what he had written. He seemed to like it as little on the page as in the air.

"What else?" he asked finally.

It seemed easier to get mad than admit her inability to come up with additional qualities.

"Well, I would think, Mr. Charter, that her being a good mother is quite possibly more germane to your inquiry than any fleeting impressions I might have about her cooking ability or talent for joke telling."

He reached a weary hand up to his crown and needlessly smoothed his steel-colored comb-over. "What do you know about Heather Pratt's personal life?"

"By which you mean her sex life. Am I correct?"

He confirmed this with an inclination of his head.

"I know what the gossip is, but she herself has never told me who Polly's father is. To tell you the truth, I'm not very curious about it. You may have noticed that Heather's taken on the entire responsibility for raising her daughter, without any help or financial support from the father. And in my view, if a man's not taking the remotest interest in his child, it really doesn't matter *who* he is. He's just a shit." She scowled at them both.

"You think it's irrelevant, then," Charter observed.

"I think it's none of your damn business. But more to the point, this is all completely beside the point. Heather didn't have that baby. She wasn't *pregnant*."

"We think she was, Naomi," Nelson said quietly. His voice retained the faintest memory of heat, but that was enough to give her an instant's pause. "Just about everyone in town thinks she was."

"Fantasy," she spat. "Absolute bullshit." She glared at Nelson.

"I wish it was fantasy." Nelson's voice was sad. "I don't think it is."

"I don't know who all these close personal friends of Heather's are, telling you this. They certainly don't hang around her much."

Charter said nothing. Maddeningly, he was waiting for her to continue, and to her own disgust, she did. "You should have seen her the other day. She had some flu, she was weak as a mouse."

Charter raised an eyebrow. "I'm not surprised. She would have given birth a few days earlier."

Naomi went cold, furious at herself. "I didn't mean . . . She wasn't . . ."

"She wasn't . . . postpartum?"

"Of course not."

"And you know this because you examined her yourself? Women's health in the hands of women?" He leaned forward. "Our bodies, ourselves?"

She sat back in her chair. "Jesus fucking Christ."

"Naomi." Nelson sat forward. "Help us out. We need to get to the bottom of this."

"Oh sure," said Naomi, her voice brittle. "I can help you out. It's an easy one. I can solve it all for you right here in my office with pure logic. If a woman can have one out-of-wedlock baby, then she's surely capable of a dozen, so that part's easy. Also, a woman who's already a slut is also a woman capable of killing a baby. So there you have it: one baby equals two babies equals dead baby. Hell"—she grinned at them—"you won't have any trouble getting a New Hampshire jury to convict based on that. C'mon, let's go over and get her now. We'll just explain to her that we've managed to eliminate the through-hikers and the gals living in sin with their boyfriends, and all the prostitutes in New Hampshire have alibis for the last two weeks, so it's her. She's from Goddard Falls. She'll understand."

"Are you finished?" Charter said, almost affably.

Naomi felt herself panic. The truth was that even though she had no deep love for Heather, it was still clearly present within her, this compulsion to speak on the girl's behalf. For whatever reason, the town had selected Heather to bear responsibility for the baby in the river, and though Naomi herself could believe no part of it, she understood the pointlessness of averting the tide. To herself was left the role of speaking for the one they had already condemned; she had not asked for it, but neither would anyone else accept it if she refused. For that alone she wanted to curse the girl.

"You say Stephen Trask brought Miss Pratt's work to you."

"Yes"—Naomi nodded—"that's right."

"And did he mention, at that time, why she was leaving the sports center?" Charter asked.

Naomi turned to him. "No, actually. And I didn't think to ask. And in any case, Stephen spoke very highly of Heather, I recall. Of her *character*."

"But you were hiring her for her needlework skills, not to teach Sunday school," Charter observed coolly. "Why do you think he was at such pains to recommend her?"

The question caught Naomi short. "I don't know," she said truthfully.

"Perhaps Stephen Trask knew something about Heather that you hadn't heard yet. Or perhaps he was anxious for you not to credit something you *had* heard."

She looked at her hands in her lap. She had hired not Heather specifically but the person who had made the exquisite work Stephen had brought her. She did not interview artisans for the collective, she included them—that was the whole point. Heather, as far as she knew, was leaving the sports center because the work there hadn't suited her. There was no mystery about it. At least, she had not known just then that there was a mystery. She shook her head.

"Mrs. Roth?"

Naomi looked up. "This is a collective of workers, Mr. Charter. I don't interview, at least in the ordinary sense. I don't 'check people out.' Heather came to me wanting work. Her work was extraordinarily good, and so she was included in the collective. I made no judgments about her personal life then, and I'm not overly anxious to make them now."

"That's admirable," Charter said dryly.

"It a pretty big leap you're making here," Naomi said, her voice steely.

He put away his pad and clicked his pen. "That doesn't make it wrong," he said.

Chapter 8

The Gene for Faith

"SO *YOU'RE* THE QUILT LADY," JOEL FRIEDMAN said, taking a glass of wine from Naomi's hand. "We heard about you. Our contractor said there was another woman from New York."

"Well, I think that about says it all." Naomi laughed. She went back to her kitchen for the Brie, then set it on the trunk that passed for her coffee table. Judith cut a piece for herself. "I've been here nine years and I'm still the woman from New York."

"Naomi came here with VISTA," Judith prompted. She had evidently told him this already.

"No kidding," he said. He sounded—astonishingly—impressed.

"No kidding. I was indeed part of that legion of light. I came with my ex-husband a year after we graduated. Well"—she laughed—"after I graduated. Daniel was supposed to be writing a thesis about Paul Robeson, but he kind of petered out after a year or two. I wanted to go to South America, but this is as far as we got." She drank her wine. The tannin bit her tongue.

"Not quite as exotic as South America," Judith said.

"No. But there was still stuff for us to do. I mean, unemployment was something absurd, like 40 percent. And the women—forget it. Daniel started a maple syrup co-op."

"He still around?" asked Joel.

Naomi shook her head. "Moved on to a higher karmic plane. Woodstock, New York." She saw that they did not know precisely what to make of this, and shrugged. "He went to live with an old college friend. Five socialists on a farm where nothing gets farmed, floated by somebody's trust fund. Revolutionary inertia: the last social disease of the eighties." Naomi grinned, disarming them. "You know, these guys, they want to change the world, but only if they can do it by their shining example. If you have to actually make an effort, that's cheating. But—and I'm sure you'll agree this is shocking—the good folks of Goddard, New Hampshire, did not turn into Luddites because Daniel Roth moved into town and built a house without a television. When I got all these women together and we started making money, he acted as if I'd become a Reaganite. Suddenly I'm a counterrevolutionary because I want a toilet that flushes! Anyway"—she sighed—"I'm sure he's happy. I have no doubt he's living a life of virtue, preaching to the converted and accomplishing absolutely nothing."

Joel smiled, a little nervously. "Well," he said, "he's bucking the trend, anyway."

"The trend?" said Naomi.

"Oh sure. They're fishing their draft notices out of the ashes, you know? Half the training program at Morgan Stanley knew each other from the Little Red School House. There was one guy I remember from college—this was a little before your time," Joel told his wife, "he led a sit-in to protest ROTC on campus. Then he dropped out to organize full-time. Then he disappeared—I think he got radical. I just assumed I'd never see him again. I swear to God"—he grinned—"I saw him in a suit on Madison Avenue a few months ago. He smiled at me. He *blushed* at me." Joel shook his shaggy head, smirking. "Like it was all one great mass adolescence and everybody just grew up."

"Hey"—his wife hit his arm—"speak for yourself. Some of us are still out there hacking away. Look at what Naomi's doing. I might get ambitious myself. Start up a New Hampshire branch of the National Abortion Rights Action League or something."

Naomi grinned. "Hate to disillusion you, Judith, but NARAL already exists in New Hampshire. This is a pro-choice state."

She was stunned. "You're kidding."

"I'm not. Always has been. But it isn't a women's issue here, it's a privacy issue. Believe me, they'd as soon hunt feminists the way they hunt deer, but they'd rather hunt the government than either of them. They loathe Washington here. That's why they love election years, cause the candidates come and kiss their butts."

"Gee," Judith said, still dealing with it. *"NARAL."*

"Oh, there's still plenty to do, don't worry," said Naomi. She got to her feet and went to check the stew. "This is a place where state-funded education doesn't even kick in till first grade," she called from the kitchen. "It's assumed that women are home, you see. Men get custody of the kids in divorces here, even when they've beaten their wives to a pulp. Lesbian parents? Forget it. Equal pay for work of comparable value? Dream on. Listen," she said, carrying the large pot to the dining table and placing it on a wooden board, "women barely speak to one another here. That's the single thing that keeps everything so static. I mean"—she ladled stew into their bowls—"of course they *speak* to each other, but they don't talk about their lives. Never. You've heard of Yankee reserve? Everybody's in their own shell, so you get gossip but no meaningful exchange."

"I guess they call it the Granite State for a reason." Joel grinned. He was older than Judith, Naomi thought, his bushy mustache and unimposed-upon hair gone early gray. He had that distracted brilliance she had always liked, the kind that could eradicate ancient diseases but couldn't figure out how to match socks. Indeed, she observed, he was staring at his socks even at that moment.

"Oh," Judith said, "*Joel*. Didn't I say you should change?"

"You said I should change my pants. You didn't say anything about my socks."

Judith gave Naomi a look that told all.

Joel frowned at his feet. "I went down to the river in back of our house. The Sabertooth River, or whatever it's called."

"Sabbathday." Naomi laughed.

"Sabbathday." He considered. "Discovered on the Sabbath?"

"Well, not exactly. These settlers were on their way to their new homes, and they stopped by the river on the Sabbath. They started thinking about what it would be like when they got where they were going, and they turned around and went home. That's the story, anyway."

"Is that true?" Judith said.

"I don't know. It's what I heard. And they named it Sabbathday in honor of their change of heart."

"Our Sabbath?" Joel laughed. "Or theirs?"

"Oh, theirs. I don't think there were too many Jews in New

Hampshire two centuries ago. There aren't that many now. And anyway, then it would be Shabbosday, wouldn't it?"

"I guess." He grinned.

Naomi surveyed the table. "I think we're ready."

They came and sat, Judith and Joel across from Naomi, an arrangement she regretted almost immediately, since it must look to them as if she were somehow interviewing them. She wasn't. Well, she was, but they had already passed.

She watched them eat. Joel threw salt over his stew.

"You know, the house you bought is beautiful. I've never been inside it, but I've driven past it about a million times."

"The last owners moved south." Judith nodded. "Virginia, I think they said. Gaylords, from Boston."

"Yes, I knew her," said Naomi. "They were up here in the summers. She bought some things from my collective." She lifted her glass. "Are you winterized?"

"We'll soon find out." Judith grinned. "The contractor thinks we might have some trouble with the plumbing."

Naomi rolled her eyes. "That's Ashley. He's always got an eye on the next crisis. I once had him in to refit a storm door, and of course we ended up with a whole wall ripped open. Water damage, he insisted. Still"—she sighed—"you can trust him. He won't make off with anything, and he won't start somebody else's job till he's finished yours." She shrugged. "Who knows. Maybe there *was* water damage. My ex-husband built this house. He sort of made it up as he went along."

Judith smiled. Her hair wound down in tight rings over her chest. Her eyes were set a millimeter too close for *Vogue*, and her nose had a convex curve another woman might have fixed years ago.

Joel was already dragging a heel of bread over his plate. "This is so good," he said, and she took the hint and got him more. "I haven't had a home-cooked meal since we moved here."

"The kitchen," Judith said quickly.

"Right." He glanced at her. "And it'll only get worse once she starts her job."

Naomi looked at Judith. Their previous conversation, amid the orange tomatoes and shiny cucumbers, had not covered this rather essential topic.

"I'm starting at a law firm in Peytonville next week," Judith said.

"You're a lawyer?" Naomi heard, and rued, the note of disapproval in her voice.

"Oh, don't look so scandalized." Judith laughed. "This firm has the public-defense contract for central New Hampshire. Indigent cow thieves, as my dear husband says. Well"—she shrugged—"at least that's one thing I never saw at Manhattan Legal Aid, though I think I saw just about everything else." She sighed and looked down at her plate. "Of course, I was going to wait awhile before starting, but I don't really see the point now. I'm going a little nuts rattling around here. And Joel's started already. So I called Peytonville and said I'd come on Monday."

"I know you're going to teach at Dartmouth," Naomi told Joel apologetically. "But I don't know *what* you're going to teach."

"Biology. Well, it's all very confusing. Genetics, specifically. And I'm technically at the medical school," he said. "I mean, my appointment's there, but my lab's in the science complex, attached to the biology department."

"And he doesn't actually *teach* anybody," Judith said dryly. "Sometimes I wonder why they bother admitting students to these places at all."

"Oh now." He smiled. "Students are fine, but I'm not a very gifted teacher. I just like to get on with things in the lab. And Dartmouth offered me less teaching for more money and a better lab." He shrugged. "So sue me."

"Genetics," Naomi mused. "Watson and Crick. Those fine gentlemen who shoved Rosalind Franklin out of the way in their noble—or should I say Nobel?—pursuit of the double helix."

He put up his hands. "Hey, no argument from me there!"

"I read somewhere that one day they'll be able to look at our DNA and tell us what kind of cancer we're going to get."

"Oh, not just cancer," Joel said eagerly, a scientist taking the bit. "Everything's there. Well, we can't prove it yet, but we're going to be able to see a whole life in a single cell. One little bit of a baby's skin and we'll be able to tell if he's going to have blue eyes, or a stroke, or a good sense of balance, or cancer, or genius . . ."

"Or bad breath," Judith said tersely. "But do we want to *know*? We've blundered along for a few thousand years without knowing how we're going to die. Why would we want to change that now?"

"Because, in the case of disease we want to treat it early, and in the case of genius we want to nurture it."

"Sounds very *Brave New World*," Naomi said affably. "I don't think I'd want to know if my child—"

"No, you would," Joel said. "I mean, if you thought about it, you probably would."

Naomi, abruptly quiet, understood that they had arrived on some hazardous ground. But she did not like the silence, so she went on as if there were no silence to break.

"Well, I'm glad you're here." She looked at Judith. "It's great news for me."

Joel, too, looked at his wife. He smiled. "She didn't want to come, but I threw her over my shoulder. After all, I'm the man, right?"

"Please." Judith rolled her eyes.

"And I don't see bringing up kids in New York."

"You have kids?" Naomi looked at them both. They were looking at each other. An entire conversation, inaudible to her, passed between them. At last Judith turned to her.

"Not yet," she said. "Maybe soon." She listlessly moved a carrot around her plate with the tip of her fork. "My mother came from Germany after the war. She was the only one in her family to make it out. She had a very specific interpretation of procreation, which she thoughtfully passed on to my sister and me. Basically, she told us that if we didn't have children it would mean Hitler had won."

Something in Naomi's stomach clenched. "That's pretty heavy for a little kid."

Judith, unaccountably, smiled. "Oh, I don't think she meant it to burden us. She just wanted us to see the world the way she saw it."

"She was a character." Joel shook his head. "Some people coming out of the camps were like that, you know. Almost hedonists. They were determined to have joy every day. Of course she hated almost everyone."

"Except her daughters," Judith reassured Naomi.

"Right. The two of you, she completely adored. You were

the reason she was saved. I mean"—he smiled fondly—"to have you."

"Yeah." Judith held her glass for Naomi to fill again. "That was the whole point to life. Life was a bunch of threads, and the threads were families, and they were dangling down through the centuries, all the way back to the beginning of time. Or Abraham and Isaac, anyway. And then someone came along and tried to cut through the threads with these big cosmic scissors, and of course he did this very efficiently, but not quite efficiently enough to finish the job, so some little threads were missed. And so now the ones he missed have to make up for the ones he cut." She shrugged. "Anyway, that's how my sister and I inherited the responsibility of repopulating the world. My sister says it's why she became a midwife."

"A midwife!" Naomi was impressed.

Judith nodded. "Rachel went and studied with those women on the commune in Tennessee. They're the ones who wrote that *Spiritual Midwifery* book that tells you how labor pains are supposed to be psychedelic and holy."

Naomi laughed. "And so, has your sister fulfilled her responsibilities? I mean, does she have kids of her own?"

Judith seemed to consider. "Well, yes," she said. Her voice was surprisingly soft. "She has two. A boy and a girl."

"That's nice. One of each." Naomi's voice was bright. It seemed awkwardly bright suddenly.

"Yes," said Judith. She looked past Naomi, her gaze fixed. Naomi fought an urge to turn around and see what was so completely interesting. But then she spoke. "So what do you think. Would a kid raised in New Hampshire just automatically grow up to be Pat Buchanan or Phyllis Schlafly?"

Naomi smiled at her. "Well, no. But you'd have your work cut out for you. I mean, I've been here nine years and I've never had a real woman friend." *Until now*, she was too shy to add.

"Well, the sixties did get to most places, in the end," Judith said. "I mean, some places it didn't turn up till the seventies, but still."

"Nope." Naomi shook her head. "They headed it off at the Connecticut River. They painted over the road signs so people kept driving till they hit Maine." She speared a carrot out of the gravy. "It just never really happened here."

"But how can that be true?" Joel said. "I mean, there's no difference between New Hampshire and Vermont, is there?"

"Actually," Naomi said, "there *is* a difference. They don't even look alike, really, if you think about it. Vermont has rolling hills and green valleys; you tend not to get them on this side of the river. A geologist I met once told me that, geologically, they're quite distinct from each other. They actually belong to different plates or something, he said. The back-to-the-land types found this particular land very inhospitable for their purposes, while the land across the Connecticut River was a bit more forgiving. There were something like a hundred communes over there. You know"—she tore a piece of brown bread and spread it with apple butter—"Vermont had about a 10 percent population hike in the sixties."

"That's a lot of hippies," Judith observed.

"Not just hippies," Naomi said. "The other reason was skiing."

"Skiing." Joel laughed. "What does skiing have to do with it?"

"Oh, skiing was terribly important in the sixties. It was new, for one thing. I mean, it had been around for decades, but now there were big centers with lifts and snowmaking, and there were the new interstates to bring people up from Boston or New York for the weekend and still get them home in time for work on Monday. A lot of folks came and got hooked, and they looked around at what was happening in society and just decided to chuck their work and do what they liked. So you had a whole state full of college graduates running snowplows and tending bar. And after a few years, when they'd gotten it out of their systems, they dusted off the old degrees and started up businesses or began selling real estate, or they hung out their shingles, and *voilà*: a state full of professionals with residual political commitments. And of course, people go where there are already people doing what *they* want to be doing. People like to be with their own kind. They want to live among like-minded souls. Unlike me, of course," she said with acrid self-deprecation. Then she smiled at Judith. "You said it yourself, you wished you'd moved to Putney."

Husband and wife exchanged a loaded look. "I would have *loved* to move to Putney," Judith said.

"Lots of great people in Putney," Naomi prompted. "They have a food co-op . . ."

"Yeah, yeah." Then Judith smiled. "I knew this woman. She was a weaver in Putney. About five years ago she decided to move to Israel. She wanted to try living on a kibbutz. So she's out in the field there, picking lemons or whatever, within shouting distance of the Lebanese border, and a guy comes up to her, says, 'Don't I know you? Aren't you in the Putney co-op?' "

Naomi grinned. "Still, I'm glad you came here. Seven more of us and we'll have a minyan."

"That's supposed to be all men," Joel said, tearing off another piece of bread.

Judith leaned conspiratorially toward Naomi. "Got him away from New York just in time. There's a religious revival going on. This charismatic rabbi near Lincoln Center's pulling 'em back into the fold like a Venus flytrap."

"Ouch," Naomi said.

"Absolutely. It's invasion of the body snatchers, the Goldberg variation. People who toasted the death of God with LSD are studying Talmud with their kids. A woman I worked with started trading cases with me so she could get home before sundown on Fridays."

"But you're a scientist," said Naomi to Joel. "How could you possibly reconcile genetics with God? You can't believe in both."

He had evidently considered this problem before. "I don't know. I think you believe what you believe. You let the details sort themselves out later."

Judith rolled her eyes. "God's a pretty big detail, sweetie."

"Well, I'm perfectly comfortable with the fact that there is no God." Naomi shrugged. Joel, pursing his lips, said nothing. "I used to say 'agnostic,' " she went on. "Then one day it occurred to me: who am I kidding? I'm not agnostic. Saying you're agnostic implies that you're engaged in the active, ongoing pursuit of an understanding of God, and truthfully, I hung up my pursuit years ago. It would be like saying you're training for a marathon when you're not even jogging around the block—it's misleading and even a little dangerous."

"Dangerous?" Joel looked at her.

"Yeah, you get to thinking you're not going to drop dead

from a heart attack because you've been doing all that imaginary training. I mean," Naomi said, "you get complacent about an afterlife because you can't admit to yourself that you really just don't believe. Like the God you don't acknowledge is going to give you points for not admitting your disavowal outright."

"But how can you be *sure*?" Joel leaned forward.

She smiled at him. "I must lack the gene for faith."

To her amusement, he seemed to take this seriously. "Perhaps you do. Perhaps it comes down to that, after all."

"You have to forgive him." Judith leaned in. "It's his version of a midlife crisis. This is what a midlife crisis looks like in a man who's basically happy with his life. Like I said, I got him out of New York just in time. In another year, I might have had two sinks, two refrigerators, two dishwashers . . ."

"But you said you *wanted* two refrigerators in the new house." Joel frowned.

"Yeah, sure. But not to keep kosher. It's to keep sane. I'm going to have to freeze all the stuff I haul up from Zabar's. And as you ought to remember, my dear husband, when I'm working, it's dinner on ice. You may have transported me to the land of Live Free or Die, but once I start in Peytonville, you're going to have to get used to defrost and reheat again." She shook a silver-ringed index finger at him. "*Much* as I love you, you know the cow thieves come first."

"I know." Joel smiled.

Naomi offered coffee and got up to make it.

"It's kind of funny," she said to Judith, who had followed her into the kitchen, "when my ex-husband and I first came here, I was just charmed by that. 'Live Free or Die' on every license plate. I was thinking: 'Born Free.' Lions in Africa. I was thinking, you know, out in the wilderness, the feeling of freedom and exhilaration. Like: go out and really *live* your life, don't just sit around and let it happen to you. Be free! You know? Then one day I was sitting on the porch at Tom and Whit's, watching these two guys stock up their car to go out hunting. They've got a Stars and Stripes tied to the CB antenna and this bumper sticker that says *America: Love it or go back to wherever you came from*. And I look at these guys driving away with their guns on the top of their car, and it suddenly hits me: 'Live Free or Die' doesn't have anything to do with being free—like, up on the mountaintops looking at the view. It means 'Better dead than red.' That's all it means." She smirked at Judith. "Isn't that pathetic?"

"The slogan?" she asked. "Or the fact that it took you so long to figure it out?"

Naomi laughed. "Both, I guess."

"But you're still here. I mean, if you felt that way, why did you stay?"

Naomi's smile faded. "I *like* it here," she said. It wasn't true, but it should have been true, so she said it and Judith appeared satisfied. After all, what wasn't to like? Goddard was the town people who lived in cities longed for, the one made of classically austere New England houses and surrounded by unbearably beautiful wilderness. The people here had made room for her, in their chill and unloving way. They had let her build a business for them without burdening her with their gratitude. Judith went out to the table. Naomi turned on the faucet.

She had stayed because of the business, though it was clear to Naomi that Flourish could easily survive her departure, or that she could have found some way to run it from another location. Or perhaps she had stayed because of what she and Daniel had begun together, since she, at least, was still committed to everything they had planned; she was stronger than that small spasm of selfish disappointment that had so easily borne him away. But that, too, had been transformed the moment she reached into the river water and touched the baby, when she saw that the truth was far more simple.

She remembered, years before, how Daniel had called out to the God he didn't believe in as that young girl fired shots from the Sabbathday riverbank: through his panic, a glimpse of something so deeply buried neither of them had even suspected it was there. Now it seemed that the baby might be like that, for her—a buried thing surfacing, a bottle with a message for Naomi alone. And when she deciphered the message, she would know what her life was to be about. She had stayed behind for this, in other words.

"I wish they *were* just cow thieves," she said when Judith returned to the kitchen.

"Pardon?" She set down the dirty plates.

"Oh, thanks. What you said before about the cow thieves?

I wish they were just cow thieves. I'm afraid you'll find it's just as nasty up here as it was in Manhattan." She pressed the button on her coffee grinder, and its whining churn filled the room. Judith waited until it was over.

"I doubt that," she said. "You have no idea how bad it's gotten. We're seeing gang stuff, like in L.A., and the drugs are out of control. Everything is just breaking down. The kids are the worst. They just don't care anymore. The boys'll shoot somebody and feel nothing at all, and the girls drop their babies down the garbage chute. It's beyond sad, really. It's just unspeakable. I got to the point where I started to think it might be better to live somewhere—"

"We had a baby." Naomi cut her off.

"I . . . what?"

Naomi got milk from the refrigerator. "We had a baby here like that."

"Like what?"

"Like dead," Naomi said, a touch impatiently. "Somebody found a baby in the river last weekend. Dead." Ashamed of herself, she swallowed. "Actually, I was the one who found it. Her." She stopped. Judith was looking at the floor. "I'm sorry to be the one to tell you, though it's all over town. I'm surprised nobody's felt the need to disillusion you about our bucolic little hamlet before me. Actually"—she eyed Judith—"I'm a little sorry *I* did."

"No, no," Judith said, her voice soft. "I'm glad you did." She shook her head. Her tight black curls caught the kitchen light.

"They have a suspect." She shut her eyes tightly, as if to render the image of Heather invisible. "But they're so wrong. I don't know what—"

"What do you mean they're wrong?" Judith said, her voice tense. "Do you know something? Do you know they're wrong about their suspect?"

Naomi reached for the handle of her kettle, and it vibrated at her touch as the water readied itself to boil. "I know the girl. She's in my collective. She had a . . . well, I guess, a *connection* with somebody. Somebody married, of course. So she lives in Goddard Falls with her daughter. She takes care of the baby, does samplers for Flourish. She doesn't bother anybody." Naomi looked up at Judith and set her jaw, in-

censed, but more and more she understood that it was herself
she was most angry at—at her own lingering hesitation to take
Heather's part. Surely she could spare the gesture of—wasn't
this the whole point?—*sisterhood* for this one girl, lost to the
fold. Perhaps Heather Pratt was only waiting for that gesture,
that offer of community, to blossom into—what? A fully self-
actualized human being? An earth mother? A warrior woman?
Of *course* it was a faintly comical notion, but why did she
keep wanting to believe it was possible? "And now they've
apparently decided that she was pregnant and she had this baby
and stabbed it, and I just—"

"Stabbed," Judith nearly shouted. "What do you mean,
stabbed?"

Naomi bit her lip against remembering it. "The baby
was . . . she'd been . . . You know." She stopped. "I'm sorry, I
just don't want to think about it. It was so . . ." She gave up.
"That poor little baby." Something in her throat condensed.

"I shouldn't have asked." She heard Judith's voice. "It must
have been terrible for you."

Wordless, she nodded. The kettle sang and she switched off
the gas.

"They've got to be wrong, that's all," Naomi said. "It's
some kind of primitive dynamic, like from an anthropology
text. A calamity hits the village, like a plague or a flood or
something, and the people turn on their local recluse or outcast
and string 'em up. It's disgusting." She closed her eyes,
preemptively weary. "I just wish I knew how to stop it."

"Why is it your job to stop it?" Judith asked. She was leaning against the door frame.

"I don't know that either," Naomi said honestly. "But it just
is. It's expected of me."

"Ah," she said darkly. "Outsider defending outcast. *Auslän-
der aus!*"

Naomi sighed. "I guess. Something like that." She forced a
smile. "Anyway, nothing's happened yet. There's still a chance
they'll get a grip and point themselves in the right direction.
Do you mind if we, I mean, could we not talk about it anymore?"

"Of course," said Judith. "I'm sorry."

"No, I am." She reached into the freezer and extracted two

pints of liquid gold. "For you urban refugees, I went to special lengths." She spoke with forced good spirits.

Judith, however, was genuinely delighted. "Häagen-Dazs!"

"Häagen-Dazs," Joel exclaimed from the dining room. "Where did you find it?"

"Oh now," Naomi laughed. "You just hang on there. You don't expect me to divulge all my secrets at once, do you?"

Joel's eyes were wide. "Oh my God. Rum raisin. Naomi, I thank you from the bottom of my heart."

"The bottom of his *stomach*," Judith corrected, carrying the coffee mugs out to the dining table. "The bottom of his ever-*increasing* stomach."

"I don't care what you say. Nobody can make ice cream like the Danes."

Naomi nearly howled. "Danes my butt. 'Häagen-Dazs' was dreamed up by some marketing person. It has no meaning at all, didn't you know that? It's words from a language that doesn't exist. The stuff's made in Jersey or somewhere."

"You're not serious." Joel looked wounded. "Say it ain't so, Joe."

"It's so. *Joel*." She grinned. She liked him enormously. The telephone rang.

"Just be a minute," she said. She went back into the kitchen. Mary Sully spoke her name as soon as she picked it up.

"Hello, Mary." Naomi's thoughts raced on ahead. She wanted to be ready.

"Naomi," Mary said again. "It's so awful. You won't be-lieve."

I will, she steeled herself. "What is it, Mary?"

"Naomi, they arrested Heather Pratt last night. For murdering the baby you found. Oh, can you *believe*—"

"All right," she said. She was amazed at how calm her own voice sounded. The enormity of her own task, the cup she couldn't bring herself to turn aside. "All right, Mary. Thank you for letting me know. But, Mary"—she took a breath before saying this, before making her public debut as the girl's de-fender—"let's not get ahead of ourselves. They may have their suspicions, but I'm sure they don't have the slightest idea what really happened. Let's just see if we can try to give Heather the benefit of our doubt. She needs our help now, not condem-nation. Let's—"

"No, Naomi," said Mary in a kind of wonder. "No, it isn't that. I mean, you don't understand. They arrested her last night and they said she confessed. Heather confessed." Naomi rocked, trying to make the floor stand still. Her hand on the phone was wet. "She did it, Naomi. She killed her baby. She stabbed it with some kind of knitting needle." Then Mary paused. A gulp of air, a twisted sob. Her new voice deep with rage: "That little *bitch*."

Part 2
Heather

My hand moves into darkness as I write, The adulterous woman lost her nose and ears; the man was fined. *I drain the glass. I still want to return to that hotel room by the station*

to hear all night the goods trains coming and leaving.

—Sarah Maguire, "Spilt Milk"

Chapter 9

The City on a Hill

NOT MANY PEOPLE KNEW THAT HEATHER PRATT had once been a matriculated student at Dartmouth College. She barely knew it herself, she had been in and out of that place so fast, and though it had taken place only two years earlier, it already seemed an immeasurably long time ago. When Heather thought of the episode at all, it was as a kind of white-and-green blur—the stark white buildings at the edges of the college quadrangle, its boundaries denuded by the trees it had lost to Dutch elm disease, but still verdant in its uniform lawn, dissected by straight white paths. She remembered the week she had spent unpacking and then rearranging her few belongings in North Massachusetts Hall, trying to find a common language with the girls from Choate or Andover or Fieldston, the nationally ranked tennis player from Palo Alto, the Olympic skiing hopeful from Nome, as they tentatively formed alliances and fanned out over the campus.

How it had all come to pass in the first place she still wasn't entirely sure. In Goddard, the high-school guidance counselor routinely pushed the top two or three in the class in the direction of Hanover, managing to get a kid in every decade or so, and the college tended to turn a lenient face to the cream of New Hampshire students—part of an academic noblesse oblige that went back centuries. When they accepted Heather Pratt, she was far too alarmed to express doubt.

Not that she wasn't clever. Heather was bright enough, and she read, but she lacked that special thing—the hunger—that served as catalyst for a mind truly going places. It had never occurred to her to go anywhere, for example. She had no sense of the world beyond what she had actually seen of it, which was basically the White Mountains only, with a senior trip to walk the Freedom Trail in Boston and consume platters of spaghetti and meatballs in the North End. Of the vast and intense variety of the earthly domain, Heather knew only enough to get by, nor did she care to know more. She did not yearn to see the few sorry icons—Hollywood, Disney World— her own country and culture had managed to drum up, and travel to other countries was incomprehensible—what possible purpose could *that* serve? The known world of the mountains, the little towns that stuck like tenacious burrs to their hillsides and riverbanks, had drawn itself around her as a reliably comfortable thing, and in Heather's experience, comfort was not to be taken as a given.

Through this myopia, the Dartmouth course catalogue— with its bulk and variety, with its heady, complex requirements for that vaguely unreal item called a bachelor's degree—was a blurred and terrifying churn. Heather, who did not make a habit of thinking in terms of what she wanted, looked around herself in her dormitory or the great chattering dining hall and could barely register that she was of an age with these avid proto-professionals. Watching them, absorbing the rhythms if not the content of their debate, she found that she bore them no ill will at all, nor was she covetous of what they had or their sheer effortlessness in this dizzying place. They were simply Other. When they paused in their revels of mutuality, she knew that they must know her for what she was not, and that they must then, with no particular rancor, purge her from their midst. Her decision, when it came, was merely to do it first.

Of course, she was not the only one of her kind at Dartmouth, but the handful of impoverished local kids—who seemed to find one another at once—had a kind of vicious tunnel vision about the college, a determination to milk the place for every drop of enrichment and future prosperity it might be inclined to throw in their direction, and she could not share that, either. For Heather there was no goal at the end of the tunnel, and nothing for her to focus on amid the blur of Fair Isle sweaters and waving lacrosse sticks. Her fellow New Englanders, those noble savages lifted to this city on a hill by the power of rank aspiration and raw tenacity, seemed to sense this about her, marking her as pariah even before the wealthier offspring of the Eastern megalopolis did.

Her two roommates were a sweet girl with a tiny Southern voice and a dazed expression, and a rough-and-ready army brat whose mission, those first days, was to figure out which ste-

reotypes of men were in which fraternities, so she could concentrate her efforts. They shared a large overheated room with
a small adjacent chamber into which their bunk and single beds
barely fit, and a bathroom with an ancient, yellowing tub.
Heather went to a freshman party and sat for an English placement exam and met her advisor, who seemed reluctant to ad-
vise. She learned the school song, with its romantic
idealization of the White Mountains—*the still north, the hill
winds*—and incomprehensible lyric about "the granite of New
Hampshire in their muscles and their brains," which everyone
giggled at but Heather found somehow insulting: *granite for
brains!* On the fourth evening, she accompanied the army brat
to Alpha Delta, where a rugby player danced with her on the
sticky basement floor, then took her upstairs to his fetid chamber. She did not know why, precisely, she went with him. Sex
was something she had always assumed she would have sometime, with somebody, but she hadn't otherwise spent much
effort thinking about it. The rugby player, Heather decided,
had known this about her, or had taken her nonchalance for
sophistication. Either interpretation pleased her, and besides,
he was himself pleasant, in a drunken and otherwise distracted
manner. He breathed malt into her brown hair, his fingernails
were clean. When he was finished, she felt altogether that some
benign but hardly earth-shattering thing had been accomplished, though as far as she herself was concerned, she felt
the same as before, essentially. They parted amiably, though
it later occurred to Heather that he might have been half asleep
at the time. In any case, she made her own way home after
midnight and, forgetting the security code at her all-women's
dormitory, was forced to wake up a girl in one of the ground-
floor rooms, thereby acquiring for herself the woman's resentment and a fully formed reputation in one swift and
economic motion.

She did not want to go to sleep. She did not want to let
herself into the tiny room that was nominally her own, with
its little beds and breathing, sleeping girls. Instead, Heather
wandered into the dormitory common room, a dingy parlor
with an old piano and battered armchairs arranged in a silent
semicircle that faced the door, like a disappointed but stubborn
audience. There were no sounds from the hallways around and
above her, and even the battling stereos that were normally

perched on the windowsills of the dormitory next door—facing out in a gesture of collegiate altruism—had been retired for the night. There was moonlight on the college green, the white chill of autumn moonlight which Heather knew well enough— it was the specific moonlight of her own home, bleak and hard and utterly familiar—and yet over the coddled lawns that moonlight struck her as discordantly alien, and she felt as if she were somewhere far away in some other country she had never sought to visit, rather than only an hour from the house on Sabbath Creek Road.

On the jutting fireplace mantel lay a small green book, pocket-sized, tooled in real leather. She picked it up and fanned the leaves against her thumb, riffling the silvery alphabet marks, the pages unpopulated but for the lines that waited to be filled with names and places and numbers. Inside the front cover was the owner's own name, written in a gesture of pure optimism, of plain anticipation of the life that was to be led in this place, among these people. For the person who had left the address book here, Heather saw, the strangers in the classrooms and the dining hall and the fraternity basements were only raw material—like whatever stuff the alchemists had turned to gold. They were the unknown quantities, not yet converted into companions, or lovers, or rivals, perhaps. Heather was suddenly, retroactively aware of the formation of a social structure within this miasma of her peers, the spontaneous divisions and connections that were occurring all around her as she herself wandered along her way, the couples and feuds, the newly minted best buddies. She tried for a moment to imagine that this was her own book, its pages crowded with ink, with men and women jostling for space, each entry suggestive of a face or a voice or some incident that was somehow pleasant to remember. She felt a heaviness grow in her, then a surge of panic. That was when Heather knew.

By midweek, she had tentatively told her roommates that what she wanted to do, really, was study physical therapy.

Physical therapy? Um, they exchanged glances, did Dartmouth offer a degree in physical therapy?

The thing was, it didn't. So Heather took herself in hand and went to the Dean of Freshmen.

Physical therapy was its own red herring, of course. She hadn't the least idea what a physical therapist did, but it sounded so exact and so concrete: a discipline. To Heather it seemed to offer an unarguable logic. "What I really want to do," she told the grim woman, whose mind was elsewhere, "is physical therapy. I know that now."

"But"—the dean glanced down at the file in her lap—"*Heather*, you know that Dartmouth is a liberal-arts institution. We offer the bachelor of arts degree only. There's no reason you couldn't go on to get a specific degree in physical therapy later, but here the emphasis is on a more well-rounded education."

Heather shrugged. She wasn't obligated to say anything, she knew. Her being here was enough to get it done.

"If you knew that you wanted to be a physical therapist," the dean pushed, a little irritated, "why did you apply here?"

"I just decided," Heather said. "I mean, it just became clear to me, you know?"

The dean did know, and Heather could see it. Lurking behind her expression of rank disapproval was the accusation that Heather might have thought this out a bit earlier, thereby allowing some truly deserving poor kid from New Hampshire to have a shot at a decent life. But no.

She was out that afternoon, and back in Goddard Falls by dinnertime.

Chapter 10

A Speck of Dust

THAT AUTUMN, HEATHER FOUND WORK IN GOD-
dard, at the sports center.

The sports center was new, a bit of the federal brass ring
the town council had managed to grab as it whooshed overhead, swinging south to Keene and Manchester and the snug,
prosperous towns scattered between them. The center had
opened that June with enormous local fanfare, but when the
summer residents headed home it became clear that townspeople considered working out in the gym, with its new machines
and shiny free weights, something of a laughable activity, and
they were disinclined to learn the gentlemanly sports of squash
and racquetball, leaving the little courts abandoned—shiny
wooden rooms hoarding stale air. Swimming was the only
draw, and swarms of kids turned up after school for group
lessons, but the center stood depressingly empty throughout
most of the day and showed little promise of ever being able
to sever the federal umbilicus.

Stephen Trask, a son of Goddard Falls who'd made it to the
University of New Hampshire and then beat it right back home
after graduation, was the director of the center, and he hired
Heather in part because he appreciated the gravity of what
she'd just done and wanted to be in a position to lean on her
about going back to school. Trask still had family in Goddard
Falls, but he lived in Goddard now, in a new ranch on a new
street near the Stop & Shop, with his wife and sons. The
Trasks—who read books and belonged to a mail-order video
service that allowed them to rent foreign films—were probably
the only Goddard residents who tried in more than a perfunc-
tory way to make friends with some of the summer people, an
effort that consistently proved frustrating to all concerned,
since the couple hoped to talk about culture and politics and
the visitors seemed to want to talk only about local lore and
the scandals of Goddard neighbors they barely knew. Celia,

his wife, worked too, at Tom and Whit's, and even though she came from Manchester, she'd done well in Goddard, where she was considered sophisticated but still comfortably native. When things got bad for Heather at the sports center, it was Celia's idea to bring the girl to Naomi.

But things didn't get bad for a long time, because in fact Heather liked her job. She liked leaving her house in the morning and waiting by the roadside for Martina, who was the center's entire housekeeping staff, to pick her up and ride her into Goddard. She liked Martina, who had been born again in a West Lebanon church made of cinder blocks, with an ARE YOU ON THE RIGHT ROAD? sign out front. And she liked the center itself, a clean white box of a building with skylights over the basketball court and a cozy lunch bar in back whose windows overlooked the slope down to the Sabbathday River. Perhaps most of all, Heather liked the fact that from her swivel chair at the reception desk she could blamelessly watch the interplay of husband and wife, of parent and child, of boyfriend and girlfriend. Her experience of what she had, since the age of reason, thought of as "normal" life was little more than superficial, since her own and her grandmother's interaction with neighbors had always been minimal and since high school had a skewed normality all its own. Here, in her official capacity, she loved the fresh tone of authority in her own voice, her ability to answer the questions asked of her. She loved introducing herself on the telephone as "Heather Pratt, over at the sports center," and hearing the "Ah yes" of recognition that had absolutely nothing to do with her. She typed Stephen Trask's letters and checked IDs and called up parents when their kids got too rowdy in the pool, and she walked the rooms and corridor with an authoritative gait, making a note of anything that needed seeing to, since who else would know what to look for?

She felt, for the first time, the satisfaction, if not the nobility, of work, the comfort of real fatigue at the end of her day. She enjoyed being able to return to her role as her grandmother's emissary to the world of the town of Goddard, a post she had filled de facto while in school. Now, for the first time since graduation, she had her observations to offer at dinnertime. She had the relative variety of her days, the relative panorama of humanity upon which to embroider her stories as she and

Pick embroidered together, and she knew the good effect of this steady, carefully regulated influx of other people into the stilted air of the farmhouse.

Pick, who had earned her nickname as a perfectionist eight-year-old (the precise incident involved a Four-Star quilt, assembled over a period of ten months, disassembled for six, and reassembled for a solid year, all because it wasn't good enough the first time), was nearly seventy when Heather came back from Hanover. She was frail, like something that had grown too tall and now buckled under its own height, but she was still up most days at dawn. When she had pain, she found something to do sitting down, and she had pain a lot, which was why the house was full of objects she had made—pillows etched with flowers, sheets crowded with pattern, every chair needlepointed and every floor hidden by some confection of salvaged cloth. Pick had taken care of Heather on her own since Ruth, her daughter and Heather's mother, had set out west from Goddard Falls fifteen years earlier, her trail turning cold shortly thereafter, somewhere west of Chicago. Heather did not remember Ruth and seldom had occasion to miss her. Pick remembered Ruth all too clearly, and so missed her even less.

In her time, Pick too had been a good student—or what passed for a good student if you were a girl when she was a girl—but she accepted with no resentment at all the smallness of her place in the world. She did not fault Heather for coming home; on the contrary, she had endured the ten or so days of her granddaughter's college career in a general anticipation of Heather's return, and she marked the happy occasion by killing and roasting one of her portlier hens (as if Heather's modest sexual foray—which she kept to herself—had somehow marked her as a prodigal). Heather unpacked her bag, and returned her clothes and books and sewing to their places with a sense of intense satisfaction, since she was back in the one place where no one questioned her oddnesses—to her face, at any rate. And she was content. At least until she saw Ashley.

Later, she would date the change in her circumstances from this moment, like some temporal guillotine crashing her asunder, splitting her from the life she had led and reeling her, at first, into a shrill unutterable joy. At first.

He was on a ladder in the women's locker room, his upper

half swallowed by the ceiling, his trousers poignantly slack to reveal—nothing so crude as his backside, but the place where his back narrowed, the sweet hairs in that most vulnerable curve. She saw, later, that her first impulse had been to touch those hairs from sheer curiosity, to *see*—in other words—if they could possibly be as wrenchingly soft, as beautifully smooth, as they appeared in that miraculous and paralyzing instant. She saw the ghost of her own hand reach up to them as she herself stood, paralyzed in her corporal bulk, watching, and the shiver came down through her fingertips into her arm, and chest, and out again, shooting to every point on the surface of her skin. There was a kind of crush in her lungs, as if each had been taken in a broad hand and squeezed like a sponge. And there were deep stigmata piercings in the palms of her hands. She was suddenly hot, and very upset.

Ashley, oblivious, groped at the back loop of his pants, for a pair of pliers. He found them, his fingers—hard-skinned but unaccountably elegant in their length, in their lines—gripping the instrument, already wielding it as he brought it up to his shoulders and past sight into the hidden gap of the ceiling. Heather had a brief, crushing vision of those fingers inside her, the wrist supple between her thighs. She had not known she was capable of such wantonness. Nor had she known she could covet so fiercely—she had seen the clear glint of gold, a thick band, on that finger as it flashed overhead.

She looked down at her own finger, baffled; then, abruptly, enraged—that he had married someone else in the first place. That he hadn't waited for her.

"Aw, fuck."

The legs shifted. One foot searched backward for a lower rung. Another four inches of chest was revealed, smooth-skinned in a ragged, open collar. The other foot came down: a ponytail of russet hair, unruly but clean and wrapped in a coil of red bandanna, a winsomely shaped ear. His chin was smooth, like his chest, with a faint point—elfin, almost. She wanted to look more closely, to stare at it, in fact, but with one more descent of the ladder, Ashley was suddenly there, in front of her, near enough for her to touch and looking at her as if he absolutely expected her to do just that. Involuntarily, Heather stepped back, and to her intense relief, that compulsion abated, at least for the moment.

"Excuse my language." Ashley shrugged. She wondered if he mistook her expression for disapproval. "I didn't know anybody was here."

"I was just . . ." Heather heard her own voice, but she didn't know what it wanted to say. She was glad it still worked, though.

"You work here, right?" he prompted. "I've seen you."

Her throat went dry. He had seen her, she thought. She had been seen, without her knowledge. By him.

"At the front desk."

"Right." Heather nodded. He was telling her all the important stuff.

"What, two, three months?"

"About that. I mean, yes."

He took hold of his ladder to rattle it down, dislodging a puff of dust, an irresistible shimmer in the wake of some bleak fairy's wand. Heather looked up.

The tear came first, then the pain. She bent over, heat searing her eye, as if some thorn had lodged there, taken root and grown: a twig, a branch, a tree sprouting agony from the optic nerve. She had never imagined anything could be so sharp. She pressed against it, uselessly, with her hands. She was weeping freely, if lopsidedly: a one-eyed geyser. Her own voice moaned. Through the blur, she saw him step close.

"Let me," Ashley said.

His hand took away her hand. He watched for a moment, his face so close. The needle in her eye jabbed with pain. Then, with two careful fingers, he spread her lids apart, splaying her open. Heather stopped cold, her tears arrested. It occurred to her that she had wet her pants. They were wet, anyway. She knew what he was going to do. She could not believe what he was going to do.

"Don't move," he said, as if she could.

Ashley opened his mouth. He breathed over the surface of her eye, then licked his own breath away. His tongue was inexpressibly soft. The thorn evaporated. He licked again, this time out of love. His tongue traced a line down her center, dividing and conquering as it went—eye from eye, breast from breast, lip from lip—splitting her open, then patching her together again with some sweet cement. She did not want the light back, or the air. She did not want him to see her face like this. Her avid eye searched the dark inside of his throat, but there was nothing visible to the eye, even the naked eye.

Then he stepped back. The light blurred in. His abundant smile focused in her line of sight.

"All right?" Ashley said. "Is it gone?"

It was gone, that grain, though a boulder had taken its place. It seemed to her now that the amorphous, irreducible thing that had always been wedged between herself and her peers, between herself and the town in which she had spent her life, had suddenly crystallized into stunning certainty. Finally, beautifully, the world had a point around which it revolved. The world had a winsome symmetry, and the music of its turning spheres was transformative. Through primitive instinct, she understood the mesh their lives would make. Her tongue knew the taste of his skin. Her skin knew the sweetness of his hands.

Ask me something else, she thought, but Ashley already knew everything.

"Your name's Heather. Steve Trask said." His voice seemed to resonate in her own throat, as if she were ventriloquizing him without conscious intention.

"Yes."

Ashley bent down to his toolbox. His ponytail fell forward, over a shoulder. A blue vein rose from the back of his fine hand.

"I think I've figured out why the air-conditioning isn't working, anyway. I need to order a part, though." He looked up at her. His confidence in her was electric between them. It made her strangely proud, as if she had indeed accomplished something rare and utterly admirable.

"Have to come back, I guess."

Heather felt her own head nod, encased in heat. "I guess so." He straightened then and looked at her. He was waiting.

"When?" she said. "When will you come back?"

Ashley smiled, his lips together, the tip of one white tooth revealing itself nonetheless. He told her his name.

"I don't have a car," said Heather Pratt.

Chapter 11

The Logging Road

ASHLEY HAD A CAR. A BATTERED VOLVO, RUSTED and unlovely, the cracked plastic of its gearshift covered with a leather cap worn to the shape of his palm. When she first sat down beside him on the frayed plastic of the front passenger seat, the body of the car seemed to close around them, defining the specific world that was to be theirs alone. It did not occur to her to begrudge the smallness of this world, its arguable tawdriness and lack of comfort. Already it was clear to Heather that whatever destinations she might reach in this car would be the most meaningful she could possibly aspire to.

That first day he drove her through Goddard and into the forest along the Sabbathday, past the place called Nate's Landing, where, already, it was too chilly for children to play in the sandbox or near the water, and then past the Drumlins, past any place she knew the name of. A logging road set off into the forest then, into the unmarked expanse, its spiky pines blazed in occasional orange or ornamented in strips of yellow plastic, like—she thought, she couldn't help thinking—the tree in that song about the prisoner coming home.

Because she was about to come home, Heather knew, the Volvo rocking heavily along its rutted path. Ashley would stop when they got there, and she would look around herself and recognize the contours of her intended place on this earth. Already that place was dear to her. Already she could anticipate nostalgia for it, intense like the nostalgia of exiles amputated from their homelands. She leaned forward in her seat, perched for a first glimpse.

The path opened near a stand of birches, then dissipated in gravel and grass. There simply was no way forward and no farther place to get to. She had never, it seemed to her, felt so thoroughly the sensation of being in exactly the right place. The forest seemed close, not claustrophobic, the air full of sap and pine. Heather felt, rather than saw, his eyes on her. She felt held, as if he were indeed carrying her over some invisible threshold. It was pleasant. It was shattering, but also pleasant. Even in the fraternity room in Hanover she had had no notion of this, of being longed for with such fond violence. Her body wasn't listening to her, if it ever had before. Glancing down at herself, she saw her own limbs move confidently in their new command. It stunned her, watching one wrist tense in the rope of Ashley's hair, the other reach with perfect aim for the narrow sway of his back, its skin electrically hot. The chill air hit her like a smack as he took away her clothing. Somewhere a zipper tore with an understated purr, and then her hips were free. Tights tangled her ankles, hobbling her like a dumb animal: she nearly howled in frustration. Ashley's shirt was gone; somebody's hand had reached back and torn it away over his head, shaking loose the ponytail. His hair was longer than hers, even. Its thick beauty shamed her. She wiped a handful of it across her face and, to her amazement and dismay, it came away slick with tears. She could not imagine a more terrible demonstration of weakness. He would hate her now, Heather thought, but she saw in his face that he did not hate her. Even she could recognize what passion looked like, Heather thought. Even she must recognize love when she saw it. "You're so beautiful," he said then, as if it had to be confirmed.

Her eyes, without warning, blurred again. She shut them. "I don't see it," her own voice said, sounding unaccountably weary.

Ashley was over her, his mouth at the lobe of her ear. "But you've never seen yourself like this," he said, and it was so sensible that she knew he was right. Heather was beautiful, so. She had wanted to be, and now she was, for him. She understood then that she would never be able to love him enough to show her gratitude.

His miraculous hand untangled her tights and they came away. She did not know where they went. All she wanted on earth was to be bare next to his bareness, and it felt to her that she was twisting wildly, as if she might rid herself of what remained in this way. A bra had never seemed such a ridiculous thing before, so utterly useless but, at the same time, so unnecessarily complicated. She scratched herself, clawing it from her skin. Ashley touched the place to his tongue, a rising welt by the nipple. He kissed the nipple with an open mouth, then he closed his mouth. Breath rushed from her. He took away her underpants and she was glad, because they were wet and they embarrassed her. She was better off without them, Heather thought, reaching for his hand, but his hand was already there.

For one crazy moment she had no thought at all, then all she could think of was that picture, the famous one where God touches Adam and brings him to life, finger to finger. Ashley's finger was in her now. She didn't know she went that deep, really. He seemed to be searching for something, and she wanted him to find it, whatever it was, because he should have what he wanted, anything he wanted. A drone filled the space between their two bodies, but every time he kissed her the sound stopped in her throat. That embarrassed her, too, but she couldn't stop. She began to conjure wants—specific physical necessities. She could not have made sentences of the things she wanted him to do. Her legs went wide around him. The strength of his hand was unbearable. *God gives life to Adam*; it made her laugh. The world turned on Ashley's fingertip. He took his fingertip away.

First it pained her, a cutting pain that flashed to the terminus of each limb with a dull depression hard in its wake. For the swiftest instant Heather saw the murky face of her other lover, her drunken, genial frat boy, and it seemed to her that there must be so little to this vast mythic act, after all, and she had been wrong to come here, even with Ashley, but then Ashley moved and the mood fled. He moved not in and out of her, but around inside her, as if he were stirring her from within, mixing some potion of her innards. She didn't know what to do, and in her frustration began pushing against him—all wrong—until Ashley, without scolding or mocking her, very calmly reached below Heather and lifted her, and showed her how she was not to trouble herself but only hang on. "Better?" He smiled. But she was already away.

Through haze: the rasp of his pointed chin burrowing her collarbone, her burning nipple cooled by his tongue, the sawdust edge to his smell. She catalogued fiercely, hurling them in to think about later, when she could think again, when there wasn't this swirl of distraction around her. His shining hair over her eyes. Her own name spoken in her own ear, like the highest imaginable praise. The pressure churning a spiral at the base of her spine, then shooting to the soles of her feet, the palms of her hands. She couldn't believe what she was hearing, how loud it was, and only the unmistakable sensation from within her own throat could convince her that the voice calling so loudly was her own. He came in a shower of sparks. He loved her that much.

It was sticky between them when he moved. Ashley laughed. Heather was mortified at the noise, which lingered still, trapped around them in the car, but he refused to acknowledge her apology. "It's like that thing in the Bible." He grinned. "Isn't it?"

"What thing?"

"You know—about the voice crying out in the wilderness."

Heather smiled at him. He slipped from her, leaving her suddenly bereft. "I wish," she said suddenly. She wiped her face. He was waiting. "I wish I was a virgin. I mean," her voice was indistinct, "for you. I wish I was a virgin for you."

It was dark now, but she could see him clearly. He took a long time to respond, long enough for her to be horrified at what she had said, but he seemed to understand this also, because he shook his head and kissed her.

He drove her home. Heather didn't say anything. He would pick her up the next afternoon—every next afternoon, from now on—and take her to the forest. He left her at the end of the drive and turned the Volvo around. She waited till she couldn't hear it anymore, then she turned and walked through the bald moonlight up to her house. It was a few minutes' walk. Technically, she was pregnant by the time she reached her own front door.

Chapter 12

A Coincidence

OF COURSE SHE KNEW HE WAS MARRIED. HE wore a wedding ring, after all, and Heather wasn't stupid. She also assumed the marriage was happy, since Ashley was too good a man to stay in a marriage that wasn't. He never lied to Heather about these things. He respected her too much for that. He never told her he would leave Sue, or that his wife did not understand him, or even that they no longer had sex together. Sue, his life with Sue, was utterly beside the point as far as Heather was concerned; the point was that, for Heather, Ashley had saved one portion of his bliss. It was a finite portion, and yet it was abundant beyond anything she had ever imagined for herself. It felt unseemly to want more from him.

He collected her every day after work. He waited for her in the parking lot, folding and refolding *The Manchester Union Leader* into wedges to read against the steering wheel, drinking from his thermos of sweet white coffee, not hiding. That he was not ashamed of her filled Heather with helium joy. She reached for the passenger door of the Volvo with a proprietary pleasure she had not felt even in her own home, and took her own seat beside him. It was the lightest moment of her day, and the moment she most missed on weekends, or on the few afternoons Ashley could not come for her. Even more than the sex, Heather thought, though she craved the sex and was harmed by its lack, as if, without it, some vital substance were draining itself from her and howling for replenishment.

It gave her grace, or seemed to. She was aware of that, swiveling over him or bending herself to his bending, as if they had trained and trained together to make this look effortless. Her naked body became a nude beneath his hands; he had, by some alchemy, charged art into her, and she moved as she imagined a woman in a painting must move, released from her canvas restraints. It gave Heather an undreamed-of power: a touch made him shudder. *Her* touch. She touched him again and he moaned. He showed her the strength in her own tongue. He showed her the reason her breasts were so soft. He showed her the way in which words could actually sound like themselves: moist, friction, thrust. His voice in her hair could make her cry out. The sweet coffee in his mouth shot its sweetness down between her legs.

And he loved her, obviously. He didn't have to do these things for her, after all. He didn't have to drive her home, or take her by the Stop & Shop if she needed something, waiting outside where he could be seen by everyone. He didn't have to hold her by the roadside before she stepped out of his car, out of the world of light, and tell her—unnecessarily, as it happened, because he had told her before—that she was beautiful. Married people seldom had as much, at least the ones Heather could see. She began to look at them now, these paired-off people, in the supermarket or the sports center, or flashing past in their own cars as Heather drove by with her lover. She saw how marriage hardened the husbands and thickened the wives, how conversation between them became competitive, then punitive, before finally crusting into silence. The couples aged separately, companionable or acrimonious, but ultimately unconnected, like horses yoked together and apart at the same time. If this was marriage, Heather thought, she was not unhappy without it.

Not that it didn't pain her, seeing Sue. She seemed to see Sue everywhere now, like a word you learn the meaning of and then suddenly begin to hear on everyone's lips. This person had been yanked from anonymity and hurled into a state of ubiquity by Ashley's brisk nod in the parking lot as she climbed in beside him one afternoon, his hushed "My wife's car. Let's go." Heather watched for it after that, and indeed it seemed to turn up regularly in the early afternoons, because Heather had known Ashley's wife for months, she realized now. At least by sight: a tall figure in a flannel shirt, with one rope-thick blond braid down between her shoulder blades and a liquid gaze that slithered past Heather at the reception desk as Sue walked through to the women's locker room. She came to swim her laps, before the kids appeared for lessons and churned up the water. Heather, who couldn't swim herself, had no way of telling whether Sue was a good swimmer, but she certainly kept at it for a long time, droning up and down her allotted lane, her goggled eyes dreamily examining the ceiling with every other stroke. Even before she had known her for who she was, Heather had envied this person, admiring her strong though inelegant legs, her bright hair, loosened from its braid afterward, stiffened with chlorine. This person who needed nothing from her, who even brought her own towels in a faded UVM gym bag, who barely deviated in her course to flash a membership card at the unremarkable person who sat behind the reception desk.

Now that Heather knew Sue, she saw Sue. She saw her at the Stop & Shop, listlessly tossing groceries into one of the rickety carts, and at the Laundromat, reading *The Boston Globe* as Ashley's clothes were purged of their evidence, and at Tom and Whit's, snapping through the pages of the seed catalogues. Heather herself found it curious that, even in her heightened awareness of Ashley's wife, she bore no special animosity toward this person. That Sue declined to take notice of her was not, in itself, an offense. She was used, after all, to being taken no notice of, and in any case, Sue was a contained kind of person. Where Ashley was gregarious, she seemed to give off a chill of courteous self-sufficiency. She had no family here, Heather reasoned, but then again Ashley hadn't either. They had come together from Burlington, where they'd met as students—not to stay, but for the summer only, so Ashley could work for the builder who'd won the sports center contract.

Heather, amazed, considered the chronology. She would have been a junior in high school, up in Goddard Falls, without a car of her own. She would barely have ventured into town all summer. She had only the sparsest memories of the sports center taking shape on its riverbank at the end of Elm Street, carapace to corpus, with its small army of bronzing men crawling over it. And yet he had been here, nearby, all along.

Then, when the work ended, he quarreled with the builder. The builder, he said, was a coarse man, and stupid. He did not know how to treat a client. He did not know how to make a building. Ashley began to find clients of his own. The following spring he'd tacked a solarium onto the back of Stephen Trask's ranch—an ugly thing, in his own opinion, but there wasn't much you could do to a ranch that wasn't ugly—and so found his way back to the sports center and a regular, if part-time, salary as handyman.

Heather looked past his shoulder, idly smelling the flannel of his work shirt. She had noted Sue's detergent and begun to use it for her own clothes. She loved to sleep in sheets that smelled of Ashley. The forest darkened earlier and earlier now, and they had to keep the motor running for the warmth. Already the windshield would be matted with leaves by the time they finished, and Heather had a vision of the forest heaving up and covering her, in her pleasure and happiness, to keep her safe with Ashley and him safe with her. But through the leaves, the skeletal fingers of pointing branches remained, awaiting their winter accusations.

She took Ashley's hand from its resting place deep in her own hair, held it to the last of the light, and kissed it. The fine thing—that thing that was not herself, and not him, but a consummation exceeding them both—had begun to thrill her, a ghost of an idea, a quickening of love, a potent and dangerous infusion of delight. Her secret.

Ashley sighed, moved lower, and, as if by clairvoyance, kissed her abdomen. "You're so great," he said, to it or to her.

"Who?" said Heather, frowning.

He laughed. "Oh, I don't know. What'd you say your name was again?"

"I haven't named her," Heather said. Then: "I mean, it. But I bet it's a girl."

The wind found a crack in a window and stole inside. The sheen of sweat between them iced over. Ashley's expression didn't change, but it edged into stone.

"How long?"

She reached down to him, to his face. To her intense relief, he kissed her finger as it went by.

"Two months."

They were two months old themselves.

Ashley said nothing. From outside, the rumble of the river as it passed them by. Nocturnal things woke up on all sides and spoke their minds. The shadow where his face had been only moments before began to shake from side to side.

"It's all right?" Heather said. "You don't mind?"

"No," he said. "But it's funny, you know."

By queer coincidence, his wife was pregnant, too.

Chapter 13

An H Like an A

"YOU HAVE SOMETHING TO TELL ME, HEATHER?"

Stephen Trask had her in the family room, a faux-pine chamber choked with matching chairs which all seemed to La-Z-Boy back. She could hear Celia in the kitchen, telling one of the boys to keep his hands out of the spaghetti sauce.

"Well," she heard herself say, "no." She wasn't leaping to conclusions here.

Stephen glared at her, and Heather was a bit taken aback. If she'd known this was to be the purpose of his invitation she would have said no, flat-out. She hadn't wanted to come home with him for dinner anyway. Going for dinner at the Trasks' meant a lost ride with Ashley, a trade-off that seemed grossly unfair. But he'd never asked before and Heather hadn't known how to refuse. Now, tense in her absurdly relaxing chair, she braced for the next assault.

"I can't stand to see you do this," Stephen said, gritting his teeth. "You know, I can't stand this."

She tossed her head. "There's nothing wrong. Everything's fine. Everything's *great*."

"Everything's not great, Heather." He stopped, regrouped, and leaned forward, his chair bowing into the room. His high, pale forehead furrowed in concern. "I know you had a rough time in Hanover. I know you felt you couldn't hack it. I understand that. But you can try again."

"I don't want to try again." She sipped tomato juice. She had asked for tomato juice because she had read that it was good for the baby, but she had no particular taste for it.

Stephen shook his head grimly. "No, I wasn't thinking of Dartmouth. I can appreciate that must have been a shock. But you could go to UNH, Heather. They'd take you in a flash. Listen," he said, urgent, "you're doing a terrific job at the center. It's worked out really well. But it never occurred to me you wouldn't try college again."

"But why?" She shrugged. "Why should I? I'm happy here."

Celia came in, bumping Heather's chair with her shin. Her blond hair was wedged back in the haircut that had not even looked good on Dorothy Hamill. She was a smugly maternal woman with two sweet chins, a torso wrapped densely in fat. She had some wine in a glass with a long stem. Noting the charged silence, she readjusted her smile into a frown of concern. Heather felt as if she were facing some kind of oral exam.

"You know how long it's been since Goddard Falls produced somebody capable of getting into an Ivy League school?"

It all felt so distant, and Heather sighed accordingly. It felt like somebody else's story by now. Her concerns were more immediate, and incidentally far more pleasant. The spaghetti sauce smelled good. She wondered what Celia put in hers; Heather's own never smelled like this. "Is that garlic?" she asked.

Celia looked at her husband.

"Heather, Christ, what the *hell* are you up to with Ashley? Where do you think that's going to go?"

To hear his name spoken aloud, his name and her own in one breath, was a rush. Involuntarily Heather smiled. "I love him," she informed them.

Celia, to her credit, did not react. Trask groaned loudly. "Oh, Heather. I really wanted more for you."

More *from* you, she interpreted this to mean.

"You're not exactly being discreet," he said tightly.

Heather sat up straight. "I've got nothing to hide. I'm happy."

"You're carrying on with somebody who's married. At least," he said gruffly, "that's how it's going to be seen."

"I don't care," Heather said, because she didn't.

"Other people will care," said Celia. Her voice was soft. She was the good cop.

"That's fine." She shrugged. It seemed as if people were usually angry at her, anyway.

"But why *should* it be fine for you, Heather?" Stephen insisted. "Why should that be enough for you, an affair with a man who'll never leave his wife? And he never will, Heather, I can assure you. You're young and you're bright, and you have a real opportunity to make something of yourself. You think your classmates could go to college like you did? You could be anything—a doctor, even. Or, I don't know, a businessperson. You could have seen something of the world."

"But I don't want to see the world. I like it here," Heather said simply. "I like my life. I like working for you and living with Pick. And she's not too strong anymore, you know. She needs my help for things. And I'm in love," she added, as if this settled things. It *should* settle things, after all. It was a vast event, dividing time, changing the course of history.

"Ashley," said Celia Trask carefully, "is very handsome. He has not been the most constant of husbands."

Heather turned to look at her. "What's that supposed to mean?" She was honestly perplexed.

It meant, Celia told her, that she wasn't the first girl he'd paid attention to, but Heather just stared. Surely Celia could understand that nothing Ashley had done before had the slightest relevance to Heather. After all, Ashley was married. If she were to be angry about anything it would be that, wouldn't it? She faced them. She felt a little sorry for them.

"It's kind of you to be concerned about me," said Heather. She paused, eyeing the quilt tacked to the wall behind Celia's head. One of Celia's own, star-patterned, pieced with ugly modern calicos. Heather wondered why you would bother to make such an ugly quilt in the first place, and then why you'd hang it on the wall. Quilts were to keep you warm, in her view. Pick had made her a quilt when she was a little girl, pieced from the dresses she'd worn and outgrown. It was a fan quilt, intricate and precise, but even so it had never occurred to her to do anything with it but throw it across her bed. Things were really so uncomplicated when you got right down to it. It was only people messing up the simplicity that got you in trouble. That got you up against *this*, she thought, letting her gaze drift back to the Trasks' intense, expectant faces.

She took a breath. "I was good in school. I mean the school part of school," Heather acknowledged. "I took it seriously, at least, because I wasn't distracted by the other stuff going on, and I was sort of interested. I was good at the tests and that, but you know, I really wasn't any more into that than I was into the, whatever you want to call it, social world." She paused. Something occurred to her. "I don't want to be a doctor!"

"You can't want to stay here all your life," Stephen said.

"What's wrong with here?" Heather said, fully perplexed.

"But—" He stopped himself, and she understood: she was disliked here. She had always been disliked here for her contented alienation. Now she would be disliked for Ashley and the baby. But it had never bothered her before, and it wouldn't now.

"I have everything I need in Goddard," she told them, beaming. "I have work I love, I have friends." She nodded to them. They did not react. "I'm happy."

Down the hall, a great thump as one of the kids leaped off the top bunk onto the floor; the frail house shuddered.

"You deserve—" Celia began, but her husband cut her off.

"Heather, look, just send an application in to Durham. It's January now. School doesn't begin till September. You'll have tons of time to figure it out, but you'll at least have the option. And you can stay at the sports center till then."

She balanced her empty cup on the arm of the tipping chair. It was filmy with red glaze, which made her smile. "The baby's due in summer," Heather told them. "I couldn't possibly go to college in September."

"*You give it back*," shrieked Phillip, who was nine. Celia, shaking her blond head, excused herself. Stephen was staring at Heather. For the first time, she felt a bit bad for him.

"It's what I want," she said instead. Then: "But I *am* sorry."

Stephen said, "Is this about your mother, Heather?"

She stared at him, wide-eyed. It had never been clear to her why she was supposed to care that much about her mother. The once or twice she had tried to explain this to people they had simply failed to accept what she was saying, but the utter truth was that Heather did not dwell on Ruth, or long for some idealized version of her mother. Ruth's reputation had both preceded her brief career in high school and lingered long after, even to the years of Heather's own enrollment. She had been the kind of girl who slept with your boyfriend and then had the temerity not to be sorry about it. She didn't stay long, in any case. She went to Boston (though California had featured more consistently in her tirades against Goddard Falls and her parents), returning only to deposit her child with Pick. Heather had not the faintest idea where she had been since. And this person was supposed to influence her life?

"It's nothing to do with my mother," Heather said. "I don't know why it should."

Celia called the boys to dinner. Heather, suddenly convulsed with hunger, wondered if it would be rude for her just to stand up and go into the kitchen. Pregnancy had sharpened her senses and whittled down her needs into basic things. "Smells good," she said pointedly.

"I'll help you," Stephen said. "Any way I can, I'll help you."

She made herself not smile and thanked him. The armchair, tipping forward, popped her up like an ejector seat. She ate three helpings of spaghetti and, much to his amusement, Phillip's broccoli. Everyone conspired to talk of something else, until Stephen could drive her home.

The night was bone clear, picked white by the chilly moon. She could not remember a more rapturous winter, Heather thought, fingering, beneath her sweater, the ridge of her gold chain, Ashley's Christmas gift a month earlier. It had a charm, too, a letter *H* shaped slightly off, with the two vertical strokes just perceptibly inverted. As if, she had thought, examining it for the first time, those parallel lines might somehow meet, at some unspecified point down the line, if only one waited long enough. To squint at it made it an A, Heather thought. A is for Ashley. It was her most favorite object.

Stephen had a truck, which rode high, and Heather felt as if she were surveying her own lands, stretching in the pale light as far east as the pine-dark Presidentials: everything hers. She rode a cushion of elation, her gold charm between her breasts, just touching, when she leaned forward, her precious abdomen. Stephen was silent until he turned at her drive and bumped down its rocky length.

"Pick know?" he said, bringing the car to a stop.

"I don't think so." She had her hand on the door. She wanted to get out.

"She'll have to know. If you're not going to give it up."

"Give it *up*!" Heather's voice was low. She flash-flooded with anger. "I wouldn't dream of giving it up."

Stephen nodded sagely. "Well, remember what I said, Heather. And call on me. You were right to say we're your friends. Now you've got to treat me and Celia like friends."

"Thanks for dinner," Heather said lamely.

"All right." He sounded grim. "Best to Pick."

It was warm inside. Heather's grandmother had long ago gotten into the habit of overheating the parlor and kitchen even as the upstairs bedrooms shivered in blue cold. Pick was next door, not quite awake in her chair, so Heather said a quiet hello and went to wash up what was left from dinner and put away the meat loaf. She always did the dishes now. Whatever agility was left in Pick's fingers went to sewing, or turning the pages of *The Goddard Clarion*, her chief pleasure. She heated up some milk for herself. Milk was good for the baby, too.

"Have fun?" Pick said when Heather sat on the couch.

"Yeah. Celia Trask puts a ton of garlic in her spaghetti sauce."

"Can't stand garlic," Pick said. She took off her glasses, pinched her eyes, and replaced them. "Can you pick up some groceries for me tomorrow?"

Heather said yes, her heart sinking a little. A grocery run would cut further into her time with Ashley, and given the lost afternoon just past, this seemed downright punitive. The lack of an automobile had an endless impact on their lives, Heather thought. Pick, who felt, with her encroaching arthritis and lagging reflexes, that she was no longer capable of driving, had sold her car when Heather had gone to Hanover and bought, with the proceeds, enough aged and stacked hardwood for the next five winters. Heather could drive perfectly well, but returned home to utter vehicular dependence—not altogether a bad thing, as it had turned out, but frustrating. Pick sometimes caught a ride with one of the Hodge sisters. But perhaps they'd been busy.

"Hands all right?" she asked, sipping her milk. Pick's knuckles seemed to be growing hourly. Just looking at them was painful.

"You have something to say to me."

"I do?" Heather said lightly. She noted a moment of déjà vu.

Pick had declined to look up. The work in her lap was something Heather hadn't seen before, or else had failed to notice: a blur of blue, tinged with pink, more crumpled than folded. Her eyes widened.

"I would say you did," said Pick, but even though she said it sternly, she also smiled, and so Heather smiled back.

"I'm not hiding anything," Heather said, and Pick put down her needle and laughed. She had always had an extravagant laugh.

"What I want to know is, how'd you have time to get up to this? You're just about always home. You go to work, you come back. You're here all weekend."

Heather crossed her legs. It was getting slightly more difficult to cross her legs. "He drives me home," she said simply. Then, because this mattered, she said, "He loves me very much."

"Is he going to marry you very much?" her grandmother asked.

"He's already married," Heather said. Then a small laugh escaped her. "Very much."

"I see," said Pick. She took up her work again, poked her needle at it, then put it down and sighed. "How are we going to do this?"

"Well," said Heather brightly, unwilling to let the mood pass, "pretty much the same way people always have, I guess. Aren't you just supposed to spread your legs and push?"

Pick looked up, and Heather caught her breath. Arthritis aside, Pick had always been only one age to her, the nether district after middle age but simply short of old. She was like one of those teenagers, Heather thought, who leapfrog up ahead of themselves to plain and broad maturity, then let the years go past, resigned to it, until they catch themselves again. Now, abruptly and before her eyes, Pick had abandoned her static berth and leaped ahead once more. Afraid to meet her gaze, Heather looked away.

It wasn't only gratitude, though Pick, she knew, had had no obligation to accept her errant daughter's child, let alone to raise it, let alone to love it as Pick had loved her. Between herself and her grandmother there had always been an essential consonance, so dissimilar, Heather thought, from the general friction of daughters and mothers. Perhaps the generation missing between Pick and herself had taken that friction away with it, leaving this pleasant, if quiet, vacuum of years. Pick's mothering—her surrogate mothering—was hardly involved. Intimate talks on the terrible beauty that was womanhood were not within her ken, let alone her protocol; but she had loved Heather utterly in her own standoffish way, feeding her first and then teaching her to feed herself, then to cook for herself, then to provide for herself, and always to be—more or less contentedly—alone, since alone was what you could count on in life. "I'm not saying this is the answer to my dreams, you know. I won't say that." She shook her head. "What is that, coffee?"

Heather looked down into her own cup. "Milk," she said. It was nearly cold by now.

"Good. It helps the baby's bones."

Her heart leaped. "I know. I think maybe it's a girl."

"Maybe a girl." Her grandmother shrugged. "Maybe a boy. We won't throw it out, either way." She sighed. "I wouldn't count on me for much heavy lifting, though. Hands aren't up to much."

"Of course not, Grandma. I'll do everything myself. I *want* to do everything." She crossed the room and sat beside Pick, then leaned close. "I'm so happy," she told Pick's white, translucent ear.

"Well, you'd better be," Pick said. She wagged a crooked finger in Heather's face. "I can tell you right now, no one else is going to be. Like mother, like daughter, they're going to say."

"I don't care," Heather said fiercely. "I just care about the baby. And—" She stopped herself.

"Him," her grandmother snorted. "Well, it's no good thinking about him, whoever he is. I don't suppose *he'll* be here at four in the a.m. when the baby has gas."

Heather giggled. Pick glared at her. "Oh, that's funny, is it? Just you wait, my dear. You'll never work as hard for anything as you will for a belch, I can tell you. And *you*, I've never known a child with so much gas!"

"Grandma!" Heather yelped. Pick unfolded the fabric on her lap. Even half finished, it was an amazing thing, impossibly pieced with tiny parts of cotton, pink and blue in a hexagon mosaic. The bits of fabric couldn't have been larger than half-inch squares, Heather thought, and the intricacy of their placement was dazzling. It was a show-off quilt, she understood, a demonstration of what Pick still could do with her unlovely hands. And it was a competitive quilt. For as much as her grandmother was enjoying this, her own thrilled response, Heather knew she would enjoy far more showing the finished effort to Ina and Janelle Hodge. The Hodge sisters, with whom Pick had walked an edgy sixty years of mutually disapproving friendship, had been virtually enshrined as local repositories of native craft, and were forever bringing round their latest clippings from *The Boston Globe* or *The New England Monthly*. Ever since that person had moved out from New York and whipped up all the women to hook rugs and make quilts, Pick was wont to say, those girls had heads on them altogether too big for their bodies. For her part, Pick wasn't interested in sewing quilts for some housewife in Milwaukee who ought to get off her duff and make her own.

"Well?" she said, admiring her own work. "What do you think? Acceptable for a girl or for a boy, so you can go on and have whichever you want. Of course, don't go having twins now, cause I don't think my hands have got another one in them."

"Oh, Grandma," Heather managed.

"You know," said Pick, "it's no terrible thing to raise a child alone. Most women do, anyway." She frowned. "I raised your mother alone, never mind Sam was here every day of it. I raised you alone. You could take the men out of the picture entirely with no loss, as far as I'm concerned, if it weren't for money and what people are going to say about you in the supermarket. But I don't know many men with that much money anyway, and I never cared much what they said about me. It doesn't put food in your mouth or take it away when you come right down to it." She peered at Heather. "You listening to me?"

She touched her grandmother's face. "I'm going to name her after you," said Heather.

Chapter 14

A Circle of Women

AFTER THAT, EVERYBODY SEEMED TO NOTICE at once, glaring at the bulk of her winter coat with, first, suspicion, then a singular expression of horrified affront. Heather, for her part, couldn't see what it had to do with these people, rooted to the spot at the far end of the supermarket aisle or staring from their cars. Who they were, she wasn't even sure most of the time, though a few she knew perfectly well: Ann Chase or Sarah Copley, or the anonymous teased-and-dyed mothers of her high-school classmates. Martina still picked her up in the mornings, honking from the road so that Heather could wrap herself up and then walk, gingerly, avoiding the ice patches, down the length of the drive, but now Martina drove grimly, hardened in her silence. Finally, toward the end of February, she told Heather that Stephen Trask was letting her go on flexible hours and he himself would be driving out to Goddard Falls to pick her up in the mornings, and so the arrangements changed—though the housekeeper seemed to arrive at the center at pretty much the same time she had before, as far as Heather could tell.

It was true she hid nothing; she was too pleased with herself for that. She beamed at anyone who looked at her, even if they happened to be turning away in distaste. She had the most intense thrill from the new weight of each step, the tight substance of her abdomen. When Heather moved, the earth beneath her was ever so slightly displaced. Air parted about her, making way for her splendid condition. And she truly felt beautiful, her brown hair shiny and thick, her belly tautly round, her breasts full. Ashley loved them especially now, and laughed that he was only helping her practice for nursing. She held his head in the crook of her arm, the long ponytail spilling over her elbow. Pregnancy had made her wanton, Ashley joked. When she came, she felt the baby leap within her orgasm, like a figure skater doing spins at the center of the ice while crowds skate the periphery.

Because it was true, what he said—her hunger for him was a constant, visceral yen. At the core of Heather's bulk and the very root of her weight, something kinetic was in perpetual plea for his fingers or tongue. Every smell was mixed with the smell of their close grapplings, the smell of her own sticky center. Her vision was incessantly blurred by some encroaching memory of straining rhythms. Even their first lovemaking had not been so charged with pressure, she thought. Now, even more than then, it became difficult to concentrate on anything at all. She woke at night from the memory of penetration and had to press her thighs together for relief. When Ashley took her into the forest he might be inexpressibly gentle, but Heather yearned for violence. She wanted to slap his hands away and bring them back rougher. When he said he was afraid to hurt the baby, Heather compelled his hand—irresistible force meets eminently movable object. The thrill of seducing him spun in continual regeneration. She had never been greedy in this way before, but she loved her greed, her catalogue of new sounds, and most of all the authority of her commands. He was awed by her transmutation, her sheen of health. Sue felt terrible all the time now, he told Heather, throwing up and having pains down her leg and something awful, he confided, as if she desperately wanted to know, hanging out of her behind. Heather was politely solicitous, but the truth was that she preferred not to hear about Sue, even about her discomfort. She preferred to be allowed to forget about Sue entirely; a reasonable barter, she thought, for the unalterable fact of Ashley's marriage, and her own dearth of demands on him.

Sue was using the obstetric service in town, Ashley said, so Celia Trask drove Heather to Hanover to see a midwife there. The midwife believed that less was more, that women should be in charge, that caesareans were a misogynist curse of the patriarchy. Heather had no idea what she was talking about. The baby was all right? she asked the woman. Of course, the baby was fine. Heather thanked her and went home.

She had no intention of stopping work. She loved her work, not least because Ashley was around so often now; the center, fresh from its second winter, had sprung a few leaks and suffered chronic flooding from the spring thaw. They didn't actually speak to each other, but Heather could watch him through the window from her chair in the lunch bar, zipped to his elfin chin in a red down jacket, excavating the retaining wall from the slope down to the swollen Sabbathday. The shock of his particular beauty had not ebbed. She might know the smells in his most hidden places and the metallic tang of his nipples, the furthest vicinities of his mouth and the most intimate grammars to his pleasure, but there remained an involuntary jolt when her eyes found his shape in the distance. That other women did not seem to stare at him, were not struck motionless by the cataclysm of his beauty, was something that gave her comfort, since it seemed to confirm that Ashley had been intended for her alone.

Sue still came to swim, but less regularly, and Heather had not needed to be told of her gestational woes to see that Ashley's wife was unwell. Where she had walked with grace, slender in her unadorned and businesslike maillot, Sue now waddled painfully in a frilled maternity suit, a kind of waterproof muumuu in falsely bright Hawaiian colors. Her legs had thickened about the ankle, and her thighs were scrawled with the magenta graffiti of varicose veins. Painfully, Sue lowered herself into the water, and painfully she moved up and down her appointed lane. Heather, peeking discreetly from the doorway, shook her head and touched, unthinking, her own belly, stroking the head of the child she had already named, and pitied her.

The winter broke. Mud season left its usual mess. Celia Trask drove her into Hanover, where she bought a vast pair of overalls at Rosie Jekes and had her hair cut blunt to her chin—Celia's treat. Celia, doubtless on Stephen's instructions, was trying to be pals, a campaign somewhat doomed by the fact that she and Heather plainly did not like each other. They went to Peytonville for baby things—singlets and undershirts, a mobile that chimed and turned hypnotically. She did not like most of the things she bought. They weren't good enough. But the choice was narrow and she didn't know when she might get a chance for another expedition like this. The important thing was Pick's quilt, and it was finished now, its border etched in the palest green meander, offsetting the precise abundances of blue and pink. Heather readied the room next to her

own and went on with her life. She was waiting for something
to happen, and then something did.

On a Friday in June, she was stooped behind the reception
desk rooting out a new box of membership application forms
when the drift of a body moved heavily in her direction, and
then stopped. The person said nothing, but there was threat in
its silence. It stood in attendance, keeping its own counsel.
Heather, already alert, climbed awkwardly to her feet.

It was Sue, naturally, her jaw slack, her face sleeplessly
white. The two women stood eye to eye. Heather was still
unconvinced. Sue might, reasonably enough, have come to say
something unremarkable—about the pool hours, for example,
or the need for a changing table in the women's locker room.
She wouldn't be the first, and Stephen was always telling people they should feel free to tell him what they wanted at the
center, that it was their center, after all, and his charge was to
serve the community. It could be that, but as the silence lengthened Heather knew it wasn't. She had never heard Sue speak,
and she used this time to wonder what Sue's voice was going
to sound like when she got around to opening her thin and
livid mouth—not what she was going to say. By now, Heather
had little doubt what Sue was going to say.

But Sue, for the moment, said nothing. Instead, she reached
slowly, with rigid concentration and commendable aim, for the
swell of Heather's right cheek. Heather thought, for one crazed
moment, that Ashley's wife was going to pat her, as one might
pat a child on the head, or a friend to say, "Wake up!" But it
wasn't a pat. It wasn't a slap either. Sue's face remained motionless, but it seemed to harden. Heather caught a whiff of
something sour—her mouth, her bitterness trapped between
folds of unwashed skin—then, impossibly, she felt Sue's fingers tighten around her palmful of flesh, dig deep, then twist.
She could not see her own cheek, of course, but she saw it
anyway, as if on television or beneath a microscope, a melon-
ball scoop of injured tissue being wrested from her body, as
if Sue were doing her a favor and saving her life by cutting
out this bad thing. She felt nothing, but she knew enough to
think that strange. From cheek to brain—why was the pain
taking so long to reach her? Sue's jaw set, but she retained a
perplexed expression, as if she, too, were in the grip of some
great and angry hand. Heather's mouth dropped open, but her

voice had rushed to the place that was being gouged from her skull, so naturally she couldn't speak. The edge of her eye saw Stephen, frozen and perplexed, in the doorway to his office, an amazed woman with her skinny daughter in matching bathing suits, the shocking sweetness of Ashley's face in stunned profile as he reached for his wife's claw, and finally, as that familiar hand met the thing that was wrenching her face, Heather felt pain. It was terrible pain.

"Mm," her throat managed. She batted at the hand, but it had fused itself to her.

Sue's voice, syrup and lead, said: *Slut*.

Ashley slapped his wife. She burst into tears and let go. The air hit Heather's cheek like alcohol in the raw places, and she pressed her palm against it hard, as if to push the flesh back to where it had been.

"Come on," Ashley yelled, grabbing Sue's elbow, his voice raw and livid. Heather had never heard him so furious, and this, at once, became more shocking than the queer, slow-motion assault that had just taken place. She gaped after him as he dragged his wife away, pushing her into her own car and climbing in after, deflecting her blows as she tried and tried to hit him.

Stephen was at Heather's side, pulling her back. But Heather did not want to stop looking at Sue. At Sue and her husband, soldered in combat behind the filmy glass of Sue's Ford—in that angry, enclosed space that was their marriage. She wanted to break the window. She took a step in their direction.

"Heather, *please*," Stephen said. He gave an unmistakable yank. For the first time Heather looked at him.

"What?" she said, her voice oddly calm. There was a crowd, she noticed now, but they were awfully quiet.

"Come into my office," he said, unnecessarily, since he was both heading there and dragging her after him. He sat her in a chair and went to the lunch counter for ice. Her face was already numb. Stephen came back with a bag wrapped up in a towel and pressed it against her. She couldn't feel a thing.

"I don't think you need stitches," he said. He was trying to be helpful.

"Of course I don't need stitches," she said tersely. "I can't believe this."

"You can't?" Stephen said. He took the comfortable seat

behind his desk. "Which part of it shocks you? That Sue Deacon isn't a dummy? Or that she isn't a wimp?"

Heather glared at him.

"What was she supposed to do, Heather? Keep her eyes closed or keep her mouth closed?"

"She didn't exactly use her mouth," Heather said, rubbing the ice over the senseless flesh of her cheek.

He sighed. "You want to know the truth? I'm pretty amazed it took her as long as it did. You're having his *baby*, for Christ's sake."

"It's got nothing to do with her," Heather shouted.

He glared at her. "Don't be stupid. It's got everything to do with her. Every time you show yourself in public it's a billboard about her marriage. How would you like it if somebody paraded your most intimate secret up and down Elm Street? You can't possibly be so naïve, Heather." He paused. "Or so insensitive."

This took her aback.

"Yes." He warmed to his argument. "Deeply insensitive. The woman is having her first child and her husband's off messing around with somebody else."

"Me too." Heather was petulant, though it was hard to be fierce with the ice against her cheek. "I'm having my first child, too. You think she'd be good enough not to show up at my job and attack me. I ought to call the police or somebody."

"That," he chided, "would be extremely unwise."

They looked at each other in silence. Then Stephen shook his head. "Listen, Heather. I wasn't going to bring this up for a while, but it seems like a good time now." He considered his own hands, folded before him on the desktop. "I don't know what your plans are after the baby. I don't know if they include coming back to work."

"Of course I'll be coming back to work," she interrupted. More irritated than apprehensive.

"Well, I think you shouldn't," he told her. "At least, not here."

"I love it here," Heather faltered. She was starting to be afraid.

"I want you to meet somebody," Stephen said evenly. "Somebody I think you'll like. She might have work for you, and you might enjoy it even more than you enjoy coming here.

And you could take care of your baby at the same time."

"Pick's able to help with the baby during days," she objected. "I can still work here." She was sounding a little panicky now. It had never occurred to her that she might be forced from the sports center. Ashley was at the sports center.

"Yes, I know. But this isn't a good place for you, Heather. People know about you and Ashley, and they know you're both here. In a couple of hours, they're going to know what happened out there just now." He eyed her. "Believe me when I tell you this won't be pleasant for you. Now will you *please* take some advice from me?"

Heather shrugged. She wanted fervently to be rude, but she couldn't seem to muster any rudeness. "Sure. Whatever."

"Get your coat," Stephen said.

Heather went to the staff room and got her coat. People were hitting the wall as she walked, glaring at her. She turned them to stone and passed them. Stephen was waiting by his car.

"Her name is Naomi," Stephen said. He drove up Elm Street and turned right out the Goddard Falls Road. "She works in the old mill."

Heather stared at him. "I'm not working in a mill!"

"No, no." He actually smiled. "Don't worry, you'll see what I mean."

She could hear the river, swollen in its rush. Stephen pulled into the parking lot. The mill was painted white and looked homey, as if somebody lived there. On the porch, in a peeling Adirondack chair, a squat woman with a long, frizzy ponytail was hunched over a folderful of papers. She looked up and smiled, as if they'd been expected.

"Hey." The woman's voice was deep.

"Naomi."

Stephen got out and went around the car to Heather's side, as if they were on a date. He helped Heather out and presented her.

"Shit," Naomi said, getting to her feet. "What the hell happened to you?"

"She ran into a rival embroiderer," Stephen said, with false buoyancy, and Naomi, picking it up right away, stopped staring. She wasn't really squat, Heather saw now. She was Heather's own middling height, and it was her thick sweater that added most of the bulk. Still, the woman gave an impression of density and a certain graceless power. Also kindness, but that was because she was smiling, probably, and walking toward Heather with her hand outstretched.

"I'm Naomi Roth," she said. "So you're the artist."

"I work for Stephen," Heather said, shaking Naomi's hand. "At the sports center."

"But you're thinking of taking on some other work, too?" Naomi prompted optimistically. "I've already seen some of your things."

Heather frowned at her, then at Stephen.

"I brought Naomi those little things you made for the boys." He shrugged. "I just thought she'd like to see them."

"They were lovely," Naomi gushed. "Your own designs, I take it?"

"What?" Heather said. "I didn't have a design. I mean, I didn't have a pattern or anything. I just made it up."

"Well, you're very talented," said Naomi. "And I'm very happy you're here, because I just lost two of my best quilters."

Now Heather was completely lost. "Quilters?" She looked at Stephen.

"Naomi works with quilters, hookers. People who do embroidery."

"I thought this was a mill," Heather said suspiciously.

"It is. At least it was. Come on," the woman said. "I'll show you inside."

Inside, the mill wasn't a mill. The front room was a snug little office with a braided rug over most of its wooden floor, and curtains made of linen embroidered in thick bands of red cloud stitch. Clumsily embroidered, Heather noted, idly wondering who'd done them. There was a heavy wooden desk covered with a fan of computer paper. Mary Sully was sitting behind the desk. Heather knew Mary Sully. Her little sister had been in Heather's class.

"This is Heather," Naomi said cheerily.

"I know," Mary said. She gave Heather's right cheek an incisive glare.

"Here's the workroom," Naomi said, oblivious. She ushered Heather and Stephen inside. The circle of women stiffened in silence. The Hodge sisters were there, a single Irish Chain quilt across their spindly laps. Ina looked at Janelle and Janelle looked at Heather.

"Heather." Janelle nodded. "Pick well?"

"Yes," Heather said. Janelle had given Pick a lift into town only the day before.

No one else said a word, but they favored her with a look of unified intent. The disapproval made her straighten. One of her hands found her abdomen and stopped there, the universal symbol for *Yes, I am with child.* Somebody turned away in disgust.

"The room fixed up great, Naomi," Stephen said.

"I know. And it makes such a difference. We were just enslaved by the schedule when we were in the church. You know, we had no more claim to the space than the Bible study group and the bingo—less, really—so all we got were two or three nights a week, and people told me that was the only time they actually worked on their projects. They looked forward to coming, but they just didn't get a chance when they were home. This way it's completely a drop-in, and people come much more often and they get much more done." She looked at Heather. "So you see, you could bring your work here, Heather. Or, if you want, you could stay home and work there. The way we're set up, it's entirely up to you. Some people like to get together and talk, and occasionally the quilters pitch in together. And some people would rather be at home so they can watch *General Hospital*, or whatever. The only rules, really, are that you have to get your orders done on time and the work has to be good. Want to go back into the office?"

Heather gave them a last, defiant look, and followed Naomi out.

"Here's our catalogue," Naomi said, taking one off the stack on the desk and handing it to Heather. "This is for winter. I'm just getting the summer one together now. I do three a year." There was a line drawing of the mill on the cover and a sepia-toned photo of the circle of women on the back. Inside were color pictures of quilts and rugs, a few crude bits of needlework.

"Most people want the quilts," Naomi said, looking over Heather's shoulder. "And usually the one they see in the catalogue's already gone by the time they call, but by then there's something else in stock, or they custom-order by pattern and colors. Then there's restoration work—we get sent the quilt or the coverlet or whatever, and we repair it using old textiles.

Rugs, too. They send us rugs you can barely hold up, they're like Swiss cheese. See here?" She pointed to a photograph of a hooked rug, WELCOME arched over a grinning golden retriever. "I think every other family in suburban Boston owns a golden retriever." She grinned. "It's far and away our most popular thing. Or they say, I want a welcome rug like that, but with a cocker spaniel. Or sometimes they send us a picture of their dog or their cat. But it's traditional to hook your pet into a rug, so that's fine with me."

"Is this supposed to be a sampler?" Heather said. She knew it sounded a little rude, but the thing was crudely done in cross-stitch, and very dull.

"I'd like to offer better samplers," said Naomi diplomatically. "It's kind of virgin territory, you know. There's plenty of old linen around. That's my job, or part of it, anyway. I go around and buy fabric wherever I can. I also plan our advertising and deal with customers." She smiled at Heather. "So tell me something. Who taught you to sew?"

"My grandmother," Heather said. "She does everything. Quilts, rugs, sewing, needlepoint. She knit all my sweaters when I was younger. When she was a little girl, she won this contest for girls. They had to make everything in their rooms— bedspreads, pillowcases, curtains. She got to go to Washington on a bus."

"How did she teach you?" Naomi said.

"Oh"—Heather shrugged—"I don't really know. She just gave me something to embroider when I was little and then she told me whenever I was doing it wrong. She said I had the finger."

"The what?" Naomi said, perplexed. Stephen was smiling.

"I guess it's silly," said Heather. "The magic finger, she said. Like an extra finger for needlework. She said you could sew all your life, but if you didn't have the finger, then whatever you sewed would be ugly, and if that was the case, then you shouldn't be sewing at all, because there are too many ugly things in the world as it is." Mary was scowling at her computer screen. Heather looked at Naomi, then shrugged, embarrassed. "That's what she says, anyway."

Naomi grinned. "I'd probably agree with your grandmother. I'll tell you the truth, I've had to turn down plenty of people who wanted to work in the collective. Though they're free to

come in, sit in with whoever's here and do their own work if
they want. And a lot of them get better that way, watching the
others. But some people don't have it. The finger." She
laughed. "Like me. I *definitely* don't have it."

"I'm sorry," Heather said, because she was.

"Oh, it's all right," Naomi told her, happily enough. "I have
other gifts. The main thing is, I can't—well, I *won't* sell something unless it's beautiful."

"My things are beautiful," Heather said gracelessly. "I'm
embroidering a baby sheet right now. I'm expecting a baby,
you know."

"Oh." Naomi nodded. "Congratulations!"

"Thank you," Heather said. She glanced at Stephen.

"I can see why you might be wanting to set up a more
flexible schedule than Stephen can offer you," Naomi rolled
along. "You know, we've got some baby things out in the
workroom, and there's a playpen we can bring down from the
attic. It's part of the collective's mission that children be absolutely welcome here—so bringing your baby to work is definitely an option for later."

From behind the desk Mary Sully clucked in disgust and
stabbed a number on her computer keyboard. Naomi frowned.

Heather looked over at the desk. Mary Sully had always
been a snob, she recalled. Her younger sister, too. Goddard
girls whose father had the snowplow contract in winter and
sat on his butt the rest of the year. Carol Sully had married
somebody from their class and already had a kid. Heather had
seen it—a wrinkled pruny thing dressed preposterously in a
sailor suit.

"May I see your baby sheet sometime?" Naomi asked.

"It's in the car." Heather went out to get it. It surprised her
how quickly this woman had become a person she wanted to
impress. Naomi, Heather thought, was somebody who would
understand about Ashley. She caught sight of herself in the
rearview mirror as she bent for her bag. The mark had faded
to pink: a four-clawed brand of pink in the middle of her
cheek, and queerly beautiful. She went back inside.

The sheet, she was the first to admit, was excessive. Edged
with bands of chain stitches alternating with bands of seed
stitches in the palest pink, its center was busy with white and
yellow flowers in satin stitch over all but a corner of the cotton

fabric. "I'll write her name here." Heather pointed to the empty place. "And her birth date. And I might overlay the chain stitches with a darker pink," she gushed, "I haven't decided. I've made her a sampler, too—just an alphabet sampler, but there's an object for each letter. Like an apple for A. It's this big." She showed with her hands. "But it's already hanging in the baby's room. I don't have it here."

Naomi was still holding the sheet, peering at it under the desk light, then holding it up to the afternoon light through the window. She hadn't said anything.

Heather was suddenly worried. "I know how to make quilts, too," she offered lamely, "but I'm not—"

"Uh-uh," said Naomi, shaking her head. "I have plenty of quilters."

"I'd love to work here," Heather heard herself entreat.

Naomi reached up behind her own neck, lifting the untidy ponytail to massage some invisible ache. She made a face. "I think when you finish this one you should bring it in for us to photograph. Then you'd better get started on another one as soon as possible. This is going to be a popular item."

Stephen chuckled. Heather was frowning. "Item?"

"Oh, absolutely. I can think of six customers in Fairfield County alone who are going to want one of these. If you can bear to stick to pink and blue that would be best." Naomi sighed. "People are such Neanderthals when it comes to gender associations. They're horrified by the idea of putting something pink on a boy or something with sailboats or baseball bats on a girl. Like an infant will suffer permanent gender confusion or instantly catch homosexuality!"

Heather stared at her, perplexed and horrified, and more than a little dazzled. Naomi, oblivious, went on.

"I like these flowers, though. They're very subtle, not cloying at all. For boys you can do, I don't know, trees or something. Pine trees? For girls I think this is just perfect. You leave the corners blank so people can custom-order. Did this take you long?" she asked Heather.

"No," Heather said. "Well, yeah, ten days, but I've only been working at night."

"Fantastic." Naomi nodded. "So, what do you think? The sheets would be wonderful. Your sampler sounds great, too.

You've got to bring it in, let me have a look. When can you start?"

Heather looked at Stephen. When could she start? Had she quit her job at the sports center? Was she fired? "When can I start?" she asked him.

"Whenever you want," he said.

"I'll start now," said Heather. She took the sheet from Naomi's hands. She took her bag. The circle in the room beyond did not exactly open for her. It was an effort, lifting a chair from against the wall and wedging open a place for herself. She looked at everyone in their turn, so everyone else would have a chance to see what Ashley's wife had done, it seemed like years before. Her belly was too big to cross her legs, so she had to lean forward a bit, spreading her baby's sheet across her knees. A bitterness broke out, and in its hush, her new life began.

Chapter 15

The Country of Childbirth

HE WAS EMBARRASSED BY WHAT SUE HAD DONE. This was why he did not call her immediately. Two weeks, in fact, would pass before he found her again at Naomi's mill, materializing suddenly in his truck with a load of new clapboard for the dilapidated rear of the building. They did not talk in depth about what had happened, but Heather could see how badly he felt. His feelings, at any rate, were unchanged, his ardor untempered, despite the fact that Heather, surging into her third trimester, grew increasingly distended by the hour. She didn't want to stop, either, and so they didn't stop.

Only two days before Polly was born, Ashley waited for her on the porch step of the mill, deflecting the incensed stares of the women who walked past with their shopping bags of cloth and thread. She felt, when she first drove off with him, the beginnings of unwell, but her greed drove most of the nausea away and his mouth on her nipple banished the rest. This latest act—the last, she must have known even then, of their life alone together—had had a quality of almost mournful solemnity, but also of fervor, as if they both were trying to get things in, or perhaps out, before the inevitable division awaiting them. Ashley's physical movements were small, but each seemed charged with object, symbol, perpetuity. She told his ear that she loved him. Their child woke and spun.

She knew, by then, that she was close, but Heather had never been given an actual due date for the baby. The midwife didn't hold with due dates—more patriarchy, she claimed, and more mystification for Heather, who, in her ignorance of the patriarchy, figured the baby would come when she was good and ready. And Polly did, a bare twenty-four hours later, in the middle of an August night and with a herald of the sharpest, most precise pain. Heather was awake in the moment before the pain, and so she was not surprised when it came. After it had passed, Heather got stiffly to her feet in the dark room and went downstairs to phone the midwife. She arrived—a brown woman with a pinched, serious face and a tendency to hum—about seven, which was when Heather woke Pick, and everybody got down to the business of having the baby.

It wasn't so bad a business, all in all. The midwife had early on declared Heather an eminently suitable candidate for a good, soul-enriching birth, with her wide pelvis and strong legs. The midwife had been to Costa Rica, where the women hung from branches and dropped their infants in the way nature intended, and she was forever urging Heather to squat over her open hands, but Heather didn't want to squat. She wanted to walk. All morning she led the two women around the lower field, pacing from the murky, mud-clogged pond down to their own modest bit of the Sabbathday—a narrow spur off where the river split a mile to the northwest—then back to the house, stopping every five minutes along the way, then every four minutes, then every three minutes. Then they went back inside.

The midwife, who had no children of her own, thought childbirth was ennobling and purifying, the ultimate expression of female power. Analgesics had no place in the ritual, not for a healthy young girl like Heather. She endorsed fluids and breathing deeply through contractions to feel the baby in its slow descent, and suggested Heather use the time between pains to visualize her cervix opening like rings on a pond's interrupted surface. To her credit, she remained pleasant and unruffled through the long day and then the long night, but Heather herself was wrung by the time it was dark. She wanted to call a halt and get some sleep, to start again in the morning with a fresh reserve, but the baby had expanded, not ebbed, in its demands. It wanted her attention all the time now, even between its assaults on her cervix, and it had turned hard inside her, like a stone dropping down away from her. What annoyed her about the pain was not its immense, battering force but its unwillingness to share her with anything else. The pain pushed everything away—every thought not relevant to itself, every optimistic groping toward when its opaque moment might pass. She could not believe the baby was doing this to her— she had been so used to loving it. To loving her.

It was the new day before the midwife said it was time to start pushing. Heather's strong legs weren't strong any longer.

She lay on her side across the foot of her bed, her arms out-flung, surrendering without protest to the agony that gripped her. She was glad Ashley was not here to see her like this, a swollen bug with spindly appendages, flailing about in a point-less frenzy of suffering. The midwife tried to pull Heather up onto her hands and knees, and when this didn't work she knelt by the bed at Heather's head and gave her a talking-to. Pick sat behind her, rubbing her back, but the truth was that Heather couldn't even feel that anymore.

Part of it, it came to her, was that she had loved being pregnant. The term of her baby's gestation had been the pre-cise term of her life with Ashley, and they had been the sweetest months she had yet known. Not being pregnant, no longer being pregnant, had about it a whiff of life without Ashley, though she knew this was irrational and needlessly hurtful to herself, since Ashley adored her. She didn't want it now. She would send it back when it came, though first she would get it out of her. Out of her first, then back where it came from. She climbed back onto her hands and knees.

The midwife crooned her hum from the country of child-birth. The baby dropped. Through the blood and cheesy mess, Heather took one look and felt a brutal, rapturous devotion. "Polly." Heather reached for her, but she was across the room, she had left the room, she was in the bathroom being doused by the midwife, shrieking her beautiful head to pieces, her newly stumped umbilicus darkening in rage. "Polly." Heather's voice was unaccountably soft, which was madden-ing, because she was actually furious. "Give her to me!"

"All right," the midwife said, laughing, passing the bundle along. "We're not quite finished, you know."

But Heather was finished. She barely followed the rest of it—the dense, livid placenta, the three stinging stitches, the sponges of water and disinfectant. She had Polly in her arms, that queer scrunched version of her father's beauty. So this was why she had never been able to conjure her baby's fea-tures from the disparate strains of mother, grandmother, and great-grandmother; Polly was Ashley's in the end; his beauty had stamped her face just as his love had set her in motion. Heather could barely bring herself to wait until the midwife had left.

By then it was fully morning. Heather made herself stay in

bed until the car was gone, and until Pick, sapped from the exertions of the day, had returned to her bed. Then she crept downstairs to the kitchen. The eyelet curtain nearly fluttered in a just perceptible morning breeze. The painted floorboards were cool under her bare feet, but the air was hot—steamy, end-of-summer heat. She held the baby between her breasts, like a pendant, and took the phone from its cradle to dial a number she had never dialed but knew by heart, regardless. She would have hung up if Sue answered, but Sue didn't answer.

"It's me," said Heather, her voice cracking with relief and euphoria. "Ashley?"

"Yes," he said.

She took a breath. "I'm calling about the baby."

His joy flooded the hush between them. She glowed, waiting for him to ask, but in that stillness something gave beneath her: the earth on its undependable axis, the legs that had crouched to deliver his child.

"It's a boy!" he crowed. "He's big—nine pounds, two ounces. His name is Joseph."

Chapter 16

Gifts

BY THE TIME POLLY HAD LEARNED THE DIFFI-cult physical skill of smiling, she was already a child who did not smile generally. She looked at things as if she knew them already and would prefer to look at something she didn't know. She learned the specific comfort of her own left thumb. She learned to beat her mother's breast with one efficient fist. Even in sleep, she made mountains of laundry. Her father did not come to see her.

Naomi came on the eighth day, when the baby had fully lost her strained and put-upon demeanor and was radiantly plump—a bit like her mother, who had lost the bloated look of her pregnancy but kept the general padding. As gifts, she brought bags of the kinds of things a non-mother gives a new mother—toddler toys and dolls with bits that could break off and frilly, complicated baby clothes. There was an embarrassing munificence of it, about which Naomi made various self-deprecating comments. Heather, who in fact had everything she needed already, felt a little badly for Naomi and wondered how friendless the Flourish circle had implied her to be, and how bleak her prospects. With Polly crooked in her arms and ardently, efficiently pulling the stiffness from her heavy breasts, she cared even less about such matters than she had before, and indeed the circle of women felt mindlessly distant from this primal, tender connection. Naomi, Heather noted, tended to avert her eyes, and so she put Polly, who was sated and dropping sweetly to milky sleep, into Naomi's arms, less as a gesture of friendship than out of some impulse to see what would happen, and indeed Naomi began abruptly, if noiselessly, to cry. Her lips brushed the fine white hairs of Polly's scalp. Then she smelled the baby's talcy smell, wiped dry her face, and made an embarrassed escape. Pick watched Naomi leave, then came out onto the back porch to take the baby.

"Surprised she has none of her own," said Pick, binding the newborn's arms tight to her sides in a swaddle. "Maybe the husband doesn't want kids. He's a strange one."

"He is?" said Heather. She hadn't even known Naomi had a husband.

"Wanted to get people into some community maple-syrup scheme. Then he put up a solar-type thing on his house and tried to get Corbet Hodge to do the same, Janelle said."

"Oh," said Heather. "Solar what?"

Pick smirked. She put the baby into her wicker cradle. "Who knows. 'Living off the land.' I'm an open-minded person, you know. I don't think I'm better than anybody. I'm not prejudiced. I just think some people are good at some things and some people are good at other things." She shook her head. "What a fellow like that thinks he knows about living off *this* land I'll never understand."

Heather wiped a drop of her own milk from the baby's lower lip. "A fellow like what?"

Pick gave her a look. "It isn't about religion, you know. I'm not saying somebody's better or worse than somebody else just because he's Jewish. People have their own place and I feel they ought to stay in their place. When somebody moves into another person's place and tries to tell them how to get along, I'm not surprised they don't get a welcome wagon saying come on in. Come on in and tell me how to live my life, cause you obviously know how to better than me that's been doing just fine until now!"

Heather frowned at her. "I didn't even know she was Jewish," she said. She was trying to think if she'd ever met anyone Jewish. Or anyone else.

Her grandmother contemplated the baby, then reached down into the crib and wiggled a pacifier against her tiny pursed lips. She had been trying to interest Polly in this device, but Polly was interested only in the genuine article. "You know, Heather," her grandmother sighed, abandoning her efforts, "if everybody could sew like you, nobody would pay a hundred and fifty dollars for a baby sheet." (This fact continued to amaze and bemuse Pick.) "I just think in life you stick with what you're used to. If you ignore your gifts, it's like you're telling God thanks but no thanks." Pick sighed. "This is what I'm saying. It's not an insult. You just should stick with what you can do. That gal came up here, and she started making money. And she's good at it, I'll grant you that. Ina Hodge said they're putting up aluminum siding on their house next month. That's a five-thousand-dollar job at least, and she and Janelle made that money themselves. And it's what I said, we're all good at something. Jewish people are good at business." She looked at Heather. "Janelle came around last year, tried to get me up to make quilts for that gal. I told her no and said it was because of my hands, you know. It's different for you. You have a baby to support. But I have no intention to sew quilts to make somebody else richer."

"Well, I don't really think Naomi's that rich," Heather said. "She wears these old clothes, and she's always saying how her house is falling apart and it doesn't even have a real bathroom. And anyway, the mill isn't like a factory at all. Naomi says it's a collective. Everybody, like, owns a part of it. There's no boss or anything."

"Who hired you?" Pick said, somewhat sarcastically. "That gal did. So she's the boss. You sew, she earns money from it. If she stops liking what you do, she can fire you. Is that right?"

Heather, who figured it was, nodded grimly.

"She can call it whatever she wants, but she's the boss, and you work for her. These things are in the blood, sweetie. You're good at sewing, she has a head for business. Now just so you understand, Heather, I'm not unhappy about this arrangement. I wasn't too thrilled with you working at the sports center." She tried to look disapprovingly at the baby, but didn't quite manage it. "But that gal isn't running a charity, and no matter what she might claim, she sure isn't turning Goddard Falls into some Iron Curtain country. Just keep it in mind."

"Okay," Heather said, but she couldn't help adding, "Naomi's really nice, though."

"I never said they weren't nice," Pick said. She frowned. "Why do you think she cried?"

Heather shook her head. The baby was sleeping now, so quietly that Heather had to touch her stomach to make sure she was breathing. She had begun to do this rather obsessively. "I don't know. I don't know her very well."

She didn't really want to talk about it anymore, so she sat down on the bed beside the crib and got out her work. Pick had been right about Naomi's business acumen, at least; the picture of Polly's baby sheet in the spring catalogue had provoked a modest phenomenon. Fourteen of her embroidered sheets had been dispatched around the country—she kept a list of the towns in her sewing basket—and there was a current waiting list for eleven more. She could sew baby sheets and baby samplers for the rest of her life, Heather thought, or at least till she got tired of it. Then she could sew something else. She could stay at home for a bit, till the fall at least, and then she could take her baby to the mill and put her down in the crib with a mobile or a toy and sit in the circle until Ashley was able to bring them home.

She could not wait for Ashley to see their daughter. She had berated herself for catching him so off guard and—with such weird timing—so soon after baby Joe was born, but of course he had told her not to feel badly and that he was happy to know about their Polly. He was pretty much tied to home, though, Ashley said, with relatives and all descending in their streams. It would not be easy to get away just now. It might be a week, Ashley said, before he could come to see them.

But it was more than a week. In fact, more than four weeks passed before he rattled his old Volvo down their drive. It began to puzzle her. She nearly telephoned again, to be more insistent about it, but the moment passed in a fresh cry for milk. Once, in the middle of the night, she even conceived the angry plan of going herself to see him, of bringing Polly to him, but by morning the impulse had been overwhelmed by practicalities and caution. Exertion of any kind was torturously difficult, in any case, since the summer's end had sunk into a steamy, enervating lull, and the extent of her movement was to bring the baby out behind the house, where they were shaded by the roof's overhang, and there they sat, still sticky hot, watching haze hang over the back field as it sloped down to its little murky pond. But it nagged her, more and more, as their daughter's beauty seemed to grow hourly, that he wasn't there to exclaim over it, over her calmly alert expressions, the premature furrow of her brow. There had been mornings she woke to find Polly staring at her, her blue gaze steady, and it had struck Heather with a paralysis of humility, the depth of that gaze—the way it made her feel so completely *known*. It seemed to her that the baby's understanding was unmarred by prejudice, and hence perfect, and that if she could herself learn to see herself in the same way, she might be free of whatever trouble dogged her, simpering at the peripheries of her awareness. Because it did hurt, what was thought of her, whatever she might have said to Stephen Trask or to her grandmother, and the truth was that she did not precisely *like* to be stared at, or thought ill of. She could not, for example, remember the austere and tired Dean of Freshmen in her small gray office without a spike of unease, the brief punch of an old but not entirely inactive wound. She could not think of her pregnant self, turning in the circle of women with her own fierce and bitter expression, without fighting the strongest—if briefest—urge to cover her face. But when Ashley finally came and stood over the crib with her, and took her hand to look down at their child, with their love, then she would be strong enough for whatever petty cruelties lay strewn in her path like bad flowers.

But when he came at last, he never got close to the crib. Indeed, he poised at the door with one foot idling behind the other, as if in preparation for a crisp about-face and sprint in the direction he'd come. Pick came to the door, scowled at the visitor, and called for Heather, but she stood her silent ground until Heather came downstairs. "This," Heather began, breathless, "is—"

"I can tell," said Pick. She threw a glare diamond-sharp at her granddaughter's defiler, then huffed away. Heather shifted the baby in her arms to cover her belly. She still felt fat. Ashley looked painfully fine.

"Well, Heather," he said, "I can't really stay."

"Look," Heather said, thrusting Polly forward. "Look at her. She's beautiful."

"Of course." He was sweet. "I told you she'd be beautiful. So. How are you?"

"I'm—" Heather began, but stopped. She had no idea how she was. "Isn't she wonderful?" she reverted. "She has your eyes." This was not precisely true. The baby had nobody's eyes in particular, and at any event, she was sound asleep against Heather's breast, with her eyes firmly shut. "Come in." She stepped back. "Come on in, we'll go into the living room."

"I can't stay," he said again, not moving, but a touch more affably. "I just came to see you. And I brought you a present."

"Oh," Heather said. Involuntarily, she glanced at his hands, but they were empty.

"You going back to work at Naomi's soon?" he asked.

"Well, I'm working already. She comes and brings me the assignments, and she picks them up. I don't need to go into the mill at all."

Ashley nodded at this, as if she'd said something considered, with deeper meaning. "Maybe that's best."

"I miss it, though." She sneaked a smile. "I miss the rides home."

Ashley smiled, his line of sight shifting slightly, past her. "Well, that's going to be harder now, you have to realize. Things are kind of a mess."

"What things?" Heather said. "Is something the matter with your car?"

"What?" he said. "My car? No, it's . . . Well, actually, I got a new car. Station wagon. Sue insisted. No, I mean, it'll be harder now. To see you. Now that I've got a kid."

In her arms, the baby squeaked and stirred.

"Two kids," Heather said, wounded. "You have two kids."

"Well," Ashley said. "You know what I mean."

"I don't actually," Heather said, because she actually didn't.

Ashley reached back behind his neck, idly twisting his ponytail around one long and elegant finger. "She wants me around all the time. She isn't like you, Heather. I mean, look at you. You're more beautiful than ever. You look healthy, and you're just a great mother, it's obvious. But Sue's a wreck. She can't do breast-feeding, even though she tried. She can't take care of the baby without a lot of help. She's got that new-mother-depression thing, so it's like she's the baby and we all have to take care of her, too." He shook his small head. His face was tight. "And that's just how it is. I get to leave the house to go to work and the supermarket, or pick up people at the bus station in White River Junction, but that's it." He smiled piteously, inviting her to feel sorry for his plight. "So like I said, it's all going to be harder now."

"But you'll still . . ." This was taking a minute to sink in. It seemed to her that she was afraid even to say it. "We'll still be able . . . *Ashley*."

"Oh," he said affably. "Well, sure. If you want."

"If I *want*!"

The word came out loud. Polly woke with a flinch of put-upon surprise. She turned her tiny face to her father and stared, her eyes broadly open.

"We woke her," Ashley observed, though he seemed to have gleaned this without ever looking at Polly directly. "Guess I'd better get going."

"Wait!" Heather said frantically. *When will I see you?* was what she wanted to know. *When are we going to . . .* "Where's my present?" is what she actually came out with.

"Oh." He grinned. "It's that." He had turned to his car and gestured.

Heather didn't see anything. "What?"

"I'm giving you my car. You need a car, don't you?"

Right away, she knew she was going to cry. Yes, of course, she needed a car. A mother with a small baby and an aging grandparent in a remote house needed a car, and just because she had been putting it off didn't mean she wasn't aware of her responsibilities. She had even planned, vaguely, to ask Stephen to drive her down to Peytonville soon, to look in the lots with her and help her pick out something serviceable. But this was something else altogether. Her lack of transportation had been the catalyst for her first lovemaking with Ashley, and as such, it was a perversely cherished thing. The car—his car, in which they had found themselves so sweetly entrenched—was a kind of holy ground to Heather, a portable Cave of Lovers in the guise of a rusted, eight-year-old Volvo with upward of a hundred thousand miles on the odometer. To drive it to the Stop & Shop seemed a kind of sacrilege. No. To drive it without Ashley in it was a sacrilege. That he even wanted her to was horrible. She felt the first tear make its treacly descent down her left cheek. How could he want her not to need him like this? It was callous, this obliteration of the circumstances that had brought them together. Callous and wounding.

"I can't take your car," she told him, between chokes.

He looked at her, baffled. "Why not? It's a good car. And I just told you, I got a new one. I don't need it. You just need to take it to Peytonville and register it. The papers are in the glove compartment. You can write that you paid, I don't know, like a hundred bucks for it, on the transfer document. It's easy." He frowned at Heather, who wept on. "I don't get this."

"When do I see you," she gasped, "if I have my own car?"

Now he got edgy. "Oh." Ashley shrugged. "Well, you'll see me."

"When?"

"Lots. When did you see me before?"

"When you drove me home!" Heather cried. Polly started to cry, too. Heather put her up over her shoulder and rubbed her swaddled back.

He let her alone for a moment; then, when he saw she wasn't going to stop by herself, he stepped close and pressed his cheek against her wet cheek. Between sobs, she smelled: nutmeg and spicy sweat, then, fainter, the sweet talc of somebody else's baby. Polly moved against her, and for a moment she wanted to put her other arm around Ashley, to hold them both equally to each other and to her, but Ashley's mouth had found her ear and was distracting her. By force of habit, his lips closed over the lobe—he couldn't help himself. Faintness fell over her. She wondered, vaguely, where she might put the baby down. "I missed you," Ashley said.

"I've missed you so much," said Heather, who kissed him first. The doorway seemed to be getting smaller, the floor buckled beneath them. It was a scratch to the most gruesome and long-standing itch, in the deepest place—finally, he was touching her again. Places not yet healed were awake and complaining, and she felt like laughing. After all, he was hers. He still came to her for this, despite his other life. His lesser life, she thought, breaking off her kiss to kiss Polly. He was making his sound, the one she loved, the one that made her crazy as he pressed her. It was like a language of hums and breaths, happy and urgent. She really wanted to put the baby down. "Heather," Ashley said.

By now Polly was notably unhappy, sputtering her small noises of distress and tensing her bundled body. Even so, it was Ashley's hand on her breast—so much harder now, and larger, and more tender—that made her think of what to do.

"Wait," she said. She put up her free hand. "She's hungry."

He seemed surprised, then a little subdued. "I should go, then."

"Don't go." Her voice was calm. "Come with me."

She led him with one hand through the front hall and then into the living room, where she sat on the blanket-covered couch and deftly unbuttoned her shirt. Polly, sensing progress, grew still and admirably focused, but Ashley, who perched awkwardly on an armchair, looked quickly away. Then he looked back.

She was good at this. She held the baby in her right arm's crook and flicked the little buckle that latched the cup to one side of her nursing bra (fastening it up again was harder, but by then you could usually put the baby down and use both hands). The panel folded down, showing her breast, round and heavy, with a nipple rosy-dark, newly recovered from the blistering first weeks of nursing. She didn't give Polly the nipple right away but held her still on her lap, looking down over her and stroking her avid face. She wanted him to see.

Only after, once the baby had latched on, did she look up. She loved this. At first it had horrified her, the way the baby's suck had made her feel. At first she had thought herself unnatural. But now it was in her face, and she didn't hide it. The fierce little mouth, single-minded and strong and made to fit her precisely, worked away, draining the tightness, the cement heaviness, from her breast. Even these weeks later, she felt her womb contract. She wondered what it would feel like to come now. She thought it might be different—richer, in a way, and more lasting, not so wildly furtive. She wondered if there would be pain and found herself hoping there might be, a little. She had been saving this for him. Heather unbuttoned her bra on the other side before Polly was ready. Her shirt was widely open, the sun warm across her chest. She knew him very well. She moved the baby to the other arm and looked up to find Ashley's eyes on her.

"I could use a lift back into town," he said, his voice low.

Heather smiled. "All right. Let me just put her down and tell my grandmother."

It was her first time out of the house since the baby. He let her drive, and it came back quickly, despite the long hiatus. She knew instantly that she loved driving this car, putting her hands where his hands had always been, sitting where he had sat. She loved looking across at him on the passenger side, his little frown. She had closed her shirt but left the cups of her nursing bra unbuttoned. The fabric was soft against her, and dampening in two dark spots over the nipples. Ashley, mesmerized, watched them. Since she was driving, she didn't even ask before turning off, taking him along for the ride. He shifted beside her, trying to get comfortable. It was hard not to touch him, to put it off even this little bit. The logging road was matted with windfall leaves, cacophonous and vivid-bright, and the tires made a choked and wadded sound. Heather drove a little faster.

"Easy," Ashley said. "We'll get there."

"I want to be there now." She laughed.

His hand reached across. The wet over her nipple grew suddenly hot. "All right," he told her. "Let's just stop right here."

Chapter 17

The Marketplace

A FEW WEEKS LATER, SHE WOKE TO NURSE HER daughter in the cool blue light before dawn and noted, as she unbuttoned her nightgown, the first real shudder of autumn. Downstairs, Pick was already at work in the kitchen, the waft of applesauce in midproduction (an annual and fairly arduous event) and the tinkle of radio voices her accompaniments. Heather perched on the edge of her bed, feeling the weight of the baby, who was wrapped thinly and balanced on her forearm as she sucked. She reached for Polly's quilt to bind her further into warmth, and the action struck her hard with the newness of its necessity.

On the chair beside her bed lay her current work, a pictorial sampler dedicated to twins unfortunately named Krystal and Kandi. Every element of this work had been specified by the client, from the hothouse pink of the thread to the inanely posed teddy bears on either side of the twins' birth date, to the injunction that only cross-stitch—surely the most uninspired and dully restrictive stitch ever devised—be used in its execution. It was demeaning, Heather thought, wondering how much of Naomi's praise she must have absorbed in order to feel this way. With each uncharacteristically harsh jab of her needle she had had to fight the urge to sabotage the sampler entirely by making it so ugly that even this tasteless client would reject it. But she owed Naomi more than that, Heather thought, exasperated. She had given one of the teddy bears an impish leer, but it hadn't helped. Polly finished nursing, burped, and drifted to rest, subdued with milky happiness. Heather unwrapped the quilt and put her in the middle of her own bed, covering her. The baby jammed her left thumb into her little mouth. For some preposterous reason, this small act of independence made Heather feel terribly depressed. Placing pillows around the baby to prevent her somehow finding the edge of the bed, she went downstairs.

Pick was at the stove, churning her apples in a pot so big it partly covered a second burner, leaving a couple of outer coils exposed and glowing orange bright. The smell was wildly sweet, a vaporous cinnamon. She added sugar by the teacup and didn't turn around.

"Smells wonderful," Heather said. "Didn't you say you were going to make it less sweet this year?"

"That was before the baby," said Pick. "A little sugar will make the baby eat more applesauce."

"Oh," said Heather, who had no idea when Polly would be ready for applesauce, or indeed for anything that didn't come from her own breast. "Well, good, then."

"There's coffee." Pick pointed with her elbow. "You're up early."

"Yuh," Heather said, pouring herself a cup. "But at least she's sleeping through the night. I'd rather get up early than have to get up in the middle of the night."

"She's a good baby," Pick observed. She threw another teacup of sugar in the pot. "But I hope you don't think she slept through the night."

"What?" Heather blinked.

"*You're* sleeping through the night." Pick was chuckling; her wide back moved under the housecoat. "I changed her, about three-thirty."

Heather shook her head. "I didn't hear a thing."

"I don't sleep like I used to," Pick said. "You get nearer the end than the beginning, you start thinking what a waste it is, giving over all that time to sleep. *You* need it, though. I know. You sleep now. You'll have plenty of time when I'm not around to get up and down all night long."

"Oh, Pick," Heather said. "You'll outlive us all. Next time just wake me up."

Pick frowned down into her applesauce. "You got that car all seen to?"

Heather had. She'd driven into Peytonville the day before, gingerly and slow on the roads already clogged with flatlanders ogling the leaves. The car, it turned out, would not pass inspection until she handed over two hundred dollars to a bald mechanic located strategically near the DMV, and the inspector himself had taken one look at Polly, whom Heather had placed on the passenger-side floor in her basket, and started

screaming, so she'd had to drive right to the Peytonville Wal-
Mart and buy a car seat she'd outgrow in another five pounds.
Altogether, the gift car had wiped out a good chunk of her
savings, but it was still worth it. She had been wrong, she now
understood, to respond so poorly to his gift. It had been hateful
of her, too, because now it was all too clear why he had given
her the car. His car. The car was known in town, after all, as
his, and in giving it to Heather he had said that she, too, was
his, and the child was his, and he acknowledged them. It was
a great gift, and she had wept over it, because she had doubted
him, which was also hateful. Sometimes she felt she deserved
neither of them, Ashley or Polly.

That said, however, she hadn't exactly felt the need to use
the car at all, especially since Ashley had developed a knack
of materializing whenever her anxiety about seeing him hit
some critical point. Such was the imperative of their connection: when she longed sufficiently, he was suddenly there:
coming up the drive in his own new car, an apple-red station
wagon with an infant carrier latched in the middle of the backseat. And he seemed to need her even more now than before,
and could barely make himself wait until they had reached
their place at the end of the logging road. He was so sweet to
her, too, and inexpressibly gentle with her hurt places. He did
not mind that her waist had not reappeared after Polly's birth,
or that her hips were marked with dark ridges, or that her
breasts leaked and hung and had ravaged nipples. She was
bigger inside, too, which she hated, but Ashley appeared not
to notice. He seemed to float in her, buoyed by contentment,
his hips slender between her spread thighs, like something lithe
and light and small on a dense, vast surface. She felt this more
now than she had during the pregnancy, which was odd, because technically she was lighter by fifteen pounds. When she
apologized about her size, he shrugged and said it made no
difference. He mentioned, once, that Sue wouldn't let him near
her.

Heather poured herself some coffee and sat at the table,
setting aside the *Goddard Clarion* Pick had been reading and
flipping a spoonful of sugar from the bowl into her cup. A few
crystals fell on the newsprint. She pulled it closer to flick them
away, and without warning he was there, next to a Stop &
Shop ad featuring a dancing potato and the reminder that it

was time to stock up before the snow fell, bold-printed under the heading *Recent Arrivals!*, subcategory Mary Hitchcock Hospital—one great big healthy boy born to Ashley Deacon and Sue Locke Deacon, a nine-pound bruiser to be known as Joseph Locke Deacon from now till the end of time, the cellulose glue between his parents who grinned on either side of him in a gray, grainy photograph, Ashley's face half covered by shadow, half by his son's big head. Heather's throat seized up.

"You okay?" Pick said. "Need a pat?"

She shook her head and whipped over the page.

"You knew about this?" Pick said archly, evading the evasion.

"Oh sure," said Heather, her voice straining for nonchalance.

Pick turned back to the stove. "You might go into town. We could use milk. And you've got a ride, anyway." This was said with some sarcasm. To Pick, the old Volvo in the drive was a reminder of its former owner's bad behavior, and indeed, she seemed to bear it a greater grudge even than Ashley himself. Perhaps she'd figured out that Polly had been conceived in the backseat.

Heather considered. She understood that the first time she appeared in downtown Goddard with Polly, telephones would ring in her wake, threading their way to the farthest points of the Goddard and Goddard Falls web. They had to talk about her, didn't they? She was, after all, their ordained example of what bad behavior looked like, and her not caring was an additional affront—a gratuitous *fuck you*.

But what could they actually *do* to her? Express disapproval? Utter aspersions? They couldn't take her child away or throw her in jail; in New Hampshire, too, these were modern times, if not quite so modern as they were elsewhere. Even her newly affixed license plate beseeched her to Live Free or face an unacceptable alternative. And she had only loved a man and borne his child—a child who was radiant and healthy and strong. And if she had the temerity to be happy and healthy herself, after doing something so unnatural, then all was wrong with the universe. But the universe wasn't her problem.

"Sure," Heather told Pick. "Make me up a shopping list."

A few hours later, she squeezed herself into the only pair of her jeans from before that accommodated her, maneuvered a still-sleeping Polly into her car seat, and drove into Goddard.

The light was shrill through the leaves, as yet unfallen but just beginning to wave their colorful farewells. She passed the mill, its small lot crowded with cars from out of state, and drove to the traffic light opposite the dingy church, where Goddard Falls Road met Elm. There was one car before her and one car behind. Her hand had unthinkingly flicked the right directional and it clicked a hollow beat. Heather looked right, where Elm veered off toward the Stop & Shop, then left, down to the town's core, such as it was: the squat Federal homes in their colonially correct colors, the new church with its spiky salvaged steeple, the black glint of the sports center where the road curved out of town. And she saw the spanking white of the snug house that was Tom and Whit's, its crammed back house and barn lined up behind it like graduated forms. The big Adirondack chairs on the front porch seemed unreasonably bright red and were filled with tourists in plumage as polychromatic as the leaves they'd come to see. In a rush, she longed to sit among them, to show herself first to this gentler jury of the wider world. She bit her lip.

The car behind her gave a discreet honk. The light was green.

She swung the car left, downtown.

Tom and Whit's was the single reason Goddard didn't get a Stop & Shop, or any other kind of supermarket, till the seventies, when there was enough of a summer community to make a stink about the lack of facilities. People used to wide aisles and elegant displays were just not equal to the idea that a little country store could possibly have the single specific thing they needed, whatever that single thing happened to be, notwithstanding the store's motto, helpfully displayed on a sign out front: IF WE DON'T HAVE IT, YOU DON'T NEED IT. True enough, but the locals were equally aware of the coda, unwritten though it was: *Sure we have it, but first you have to find it*. They could hardly be blamed for feeling dubious, or just preemptively exhausted at the prospect of looking. The space immediately accessible from the street was an unassuming general store, not terribly large and not terribly crowded, with a central tourist-friendly table laden with local honey and homemade muffins (later a coffee maker), and a corner given over to paint. To get the rest you had to go—oh, they used to joke about this—behind the green door.

It really was green. It led to the back house, crammed with bulk foods and animal feeds, which itself led to the barn, so crowded it seemed as if whole farmhouses had been disassembled for parts and packed away here. Clothes were in the basement (Whit Chase had to show you the way himself), and the attic was divided between hunting and fishing things and regulation supply for the National Guard (Whit was a colonel). The farther in you went, the more vast and the more plentiful, but getting what you needed out of Tom and Whit's required a kind of stubborn, homegrown Zen. For just about everyone else, it had got to be a pain, driving to Hanover or even Peytonville just for the same grocery run the whole rest of the world had around the corner.

Heather parked on the road and scooped Polly out of her car seat. She was stirring, making little puckers with her mouth, slowly formulating the concept of what she wanted next from life. There was avid interest as she crossed the porch, and Heather agreeably showed the baby, turning to the "Oohs" around her as she threaded through the Adirondacks to the front door. "What a cute bitty thing," one woman said, leaping to her feet. Unbidden, she tickled Polly's chin, then poked at her tummy through the baby blanket. Polly, wide awake now, gaped in mute disbelief. "What is she, two months?"

"Two months," Heather confirmed.

"What a sweetheart!" said the woman. "I've got a little grandniece the same age." She poked again. "And what a sweet little dress."

"Thank you," Heather said warmly. "I made it. I make all her clothes."

"Well, my word," the woman said. Her hair was the color of brass, and—it looked like—the texture. "My niece, she couldn't sew a button! Y'all from around this town?" She peered at her companion, a rotund man in a new down jacket zipped up tight. He sat in one of the Adirondacks reading USA Today. "What's this town?"

"It's Goddard," said Heather. "Yes, I'm from Goddard. Well, from Goddard Falls."

"Why, you lucky thing," the woman said. "Imagine living in a sweet town like this. You lucky thing."

"Thank you," Heather said, though she wasn't quite sure that she was authorized to give thanks on behalf of the town. Polly turned her head to nudge Heather's chest. "Excuse me," she told the woman.

The first thing Heather saw when she went inside was Celia Trask's behind, large and upturned as Celia rummaged in a box under the coffee table. The second thing she saw was one of her own baby samplers hanging in the corner next to a hooked "Welcome" rug and a large notice inviting tourists to stop by the mill. She hoisted Polly a bit and stepped over to the corner.

It wasn't her original sampler, which had been photographed and returned and was now back home, hung by a nail over Polly's crib. It was the second or third she had done for Naomi, about 20 by 20 inches, with "A is for Apple" leading off in the top left corner and a name—Olivia Michelle Kuenne—in the lower right. She remembered this one especially because she had thought the name was beautiful, and because a photograph had been sent with the order: a little girl, dark-eyed and lighter than air, coaxed for an instant into a smile larger than herself. Heather had thought the sampler was long gone to Princeton by now, and yet here it was, still in Goddard.

"That yours?" Celia said, behind her.

"Yuh," said Heather. "I was just wondering what it was doing here."

"It's been up for a week or two. Naomi always has something up." She rolled her eyes. "You wouldn't believe how many tourists go straight for that corner. I told Whit, we ought to start charging for directions to the mill."

"That's great," said Heather, who supposed it was.

"Well," Celia said, a little grudgingly, "it's a good piece of work, that sampler."

"Thanks." Heather smiled. "Stephen well?"

"Yuh," she sighed. "So, you need something?"

"Milk," said Heather. "And I thought I'd have a little coffee and sit out."

Celia looked at her. "Out?"

"Out there." She used Polly's head to point. "You know, like them."

Celia frowned. "But why?"

Heather couldn't think of why, precisely. She took her coffee from Celia. Polly was butting at her, getting antsy.

"It's just," Celia said, "you know, Whit and Ann just stepped out. They went up to the bank. They're coming back."

She was saved from responding by Polly, who chose this moment to open her dainty mouth and wail. Heather dropped coins into the basket on the coffee table. "See you," she told Celia. She stepped outside and kicked the door closed with her foot. There were two Adirondacks free now. She put her coffee down on the armrest of one and sat, maneuvering Polly. She hadn't really done this in the open before. Some things had to be pushed aside, others pulled down, and others raised. Polly arched. The man with the *USA Today* glanced up, gaped, reddened, and looked stiffly away; his wife read a map of the White Mountains. The baby sucked hard, the world subsumed. Heather felt the familiar jolt of pain on the edge of pleasure and closed her eyes before smiling, so that no one would see her. Polly's mouth pulled the milk away, tireless and determined, her fist beating the breast to make it come faster. Heather drew her jacket across the baby, so that the only part that showed was that small place where they connected. They sat that way as the minutes passed. She had never felt more peaceful, or more modest.

The cold air hit her nipple as Polly released her. She rummaged under her jacket, moving her clothes around, then shifted the baby to her other arm and the open shirt over her other breast.

"Oh my God. Whit, for Christ's sake!"

Heather saw to the baby first, then she looked up.

Ann Chase was back. She stood beside her husband's truck, staring in disgust. Whit was climbing out the driver's side. He didn't hear his wife the first time, so she said it again.

"For Christ's sake, Whit. *Do something.*"

Whit didn't seem to know what to do. Heather, realizing that she must be near enough this outrage to see it for herself, looked around, but everything seemed normal. The tourists, who had been reading or rocking or both, were starting to look up. Now, inexplicably, they were starting to look at Heather.

Heather looked at herself.

At her elbow, the coffee still steamed. Polly's soft head

moved, but more slowly. Soon she would stop altogether and turn one sleepy cheek to the nipple. She liked to drift off this way, with this moist thing abutting her, pressing her cheek into her toothless mouth. It was a posture that expelled any notion of wrongness, that was so opaquely good that Heather could not seem to make a connection between the ugliness of Ann Chase's voice and herself—the apparent irritant.

"Well, sweetheart," said Polly's earlier admirer suddenly, "don't you think y'all ought to do that someplace warmer?"

Whit Chase was climbing the steps, his livid wife behind him. "You cover up, young miss." His voice was tight.

"I'm sorry?" Heather found her voice.

"You should be," said Ann.

Heather heard Celia open the door to the shop.

"What's the matter?" said Heather.

"You think this is some kind of street corner, is that it?" said Ann, who was shaking now.

"No," Heather said. Then, somewhat in disbelief: "Street corner?"

"You advertising your wares?"

"I'm feeding my daughter," Heather said, declaring the obvious.

"Whit," snapped Ann, without turning her head or breaking her stare, "get Nelson on the phone."

Heather, who did not know who Nelson was, didn't react to this.

"She was hungry," she said instead. "Look, I'm almost finished."

"You're finished *now*," Ann hissed. Whit moved past them and slammed the door.

The tourist, who had watched this exchange, put her White Mountain map in her handbag. "Come on, honey." She took hold of her husband's arm. "We're leaving."

Ann glared at them, too, as they stepped by her; then she turned back to Heather. "Who told you you could do that on my porch?" She took a step closer to Heather, who was holding her jacket across Polly's head.

"Well, no one," Heather said truthfully. "But it didn't occur to me there'd be a problem. I mean"—she gave Ann a cautious smile—"you kind of have to do it when they want it, not when it's convenient. Even if you're in public, you know?" She

noted, and resented, the supplicatory tone that had crept, un-
invited, into her voice.

Ann was shaking her head. Her wide cheeks were ruddy
now, and her straw-yellow hair was motionless in the light
wind. Vaguely, Heather wondered how she managed *that*. "I'll
tell you what I know, young lady." Her voice was low and
clear. "I know you can't bear to do a damn thing unless it's
in public. It'd never occur to you to do something if the whole
world isn't there to see you do it. You think we want to see
you takin' off your clothes and stickin' out your chest like
something in a zoo?"

There was a little smacking sound as the baby released her.
Heather wanted to pull down her sweater, but she suddenly
cared more to hide her baby than to hide her breast. Ann's
eyes dropped and she grimaced. Heather was abruptly enraged.

"I don't understand your problem, Mrs. Chase," she said
tersely. "Breast-feeding's good for the baby and all. I mean,"
she said, clarifying herself as if she were explaining things to
a child not much older than Polly, "it's natural."

"There's nothing natural about this baby," Ann said. "Don't
you hide behind that. You think you can get away with whatever you feel like. Well, it's a free country, I guess. But don't
you kid yourself that the rest of the world is just going to look
the other way. There's plenty of people who care about decency, even if you're too busy being *natural* to think about
such a thing."

Heather, shocked, wanted to hit her. Out of the corner of
her eye, she saw more colors. More people, still and listening
to them.

"I'm sorry if I've offended you," she said, shrugging her
jacket closed. Polly was asleep, but her jaw still moved in
rhythm, nursing at some dream-breast. Heather made to pick
up her bag.

"Oh no," said Ann, stepping up beside her and placing a
claw on her arm. "No, you don't. You're waiting for Nelson."

Heather stared at her. "Who's Nelson?" she asked. People
seemed to be collecting at her feet, streaming toward her, from
all the corners of the world, in their cars. One stopped as she
watched, a rusted white pickup with two hunters in front and
a big matted mutt in the back.

"You won't listen to me, that's fine," Ann was saying. "You

won't listen to your own conscience, cause you don't have one, fine. I'll even go so far as to say maybe it isn't all your fault. Your mom wasn't much of an example. But you'll sure as hell not make a spectacle of yourself after this."

"God, you're a bitch," Heather said. She said it thoughtfully, because it was a kind of discovery, and quietly, because she only meant to say it to herself.

Quick as water, Ann reached out and hit her with an open hand. The blow landed flat on Heather's cheek.

"Now, Ann." A broad white hand reached out and took Ann's hand away. Heather's cheek flared with heat. She pressed it with the hand that wasn't holding Polly. The man standing between them now was pale and soft, with a face that was kind even as it frowned. "Ann, I came right over," he said to her, his voice soothing. "Now, what's up?"

"She's up," Ann said, a ribbon of hysteria threading her voice. "She's up on her damn throne, like she's some kinda queen and we all have to pretend she's not just your average whore. Flouncing around like she owns the ground under all our feet!"

For the first time, the man glanced at Heather. He wore a tan uniform with dark brown cuffs and a collar. The pin over his left breast read: *Erroll.*

"I'm not," Heather said, pointlessly.

Ann turned to the people grouped on the stairs and at their foot. "She had her shirt up!" she yelled. There was a general clucking. Heather stared at them.

"Well . . ." Nelson said. He was red and seemed to be considering. "Ann, this sounds like something that ought to be taken care of in private."

"Hear! Hear!" someone said, laughing, from the street.

"I couldn't agree more," said Ann. "Now, we have a public decency law, don't we?"

Nelson bit his lip. "Well, I don't really know, to tell you the truth."

Heather looked at him. "I can't believe this! I was only feeding my baby." She glared at Ann. "Maybe you don't want me to feed her at all. Maybe you'd like me to just smother her or something, or get rid of her."

"There's no call for that," Whit said from behind her, but down on the street there was a distinct clap.

And then Ann's voice again, low and calm and almost confidential, so much so that Heather really listened to her. She said, "What right do you have to be so arrogant?"

Heather looked down at the people before her. There were fifteen or twenty now, a veritable crowd by local standards. They were what loosely passed for her neighbors, though they were far from what she knew neighbors were supposed to be. She knew their faces, or most of them, or she saw in their faces other faces that wore some version of their features. They were pasty and roughly edged, and they looked queerly the same, it seemed to her, like the faces of television, though naturally less perfect, with unremarkable eyes and average noses and chapped mouths that called no special attention to themselves, except that just now they were all arranged in angry expressions. It occurred to her that people were supposed to be different, that everyone always spoke about different people, and how different people were supposed to be brought together in spite of their differences, but when you got right down to it, there was only this angry sameness to almost everybody she knew. That they stared so hard at her made her abruptly, perversely elated, because it must mean that she was not one of them, and her daughter was not one of them. And this, she thought to her pleasure, was how she came by her arrogance. Because there was simply no one worse than these people, and that meant that she was better.

Then, as she looked out over the crowd, she saw him, in his bright red car, pulled over to the opposite side of the road and idling while he watched her. She couldn't see him clearly, because there was glare on his window, but it seemed to her that he must be proud of her, seeing her like this, refusing to betray him, or herself, or their child, by feeling the shame they seemed so determined to make her feel. And she felt, to her surprise, suddenly beautiful then, taller than she was, and with the leanness she no longer had. And with this new, remarkable idea, she looked again at some of the men in the road and saw plainly that, even at this moment, they wanted to put their hands on her. She smiled at them, to let them know she knew, then she turned to the policeman. "I want to go home," she said. "Can I go home?"

He looked relieved. "Well, sure," he said in his kind, baffled voice.

Heather took a step. Ann objected.

"What do you want me to do?" he said in exasperation. "Put her in prison? For breast-feeding?"

Ann sulked. "Can't you give her a fine?" Her voice rose to outrage again. "You think it's okay what she did? You think it's okay for her to come up on my porch and take her clothes off? This is our busy season, you know! We've got a business going on here. Do I have to let her use my business to make a display of herself?"

"I don't think—" Nelson started, but Heather, incensed, started moving off. The men let her brush them as she passed. She held Polly a bit aloft, to keep her clear. A single hand—unmistakable—touched her breast.

"Fuck you!" Heather snapped over her shoulder.

"Hey!" said some indistinct woman. "You watch—"

"Can't you just leave us alone?" said Heather.

She stepped onto the road and looked up. She was glad he was gone. Someone edged in front of her, a human impediment.

"I'm just trying to get home," said Heather.

But she was already home. That was the point, entirely.

Chapter 18

Polly Catches Cold

HE WAS IN AWE OF HER. HE AS MUCH AS TOLD her this. She did it all well. She made it seem effortless: her mothering, her beautiful work, her strength, and above everything, this—her consummate lyricism with the instrument that was his body. How deeply they were connected, he as much as said, trying to touch that place, that specific place, where they met. These were the only times, Heather thought later, when she was not confused. He banished the imprecise with his fingertip. He made her the very things he said she already was.

That first foray into Goddard had left her depressed, but oddly energized once the depression wore away. This was how it was to be, after all, Heather reasoned, and after all, it wasn't so bad. She had lost no actual friend, at the end of the day, or the good opinion of any person whose good opinion she particularly valued. Now that the ice was broken—well, shattered—she began to bring Polly along on more frequent excursions: to the sports center, where she dangled her before Martina, who cooed reassuringly over the baby even as she avoided Heather's eye; to the Stop & Shop, where she nodded placidly to her neighbors and then pointedly ignored them.

And to the mill, where Naomi did indeed have a playpen up in the attic, though it had not been much used. They had gone up together, the first time, Naomi leading, chatting backward over her shoulder about how she'd hoped to have more kids around, she liked kids, but after a year of its sitting vacant, taking space in the workroom, she'd stowed the playpen here. The banister jiggled. Polly was in the office, asleep in her car seat under the glare of Mary Sully. The attic was jammed with overflow brochures and crates of order forms, filled but unfiled. Also a mountain of shopping bags and supermarket cartons of material: old woolen pants, torn sheets, shredded quilts. "I know, I know," Naomi groaned. Heather was staring. "I've got to get it all sorted out. Maybe after the holidays. What I want," she told Heather, "is to build a whole wall of shelves here"—she spread her arms. "I mean, have it built. Then I'll go through everything and sort by color. For restoration work, it's the only way. Now it's a nightmare. People are wasting all their time rooting around in these bags for what they need. It isn't Ashley's fault." She frowned, hands on her wide hips. "He says he'll do it whenever I'm ready, but I just can't face the mess. Out of sight, you know." She smiled. "Well, I think I see it."

They maneuvered the playpen between them, lifting it down the staircase; then they put it in a corner of the workroom. It was early, and Heather was the only one there. "Are you sure about this?" she asked Naomi. "I mean, are you sure it won't distract people, having the baby here?"

Naomi shrugged. "If it does, it does. We'll cross that bridge when and if. But, I mean, this is my point. You should be *able* to bring your baby to work. I know you have your grandmother and all, but what if you didn't? You'd still have to make a living, wouldn't you?"

"I guess," said Heather, wiping the dust off the playpen with a rag.

"So don't you think women should have universal access to child care? I mean, it's a women's issue, isn't it?"

Polly woke in the office and bleated in protest at the unfamiliar surroundings.

"Lunchtime," Heather said brightly. "Or is it afternoon snack?"

It took Naomi a minute, then she perked up again. "That's another thing. How do you breast-feed if you have to go to work and your baby can't come with you? Maybe if more women could take their kids along, then more women would breast-feed. And that's better for everybody."

"It is?" Heather said. "How come?"

"Well, medically. Isn't it? That's what they tell me, anyway," Naomi said. "It's what I'm going to do." She went abruptly red.

And then they were uncomfortable in tandem, each looking over the other's shoulder with wordless symmetry.

"That's good," Heather said finally. She went out to her daughter.

Polly, as much as Heather could tell, loved coming to the mill. She was fascinated with human faces, and stared and stared, even when they refused to stare back. Heather brought the baby almost every morning, around eleven, and stayed until it was dark outside. Pick, she thought, liked the peace at home, and Heather did not doubt that it was good for the baby to be out in the world. She was too good for the women in the workroom to make any justifiable complaint at her presence—she cried only to get Heather's attention when she was hungry; then, her goal attained, she stopped crying—and Heather watched with some bemusement as the women struggled to maintain their resentment in the face of this irresistible child. To Heather herself they behaved as if she were not there, but this was what she was used to anyway.

Ashley came often, usually in the late afternoons. He was re-siding the back of the mill, picking off the spongy clapboards and baring the bees' nests beneath them to the hard winter sun. Of course he was discreet when they met. He gave none of those bitter, watching women the satisfaction of his attention to her, and she could only admire the restraint with which Ashley held himself in check before this audience, the skill of his perfect indifference. Heather herself was not so skilled; when Ashley was near her, her eyes were compelled to him. She sat near one of the windows, the better to see his legs spider past, his hot breath fog the panes. Even this far into their pairing, she thought, even with all that had happened, the year gone by, the child they had made, it had not lessened at all for her—this shudder of pure, sweet shock at the plain beauty of him. She liked to recall her first sight of him, half hidden in the ceiling, with only his legs reaching down to her, his narrow back descending, his long hair tied behind in a frayed red bandanna. The memory of his tongue, touching and traveling the hurt surface of her eye, still had the power to hobble her for an instant, and it occurred to her that, in her own case, love had indeed begun in the eye of the beholder.

She began coming when he came, in the afternoons, and staying until most, if not all, the other women had gone to their homes. Polly slept about this time, and Heather would lift her, inert and heavy, from the playpen into Joseph's car seat in the back of Ashley's shiny new car, where she slept on. The back of the station wagon felt inexpressibly luxurious

to Heather, who for the first time could stretch her whole
length out beside Ashley once his tools and ropes had been
pushed aside. With even this small increase in available space,
she felt some of the urgency of their coupling dissipate and,
in its place, a feeling of leisured sensuality. It was far from
comfortable still, but there seemed just slightly more time now
than there had previously been—time, for example, for some
random touches, some kisses without particular purpose.
Heather thought she had never been so happy as when he
touched or kissed her this way—for the sake of those gestures
themselves and not as precursors to something else.

And through this—the sounds and motions and even the
smells—Polly slept. She went deeply down into herself and
became almost stony, her eyes moving steadily, contentedly,
behind their eyelids, reading the text of them while behind her
her parents thrashed and spoke. It occurred to Heather, at
times, that this was not, probably, good for Polly—to hear this,
to know this was happening just out of her sleeping sight—
but the baby seldom woke, and when she did, she sat still and
uncomplaining until her mother noticed her.

Between Polly and her father there was a détente not so
much chilly as simply devoid of warmth. The baby saved her
most persistent staring for Ashley, Heather noticed, as if she
were compelled to memorize him and determined not to break
her gaze. She stared impassively but steadily, her huge blue
eyes affixed to this permutation of her own beauty, but she
never lifted a finger in his direction, and when Heather tried
to propel her toward him, to lift her into her father's arms, the
baby stiffened noticeably and clung to Heather's arm.

Ashley appeared not overly distressed by this. He seemed
content to admire his daughter from this small distance, and
to attribute her sweetness and loveliness to Heather entirely,
as if she had been singularly responsible for Polly's composition. He saw none of his own features in her, despite how
assuredly Heather pointed them out, and appeared not eager
to hear the baby praised. *Look*, Heather would say, holding
Polly's first hair to the light of the car window, where it shone
white-gold. *Isn't it gorgeous?*

Like yours, Ashley said, pulling her down again.

And her skin, my God, Heather said, lifting the baby's

sweater to show an alabaster back. *I'm not surprised*, said Ashley. *You have beautiful skin.*

She wondered if it had to do with Joseph, his boy with Sue, but Ashley never mentioned Joseph either, except to say that he had not slept well the night before, or that he hadn't had clean clothes in days because the baby took so much work. She had heard of fathers for whom their children did not really seem to register until they were of an age to have conversations and play sports, but she wondered why Ashley did not indicate this if it was the case. It did not bother her for her own sake, but she had not realized until now how closely enmeshed with her love for him was her wish that he love their child, and this small chill of disappointment began to work at her, just slightly, then just slightly more.

The holidays arrived, clad in ice. Heather, during the first round of storms, kept the baby home and herself harried with work for the Christmas rush. Polly learned to roll at will. A first strata of her clothing no longer fit, and Heather tearfully consigned these things, much of them her own work, to a box in her closet. Every year, Pick—ossifying in unsentimentality—expressed indifference to Christmas, but every year, quite by coincidence, she also managed to end up serving turkey on the day itself (Janelle Hodge, Pick would remark, had happened to mention it was on sale at the Stop & Shop) and baking a pie with the last of her apples, their mealy texture compensated for by extra sugar and, Heather was fairly sure, a substitution of rum for the usual vanilla. This had been the norm always, even when Heather was a child, but she had not really begrudged it until now. Polly, Heather thought, must have all of it: the feast, the gifts, the tree. But she understood that the most elaborate celebration would only be lost on a four-month-old, and she was content to let this first Christmas pass without too much fuss.

The cold hiccupped abruptly after New Year's, the snow breaking down to premature slush. For the first time, the logging road into the wood was not navigable and the wagon only churned its wheels in gray mud. Heather sat, frustrated, as Ashley got out of the car and pronounced it hopeless to continue, and they had to go back to Nate's Landing, where someone—some teenager, most likely—had spread around gravel. When Polly slept, lulled by the spinning of wheels, they fucked on grit, but briefly. Heather did not like the openness of the trees, the bald stretch of the Sabbathday River rushing away beneath its caul of blue ice. She wanted her time with Ashley, but she wanted to leave, and he obliged her, driving her back to the mill, where she put the baby back in her own car and drove home to supper, her thighs sticky against the wool of her pants. Four months on after the birth and she was still heavy, her belly a smaller version of its rounded, pregnant past, her thighs thick. She caught unwelcome glimpses of herself each morning in the mirror affixed to the bathroom door, stepping laboriously out of the bath and trying all ways to get her towel to wrap around herself. The weight had wrapped her lower half, laying claim to it while leaving her arms and neck slender to taunt her. The milk, she decided, lifting one of her dense and tender breasts to examine a calloused nipple, was keeping her like this, but she loved nursing Polly and dreaded the day her daughter might prefer food from another source. And anyway, there were other advantages to nursing, Heather mused. It had held off her period, and with that, she knew, her fertility. She could happily forgo her waist for that.

On the morning of the day that would change Heather's life, she did not have time for a bath. Polly had coughed through the night. She breathed raggedly through her mouth, and finally wept at her own discomfort. Her nose ran green and thick, and Heather spent hours trying to make her comfortable. The fever—if there was one at all; she was bad at telling, and she didn't want to wake Pick—never got too bad, and she was more regretful for the baby than concerned. Toward dawn, Polly fell into exhausted sleep on Heather's belly, and so Heather lay, still, despite a full and throbbing bladder, through the next hours, recalibrating her day against the new mandate of Polly's cold. When Pick rose, later than usual, she was not well herself, and stood in the doorway with one palm pressed against her right temple, as if feeling for the source of her pain.

"Maybe I ought to run you into town," Heather said softly, keeping her diaphragm as still as possible.

"No. It isn't too bad. Just a headache." She smiled ruefully. "Doctor'd just tell me to go home."

Polly coughed in her sleep. Heather stroked the back of the baby's head, where white hair—rubbed off from months of turning her head against the crib mattress—was growing back shiny, dark, and fine. "I won't go in to work today," she said.

Pick shook her head. "No need for that. You go on." She paused. "I know you like to go. I'll watch her."

"Oh, I couldn't," said Heather. But already her mind was working. She could. She could leave her sick baby with her sick grandmother. To have that extra hour with Ashley, the hour after Polly woke up and wanted her, for food or distraction, to have that small but irreplaceable freedom to make noise, to move in ways they couldn't move normally for fear of waking the baby—surely Pick wouldn't offer if she didn't feel up to it. And Pick could always call the mill if she started to feel poorly, and Heather could just tell Ashley she had to go home. Otherwise . . .

"I couldn't," Heather said again, just to stay her conscience.

"Don't be silly," said Pick, who carefully extricated the still-sleeping Polly from Heather's stomach, allowing Heather to escape to the bathroom. She was already expertly holding the baby's forehead against her own cheek, pronouncing her "cool as a cucumber." "Just a bit of a sniffle. Nothing to get nuts about."

"Sure," Heather said. "I know."

Pick put the baby down, gingerly, in her crib, where, to Heather's amazement, she did not wake instantly and start to howl but turned her other cheek to the blanket and continued to breathe, evenly, if still rather wetly.

"Okay," Heather said. "I guess it's fine. And you're fine."

"I am fine," said Pick. "You worry too much."

But Heather didn't worry too much, that was the problem. She should have worried far more. If she had called home, she thought afterward. If she had stopped work early and gone to check. If, for once, she had told Ashley that today was not a good day for them to drive to the woods, then how differently everything might have unraveled for her, for Ashley, for Polly and Pick, even for Naomi Roth, Heather would think too many months later. But she was greedy. Her greed ran through her where blood should have been, and her common concern, this drug hunger for the man whose touch was the one thing she had deemed worth pursuing in the known universe. How thoroughly the world had shrunk to this, she thought, leaving her sick house without a backward glance, revving the car like the heat-seeking missile it was, and setting off.

She worked through the morning and went grocery shopping at midday, enjoying the freedom of maneuvering her cart without having to be careful of jarring the baby. She bought eggs and milk, a bag of anemic oranges, a pot roast for the weekend, when she generally took over the cooking from Pick, a new size of diapers for Polly. She bought yogurt and a roll for her lunch and took them back to the mill, and Ashley was there, painting the new clapboards with a foul-smelling paint, working without gloves so his raw hands were spattered white. Heather sat by the window and had her lunch, listening to Sarah Copley talk about her husband, Rory, and his habit of leaving empty ice cream cartons in the sink, as if expecting her to wash them out and reuse them. *The man simply can't stand to think of anything going to the dump! It's bad enough he's got every issue of* The Clarion *back to '68.* The women chortled and murmured their own stories. Heather put her yogurt into the trash and went back to her sampler. She was waiting for Ashley now, and for the women to leave. She didn't mind the wait. She was anticipating the extra time later, the freedom she had grown unaccustomed to since Polly's birth. If she thought of Polly or Pick at all, it was without anxiety—her grandmother would call if there was trouble—but with a sweet lift of her spirits, and gratitude that the women in her life would make this space for the man. Ashley was right: she did have everything, and the parts of everything all worked in concert to give her the greatest possible happiness. It occurred to her, for the first time, that the bad feeling lingering between her and so many of her neighbors had less to do with pity or condemnation than with sheer resentment. They scorned her choices, but at root, they wanted what she had, and if what she had did not include a husband who filled her sink with refuse, then there was that much more reason for them to envy her, and that much less reason for her to care.

Ashley finished around five and packed away his tools in the back room adjacent to the office. Heather folded her sampler carefully into her bag and walked into the office. Naomi was working at the computer, her head bent forward so the green glow from the screen played out over her face as she stared deeply into it. "We have any more of that linen thread?"

Heather asked. "You know, that white? I think I'll be okay, but I might run out of what I've got if I have to put in all these extra flowers."

Naomi looked up. The green fled from her face, leaving it streaky red. Her eyes were red, too.

"Oh, hey," Heather said. "Are you—"

"Okay," Naomi said quickly. "I'm fine."

Heather was staring. She wanted to stop staring, but she couldn't figure out how. Naomi, for her part, didn't look away either.

"Everything's fine," Naomi said finally. "I didn't realize anybody was still in there."

"I'm waiting," Heather said. "I mean, I was just finishing up." She stopped. "Can I help you?"

Naomi gave a sour little smile. "Oh no, I don't think so. It's just my . . . Well, Daniel and I decided to call it quits this weekend. It's normal to be sad, right? I mean, we've been together for like . . ." She looked up, calculating, then found the answer and sighed. "Anyway, I'm just fine. Thanks for asking."

"You don't look fine," Heather said bluntly. Then she blushed. "Oh, I didn't mean that. I'm sorry."

"No, no." Naomi shook her head. "I know I look like shit. This is what you look like when you stay up all night screaming at your so-called life partner while he's pawing through a box of records, trying to remember who reached into whose pocket on Bleecker Street in 1974 to pull out the dollar that bought 'Are You Experienced?' off some wino's blanket. Charming, huh?"

Huh, Heather thought, staring.

"Well, that's life, I guess," Naomi went on. "I mean, they say you should never go into marriage without making sure you want the same things from life, but they don't tell you that wanting those things and getting those things are two distinct concepts. So, God forbid you should *achieve* anything, right? Achieving just interferes with the almighty *striving*, doesn't it?"

"I guess," said Heather softly. "I never really thought about it."

"Who *thinks* about it? That's my point. Nobody thinks about this stuff. They just do what they're told. What do you think

I'm doing with myself, Heather? You think I'm enjoying this? This!" Naomi pushed out her hands, sharply, as if urging more from an imaginary orchestra around her. "I am not enjoying this." Her voice dropped to a hush, as if she were telling herself a secret. "I am not enjoying this. I'm just doing what I'm fucking told."

Heather swallowed. She searched fervently for something to say, but she couldn't seem to grasp anything.

"So don't mind me," Naomi said ruefully. "I'm just fine. I'm just not as fine as I'm supposed to be, so the light of my life is off to find somebody who hasn't taken the code of enlightenment quite so literally as I apparently have. Somebody who meditates more and does less, I guess. And maybe has some unearned income; that might help. Also is happy to shit in a bucket and grow hair on her legs—but not under her arms! Because that grosses him out! And never, never, never wants to do something so insufferably self-indulgent as have a baby in this evil, fascist world, because, among other things, that would make him a father, which would make him *not* the baby anymore."

Heather stared at her. An idea pricked her consciousness. "Do you . . . are you pregnant, Naomi?"

"No!" the older woman shrieked. Fresh tears flew from her eyes. She sighed then, a rasp of unhappy breath. "I mean no. I'm sorry. No." She shook her head. "I thought I might be, but I'm not. Lots of rejoicing *chez* Roth over that one," she said tersely. Then she looked up at Heather and frowned. "I really admire you, you know," Naomi said softly. "I do, Heather."

Her face went a little numb. "You do?" This was a fresh concept. "You admire *me*?"

"Yuh." Naomi nodded. She swiped at her cheek with the back of her hand. "You don't take shit from people. And this town's full of people who would dearly love to give it to you, for whatever half-assed reason. Like it has anything to do with them! But you won't take it. It pisses them off, you know."

"I know." Heather nodded.

"And I'm not asking for details, believe me. But I think it's great. You walk so tall. It's a great example for your daughter, you know."

"Do you think so?" Heather said, amazed.

"Sure! You don't wait for people to tell you how to live your life, you just get on with it. You're the only homegrown feminist I've met since I moved here, you know. You ought to be proud of yourself."

But Heather did not feel proud. She was brooding about being called a feminist. She didn't want to be a feminist. She wanted to be beautiful for Ashley.

Naomi got to her feet and snapped off the computer. "This is stupid," she said, addressing the dimming screen. "I'm just putting it off. I've got to go home sometime."

Heather looked at her, then past her, out the window. Ashley was loading his car.

"I have to go, too," she said. "Are you sure you're all right?"

"Sure." Naomi grinned, her face streaky. "All right. Oh"— she frowned—"you said something about thread?"

"Oh, nothing! It's fine, I'm sure I've got plenty."

"Because we could look upstairs." Naomi gestured toward the attic stairs.

Heather checked the window. Ashley was in his car, waiting.

"No." She moved toward the door. "See you tomorrow."

"Tomorrow," Naomi said, behind her. The door shut between them.

Ashley had the engine going, and the car was warm for her. He moved a drill off the passenger seat and hoisted it into the back. "Sorry."

"All right." She stared forward.

"What's the matter?" Ashley said.

"Naomi just told me she's getting divorced from her husband. She looks sad."

"Yeah?" Ashley said. "This just happened?"

"I guess. She said, over the weekend."

He nodded. The river was sluggish today, overflowing its own ice at a thousand different points. It bugged her, the stop and go of it, the failure to hold itself back or let itself go. She hoped they would make it onto the logging road today and not have to resort to Nate's Landing.

"He was a jerk," Ashley said. "I always thought so."

"You did?" She turned to Ashley. There was a smudge of paint on the straight edge of his nose.

"He didn't know shit about building houses. I had to go out

there and fix everything he did. Not that I minded." He smiled. "I mean, cause she paid me." He turned to grin at Heather. "But still. He put this junk on the roof that was supposed to be for solar power, but it leaked like a sponge, and he refused to cut down any trees to give the house more sunlight, so Naomi had to heat water on the stove if she wanted to take a bath that wasn't freezing. That's one thing for a guy, but women like to be clean." He laughed to himself. "She always said, if guys got periods like women, they'd be the first ones to demand hot and cold running water. And he wouldn't even let her have a toilet. He had this creepy compost thing that was supposedly better for pollution or something." He sighed. "Maybe she'll want a toilet put in now."

"Was he nice to her?" Heather asked. "I mean, aside from the toilet and that stuff?"

Ashley pursed his lips. "Well, I guess. He didn't beat her up or anything."

They turned off from the river. The road, to Heather's relief, looked good. "I like Naomi," Heather said. They were driving slowly into the diminishing light. She felt as if they were hiding themselves, sweetly and slowly, crawling in tandem to their warm destination. "I don't really know her."

"Who knows anybody?" said Ashley. He stopped the car and killed the engine. There was a sound like crinkling as the wagon settled in snow, in its black ring of winter woods. The engine ticked over a bit as it cooled. She reached for his hand.

"Heather," he said. His voice was musical and far afield.

"That's my name." She leaned over and took his lobe between her teeth, gave it a little tug. Her hand turned his face to her. "Make me cry out in the wilderness."

In the darkness, she heard him laugh.

"Well, since we're here . . ."

She helped him take off her shirt. Her breasts were full of milk, hard and high, and he fell on them as if he'd never seen them before. His skin gleamed white, though what light there was seemed to drain from the car, minute by minute, taking the warmth with it. But Heather was hot. Her hands and feet, her face, her back suddenly bared and pressed back against the brown carpet of the wagon floor—all were suffused with heat and drumming the persistent rhythm of her heart and breath. He was making her make noise, all right, her greedy noise. The windows fogged white, so thickly obscured that she could not have seen out even if she thought there might be someone there, and even if there had been light to see them by. The world had wrapped them up in their own heat and sweet darkness. If there was an outside at all, she simply didn't want to know about it.

Her noise, his grunting and whispers, seemed to swallow up the other sounds, and so, at first, it did not occur to Heather that anything was happening. There were, for example, any number of explanations for those shrill human voices, the pounding of fists against metal. She might be giving voice to the voices inside her, say, or he might be kicking back against the side of the car, trying to climb faster and harder into her. Heather closed her ears and eyes and pulled him tighter, imagining faces at the window watching them, and smiled. A fist cleared fog from the glass. A woman screamed, and Heather did not recognize her own voice, or the word it said.

"My . . . *fuck*." He bucked out of her. Heather gaped at him. A fist hit the glass near her head. She lay, numb and shocked, with her legs apart, as if they had been pinned there by the beam of light through the wagon's rear window. "For . . . Jesus, Heather, cover yourself up!" he yelled. Then, when she didn't move, he took her bra and pulled it roughly down. She winced as the fabric scraped her nipple. One of her shoes was half off. Outside, in the woods, someone was crying and crying. "Jesus fucking Christ," said Ashley, yanking his sweater down over his head. "That stupid cunt, that *cunt*."

A hand was fumbling with the door latch.

"Just wait," Ashley yelled. "Just give me a fucking minute here."

He twisted away from Heather, who had forgotten how to button the buttons on her shirt and was pointing them at the holes, as if she expected them to jump through by themselves. Her hands seemed huge and arthritic, like Pick's, suddenly useless and full of pain.

"*I told you,*" a woman screamed. There was air in the car now, dark and cold. It ran over Heather's chest and she pulled together the two halves of her shirt. "*I said!*"

"What do you think this will accomplish?" Ashley yelled back. "Now you're going to be happy?"

"You promised me!" Sue sobbed, her cheeks plump and

ravaged by tears. "What are you doing to me?"

There was a woman beside her, shorter and darker but with the same face—Sue's mother. She had one thick arm around her daughter's shoulders as she glared at Ashley. Behind them, around them, more dark faces. Eight, Heather thought. Maybe more than eight. She couldn't see. The one holding the flashlight was tall. She wondered if she knew anyone that tall.

"You don't need my help to be miserable," Ashley was speaking. "You're doing great on your own. Don't you lay that shit on me. I'm just—"

"Now listen," someone said. Heather turned her face to the noise, a voice she sort of knew but didn't know. "Where do you get off treating your—"

"Who are you?" asked Heather, and everyone turned to look at her. She had been looking at that point in the darkness where that vaguely recognized voice was standing, but it was Sue who stepped forward, shoving Ashley away; she came near Heather, one hand reaching for the open flaps of her shirt collar. Involuntarily she reached for her own throat, touching the necklace he had given her.

"I'm his wife," Sue said bitterly. "And who are you?"

"Sue," Ashley warned.

She was close now, her face white except where the cheeks were hollow and the circles under the eyes, the color of smoke. Her long braid looked dirty and uneven, as if it had been lived with for days, untouched. She stared with mean, dark eyes, her mouth hard and slightly open.

"Sue," he said again, even more tersely. He reached, with one cold hand, for Heather. A bolt of heat began at the place his finger touched her arm. Sue stared, then wept. He stepped nearer to Heather, thrilling her. His arm came around her shoulders as his wife howled in pain, untouched. Heather crumbled in gratitude. He was choosing her. He was picking her.

"I told you," Ashley said. "I always told you, you get the thing you deserve to get."

Sue sobbed. Her mother held her. The flashlight jerked from Heather's face to his.

"So too bad you all had to come out," he addressed the crowd. "Too bad my wife had to put on this little show, but that's all there is, folks. Now, if you don't mind, I'd like you to move your cars. I'd like to leave."

There were three cars, Heather saw, parked single file behind the station wagon, nose to tail on the narrow track. They would all have to back out, like a weird caravan en route to the past. It would be funny to be last in line.

"No way," said the tall person with the flashlight. "You got something to settle with your wife. You got a kid to think of."

Unthinking, Heather spoke up: "Two kids."

Sue wailed anew. "How do we know it's his?" said that known voice again, and Heather looked, abruptly recognizing the shape in the darkness: Ann Chase.

"Of course it's his," she said hotly. "Of course she's his, Ann."

"Not that it's any of your business," Ashley said, and Heather flooded with love. "Now, are you going to get in your cars, or do we have to walk out of here?"

"I'm not leaving!" Sue howled, and even in the darkness Heather could see Ashley's face tighten in rage. He had never looked at *her* like this, she thought, her heart racing as this small idea was added to the weight of revelation: he wanted her. He wanted her more than *that* person. He was picking her over *that*.

"All right, then," Ashley said, his voice small and bitter. "Let's go, Heather."

She looked up at him. His arm was heavy across her shoulders. She no longer felt the cold, though her shirt was still mostly unbuttoned, and one shoe unlaced, and one pant leg hiked awkwardly up to just below her knee. He took a step into the snow, pulling her after him.

"Wait." Heather went to the front seat of the wagon, unlatched it, and reached in for her bag. She wanted them to see it was her decision, too, that he wasn't just taking her along, and paused for a brief survey of the darkness. "Well then," Heather said. "Good night."

Whore, someone said. Heather smiled. Ten minutes earlier, she had been placated by what she was, untormented by what she was not, but now he had placed her above his wife, and far from shaming her, this unsought tribunal had seen the proof of Ashley's love. She had never felt so elated, so heady with pride. She took his hand again, and they walked into the woods as the crowd behind them seethed, conferred, and raced for their own cars. But she and Ashley were off the path by then, and the moonlight was beginning to light the snow as the trees thinned nearer the river. The snow was deep in places, but he supported her, one hand beneath her arm, and she didn't really feel the cold. He said nothing but "Watch" or "Step here," but he said them easily enough, as if there were nothing at all on his mind, as if they were just out for a night walk through snowy woods.

They came to the river's edge. The water rumbled somewhere, softly, beneath its skin of ice. For the first time, Ashley paused. They had left the logging road to their left, and there was nothing here, only the faint suggestion of a kind of path beneath the snow. Heather's right foot was very cold now, but she did not begrudge the cold. Ashley's breath and her own filled the air with mist. Far away behind them, a car labored out of the woods.

"Where are we going?" Heather said, as if she cared.

"To the mill. We can cross up here a bit."

He led the way upstream to the Drumlins, where the water was low enough to expose the rocks. They were slick with ice, dark and scary. For the first time, Heather held back.

"Are you sure?"

But he had already gone first, feeling with his boot for a rough place. There was light now, lunar-white and cold. He was nimble, the way he moved, and graceful. He made it look easy.

"Come on," said Ashley. "I can see the mill from here. It's all right."

It was all right. She took his hand, slipped a bit, but caught herself. Her hands were very cold and couldn't grip well, but he supported her and she went, dreamlike, fording the river. She amazed herself, but then, Heather thought, everything was to be different now, and her own clumsy self was cast off with that other carapace-self of Ashley's secondary woman. Now his own light would infuse her, and it only surprised her that it had taken her so long to understand this about herself—that she *was* as extraordinary as he had always said, that he *would*, given the choice, choose her.

Now he had left his wife and set out with her, even into this wilderness, even though it would have been so much eas-

ier the other way. He could come and live with them in the
farmhouse on Sabbath Creek Road. They could marry, too, if
Ashley wanted, though Heather didn't really mind; the important thing was that they would bind their lives together, day
by day and moment by moment, in the pleasure and love that
was so obviously abundant between them. Pick would learn to
accept him, and Polly would grow up with her father. How
she would love her father! He would toss her into the air, and
sing songs with her, clapping her little hands together, and take
her on his shoulders so that she could see over the heads of
other children. And other children! There would be more, perhaps: beautiful, like Polly, healthy and smart, alight with the
adoration of their parents. She watched his narrow back, a step
before her, one hand trailing behind to grip the hand she
reached forward. "I love you," she said, thanking him.

She saw the dull glint of her own car, alone in the mill's
lot, and was relieved, but he held her back when she tried to
go to it and pulled her tightly against him. She felt him right
away and caught her breath. "Come up with me," he said, his
mouth against her neck. He was holding her tightly. "Come
up. Jesus Christ, I want to fuck you."

"Up where?" She could barely speak. Then, understanding,
she said, "We could go to my house."

"No. Here. I can't wait." He felt in his jacket pocket. "Shit.
My keys are in the car." He eyed the building, then grinned
and took her around back where his ladder still rested against
the rear wall. "I'll just end up fixing it anyway." He laughed;
then he took a fist-sized rock and smashed a pane of glass.
The shards fell in around the legs of a chair—the one she'd
pulled to the window so many hours earlier, she thought, to
watch his legs climb past on the ladder—and he reached in
and unhooked the latch. The window slid up. "Good thing I
haven't put an alarm system in yet," Ashley said. "Come on."

He shimmied in first and turned to lift her. She felt bad for
Naomi, but the thought fled in her rush for him.

"Sorry," she said, embarrassed, as he hefted her weight over
the sill. The glass shards crunched as she found her balance.
The room looked queer, bereft of women and light, and it
occurred to her not to touch anything, because now, in the
same room where she had spent most of the day, she was an
intruder.

"Come on," Ashley said. He was pulling her again, across the room and up the stairs to the attic, where the air smelled of dust and stale fabric. There was cold light from the single window under the eaves, enough to make their skin turn gray. Ashley was dragging his shirt over his back, leaning forward to pull it down off his head. The ponytail flipped forward over his chest and lay there, almost feminine. "Take off your clothes," he was saying. "Come on."

But she couldn't move very well. She was watching, instant by instant, more of his skin reveal itself; the shirt he had always unbuttoned but kept half on for warmth, the pants that were always pulled down to the backs of his knees . . . He was taking them away entirely now, baring his whole body. He unlaced his wet boots and put them aside, and then climbed neatly out of his underpants. Finally, he dragged away the bandanna from his ponytail, letting his hair hang loose to his breast, its untrimmed ends feathering one tiny nipple, and then there was nothing left. She stared at him, shocked as a virgin.

"What?" He laughed, stepping close. "You look . . ."

He had a hand in the back of her pants, but there wasn't much room. She felt immense next to him, and ashamed. He was pulling at her. The other hand made a fist at her crotch. "Wait," she said, "I just . . ." She just wanted to lie flat, she thought, so she wouldn't seem so, so her body wouldn't be so . . .

"Come on." It was a litany. He pulled her down. "I want to see you. I've never seen you." It was incredible how he moved, given this room to move. He was feline with claws, but sheathed claws, and everywhere he bared her skin it became as beautiful as his own. She felt herself twist off her pants, but he wanted to take off her underpants himself. She was still sticky from the car, from the walk. He made his hand hard and put it between her thighs. For the second time in an hour, he dragged her bra across her nipples and went for them, his mouth tender but frantic. Her milk let down instantly. The bra, the last scrap of fabric between them, he threw away across the room.

So this is what it looks like, Heather thought a moment later, this thing she had always done by heart, by touch. Always before, this sensation of lying beneath him, of being fucked, of reaching across his back or farther down, pulling him into her, had made its own kind of image—of something encased, she thought, and dark, and tightly wound. But now she could see the individuality of Ashley's limbs, the hands moving at will, the legs searching separately for purchase. And she saw that she was not only lying under him, not just blankly receiving him, but that she had an agenda of her own, and a talent, and a grace. She had always loved to touch between his legs at just this moment, for instance, to heft the tiny but limitlessly meaningful weight of his scrotum, but now, for the first time, she could see how her hand was touching him in its accustomed ways; she could see the elegance of her hand as it moved, and its confidence, and the sight moved her deeply. She saw how, fully naked, he became a whole, a single form united in purpose, and that this purpose was herself. She was moving faster against him, but he kissed her and pulled away. Heather watched him, bereft but waiting. "Turn over," Ashley said.

It made sense, she thought, when her shock passed. This made perfect sense, because wouldn't he want to make some gesture of novelty, to do something never before attempted— at least by them—to signify that they were setting out anew together? That everything was different now? She let him guide her. She didn't say no, though it hurt this way, though it wouldn't have occurred to her, on her own, to suggest this. "Do you mind?" he said hoarsely, after a moment, and she shook her head no, because she was finding, gradually, that she didn't, that the tightness of his front against her back felt good to her, that even in this most intimate of her openings the sensation he made was one of safety, and even, somehow, pleasure. She closed her eyes in amazement and pushed back against him, which took his breath away. There was nothing at all between them, Heather thought, and there was everything between them. She came in his open hand, elated and lost.

And then, in the luxury of this space and warmth, they stretched out, side by side, in silence. Outside, the river was muted to the point of imperceptibility, but she liked to think of it there nonetheless, as the barrier they had crossed to find this good place. Ashley had one arm thrown across her chest, the other crooked beneath his own head. The bag of fabric beneath her was soft, but the plastic felt sticky against her bare back. She turned her face to him. "I'm so happy," she said.

Her voice was soft, sated and heavy. "I love you so much."

He smiled vaguely. His eyes were closed.

"I can't believe you did that for me."

"Yeah?" he said. "If you'd wanted it, you could have asked before."

"What?" Heather said. Then she laughed. "No. I mean, I can't believe you chose me that way, in front of them."

Languidly he turned his head to her. "What do you mean?"

"You know." She brushed his long hair back off her face. She loved his hair, though it smelled faintly of paint. "Instead of Sue."

"Sue was wrong to follow us," Ashley said simply. "She can be such a bitch. She knew when she married me I wouldn't put up with that." He was quiet for a moment. "Still," he said thoughtfully, "it's clear that this is really getting to be too stressful for her. Maybe for us, too. Tonight's made that clear."

"Oh, I agree," Heather said. "It's a turning point." She waited. In the gloom she watched her own chest rise and fall beneath Ashley's arm. *Say it*, she was thinking. *Say the words.* She was willing them into the realm of the audible, conjuring them out of silence. *Tell me*, she thought.

But he didn't. For long moments he said nothing at all. His profile frowned up at the rafters. Outside, a car drove by, and then another. The sounds faded. "Good," she heard Ashley speak. "I'm glad you agree. I've been wondering how to end things."

"I'll help you," said Heather eagerly. "I'll do whatever I can."

"Your support is the main thing. Just knowing you agree with me, that's what's important. And we'll be friends, of course."

"Of course," Heather said. "Of course. There's a child, after all."

"Well, yes," said Ashley. "Heather. You're really great, you know."

She nodded. She was crying, but quietly. She was full of joy.

"I didn't think you'd react like this," he said. "I thought . . . I thought you might be upset."

A nagging idea at the back of her throat. She shook it away.

"Oh no. Never upset. I would have been happy to go on as

we were. But I love you. And of course I want to be with you. I want—" She stopped herself. He hadn't said this, precisely. But hadn't he meant it? "I mean, if you want to, someday maybe, not necessarily soon, but when we're settled and everything, I'll marry you."

That nagging thing. In the small moment that followed, it came back.

Ashley pulled himself up. He seemed weary suddenly, but his face was taut. He looked down at her, wary and amazed. "Heather." He shook his head. "Heather, I'm already married."

She considered the meaning of this. She couldn't make it out.

"Well, I know that, but after."

"I'm *married*. Married!" He sounded unaccountably angry. Heather frowned.

"Yes, so not right away. But after you get . . ." *Unmarried*, she was thinking. What was that word again? And why did he seem so . . .

"I won't," said Ashley. "I'm sorry, but that's just out of the question. I thought you understood this." He stared at her, his eyes tar-dark. "This is like a basic thing about me, Heather. How can you not have understood this?"

"Fine, it's fine." She tried to sound soothing, but there was panic in her throat: that nagging thing, working its way into her voice. "We don't have to get married. It's not important. So long as—"

"*What?*" he shouted. "So long as *what*?" He was furious. Heather sat up and crossed her arms over her chest. All of a sudden she didn't want him to see her breasts.

"So long as . . . we're together?"

He reached for his shirt and yanked it down over his head. "But this is what I'm telling you. Christ, are you thick? *We're not going to be together*. This is it, tonight. And I'm sorry. Of course I'm sorry. I should have done it ages ago. So I'm a bad guy, so what! You always showed me you could look out for yourself, Heather."

Speechless, she gaped at him.

"You always handle things. So don't get crazy on me now."

"But you said," she stumbled into speech, "you said you were going to end things."

"*I am ending things!*" He got to his feet. He yanked his

underpants up. "Come on. This isn't doing either of us any good. We're . . ." He seemed to abandon the thought. Then he shrugged. "I've always liked you, Heather."

"*Liked* me?" Her entire relationship with language seemed to have abandoned her. Even the parroting of his own words was meaningless.

"Yeah. I liked you. So I beg your pardon." He seemed angry again. He zipped his jeans with a rasp. "Come on. It's not like I said I was gonna sweep you away or anything." Ashley peered at her. "Did I say that?"

He hadn't said it, she thought suddenly. He'd only done it. "*Did I?*"

But she couldn't answer. The expanse of her belly was broad and sickly-white. It felt abruptly obscene.

"Wait," she whispered. "Just wait."

"But why?" He was sighing. "I mean, what's the point. Nothing's going to change. Everybody's dug in, you know? And I can't make anybody happy, so there's no sense in trying, is there?" He peered at her again, magnificent in his height. She gaped up helplessly. "And I'll tell you something else, Heather. You've got some share in this, too. Oh, you can make out it's all me, but you're not just some slouch going along with things. You knew what you were getting into. You're strong, even if you're not strong *enough.* And that's not my fault either, by the way." He glared at her, briefly, but with a clear white heat. "I'll admit to my own shortcomings, sure, but I'm not about to take the blame for your problems."

He waited for her to ask, but she'd been left impossibly behind by now, dead weight at the roadside. She couldn't even have formed the question, so he did it for her.

"You want to know what your problem is? I'll tell you, if you want to know."

She didn't want to know. She didn't want to know anything else.

"You act tough, but it's all surface with you. Inside, you're just . . ." His vocabulary dissipated in disgust. He shook his head. "If you weren't, maybe I *would* leave Sue for you. If you compelled me. If you . . . I don't know, if you, like, took me and *compelled* me to do it, if you made me feel I just *had* to be with you and not her. You understand? But you can't quite do that, can you?" He glared in accusation. "You're not

even close, to tell you the truth." Ashley groped for his sweater
and twisted into it. He wrenched his long hair out of the collar
and tied it up with the bandanna. Then he looked down at her
again. "I could fall in love. I'm not incapable of that. I'm not
just some asshole who likes to get laid—that's a little too easy,
I think. But you want to think that to make yourself feel better?
Fine."

"I—" Heather tried to break in. *Wouldn't*, she was thinking.
Even now. *I wouldn't think that of you.*

"But don't ask me to go along with it, because I won't."
Ashley shook his head, his lovely curls impossibly blue in the
lunar light. "You know," he mused, suddenly contemplative,
"sometimes I wonder which of you I'm more pissed at. You
yank me around, both of you. You just squabble and complain,
but you're both too weak to actually do anything about the
situation. Each of you, too weak to pull me away from the
other one." He shook his head, furious and put upon. "Then
you make out it's all my fault. You poor *women*."

Heather felt, from some impossible distance, the wetness on
her face, the cold wetness beneath her arms, between her legs,
behind her knees. She was seeping, she thought, like a tree.
She would wither away, it seemed to her, another husk in
another hayloft. Certainly she would never actually leave here.

"I'm going now," Ashley said. "Listen, I *am* sorry."

A tin coin tossed from a gilded carriage. She tried to speak,
but it came out a kind of formless breath.

"What?" He was impatient now. He was on the move.

"Where are you going?"

"Home, naturally. Now I have to deal with my *wife*."

And so he went, agile and light, a small man with beautiful
legs and a ponytail flipped casually over one shoulder, the
point around which the world would turn if there still were a
world. Heather did not move. For the longest time, for minutes
made malleable by grief so that they passed with granite slowness, she did not move, but her mind was alive and her
thoughts careening. Always, it seemed to her, she had known
that there was such a thing as pain—deep pain, and psychic
pain—and that people felt it and suffered from it, but she had
not had any idea of its dimensions or its capabilities. Now pain
infused her, spreading like oxygen through her lungs and moving freely along each limb, then permeating her skin and leap-

ing out into the air, where she only breathed it in again. It suspended her, this pain. She had never known anything like it, so vicious and so relentless. Her life, the sweetness of her life, was past. Her life was past.

Heather held up one hand experimentally. The fingers moved. She brought them to her nose and smelled, but there was only the cold, which blotted smell, or perhaps the ability to smell at all was gone, too. Not that it mattered. Her curiosity was merely clinical; she just wanted to know what her new demarcations were, what it would feel like, now, to be alive for the many years left that she would have to be alive.

Because of Polly, who even in this great haze of anguish could not entirely absent herself from Heather's awareness. She was Polly's mother, though now she was nothing else, not anymore. She had to get up and go home somehow, and somehow learn to navigate time with her new husk-self. She had to learn to coexist with this howling thing that wouldn't shut up and that ached so hard, and she had to learn to do it so well that no one would see it or—God forbid—guess its cause.

She wasn't strong enough. She wasn't strong enough to make him love her.

She had passed into her own future, a tintype landscape of false colors and blank, rigid expressions, where people moved about in brittle unhappiness. And the worst part was that Heather hadn't even noticed the wall she must have crashed through to get here, but it was behind her now, dense and high and vigilant, blocking even the memory of those few joyful moments when she had thought he had chosen her. And she would never get back. And this would always feel the way it felt right now, which was terrible.

A naked woman, breathing quickly, clammy with cold sweat and crusted with semen, lying on a plastic bag of shredded wool in the attic of an old mill on the bank of a frozen river. Her life.

She felt for her clothes, holding up what turned out to be her shirt, for the longest time, trying to figure out how it went on. Heather put it on. And her sweater. She couldn't find her underpants. She put her legs into her jeans, but they felt strange—the fly, it turned out, was in back, which was wrong. She took the pants off and put them on again. She discovered that it wasn't difficult to do these things. You just thought them and they sort of happened, even if you couldn't feel them the way you'd felt them before. She would learn. She went downstairs. She went out the office door, closing it behind her, listening for the click of the lock. The world was still and the moon high and huge. She would go home now, and not think. She would put all of her effort into not thinking.

Heather started the car. Her breath frosted the windshield from the inside—empirical evidence that she existed. The steering wheel was freezing and she held it pinched between forefinger and thumb, her pinkies out in a posture of absurd gentility. She drove without intention, but the roads were clear and there were no other cars. The clock's hour hand was fixed somewhere between eleven and twelve; there was no minute hand. The earth was unpopulated. Only the ends of sodden sticks and logs and rocks broke out of the snow. The white fields fell away behind her, and the few still, dark houses. Where was he now? she thought, forgetting that she was supposed to be not thinking. She took the stab of new pain that followed as her due. Her cold foot groped for the brake. She turned onto Sabbath Creek Road.

The house was black and silent. For one queer moment, she wished herself back—through the night and the great wall into that warm swirl of transient happiness—into the mill attic, even alone, even after he had left, because at least there lingered there some remnant of him, but here, in her own house, there would be nothing. She did not want to go inside. At least not yet.

So she walked out behind the house, her shoes packing down the brittle ridge of ice, sinking two, three inches into the dense powder beneath; she moved slowly down the hill of the back field, all the way down to the bottom, where the slope sank to the small pond, its muddy water frozen now the color of steel. The moon seemed to rain down bone-whiteness on the field, a bleached-out planetary light. It reminded her, with a jolt, of that night so long before when she had walked home to her dormitory across the college campus, having left her virginity behind in the bed of some sleeping fraternity brother. How much more had she left behind tonight, Heather thought, and yet, for the first time, she felt a kind of perverse virtue to her unencumbrance. She was light, too, after all, and stripped clean, purified by sadness. And alive. All around her, the snow

slept beneath ice, the earth beneath snow, and below that, in-
numerable creatures—all sleeping, each dug into the dark,
rolled tightly into themselves. All around her in their houses,
people were sleeping, and even here, somehow under the
muddy, half-frozen water, there were probably things not quite
dead but sleeping.

She did not know how she had come to be the only person
awake in the world, but if it could just stay this way, if they
could all just stay asleep forever, it occurred to her that maybe
it wouldn't seem quite so insurmountable, this ordeal of keeping on living.

Later, Heather would rue this thought. She would blame
herself, and entirely without reason. Pick, after all, had been
dead for hours by that time, cold on the couch before the
fireplace, which was also cold, her tangled fingers by now
hopelessly unyielding. Upstairs in her crib, Polly was cold, too,
and wet—the skin of her thighs already blossoming in raw red
patches—and still sick, naturally, since her chesty cough had
gone untreated and uncomforted for many hours. But mostly
hungry. She was so hungry, in fact, that she had only recently
fallen asleep after a long, ragged evening of crying.

It was particularly cruel, Heather would think much later,
that this vision of herself—alone and alert even as the world
was sleeping—had made her feel as if she saw things clearly,
as if she were somehow, finally, in control. Afterward, she
would think of this moment only with shame, for her pre-
sumption. By then, the enormity of her ignorance, the *knowledge* of her ignorance, was crushing.

Of her dead grandmother and unhappy child she was unaware, of course—how, from where she crouched, at the bottom of the long hill and the edge of the dark pond, could she
have known of them?—though she would make those discov-
eries soon enough. Nor could she know that eight months
hence she would be here again, in this precise place, and even,
almost, in this same posture, squatted in pain and wrung with
misery. And as to the other thing—her conceit, naïve and arrogant, that she was utterly alone on this bleak point of the
deserted earth? The truth is, Heather could not have been more
wrong about that, either.

Part 3
The Second Baby

If you drained the ponds
in your back yards
you'd find more than you bargained for.

—*Peter Fallon, "If Luck Were Corn"*

Chapter 19

A Word with Heather

JUST OVER NINE MONTHS LATER, THEY LED HER into the bland and undersized interview room down the hall from Nelson Erroll's office.

They had come for her in the late afternoon, in three cars following one another up the little lane of Sabbath Creek Road, slowly, sturdy vehicles painted dark blue with matching flashers turned off. She had looked out the window to see them come, not really surprised, but not afraid, either, because it had not occurred to her what might actually be about to happen. Polly was next door in the living room, playing with cards by smearing them about over the couch and turning them over, one by one. She had found the cards earlier in the week, in one of Pick's drawers, and had been instantly enthralled, particularly with the kings and queens. Heather half listened to her, and half to the radio, which said the fair weather was likely to hang on for a bit, good for the homecoming football game in Hanover, where the station was located.

She was cooking, the first time in weeks she'd felt up to it. There were two chickens nearly done in the oven and a pot of potatoes boiling on the stove for Polly, who loved them mashed, and apples cut up in a bowl and covered with brown and white sugar, which was about all she could remember of how Pick had made Brown Betty. She felt good. After months, it seemed, of feeling terrible, one way or another, she had finally made her way through to this afternoon when she could stand in her own kitchen and feel, if not strong, then at least not unwell, and, if not happy, then at least not cataclysmically bereft. She heard Polly interrupt her baby solitaire with a sputter of discomfort. She needed a change, though she hated to be changed and tended not to complain until the problem was unignorable. From the living room she heard her daughter's single word: "Mama!" Heather smiled. She put the lid on the pot and lowered the heat under the simmering potatoes. Then she heard cars on the lane.

Now Polly was calling again. Not scared, really—she was too fascinated by human faces to be scared easily—but concerned. The police station wasn't big; she had driven past it all her life and knew it was only the size of a ranch house, but she hadn't ever been inside and she didn't know where Polly was. The cinder blocks let sound in, though it was muffled. She could have been on the other side of the wall.

"What happened to my daughter?" Heather said.

The man, Robert Charter, was writing something on lined sheets in an open folder. He didn't answer her, and some instinctive thing made her not ask again.

The clock showed it was nearly six. Polly hadn't eaten, of course. They hadn't even let her bring food from home. They'd only turned off the stove and left it all there, and the chickens would probably be dried out by the time she got home, and the potatoes stuck like glue to the pot. Charter frowned down at what he had written. Then he looked up at her.

"What did you say?"

"I said, what happened to my daughter?"

He seemed to give this an inappropriate amount of consideration. Then he sighed. "Well, frankly, Miss Pratt, that's exactly what we're hoping you can tell us."

She stared at him. From beyond the cinder-block wall, Polly burst into a wail. Heather leaped to her feet. "Let me see her."

"Officer Franks is with Polly," Charter said calmly. "Lucy has two kids of her own. She brought some food in for Polly earlier. She knows what kids like; not to worry." He actually smiled. "I'm glad you could come down, Miss Pratt. I've been wanting a word with you. Appreciate your coming in voluntarily."

"Voluntarily?" said Heather. "There were three police cars at my house. You said if I didn't come—"

"But you did," he said simply. "And voluntarily, as I said. And I appreciate it, as I also said."

"So I could leave," Heather said, as if it were a question.

"But naturally. Only then we'd have to go right back and invite you to come in again. Better to just have our talk now, wouldn't it be? Then we can all move on."

"I don't know why you want to talk to me," she said plainly. "I'm just telling you."

He studied her. It was remarkable, the degree of blankness he managed. She could read nothing from him, which scared her. But if he was really willing to just say whatever it was he seemed to want to say, then it was worthwhile for her just to listen to it now.

"All right," Charter said. Then he went blank again.

She thought he was very ugly. Not just without beauty, the way nearly all men—all but Ashley—were without beauty, the way men like Stephen Trask were fine, plain, unobjectionable but without beauty. She thought he was actively, strenuously ugly, with his florid face and ridged, combed-over gray hair. He sat with his stumpy fingers splayed on the tabletop, a thick gold ring on the left ring finger, a chunky gold school ring on the right. She frowned at the school ring. She had always thought they were stupid things.

"So, fine," Heather prompted at last. "Say your piece. Then I have to get home."

He considered her for a minute before speaking. "Tell you what. I'll just get a little background first, okay? Like your name. Full name."

Heather Ruth Pratt, she told him. The clock said ten past six.

"And date of birth?"

"May 1, 1965."

He looked down at the page. "Your employment."

"I work for Naomi Roth's collective. It's called Flourish. I make samplers for her, but I can work at home, too."

"And did you have any other employment before that?"

She hesitated. "Well, I worked for Stephen Trask at the sports center for a few months."

"About five months, that would be?"

She stared at him. "If you know, how come you're asking me?"

Charter smiled, as if this were funny. Then he put down his pen. "Shortly after you began working for Mr. Trask, you made the acquaintance of a married man named Ashley Deacon. You pursued him and began a sexual relationship with him. You became pregnant. You were proud of your pregnancy, even though it was the result of an adulterous affair.

In fact, it's generally felt that you flaunted this pregnancy. In any case, you neither hid it nor denied it. You had the child in"—he flipped over the slender top file to a somewhat thicker file beneath, opened it and rummaged, and read—"August of 1984. Your daughter Polly. You flaunted the child, too. You went up on the porch over at Tom and Whit's and opened up your shirt and started to breast-feed, and you continued to do so even after people asked you to stop. You are hardly demure, Miss Pratt."

Heather, struck dumb, could only gape at him.

"Shortly after your daughter's birth you recommenced your affair with Mr. Deacon, although by now he had also begun a family with his wife." Charter paused. "Was that smart?"

"I want to go," Heather managed. "I don't have to listen to this!"

"Is any of it untrue?" he asked, looking concerned. "Are my facts wrong?"

"Why am I here?" she shouted.

"To help me," he said. "I need your help."

For an instant, her panic abated. He did look concerned, even a little needy.

"What help?" she asked. "About what? You obviously know all about me already. What else do you want to know?"

Charter reached up to his own head, patting the wave of hair thoughtfully. "About the baby," he said evenly. "Tell me about the baby."

"What?" Heather nearly shouted. "She's not even a baby anymore. She's fourteen months old." A thought occurred to her. "Is this, like, a child-abuse thing? Did someone tell you I'm not a good mother or something? Because I am a good mother. I'd like to know who said that!"

"No one has said you aren't a good mother, Heather." Charter's voice was soothing. "In fact, people have gone out of their way to tell me what a good mother you are."

"People? What, are you doing a survey or something? On what kind of a mother I am? What kind of detective are you, anyway?"

He leaned back in his chair. "I'm no kind of a detective. I'm a district attorney. I work in Peytonville. I'm just here to find out about the baby."

Heather went chill. She had finally realized what this might mean.

"The baby," she said, her voice hushed. "You mean that baby Naomi found." She waited for his confirming nod, then permitted herself a small moment of relief. "But, Mr. Charter, I don't know anything about that baby."

He nodded, as if he'd been expecting these very words. "Then you're denying you gave birth to that baby. The one Naomi Roth found in the river."

"Well, of course I am. Of course I am!"

He wrote something down. She tried to make out what it was, but he flipped the folder over it. Then he looked up again. "But let me get this straight. You're not denying that you *had* another baby. Not your daughter Polly. A second baby."

She tried to keep her face still. "I do deny that, yes."

And why shouldn't she? What business was it of his? It's not as if he could change anything.

"You absolutely deny it." He waited, intent.

The clock said six-thirty.

"Let's go back," he said, resuming his easy tone. He never took his eyes off Heather. "Let's talk about Ashley, all right?"

"Will it get me out of here faster?"

"Very probably. Did Ashley make it clear to you that he was married?"

"He never lied to me," Heather said, since she still felt that to be true.

"But that didn't stop you from pursuing him."

"I didn't pursue him," she said hotly. "We fell in love. We both did."

"You no more than him?"

Heather shrugged.

"Who initiated sex?" He looked at his hand as he wrote, not at her.

"We made love," Heather said with strained dignity.

"In his car," Charter noted.

And other places, she started to say, but there was only the mill attic, and Heather didn't like to remember that time. Certainly she didn't want to talk about it now.

"And what contraceptive were you using?"

"Obviously," she said tightly, "we weren't using any."

"And whose idea was that?"

She paused to collect her thoughts. "Well, we were both happy about the ... about me having Polly, if that's what you're implying."

He put down his pen. He looked affronted. "But I'm not implying anything, Miss Pratt. That's not my job, either here or in court. I just have questions and I think you might have answers, that's all. So I ask and you answer, and then everybody can leave. Is that all right with you?"

"Fine," said Heather. "You want to know all about my love life, you ask any question you want. But I don't know anything about that baby, so if you're trying to find out about it, you're going to be pretty mad about wasting your time with me."

"Well, that's all right." Charter sighed. "Don't you worry about that. Now tell me, was Ashley supportive of your pregnancy?"

"Of course. He saw how happy I was, and that made him happy, too."

"So the idea of having children by his wife and his mistress born within a week of each other, that didn't seem to bother him, then."

"You'd have to ask him," Heather said evenly.

Charter went to his thick folder and dug in. Delicately, he searched. There were many sheets of yellow paper. Heather, realization dawning on her, looked on in horror. Pages of words, about her and Ashley. People who had sat and talked about her, about her personal things, to this ugly man.

"Yes," he said, evidently confirming his own memories. " 'Sure it bothered me. But I couldn't do anything about it. And it was up to her. If she'd gotten rid of it I would have been happy, but I wasn't going to make a big thing.' "

Heather couldn't speak. Her eyes were wet suddenly, and uselessly she willed herself not to cry.

"I've upset you," Charter observed. "I am sorry."

Heather said nothing.

"Not very gentlemanly, was he?"

Fuck you, she thought, surprising herself.

"Still, he was more than willing to go on having sex with you, anyway. A lot of men probably wouldn't even have done that."

Heather wept. She couldn't help that. But she wasn't going to give him the satisfaction of answering him.

"And when the baby was born, was he there? Oh no . . ." He consulted the same papers, flipped a page ahead. "His own son had been born a week earlier. It would have been hard for him to get away, I suppose. But surely he contributed to Polly's upkeep? Even if he couldn't spare time away from the wife, he would surely have given you some money to help out. Just," Charter said, "to demonstrate his responsibility."

"No money," Heather managed. "I wouldn't have asked."

"Just to demonstrate . . . his paternity, then."

Through her tears, she seethed. "Ashley knew he was the father."

"Did he?"

From afar, Polly wailed. Heather leaped to her feet. "Give me my daughter!"

"No," Charter said simply. "Not right now."

"Right now!" Heather screamed. "Right now!"

He sat, impassive.

"Polly is crying." She waited for him to deny this, but he didn't.

"Nonetheless, Lucy can take care of her. I'm sure we won't be much longer."

This gave her pause. She felt this bright thing—home, her own child in her own arms—dangling before her. Anything was worth that. Even this. She glanced at the clock. It was seven o'clock. Polly's bedtime was seven-thirty. She could still make it back to the safety of her own routine.

"All right." She breathed deeply.

"Five months after your daughter's birth, you and Mr. Deacon were having sex in his car in the woods near the Sabbathday River. His wife and some of her friends followed you and confronted you. You fled the scene—"

"Fled the scene?" she asked incredulously. "I left. With Ashley."

"Yes. Shortly thereafter, he terminated your association and returned to his wife. Sue Deacon has just had a second baby. Maybe you knew."

Heather nodded, though she hadn't heard. She'd seen Sue once, over the summer, from her car. She'd known Sue was pregnant.

"And you, by coincidence, were also pregnant."

"No," Heather said. She shook her head once, twice. Then she said it again. "No."

"You were pregnant a second time, with Ashley's child."

"No."

"Conceived at the end of your affair. Perhaps even at your last sexual contact with him."

"I said no. How many times?"

"This time, it seems to me, you wouldn't have been so happy about being pregnant. Your boyfriend had gone back to his wife. Your grandmother, I understand, had passed away. You were all alone, and you were pregnant."

"This is completely untrue." She gave a choked laugh.

"This time you did not flaunt your pregnancy. You didn't tell anybody about your pregnancy. Not even the father of the child. Conversely, you did not choose to terminate your pregnancy. May I ask why not?"

"Because there wasn't one," she said tightly. "I wasn't."

"You did not seek medical help. The midwife who delivered your daughter did not hear from you. Over these past few months you stayed mostly at home, and when you went out you wore large shirts and sweaters, even in the heat." He paused, and even smiled. "That must have been uncomfortable!"

"I never lost the weight," she said, her voice ragged. "From Polly. I never got it off. And I . . . I'm still nursing my daughter. You know, not all the time, but once or twice a day. It keeps you fat. I read that."

"Really," Charter said. "I didn't know that."

They looked at each other. Heather was starting to get her face under control, though it stung a bit.

"Well, I must say, you don't look fat to me," he offered.

"I've . . . I had the stomach flu last week. I didn't eat for a few days. And I threw up," she added.

"How awful for you," he said dryly. "And still you didn't call the doctor?"

"Well, no. It was only a stomach flu."

She looked up at the clock. Polly would not make her bedtime.

"Would you like to see a doctor now?" Charter said. His voice was quiet but his tone intent. Very carefully, Heather shook her head. "But why not? Stomach flus can be very un-pleasant."

"No, thank you. I'm fine."

"And Polly didn't catch your flu?"

"No." She smiled brightly. "Lucky."

"Very." He frowned down at his hands. "Oh no, Miss Pratt. How long are we going to go on like this? How much time are we going to waste?"

"Listen," she said, "I want to go to the bathroom."

He looked at her blankly, as if he didn't understand.

"The bathroom." She felt as if she were in school. Was she supposed to raise her hand? "Please."

"Are you ill? More of your stomach flu, perhaps?"

"No. I just . . . I need to use the bathroom." She felt her face get hot. "To pee. All right?"

"Soon," he said. "Let's try to move forward."

"Forward to *what*? I don't even know what's going on! I told you I didn't have a baby, and I sure don't know anything about that baby Naomi found. It wasn't mine!"

"Well, possibly you have some idea whose it was, then."

"I have no idea!" she shouted. "I don't know whose. It could be anyone's. It could be . . ." She knew she shouldn't say this, but couldn't interrupt herself. "It could be Sue Deacon's, for all I know. Did you haul *her* in here?"

He got to his feet slowly and looked down at her. He was not tall, but dense, graceless beneath his good gray jacket and slightly frayed tie. For the first time, something in his look made her feel irreversibly powerless, as if she had already been locked away for life at his specific mercy, and he a merciless man.

"Please tell me," Charter said, "that you are not accusing Sue Deacon of murdering that child."

Then, in addition to her fear, she felt ashamed.

"I need a little break, Miss Pratt. I'll be back in a few minutes. Please think carefully about how we are going to proceed."

And he left her, sweeping the files away from her off the table as he went, closing the door deliberately behind him.

The room had changed in the past hour. It had seemed small when he led her in, a great table with a channel of space around the edges, and no windows, but now it felt downright stunted, as if it had been made for a person of abnormally minuscule dimensions. What could you do in such a little place but imprison people, or frighten them? Her bladder ached. She moved her feet beneath the table and brooded over its surface: beige flecked with other beige. The cinder blocks were painted beige, too. She watched the second hand sweep around its course a few times. She was trying not to think about any of this.

But the quiet prodded at her, the absence of human voices. She even, for a moment, missed *his* voice—Charter's. There was not silence, precisely, but a hiss of air from the walls, through which no sound percolated. The clock, she thought, could no longer tell her exactly what time it was, since she found that she could no longer completely trust what it said. Not without evidence—*something*, some glimpse of the world. The world could have disappeared, she thought. It could have just gone away, as he had gone away, shutting the door behind it, leaving her in this beige tomb lit with fluorescent glare and lacking a toilet, and she wouldn't ever see Polly again.

So Heather started to cry, but softly, only for herself. She had yet to make any sense at all about this—not only about this man and this room and the police coming to her house, but about the baby herself. And the baby herself had begun to leave her, mercifully. Whatever parts of Heather she had taken along were justifiable losses, too, so long as the baby went and did not return. And Polly . . .

Panic surged inside her. She jerked to her feet. She hadn't heard Polly in . . . Oh, the clock was useless! Polly was gone. They had locked her in the room and gone away with her daughter. *She had to get out.*

"Hey!" Heather shouted, first experimentally, then again, louder. She went around the table to the door. She banged on the door with her fist, then tried the knob. The door was locked. "Hey! I need to go to the bathroom!"

Silence. Dread ran through her, but she backed away from the door, determined not to compound her fear by trying again, and again hearing nothing. She walked back around the table, one arm braced above it for support, and sat in her chair again. Then she put her head down. All this . . . this thing, this weird episode she was mired in, would pass away if she just kept going forward, and she would remember this night—it was night now, if the clock was even remotely right—as some strange and obnoxious inconvenience, like one of those nights when Polly was little and up at strange hours, reading darkness for day. Like an airplane trip must be, she thought, taking off in the night and arriving in the day, or vice versa. It wasn't terrible, after all, but she wanted it over. When he came back, she would do whatever she could do to make it over. Whatever he wanted her to do. Her palms, cupped, made a bed for her forehead. Both were clammy. The door opened.

Charter came in, followed by the sheriff, Erroll. Erroll was bigger, but he hung back and looked a little unsure. He even stood till after Charter had sat in his seat again. Charter slapped down the file in its place and flipped the top cover open, beginning to read, nonchalantly. Heather noted, with disbelief, an abandoned crumb in the corner of his mouth. Then Erroll closed the door and took the seat next to him.

Heather said, "Listen, do I need a lawyer or something?"

Nelson looked at Charter. Charter frowned. "I don't know. *Do* you need a lawyer? Have you done something wrong?"

"No!" said Heather.

"Then why would you need a lawyer? I don't understand."

She didn't understand, either. But she was scared. She wanted Polly, and she wanted to go home. She'd thought when you mentioned a lawyer they were supposed to stop, but he looked as if he had no intention of stopping.

"All the same," she said bravely, "I think I'd like to talk to one. If you don't mind."

Heather saw Erroll lean close to Charter and speak in his ear. Charter's face never changed. He expressed himself with one dismissive grunt.

"I don't think you understand, Miss Pratt. It's certainly appropriate to call a lawyer if a person is under arrest. But that's not the case here. You're helping us, and as soon as you are finished helping us, you can go home. Don't you want that?"

"Yes," said Heather poignantly.

"All right, then." He was complacent.

"Where is Polly?" Heather said. Her voice came out harsh, but really she was just trying to get the words out.

"Fine," Charter said. Erroll glanced at him, then at the table. "Not *how*. *Where?*"

He looked up. "I said she's fine. Don't worry." And when

he saw, to his apparent amazement, that even this wealth of information did not placate her, he sat back in his chair. "I've arranged for Polly to spend the night at Officer Franks's house. She'll be just fine."

Heather stared at him. Monologues of outrage raced over her tongue and fled, unspoken, leaving her depleted of language—even, incredibly, of anger. It was only as she had thought. They had taken Polly away, that was clear. It wasn't as if she didn't know what she had to do.

"I had a baby," Heather said.

Charter pursed his lips. "Really."

"I had a baby. I'm sorry I didn't say so. But it died."

"Did it, now?" He reached into his breast pocket and extracted a pen. "You don't mind if I write this down, do you?"

She was breathing deeply. It hadn't been hard, after all. Not as hard as she'd thought. So someone knew—the earth hadn't blown apart.

"We have a tape recorder in the office." Erroll spoke for the first time. "I could—"

"No," said Charter. "Not necessary." He turned back to Heather. "Your baby died."

"It was a miscarriage," she said, because it had been, sort of. That was how she had come to think of it, these past weeks. A miscarriage of life. Wasn't any death really a miscarriage of life?

"And this occurred when?" he said, nodding slightly, as if he were only sympathizing with her.

"Oh, a while back. Few months? Maybe. I don't really remember. It was summer, anyway."

The pen waited. "In the summer," he mused.

"I was . . . I had it in the toilet. I felt sick in the middle of the night, so I went to the toilet and it . . . came out. I felt terrible," she said, a little desperately.

"I'm sure you did," Charter said. "Can we go back, please?"

Back, Heather thought dimly. There was no back.

"When did you discover you were pregnant with this second child?"

"Just after . . ." Just after her life had tacked in its course, she thought. Just after Pick had fallen asleep on the living-room couch and never wakened. Just after Ashley had told her she wasn't strong enough to take him from his wife. Just after the before of her life had ended and the after had begun. "I don't know exactly," she said instead. "January?"

"And whom did you tell about this pregnancy?"

She had told no one, but he knew this already. Not the midwife, not Stephen Trask or Celia Trask, not Naomi Roth, who had thought she was such a good example to her daughter. Certainly not Ashley, who turned away from her now when they met, who crushed her heart with his jagged indifference. The truth was she had barely told herself about the baby inside her, there was so much mourning in the aftermath of that night. The baby, set ticking by so much sadness, was like a measure of the reach of that sadness out of the past, and it only got bigger instead of lessening and loosening its grip on her. She might have been getting better, but it only grew, taking up space and reminding her of what she had lost. She could not bear to think about it, but when she did it was with bitter resentment; how much more had she wanted back the things that had left her life, in place of this thing that had come?

"I'm not really close to too many people that way," she said now. "I can't think of anyone I told."

"That's a shame," said Charter. "And you didn't go see a doctor either, is that right? Good mother like you?"

"I felt fine," Heather said. "I did."

"Until your miscarriage, that is."

She looked up at him. "Yes, Until then."

"And you can't remember when that was, exactly?"

"No." She looked for the crumb. It was still there. Staring at it helped her avoid his eyes.

"Could it have been more recent than the summer? Last month or so, for example?"

Heather shrugged.

"Like, during your stomach flu, maybe? When you did all that throwing up and lost all that weight you never lost from having your fourteen-month-old daughter?"

She swallowed. "I really need to go to the bathroom."

Erroll started to get to his feet.

"Answer the question!" Charter shouted.

Heather's eyes filled with tears. "Yes. Sure," she choked. "Now can I go?"

"Take her," he said nonchalantly. He was writing. Erroll

opened up the door and waited for her to come around the table.

The station was quiet but not empty. A policeman she recognized from her house was leaning against the wall of the corridor, merely watching her. Others were in a room she passed, talking softly, even laughing, drinking coffee, but not precisely *doing* anything. As if they were waiting, she thought vaguely, which was of course exactly what they were doing. They were waiting for her. The bathroom was on the other side of the entrance area, a single stall in a little room, not designated for men or women. Erroll reached in and turned on the light. He wouldn't let her shut the door all the way.

"I'll just stand here," he said, as if that were completely normal.

She was too tired to argue. She went into the stall and pulled down her pants, checking reflexively for blood, but there hadn't been blood for a few days now. She wondered when she would stop checking, or whether she would ever stop checking. She barely felt the relief of her bladder letting go. She could sleep, almost, or not so much sleep as just fall away from herself, right here. After a while they would come in and get her.

It had been stupid to say she'd had the baby in the toilet. You couldn't flush a baby that big away—they knew that, of course—so there was nothing gained by doing it. She still would have had to take the baby out of the toilet and put it somewhere. Charter would ask about that next. She had to use this time. This time out of his sight was precious. She had to think what to say when he asked her.

"You all right in there?" Erroll said.

Heather shuddered. She could barely remember what she had said already. She couldn't imagine what she would say next.

He walked her back to the room, back through the gauntlet of attendant policemen. She wondered where they had all come from. As far as she knew, Goddard itself only had one, or maybe two. When Erroll pushed back the door, Charter had a form in front of him, flat atop the manila files. He was tapping it with his fingers.

"Like to send some of these men out to your place," he told

Heather without preamble. "Just informal. To have a look around."

"But why?" she said. "What are you looking for?"

"Oh, nothing in particular," he said evenly. "Like I said, it's just informal. You'll need to sign, though."

"Sign what?"

He held it up, from where he sat, as if she could read that far.

"Shouldn't I have a lawyer if I need to sign something?" she asked.

"Oh, I don't see why," said Charter. "A miscarriage isn't against the law. Maybe a doctor, sure, but I don't see what a lawyer can do about a miscarriage."

"Can I see it?" Heather said.

He slid it across the table. It gave the police permission to search her house for any materials or objects relevant to the investigation. For the first time since she had told him about the baby, her heart leaped a little. She knew there was nothing to find.

"I'll sign this," Heather said. He skitted his pen across the table, and she did. Charter handed the sheet to Erroll, who went out.

"I'd like to talk a little more about the baby," he said when they were alone again. "Bet you felt pretty bad about having a miscarriage."

"I did," Heather said.

"Especially when the baby was so far along."

She shrugged. She didn't really think it mattered how far along it was.

"So . . . what did you do when it happened?"

Heather thought. She couldn't think. "I don't really remember," she said finally.

"You don't remember," Charter echoed. "You don't remember what you did with the body of your baby."

The miscarriage, she noted dully, had become a dead baby. It seemed not much of a difference. Not worth fighting over, anyway.

"Well, I was upset. It was the middle of the night. I don't really remember."

"You remember it was the middle of the night, but you don't remember what you did with the body of your baby."

He regarded her.

"Did you, for example, take it out of the toilet?"

"Well, I must have." She tried to smile. "I mean, I couldn't have left it there."

He didn't smile back.

"But you don't exactly remember, because you were so upset."

"I was upset," she recalled.

"And maybe . . . well, I'm just thinking aloud here. Stop me if I'm off track. I'm just thinking how I would maybe have felt about having the baby in the first place. Like, sad, for example. Maybe even angry. After all, you had a lot on your plate. You already had a little kid to take care of. You knew your boyfriend was off having kids with his own wife and wouldn't be around to help you. Plus your grandmother was gone. Understand she helped you out taking care of Polly. Freed you up in the afternoons, for example."

Heather looked at him. She noted, with a whiff of pride, that she had passed beyond being insulted by him.

"And now that was all gone, and all you had was a dead baby in the toilet."

"Miscarriage," she muttered.

"Sure. But dead, right?"

"It was dead," Heather confirmed.

"And you knew this for a fact, because . . ."

She gazed at him for a moment, uncomprehending.

"What do you mean?"

"Well, it just occurs to me, you must have medical training of some kind, or you wouldn't be exactly qualified to pronounce a baby dead. But maybe I'm wrong." He shrugged.

"It was *dead*!" Heather shouted.

"Yes," said Charter. "But before you killed it? Or after?"

Her mouth went dry, then—it felt like—her whole head. She could not have spoken even if, by some extraordinary chance, she'd been able to think of what to say.

"That's the question," Charter said. "That's what I'm wondering."

"Listen to me," said Heather, barely recognizing the steely timbre of her own apparent voice. "You can send every cop in New Hampshire to my house, but you're going to be pretty disappointed. There is no dead baby in my house."

He gaped at her, sincerely amazed. "But of course there isn't, Miss Pratt. How could there be? Your baby daughter is in a freezer in Peytonville. And whenever you're ready to tell me how she got there, I'm ready to listen."

Chapter 20

The Pond and the River

AT SOME POINT THEY LET HER SLEEP. DOWN AT
the other end of the building, as far as you could get from
Erroll's office, which, given the size of the station house itself,
wasn't all that far, was a single room. A cell, she supposed,
numbly. Not that it mattered. She would have taken a box,
just to get away from him.

The horror of what she'd been accused of doing refused to
thoroughly sink in, but she hated him for saying it, nonetheless. For those first hours of the night they had remained this
way, intractable on either side of the table, like heads of state
who arrive at a negotiation determined not to negotiate. After
a while, she simply refused to keep speaking, to answer even
the most mundane of questions. Then she put her head down,
literally, on her arms, and to even her own amazement fell
promptly asleep. When she woke, it was because two men
were half-leading, half-carrying her here.

The sleep was merciful, dreamless and opaque. She barely
distinguished the little room with its steel-framed single bed
and scratchy wool cover, but dove back into oblivion, refusing
any stray fragments of thought—her daughter, the unnamed
baby—until she was numb and away. There was no clock in
the room, of course. A policeman sat in a chair by the door,
and the station was quiet. She hoped they would never come
back.

When they came back, it was still night. Heather jerked
awake, adrenaline rushing through her body. The man at her
right elbow seemed angry. He gave a tug and she got unsteadily to her feet. He was a different man—not the one who had
sat outside the door. He was one of the ones who had left to
go to her house. She wondered how long they had let her rest.

Charter was back in the room, waiting for her, his thick
back to the door. Erroll, who sat beside him, looked over his
shoulder to give her a little smile when she reached the door-

way. She walked around them, back to her place, without asking. The table was covered with objects, but she had to squint
at them to see what they were because they were shiny from
being put in plastic bags, the same zip-lock type Pick had used
for freezing her applesauce. Heather peered at them and saw,
to her mild curiosity, that they were all spikes. Long thin nails,
some rusted; an awl with a faded wooden bulb; an ice pick
with an apple-green handle, indistinguishable from her own,
at home in the kitchen; and a metallic array of thin knitting
needles, multicolored, just like the ones in Pick's sewing basket at home, sharp and glittery like pickup sticks. She had kept
her basket by the couch, for her tools and whatever lovely
thing she was making. Since Polly's quilt there hadn't been
much. Her hands, she said, and she preferred to play with the
baby. There was one sweater she did make, Heather remembered: lavender, with sweet white cuffs and collar, but Polly
had already outgrown it and there wouldn't be anything more.
Where was the basket now? It suddenly seemed awfully important to remember, but Heather couldn't remember.

"I hope you were able to rest," Charter said. "I think you
did need a rest."

Heather looked at him.

"And you're ready to continue, I assume."

Continue, she thought. She looked at the spikes.

"You recognize these?" he said evenly. "It's a lot to take
in."

She peered at them again. She wasn't sure she understood
the question.

"Do I recognize them? They're all different. It's knitting
needles and an ice pick."

"Well, I'm glad you're not going to disagree with me about
that," he said genially.

"Are they mine?" Heather said. "Are they from my house?"
She stood up and leaned forward across the table. A couple of
them she didn't recognize. "Those aren't mine," she said,
pointing at the awl and some of the nails.

"They were all collected from your own home, within the
past two hours."

"Really?" Heather said, perplexed. It was possible, she supposed. After all, Pick had been much more handy than she.
She never used half of Pick's things in the cellar, and she

hadn't bothered to clean out the tool area, either. "Well, all right."

"So then you agree that these are your things."

"Do I *agree?*" Heather frowned. "Why are you asking me about this?" She felt disoriented now, as if she had missed some crucial turn in their drama. She had told him about the miscarriage, and he had accused her of killing her child. That was bad enough, but what did it have to do with spikes?

"It's important for us to know," Charter said, his eyes on her face. "I know you don't really want to think about these things, and believe me, I promise I won't make you go over and over it. But we need to know exactly what happened, and that means we have to know which one of these you used. Or maybe the one you used isn't here at all. Maybe you put that one somewhere so you wouldn't have to see it. We need to know that, too."

"Used," said Heather, testing the word. "Used for what?"

He looked at her. His thick forefinger tapped the top of his file. The file, she noted vaguely, had grown.

"I used this one for defrosting the fridge," she said, sounding, to her own ears at least, just the tiniest bit angry. Or was it desperate? "The nails and stuff I don't know. I'm not very handy. The knitting needles were P—my grandmother's." Charter did not react. "See these? These are for big stitches, with wool. The littler ones make finer stitches. She made a sweater for Polly with them. It was a lavender sweater. It's already too small for Polly." Even to her own ears she sounded strange, but she couldn't stop herself from talking. "Those"— she pointed—"were for making socks. You use four of them. You make a triangle and the fourth is to knit."

"I don't need knitting lessons," he said sharply. "Which of these did you use to kill your baby?"

Instantly she was fully awake. "I didn't kill her," Heather snapped.

Charter raised his eyebrows. "The baby had a stab wound, as you know."

As she knew? Heather thought. Had Naomi said this to her? About the baby from the river?

"It was not an accidental stab wound. Unless"—he leaned forward—"that is what you are telling us, Miss Pratt. That your baby's stab wound was somehow accidental?"

"I didn't stab her," Heather said. "I *never* . . ." She stopped. Never, never. She couldn't.

"Are you unsure?" he asked. "Do you need to think?"

"No," Heather said. "Look, you said a miscarriage wasn't a crime."

"That's true," he agreed.

"I never stabbed a baby. That wasn't my baby!"

He sighed deeply. "Don't you see that this isn't helping? You are only wasting your energy, Miss Pratt. My time, you're free to waste. I've got plenty. But your energy . . . It seems a shame. We could be helping you, you see? We could be starting to do all the things we want to do to help you, but you are making it so hard for us. Please. Make up your mind to tell us only the truth from now on. We won't judge you."

She looked into his face. His features were easy, untroubled. This, she saw, was only bureaucratic work for him. The period of his judgment was indeed long past, and there remained only the filling out of forms. He wouldn't stop until every line had its quota of confirmation.

"You're lying," Heather said, enraged.

Charter leaned back in his chair. His face was tight, and beneath their ragged brows his gaze was tight, too, and fixed. "I'm lying," he said carefully. "I'm lying." He shook his head. "Do you know how long I have been doing this, Miss Pratt? Talking to people who are accused of crimes?"

"You said miscarriage—" Heather shrieked.

"Not miscarriage. Murder. Murder, by stabbing, of an infant baby!" His ugly face was suddenly made more ugly by the blood beneath his white skin. Almost comical, she thought. Did he know he could change colors?

"I never!"

"Twenty-one years, Miss Pratt. As long as you've been alive. And here are three things I've learned about talking to people who are accused of crimes. Even in this big world, full of all kinds of people, there are three things that always happen when somebody's accused of a crime." He was seething. She pictured his heart pumping rage into his voice. "First thing: they lie. Second thing: they lie. Third thing." He glared at her. He slammed the table with the flat of his hand. "They *lie!*"

The sound took a long time to dissipate. No one spoke.

I want to go home, she thought pointlessly. If they let her go home, she would stay there forever. She would never show her face. Surely that would be enough for what she'd done.

"Heather," said a different voice. Heather looked up at Erroll. "You tell us. In your own words. I know you remember, and I know it hurts to remember. But you know we have to know." He glanced at Charter. "We won't interrupt you. That seem fair?"

Fair? Heather thought. None of this was fair. They didn't know what it was like to be so weak your lover could no longer love you, or have a baby inside you whose face you couldn't bear imagining. They didn't know what it was like to be out there in the back field, in the night with all those stars watching to see what would happen.

"I'll tell you," she heard herself say. "This is the truth." She looked at Charter. Without taking his eyes from her, he felt for his pen.

"I was sleeping," she started. She had no idea how she would tell this story. "It was the middle of the night. Tuesday night. Don't ask me what time, all right? And I woke up sick. I felt . . . it wasn't like with Polly. It was just, like it was suddenly there. No preparation. I was just going to have it. And I wasn't ready, you know." She looked at their faces. Charter was writing. "I hadn't told anyone, so I was by myself. I felt really hot. You remember," she said, trying not to sound so ragged, "it was hot."

"A couple weeks ago," Erroll said. "Yes, it was pretty hot."

"I just . . . I suddenly didn't want to be in the house. I didn't want Polly to wake up and hear me. She can get out of the crib sometimes. I didn't want her to hear me and get out, and come in and see . . ." Heather shrugged. "So I went outside. It was cooler outside." And the stars, she thought. Like bullet holes people up there were peeking through, watching her. "I didn't know what would happen. I never meant for anything bad to happen."

"I'm sure that's true," said Erroll. Then he waited for her to start again.

"I went down the hill. There's a pond back there at the bottom. Well, not a pond, really. It's mostly mud with a few big rocks around the edge. I don't know why I went there. I didn't plan that." She looked at them. "I just was walking through the . . . cramps. You know?" But they couldn't know, she thought bitterly. "And after a while, maybe a few minutes, like ten, down at the pond, I just felt like it was time to . . ." She stopped, suddenly embarrassed. Because it had felt just like going to the bathroom, really, and at the time she hadn't been sure it was the baby at all, only this other thing that she had to do before the baby could come out. "I got down," she told them. "Like crouching, all right? And I pushed, and something came out. But I didn't realize it was the baby," she said quickly. "I thought it might be . . . something else." She wasn't looking at Charter at all anymore. Erroll seemed intent. He nodded. "But I felt better, so I just stayed like that for a little while." She closed her eyes. "I don't know how long. Because I thought if I moved, it would start the pains up again. And it was only after that I looked down and I saw the baby."

Charter stopped. He looked up. His face was wooden.

"Your baby," he said, after a moment.

"Yes." Heather had tears in her eyes. She hadn't felt them come, but she felt them fall. "She was dead."

He put his pen down.

"Just like that," he observed.

Erroll turned to look at him.

"You're saying the baby was born dead," said Charter. "I want to make sure I understand."

Heather, desperate to finish, nodded quickly. "She never moved. She didn't cry. I'm not a doctor or anything, but I know she was dead! Polly cried right away. Babies cry! But this one just . . . she never." She glared up at them both through her tears. "She was just dead! I couldn't do anything about it."

"What *did* you do?" asked Erroll softly.

"I stood up. I . . . That other part came out, too. I felt really dizzy, like I was going to faint. I wanted to go back up to the house. I was afraid of fainting out in the field. I was afraid Polly would wake up and call and I wouldn't come." *Like the other time,* she wanted to explain, but couldn't. Like the time Polly had called and wept all day, pleading for the dead to return and comfort her. "So I went back. I went on my hands and knees for a bit. Then I got up. I walked up. I got back to the house and I got back into bed. I couldn't think about what . . ." She shook her head. "Because she was dead. I couldn't help her anyway. And I couldn't stay awake. When

I woke up, there was so much blood on the sheets. The mattress, too. I didn't know what to do. I had to take care of Polly."

"And did you?" Erroll said. "Is that what happened?"

"I took care of her. I got breakfast for her. I rolled up a towel and put it in my underpants. I tried to eat some stuff, but I kept throwing up. It was like that all day."

"What happened then?" Erroll said.

"I put Polly down for her nap in the afternoon. About two. That's the time she usually goes, anyway. And I tried to sleep, too. On the couch downstairs. But I kept thinking of it out there. I couldn't remember so much about what happened. I thought maybe none of it had really happened. I mean, I knew something, but I couldn't be sure."

"So you went out?" Erroll said helpfully.

"Yes. I walked out. It was warm again. I went down to the pond." She started to cry again. She swatted at her eyes. "I saw it on the ground. I saw it was a girl. That's the first time I knew it was a girl. It had"—Heather swallowed—"this shiny thing over it. It was all gray. And there were some flies. I couldn't stand that. I didn't want flies."

Erroll nodded. Charter had his head down.

"I thought I should bury it. I kept thinking of that phrase 'proper burial.' I didn't know what that meant. I'm not sure I know what it means now. What's proper about putting something in the ground? Just, you know, digging a hole and putting it down there? I didn't think I'd feel any better if I did that."

"And that's what you were trying to do?" Charter said, a little caustically. "Feel better?"

"No, I . . . well, I don't know. Maybe," said Heather. She took a breath. There wasn't much more. "So then I just . . . My eye sort of fell on the pond. It was right there. It was so dark. You couldn't even see into it. And the mud on the bottom was really soft. I remembered from when I was a kid, I used to get all mucked up in it on really hot days, and the mud in between my toes." She felt abruptly embarrassed by this, as if it were, in a way, even more intimate than the other things she had said. "It was . . . it seemed as if it was just like the ground in a way, but it was right there, and I wouldn't have to carry . . ." She looked helplessly at them.

Charter had stopped writing. He stared at her in distaste.

"What are you saying?" His voice was soft but fierce. "Are you saying you put your baby's body into this pond? And left it there?"

She nodded eagerly. She felt the weight lift, she wouldn't have to say any more. There wasn't any more to say.

"And this is your statement?"

"My . . . ? It's what happened," Heather said. "It's where I put it. It's still there."

"I thought," Charter shook his head, "you weren't going to lie to us anymore. I thought we had reached an understanding, Miss Pratt."

"I don't know what you mean. I've told you."

"And your baby daughter"—he seethed—"then rose of her own accord, fell once upon a sharp object, and crossed half a field to drop herself into the Sabbathday River."

There was a shriek inside her head. It kept getting in the way of things people were saying in the real world, messing up the meaning of their words. She just couldn't understand him. She just couldn't understand what he was saying to her.

"I'll show you," Heather offered.

He had turned his shoulder to her, like an indignant classmate, circa fourth grade. He had turned and was pouting at the door when she called him back.

"Show me what?" Charter barked.

"The baby. My baby. I'll show you."

He was silent. Heather got unsteadily to her feet. "Come on. Let's go now."

"It won't work," he said. "Just save yourself the trouble."

"But it's there," she insisted. "I know it is. I checked. When Naomi told me about . . . well, what she found. I knew it wasn't mine. I mean, how could mine have gotten into the river? I knew it wasn't mine, but I had to check, anyway. Wouldn't you have checked?"

He seemed disinclined to answer this.

"I went down with my flashlight. I felt in the water. I touched it. She was there."

She stared at them.

"I touched her!"

Charter shook his head. He seemed amazed by her.

"I never stabbed my baby! She was already dead!"

"Maybe you wanted to make sure," he said quietly.

"What?"

"Well, you were pretty sure she was dead. But you just wanted to make sure. Is that possible?"

Possible? Heather thought. It was crazy. Why would anybody stab a dead baby?

"You see," he said, almost kindly, "if you did that, you could be sure it was dead, in a way you couldn't be sure just by, say, leaving it on the ground. Yes?"

Yes? Heather thought. Yes to what?

"And you wanted to be sure, didn't you? That's why you went back to look, wasn't it? You couldn't stand that little chance that you were wrong and your baby daughter was just lying there in the grass, crying out for you?"

She nodded, through hot tears. This was, after all, so absolutely true.

"And maybe when you went down to see the baby you took something sharp with you. Just to make sure. Since it probably wouldn't hurt her, because she was probably dead already. And you could rest easy afterward."

"No, that's—"

"Let me finish. And the baby seemed dead to you. Though, as you said yourself, you're not a doctor or anything, so it's not like you could be absolutely sure. But one little poke, just to settle the question. And then this baby you never really loved—not like you love your daughter, your little girl who you were pregnant with at the same time you had your boyfriend keeping you company all the time—this baby you never told anybody about and nobody would ever miss, would just sort of go away. I can certainly understand why you felt that way."

She had no words. She shook her head.

"And then when you were finished, maybe you did put the body somewhere. But not in that pond, I don't think. Because you didn't really want it so close to your house, did you? You sure didn't want to look out your window and see that pond and have to think about what was inside it. You wouldn't want your daughter to go out and play there, just like you played there when you were a little girl, and put her toes down there into all that soft mud and feel the body—"

"No!" Heather screamed. "Don't say that!"

"So I *understand* why you wouldn't want to leave it there," he said, as if stating the obvious. "It's what I would feel, too. And I'll tell you, if it were me, I would want to put it pretty far away. At least as far as the river. Yes?" He looked for confirmation, but went on without it. "I'd take it straight to the river, is what I'd do. Because the river would take it away, wouldn't it? The river would take your baby downstream and away from your life and your daughter's life, and you wouldn't have to think about it again." He sighed, contemplative. "That must have felt wonderful to you."

Heather shook her head. She was weeping openly now, messy and loud. She no longer had the strength to wipe her face.

"Could I . . ." She trailed off.

"Yes?" Erroll said.

"Could I *please*," she sobbed, "just take you out? I'll *show* you. I put the baby into the pool. It's still—"

"But why?" Charter said wearily. "Aren't you tired? Aren't you tired of all this?"

She was. So tired.

"Miss Pratt," he spoke in yet another voice, "I have to tell you something. I admire you. And I know you've been through a lot, and without any help. Know you're smart, too. I heard you'd been to college, and I can see why. But this won't go away just from your being strong. Can I explain this to you?"

She looked up, her face streaked and running.

"I know what you're thinking," Charter said. His fingers were interlaced. He had put his pen aside. "You're thinking, I can get through this. You're thinking if you answer my questions right, you can somehow find your way through this night and this problem we have, and you'll get to leave here and go back to your life. But you won't. It isn't going to be like that. Your life is going to be different from now on, no matter what happens in this room. No matter"—he put up his fingers like quotation marks—"how *you do*." He gazed at her steadily. "You can't think about getting back to your old life now. It's gone."

He paused. They all listened to her weep.

"Also, you can't stay here. Well, we can't stay here forever, you know that. We're all tired, and we need to have progress. I only interrogate a witness once. I can't just keep coming back to you and waiting for you to do this right. You have to do it right this time, Heather." He looked at her. "So we can't go back and we can't stay here." He shrugged. "You see, this isn't really very complicated, because what I'm saying isn't the same thing as saying your life is over. Your life, Heather, is far from over. You can have a long life, and a good life. It just isn't going to be the same life you had before. Your job now is to go forward."

"How?" she stumbled. "How am I supposed to do that?"

"Well, think about it. Your baby is dead. Nothing's going to bring her back. And people . . . well, people are going to think what they think. There's nothing you can do about that. Certainly, nobody's going to think better of you for doing what you said you did with the baby than for doing what you really did, but people respect you, at least, for telling the truth. And if they can't be compassionate about how bad it was for you, and maybe how confused you were, then that's their problem. So you see, there's really no reason not to just get it all off your chest."

"No." She was stiff, her head, the muscles of her face pinched and hard. "There's nothing."

"There is," he said. He seemed to sigh. "Listen. Can I tell you something about myself?"

She didn't really want to know anything about him, but she knew the right answer to his question. She nodded.

"There are things I've learned. About guilt, Miss Pratt. I've learned about guilt because no matter how many different kinds of wrong there are in the world, there is only one kind of guilt. Its dimensions might change. Its magnitude. But in essence there's just one guilt. For example, I step on your toe. I feel bad about it and I apologize. The next day, I get behind the wheel of my car while I'm inebriated, and I run into you and kill you. What I feel in the second case is precisely the same emotion as the one I felt for stepping on your toe. But"— he leaned forward slightly—"but it's grown. It's the same gall. The same distress, but vaster, denser. Guilt is internal, Miss Pratt. It doesn't depend on other people telling us how wrong what we did was. If you don't feel it to begin with, it doesn't matter how many people line up to say you were wrong— you'll never feel it. But if you do feel it, you'll feel it whether it's my foot or my life. Or your baby's life. This is what I'm trying to say."

The bright sheen of his forehead. She saw the glint of scalp through his skein of steel-colored hair.

"The people who never feel it? I don't know what it is about them. Something chemical that's off in some way. Maybe it's genes. They say everything is genes. But thank God, it's rare to find a person like that. You're not a person like that."

Heather frowned. Was that good, then? To feel guilty?

"And here's the other thing I want to tell you about guilt. If you feel it, and you hide that feeling, guilt destroys you. It *destroys* you. Believe me, I know about this, Miss Pratt. It's terrible to watch a person tear themselves up. They go around, denying, denying, but inside it's killing them. But you think, What else is there to do? I mean, what's the point of confessing your guilt? It doesn't undo the crime, right? It can't give you another chance not to do the thing that you feel so bad about. No. But it does something else."

"What?" Heather said.

He leaned forward, his palms flat against the wooden tabletop. She watched his fingers spread.

"It makes you strong. It makes you healed." Charter shook his head solemnly. "I've seen this, not many times, it's true, because not many people are brave enough to own their guilt. But those few times, it's been like salve to a wound. The wound of their guilt," he said. "The person who says, Yes, I've done this. Yes. It was wrong and I know it was wrong, and I'm sorry. This person will be forgiven by the person whose forgiveness she needs most of all, and that's herself."

"But," Heather said, perplexed, "surely the person who ought to forgive her is the one she hurt, right?"

"That's important," he said, pleased to have engaged her at last. "But don't underestimate the importance of forgiving yourself. And you need to ask forgiveness before you can get it. And you need to admit what you did before you can ask forgiveness. It's so simple, Miss Pratt."

Heather stared at him. Her bearings were gone. She wanted forgiveness. She wanted sleep, and her daughter's warm back under the palm of her own hand. God, she wanted to be done with this.

"I didn't do anything wrong," she whispered. "Oh, I didn't. I'd say so if I did. And I'd ask for forgiveness, too."

Charter closed his eyes. He shook his head, frowning. For

a few long breaths he said nothing at all. Then he sat back in his chair.

"There's something else," Charter said. "I mean, I think you deserve to know."

Heather looked up, not hopeful, but mildly curious.

"Well, there's Polly." He shrugged.

"Polly," she said dully.

"Well, yes. I can hardly see how they'll let you just take her home again, without our getting this cleared up."

Erroll turned to look at him. Charter put a hand up without turning and continued.

"They couldn't do that. You see that, don't you? We have to get this settled first, and telling the truth about what really happened is a big step to getting it settled. The sooner you do it, in other words, the sooner you'll be able to move ahead with things. But until then . . ." He sighed.

"I can't have Polly back?" She was numb.

"We need to do this, Miss Pratt."

"I want—"

"I know," he said reassuringly. "I know that. But first we need to. Remember what I said. We go forward now. We don't go back." He paused. "You see, a lot of people would feel that a mother who had the kind of experience you had really had to have been suffering, and she might need a doctor's care. They couldn't feel right about letting her go back to taking care of a little child until a doctor said it was all right. You understand?"

"No," Heather said bluntly.

"You love her," Charter said.

She nodded. She loved her. Polly was the only thing she could love now.

"And you want her back, don't you?"

"Yes. Please," she cried.

"Then you know what you need to do, don't you?"

And she did. For the first time, clear as water, she did. Whatever it took. "All right," she told them.

Charter got to his feet and opened the door. A minute later he was back with a little man and a typewriter. They all watched the man plug in the machine and roll the paper up.

"We're going to take your statement now," Charter said

affably. "Do you want to do it yourself or do you want me to help you a bit."

"Help me," said Heather.

"Okay. I'll say something and you say yes if it's true. Remember that this is your sworn statement, and you'll be signing it. So it's important we don't put anything in that didn't happen just that way. You understand?"

She understood.

"My name is Heather Ruth Pratt and I was born May 1, 1965. Correct?

"Yes."

"I live in the farmhouse on Sabbath Creek Road. This is the house left to me by my grandmother"—down at his notes—"Mrs. Polly Bates Pratt."

Heather nodded.

"This is correct?" Charter said, a little peevishly. "I want to be sure."

"It's correct," she said. Charter looked at the man, who typed.

"I am employed as a craftsman at Flourish, Incorporated, in Goddard."

"Yes," Heather said.

"I had a sexual relationship with Ashley Deacon, who is a married man, from October of 1983 to January of this year, 1985. I am the mother of a daughter, Polly Pratt, born in August of 1984, now fourteen months old."

Heather nodded. The little typist worked, his head down.

"At the end of last year or the beginning of this year, I became pregnant for the second time. I did not seek prenatal care for this child. I did not tell anyone I was pregnant."

"No, that's right," Heather said. It all felt so far away.

"On the night of . . ." He took out a pocket calendar and studied it. He looked up. "Does September 17 sound about right? That was a Tuesday night."

Heather shrugged. "It sounds right."

"On the night of Tuesday, September 17, I went into labor in the middle of the night. I went outside into the field behind my house."

"The back field," Heather corrected, as if this were important.

"The back field," Charter agreed. "I had my baby alone and unassisted."

"Yes," she said. "That's right."

"I did not bring my baby into the house after it was born." Heather looked at him. "What?"

"Oh, was that wrong?" he said. "Did you bring the baby into the house?"

"Well, no. I said what happened."

"So all right. I did not bring my baby into the house. I returned to my house without the baby."

"You forgot to say that it was dead." Heather frowned.

"But you need to confine the statement to what you know," Charter explained. "You said yourself, you're not a doctor. Didn't you say that?"

"I'm not a doctor," Heather agreed.

"So then we can't enter an opinion about that. Now let's go on with the statement, yes?"

She nodded.

"I went back to the field with a sharp object, to make sure the baby was dead." He paused. "Which one?"

"Excuse me?" She looked confused.

"Which one of these?" He gestured, as if he were trying to sell her one. "Will you show me the one you used?"

"I don't remember," she said, because the fact was she didn't remember anything about a sharp object at all.

"Try," he said stiffly, and of course she wanted to please him. After all, he was the one who was going to get Polly back for her. She leaned forward out of her chair and looked at them. They were so hard and pointed. She didn't like the look of any of them. Pick had not liked her using the ice pick on the refrigerator; she'd warned Heather that she could get electrocuted that way. The nails and the awls she didn't recognize. But the needles—Heather remembered how they'd flashed in the firelight when Pick worked, and that lavender sweater twitching, growing as the two needles clicked. Blue needles, Heather recalled, that time. She thought of her grandmother's hands on those needles, misshapen and stiff, but moving, clicking. If Pick were here, she thought, this would not be happening. Whatever this was, it would not be happening.

Heather got up out of her seat and touched one of the blue

knitting needles. She felt its round chill inside the plastic, intractable and hard.

"Thank you," Charter said. He picked it up by the corner
of the plastic bag and hurriedly jotted something on the label.
He turned back to the typist. "I stabbed the baby once in the
chest. Yes?"

Heather shrugged.

"Yes? I think you'd better say yes or no."

"Yes," said Heather.

"Then I carried the baby's body across the field to the Sabbathday River." He paused. "Did you throw it in? Or just lay
it in?" He waited. "I don't want to get it wrong, Heather."

She looked up at him. It was the first time he had used her
first name. It must mean he liked her a little, she thought,
utterly grateful. She didn't want to disappoint him now.

"I laid it in. Like . . ." She trailed off.

They all waited silently.

"Like Moses," Heather said. She started to cry again. "When
she found that baby, Naomi, I just felt so . . ." She pushed at
the tears, moving each out of the way for the next. "I felt it
was mine. I knew, deep down. I felt . . ."

"Sorry?" Charter suggested.

"Oh, God," cried Heather. "I am so sorry."

They listened to the typist finish his clatter. He rolled the
statement out, and Charter looked it over. "You'll need to
sign," he said, sounding tired. She felt awful to have put him
through this, all of them. The men who'd been out at her
house, and Erroll, who was pale from going without sleep.
And Naomi. What would Naomi think of her now?

"What's going to happen?" she said.

"We'll take you down to Peytonville," said Charter. "You'll
be able to rest, and see the doctor."

"And Polly?" For an instant, she wondered if they would
let Polly come with her.

"We find a place for Polly till this is over," said Erroll,
breaking in. "Maybe you know someone."

"There are channels," Charter said icily. "Proper channels.
We can't just—"

"But it would be better for Polly to be with someone familiar. I think we can all agree on that." He didn't look at his
superior. He looked at Heather.

"Thank you," she said. "It would be."

"But who?" Charter was sharp. "You said yourself you don't have any friends."

Heather started. Had she said that? Was it true?

She tried to think. Celia and Stephen would take Polly, of course, but Heather didn't think Stephen would help her now, and Celia didn't like her. Heather closed her eyes.

Even Naomi would be ashamed of her now. Especially Naomi, Heather thought. And yet the memory of Naomi's words to her nine months before suddenly came back again, unbidden. About how strong she was, and what a good example. A homegrown feminist, Naomi had called her, not that Heather was wild about that word. For the briefest moment something inside Heather surged with hope. If only there could be someone to say these things to Polly, too, even though Polly was too young to really understand. Someone to speak well of her, though it seemed incredible that anyone ever might.

But Naomi was from another place. Not from here. It wasn't, she knew, a place where people stabbed their infants and laid them in the river, but even so Naomi might understand what Heather had done. It was more than Heather herself ever would.

She held the paper in her hand, but the words blurred before her, obscured by the one good thing she could do. It made her blindingly happy.

"I want Polly to go to Naomi Roth," she told them. It was not a request. She smiled easily. Then she took a pen and confessed to the murder of her child.

Chapter 21

The World Overhead

THE DINNER PARTY ENDED EARLY. NAOMI would have denied it, if asked, but she keenly wanted Judith and Joel to leave, and soon they did. She couldn't have blamed them; there'd been a damper on the evening since Mary Sully's call, and Naomi, in her bitterness and disbelief, had tumbled out all the story she knew to her guests, alternately raging and mourning. Heather was marked, she told them, by being different. Only that. She saw how the women at work threw themselves into shunning her, and how Heather merely ignored their judgment. She saw how Heather, while not precisely beautiful, had that indefinable shimmer that drove women wild. Heather, she told them, could not possibly have done what Mary said she'd done. Heather was the town's designated sacrifice, its lottery winner under a shower of stones.

They stared at her, looked at each other, and said good night.

Once they'd gone, she piled the dishes, running the melted Häagen-Dazs down the drain and shoving the pot of leftover stew straight into the fridge. In the aftermath of the ruined party, her house seemed small again, its absurd shape and proportions restored from the brief interlude of voices and laughter and shared food to this, its customary detachment. It had always been one of the features of her A-frame that it sat in its wooded depression unseen by any other house, as if the world had passed overhead while it—while she—sat here, hunkered down in hiding. She thought, sometimes, of how the immense iceberg had covered all New England before retreating—"retreating" was the word they used—back to its lair in the polar cap, carving mountains out of the land in its wake. She imagined what it would have been like to live down here at that long moment and look up into the great ice overhead, a frozen caul over the world with a single, tiny living thing hidden away beneath. In planetary time, Naomi thought, looking dumbly at the smears of stew, the crumbs of bread on her dining table, this wouldn't figure much. But Heather.

She shook her head. It came to her that she might just do nothing, but she couldn't seem to hold the thought. She got her coat and keys, and went outside.

Nelson Erroll lived on the far side of Goddard from Naomi, south of the town center itself and en route to Haverhill, in a yellow farmhouse that had been his father's. The house had a barn with three huge but withering silos that shot up like a colossal trident. It sat just off the main road, pretty but a little lost, as if no longer sure why it was precisely there; its many acres—once given over to sheep—were long gone, sold to a Boston academic who feared development around his summer retreat farther up the mountain. Nelson lived alone, though he had once had a wife and twin sons. These, too, were long gone, since Carol Erroll had moved down to Keene with her second husband, and only a succession of school pictures, framed in a line on the piano top, gave immediate evidence of the sheriff's earlier life.

Naomi drove her car around the back of Erroll's house and parked out of sight of the road, alongside the silos. By the time she reached the kitchen door he was waiting for her, peering out into the dark and looking, if not concerned, then mildly curious. He made her out on the second step and nodded, without exactly smiling. Naomi didn't feel like smiling, either.

"Sorry I didn't call," she said when he opened the door.

"Doesn't matter," Erroll said. "I wouldn't have heard the phone. I've been sleeping."

She looked reflexively at her watch. "It's only ten."

"I was up all night." He shrugged. "Slept most of the day today."

"Up all night," Naomi said viciously. "And doing such hard work, I'll bet."

He frowned at her. They stood in the kitchen. The air, suddenly cold, wafted in the open door.

"This is such shit," Naomi said.

Erroll sighed. He shut the door. "I was going to make some dinner," he said, his voice tired. "Want something?"

"I've eaten. Nelson, this is completely insane. Don't tell me there's anything to this."

"Sit down," he said, and Naomi did. He went to the refrigerator and rummaged, eventually extracting a single steak in its foam Stop & Shop tray. He dug the plastic away with his fingers. "Sure you don't want one?"

"No," she said. "Thanks."

He took down a skillet from over the stove and put it on the electric coil. He filled the kettle and it hissed when he turned the heat on beneath it. Then he came to the kitchen table and sat down opposite her.

"Tell me," Naomi said. "*Explain* this to me. You *can't*, I bet."

"I can't," Erroll admitted. "But that doesn't mean it's not true. I was there, Naomi. I was in the room. She did it." He shook his head. The top of his head shone in the fluorescent kitchen light. "I didn't want to believe it either, but it's true."

"It can't be. Now look, I'm *not* being naïve. But Heather loves her daughter so much. She would never hurt a baby like . . ." She closed her eyes, the better not to see that single, perfect hole over the infant's heart. "She couldn't."

Erroll shrugged. He got up and put his steak into the skillet, then poked it once or twice with a fork.

"This fucking town. They just *decided* it was her. Because she's a single mother and they can't deal with that. Because she doesn't go around beating her breast with shame all the time!"

"Because she was pregnant, Naomi. Because people knew she was pregnant and then suddenly she wasn't pregnant anymore and there was no baby. Because we had a baby without a mother and a mother without a baby! That's *all*."

"She wasn't pregnant," Naomi insisted. "She just put on some weight over the summer." She paused. Nelson was looking at her. "She was just depressed and she gained weight! It isn't a crime. I mean, her grandmother died and she didn't have anybody. Wouldn't that make you depressed?"

"Sure," he agreed. "But that isn't the point." He frowned. "You've got to understand, Naomi. After you brought the baby's body in, and word about it got out, the phone started to ring. Within forty-eight hours we had fourteen calls about Heather. Especially from women who insisted she must be pregnant. We were looking at all kinds of possibilities—"

"I *heard*," Naomi snapped. "Like through-hikers. Women on welfare. Women living in sin."

He shrugged and flipped his steak. It spat grease into the air. "We had to. We wanted to be thorough."

"Lesbians. Single mothers. Women who live alone." *I'm surprised you didn't accuse me*, she almost said. But then she remembered: they had accused her. They had accused her first.

"Naomi, we had to bring her in. After all those calls. And we talked to Ashley. We found out the dates and everything. She could have been pregnant. And the fact that she didn't tell him about it, or anyone else." He looked at her. "You have to see that was, at least, suspicious."

"It wasn't her. Jesus, Nelson, we're talking about a *stab wound*!"

"She showed us the weapon, Naomi."

Naomi, stunned, looked at him.

"She showed us the weapon she used. It's her, Naomi. I'm sorry." He speared his steak and dropped it on a plate. "I know you like her, but it's her."

She watched him eat, his head down, the skin of his scalp alive with reflected light. He seemed famished. She didn't begrudge him his meat.

"Just like that," she said, more to herself than to him.

Erroll looked up. "Sorry?"

"Just like that? You sat her down, she said, 'Yes, I killed my baby with a knife'?"

"No, not just like that." He shook his head. "I can't really discuss the specifics of what was said, Naomi, and I'm going to count on you not to let this go any further. But I will tell you that at first Heather did deny being pregnant. She later admitted she was pregnant and said she'd had a miscarriage, but it seemed pretty clear to me that 'miscarriage' was a term she'd taken on to make it a little easier for her to live with herself."

"What are you, a psychologist now?" She regretted it as soon as the words were out, but she couldn't take it back.

"No, Naomi. I'm not a psychologist. It's only my opinion. A layman's opinion, all right?"

"Sure," she said.

"It just seemed to me that she was sad. She was sorry for what she'd done. At one point she even told us she'd had this miscarriage, and put the baby's body in a little pond in back of her house. So the baby you found couldn't have been hers." He shook his head. "I think it made her feel better to think that." He sighed. The skin under his eyes was barely there, so thin, like tissue bared to bright light. It pulsed, tightening and opening, as he looked at her, and she unexpectedly found herself listening to her own breath. "I feel awful about this, you know."

"I know," Naomi said. "I can see that."

They looked at each other.

"I'm glad you came over," he said. "I mean, I know you didn't—"

"I was furious," she cut him off. "I'm still furious. God." She looked out the kitchen window. The moon glinted off the silo-trident. "What're they going to do to her now?"

"I hope she'll get some help," Erroll said, pushing his plate away.

"Help," Naomi said with disdain. "You know the kind of help they'll want to give her. The stake at dawn."

He smiled a little. "Hey, we've moved on a little bit since that kind of thing, no matter what you city types might think."

She nodded. She hoped it was true.

"Where have they got her?" she asked suddenly.

"In Peytonville," Erroll said.

"Can I see her?"

"In a few days, I'm sure it's possible. And I think that would be nice. I think that would mean a lot to her."

"Good." Naomi nodded, instantly regretting the offer. The truth was that she didn't want to see Heather. In fact, she desperately didn't want to see Heather. The hand that had raised a weapon over that baby—she didn't want to see that hand. But nobody else would go, Naomi knew that much. And maybe Heather needed to see that Naomi, who had after all taken the baby from the river, could be forgiving of what she'd done.

"There's something else," said Erroll. He was pouring water out of the kettle and spooning in instant coffee, two cups. "I was going to call you in the morning, anyway."

Naomi took a cup and asked for milk to cover the taste.

"It's Polly. Heather wants you to have her."

She sat there, overwhelmed. The brownish bubbles of the instant coffee gathered on the surface.

"She wants *me*?"

"She asked for you. I think she knows that you sort of believe in her. I mean, believe she's a good person, whatever she's done. Anyway, I didn't ask her why, but she was very clear about it. Of course," he looked at Naomi, "you don't have to agree. You can say no. They can find a foster arrangement for Polly. It's not like you have kids of your own and it's just one more." Naomi's throat caught. She took a scalding gulp and coughed. "And, you know, we don't know how long we're talking about here. That's another thing."

He paused. He ran one hand through the ridge of his pale hair. It came to rest on his thigh.

"You think about it," he said kindly. "Nobody expects you just—"

"I'll take it," Naomi said. "I mean Polly. I'll take Polly. Of course I will." And she got up and left before he could see her face.

Chapter 22

Somebody in Her Corner

FOR THE FIRST WEEK, THEY WOULDN'T LET HER visit Heather. She was "under evaluation," they said, in some kind of medical wing adjacent to the jail outside Peytonville, and Naomi couldn't seem to find a single person who had authority to explain the situation. The jail itself, when she called, referred her to the press office, where she was told that the accused murderess could not be permitted to speak with nonfamily members without the permission of Heather's lawyer. Heather's lawyer was, officially, the Public Defender's Office in Peytonville. So Naomi called Judith.

"I just started," Judith said, laughing. "I'm barely up on the coffee-maker instructions. I don't know anything about what's going on with this!"

"I want to see her," Naomi said. "I feel awful that I haven't been to see her. You know I'm going to take care of her little girl."

"I didn't know," Judith said, and Naomi explained that Polly was still with a foster family in Peytonville, until the paperwork got sorted through. "Are you really up to this?" she asked.

Naomi couldn't say that she was. At night, when she was alone and looked around her little house, trying to imagine having Polly with her, she didn't know how she might be able to do this, how she could possibly meet the unimaginable needs of a fourteen-month-old child. It would be like bringing an exotic animal under her aegis, she thought. What would it eat? And how would she keep it alive? She only had to believe that she would learn. She remembered something her mother had told her when Naomi, native New Yorker that she was, had finally, in her early twenties, taken on the task of learning to drive. She'd been terrified of the power of driving, the responsibility of guiding a lethal weapon through crowds of other people in other cars, and sure she wouldn't be able to understand road signs or respond to the mutable and constant requirements of the highway. "Listen," her mother had said, the night before Naomi's first lesson at Ithaca Triple A, "people much stupider than you can do this. You can do it, too."

Now she was a good driver. And like most other late converts, she liked to drive.

"I'll be okay," she told Judith. "Polly's sweet, and it's what Heather wants. So how could I say no?"

"All right," Judith said. "Look, I'm a little harassed right now. Can I look into this for you? I'll find out who's got the case and see if I can't get you on an approved list. Is that okay?"

"Okay," Naomi said. She hung up the phone and called Erroll.

"I'm glad you called," he said. "I was going to call you."

"You always say that," she observed. "But you never do."

He paused. She could imagine him frowning into the phone, completely incapable of response.

"Nelson, I'm going to have to get out to Heather's house. I need to pick up things for Polly. Like a crib, you know?"

"I see," he said. "Well, I don't know if that's possible."

"Work on it, will you?" she said, a little irritated. "I mean, this poor kid doesn't know what's hit her. And we're going to move her again. The least we can do is get some of her own things, you know? Like her toys, Nelson." She waited, listening to the silence. "I'm not going to go around collecting *evidence*, okay?"

"You'd need an escort." He sounded wary but relenting.

"Fine."

"You couldn't go out on your own. It's a crime scene, Naomi."

"*Fine*. Whatever. Will you please work it out?"

He said he'd try, and Naomi, aware that she wouldn't get any more out of him, let it go at that.

Judith called her at home that evening.

"You're on," she said. "You can visit any weekday afternoon, from two to four-thirty. Just call in the morning and say you're coming." She gave Naomi the number. "No tape recorders, no cameras. Any gifts have to be checked by the guards. She's on a suicide watch."

"How surprising," Naomi said dryly. "What she's been through, I can't imagine why."

"Yeah," Judith said vaguely.

"So . . . who's in charge, then?"

"What?" said Judith.

"You know, who's going to defend her?"

"Well, nobody yet. No one in particular." Naomi heard her sigh. "I don't think anyone wants it, to tell you the truth. Most people in the office are just generally freaked out by the whole thing. There are only two other women, and as far as I can tell, they can't handle the material at all. They both have kids," she said in explanation.

"And the men?" Naomi asked, her heart sinking.

"Well, one or two seem pretty excited about getting a high-profile case like this one's bound to be. I mean, already the calls from reporters—they've never had anything like it. They'll probably give Heather to one of those guys."

It sounded primitive. Naomi winced.

"Hey, Judith?"

"Hmm?" She sounded distracted. "Sorry, I'm rinsing. They're not hooking up the dishwasher till next week."

"Well, I was just wondering. What about you?"

"What about me what?" She sounded wary. "Oh no, you mean Heather? Oh, Naomi, no. There's no way."

"But why?" she asked.

"Because I'm the new kid," Judith said, amiably enough. "I can't just waltz in and ask for the biggest case in years!"

"You can if nobody else wants it," suggested Naomi. "Or if you're better qualified to handle it. I mean, maybe you had something like this before. In the city. You said—"

"I said it was happening," she spoke tautly. "I never said I'd had a case like that myself."

"But you could say you were aware of cases like that, in your office. Maybe you assisted on them or something, even if they weren't yours specifically. Couldn't you?"

"May I ask why you're saying all this?" Judith said. Naomi heard the water shut off in the background. "Why are you asking me to do this? And are you in a position to ask me to do this?"

"No," Naomi said. "Of course, officially, I'm not in a position to ask anybody to do anything. I just want to see somebody in her corner, you know? Not somebody who has to defend her but somebody who really wants to see her get what she deserves, and not somebody who doesn't care about her but just wants their own picture in the paper. She needs a friend."

"A lawyer isn't a friend," Judith said carefully. "A lawyer shouldn't be a friend. Sometimes a friend is the *worst* kind of advocate."

"Even so," said Naomi, who couldn't quite parry that, "she needs help."

"She'll get it. In the hospital."

"Oh, right!"

The silence built between them.

"Listen," Judith said finally, "I hear what you're saying. And I promise to think about it. That's not the same as saying I'm going to ask for the case. But I'll think about it. *Basta*?"

"*Basta*. And thanks."

"Don't thank me. It's unlikely they'd even consider giving it to somebody so new, no matter how many big-city murderesses I've defended in the past. And also, I've got family stuff I've told them about. They know I'm going to be running up and down to Providence a lot over the next couple of months."

Naomi considered. "Providence?"

"My sister. She lives there. Her son is ill."

In the way she spoke it, there was finality. A door shut between them.

"I'm sorry," Naomi said.

"So it's unlikely. That's all I'm saying," Judith said. Naomi heard Joel around her, faintly. They were speaking.

"I understand," Naomi said. "But thanks." She said goodbye.

Chapter 23

The Language of Mothers

THE NEXT DAY, SOME HIGHLIGHTS OF HEATHER
Pratt's confession were published in *The Manchester Union
Leader*. Naomi read this sidebar, and the large article it accompanied, while she sat in a restaurant near the jail and
waited for visiting hours to start. There was a photograph of
the baby, draped in sheeting like a football under a shroud, in
the arms of the medical examiner, and a close-up of the knitting needle with its metal sheen. Naomi's tuna melt, untouched
since she had turned to this particular page of the paper, sat
congealing in grease on her plate, the twisted wedge of sliced
orange going dry. Naomi felt sick. She rubbed her forehead
as pain erupted behind her sinuses. Now, even after she had
maneuvered so doggedly for permission to visit Heather, it
seemed to her that there was no question of going through
with it. How she would face the person who had inflicted such
an injury on such a victim, then sent its body downriver into
her own hands, was unfathomable. And what she might possibly say . . .

The waitress came to pour more coffee. It tasted foul, but
Naomi drank it.

"Something wrong with your sandwich?"

She seemed affronted. Naomi apologized for her own lack
of appetite.

She had been to see Mrs. Horgan, the foster mother in Went-
worth, just north of Peytonville, and spent the morning making
tentative overtures to Polly. The little girl seemed dull but not
unhappy. She watched the two older boys, Mrs. Horgan's
grandsons, while they watched television, far more consumed
by their faces than by the bright colors on the screen, and ate
pieces of cheese and carrot sticks cut thin for a morning snack.
Naomi tried to appear competent, but she took notes frantically, asking for recipes and advice and instructions for every
medical scenario she could think of. Polly did seem to rec-

ognize her, Naomi thought, though the girl didn't exactly seek her out. Naomi would come back to pick her up the following afternoon, she told Polly, hearing herself speak, for the first time, in the language of mothers—the high pitch of maternal concern. She was thrilled by the sound of her own voice, and thrilled when Polly did not automatically turn away. I can do this, Naomi thought. Delivery first, then content. Imitation, then authority. I can do this, too.

She was meeting Erroll at five, at Heather's house. She would collect, under his watch, whatever Polly needed.

At two o'clock Naomi went to the main entrance of the Peytonville jail and was directed through a confusion of identical white corridors to the medical wing. There seemed little overtly medical about this place, no nurses in uniform or guards who looked any different from the guards she had seen in the main part of the jail. Behind the desk, a man with a holstered gun sat before a bank of closed-circuit television screens, some blank, a few with blurry, motionless figures. She squinted to see if one was Heather, but by then the guard was staring at her distrustfully.

"You from the press?" he said, when she told him whom she was there to see.

"Just a friend. I called before. It's okay for me to come."

He didn't believe her, though her name was indeed on a note attached to Heather's file. He called his superior, and then the Public Defender's Office, and then his superior again. Then he asked if she had brought anything with her.

Naomi put her bag on the desk and watched as he went through her keys and bunches of used Kleenex and date book, jammed with stray and unsecured pages. He took it behind the desk and said he'd hold it till afterward. Then he went through the things she'd brought for Heather: a sweet-smelling fancy soap and a Whitman's Sampler. Both things were choices of desperation, and she felt a little embarrassed watching the guard pick over them. Both were unallowed, he told her. Naomi shrugged, too preemptively exhausted to even be angry.

He took her to a small room sliced in two by steel mesh. There were tables on either side of the mesh, and hard plastic chairs behind them, and doors with small windows in the upper half. She waited there about ten minutes, needing to go to the bathroom but irrationally afraid that, if she went, she might miss her chance to see Heather. She crossed her legs and idly fingered the knee of her jeans, which was buttery soft, about to break through to the skin. She didn't want to be looking up when they brought her in. She wanted that extra instant, to be ready, but not before it was necessary.

When the door squealed open, she closed her eyes.

Heather took the seat opposite, shapeless under a blue hospital gown with loose pants. She put her hands on the table and looked calmly at Naomi. Naomi could not look calmly back.

"Oh, Heather. Did they make you do that?"

Heather's hand went to the back of her head. "No. I asked them to. They said I didn't have to."

"But your hair." She knew she shouldn't say this. It was cruel to say this, Naomi thought.

"It's all right. It's less worry like this. And it will grow back. My head feels light."

"That's good," Naomi said. "Well, you look very well."

"I do?" Her voice had always been thin like this, Naomi thought. She was Heather still—a pale and formless person, a blank where a person was supposed to be.

"I brought you things," said Naomi. "I brought you some soap and some chocolates. They said I couldn't bring them in. I'm so sorry."

"It's all right, Naomi. I'm fine. I don't need anything."

You need a shake, Naomi thought, before she could censor herself. She stared at Heather. Only a few weeks had passed, it came to her, since she had last seen her, out at her house with the kitchen smelling of applesauce. She had gone to bring another sampler kit, she recalled now with a stab of resentment: that first sampler sacrificed to be a shroud for a dead baby.

"You've seen Polly?" Heather asked, and Naomi nodded.

"Just this morning. She's fine, you know. Eating, playing." She paused. What else was there to report? What else did children do? "I'll pick her up tomorrow and bring her to my house." She paused. "That is, if you still want me to look after her."

"I do," said Heather, showing some animation for the first time. "Oh, I really do. If you will."

"Of course I will. For as long as it's necessary."

They looked at each other, exchanging the same grim thought.

"I'm going out to your place later on today, to get stuff for Polly. Can you think of what I need?"

She hadn't been allowed paper and pen, of course, so Naomi closed her eyes and tried to memorize: the crib, the special blue elephant, the plastic mat that attached to the bathtub with suckers, the plate with Snow White and the cup with Dumbo, the striped red blanket, the zip-up pajamas with little Christmas trees, even though it was big for her, the No More Tears shampoo. There was so much. There was too much to carry.

"Naomi," Heather said, "I can't thank you."

"It's all *right*." Naomi shook her head. "Please, let's not—"

"But what you must think." Heather's voice cracked open. Naomi saw, to her great dismay, that she was beginning to weep, and freely.

"Heather, don't." It was all she could think of.

"But it's so terrible, it's all so terrible. What I did!"

"Don't *tell* me," Naomi said sharply. "Heather, I can't."

"You thought I was such a good mother. You told me."

"You *are*," Naomi heard herself say. "Polly has a wonderful mother."

"But the other one. You see, it was Ashley's, too. I should have loved it, too."

Naomi felt herself lean back, away from the table. Heather was crying still, her nose running. Naomi looked down.

"You'll be able to forgive yourself." She was choosing her words as carefully as she could. "One day you will. I know it. And things will get better."

"No, you don't see!" Heather said sharply. "I didn't *do* anything to the baby. I just didn't love it. That's what's so bad, you see?"

Naomi didn't see. She wanted to go. She glanced behind her shoulder at the window.

"That stuff they made me say, about the needle and putting it in the river . . . none of that happened!"

Naomi almost missed it. Then, slowly, she looked back at Heather. The girl's chopped hair was ragged around her ears, but her ears, Naomi noticed, still stuck out a bit. She had no idea how to respond.

"I never hurt my baby!" Heather said. "I didn't!"

"Well," Naomi spoke, "I can't—"

"They made me say it. They wouldn't give Polly back if I didn't. And now . . ."

She trailed off, bereft.

Naomi shook her head. "But, Heather, it was your baby. It *was*." She frowned. "Wasn't it?"

"I had my baby in the field behind my house. I *told* them it was dead. It was dead when I had it. It just lay there on the ground. It didn't *breathe*!" She looked to Naomi as if for confirmation. None was forthcoming. "So I put it in the pond there. It's a muddy little pond at the bottom of the field. I put it there. I never moved it again, and I never . . . with a *needle*!" She glared at Naomi. "Never!"

Naomi was feeling sick again. Her sinuses beat some deep, resonant rhythm. She thought she might go mad if she didn't get out of the room soon, but she had unfortunately lost the strength to get up and move away. From Heather, who was truly divorced from rational thought, Naomi thought—from the realm of the rational in which she, herself, was trying only to navigate. She couldn't listen anymore. She had to leave.

"I'd better go," she said, concentrating on the words, making them come out right.

"Naomi, listen." Heather poked her fingers through the grate and grabbed at the mesh: the nails were short but with rims of dirt, anyway. Naomi flinched. "Listen to me, Naomi, please. At the house. The pond at the bottom of the field. Remember! It's there. I know it is. I *didn't move it*." She stared out from behind the wire. "I checked, Naomi, it's there!"

Naomi was overcome with pity. How terrible it must be, she thought, to do what Heather had done and find your life was not even over, that you could not even escape your own sadness and guilt by being dead yourself, but had to stay alive to face the blame of others. She would have to not blame Heather, she suddenly understood. Heather deserved that at least: one person, her whole life, who would not blame her.

"It's all right," she said. She was amazed by the softness of her voice. She said the same words again, and again they were soothing, sweet, infused by a caring she didn't at all feel. "Heather, try to rest. And let the doctors help you. They want to help. I'll get Polly settled and come back soon to see you. I'll bring her, too, if they'll let me."

"Yes, please," said Heather. She seemed depleted. "I want to see her."

"And try not to think about any of this. None of it can be helped now. There's nothing we can do to change what happened." She got to her feet. "Take care."

"Naomi."

She was leaning forward, to the mesh. So close it cut into her forehead, making a lattice of indentation.

She whispered: "Please."

Naomi, who wished fervently not to do this, leaned forward. Their heads were close, touching not each other but metal. "What?" she said.

"Remember. The bottom of the field. It's small. Don't miss it. *Please.*"

Naomi took a step back, repelled. Heather smiled, her face weirdly strained. The two women stood in this way for a moment, suspended in tandem but separated by space and metal, and circumstance. Were it left to Heather, Naomi thought suddenly, she would not be allowed to leave at all. Anxiety surged inside her. She found her own legs and jerked them to life. Then she turned to the door behind her, banged on the square of glass, and made good her escape.

Chapter 24

All of the Worst Things

BY THE TIME SHE DROVE OUT TO HEATHER'S house later that afternoon, Naomi had managed to winnow her memory of the interview to a vague impression of the girl's shorn hair and a detailed list of Polly's necessary things. This, transcribed over a Flourish order form, lay on the passenger seat as she turned onto Sabbath Creek Road, and Naomi drove, leaning forward, eyeing with suspicion the darkening sky.

"Looks a little nasty," she called to Erroll as she pulled up next to his car. They both got out.

"It's supposed to storm," he told her. "I can't stay too long."

"Fine."

Naomi reached back into the car and retrieved her list.

"You been to see her?" he asked.

Naomi nodded. They were walking around to the front door. "This afternoon. They've cut off all her hair," she said accusingly, as if Heather had not made the request herself. It occurred to her that she wanted him to feel bad.

"No kidding," Erroll said. "I hadn't heard that."

"And they wouldn't let me give her the gifts I brought. A bar of soap, for Christ's sake!"

"There's probably a reason," he remarked. He looked, she thought, paler than usual, a blue cast to the skin around his blue eyes. "Look, I'm not going to keep saying I'm sorry about this, Naomi. I'm not happy, but there's no question, you know?"

He paused, waiting for her.

"I know you know that, Naomi."

"Fine, fine." She nodded impatiently at the door. "Let's just get on with this. I've got a whole list." She brandished it. He sighed and fished the key from his pocket.

"No one's been here since the night we interviewed her," he commented. They both stepped in, smelling the sharp air.

"Yuck," she said involuntarily. "What'd you do, leave a stink bomb?"

Following the smell, she walked directly to the kitchen and flung open the oven door.

"Nelson," Naomi said. "Jesus Christ."

He came up beside her and they looked at the two rotting chickens as they breathed through their mouths.

"Where's the garbage?"

"I took what was in the bin back to the station that night. We had to go through it. Then we threw it away."

"Help me find some garbage bags."

She rummaged in the drawers until she found a roll, then she threw away the chickens, pans and all. On the top of the stove, a pot of potatoes had fossilized into sculpture. Naomi threw that away, too, and the perishables in the fridge. Then, consulting her list, she started putting Polly's plates and utensils into a shopping bag.

Through the kitchen were signs of disarray: drawers pulled out, cabinets emptied onto countertops. Erroll stood in the center of the room, watching her without comment. By the time they moved into the next room, it was too dark to see without light.

The living room was even more disturbed, with cupboards open and chairs upturned. Playing cards were spread over the living-room couch. Naomi frowned at them, then gathered them up.

"What were you looking for in the cards?" she asked him sourly. "Did you think she killed her baby with a joker?"

"They were there already," Erroll said. "The little girl was playing with them."

The playing cards, the chicken in the oven. "You just moved them right out, didn't you?" she said harshly. "Just came on in and moved them out, whatever they were doing."

"Heather came voluntarily," he said, sounding tired. "Naomi, I'm not going to discuss this with you." He glanced at his watch. "Can we keep going, please?"

"*Sure.*" She moved past him upstairs, gathering Polly's toys from the steps. In the upstairs bathroom she took shampoo, the pajamas hanging on a peg over the tub, a bath mat, and everything that looked baby-specific from the medicine cabinet.

"You're going to need another bag," he observed. "I'll bring one up." He turned and went downstairs.

In Heather's bedroom the bedclothes had been flung back and the denuded mattress actually cut open. She stared at it without even rudimentary understanding. The books had tumbled forward off the bookcase: paperbacks, a thick Norton anthology that looked pristine, a couple of child-care reference books which Naomi gratefully picked up, a small green address book with some kind of gold crest on the cover. Clothes in the closet had been pushed roughly aside on their hangers, and objects on the floor picked up and dispersed. She felt, in this room more than any other, the invasion of Heather's privacy, the exposure of her life. She felt how even the image of such hands in her own things enraged her, and then, eyeing one partially untwisted wire hanger at the foot of the bed, of how suspect any person's belongings could be made to seem. There was nothing in here for Polly, at any rate.

He helped her with the crib, lifting and twisting it down the stairs and out the door, where they placed it in the back of Naomi's wagon. She was glad they hadn't had to break it down, since it looked complexly put together and she wasn't at all sure she could manage it on her own. He brought out the high chair from the kitchen and wedged it into the backseat. There was a separate bag just of Polly's clothes, and Naomi, remembering that the little girl loved applesauce, took the last of the batch from the freezer in the basement. This act in particular gave her a brief jolt of optimism, and she was glad she'd thought of it. Erroll turned the heat back down and walked through one final time on his own—to make sure, she thought bitterly, that nothing deleterious to Heather had been removed, and nothing beneficial surreptitiously planted—then he got into his car.

"Naomi."

Erroll had rolled the window down. She was standing a few feet away, digging for her keys.

"What?"

"Has anyone said anything to you? Any calls you want to tell me about?"

"What calls?" Naomi said.

He sighed. "I just want you to know, we're here to make sure people behave themselves. You and that little girl deserve to be left alone, is what I'm saying. I take that seriously."

She looked dumbly at him. "Has someone made a threat against me, Nelson? Or Polly?"

"Not at all," he said. "And anyone who does is going to be sorry about it. There's just grumbling about the situation. Well, you knew that." She waited. He looked regretful. "You know how people feel about all this, Naomi. They're bitter about Heather. And anyone who defends her . . . well, some people— not most of them, I'm saying *some*—would naturally feel angry at anyone who defended her."

"How sweet," she said caustically. "You're worried I'll lose my many dear friends in Goddard."

"I'm not worried," Erroll said. "But I want to know right away if anyone does say anything to you."

"Well, I'm not worried, either," she said. "Christ, what paragons of virtue!" Naomi rolled her eyes. "Listen, anyone who could turn on a little girl like Polly who never hurt anyone, they don't *deserve* to have me for a friend!" She looked back at Erroll.

"You call me any time, Naomi. All right?"

"Sure," she said. He started his car and drove back down the lane. She stood for what seemed a long time, watching him go, and numbly unbalanced by this confirmation of how completely she was alone. The first drops of rain fell on her, hitting the part in her hair. Naomi looked up into roiling skies. She got into her car.

The engine rumbled to life. She swung the wagon in a backward arc, her arm behind the headrest of the passenger seat, her neck craning to the rear. Through the slats of the crib and the dirt of the rear window and the skein of falling rain, she took in the briefest glimpse of Heather's back field, its long slope down. And then, with an unwelcome rush, it all came back to her: the jolt of cold metal pressed against her forehead, and Heather's forehead pressed to the same metal, and her whisper. Naomi stopped, her foot on the brake, her hand about to shift. She shook her head. The very idea.

"Oh, *please*," she said, softly but unquestionably aloud. "Don't even *think* about it."

Except that now she couldn't *not* think about it. And what was there to think about, in any case? A mad girl's fancy, the crazed, irrational hope of the guilty that some stray thing would show what was unalterably true to be, after all, unalterably false? It didn't bear the smallest effort. And she was late, and now it was raining.

"Shit," Naomi said. This time her voice was not soft. She jerked back the ignition, furious, and got out of the car.

In the three minutes of her indecision, the rain had grown strong and the sky virtually dark. She set off quickly, rounding the back of the house, intent on doing only a quick survey and setting this ridiculous uncertainty to rest. Uncertainty about what? She upbraided herself. That Heather had told the truth about a hill behind her house, and a pond at the foot of the hill? And if she had, so what? Because Naomi, mortal that she was, could not ever hope to make sense of the sad and tangled things in Heather's mind, nor ease those things at all, so this— this crazy search for nothing—must be for something else. Would she feel worse or better if the pond was there? She didn't care. She wanted to go home.

It wasn't there. Naomi stood at the top of the slope and peered into the rain. There was nothing at all, just a a kidney-shaped depression clogged with muddy water. Not a pond, by any means, or no more a pond than, say, the fire escape of her College Town apartment had been "The Riviera," and yet that was what they had called it, she and Daniel and their house-mates, stripping to the waist—herself along with the guys, because feminine modesty was inconsistent with feminism—and oiling themselves to attract the melanoma-rich waves of light. Local parlance, not serious. She squinted at the little place, its surface just discernibly pocking with rain. *The pond.*

It's small, she thought. As Heather had said. Naomi, unable not to go closer, went closer. With a curse for each step, she let the slope make it easy, her running shoes squelching the mud. It got bigger as she came near, but not much. Even up close, Naomi thought, it was a stretch to call this anything but "the puddle" or "the mud hole." The red herring! She chided herself. Or the clothes on the emperor who happened to be naked. My personal waste of time.

All right, so it was a little pond—big deal. A rectangle of thick water, but tapering at the end nearer her, like a love seat built to stick out of a corner. At its edge were three stones, each the size of a human head, but tipped over, as if the eyes were looking down into the muddy ground. It looked unsavory, a bathtub promising only additional filth, a sorry little landmark. Naomi turned back to the house and was surprised by how far up it seemed, how steep and high above her.

So Heather had told the truth, she mused, and Naomi was glad to know it. This, it seemed to her, was ample payback for having had to come down here: the girl was not so mad her madness was unanchored by truth. And yet, really, Naomi knew that much already. So what was gained by this? And how could she go back now and feel that she had settled anything at all? The pond before her, pebbled by rain, had given up nothing but its existence.

Because—now, honestly—it had to have happened as Heather finally admitted. There weren't other possibilities, and even Nelson had understood that Heather somehow preferred to think of her baby here, in this filthy water, than zipped into a body bag in a Peytonville freezer. How surprising! Naomi thought, staring glumly into the pond.

But, then again, why down there and not some other place? Why not—she looked around—underneath those trees, or farther across the field where the Sabbathday was edged in stones? She pushed back wet hair from her forehead and noted, for the first time, how cold she was and her sweater wet through in the sleeves. She wanted fiercely to leave, but by now it was clear what had to be done before that could happen.

There was a bubble, as from a frog.

It amazed her how quickly her heart clutched. She nearly wept.

Leaning forward, still crouched but bracing one hand on the largest rock, she touched that place where the bubble had come and spattered and made the surface break in circles.

It was like reaching through mirrors, or the arm that rises out of water to catch Excalibur, or the flailing arm—not waving but drowning, as she'd read, long before, in a poem. *There was nothing down there at all.*

She thought this, even as her finger touched a finger.

Naomi jerked, slipping. The hand braced behind her came off the rock and slapped mud. The ground was soft, unclean but forgiving. The hand before her dripped black water over the little pond, the fingers clawed and stiff, nearly touching their own reflections. She was shouting, but the rain took her voice away, and Naomi was glad. She didn't really want to hear what she had to say.

Because she knew, now that all the worst things were here, even at her feet, though just past sight. All the unspeakable things, the ones you must turn your thoughts from at any cost: the children in the robes of Scrooge's second ghost, the children in the cattle cars, calling out in racked unison for a myriad of lost mothers, the child lost by accident in an unforgiving instant, the child supine beneath his father's raised hand. The pain at the center of the universe. She reached out again, bending forward, slipping on a deep glove of water. Her hand touched a tiny hand, reaching up. Her elbow wet, the sleeve, up to the shoulder now. She smelled drenched wool. Not this, Naomi thought. A muddy branch, the most repellent animal, a water snake pretending to sleep: make it anything but this!

But it could only ever be the thing it was. It was innocent of everything, that included. It had not made itself. It had not put itself here.

She thought of how Daniel had run behind her in the Sabbathday River, shouting for God and denying it after. She would not deny it, Naomi thought, frantic. If only it could not be this, she would never deny it.

"Oh, please!" she shouted, looking up, in case God was there, after all. But if he was, she could never stop despising him now.

For one final moment she waited, holding its hand in a place she couldn't see. And then she drew it up—so weightless, even rooted by the fallen parachute that trailed behind—into the world of air, the rain, the day with no more light: this fragile thing, this glacial thing. The second baby.

Chapter 25

Dustin Hoffman in *The Graduate*

WHEN POLLY NAVIGATED THE RIM OF HER CRIB
and dropped to the floor, Naomi woke up with a shudder. She
hadn't been quite asleep, anyway, only lying on top of her bed
in a kind of wrung, exhausted inertia. Because, on top of surrogate motherhood—which was utterly depleting—and the
bleak offensive of her depression-in-progress, the phone had
been ringing and ringing for days.

She picked Polly up and put her under the covers. The little
girl seemed reluctant to rest, but Naomi didn't mind. 6 a.m.
or not, neither was likely to fall back asleep, and entertaining
Polly was an excellent way not to think about what had happened. She was amazed by Polly, anyway, and thrilled by the
girl's total acceptance of her. Was it possible that she had no
memory of Heather? Naomi tried to remember the earliest
things in her own life, but could go no further back than the
playground on the roof of the Ethical Culture Society building
on the West Side of Manhattan. She'd been four then, Naomi
marveled—everything before that was lost to a kind of nar-
coleptic swirl. Polly, who had reached her arms around Naomi's neck when Naomi had come to collect her at Mrs.
Horgan's, who had calmly lifted her arms and waited for Naomi to figure out the car seat and strap her in, seemed to begin
her little life anew with each hour, placid and accepting. Naomi, who thought occasionally that she really ought to hold
back in these matters, that her role was to care for without,
particularly, caring, could help herself less and less from giving the little girl random hugs. She loved her. Already, she
loved her.

She was amazed by what Polly could do—make the sound
of a boat in the bath, roll a rubber ball under her palm. She
was amazed by the specifics of Polly's taste, her willingness
to eat applesauce but not apples, and small pieces of pasta but
never spaghetti or linguine. An able walker, Polly only seldom

bumped a table, and Naomi had quickly consigned to the annex—her only Polly-free zone—any object in her possession
which might hurt the toddler.

She was capable at this, which was perhaps the most amazing thing of all. Naomi's arms, after the first or second try,
knew how to lift Polly up, and her hip knew how to lean itself
between Polly's legs, balancing her with one arm to keep the
other free. She walked around this way, making tea and stirring
it until it was chilly, washing Polly's dishes and setting them
in the rack. She hadn't left the house, of course, and after the
first couple of days the tape of her answering machine had
filled and refused to even listen to subsequent callers. She'd
stood, one evening, with Polly asleep in her own bedroom,
cutting off each message as soon as she got the gist.

*"Its Nelson. I wanted to let you know they've taken it to
Peytonville. Naomi, I know how you must—"*

"Naomi? It's Judith. Listen, I heard—"

"Yeah, Boston Globe. *The number is—"*

"Ms. Roth? My name is Chris Fahland at The New York
T—"

"Naomi, please, call Judith."

"This is Sarah Copley. My God, we don't know what—"

"Yeah, Boston Globe. *I'm on a deadline here. I need—"*

She only vaguely listened, hearing the voices as a kind of
filler between strident beeps. There were too many people out
there, anyway, and she was really happy just to stay here with
Polly. There was plenty of food, and everything was interesting. Out there, she thought grimly, there might only be more
babies to find.

For a week they didn't come. They left her alone. But late
one afternoon she heard the rumble of a car turning down her
steep drive. With a sinking heart, she took Polly on her hip
and went to the door. It was Judith.

"Shit," she said, climbing out the driver's side door and
reaching back in for her bag. "I've been calling you for days.
Didn't you get my messages?"

"Sorry," Naomi said. "I just couldn't talk about it."

"I'm not surprised. Jesus, what a hell of a thing." They stood
looking at each other. Judith's hair was wedged ineffectually
behind her ears, the kinks and curls freeing themselves. One
earring, like a small silver spoon hammered flat, was dangling

flat against her hair. The other, its fork mate, was tangled in strands of hair. Naomi felt herself stare at it. She felt it sting when she moved her own head. Finally, Judith said, "Look, can I come in? I won't stay long."

"Oh, of course," said Naomi. "I'm sorry. I'm very rude."

"You're not at all." She walked into the living room and surveyed the impact of Polly. "Naomi, God, what an ordeal for you."

Naomi promptly burst into tears, which very much surprised her.

"I'm sorry."

Judith put her arms around her. "Don't be. It's all right."

"I'm sorry!" Naomi said again, weeping. Polly wriggled and Naomi put her down.

"So this is Heather's daughter?"

"Polly," Naomi said. "She's doing well. Come on, I'll make tea."

There was a shelf of herbals. Naomi put on the kettle while Judith prowled around. "Your choice," Naomi said.

"To tell you the truth," said Judith, "I never really liked herbal tea. I know it's awful, but do you have any Lipton?"

"Shock and horror!" Naomi laughed. When she heard herself laugh, she smiled. They settled on Constant Comment.

"We used to call this Constant Commie in college." Judith smelled, entranced by nostalgia.

"So did we! I thought we invented that."

"Maybe there are no original ideas, after all." The bag was more of a briefcase, Naomi noticed. She frowned at this.

"Are you coming from work?"

"Yes. I need to talk to you about all this."

Naomi looked at her. She did not want to hope that this meant what it suddenly seemed it might mean.

"Have you seen Heather?" she asked instead.

"Yesterday afternoon. She's overjoyed. She wants to come home." Judith sipped her tea. "It should be that simple, but it won't be."

"All right," Naomi said. "Tell me what's going on."

"Well, it's perfectly clear to everyone at my office what happened. Heather had her baby just as she told you—by herself, outside. The baby didn't live, and she panicked and threw it, and the afterbirth, in the little pond. Well, she called it a pond. I haven't been out there yet."

She paused to sip her tea. Naomi waited.

"Obviously, she was tremendously guilty about this, so when they arrested her it wasn't difficult to get her to admit to anything. Maybe she even thought there was some bizarre way that *was* her baby in the river. I don't know. Guilt is powerful. We'd all crack under that kind of pressure, I'm sure. But the key is that she asked for a lawyer. At least twice, she says. And they wouldn't let her see one. The interrogation should have stopped right there, so everything afterward shouldn't be admissible. Only of course Charter denies that she asked for a lawyer, and he says there's no mention of it in his notes. How surprising!" Judith laughed grimly. "Also, she offered to bring them to the pond herself, and they weren't interested in that, either. So that could have ended it, too. And finally, Heather says they basically told her she'd never get Polly back if she didn't confess, which is," Judith said viciously, "absolutely reprehensible."

"Judith," Naomi said, very carefully, "does this mean you're going to be Heather's attorney?"

Judith turned to her. "But I told you already. In my message."

"I didn't listen." Her heart leaped. "Oh, I'm so glad! But what made you change your mind?"

She shrugged. "I couldn't stand what was happening to this girl. I mean, who knows what she did, but it's clear as hell what she didn't do. And she still doesn't know what hit her. It's incredible—she has very little grasp of the situation. She needs someone looking out for her."

Naomi nodded. She didn't trust herself to say anything. She thought she might not be able to contain her gratitude.

"Now, anytime you have a confession to a crime the person didn't commit, you have the potential for a lawsuit, so that's a powerful lever here. I haven't been to see Charter yet, but I won't hesitate to threaten him if he doesn't back down. It might not happen as quickly as any of us would like, but I don't see how else he can possibly deal with this. I mean, what's he going to say, she killed both of them?"

"And they won't just sort of switch it around and charge her with killing the second baby?"

Judith shook her head. "They can't. The second baby had no puncture wound. Charter might like to just take her confession and edit it to fit the second baby, he's not going to be able to do it." She smiled tightly. "It'll work out."

Polly waddled up to Naomi and Naomi went to find crackers for her. She put the baby on her lap and they watched her eat.

"She's sweet," Judith observed, but she said it flatly, without warmth.

"Yes. But I'll be happy to give her back if this can get settled soon. Oh, Judith, I really can't thank you enough."

"But it's my job!" Judith laughed. "And anyway, when that second baby turned up, the couple of guys who wanted the case were totally freaked out. I was just about the only one still functional on the issue. Because I can't stand the way they *blame*, you see? And always a woman. You didn't see them running around questioning men, did you? They just picked up on this girl because she'd had some problems and done this appalling thing by having a baby with a married man, and so they hauled her in and manipulated her and threatened her until she would have admitted to sinking the *Titanic*." Judith shook her head. "I find this personally offensive, Naomi. I consider myself responsible for righting this. On Heather's behalf, but also on ours. You see?"

Naomi, who didn't quite, nodded anyway.

"But what about your . . . family thing?" she said. "I thought you said you couldn't take on a big case."

"Well, with luck"—Judith smiled—"this won't be a big case. I'm going to see Mr. Wonderful on Monday. Give it a week or two for red tape and we can all get back to normal." She drained the end of her tea. "You, too."

"Me," Naomi said sadly, "maybe not. You can't imagine."

"Oh yes," said Judith.

"It's like I'm some gruesome Little Jack Horner. Except every time I stick my finger in the pie I pull out a dead baby. Where will I find the next one, you know?" She squeezed shut her eyes. Already they had begun to blur, those two little bodies—both sleek with water, both stiff with death. The faces she had turned so quickly away from, in order not to see, were nonetheless inescapably immediate, as if their outlines had been transferred to a skein between Naomi and the world, so that she was now forced to look through them at all times.

Those little sisters, twinned in death if not in birth, had become all the dead babies who had ever not breathed. And she had held them, each, and carried them in her arms. Naomi, feeling their little weight even now, shook her head. "You know," she heard herself say aloud, "I had an abortion when I was at Cornell."

"Really," said Judith quietly.

"Daniel came with me. Well," she said darkly, "he waited outside. We both agreed it was the right thing, but all the time I really hoped he'd stop me. Take me out of there. Like"— Naomi smiled—"Dustin Hoffman in *The Graduate*. She'd be thirteen now."

Judith waited.

"Well, if it was a girl. She'd be thirteen." She sighed. "It's what broke us up finally, I think."

"The abortion?" said Judith.

"No. But I wanted to have a baby, and he didn't want to. Last winter."

Polly broke her last cracker into crumbs and brushed them along the table.

"I'm sorry," said Judith.

They sat in silence for a moment.

"Naomi," Judith said, "I want you to come with me when I see Charter."

She looked up, alarmed. "But why?"

"Well, you're as close to a next of kin as Heather's got. And if you bring Polly it might help to give him a little kick, you know? Get him to hustle things along so this mother can get back to her baby. Plus, you've met him, and you're the one who told him in the first place he was barking up the wrong tree. It might guilt-trip him a bit, you know?"

"It might make him more determined not to be wrong."

"But he *is* wrong." Judith smiled. "He can't change that, and neither can we. We'll appeal to his sense of fairness. You know—win some, lose some, in spite of the best intentions. We'll say we respect his determination to bring the person responsible for the first baby to justice, and the sooner we get this Heather business out of the way, the faster we can get on with that. Also," she paused, "I want him to see that there's support for Heather among women. And if he tries to drag this on, he's going to have to deal with that, too."

Naomi couldn't stop herself from laughing. "Support from women!" she cried. "Oh, Judith, dream on. You live in New Hampshire now. They won't see that this has anything to do with women. 'Feminist' and 'Communist' mean the same thing here. It just won't happen."

"It might," Judith said. "You never know. When they see how she got railroaded they'll put themselves in her place. They'll think, Well, I might have cracked under those circumstances, too." She considered. "Naomi, I really feel they'll forgive her. I have that faith, you know?"

Naomi frowned and slowly shook her head. "Not her, not us. Not anyone who touches this." She looked at her friend. "Look, I'm a lost cause here. I've done too many things already, but you should be clear about what will happen. She may be innocent, but they still won't applaud you for getting her off. They'll just be irritated that someone prevented Heather from getting what was coming to her."

"And that is?" Judith said archly.

"Well, losing her child for a start. A woman like that should hardly be a mother, after all. And jail time, too."

"But why?" Judith cried. "What's the point of that?"

"No point. Just that people have been working up to this for so long, and now, just on the verge of all of their general dislike being spectacularly justified, it'd be anticlimactic to have to back down." She paused, stirring the cold tea in her cup. "There's a line from *Anna Karenina* I always remembered: 'They were already preparing the lumps of mud they would fling when the time came.'" She smiled sadly. "It's been like that."

"You can't be sure," said Judith.

But she could, and Naomi was tempted to say it, citing her tenure as resident alien in Peyton County. There would be blame in abundance, as she knew perfectly well, and neither she nor Judith, nor anyone who took Heather's part, would be forgiven for it. But had she been Judith, Naomi thought afterward, she wouldn't have wanted to hear it either, so Naomi shrugged and said no, of course she couldn't be sure, and naturally anything could happen when people understood how badly used Heather had been. Then she agreed to go see Charter, and they talked no more about it.

Chapter 26

A Woman to Blame

THE OFFICE OF THE DISTRICT ATTORNEY TOOK up a sizable section of a gray granite building adjacent to the Peytonville courthouse. This charmless display of local stone and unoriginal design had been solemnly composed and dedicated in the 1960s, and though the building had been outgrown many times over, and the overflow of victims' services and parole and child welfare had been shunted off to even less lovely buildings on the outskirts of Peytonville (with—it seemed, nonetheless—little impact on the general crowding inside), the district attorney had always held on to the same suite of offices in the building's back corner. There was a small park outside the entrance, and Naomi and Polly waited there for Judith to arrive for their meeting with Charter.

The little girl's parka from the previous winter did not fit, so they had stopped in the Peytonville Wal-Mart to buy a new one, and the significance of this—of her first purchase for Polly, the first expression of her own preference for how Polly should live—had not escaped Naomi. She watched with barely tempered satisfaction as Polly ran around and around the small garden, circling a dying floral display and chirping her new word in melodic sequence: "Go, go, go!"

Even more than Polly, Naomi wanted to go, but Judith had called again the night before, reminding her of the appointment with a very pointed tone. She was only just beginning to feel ready to go out at all—apart from the drive to pick up Polly, she had not even been to the supermarket since finding the second baby—and an interview with Charter did not promise a gentle reintroduction to human society. She was doubtful, too, of what good her being here could possibly do. Charter disliked her—she brought him dead babies to contend with, for one thing—and had as much as accused her of infanticide the very first time they'd met. These things did not augur well for restrained, productive interchange, and Naomi only hoped that her own undisguisable resentment would not do Heather more harm than good.

Judith arrived, dressed beautifully in a brown suit, swinging her briefcase. Naomi marveled, watching her come up the walk, barely recognizing the woman in Reminiscence overalls she'd first seen in the produce section. Her hair was shorter, her figure professionally trim. She was full of respect for how capable Judith must be, to appear so competent with such apparent effortlessness. If she herself had ever gone to law school, Naomi thought, it was this polish that would have eluded her, far more than any intellectual shortcoming. She simply could not project herself into a picture of appropriate attire and behavior, of well-tended hair and simple, understated clothing, of panty hose and unobtrusive jewelry. How lousy to be defeated by such irrelevancies! she thought, surveying her own disorder. Polly squatted down and threw a fistful of white pebbles into the air.

"Whoa!" Judith laughed, dodging the spray. "Okay, we're late."

She slowed but didn't stop. Naomi swung Polly up onto her hip and jogged after.

"Still think this is a good idea?" she asked.

"I do. I'll do the talking." She looked at her watch. "You just look at him. Don't say anything. Though if I give you a meaningful stare, you can consider yourself unmuzzled."

"Unmuzzled?" Naomi said. "This because he already thinks of me as a bitch?"

"Ha, ha," Judith said flatly. "Come on, it's over here."

The door at the end of the hall was open, and through it they could see Charter standing behind his desk and leaning over, dialing a number on his desk phone. In this posture, the ripple of his combed-over hair was presented flat, like the drawn-on ocean waves a child might make. He wore, Naomi thought, the only gray suit she had ever seen him wear, or perhaps he had a closetful and rotated them. His right hand, with its chunky class ring, drummed the tabletop.

"Hello," said Judith brightly. "We're here for our ten o'clock."

Charter looked up and frowned. Then he looked regretfully at the phone and hung up.

"Welcome, Mrs. Friedman. Mrs. Roth."

Ye Daughters of B'nai B'rith, Naomi thought obnoxiously.

They went in. Charter's eyes went right to Polly, who looked calmly back.

She pointed at him. "Mama."

Everyone tensed. Naomi put her down on the floor and fished the magic blue elephant out of the diaper bag.

"Is this necessary?" Charter said tersely. "I hardly think it's appropriate to bring a child here."

"This is Heather Pratt's child," Judith said, her voice calm.

"I'm well aware of that, Mrs. Friedman. But how that has bearing on her being here I can't imagine."

"Well"—Judith smiled—"I certainly don't want to inconvenience you. Let's just get this sorted through quickly, and then we can leave you in peace."

He took his seat. "I'm not sure what we can sort through in such a short amount of time," he said. "You asked for the meeting, so why don't you let me know what you have on your mind?"

Momentarily silenced, Judith rallied. "Well, why not begin with the second baby. What's the status there?"

"Deceased," he said bluntly. "Next?"

"Mr. Charter," she said carefully, "I don't think that's helpful."

"The second baby is still being examined by the coroner. Time of death can only approximately be determined, but he feels he can narrow it down to the period two days before to one day after Mrs. Roth found the first baby. Naturally, that includes a date and time of birth identical to that of the first baby."

Naomi, who didn't exactly understand this, but didn't like it anyway, frowned at him.

"So it's clear to everyone that this second baby was indeed Heather's baby."

"Nothing is clear to me, Mrs. Friedman. We will continue to investigate."

"But it's obvious that this is the baby Heather admitted to bearing. This is the baby whose body she admitted putting into the pond on her own property."

"That may be," he said, pursing his lips. "Or not."

For a moment, there was silence. Judith, Naomi saw plainly, wasn't happy about how this was going.

"Mr. Charter," she said suddenly, "I hope you're not planning to file criminal charges against Heather in connection with this second baby. This is a case of a tragic stillbirth, clearly."

"That is certainly possible," he said sagely.

"I feel I should tell you that pursuing criminal charges against a grieving mother can hardly enhance your public profile."

He glared at her. "I thank you for your concern about my public profile, Mrs. Friedman, and ask you not to trouble yourself about it any longer. I will file charges against people I suspect of committing crimes, which, along with proving those charges, is my job. After that, it will be up to a jury."

Naomi couldn't hold herself in check any longer. "I don't believe I'm hearing this," she said. "She *told* you what happened to her baby. I mean, Jesus, what crime do you think you can prove Heather committed?"

He looked at them both. He seemed to find this moment pleasant.

"Murder, Mrs. Roth. I think she committed murder."

Naomi stared at him, then at Judith, who was also speechless.

"You've got to be kidding," she yelled. "Have you been keeping up on current events, Mr. Charter? That wasn't Heather's baby in the river. We don't have any idea whose baby it was! And just because you wasted your whole investigation making up your mind it was the wrong person, and just because you didn't have the decency to listen to Heather when she told you you were wrong, that doesn't mean you get to go after her. It's your assumptions that turned out to be wrong!"

"I did make assumptions," he admitted, examining his fingers. "But given the information I had at the time, I made appropriate ones."

"And what assumptions," Judith said tightly, "were those?"

He swayed his head back and forth for a moment, as if considering. Then he looked at Judith again. "I assumed," Charter announced, "that she had had only one baby."

Naomi, who dimly sensed Polly playing with the laces of her hiking boot, felt energy drain from her. Beside her, Judith, too, was having difficulty recovering.

"This is," she managed. "The most. Outrageous." Then she gave up.

"I wish I could agree," he said, triumphant but serious. "But you see, Heather in effect admitted both acts to us—the act of stabbing the first baby and the act of giving birth to the second, and disposing of its body. We expect, moreover, that when we complete forensic tests we'll have independent evidence for each of the acts. And please don't forget, Mrs. Friedman, that Heather Pratt was the *only* woman we ever discovered, within at least a sixty-mile radius of Goddard, who had recently had a questionable pregnancy." He looked from one to another. "By which I mean a pregnancy that did not result in a recorded birth—live or dead."

Naomi found her voice. "Impossible. She would have been huge if she was carrying twins."

"Not necessarily. The doctor who examined her says it depends entirely on the position of the fetuses. And please remember that, by her own admission, she stayed close to her home over the summer months and wore loose clothes."

"So . . . what? She had two babies, stabbed one and threw it in the river, then put the other in the pond? Jesus, *that* makes sense!" She was shaking. She looked to Judith for help, but Judith was very still.

"I don't expect it to make sense, Mrs. Roth. In fact, I doubt it ever will." He frowned at his hands, splaying the short fingers. "Not only that, I want you both to know that I don't consider myself responsible for conferring justice on Heather. It isn't my place to punish this woman."

"How noble!" Naomi cried, lifting Polly onto her lap. "As if you weren't punishing her right now. What about her *daughter*, Mr. Charter? Every day this drags on is a day Polly is prevented from being with her mother, where she belongs. Granted, she's young, and she doesn't understand the niceties of what's going on, but I can assure you she knows something's wrong. How is this fair to her?"

"It may not be fair." His voice was even. "But it may well be appropriate. It may be that Heather is by no means a fit parent and ought not to be raising a child, particularly on her own."

Naomi looked at him, blank with rage. For the first time in her life, she stifled an impulse for violence.

"This is absolutely reprehensible," she managed, finally.

To which he smiled, a little sadly. "Forgive me if I suggest that a woman who kills babies is an unfit mother."

"All Heather did was maybe not get prenatal care for her pregnancy," Naomi said bitterly. "She had no obligation to tell anybody she was pregnant. Not even the father, for Christ's sake! And certainly not you. Then she had a stillbirth. That was *hardly* her fault! She doesn't deserve to be locked up for either of those things. And the other stuff is crazy! You're just *doing* it to cover up your own mistakes."

"My mistakes," he said blandly.

"Well," Judith broke in, her voice amazingly calm, "there *is* the small matter of this graphic confession to a crime my client absolutely did not commit. It seems to me that all this nonsense about twins is a very elaborate way to deflect questions about that confession. But I won't be deflected, Mr. Charter. I think you know that."

"The confession was entirely proper, Mrs. Friedman. And it was witnessed, as you know."

"My client tells me she asked to see a lawyer. More than once."

"I have no recollection of that," he said.

"She also, as I understand it, offered to take you—even *begged* to take you—out to her house and show you where she'd hidden the body of her stillborn infant. A plea you ignored, according to her. I wonder why."

"She appeared hysterical at that time. The request seemed hysterical."

"Hysterical!" Judith was enraged. "Jesus, you have gall."

"The confession was proper," Charter said again, though tersely this time. "And I resent your inference otherwise. Our only *mistake*, as you put it, was conflating what were actually two confessions into one event, but this was in keeping with the information we had at that time."

Judith stared at him. She seemed to be thinking. Then she sat forward in her chair. "Forensic tests on both babies are continuing, I assume?"

"They are," he said. "But I can assure you that the knitting needle Heather identified is entirely consistent with the wound the first baby received, so I wouldn't place too much hope on—"

"I was thinking more of serology," Judith broke in. "I expect you'll be trying to establish maternity through blood type?"

"And paternity, yes. We took a blood sample from Ashley Deacon several days ago."

"Well then—" Judith smiled. "If, as I very strongly suspect, you discover that Heather Pratt does *not* have a parental relationship to the Sabbathday River baby, you will naturally cease this ridiculous attempt to pin a gruesome murder on my client and use a coerced confession to make it stick. And since your only 'confession,' as you call it, was to the murder of the Sabbathday River baby, then you won't have any evidence at all on the baby found in Heather's pond."

He smiled. His elbows were planted on the desk, and his palms together before his face, as if he were saying a bedtime prayer. "All that is true, Mrs. Friedman. But unlike you I have every confidence that the serology will show Heather to have been the parent of both babies. We have an arraignment date, incidentally."

"Excuse me?" she shouted. "You couldn't get an arraignment date without an indictment!"

He nodded in agreement and began looking around his desk, lifting stacks, riffling through the In box. "I would have sent it," he said with deeply insincere courtesy, "but I knew you were coming." He handed it over. "Grand jury met on Friday," he said affably as she read, her face a mask of incredulity.

Then Judith looked up, and slowly she shook her head.

"There's always a woman to blame, isn't there?"

He considered this. "Always? No. But in this case, yes. There is a woman to blame."

"You could stop this right now, but you're too proud to do it." She was staring at him, as if he were some rare creature from a distant place, transported an imponderably vast distance only for normal people to gape at. "Well, it's your mistake, Mr. Charter. I expect you'll think back to this interview very soon and wish you'd stopped it. You'll be a laughingstock, you know. And very much hated. But very famous, too, if you take this on. Well, I guess you know that already. Though maybe you don't know what you're going to be famous *for*." Judith picked up her briefcase. Naomi, following her lead, got up with Polly and slung the diaper bag over her shoulder. The girl was sucking an ear of her elephant, her gaze gray and steady on Charter. "Women won't stand for this," Judith said. It sounded, to Naomi's admittedly stunned ears, like a warning.

"Women!" He put his head back and choked out a single laugh. "What does this case have to do with *women*?"

Chapter 27

Over the Edge

HEATHER STAYED IN JAIL. POLLY STAYED WITH Naomi, who grew even more attached to her. Judith made an effort to get some kind of bail for her client, but Charter produced a psychiatrist to proclaim Heather a threat to her own safety. Ultimately she was moved to the locked ward of a mental facility east of Peytonville, in the lake region, where, according to Judith, she lapsed further into depression. Polly was no more permitted to visit her mother in the hospital than she had been in the medical ward of the jail, so Naomi sent photographs and tape cassettes of Polly's words as they came, and crayon scribbles. She had no idea if any of it was delivered. Judith, with a trial date of March 2, was forced to temper her indignation and apply herself to other cases. The number of these surprised her. The fact that none of them involved the theft of cows amused her husband.

And, as she had warned Naomi, she did indeed disappear every couple of weeks, always returning depleted and reticent. Naomi would sometimes learn of these trips only in retrospect, though she saw Judith often and though, as the weeks passed and the fall sank into early, hard winter, the connection between them grew both easier and more complex. In the openness of their friendship, Judith kept this one door tightly locked, and Naomi respectfully did not knock. It wasn't unusual, for example, for the two women to spend an evening at Naomi's or Judith's house, cooking and talking, often at the expense of husbands, past and present, and take leave of each other in some small hour of the night, and then for Naomi to call the next day and learn Judith was gone—down to Providence for a weekend or a week. The more time passed, the less able Naomi felt to broach the subject.

Not that her curiosity took too much time away from other things. Her life with Polly consumed her, wearied her, and amazed her. She had not imagined how satisfying she would

find the most mundane acts involved in caring for Polly: the
diapers and baths, the endless rotation of a handful of acceptable foods. She enrolled them in a baby music class and drove
down to Hanover once a week to watch Polly bang a drum
and ring a bell while a woman led them in silly songs. She
took Polly to the sports center for parent-toddler swimming,
moving her little limbs in the water while the little girl shouted
and smacked the surface. She loved the routine of taking Polly
to the supermarket, telling her the names of things, the colors
of the bright boxes. And she took Polly to work, setting her
down in the office with her toys, or sitting her on her lap while
she used the computer. It seemed, as the weeks went by, that
she brought less and less of herself to maneuvering her own
adult life within the community. This was perhaps no bad
thing, Naomi thought, when she thought about it, because her
life in the community seemed more perilous than ever before.

In this empty period between confession and trial, the town
seemed to settle its own mind on what newspapers were now
pretty consistently calling the Goddard Babies Case. Heather
Pratt, the mother of twins, the murderer of twins, was a topic
few needed to discuss, because there was nothing but agreement on the matter. Whatever bitterness was being vented had
to do more with what this meant for the town itself. Whatever
tears were being shed were not for Heather, nor even for the
babies, but for the town's new and now inescapable slogan,
cleverly penned by a wag on *The Boston Globe*: "Goddard,
New Hampshire—Dead Baby Capital of New England." The
women, in particular, were incensed. Naomi remembered with
grim humor Judith's theory that women would support
Heather, that they would identify with her and come to her
aid. But in the weeks following Heather's imprisonment, there
was not a single gesture of support, not even an insincere one.
Naomi received no offers of help with the baby, and Judith no
calls saying how awful it all was. Even Stephen Trask turned
away from her when Naomi passed him at the sports center.
He seemed, to her annoyance, to take Heather's situation as a
personal failing.

Judith met occasionally with Heather and reported her spirits
as stable, though not particularly good. She was refusing to
discuss her experiences with the psychiatrist assigned to her,
but she was forthcoming with Judith, at least in responding to

questions, though never exactly volunteering information. She told Judith about her brief experience at college, her passion for Ashley, her joyous first pregnancy. She admitted not caring that Ashley was married, or that the affair had plainly become common knowledge, or that she herself seemed to be apportioned the full blame for it. She answered the most rudimentary queries about her grandmother, whom she loved and missed, and her mother, whom she had not seen for many years, and the work she did for Naomi and the collective. What Heather really wanted to talk about, of course, was Ashley. She wanted to know how he was, how his children were. She wept when Judith showed Heather his name on the prosecution's witness list, though Judith tried to explain that this did not mean he was "against" her, per se. Naomi's name, after all, was on the same list.

All told, there were few surprises in the district attorney's emerging case. In addition to Ashley, various observers of his and Heather's affair would report on her wanton behavior, and Sue Deacon would take the stand to portray the wronged wife. Heather's midwife and the doctor who had examined her after her arrest were due to testify, as was Nelson Erroll—who, Judith assumed, would introduce the confession—the medical examiner, and a forensic serologist. It was the serologist who most concerned Judith. As the weeks passed and no report on the babies' (and their putative parents') blood types arrived in her office, she bombarded Charter with demands for disclosure, but he only said that tests were not yet complete. Even Judith, who had seemed to have complete confidence that the first baby's blood group would be incompatible with those of Heather and Ashley, began to worry, and the trial date approached with no sign of Charter backing off.

A second formidable obstacle was that Heather would not agree to testify. The very prospect terrified her, she said, and she would not listen to Judith's claim that her own words were her single greatest asset. Heather must be able to respond to the moral condemnation the prosecution would offer, Judith said, and with the plain language of human love and frailty; she was, Judith reminded her, not at all a calculating and uncaring mistress, but a young girl who had fallen deeply in love with a man—a man, Judith said harshly, who had then abandoned her with one infant and a second on the way. Heather must herself tell the jury of her intense distress and her fears, and the confusion and panic she felt as the new baby's birth approached. She must tell the court how she had never intended harm to her baby, but that when the baby appeared dead at birth, she had made the bad decision to hide the body and try to recover from this trauma in private. Her own words were the magic that would undo this hasp. Judith explained this clearly, and without giving in to a strong temptation to yell at the girl. Then she gave in to temptation and yelled, but that didn't work either. Heather refused to testify.

Every day Naomi and Judith expected Charter to call. Every day they were sure it was imminent, his sheepish admission that, having now ascertained that the Sabbathday River baby was not Heather's—had no connection to Heather at all—his office would be dropping one of the counts of second-degree murder. Moreover, given the lack of confession in the matter of the second baby, not to mention the lack of evidence that the second baby was anything but a stillbirth, those charges would be dropped as well. But the days passed and the call didn't come. Judith's own calls went unanswered. She grew first concerned, then suspicious. Finally, she waited for him in the morning outside his office, watched him walk in, then followed. This was February, less than three weeks before they were due to go to trial.

That afternoon, Judith stormed into the mill, flung her heavy overcoat on a chair, and told Naomi she had to speak to her.

Naomi nodded dumbly, immediately tense. She was at her desk, working at the computer. In the workroom half a dozen people were sitting in a circle. There was laughter, Judith noted, and this enraged her further.

"I went to see that bastard. That *bastard*!" She glared at Naomi. "He wouldn't return my calls. I kept asking for the serology report, and he wouldn't send it."

"The serology report," Naomi repeated.

"And the trial's less than a month away! I don't even think I've got time to get a defense expert without having to ask for a delay. Not that he'd even give me the babies' blood samples. He'll probably claim they were entirely used up in the testing. Jesus!"

"Judith," Naomi said, "I don't know what you're saying."

She took a breath. She was trying to get herself under control.

"All right. These are the prosecution's serologist's results. For baby number two—the baby from the pond there is, quote, high probability that Heather and Ashley are the parents."

"Right," Naomi said. "As Heather said."

"Right. Now listen to this. For baby number one, the river baby. Heather's blood type shows her to be a 'possible' mother, but Ashley's paternity has been definitively ruled out."

Naomi brightened. "So that's great. That's what we were hoping. He isn't the father, so it isn't Heather's."

Judith set her jaw. Slowly she shook her head.

"What do you mean, no? No *what*?" Naomi said.

Judith, unable to speak, kept shaking her head.

"Just tell me," Naomi said, baffled and impatient.

"Think, Naomi. *Twins*. No," she corrected herself. "Don't bother thinking. Thinking implies it will make sense, and it won't. That crazy bastard. He's tilting at windmills, but he hasn't got an ounce of honor."

"Twins," Naomi repeated. "I don't get it. Twins have the same parents."

"One would think," Judith sneered.

There was silence as this, with excruciating slowness, gradually became clear.

More than anything she wanted to laugh. It had all gone over the edge now, into some immense absurdity.

"It even has a name," Judith was saying. "Listen to this: superfecundation. This is what you call it when a woman has twins by different fathers."

"It's impossible," said Naomi, who was still laughing inwardly.

"It is not quite impossible. It is very nearly impossible. Statistically, yes, it's so far out that you could call it impossible, but there exists the minuscule chance. This is where reasonable doubt comes in," she said with great exasperation. "Juries say they understand it, but they don't a lot of the time. You tell them, Well, you don't have a *reasonable* doubt that the sun will rise tomorrow, do you? And one idiot will think, *But it might not*. That's all it takes. Oh, Naomi, this is so, so crazy."

"But"—she still couldn't seem to catch on—"I don't understand who they're going to say is the other father. There was only Ashley. And wouldn't a second father have had to sleep with her like at the same time?"

"Oh no," Judith said lightly. "I've just been given a mini-course in this nonsense. Within twenty-four hours, before or after. The woman releases two eggs—well, it's true, that happens all the time. But then there are two *fertilizations*, each by a different father. *Voilà*! And here's where it's so terrible. They've got a whole gang to go up there and say Heather was a woman of no morals. What's a second lover! What's having sex with two guys within twenty-four hours! I don't think it matters if they come up with a name or not. By the time Charter's finished his case, she'll be the Whore of Babylon."

"God." Naomi was horrified. The weight of this was hitting her now. She looked involuntarily at Polly, who was napping in her playpen next to the attic stairs. "But . . . Judith, I can't believe the attorney general will let Charter mount a case like this. I mean, claiming that this girl had twin babies by different fathers, chucked one in a pool of water and stabbed the other—it just defies belief on about eight different fronts at once. He'll put a stop to it. He won't want to be associated with something so nutty."

"That's what I thought," Judith said with renewed wonder. "I said that to him, and you know what he said? 'I assure you that I have the full support of the attorney general on this matter.' "

"Maybe he's lying," Naomi considered. "Maybe he hasn't told his boss what he's got planned."

"Maybe he has," Judith shot back. "Maybe the whole world's crazy. Except us."

"Oh God," Naomi said, shaking her head. "Poor Heather."

"Poor *Heather*." Someone spoke from the doorway. They both looked up.

Ann Chase surveyed them with raw contempt, swung on her heavy heel, and flounced back to the circle beyond. Her rug in progress, a blue kitten in burlap, flounced behind.

Naomi and Judith looked at her, then at each other. Naomi felt anger surge inside her, and she welcomed it. It felt powerful to have an object for her hatred, almost deliriously sweet. She got to her feet.

"What are you going to do?" said Judith.

"Something I've been dying to do for ages," Naomi said, leaving the room. She walked back into the workroom and up to the circle. Janelle Hodge's chair was directly before her, and she saw over Janelle's shoulder a crib quilt in pink and blue—a customer preparing for any eventuality. Next to her, Mary Sully was making a charmless quilt, for her sister, Naomi knew. Mary's talents were clerical, and it was just as well she'd never offered her needlework services to the collective. Ina was there, and Sarah Copley, and all the others—her most inner circle. *Good*, Naomi thought. *I want everyone to see*.

She walked around the ring and laid a hand on Ann's shoulder. Ann studiously did not look up.

"Ann," said Naomi, "you've got something to say?"

Ann yanked at the wool in her lap, ignoring her.

"I feel you do," Naomi said again, her voice a little harder, "have something to say. I'd like to hear it."

"You don't want to hear what I've got to say," said Ann, her head down. "You don't want to think about what that girl did. You're too busy caring about her *rights*!"

"I do care about her rights," Naomi said. "Her rights are the same as my rights. And yours."

"Oh no." Ann shook her head, looking up for the first time. "No, thank you. I don't need the right to go root around with somebody else's husband in a car, or have kids with him while his own wife is right there. I don't need the right to throw babies in ponds or kill them with knitting needles. You just go and take away that right. I can live without it."

"Heather didn't kill either of those babies, and you all know it."

Ann gave her a slow, sour smile. "Fine. You think that? *Fine*. Now leave me alone. I have my own opinion."

Carefully Naomi stepped into the circle. She faced Ann Chase and looked down at her, stiff hair the color of straw, her face hardened but unwrinkled, also the color of straw. It struck her that she had never, until this moment, recognized Ann Chase for what she was, or at least what she represented to Naomi. This face and this set of brutal features were the ones she had been trained to recognize and isolate and convert with love and holy nonviolence. Naomi knew she was supposed to respect this woman. She was supposed to show courtesy and regard for her opinions, all the while demonstrating the quiet dignity of her own, correct, philosophy. She remembered how Mickey Schwerner had consoled his murderers before they tore him apart—"Sir, I know just how you feel." But Naomi found, to her astonishment, that she wasn't that kind of person anymore. The truth was that she had always hated Ann.

"I'm glad she's in jail," Ann said contemptuously. "I hope she stays there."

"You're fired," Naomi said.

All the women seemed to jerk at once. Only Naomi, who had known what she was going to say, was still.

Sarah twisted around to look at Ann. Ann was staring. "Excuse me?" Her rough voice rose in outrage.

"I'm sorry," Naomi said, glaring. "I'll speak more clearly. You. Are. Fired."

Ann seemed glazed but livid. After a moment, she found her voice. "Who says?"

"What, you don't know who I am suddenly? I'm the person who brings you commissions and sells your work and gives you the money. But not anymore. You're out."

"And you're the boss lady!"

"This building is my property." Naomi sounded calm. "If you trespass on my property, I will file charges against you. Go on," she said, freshly angry. "Get up. Get out."

"I don't believe this."

"You were always a bitch, Ann. But there's no law that says we have to like each other. And, believe me, I'm not telling you you can't have your own opinion. You can, of course, even if it's asinine. But I won't have this kind of viciousness against a coworker."

Ann got to her feet. "I thought this was a collective! I thought nobody was the boss!"

"In ideal circumstances, maybe. These aren't ideal circumstances." She didn't want to hear exactly what she was saying, it occurred to her suddenly. If she didn't pay too close attention now, she couldn't reproach herself later.

"If that isn't the most hypocritical—"

"And anyone else," Naomi cut her off. She turned to look at the rapt faces ringing her. "If you want to leave, if you think I'm being unfair, or punishing Ann for how she feels about Heather, if you want to walk out to show solidarity with her, if you want to go on strike or just stop working—*fine*. You can do that. Or you can tell me how you feel and I'll listen. Or you can think what I think, that Ann was very cruel and very unpleasant and her presence here made it difficult to be around her, so it's fine that she's gone. You all know I've never done this before. I've never felt it was necessary. But it's necessary now." She looked back at Ann, who still stood, her kitten rug at her side. There was something electric in that blue, Naomi thought, peering at it. She wondered if Ann had been sneaking in acrylic fabrics. This idea made her even more furious. "So that's it." She looked at Ann. "Get out. I'm not going to ask you again. You leave now or I call the police."

"The police!" Ann protested. "You're insane."

Quite possibly, Naomi thought. She knew how this would fly around Goddard.

"You know," Ann said, stopping to yank up her big bag of wool, "I always thought it was strange you found both those babies. How'd you know where to find them, anyway? It seems to me you *knew* where they were!"

"Meaning what?" Naomi yelled. "Oh, never mind, just get lost."

But she stood for another moment, looking around the ring of frozen faces. No one else had gotten up. *"Well?"* Ann demanded after a moment. Then she turned to her right. *"Sarah?"*

"What is this, high school?" Naomi shouted. "If you get cut from the team everyone else has to quit, too?"

"Let me think," Sarah Copley said. "I'll call you tonight."

"You *better* call." She knocked her chair aside. "Well, I'll be glad not to have to see *you* every day," she sneered at Naomi. Then she noticed Judith, who was in the doorway and had been watching. She stopped, and shook her head. "Your kind really sticks together, doesn't it?"

From across the room, they all heard Judith mutter: *Jesus Christ.*

"What would *you* know about Jesus Christ!" Ann yelled. She crossed the room with short strides, pushing past Judith. Then she stopped. "You get her off," Ann said, nodding. "You do that. You make her out like some poor victim. Don't think about what she *did*."

"I think about it," Judith said, her voice even.

Ann was gone. The slam of the door woke Polly, who cried immediately. Naomi lifted her and put her own face against Polly's cheek, swaying and hugging the little girl. She was crying, too, she felt now. Judith came up behind her and put her arm over Naomi's shoulder. They stood like that for a while, in the numb silence. She felt Judith kiss her, and smiled. Then she heard Judith speak, though her voice was soft. "It's all right," she said. "We'll sort this out."

But it wasn't, and they wouldn't, and both of them knew it.

Part 4
Mud Season

A Polish midwife was assisting at my birth.
And I gave birth to a beautiful girl.
There on the stones. In my own filth.
No soap. No cotton wool. Without hot water

I went to my cot. No mattress, just a cover.
And in the morning, Mengele.
My breasts were bandaged up:
to see how long a new-born lives

deprived of food. I had no choice.
Each day I chewed my bread
and wrapped it in a scrap of cloth
I soaked in soup. A peasant dummy.

With this I fed my child. My God.
The child lost weight
and every day came Mengele.
Soon she had no strength to cry.

She only whimpered, and my milk got up.
I couldn't give her anything.
Except, about the sixth or seventh day,
the syringe of morphium.

Cut slanted like a quill.
And warm from Matza Steinberg's hand.
I can understand ghosts.
How they have to come back.

What it costs to return
through the bricks of a house.
Eyes tight shut.
Weeping, broken skin.

 —*Craig Raine, "Skeol"*

Chapter 28

The Farthest Edge
of the Diaspora

IN MUD SEASON NAOMI NEVER FELT COM-
pletely clean. The dank communal depression from first melt
to the first bud on the first deciduous tree was a foil to the
New England calendar, an annual humbling for a region unused to ugliness, if not downright spoiled by beauty. It was,
Naomi felt, like a yearly rewind of seasonal change, a necessary pause before the familiar, spectacular film could start
again with its usual sweet variety of warmth and cold and color
and starkness: lush summer, inexpressibly lovely autumn, then
winter—chill, pure, and white. This mud season, like each one
before it, the steep drive down to her house got boggy, but
this year she was terrified of skidding down the hill with Polly
in the car. She took to parking her car up at the top and fer-
rying her down her loads—groceries, work, baby—cursing
Daniel every soggy step of the way. She forgot what it was to
trust the ground, to believe in its faculty for holding her up.
Water rose underfoot, summoned, it seemed, from the very
depths of the earth to pull her back, or at least to cake her
boots with dirt and soak the cuffs of her jeans. The sky was
unchanging gray, only pausing in its somber monochrome to
spill rain now and then. This time of year, it seemed to her,
the people who actually lived in New Hampshire were too
much left to themselves: devoid of distractions, mired in muck,
bitter at winter taking so long to clean up after itself. Left to
themselves, with too much mud underfoot and too intense an
urge to sling it elsewhere.

By now, Heather's self-proclaimed lovers were legion, a
happy chorus spouting salacious praise of her charms. There
was almost, Naomi thought, a kind of cads' agreement that
everyone had slept with her. Confident looks and offhand
shrugs were engaged whenever men were present and the topic
of Heather and her dead babies arose. *What could you expect,
a girl like that who didn't even care who she did it with?*

Naomi heard that Heather had a virtual boudoir in the utility closet in the high school's north annex. She heard Heather had fucked Ashley and other men at the sports center, in the staff bathroom, which could be locked from the inside. She heard Polly was not Heather's first child, and that Heather had given three or four of the guys on the basketball team VD. People seemed to take it upon themselves to tell Naomi these things, and with a spirit of almost sympathetic neighborliness, as if she alone was not aware of what Heather had been up to and could therefore be forgiven her bizarre support for the girl. At first, Naomi had taken a shot at a few of these kindly messengers, challenging them for dates and locales, for any shard of proof. Was So-and-so, Heather's newest self-proclaimed swain, planning to testify about their wanton past at the coming trial? Well, no. None of them would get up in court and say openly what they were saying over at Woodstock's, and no one else seemed to think there was any call for them to do so. On the contrary, there seemed to be some kind of tacit agreement that the dates and settings of these carnal events were not relevant to Heather's infamy. It had all happened *before*.

Amazingly enough, for a girl with such ravenous appetites, no one could recall having sex with her lately. Say, after last January or so. Heather's mysterious second lover, the theoretical father of the theoretical twin Ashley had not fathered, remained elusive.

This did not deter Goddard from embracing with great gusto the theory of the second lover, which had the benefit of attributing an even higher concentration of baseness to the woman awaiting trial in Peytonville, and lessened the already minimal portion of blame assigned to Ashley. He'd been duped by her, too, the theory went. More, perhaps, than anyone else. To cheat on a lover who was cheating on his wife! The fugitive second lover was Ashley's entrée into the fellowship of the betrayed, and Naomi watched with horror as he took up his role. She began to not call him when she needed his help. She began to despise him.

People who had never talked to Naomi before went on not talking to her. That didn't matter. People whose nodding acquaintance had always sustained her fantasy that she was in fact a member of this community went on nodding, but curtly.

That didn't matter, either. Ann Chase's bitter departure from Flourish swept two or three of the lesser rug hookers out on her coattails, but Sarah Copley had hung on, and more—she had her mother hooking now, from a nursing home up near Warren, and the mother's roommate had started a schoolhouse quilt just to see if she could still do it after all these years. (Nursing homes! Naomi thought, shaking her head. That she hadn't thought of it herself made her a little cranky.) So Flourish flourished even as Goddard hardened its heart against her.

None of it mattered. For the first time in years, Naomi had a real friend. She had forgotten what it felt like, to pick up the phone and hear not some formal query but only a gruff "Hey, it's me." She had forgotten the stopping by, and the hanging out, and what it was like to stay up late to gab over nothing laced with humor. She had forgotten the rhythm of falling in with another person's routine, and of another person knowing what she herself was doing at eight in the morning, or noon, or seven at night, and not having to catch up with the news of a husband's new thesis topic or a kid's triumphant school report before having to offer the lame excuse for oneself— *What am I up to? Not much.*—because it never exactly seemed newsworthy, your own life, especially when compared to the news bulletins from the other end of the phone. But Judith knew. She admired Naomi for the small and everyday events that were her occupation in these muddy, suspended months between Heather's arrest and her trial. She was the only person Naomi could crow to over Polly's new word, or complain to about Ann Chase's brutal small-mindedness.

And she helped Naomi recover the dialect of sarcasm, a language that had atrophied from lack of use. It amazed her how pleasurable it was to speak this way. It made her remember nights in college, in crowded rooms lubricated by marijuana and noisy with students who couldn't quite pronounce the names of their great-grandparents' *shtetl* ("I'm pretty sure it was called Anatevka," one pathetic girl had actually said) but thought it was somewhere in Russia, or where Lithuania used to be, or was it Latvia? She remembered a guy one of their housemates had brought home their senior year, a political scientist with a beard, mustache, and shag of hair that all seemed to merge over his head. "There's a town named after my family back in Poland somewhere," he told them over vegetarian chili. "I think it might have been the other way around," Naomi had responded. Chattering their language of *Men are meshugenneh* and *What, this surprises you?*—this was the dream of a common language, Naomi thought now, because it *was* dreamy, like speaking in tongues must be. Their pitch had taken generations of a conjoint heritage to perfect, and yet she had lost it willingly over this past decade, or at least without putting up a fight, and only now did she feel the cost of that, as she felt the intense gratification of hearing herself think and think aloud. One afternoon, she had stood with Judith behind a woman at a pay phone in Peytonville, waiting for their turn so that Judith could call her office, and the woman, despite glances back at them, had gone on and on to her invisible interlocutor, about nothing—television programs, a friend's bad taste in carpeting—before at last turning to look at them and asking, with deep insincerity, "Oh. Are you waiting for the telephone?" Judith and Naomi had looked at each other and rolled their eyes in unison, then spoke in a single caustic voice. "No. We're just standing here."

Her admiration for Judith was unqualified. It amazed her that one woman could do so many things and be gifted in so many individual ways. Judith was fierce in her role as Heather's advocate, thoroughly cool even as she ran a frenzied circle around this sluggish, lackluster girl, and as she dealt cordially, tactically with Charter, whom she despised. She could rage at will, then pull herself up to perfect pitch for the strategy at hand: fluid, brutal, transmutable. At the same time, Judith was serene—in her off-kilter beauty, the close eyes and high, rounded nose, the widely placed hips that, alone, took her out of single-digit skirt sizes. She was serene in her willingness to be still, without entertainment, and in her willingness to age—once, that is, the requisite attention had been drawn to a new wrinkle or a suddenly gray lock woven into her curls. She could cook, too. Naomi, who was not a very accomplished cook, who viewed cooking as something like a laboratory experiment, loved to watch Judith chop things and fling them into tians and casseroles. She kept two great copper pots on the stove, threw chicken carcasses and vegetable ends into one for stock, and the shells of shrimp into the other for risotto. She read cookbooks for pleasure and kept a stack in

the downstairs bathroom (this never failed to amuse Naomi),
but she never used them for actual cooking.

They fell into routines: Friday nights at Judith's, where Naomi brought her week of laundry (to her shame, she had soon
abandoned cotton for disposable diapers, but Polly still produced an imponderable volume of dirty clothes) to wash while
they ate, and Mondays at Naomi's just the women, a six-pack
of Rolling Rock, and pizza brought over after work from Peytonville. Even after all these months, she had not quite gotten
over her relief at Judith's appearance in Goddard, or Judith's
nonchalance at being here, as if it were the most normal, in-
consequential thing imaginable for two women like themselves
to be settled where they were—up here, at the farthest edge
of the Diaspora, and in these craggy, inhospitable hills.

So wide were the vistas of their conversation that Naomi
learned not to begrudge those few things that seemed never to
come up between them, the things she could not seem to get
herself to pry about. She wondered, for example, why Judith,
who had said after all that she wanted to have children, had
not told Naomi that she was pregnant, or that she was trying
to be pregnant, or that she was trying but could not seem to
succeed in being pregnant. She wondered why Judith, for all
her emphasis on the necessity of having children, did not ever
extend herself to Polly, nor even warm with Polly, nor even
very interested in Polly, and touched her only stiffly when she
had to touch her at all. Joel, too, seemed not to notice Polly,
nor did he talk about having a family. Maybe it was a disagreement between them, Naomi theorized, but Joel, like Judith, apparently had nieces and nephews whom he loved and
whose photographs he kept pinned to the bulletin board in his
office. Of Judith's own nephew, the one who was sick, Naomi
heard nothing, and only once asked, when Judith phoned to
say she had to cancel their Friday night because she was going
to Providence.

Your nephew. Naomi made it offhand, like an observation,
but with a smack of concern. *He's still sick?*

He was still sick, Judith had said, and before Naomi could
stop herself, and because she wanted to know, and it seemed
so odd to her that she didn't know, asked what was wrong
with him.

You've never heard of it, Judith said.

But if Judith and Naomi talked of everything—or nearly everything—Heather remained intractably uncommunicative with her lawyer. Even as the time for her trial came near, Heather said little about what was ahead, and nothing at all about her baby. She dug into her silence. She fell over it as over some object she had elected to guard with even her life. It was as if, Judith sometimes told Naomi, bitter in her frustration, the girl had to be repeatedly reminded what this—this baffling incursion in her life, this brutal separation from Polly—was after all about.

Nor, to Judith's disbelief, would Heather agree that Ashley might at least be held to account for having left her so harshly, without accommodation for the child that already existed or the one to come. What had happened between them to make him leave her, Heather insisted, was first of all private to them, a matter of intimacy, even as their passion had been, but beyond that her own ultimate fault. Enraged, Judith tried to assault this claim, but Heather would not part with her rendering of a perfect Ashley brought low by her own imperfection. She dreaded the trial for *his* sake, she admitted to Naomi one day, and Naomi, to her own surprise, understood this immediately. Heather wept and withdrew in preemptive shame, unable to bear the thought of him up there, having to admit to the degradation of loving her as he had. She wanted to save him that. She could not understand why things were moving so steadily forward in the wrong direction, or why Judith couldn't stop them. She could not understand what she had to do with that other baby, the one from the river, or why Charter was insisting on making her its mother. She had enough to answer for with her own baby, Heather complained, but in a tone that did not imply she was thinking overly much about this, either. Above all, she could not understand this great disaster that had grown up around her, and ensnared her, and taken away her child, and laid terrible, intolerable crimes at her feet.

Heather would never understand, Naomi told Judith finally. She would never see that it was about so much more than herself, and her own act, whatever it might have been, alone in a field. If they waited for Heather to confront the symbolic weight of the story she inhabited, they would wait forever, so if this was important to Judith, Naomi urged her to move forward alone, or at least without an active protagonist. Judith considered this. Then, the following week, she brought a woman named Nan Rubin up to see Heather. Nan was a Planned Parenthood friend from the city, and from Camp Thoreau before that, Judith said. She wrote for *Ms.* She spent three long afternoons with Heather in the little visiting room at the hospital, and was a little dazed when she emerged. She told her old bunkmate that she had never met such human opacity in her life, and went back to New York to write her piece. Almost immediately, the magazine sent a photographer to take Heather's picture through the mesh of the hospital interview room, and Naomi, when she saw it, was amazed at how lovely Heather was made to look: ethereal and hunted, like a doe gazing into headlights.

Was it going to be a slaughter? Naomi was afraid to ask. She was unwilling to burden Judith with the weight of her own fear, or—more subtly now, more problematic—the burden of her own ambivalence about Polly, and the thrill entwined with her rage when she thought about Heather convicted, Heather sent away forever, and Polly hers to watch and love. She had shameful fantasies—shameful on more than one level—of taking Polly, redolent in frills and patent leather, to *The Nutcracker* at Lincoln Center, or watching her sing slave spirituals in the immense auditorium at the Ethical Culture Society, her sweet face, aged six, aged ten, amid the sweet faces of other children.

Polly was dredging language from the air around her now, pulling it to herself, greedy to make herself known. Naomi, looking into her eyes, saw the exponential surge of intelligence, and only sporadically remembered to feel regretful that Heather was missing this. Polly never asked for her mother, and Naomi noticed that the little girl did not appear at all confused by the shift in maternal personnel. Early on she had endowed Naomi with a name that sounded like "Neema," a collaboration, she thought, of Naomi and Mama. "Neema up," she would instruct. "Neema juice." She was not affectionate, particularly, but she liked to lay a proprietary hand—often sticky with apple cider or gritty with crumbs—at the base of Naomi's throat, patting the revealed triangle of winter-pale skin. It was a sweet gesture, a little baffling, but in lieu of kisses or baby hugs Naomi welcomed its reassurance. As for herself, she kissed Polly whenever she could, and took as her chosen lullabies Meg Christian songs, which even Meg Christian might not have found appropriate for an eighteen-month-old: *So many years I've been bitter, wanting to be someone else. Nature had formed me, and the world had conformed me into thinking I must be less than the bravest and the best, better find me a nest to take care of, and let somebody stronger take care of me. But now I'm glad to be a woman . . .* Sometimes she caught herself like this, crooning feminist anthems, dressing Polly in black coveralls and peasant shirts made by peasant collectives in Central America (these had to be specially ordered from New York), and was sufficiently acute to find herself a little ridiculous. If she were mine, Naomi thought, this is how I would raise her, that's all, to grow up and write her name on the world. But when she thought—when she made herself think—of Heather triumphant, Heather exonerated of this cruel absurdity, and Polly restored to that house and that mother on Sabbath Creek Road, she knew instead that Polly would grow up to be like Heather, a slate on which the world wrote.

But this was far down inside her, deep and safe, obscured by the great weight of her fury at the injustice Heather was suffering, and Polly—who after all deserved her mother—was suffering. Naomi found herself calling old friends, at night after Polly was asleep, reporting the outrage unfolding up here in the remote north, beyond the safe pales of their academic groves. After these months of local myopia, it seemed incredible to her that anyone could know nothing about this, about what was happening in Goddard, and she heard herself shrieking Heather's story over and over to these women she had once known so well, until the story seemed reduced to its essence: a working-class woman, a single mother, seduced and abandoned by a classic male user and left alone to raise a child unacknowledged and unsupported by its father, a strong woman indicted by a community intolerant of her independence, a woman whose sexuality was abhorred, whose fertility was suspect, and whose child was shunned, a scapegoat accused on the flimsiest of nonevidence of the most heinous of acts, preemptively convicted, preemptively condemned to be locked up forever and to lose her daughter. Unspeakable. Repellent. Horrifying.

She didn't know what she expected. Surely she did not think

they would all charter a bus and set off from their own lives to insert themselves into this unfolding disaster. She was not thinking that, no. Because they were all tired, these busy women. They were studying for bar exams, and forming Womanspirit covens, which convened on Boston Common or the Sheep Meadow at dawn, and finding black children—that is, the right black children, the black children of Afro-American Studies professors and civil rights attorneys—for their own white children to play with, so that their children would not have the ethnically homogeneous childhoods they had had themselves.

So what else was going on? they wanted to know. And Naomi, thwarted, told again the old, old stories of the dissolution of her marriage, which most of them knew already. It surprised her how stale this felt, and far away.

And did she ever hear from Daniel now? And did she know what he was doing?

What *was* he doing, Naomi thought, because this was asked with a bit of an edge, as if they were asking about a specific thing, and whether she knew it or not. And so she let them tell her, and it turned out to be not that big a deal. Daniel was living with a woman named Katrina Frosch. This was said with some rather irritating respect.

Evidently it was generally known that Katrina Frosch had once lived with a guy who had once been a Weatherman.

Naomi hung up the phone and howled with bitter laughter. Ah, Daniel. Always the terrorist groupie, back to the very beginning. She remembered his abandoned Paul Robeson thesis speckled with "Amerika"'s, and his evasive, self-effacing murmurs of support for Bernardine Dohrn and her demented crew, as if he were in constant contact with them, a lone plant left to linger aboveground for purposes implied but unrevealed. She remembered the *Uncle Che Wants You* poster he had brought home in Ithaca one day, for the bathroom (at least they'd *had* a bathroom). How nice for him, Naomi thought meanly, that he finally got somebody with the proper radical credentials, not another materialist *hausfrau* who just wanted to shit in a capitalist toilet.

The trajectories of history, it occurred to Naomi, always look so much straighter in retrospect. And powerful! As if your life knew where it was going the whole time, even though

back then it all felt so, well, flaccid and unsure of itself. But
if Daniel was still on the path, Naomi mused, if he was passing
the time down there in Woodstock doing what he'd always
done, and if she was *also* still on the path, and had never
changed her mind about anything that felt important, then how
had they begun in the same place and ended up so far apart?
They couldn't both be right, she thought. But was it possible
that they could both be wrong?

It seemed to Naomi now that she no longer quite *knew* the
things she had known so effortlessly in the past. It seemed to
her that she had operated on the gentle dinner-table indoctri-
nations of her childhood and the rather more energetic ones
of her student years, and beyond these—because she was not
only a vessel for other people's ideologies, surely not—she
had operated on pure instinct.

Naomi had some faith in her instinct. Instinct told her she
had not lived—was not living—*badly*. Instinct told her that
what was happening to Heather was wrong—as plainly, reassuringly wrong as segregation or women denied control of
their own bodies. In the distracted voices of her old friends,
above the chatter of their children and spouses in their far-off
kitchens, Naomi had expected to hear at least an echo of her
own outrage, but she had heard only sighs and regret, a kind
of *yuck yuck well that's patriarchy for you!* It seemed impossible that she was the last one out here, she thought, putting
down the phone, the last little child in the hide-and-seek game,
valiantly, rigidly, stubbornly, *stupidly* enduring the mud and
the cold as night fell around her and all the other children
went in for dinner. And she hated this. She hated the burden
of pretending there were other people holding the banner and
not just her, when it *was* just her—trawling along with this
long white flag behind her and no one to pick it up out of the
mud. Always a bride! And here she comes, Naomi Roth: army
of one, inheritor of the Fannie Lou Hamer mantle of honor,
founder and sole member of the northern New Hampshire
chapter of Sisterhood Is Powerful . . .

Sisterhood, she thought, is pathetic.

Sisterhood, she observed, could not be enforced.

Moreover, she really didn't want to have Heather Pratt for
a sister, anyway.

But the trial was near now, and her seat was assigned: left

of the aisle (of course!) and foursquare behind the accused.
Judith was counting on her, and Heather, too, she supposed,
and in his own way Charter and his hordes of the righteous.
It was all so old and tired, Naomi thought, and she was old,
and too tired for this now, and for all the efforts she had made,
her hands—this time of year, always at this time of year, and
nothing to do with the babies she had touched, Naomi told
herself—were not quite clean.

Chapter 29

Theme and Variation

DON'T COME FOR JURY SELECTION, JUDITH HAD said. Why get depressed before it's absolutely necessary?

And it was as bad as she'd warned, she told Naomi, reporting in nightly phone calls, her voice wrung with exhaustion. Four days in a row the prospective jurors had come through the courtroom and the jury box, like sheep through a dip, bobbing along in their bland prejudices. Many of them glared at Heather outright, and one woman, plainly pregnant, said she didn't think she could stand to be in the same room as the girl, as if there were some awful thing coming off Heather, some pestilent fog like Cecil B. DeMille's Angel of Death in *The Ten Commandments*, that might poison her own bright child. Only a few had not heard about the case, and those, when they gleaned the elements involved, seemed so horrified that they looked pleadingly at the judge to release them. Judith only wished she herself might be released so easily.

There were a few, she said to Naomi, who seemed capable of distinguishing fictional from factual, and these Judith accepted, even in cases where they acknowledged reading about the case. One social worker she desperately wanted was dispatched by Charter's peremptory challenge. Another prospective juror, an amiable gay man who taught at a junior college near Warren, dashed her hopes when he said that he honestly didn't think he could put aside the opinion he'd already formed, that Heather Pratt could not possibly have committed the crimes with which she was charged, and that therefore some police impropriety must have played a part in her interrogation. He was out of the courtroom within seconds of having spoken these words. Charter did not even have to use one of his peremptories.

Judith, for her part, shot through most of her allowed challenges on the first day, and the rest on the second, watching the number sink, like somebody waiting for her money to run out and calculating when she must begin to starve. She had no choice; they were so terrible, these people, with their palpable disgust for Heather and for Judith herself. They looked at Charter even as Judith was asking them questions, they were that unwilling to engage with anything she might bring to bear on the issues at hand. She began to lower her standards: ignorance was acceptable, imbecility not; distaste for the accused was preferable to outright, visible revulsion; people who had read about the case in the newspaper were better than people who'd heard it through the grapevine. And so, inevitably, they began to build a jury. Open-minded? Let's say, not closed entirely. Capable of hearing the truth? Naomi asked, and she heard Judith, far away on the other side of Goddard, sigh into the telephone. Whatever *that* was, Judith said.

On the Tuesday they were set to begin, Judith telephoned Naomi early, even before Polly was awake, to tell Naomi she should wear a skirt. And stockings.

"Stockings?" Naomi grumbled, half asleep. She hadn't owned any in years.

"It's important. You're going to be sitting behind us. You need to be completely unobjectionable."

"That's disgraceful," Naomi said. She regretted it instantly. "Listen, of course, I'll stop on the way into town and get something."

"I wouldn't ask if it wasn't important," Judith said shortly. "You're perfectly right that it shouldn't matter, but it does. So if you're going to come at all, you've got to promise me that—"

"I know." She sat up. "I know. I'm sorry. Christ." She noted the clock. "You're up early."

"I've been up for a while," Judith said. "I'm not a natural at this, you know."

"You *are*," Naomi soothed. "Heather couldn't have a more suitable advocate."

Judith was silent. Then Naomi heard a small dark laugh. "I don't know if that's a compliment."

"Of course it's a compliment," Naomi said. "I mean, think what you've been able to accomplish already."

What Judith had been able to accomplish already was a showdown over Naomi's appearance on Charter's list of po-

tential witnesses. She'd argued, in a pretrial motion, that Naomi's experience of discovering the bodies of the two infants
had no bearing on the issues being decided at trial, and that
Charter had only listed her in an attempt to remove her from
the courtroom and deny Heather the support of her only friend,
the woman who was caring for her child. Not so, Charter had
claimed. He counted on Naomi's testimony to help jurors "discover" the babies' bodies as she herself had discovered them,
to impress upon the jurors the extent of the babies' injuries.

But surely the medical examiner would be able to establish
this, Judith countered. Surely there was nothing a layperson
could add. And with so few potential benefits, she hardly
thought Charter would call a witness whose antipathy toward
the prosecution was so well known to him.

The judge, Hayes by name, corpulent and with a tendency
to plant his lantern jaw atop his two thumbs in a posture of
concentration, turned to Charter. Was this in fact known to
him? he asked.

Charter said that he did not consider Naomi's feelings to be
relevant, one way or another. He would not be denied such an
important witness just because the defendant needed a cheering
section.

Then could Mr. Charter explain why, with the trial about to
begin, he had never contacted his important witness to go over
her testimony?

"I'd like an offer of proof, your honor," Judith said, facing
the judge. "It is important to my client to have her friend here.
I'd like to know exactly what Mr. Charter hopes Ms. Roth's
testimony will reveal. Perhaps we can stipulate to some information and save everybody some time."

Which sounded reasonable to the judge. He looked to Charter, but Charter wouldn't budge.

Or, Judith suggested brightly, as if she were only now thinking of this, they could compromise by having Charter agree to
call Naomi as his first witness. After that, Naomi would be
free to remain in the courtroom for the duration of the trial.

Charter glared at her, and Judith smiled. He had no wish to
call Naomi at all, of course. But now, just possibly, he might
be forced to. And if he went first with Naomi's testimony,
Judith would be able to establish some positive impressions of
Heather's character at the outset.

"Well, that's an interesting suggestion," said Hayes with approval. "And I would think that's probably the place for this testimony, if it's about discovering the bodies. Right at the beginning should work well for you, Mr. Charter."

Grimly, Charter smiled. Judith smiled, too. Then she went back to her office and broke the news to a horrified Naomi, who hadn't even known about the witness list.

She didn't want to testify, Naomi insisted. And there was nothing to testify *to*! She'd only found them; she didn't know anything *about* them. Judith made soothing noises. Charter didn't want her to testify either, but now he had to put her on the stand. And then she proceeded to list a few of the points Naomi would make when she got there.

"We might not get to you today," Judith said now, "but even so, you need to appear conservative."

"Of course," Naomi said ironically. "I'm a prosecution witness, after all."

"You're Heather's witness. And he'll try to bait you, but you need to keep cool. Your character has to vouch for her character, all the time."

All right. Naomi hung up the phone and took advantage of the continuing silence from the next room to hunt out Polly's things for the day. Mrs. Horgan was being very kind about the arrangements, and Naomi appreciated her sensitivity, but her idea of suitable toys was a Barbie in the hand of each little girl and a plastic gun in the hand of each little boy. Naomi was sending Polly off with her own suitable books and gender nonspecific stuffed animals, and a *Free to Be You and Me* tape to be played at nap time. There was no way around Mrs. Horgan's American cheese and Wonder bread, but Naomi filled a bag with apples and dried apricots and bottles of organic grape juice. Polly slept on soundly, even as the first day of her mother's trial began.

Naomi washed her face and wound her hair into a heavy bun, sticking it into place with a fistful of metal hairpins. She dressed in a black wool skirt, a little snug across her rear, a thin white sweater, and a black wool jacket that didn't quite match the skirt; that black always goes with black is a myth propagated by urban dwellers, she thought. She did not recognize herself, exactly, though there was a certain resemblance, like a variation on a family theme. She looked unobjectionable, and a little old. She went to wake Polly.

Naomi had not been to a trial since her own, years before, on charges of disturbing the peace in Ithaca—a lie-in at Day Hall over CIA recruitment on campus had gotten nasty. She walked up the granite steps of the Peytonville courthouse with a set jaw and a staunch refusal to acknowledge any grandeur in her surroundings. The shoddy behavior of shoddy men must not be in any way elevated by the presence of polished stone, or massive plaques of the names of local boys gone to soldiers, or fierce patriarchs chiseled out of boulders. This thing stank, irredeemably, and it galled her that she was obligated to dress for such a sham of truth seeking and justice, and to respect its rituals. She saw Judith at the top of the wide staircase, just inside the lobby, immaculate in a severe gray suit. She looked beautiful, Naomi thought, and she kissed Judith and told her so.

"Opening statements are important," Judith said. "Juries remember you this way."

"Nice pearls," said Naomi.

"Thanks. Nice stockings." She smiled. "Hey, it's for a good cause."

There was press around, Naomi saw, the local writers looking cowed by their national counterparts, and there were faces from Goddard, some of which acknowledged her. Then Charter came through, trailing staff and reporters, signaling his stature with the intense cadence of his gait. He stopped before Judith and Naomi and nodded. "Mrs. Friedman."

She gave him a cool look. "I prefer Ms., Mr. Charter."

"Well"—he smiled disingenuously—"I'll do my best. Old habits are sometimes difficult to break." He turned to Naomi. "*Ms*. Roth."

"Hello," Naomi said. She was embarrassed to hear the smallness of her own voice.

"Ordinarily, as I'm sure Ms. Friedman has explained to you, you would not be permitted to enter the courtroom until you were called to testify." He waited for her reaction: the flash of alarm, the glance at Judith. "But because I am going to call you as the state's first witness, I'm going to let the formality pass. You are welcome to hear opening arguments."

He was extending himself, she realized. He wanted her to feel grateful to him when she testified. Naomi smiled. "Well, thank you."

"I will be asking you simple, specific questions," he went on, his goal evidently attained. "If you could direct yourself to them, I would appreciate it. There is no reason to bring your personal feelings about either Miss Pratt or myself into your answers. We all want the same thing here."

She started at this extraordinary statement. "Mr. Charter—"

"It's not for you to decide. It's not for me to decide. We'll give *them* the information"—he dipped his head to the side, as if the jury were arrayed before them in this crowded hallway—"and they'll do the deciding. Please do not contaminate this process with your opinions or your ideology. If you can assure me that you will do that, then I will make the same assurance to you."

"Naomi will answer your questions to the extent of her abilities," Judith broke in. "She will make no unsolicited comments. And I thank you for your sensitivity to her situation." She placed a hand on Naomi's arm. "Let's go inside."

They walked past him. Naomi was dazed. "What was that—"

"Damage control," Judith whispered. "It's all right. We talked about what might happen when you're up there. It's going to be fine."

They moved forward, through a courtroom already dense with people. It was not a large room, but it was made to seem so by its two large windows, which gave it a lofty air, and by its ceiling, which was also high, though dangling a symmetry of silver vents and pipes. Naomi took an empty seat behind the defense table to the left of the judge's bench, and the wood joints of her chair gave an ominous creak. Judith unpacked her briefcase. Charter appeared not to have a briefcase of his own, though his aides were unpacking the ones they had carried. There was so much paper, Naomi thought, looking at the piles and stacks of files, and the protruding bits of black-and-white photographs. So much from so little, and all of it brought into being by her. How she wished she could take it back now. She wished that she had pushed them back into the water, those babies, weighting them down so that they would never surface and be known, or be photographed and fought over and used to wreck the lives of living people. If only she had left them there, and the water had taken them away downstream or buried them too deeply for her to touch. If only, she thought grimly, they'd been just a little farther out of reach, or she'd been a little less intent on reaching out; but then she was always sticking her fingers in, wasn't that the point? And her nose, where it wasn't welcome. The point of a hairpin pricked her scalp, and she reached back to adjust it.

Then Heather was with them. She wore a tan dress Judith had bought for her, high-buttoned and with blue embroidery around the neck, and her cropped hair had filled in a bit, softening the shock of her small head with its defined bones. She was thin now, Naomi saw, and for the first time it occurred to her to berate herself over not having recognized Heather's pregnancy the previous summer. The extra flesh of her torso, the aftermath of Polly which the second baby had inherited, was gone now, leaving a figure not so much lean as downright feeble. She reached for Heather's shoulder. "Hi," Heather said, turning.

"Hi, Heather." Her voice sounded unnaturally jolly.

"How is Polly?"

"She's doing great," Naomi said heartily. "She calls me 'Neema.' " It was meant as a reassurance that Polly knew her own mother and Heather needn't worry about being usurped, but Heather looked as if she might cry, anyway.

"Oh, don't," Judith broke in, putting her arm around Heather's shoulder. "Just sit down, yes?"

Heather turned and sat. The judge was announced, and Naomi, seeing him for the first time, thought him effortlessly authoritative, broad and physically dense in his black robe, and sporting a natural scowl. Born to judge, she thought grimly, as Hayes exchanged the kind of studiously impersonal nod with Charter that could only imply the closeness of their friendship beyond this room. He welcomed the audience and preemptively castigated them for the variety of bad behaviors they would henceforth refrain from. Judith was writing on her legal pad, her head down. When the door opened, she sat up, shifted in her chair, and placed her hand over Heather's. Naomi could not see Heather's face, but she did see the small jerk of her shoulders as those two hands met, and the discomfort that lingered after it. Perhaps this, too, was part of Judith's intention, that they should see Heather first like this: the woman whose sensuality had supposedly overbrimmed to murder, unwilling even to be touched.

The jury was welcomed, then thanked, then charged with the solemnity their task required. The gavel was raised and brought down sharply in a theatrical gesture for their benefit, because they all expected it. Charter got up, and ritually shot his cuffs. This was to be a habitual gesture, the first note of frailty she had ever seen in him, but it did not make her like him better.

Charter walked to the jury and placed a hand on the bar before the first row of their chairs. A finger tapped the wood. He seemed to be considering.

"Ladies and gentlemen"—his voice was uncharacteristically soft—"I think you'll understand what I mean when I say that I am sorry to see you here today. I'm sorry"—he waved his hand behind him at the spectators, but kept his eyes forward—"that any of us are here. Indeed, in my many years of prosecuting men and women accused of crimes in this state, I have never been involved with a case that filled me with so much regret, that made me so heartbroken. And I sincerely apologize to you for subjecting you to the sad and terrible things I am going to have to tell you about."

He sighed, and touched the ridge of his curious hair. "Now, some of you are parents. Some of you aren't. I'm not a parent myself, but that does not protect me from the horror of a dead child. I feel that horror, ladies and gentlemen, and I know you will, too. But your job is harder than mine, or indeed anyone else's. Because you cannot let yourselves stop at the horror at the heart of this case. You have to go forward, to go through it. And you have to do it professionally, and intellectually. You have to consider the testimony that will be given here, both by our witnesses and by my opponent's witnesses, and not give in to grief or recriminations. Because your job is to tell us how we should confront these terrible events. This terrible crime." He sighed, then turned slightly. He was looking at Heather. "Please understand that I am not asking you to explain this crime to us. The murder of two infant girls is an incomprehensible act, and I don't expect you to be able to comprehend it any more than I will ever be able to comprehend it myself. We must be very clear about the distinction between understanding *what* happened and understanding *why*. Put *why* right out of your minds, ladies and gentlemen. *Why* is between Heather Pratt and God."

Naomi saw the stiff, minuscule shake of Judith's head. Her own hands twisted together in her lap.

"Heather Pratt is on trial today for the murders of two infant girls. The girls were twin daughters, born in secret. Heather was their mother, and you will be hearing soon about their paternity. But first you'll hear about what was done to these little babies, how they were heartlessly killed, then left for someone else to find. What kind of woman would do this? Well, I don't know that I'm able to answer that question, but I can answer the question of what kind of person Heather Pratt *is*. She is a woman who was brought to the attention of the police for disrobing in plain sight, in a public place. She is a woman who thought nothing of having an affair with a man who was married to someone else, and nothing about having his baby. She is a woman who wantonly continued the affair, even after the married man made it clear to her that he would never leave his wife. She is a woman who hid her pregnancy, who didn't seek prenatal care for her child, who had her babies in secret and disposed of them in secret. And if they had not been found—at different times and in different places, but ironically by the same person—none of us would be here today."

He shook his head distastefully, as if that irony were Heather's fault, too.

"But more than anything else, ladies and gentlemen, Heather Pratt is a woman who confessed to this crime. Who gave details. Who showed us the weapon with which she murdered one of her daughters. Who knew it was wrong to do as she did!" He let this sink in, making sure each of them got a long look at his anger. "You're going to want me to explain that to you, and I can't. You're also going to want me to explain why Heather Pratt, who is by all accounts a good mother to the daughter she had eighteen months ago, should turn against the twin daughters she had last September. And that I think I *can* explain. I think Heather loved her first child because, at the time of her first pregnancy she thought her lover, her married lover, would leave his wife and marry her. But by the time of her second pregnancy, she knew better. She knew because her lover had made it clear to her that he would never leave his wife for her, and so she hated the child, or children, she was carrying. She told no one that she was expecting these children. She didn't notify the midwife who had delivered her daughter Polly, and when the twins were born, she did what was necessary so that no one would ever find out they existed." He waited for this to sink in. A few of the jurors, Naomi saw, could not look at Charter now, or at Heather either. Charter sighed, milking the moment. "I cannot know her state of mind at this time, but I'll tell you what I honestly believe. Heather's state of mind is secondary to the brutality of her acts. This woman"—he turned from the railing. He pointed, a jab in the air—"gave birth to two beautiful, healthy baby girls and immediately put them to death. Now, some of you may feel she deserves our compassion, and I don't say that's untrue. What I do say, ladies and gentlemen, is that those babies have the first claim on our compassion. We are here for *them*, because *they* are not here. It is not our job to succor their mother, who *is* still here among us, healthy and strong. Let us leave Heather to her conscience, and to God."

He turned back to them now, the preacher to the captive converted. "Now, as if this story weren't amazing enough, there is a further twist. The evidence will show, ladies and gentlemen, that these two little girls, twins born to the same mother, were in fact only half sisters to each other. Yes." He nodded sagely as they looked at him, incredulous. "It's true. No, you don't hear about it all the time, but that doesn't mean it doesn't happen. It happened here. There is a doctor who will tell you about this process, which has a funny-sounding name: superfecundation." He kept, Naomi noted, a very straight face. A poker face. If she didn't know better, she thought, she might believe him herself. In the jury box, however, it was a different matter. Their eyes widened. One or two looked stunned, another grinned. "Now, for this to take place, a woman must have sexual relations with two men in a given time period, which is precisely what Heather Pratt did. She had sex with her married lover, and then she had sex with a second man. We know the name of this man, and you will learn it soon."

Naomi, despite herself, looked at Heather. A second man? It was not possible. How could that be possible? Then, furious at herself for even entertaining the notion, she gave an exag-

gerated sigh, shook her head, and earned a glare from Judge
Hayes himself.

"Hard to believe? Of yourself, maybe. Of your friends, your
wives, or your daughters, absolutely. But hard to believe of a
woman who was quite comfortable with her promiscuity? Who
saw nothing wrong with pursuing her affairs? I think you will
understand, once you learn of Heather Pratt's history, why I
am confident that superfecundation took place, and that she
gave birth to twin half sisters.

"Now"—Charter folded his arms in an uncomfortable ap-
proximation of a casual posture—"before we begin, there's
something I want to say to you about what might happen
here." He eyed them, looking grim. "All of us say that we're
here to find the truth, that's what a trial is for—finding the
truth. It's a nice thought, but I've got to warn you that, for a
process devoted to truth, there's a fair amount of—well, let's
call it 'distortion,' involved. I'm not saying my opponent is
going to lie to you." He stepped back and put up his hands.
"Not at all. But what she might well do is try to get you to
forget who the victim is in this case. Except I know that you're
stronger than that. I know you won't forget," he said approv-
ingly. "I know that you won't forget, as my opponent speaks
to you, and tries to create sympathy in you, for her client"—
he lifted a warning finger—"as I can assure you she will try
to do, that Heather Pratt is not the victim in this case. The
victims in this case are not in the courtroom with us today,
but they aren't far from where we are sitting, either. They are
in a freezer in the basement of this building!" Naomi surveyed
the faces in the jury box. To her dismay, they were riveted,
grim, and a few were visibly stifling tears. "Two little girls!"
Charter thundered. "Two little girls who will never grow up
to play with a doll, or have a sweet-sixteen party, or be brides,
or indeed have babies of their own. Beautiful newborn infants,
healthy in every way. One stabbed through the heart and
thrown into the river that runs behind Heather Pratt's house.
One drowned in a little pond in Heather Pratt's back field.
They came from the same womb, ladies and gentlemen, and
they were murdered by the same hand."

One juror, a woman Naomi's age, with hair already gone
gray, had lost the fight. She wiped at her tears with the back

of her hand, but kept her eyes on the D.A. Naomi groaned inwardly.

"It isn't easy to judge someone's guilt or innocence, no matter how clear a case seems. I want you to know that I'm mindful of that, and I don't belittle the difficulty of what your job is here. I appreciate the work you're going to have to do, and I know it'll be hard. I'm not saying you have to feel nothing at all for this young lady who's on trial, but it's far more important that you keep your mind on what you know is true, what you know she did, and more than anything else, on who she did it to. *That* is truth, ladies and gentlemen. And that is what I know you will affirm to us once this case is over. I thank you for all the hard work you're going to do."

And he turned and walked back to his seat and sat down.

Judith looked over at him, her disdain evident to Naomi, even in profile. She gave Heather's arm a comforting squeeze and performed a small, disbelieving shake of the head for the jury's benefit before getting to her feet. Then she stood, looming over Heather. Her height made Heather seem small, and though Naomi couldn't see Heather's face, she was able to discern the dejected sag of her shoulders. "Ladies and gentlemen," Judith began, "I share Mr. Charter's skepticism about finding truth in this trial, but for a different reason. It's a reason that has nothing to do with you. You are a fine jury—intelligent, and capable of the difficult task that's required of you here. But we begin with a terrible story, with a terrible fact at its center: two little babies, dead. And that's about the only thing District Attorney Charter and I can agree about." She paused. "You see, usually, when a case comes to trial, a jury gets to hear two sides of the same story. Two variations, I guess you'd call it. Like, variation one: Dick shot Jane because he hated her for having an affair with another man. Or, variation two: Dick didn't mean to shoot Jane; it was an accident, because he thought there was an intruder in the house, and he made a tragic mistake."

She shook her head. "Not in this case. In this case we can't even agree on what the story *is*. You're not going to hear two possible ways of telling what happened. You're going to hear two *completely different versions* of the events that have brought us all to this courtroom today. And you're going to have to decide what makes sense to you. What feels like a rational account and what feels like a fairy tale.

"Now, before I get into that," Judith said, her voice dropping from the strident to the mournful, "I want you to understand that we're *all* affected by those two poor little girls. We *all* want to understand what happened to them, and yes, we want to blame the people who harmed them. But that's not why we're here."

She stepped around her table and leaned back on it, her legs outstretched, but crossed at the ankles in a delicate way.

"We're here because of one man's fantasy." She shrugged. "It sounds bad, believe me, I know. But it's true. We're here because one man made up his mind about this case a long time ago, and he refused to admit he was wrong when the evidence clearly indicated that he was. He couldn't admit that he had made a mistake, and as a result of that, this young woman"— she touched Heather's hand—"has spent the last five months in prison, separated from her baby, whom she loves deeply. She's spent those months waiting for this court case. Dreading this court case, which terrifies her. And I'll tell you something else. Heather Pratt has no idea what the case of a murdered baby found in a river has to do with her. But she has a very good idea of what it can do *to* her."

Judith sighed. "Let me be clear about something. I'm not saying that the district attorney went out of his way to make a mistake, or that he set out to railroad my client, a young woman he'd never laid eyes on before last fall. Mr. Charter is a decent man, and I'm sure he embarked on his investigation with every intention of getting to the bottom of a terrible crime. He made some mistakes, but I don't fault him for them. But he refused to acknowledge those mistakes, and I certainly do fault him for that.

"Now, let me see," she said, cocking her head, "let me see if I can find a way to explain to you what I mean." She sighed, and appeared to think, but Naomi knew Judith far too well to imagine she was just working this out now. "Let's say," she said, "you wanted to glue something on your living-room wall. Like . . . let's say you went down to New Orleans on vacation and you brought back one of those masks they have down there in the souvenir shops. They're made of ceramic, and they're painted black and white and decorated with paint and feathers, and sometimes glitter. You know the ones I mean?"

She eyed her audience and waited for nods: tentative rapport.
"So you bring it home and you decide to glue it onto your
living-room wall. But unfortunately the glue doesn't stick very
well. Maybe it holds for a day or two, but the mask is heavy.
It needs strong support, like a nail or a shelf to keep it up.
The glue's just not up to the job. So the mask falls off onto
the floor. But you try again, because you want that mask on
your wall, and it looks great where you put it, and you're not
going to be defeated by a little bit of glue. But you know, this
time, when you put the mask onto the wall, it doesn't really
look quite as nice as it did the first time. You've got some of
that old glue underneath the new glue, and it shows around
the edges, and what's more, the mask doesn't really sit flat
against the wall anymore. But hey, at least it's sticking."

She pushed off the table and walked toward them.

"Then it stops sticking. It falls off again. By this time,
maybe that mask is trying to tell you something, right? Like
it just isn't meant to be hung up on walls with only a little
glue, right? But you are really determined by now. *Damn it,
that mask is going right back on the wall!* So you throw on a
little more glue, and by now the whole thing is a real mess. It
looks like an amateur job, with the old glue and the new glue,
and it's kind of crooked. Well, how long is it going to last
this time?"

She leaned forward, touching the railing.

"That's what you're going to have to tell us." She eyed
them, letting her gaze drift from face to face. "Now usually a
defendant will be brought to trial for a crime when there is
evidence linking him or her to that crime. That is not the case
in this trial. We're not here," she said, her voice heating up,
"because a trial of evidence pointed to Heather Pratt. Mr. Charter did not lay a foundation for his accusation on this most
serious of charges, I'm sorry to say. He just hung his mask in
the first place that felt right to him. But when it fell off the
wall, when it became clear that he'd accused the wrong person,
did Mr. Charter get to work finding a better place? A more
appropriate person to stick it on? He did not. He just threw on
a little more glue and tried again. And when it happened the
second time, he tried *again*, and every time he redid his original bad job, it got worse. Because no matter how nice that
mask looked where he put it, there were other forces at work

here, and they were much stronger than the little bit of glue, of conjecture, and of suspicion. And of dislike, ladies and gentlemen." She stopped and shook her head briskly.

"What was stronger? Well, gravity, for one thing. Reality. The truth."

Naomi looked at Charter. His cheeks were flushed, as if two blazes of livid red had been applied by some unsubtle cosmetician. He sat rigid, the fingers of his left hand splayed and stiff.

"We are all here today for only one reason. My opponent in this case, a decent man and a well-meaning man, made a rush to judgment based on his own moral prejudice, and in so doing, he has destroyed lives." She paused. She wanted them to see that she would not take this back. "This is a terrible accusation, I know, but I have to make it. Mr. Charter was driven to find the perpetrator of a crime we all abhor, and so he turned to a woman whose *morality* he abhorred, and he made her into a murderess. He accused Heather Pratt of murdering the infant girl found in the Sabbathday River on September 22. When she denied that she had done this, he didn't believe her. Well"—Judith shrugged, a half smile—"I guess I wouldn't say that's uncommon, to deny a crime." Then her face hardened. "But then Heather told her interrogators that she *had* had a stillborn child a few weeks before, and she begged them for the chance to show them the body of that child. They ridiculed her. They would not allow her to take them to the place where her own child's stillborn body had been put. And when that body was discovered—and it was easily discovered! There was no criminal attempt to hide the body. It was found simply by looking where Heather said to look—when it was found, Mr. Charter did not even pause to consider that he had been wrong about Heather, that there was in fact a real murderer, still unidentified, still out there. No. He simply affixed a new charge to his accusation. Heather Pratt had murdered not one baby but two! She had, we were asked to believe, given birth to *twin* daughters, murdered them in *different* ways, and disposed of their bodies in two *separate* places. He was that determined not to be proved in error! Being right, ladies and gentlemen, was more important to him than preventing the absolute destruction of this woman's life." She paused for effect, but to Naomi's eye, the jurors still looked dubious. They didn't trust Judith, she saw. And they didn't like her accusatory tone. Naomi's stomach clenched. She wished she could speak to Judith, but it was too late.

"Still," Judith went on, almost jauntily, "that was nothing compared to what happened next. *Next*"—she shook her head in exasperated disbelief—"some genuine evidence entered this investigation. Forensic evidence that had nothing to do with what kind of person Heather Pratt is, or what Mr. Charter thought of her. And this impartial forensic evidence, which Mr. Charter himself will be telling you about, proved to him that Heather Pratt's lover—the father of her daughter Polly and of the stillborn daughter born last September—could not have been the father of the infant found first, in the Sabbathday River, if, by some chance, Heather was its mother. Did this indicate to Mr. Charter that he might have made a mistake? After all, hadn't he believed, prior to this report, that Heather had had twins in the normal way?"

She regarded Heather, then turned back to the jury and shook her head with an *isn't this crazy?* expression on her face.

"Well, that was before he had this actual *evidence*. Do you know what he wants us to believe now? He wants us to believe that Heather—who claims that she gave birth to one child, a child who died tragically at birth, a child whose blood type is consistent with that of Heather's lover—actually had twin children *fathered by two different men*." She let the sound of her incredulity linger.

"Anywhere else," Judith sighed, "this might be a comedy. But here"—she gestured with her hand—"it's a tragedy. Because this young woman, who has already suffered the hardship of being abandoned by her lover while pregnant with his second child, who has already struggled alone, without any emotional or financial support, to raise the child she already had, and who has already experienced the devastation of a stillborn child—this young mother has now been declared a murderess. She has been deprived of her livelihood, thrown in jail for nearly six months. She has had her daughter—whom she adores and to whom she is an excellent mother—taken away from her." She stopped, letting them see her disbelief, and her compassion. "And why? Why Heather Pratt, out of all the women he might have accused? What made Heather Pratt such a perfect candidate for a murderess? Well, it's very simple. Heather was a bad woman. She did bad things. She had an affair with a married man—terrible! She had a child without being married. Also terrible! And she refused to apologize for it, or be shamed by it. She showed her first pregnancy in public. Later, she showed off her daughter Polly. She refused to take the hint when people let her know she ought to go off and hide." Judith shook her head. "They never forgave her for that.

"Now," she went on, stepping back a bit, "it may well be that you don't approve of everything Heather Pratt has ever done. I'm not sure I approve myself. Heather made a lot of mistakes, I'm the last one to deny that. For starters, she fell in love with a heartless jerk instead of a decent guy. She wasn't responsible about birth control and she got pregnant. She continued the affair against all the evidence that her lover would never leave his wife and live with her, and she continued to be irresponsible about birth control, even though she must have understood, by this time, what the result of such behavior might be. So when Ashley Deacon finally broke off their relationship, and when Heather discovered that she was pregnant again, you can understand how unhappy and depressed she must have felt. That's no excuse for what happened next. Heather had an obligation to make some kind of preparation for the birth of her second child, and she didn't do it, with fatal results." Judith turned and looked at Heather squarely, but Heather did not look back. She was examining her hands, cupped open before her on the table, as if she were trying to read her own fate in the lines. She was also crying, but silently. "And those, ladies and gentlemen, are the crimes of Heather Pratt. They are serious crimes, but they are not the crimes with which this court has charged her. And I know you know that there's a world between Heather's actual failings and the murder of two children."

She paused for a moment. She looked pointedly at Charter, then back at the jury, intimate but firm. "Now, from all this conjecture, you must think there's very little actual evidence in this case. You'd be wrong to think that, ladies and gentlemen, because there is evidence. You won't hear it from the prosecution, because it interferes with their myth of Heather the murderous mother, but I can assure you that you're going to hear it from the defense. The *evidence* will show that there was no second man in her life, no phantom father of her phantom twin. The *evidence* will show that Heather was pregnant with one fetus only. The *evidence* will show that it is entirely possible that Heather's baby died naturally, if tragically, at birth, precisely as she told the police it had. The *evidence* will show that we can never even know whether Heather's infant achieved life." She shook her head, grave. "*It might never even have lived.* No life, no death. Certainly no murder. No *crime*, ladies and gentlemen. Heather's child was stillborn, and she buried the body herself, with her own hands. Was that proper? Probably not. But it hardly warrants the treatment Heather has received, and it certainly isn't a double murder."

Judith went back to her place, and there she stood, her hand at Heather's shoulder again. Naomi was close enough now to see that shoulder twitch at the touch.

"Mr. Charter chose to affix the mask of a murderer to Heather Pratt. But he chose the wrong person. The mask doesn't fit. It's *wrong*. It's held in place only by the condemnation of people like himself, people who don't approve of Heather Pratt, and that, ladies and gentlemen, is far too weak a glue to make a multiple murder stick where it doesn't belong. I know you won't let that happen. I know you'll see truth where you're asked to see a fairy tale. I know you'll understand that we cannot avenge the deaths of two innocent babies with the life of one innocent woman. I know you'll be the voice of reason in this terrible case, where there has been so little reason until now. On Heather's behalf, I thank you for that."

She sat down. Naomi stared at Judith in blank awe. For a moment it had seemed to her that the jurors must stand in unison and walk out of the courtroom in protest, but instead they regained their individual composures and looked to the judge for guidance. And Judge Hayes, despite the burden of reason, did not rap his gavel and release them all from this realm of the absurd and the unjust. He called for the prosecution's first witness, and the trial began in earnest.

Chapter 30

So Help Her God

SHE COULD NOT IMAGINE WHY THEY CALLED IT the witness stand—Naomi would actually have preferred to stand, or to have the option of standing at least. But the seat she was directed to take was utterly ordinary, a plastic bucket on splayed metal spikes, even cracked in places and grubby everywhere else. It was not at all elevated but sat on the courtroom floor to one side of the judge's bench, diagonally across from the jury. Naomi looked at them and smiled nervously, but they were nervous, too, she saw, and did not smile back.

At the bailiff's request, she said her name. Then somebody held out a Bible.

Naomi gaped at it. Vaguely she understood what they wanted her to do, but she couldn't do that. Could she put her hand on her heart, maybe? Or pledge by something else, if she could think of something fast? Would they let her do that? The moment lengthened interminably.

"Ms. Roth?" somebody said.

Naomi looked up. Judge Hayes was frowning over at her.

"You need to swear."

"I swear," Naomi said. "I do. But . . ."

The bailiff was frowning at her. "You need to say it with your hand on the book."

"But I don't—" She looked over at Judith, who was glaring at her, frantic.

Instantly Naomi placed her palm on the cheap leather binding of the Bible and swore to tell the truth, *so help her God.* For about five different things at once, she was ashamed of herself. She looked at the jury, embarrassed, and hoped they would forgive her for Heather's sake.

Charter, still in his seat, milked the moment a bit, shaking his head in wonder. She tried to pull herself together, but her thoughts raced on, heated and bitter. It took all her strength to make her heels stop drumming the floor.

"You did not want to testify today, did you, Ms. Roth?"

"That's true," Naomi said, grateful at least that they'd begun, though a little perplexed by this opening volley.

"Am I right in thinking that you are not particularly in sympathy with the prosecution?"

"Yes," she said, growing more confused by the moment.

"And yet I have decided to begin my case against Heather Pratt with the testimony of a person who thinks I'm wrong about her. Why do you think I'm doing that, Ms. Roth?"

It occurred to her that she should laugh, but she couldn't muster the humor. "I really don't have any idea."

He sighed, as if she had disappointed him. "Well"—he got painfully to his feet—"why don't we talk about some things we *are* in agreement about. Would you please tell the jury about the morning of September 22 of last year."

"Oh," she said stupidly. "Of course. I was at the river. I mean the Sabbathday River. Just south of Goddard."

"And what were you doing at the river?" Charter said.

"Running. Well"—she blushed—"jogging, really. I don't run very fast."

"You're a regular jogger?"

"No. I should do it more." The truth was, she hadn't been jogging at all since that day last fall.

"And where were you, precisely?"

Naomi closed her eyes, then opened them quickly. She did not like what she saw when her eyes were closed.

"Near Nate's Landing. I'd say half a mile upstream."

"And did something make you stop in your jogging?"

Naomi paused. Powerfully, irrationally, she wanted to say no. No, she had seen nothing. No, she had found no dead baby. There was no Nelson Erroll, no medical examiner, no Robert Charter, no Heather Pratt. They could all rise and go home and laugh at their shared delusion of sin. She looked at him. He was waiting.

"I saw something," Naomi said.

"What did you see?"

She remembered, and shook her head slightly. "I thought it was a doll. It made me think of a doll I'd had when I was little."

"A doll in the river." He seemed to consider. He was leaning over his desk, his weight on his braced arms. "And what did this doll look like?"

She knew what he wanted, but she wouldn't give it to him. "I couldn't see very well."

"And yet you were intrigued enough to go closer."

"I was, yes. I thought someone must be missing the doll. I could get it back for them."

"You thought someone had left a doll in the river and you were going to get it back for them?"

It sounded much stupider in his voice. She frowned. Naomi nodded. "Yes."

"Was the . . . object close to the shore? So that you could reach out and grab hold of it?"

"No." She shook her head. "It was in the middle of the river. I had to pick my way over the stones."

"And the water would have been cold in late September, too, I imagine."

"Yes," said Naomi.

"And yet you say you thought this was only a doll some careless child had lost? And you were willing to slip on the rocks and get wet in the cold water? Just to retrieve a doll?"

"It wasn't a big deal, really."

"But rather excessive lengths to go to, for a *doll*, I think."

"Well, that's what I thought it was. I didn't think . . ."

"You didn't think what, Ms. Roth?"

"That it was anything else," Naomi said lamely. Then she looked him squarely in the face. "I didn't think it was a baby, Mr. Charter. I just thought some little kid might be missing her doll." So *sue me*, she thought. And, purely for her own satisfaction: *Go fuck yourself.*

"And yet"—he sighed—"as we all now know, it was indeed a baby. Will you tell us please how you made this discovery?"

She concentrated, trying for a dispassionate, clinical pitch. "I touched the leg. It was very cold. I turned it over. She was . . ." And here words failed her abruptly. She was . . . what? Butchered? Incised? Pierced? Put down? "I knew," she finally said, "that she was dead. A dead child."

"And a girl," he prodded.

"Yes. She was a girl."

"Ms. Roth," he said disingenuously, "I imagine this must be difficult for you, but I'd like you to tell the jury what you remember about the baby you found. About her face, for example."

Her face? Naomi squeezed shut her eyes. She could not look very well at the face of the baby, its points of white flesh and open gray eyes, the dark hairs floating in water around the baby's head. She realized now, after many months, that her understanding of the baby's face had been first forgotten and then reassembled, a composite both antiseptic and impersonal: generic baby. Probably the baby she might describe would owe as much to the Gerber label as to what she had seen in the Sabbathday River. For the first time, she truly understood the vulnerability of memory. If Charter wanted pathos for the jury, she was incapable of delivering it, and not out of spite, either.

She looked at him now. "You know, I don't really remember the baby's face very well. I'm trying to, but I've sort of forgotten and I don't want to remember it wrong. She was very small and still, that I do remember. And very white."

"The experience of finding the body must have been unpleasant."

Naomi nodded in agreement, though she did not trust the sympathy in his voice for one instant.

"It was. Awful."

"And what did you do when you found the baby's body?"

"I picked it up, of course. I ran to the road, back to my car. Then I wrapped it up and drove into town, to the police station."

"What did you wrap it in?"

For a moment she stared at him, perplexed. Then she remembered: the sampler. *A is for Apple.* Grotesque, but surely a coincidence. Surely he wouldn't try to make anything out of that.

"I really don't remember," Naomi said bravely, and Charter smiled at her and went to the evidence table. He took his time, hovering over the plastic bags, gazing down in particular at the knitting needle placed at the end nearest the jury, all very unnecessary, since Naomi herself could see the sampler perfectly well from where she was sitting, one slash of red over faded linen. *That's it over there*, she almost pointed.

"Would this have been it?" Charter lifted the bag in question. The red ghost of an A under shining plastic.

"Very likely," Naomi said dryly.

Charter entered the bag into evidence. The court reporter clicked. He held it out to Naomi.

"What is this, precisely, Ms. Roth?"

Well, *it's a contemporary example of American folk art, Mr. Charter*, Naomi thought, *a testament to the national character, and to artistry even in the face of deprivation, a form of expression available to girls and women who were denied education and sexuality, not to mention the right to work or control their own bodies or direct their own lives or leave fathers who beat them or husbands who beat them and probably, when you got right down to it, sons who beat them, too. And isn't it amazing that at the end of a long day of toil in a society that did not value her at all, a woman might have used the last hours before sleep and risk ruining her eyes to create something so useless and lovely as this sampler?*

"It's a sampler, from my company." She looked apologetically at the jury. "I direct a collective of artisans. We make these. Samplers." She gestured lamely. "This one just happened to be in the backseat that day. I grabbed it and wrapped the baby up in it."

"But the baby was dead. Surely you knew that."

"Yes, of course."

"Then why bother wrapping it up?"

"Because," Naomi began, and then she heard what she was about to say and shuddered. *Because it was cold. Because I wanted to save her, for myself.* "Oh, it was just a stupid thing to do."

"Did you perhaps think, I can help this poor baby? I can save her?"

"I knew I couldn't save her," she told Charter crossly. "She was dead."

"Then why not just toss her in the backseat?"

"She was only a *baby*," Naomi said, horrified. Then she was horrified for a different reason. So easily trapped, after all. She did not look at Judith. Her face was hot now, and she could feel the shake in her jaw, tiny, then seemingly less tiny.

"Only a baby," Charter said cruelly. He walked back to his table and half sat, half leaned on it. "Just out of interest, which of your artisans made this particular sampler?" He touched it. The plastic crinkled.

"Listen"—she leaned forward—"it only happened to be there. It doesn't mean anything."

The judge leaned over. "You need to answer the question, Ms. Roth. Don't anticipate, please."

"Thank you, your honor," Charter said affably.

"Well, as you know," said Naomi tightly, "that particular sampler was made by Heather Pratt. I'd picked it up a few days before and hadn't gotten around to bringing it in. I probably had a few other people's work in the backseat, too, but I just happened to touch that one first."

He nodded sagely.

"Well, let's talk about Heather Pratt," Charter said, as if the subject had come up naturally, and out of the blue. "How long have you known Heather Pratt?"

"I've known Heather for about two years. Her work was brought to me by Stephen Trask. Heather had been working for Stephen at the sports center, but she wanted to change her job."

"You had not come across Heather before that?"

"No reason I would have. She was in high school."

"Did Stephen tell you why Heather was interested in leaving her job at the sports center?"

"No. But he would hardly be recommending her to me if there was anything terrible, would he?"

"I suppose," Charter said thoughtfully, "that depends on what you might call terrible."

Naomi frowned.

"He didn't, for example, tell you that Heather was an irresponsible employee?"

"Absolutely not." She sounded affronted, at least to her own ears.

"Or that she had stolen from the sports center during her time there?"

Naomi glared at him. "No. And I wouldn't believe that."

"Or that she had engaged in physical altercations with clients of the sports center?"

"No. I seriously doubt that," she said harshly.

"You do? That's odd. Didn't Heather Pratt have a very prominent mark on her cheek the first time you met her?"

Naomi stopped short. Oh God—that was true. *She ran into a rival embroiderer*, Stephen had said. Damn Stephen Trask, she thought bitterly. What else hadn't he told her?

"That's true," she said quietly. "But I don't have any idea how that happened."

Charter nodded. He seemed ready to move on.

"And was there anything else noticeable about Heather Pratt when you met her? Anything physical?"

Naomi squared her shoulders. "She appeared to be pregnant. She told me she was pregnant."

"Yet she was unmarried, wasn't she?"

"A marriage license," Naomi said tightly, "has no effect on fertility that I know of."

But this, too, she saw right away, would not help Heather.

"I mean, I didn't know whether she was married or not. I didn't feel it was any of my business." *I still don't*, she thought.

"You employed Heather Pratt from that time, spring of 1984?"

"Yes. She was . . . she *is*, an excellent employee. Responsible, considerate. She is extraordinarily skillful at needlework, and her work has become enormously popular. I think everyone who sees one of her samplers wants one for herself. She's the only artisan at Flourish with her own waiting list, do you realize that? And she works hard. Very hard. She's never been late with a single assignment. I'm glad I had the opportunity to hire her."

"Are you finished?" he said quietly.

Naomi started. "What?"

"Are you finished? Because you may have heard that this person has been accused of murdering two newborn infants, not being bad at sewing. She is, in fact, on trial for murdering two newborn infants, even as we speak. We are not here to talk about what a good employee she was."

Judith was on her feet. "In point of fact, your honor, it was Mr. Charter who brought up my client's employment record with regard to her work at the sports center."

"That's true, Mr. Charter," Judge Hayes said. "Why don't we all try not to overreact and just move along."

Charter, who could not glare at the judge, for his own sake, and could not glare at Judith without the jury seeing, glared at Naomi. Then he let it go.

"Did there come a time, Ms. Roth, when you learned the

identity of Heather Pratt's lover? The father of her child?"

"I was aware of rumors," Naomi said. "I heard some of the other women speak about it. But I didn't think it was their business anymore than it was mine."

"Whom did these women name?"

"Ashley Deacon," Naomi said.

"Someone known to you?"

"Yes. I knew Ashley." She paused. "He did work for me sometimes. Repair work. You know, contractor work. Both at home and at the mill. My office," she said in explanation to the jury.

"And did it seem likely to you that these rumors were true?"

Naomi looked down at her hands. "I thought they might be true, yes. Certainly it seemed possible to me."

"Was Ashley Deacon a married man?"

"Yes." Naomi didn't elaborate.

"Your new employee was pregnant by a married man?"

"Well, as I said, I didn't speak to Heather about her private life, but that was the consensus, yes."

"And this did not detract from your good opinion of her, I take it."

"I've always felt," she said archly, "that there was something to that saying 'Judge not lest ye be judged.' "

"But judging aside," Charter was smooth, "you obviously took an interest in this person. Did you not feel you could speak to her about these rumors? Or offer her help in some way?"

"Heather didn't need my help. She was perfectly independent. She was happy to be pregnant and looking forward to the birth of her baby. And she became a wonderful mother to her child."

"But becoming a mother, even a *wonderful* mother," he said sarcastically, "did not prevent your friend from continuing her affair, did it?"

"The affair continued," Naomi said. "Though, again, I had no personal evidence of it. I understand that to be true."

"You understand that to be true." He smiled. "Are you aware that Heather Pratt met Ashley Deacon almost daily at your own office and drove from your own parking lot into the woods, where she had sex with him?"

"No," Naomi said, but she rolled her eyes. *So what?*

"Are you aware that this *wonderful mother* would take her daughter Polly along with her on these occasions? That the baby would remain in the car while her mother had sex a few feet away?"

She glanced at Heather, whose eyes were wild. "No." Naomi's voice, slipping from her control, was softer.

"Are you aware that shortly before 11:30 on the night of January the sixteenth of last year, Heather Pratt broke into your own mill, your place of business, in order to have sex in your attic?"

Her face was numb, really, Naomi thought. She had better pinch it before it disappeared altogether. Judith was nodding, little nods, soft at the bottom and the top. Like: just get on with this, just get this over with, and so Naomi did, but really all she wanted was to go home now. "I didn't know that," she said. "I'm sorry to hear it."

"But forgiving."

"Certainly I forgive her. I can't begin to imagine what the circumstances must have been."

"Does it really matter what the circumstances were?" he said. "Isn't it enough that she broke into the office of her friend, who had supported her, to have sex?"

"Circumstances always matter," Naomi said shortly.

"And you felt sorry for her, a little bit, didn't you?"

"I felt badly that she was receiving so little support from the community, and from her child's father. Especially after her grandmother died, she got no support at all. So yes, I felt sorry for her, and I wanted to support her."

"You were her friend."

Naomi hesitated. If she said yes, he would get her somehow, because the true answer was no, and Charter knew that. But she had to say yes, otherwise they would wonder what she was doing here. He was drumming his fingers on the tabletop, enjoying her hesitation.

"I was her friend. Not—" *Close* friends, she was about to say, but he cut her off.

"Really her only friend, I think. Certainly one of very few."

"I think so, yes."

"And yet Heather really told you very little about herself, is that right?"

Not that kind of friend, she almost said, but what other kind was there, really? "Yes," she agreed.

"She didn't, for example, ever admit to you that she was involved in an adulterous relationship with Ashley Deacon, or indeed with anyone else."

"Anyone else?" Naomi said, her voice unmistakably snide. She was proud she'd had the wherewithal to muster this.

"Yes, Ms. Roth. Or anyone else."

"I don't believe there was anyone else, Mr. Charter," she said tightly.

"Ah," he said archly. "But unfortunately, your beliefs are of very little value when it comes to your friend Heather Pratt. In fact, it's rather remarkable how very little of her life she chose to share with you, her only friend. Let's see," he went on with great disingenuousness, "she did not tell you who her daughter's father was, am I right?"

"Yes. I mean no." Naomi shook her head, flustered. "She didn't tell me."

"And she didn't tell you that her affair ended in January of last year, is that so?"

"Right," she said.

"And she didn't tell you who else she was seeing at that time."

Naomi started to shake her head, furious, but Charter spoke again. "Did she tell you or not?"

"She didn't tell me about anyone else," Naomi spat. "Because—"

"Did she tell you," he thundered, and Naomi went silent, "about the other man in her life? About Christopher Flynn?"

Christopher . . . Naomi's thoughts spun, catching on air. *Christopher Flynn*. She couldn't think. She didn't know anyone whose name was Christopher Flynn. Was there a Christopher Flynn, and if there was, what had he said? She looked over at Heather, who was shaking her head, amazed. What did *she* know about Christopher Flynn? Abruptly, Naomi hated Heather.

"I don't know anyone by that name," she said finally, her voice weak.

"Come now," he said, smiling. "You must know Christopher Flynn, the man who overlapped in your great friend's life with her other lover, Ashley Deacon."

"I don't know anyone by that name," she said again. "I swear, I've never heard it before."

Charter shook his head. "Somehow I'm not surprised." He sighed dramatically. "Well then, given the fact that Heather evidently told you very little about her life, I don't suppose she shared with you her very important news last January, that she was again pregnant. That she was expecting a second baby, or indeed twin babies, in September of last year."

"No, you're right. She didn't tell me that," Naomi said.

He nodded. "And yet many of your neighbors, even those who were not intimate friends of Heather Pratt, *did* know that she was pregnant. Is that so?"

"Evidently," she conceded. She could not look at the jury now. It was humiliating, a gradual strip search before a captive audience.

"In fact, when I came to see you in the weeks after your discovery of the baby in the river, in order to question you about Heather Pratt, it was because so many people had contacted me to let me know that Heather Pratt had recently been pregnant, and that she was no longer pregnant but that there was no baby, you insisted that I was wrong, didn't you? You insisted that I was mistaken about Heather being pregnant a second time, didn't you?"

"I did," she remembered, her hands pressing the sides of her thighs. She remembered that. Because he *had* been mistaken, even though he had apparently been right.

"*No*, you told me. Heather Pratt had *not* recently been pregnant. And you knew that for a fact. Because you saw her every day, and she was such a good mother. Correct?"

"I'm going to object," Judith said loudly. "There's no call for Mr. Charter to bully the witness this way. She's trying her best to respond to questions."

"Yes," Hayes said. "Sustained."

Charter smiled. "May I ask," he said in a parody of chivalry, "whether you still feel that Heather Pratt was not, in fact, pregnant a second time?"

Naomi swallowed and looked up. "No. That was wrong. I mean, I know I was mistaken about that," she said quietly, with what she hoped was dignity.

"You were mistaken," he said happily. "Anything else you were mistaken about?" He waited for her, then he went on.

"For example, that this girl who broke into your office was a good employee? That this girl who brought along her child when she had sex was a good mother?"

"I don't know," Naomi said lamely. That was all she could come up with.

"You thought I had arrested the wrong person for this crime, didn't you?"

"Yes," she said, trying to summon her outrage. "I still—"

"You thought this good girl, this good employee and good mother and good friend, who would surely tell you, her only friend, if she got herself pregnant again, could never slaughter her children and get rid of their bodies, so that no one would ever know they existed. You thought that, didn't you? But your track record's not too strong, is it now, Ms. Roth? Not when it comes to what actually happened. You don't really know a thing about Heather Pratt, do you?"

And she wanted to answer, but Judith was screaming, at least in Naomi's head. In the courtroom Judith's voice was hard but not loud, and it was the judge shouting at Naomi not to answer, and Charter speaking softly, but somehow audibly over the other sounds, saying that he had nothing more to ask.

Chapter 31

Friends Like These

"WHO THE FUCK IS CHRISTOPHER FLYNN?" JU-
dith said later, when they stopped for lunch. "Heather says she
never heard of him."

And you believe her? Naomi almost said. She felt dreadful.
She sat with Judith in the diner across from the courthouse,
letting her hamburger sag into its greasy bun and taking scalding sips of her tea. "I've never heard of him either," she said
instead. He's nobody I've ever met, but I know more women
than men in the town. Could be one of the local Lotharios who
can't stand to be left out of the fun," she said bitterly. "That's
all I can think of, anyway."

"Do you think it's possible there was somebody else?" Judith said, her voice so low Naomi had to watch her lips. "You
know, somebody else besides Ashley? Maybe just because she
felt especially lonely around the time he left her?"

"I don't think so," Naomi said lamely, but she wanted to
add that she was evidently the last person to consult on the
subject. "Heather says no?"

" 'Only Ashley, only Ashley,' " Judith intoned, with melodic
sarcasm.

"So what is this, then?"

Judith took a bite of her sandwich, made a face, and put it
down. "I have no idea. Some kind of smoke, obviously. But
the kind with fire or without?" She shook her head. "I can't
tell yet." She sighed. "Anyway Charter was pretty good."

Naomi groaned.

"No, you did the best you could. And who knew he had it
in him?"

She herself, she told Naomi, had assumed he'd want to get
rid of his reluctant witness as quickly as possible; she'd never
dreamed he would get as much out of Naomi as he had. That
stuff about stealing from the sports center? Heather had said,
grudgingly, that she might have taken a towel once or twice.

For the car. But the rest . . . her taking Polly along for her trysts with Ashley and breaking into the mill—*that bastard Ashley*, Naomi thought; he hadn't said a thing, just gone ahead and repaired the damage—Naomi didn't want to know anything more.

She mustn't beat herself up, Judith said kindly. Clearly Charter meant to assassinate Heather's character first and worry about the actual charges later, and after all, they'd been able to salvage something when Judith had her turn. With Judith's guidance, Naomi had talked again about Heather's fortitude, her love for Polly, her utter lack of other friends and the constant assault of bad opinion from all sides. She talked about how horrified Heather had been when Naomi visited her house and described the baby in the river—not guilt, not evasion, but horror that someone could do that to a child. Naomi told how she had seen Heather walk out behind her house in the darkness that night, and then what she herself had found behind the house, in the pond, precisely where Heather would later tell her to look: Heather's own child, her baby, born dead. She told of her interview with Heather after her arrest, and how vehemently the girl had rejected any responsibility for the baby Naomi had found in the Sabbathday River, and how Heather had told her where to find her own baby, the one born dead in the field behind her house, and how Naomi had found it just there.

And had Naomi herself formed an opinion on Heather's connection to the baby found in the river? She had, Naomi told the jury. There wasn't one.

And the baby in the pond behind Heather's house? A stillbirth, Naomi said. And judging from Heather's tears, a mourned one.

Even so, Naomi felt terrible about the morning. She pulled the pins from her hair and massaged her scalp: bruised. "You have the best hair," Judith said, watching her. "My sister has hair like yours."

"Ashkenazi deluxe," Naomi said. "One of my housemates in college called it that. Something in the density, not to speak of the waviness factor."

"Well," Judith said, "it was cold out there in Eastern Europe. We had to keep warm somehow."

"Evolutionary adaptation?" She smiled, feeling, for the first time, a little lighter.

"It's what my mom said about hairy legs. My sister and I were cornering the local Nair market, right? And my mom used to say, 'In the camps it kept us warm, girls!' "

Naomi laughed. She stirred her tea. From their booth, she could see Ashley climb the courthouse steps. "Oh no," she groaned.

"It's all right," Judith told her. "I'm ready for him. By the time I'm finished with darling Ashley, they'll imagine he slept with everything in town."

Naomi pursed her lips. "That's pretty close to the truth, actually. He had that way."

She was looking at her tea. Never in the history of tea had tea been so mesmerizing.

"Naomi," Judith said.

"A beautiful man," Naomi considered. "Who loves women and doesn't get insane about them. Isn't that what every girl needs? A beautiful man who doesn't get on your case about anything? He arrives. He courts. He compliments. Hey, maybe he fixes the sink. He seduces. He satisfies. *And how.* Because he really adores this, you understand? It isn't about getting laid, it's about pleasure, the more the merrier. And then he leaves. *Whew!* Out the door before he can say anything awful to make you feel like shit. Now, that's what I call the perfect man."

"Jesus, Naomi." She was shaking her head. "You might have told me."

"Why? What's the difference? *He* was promiscuous, not Heather."

Judith was looking out the window. Her crooked nose made a Picasso shadow across her cheek.

"He was always available, you understand. *Always.* It's like he wore a sign: ANYTIME YOU WANT, YOU JUST LET ME KNOW. But I was with Daniel, which was fine. Then Ashley came around a lot after Daniel left. I'd hired him for stuff, like the bathroom. And my addition. But sometimes he came on his own. You know: 'I thought I'd have a look at the roof again. It seemed a little spongy last time.' Or he'd bring something he'd salvaged from another job, like a window, because he thought the ones Daniel put in were shit, and if I wanted he could just do a quick swap. What can I say?" Naomi sighed, meeting Judith's eyes now. "There are some times in a woman's life when she can really use a cad."

"*Use* being the operative word in that sentence," Judith said dryly.

"He didn't suffer." Naomi picked up and sipped her tea. "Anyway, it was only a few times. And then he stopped." She pushed her teacup away. "Which was also fine. I was actually interested in somebody. I guess he knew that."

"I see." Judith picked up the check and went to pay it. Naomi pulled on her jacket. Then she wound up her hair and pinned it again. "Are you sorry I told you?" she asked when Judith came back.

Judith looked surprised. "No. Not at all. I just don't want to be late back."

So they returned to the courthouse, Naomi conscious now of gazes fixed on her and how people stopped saying what they were saying to turn and note her passing. She saw Ann Chase and her husband and withstood their glares, then Stephen Trask, who looked resolutely past her, which was somehow worse. Judith went ahead to see Heather, but Naomi went up to Stephen, right up to him, and made him look at her.

"Thanks a lot," she said.

"You're welcome," said Stephen, falsely bright. "What for?"

"Oh, take your pick. Telling me all about Heather, for one thing. I looked like an ass up there. You bring her to me with a great big bruise on her face, you don't even bother to tell me she's just been in a catfight with her boyfriend's wife."

"I didn't think I had to pass on every sordid detail, Naomi. Heather and Sue Deacon . . . you know, it just didn't seem like my place."

"Fine," she said. "But that's between you and me. What about what's between you and Heather?"

He started. "What do you mean?"

"I mean, why haven't you been to see her? Why haven't you shown her any support? When she saw your name on the prosecution's witness list, she asked Judith if you hated her now."

He was red, his jaw set. "I don't hate her. I just can't see her."

"Why can't you?" Naomi said harshly. "Why am I out here

alone? You believed in Heather enough to give her a job. You brought her to me and praised her to the skies. You had her over to dinner at your house. Now nothing. And now's when she needs her friends."

Stephen was shaking his head. "I wish I could help her, but I can't help her now."

She put her hands on her hips. "And what's that supposed to mean. This is all ludicrous, Stephen, and you know it. *Twins by two lovers!*" Naomi snorted "*Ridiculous*. It would be ridiculous even if she'd *had* two lovers, but you know perfectly well she was madly in love with Ashley. Robert Redford couldn't have gotten her in bed."

Still, he wouldn't look at her.

"Look," she tried one final time. "I don't know what Charter's said, and I'm not going to try to find out what your testimony is going to be. But please, Stephen. Just go and see Heather. Just show her you're still her friend."

He looked at her, and for a moment Naomi thought he was about to say something, but then he turned his mouth away, still pursed. "I'm just not able to do that, Naomi." He nodded, as if reinforcing himself. "That's it. And I'm sorry."

He put out his arm, as if she had stepped in front of him and he had to deflect her. Then he walked past her and past the open door of the courtroom into the hallway beyond. Naomi stared after him, swaying in disbelief.

Dimly, she saw that they were all passing by, though not without slowing to look. Rubbernecking, Naomi thought vaguely, like what people did on the roadway when there was an accident, except that she was the accident here, or Heather was, really, but Naomi had somehow become the unlucky passenger along for the ride, and no one seemed willing to stop and help them. Charter, sweeping by and through into the courtroom, nodded to her, evenly and without rancor.

For a moment she could not remember which side she was on.

Naomi roused herself and went into the courtroom, taking her seat behind Judith.

Judith was talking with Heather, their shoulders near but not touching.

"No," Heather said, too loud. "I said *no*, I have no idea. It's all . . ." Bereft, she shook her head.

"Fine," said Judith, her voice chilly.

The jury was called. Judge Hayes came in and took his seat.

From where she sat, the witness chair bore scant resemblance to the hot seat of Naomi's experience earlier that day. Now, watching Stephen Trask smoothly recite his oath, lift his hand from the leatherette Bible, and sit down in the same cracked plastic bucket of the chair, the whole episode of her testimony felt surreal, as if it belonged to some childhood embarrassment she had never successfully eradicated from her self-image. Stephen sat calmly enough, his hands flat on the thighs of his crossed legs. He told Charter how he had first met Heather, and how he had employed her, and what kind of employee she had been.

"Well," he said carefully, "Heather isn't really a very outgoing person. I've always thought she was shy. And I think working at the reception desk in particular was good for bringing her out of herself a little bit."

"So you were concerned for her," Charter prompted.

"Well yes, I was. I was hoping she might work for a short time and then find her way back to college. You see"—he turned, perhaps instinctively, to the jury—"she had had a chance to go to a very good college. She's really a good student. But I think it just didn't work out because she just wasn't ready for the . . . the *interpersonal* challenge of it. Her social skills." He finished.

"Her social skills?"

"Sure. As I said. They were . . . she wasn't easy with people." He looked at Charter, waiting for a nod which didn't come. "I think she'd been alone a lot. She wasn't used to dealing with people."

"But wouldn't you say that dealing with people was the primary requirement of the job you hired her for?"

Stephen agreed that it was.

"And yet you hired her despite her deficiency in this area."

"Yes. Because I thought it would be good for her."

"Ah." Charter nodded. "You were thinking of her even more than you were thinking of the job."

"I suppose." Stephen shrugged. He seemed uncomfortable with the praise.

"And was your faith in Heather rewarded?"

"Rewarded?" He considered the word. "Well . . ."

"Was she, for example, an honest employee?"

Stephen, after a moment, shook his head. "No. I'm sorry, but no."

"Could you perhaps elaborate on Heather's dishonesty?"

"It's only a small thing, but a few items went missing that I believe she took. Towels," he said, looking uncomfortable.

"And Heather would have had access to these towels?"

"Sure. Yes." He uncrossed his legs, but didn't like sitting that way either, and crossed them again.

"Was there something else?" Charter nudged.

Stephen straightened. "I considered it dishonest that Heather pursued an extramarital affair with a fellow employee. I considered it dishonest that they used the sports center to meet and plan their trysts. I also considered it dishonest that they should continue their affair even after it became evident that the affair was disruptive to a harmonious work environment at the center." Having huffed through this speech, he promptly looked uncomfortable again.

"Disharmonious," Charter considered, as if for the first time. "In what way did this disharmony show itself."

"There were complaints. Other employees came to me. Well, one did. It was uncomfortable." He stopped. "I was uncomfortable."

"Who, in your opinion, Mr. Trask, was Heather's counterpart in this affair?" He was standing at his chair now, straight but at ease, one hand resting on the seat back.

"Ashley Deacon. My handyman."

"And Ashley was married at the time?"

"To Susan Deacon, yes."

"Did Heather know Ashley was married?"

Stephen nodded. "Yes. We had a conversation about it. Heather said she didn't care."

A movement made Naomi glance at the jury. One woman was shaking her head.

"She didn't care that he was married?"

"Well," he amended, "she thought it was really no concern of mine, or anybody else's, either. And I told her I didn't see it that way. See, I was trying to help."

"You were advising her that, in your opinion, she was making a mistake."

Stephen sighed audibly. "It was a big mistake for her. I said he was never going to leave his wife, but she didn't seem to care about that, either. And then she got pregnant. This was back in the fall of '83. She still kept on with him."

"And what was your reaction to the pregnancy, Mr. Trask?" Charter said.

"Just"—he shook his head—"disappointed. I knew she wouldn't get back to college if she had a baby. She'd never get anywhere. And Ashley wouldn't do a thing for her. He was having a baby with his wife at the same time. Which Heather knew," he finished bitterly. "It was just a mess."

Charter let this word linger, and busied himself turning the pages of his legal pad. When he found what he wanted, he walked around the table and across to Stephen.

"I'd like to talk about something that happened in the Goddard Sports Center, on Friday the fourteenth of June, of that year. This was about six months into Heather's pregnancy with her daughter Polly. Do you remember a significant event on that date?"

Stephen nodded grimly. "I do. There was a confrontation between Heather and Sue Deacon. At the reception desk."

"A confrontation," the D.A. said eagerly. "Can you be more specific?"

"They were going at each other. I went running when I heard the screaming. They were grappling with each other. There was a lot of noise. And blood."

"Blood!" Charter sounded shocked. "Your employee was having a physical fight at the reception desk?"

"Yes," Stephen said. "People were standing and watching. Nobody seemed to know what to do. And then Ashley got between them and pulled them apart."

"So Ashley Deacon himself separated these two women?"

"That's right," he said. "And after that, I really felt Heather should not continue to work at the sports center. I took her to meet Naomi Roth, because I knew Heather was very talented at embroidery. I thought they might be able to work together."

Charter nodded, as if in praise of Stephen's perception. Then he cocked his head. "Mr. Trask, it seems to me that you made every effort to be of help to Heather. But even so, she was not very open with you, was she?"

"I'd say she wasn't," Stephen agreed.

"Did she, for example, inform you when her relationship

with Ashley did finally come to an end in January of the following year, 1985?"

He shook his head sadly. "No. I found that out from other people. It was pretty common knowledge around town."

"Did she tell you that she had again become pregnant at around this same time?"

"No. She didn't tell me. But I saw her the odd time over the summer. Last summer, that is. And I knew. Looking at her, I could tell she was pregnant. I'd seen her every day almost during the first pregnancy, after all, so I knew."

"Did you ever confront Heather about this?"

"Once," he said. "It was in the parking lot at the supermarket. But she denied it. She said she wasn't pregnant. Only that she'd put on a few pounds because she didn't have her grandmother around to cook for her anymore, and she wasn't eating very well. That's what she said. And I thought, Well, I can't do anything about it if she won't tell me the truth."

Charter nodded sagely. "But you knew that she was no longer seeing Ashley by this time. Did you wonder who the father might be?"

"Sure," he said uncomfortably. "But she wouldn't tell me."

"I see," Charter said. "So she didn't volunteer the names of any of her other lovers."

Judith was up, lightning fast. "I'll object to that, your honor. We haven't heard any evidence about any other lover, as Mr. Charter is perfectly well aware."

Hayes looked irritated, too. "That's sustained, Mr. Charter. Care to try it again?"

"Thank you," said Charter, as if the judge had only meant to be helpful. He looked to Stephen again. "Did Heather ever mention another lover whom she was seeing simultaneously with Ashley?"

"I really can't remember," Stephen said. "I couldn't say absolutely, one way or the other."

"Did she ever mention the name Christopher Flynn, for example?"

Stephen frowned. "Well again, I'm not sure. But it's possible, I guess." He looked briefly at Heather, then away.

"So you say it's possible she mentioned the name Christopher Flynn to you?"

"It could have happened. I don't remember a specific time, but it could have happened."

Heather's back was stiff, her head moving slowly, side to side.

"And do you know who Christopher Flynn is?"

"I've never met him," said Stephen, and with that his direct testimony ended.

With friends like this, Naomi was thinking. It had been increasingly difficult to look at Stephen over the course of his testimony, and now, without Charter to deflect their attention, she understood that they could not look at each other at all. He understood this, too, she saw. He used this moment before Judith rose and addressed him to look studiously at his hands; then, when that was exhausted, rather aimlessly over Naomi's head. Her friend, or what had always passed for her friend, now irrevocably gone.

One of Judith's hands reached back to tug at the tail of her jacket. This was her habitual preparatory gesture, her small betrayal of nerves. She was getting to her feet.

"Mr. Trask," she said evenly, "from your description of my client's thievery, I take it Heather was the only person in the sports center who had access to towels. Would that have been the case?"

He looked taken aback. "Well no. Of course not."

"Really? Who else might have been in a position to steal towels?"

"Another employee, I suppose."

"What about a client? A person who came in to swim or use the squash court?"

He shrugged. "Possible."

"Maybe one of the moms. You have a lot of moms, don't you? I understand your infant and preschool swimming lessons are very popular."

"They are," Stephen agreed.

"Moms can get pretty distracted, trying to get their kids dressed after a lesson. Is it possible somebody inadvertently threw a towel in her bag now and then?"

He gave her an unmistakable glare. "It's possible."

"In fact, we may not even be talking about the theft of a towel, now that I think of it. Don't things just occasionally disappear?"

"Oh no," Stephen said, but he already sounded trapped.

"No?" Judith grinned. She turned to the jury and grinned again. "Am I the only one that happens to? I always thought there must be some law of the universe that says when you put a pair of socks through the wash you end up with only one sock at the other end."

She rolled her eyes. The jury, appreciatively, tittered.

"In fact, Mr. Trask"—Judith turned to face him again—"you don't have the slightest bit of evidence that might indicate my client was responsible for the loss of a single towel, do you?"

"She might have taken one," he said stubbornly. Naomi, in disgust, looked away.

"So might I, the last time I was over at the Goddard Sports Center. In fact," she grinned rather suddenly, "I think I did." Judith turned to the jury and shrugged. "By mistake, I assure you." Then she went quiet, letting the temperature plunge. "But what I don't understand is what on earth a few missing towels have to do with these horrific and outrageous charges against my client. Or is that all the evidence her accusers can muster against her?"

Charter shot to his feet. "Your honor!"

"All right." Hayes put up his hand. "Ms. Friedman, you know better than that."

"I apologize, your honor." She turned away, and Naomi caught the most fleeting of smiles.

"Mr. Trask, you've told us about the confrontation that took place between Sue Deacon and Heather Pratt two years ago. I believe you testified that you were summoned to the scene of this confrontation by the commotion. Is that right?"

"It is," Stephen said.

"So if you were responding to the noise of what was already in progress, then I take it you were not present to witness the beginning of the conflict."

He nodded agreement, slowly. "No."

"So then, you didn't actually *see* the beginning, did you?"

"No."

She turned her head to look at the jury. "Well, that's interesting. Because from the way you described it, you seemed to know a lot about what actually happened between these two women."

"I only knew what Heather told me."

"And what was that?" Judith said. She seemed willing to take the risk, though why, Naomi couldn't imagine.

"Well, what she *said* was that Sue just attacked her. But I mean, she *would* say that, wouldn't she?"

"Oh," Judith considered, "you mean, she lied to you about what happened."

"I didn't say she lied!" He sounded affronted.

"Well, you must have thought she was lying, otherwise you would have asked Heather why she had initiated the fight, wouldn't you? And if you *had* asked her, I'm sure you would have told us what she said to you."

He was working it through. Naomi, who was a mite quicker, was filled with admiration for Judith.

"I guess I thought it was possible the fight could have happened like she said."

"I see. And has something happened since then to make you change your mind about Sue Deacon initiating the fight?"

He shrugged. "Well, not really."

"Then what are we talking about, exactly? A person comes into your sports center and attacks one of your employees, and here we are blaming the person who got attacked? Is that it?"

"They were both fighting," he insisted a little fiercely. "Heather had her hands on Sue's arms. I saw *that*!" His voice was harsh.

"Well, isn't that where her hands would be if she was trying to hold off an attacker?" Judith asked innocently. "But you mentioned blood, I think."

"Yes, there was blood."

"On both parties? Or only on Heather?"

"I only saw Heather. I was taking care of Heather."

"So you wouldn't know if Sue Deacon was even hurt at all in the confrontation she initiated."

"I only saw Heather," he said morosely. "She had blood coming off her cheek."

"In fact," considered Judith, "Heather wanted to report the assault to the police, didn't she?"

"That's right," Stephen said. "She said that."

"But you talked her out of it, didn't you?" Judith, it occurred to Naomi, was enjoying this.

"Yes. But I thought she'd behaved very badly herself. I thought she was disgraceful."

"*Really.*" Judith smiled. "That's odd. Because within an hour of this attack, you were with Heather at Naomi Roth's place of business, praising her work and her integrity as an employee. I wonder that you would recommend such a violent and dishonest person so highly to another employer."

He looked studiously at the floor. He did not respond.

"Mr. Trask," Judith pressed, "you were very supportive of Heather, and helpful to her, even though you disapproved of her attachment to Ashley Deacon. Am I right in saying that?"

Stephen, for an instant, caught Naomi's eye. "I tried to help her."

"Were you angry at her for involving herself with such an unsuitable person?"

"Well, not *angry*."

"Were you upset with her for blowing her chance to go to college, coming home and getting herself pregnant by a man who wasn't going to take care of her?"

He nodded hard. "You bet."

"When you saw her last summer, in the parking lot, and thought she might be pregnant for the second time, you must have been doubly disappointed."

"I thought she was just throwing her life away," said Stephen. "But she lied to me about being pregnant. She said she wasn't pregnant."

"Did that make you angry?" asked Judith, and Naomi thought he would dismiss the idea, and quickly, but Stephen seemed to give it sober consideration.

"Yes," he said quietly, and Naomi was taken aback. As if it had anything to do with him!

"I see," Judith said. She walked to the front of her table and sat back against it. "Mr. Trask, Heather is an independent person, is she not?"

"Yes," he said sadly, "I'd say she was."

"Did she have supportive parents, for example?"

Stephen shook his head. "No parents. Heather's mother left her at home with her grandmother. I don't think the father was ever in the picture."

"So Heather grew up alone with her grandmother?"

"That's correct. Until Pick's—that is, Polly's—death last year."

"How old was Heather when that happened?"

"Oh . . ." he thought, "I'd say nineteen."

"And since her grandmother's death, since the age of nineteen, Heather has been completely on her own, no family of any kind?"

He nodded. "Yes."

"Any friends that you knew of?"

"She came to work with another employee, Martina Graves, for a while. But no, not many friends. If any," he amended.

"So basically we're talking about a young woman with no family and very few friends, trying to bring up a daughter in virtual isolation?"

"Her life was very hard," Stephen said. "I know it was."

"In your opinion, was Heather a good mother to her daughter Polly?"

He glanced at Charter. "Well, I've heard some things I certainly disapprove of."

"We've all *heard* things, Mr. Trask," Judith cut him off, "but what I'm really interested in is what you actually observed."

"She was a good mother."

"She get much help from Ashley Deacon, the father of her child?"

"None I know of."

"No financial support? No help around the house?"

Stephen looked down. "He was pretty uninvolved, as far as I'm aware."

"But he continued the affair, even after Polly's birth, didn't he?"

"Yes."

"Tell me, Mr. Trask, when—in your understanding—did the affair between my client and Mr. Deacon come to an end?"

He looked briefly at Heather. "That would have been last January. There was some kind of ruckus in the woods. I think they split up that night."

" 'Some kind of ruckus,' " Judith considered. "Can you elaborate?"

"I can't really. I wasn't there, so I can't say what happened."

"All right. But you're fairly certain that this 'ruckus' coincided with the end of the affair."

"Yes." Again, he looked at Heather. "I went to see her the next day. It was the day after her grandmother died. I went over to the house. She told me it was finished between her and Ashley."

"Hm." Judith got up and walked over to where Stephen sat. She planted one elbow on the ledge by his shoulder and turned, so that they, conspiratorial almost, could consider Heather together.

"How did she feel about the breakup? Was she relieved it was over?"

He looked at Judith as if she was crazy. "No. She was . . . she was in terrible shape. She knew he wouldn't change his mind, but she was devastated."

"Oh, so I infer, then, that the breakup was Ashley Deacon's idea?"

"Very much so," Stephen said.

"The man she had devoted herself to, in spite of the fact that he had used her for sex, gotten her pregnant, and refused to take any financial or personal responsibility for his child, just one day decided he'd had enough of her and dropped her?"

"That's about it," Stephen said cruelly. "What a prince, huh?"

"Objection!" Charter shouted. Judith suppressed a smile. Judge Hayes leaned over Stephen.

"You should just answer the question, Mr. Trask. No editorial comments, okay?"

"I'm sorry," he said softly.

Judith picked it up again right away. "And, as you said before, Heather didn't have any family at all, and very few friends?"

"No." He shook his head. To Naomi, he looked pained, as if this were all somehow his fault.

"And can you imagine how much worse this already terrible state of mind must have become when Heather discovered she was again pregnant?"

"She didn't have to lie to me!" he thundered. "She could have told me the truth when I asked her. I thought I had a right to know!"

"And why," Judith seemed taken aback, "did you think that?"

He looked surprised himself by what he had said. He eyed all three of them—Judith, Naomi, Heather, in turn—and then glared at Charter, who glared back. Then he apologized, though for what Naomi couldn't quite work out, and Judith, as if in forgiveness, let him go.

Chapter 32

Some Kind of Paragon

ASHLEY'S TESTIMONY WOULD WOUND HEATHER, whatever it consisted of. Naomi did not know what Judith said to prepare her client the following morning, but she hoped keenly that whatever it was, it would not make the situation worse. Naomi had noted her friend's disdain, her disapproval of Heather's heartfelt subjugation, of Heather's choices, even of Heather herself. Judith was not a soft person, that much was clear, though it did not deflect Naomi's love for her. She could not condemn a brittleness that came from admirable, unenviable things she herself had not endured, like a mother's wartime fortitude or a career of defending the indigent. Sometimes, she thought, finding her seat before the morning session began, Naomi felt herself a kind of human barrier between Heather's fragility and Judith's angry disbelief, loyal to both but never allowing herself to hope that there might at some point be a synergy, of understanding, of—oh, that elusive—sisterhood among the three of them, in spite of the fact that the world now viewed them in precisely this way: three witches over their cauldron, three crones busy at their blood-libel, their slaughter of innocents. She crossed her legs, the panty hose grating her skin; this, the second of her three-pack, already had a string-bean-length run at the ankle. She had seen Ashley out in the hallway, absorbed in *The Manchester Union Leader*, the paper folded back on itself into a neat wedge. He was reading an article about himself.

Heather began to cry immediately when he was brought in, but discreetly, as if she did not want to burden anyone with her unhappiness. As he walked, he looked past the frantic stare of the mother of two of his children to Naomi, whom he smiled at warmly and nodded to, as if they were meeting in the supermarket or the parking lot at the mill. "Hello," he even mouthed, with that benign sweetness in his eyes. She thought again of the window he had broken and then wordlessly repaired, and turned away.

Amiably, he walked to the witness seat, and lifted his hands, and said the words of the oath with a kind of breathless wonder. He turned and sat, crossing his legs. His hair was back, but his habitual bandanna had been replaced by a discreet rubber band, and he wore a tan corduroy jacket over a white shirt buttoned up nearly to the top. Charter was flipping the pages of his legal pad, but Ashley waited calmly, his eyes over their heads to some unknowable point at the back of the room.

When the D.A. straightened at last, Ashley related for them all the points of his life: childhood and college, marriage and work. He had helped build the sports center in Goddard, then remained on call to maintain the plant. He had married Sue Locke in 1980, when they graduated from the University of Vermont. Now they had two children. It sounded so utterly unobjectionable, Naomi marveled, and indeed, Ashley sat easily in the witness chair, without even showing the physical discomfort Naomi knew it engendered, as if he feared nothing at all, regretted nothing at all. For the first time in her life, she understood that charm was not necessarily a positive attribute.

"Can you recall for me," said Charter, "the circumstances of your first meeting with Miss Heather Pratt."

Ashley pursed his lips. "I was working at the sports center," he said evenly. "This was, oh, I guess November of '83. The place had only been going about half a year."

"You were on staff at the sports center?"

"Well, on staff, no. But we had kind of an agreement. I mean, myself and Stephen Trask. He called me if there was anything to do, and there was always something to do. The builder on the job wasn't very good, in my opinion."

Charter spoke from his seat. "And did Mr. Trask introduce you to Heather Pratt?"

Ashley shook his head. "No. He never did. She came to me by herself."

"Can you describe that meeting, Mr. Deacon?"

"Sure." He nodded. "I was up a ladder. When I came down, there she was, looking up at me. She said she had something in her eye and she wanted me to help her get it out."

Charter looked meaningfully at the jury.

"Something in her eye," he said encouragingly.

"Just a speck." Ashley shrugged. "Then she asked me for a lift home."

"Did you think she only wanted a lift?" Charter leaned forward.

"Well, no." He grinned. "I mean, she made herself clear."

"And you gave her that lift?"

"I did," he said.

"But you didn't take her straight home."

"No. We went to the woods."

"For what purpose did you go to the woods?" Charter asked.

Ashley gave him a look, incredulous, but not offended.

"To fool around," he said. "Obviously."

"Did you get the impression that Miss Pratt had done this sort of thing before?" Charter said innocently.

Judith got up, "Object, your honor. I don't think we need to hear Mr. Deacon's unsubstantiated impressions of my client's history."

Judge Hayes nodded. "True. Sustained."

Charter pursed his lips. "Let me ask that a different way. Did anything occur on that first occasion that led you to form an opinion of the defendant's history with men?"

Naomi looked at Judith expectantly, but this time she didn't rise. Ashley said, "Well, she said she wasn't a virgin. And she didn't *act* like a virgin, if that's what you're saying."

"What, specifically, are you referring to when you say that?" said Charter.

"Oh . . ." He shrugged. "She was . . . I could just tell she'd been with lots of guys. The way she moved. *You* know. And then she came out and told me as much."

"That she wasn't a virgin?"

Naomi winced. How many more times would he manage to get this said aloud?

"Yeah."

"Did Heather actually name some of the other men she'd been with?"

"No. And I didn't ask." He said this, Naomi decided, out of some kind of warped chivalry.

"Would you tell us," Charter rose now and walked over to where Ashley was seated, "of the routine your affair with Heather fell into."

"Sure." He was affable. "Well, I would pick her up after

work and we'd fool around. Then if she had an errand or something, I'd take her. She didn't have a car, and I felt sorry for her. Then I took her home."

"You did this how often, would you say?"

"Oh, four, five times a week."

"You did this despite the fact that you were a married man."

Ashley rolled his eyes. "I didn't say I was proud of it, but it didn't feel like it was anybody else's business."

"And Heather was aware that you were married."

"Oh yeah." He seemed animated for the first time. "Oh sure. From the beginning."

Charter paused. He considered his witness. "Mr. Deacon, did you ever, at any time, tell Heather Pratt that you intended to leave your wife and live with her instead?"

Ashley shook his head vigorously. "No way. She knew I wasn't going to do that."

"Just think for a minute. Is it at all possible that Heather might have got that impression, mistaken though it was, from something you said or did?"

"If she thought that," he said fiercely, "she was dead wrong."

"Because you were always open about your situation, weren't you?"

"Very much so," Ashley agreed. "My marriage always came first."

From the jury box, a snort of laughter, quickly stifled. Naomi caught it: the woman, middle-aged, in the back corner. An alternate. But even so, she felt a flurry of optimism.

Charter, too, stifled a reaction. "Did Heather ever tell you about the other men she was seeing?"

Jesus, Naomi heard Judith mutter. She shot to her feet. "Objection. Assumes facts not in evidence."

"It certainly does, Mr. Charter," Hayes said, visibly angry. He turned to the jury. "Please disregard the last question."

But they wouldn't, Naomi saw. That was the point.

"Is it possible that Heather was seeing other men at the same time she was seeing you?"

Ashley nodded. "Sure. I mean, I was only with her for a little time each day, and not on the weekends at all. I have no idea what she did the rest of the time."

"So when Heather told you she was pregnant, in the winter

of 1984, you really had no way of knowing whether the baby was yours, did you?"

"Well." He shrugged philosophically. "I figured it was Heather's baby. I mean, it was up to her what to do with it. Besides," Ashley said, "I was having my own kid. I mean, my wife was."

"Your wife was, in fact, pregnant at the same time Heather was pregnant with her daughter Polly."

"Yeah. So, she knew what the priority was."

"I see," Charter said. "Let's move forward a bit, to August of 1984. Heather had given birth to her daughter. How did this event affect your relationship?"

Ashley frowned, remembering. "Well, it didn't much. I mean, she was at home more, with the baby, so I didn't see her as much. Actually," he said brightly, "I kind of tried to end it."

"You tried to end the relationship?"

"Yeah. I went to her house. I sort of hinted maybe we'd better stop." He considered. "I gave her my car, you see. I said it was a present. Which it was," he said defensively, as if he had been challenged on this point. "But I thought, see, that if she had her own car, she wouldn't need lifts from me."

"And what was Heather's reaction to this?"

"Oh, she cried," Ashley said. "She didn't want to stop seeing me. She did take the car, though." This was said with an edge, as if it were some kind of vindication.

"So you kept on seeing her, then?"

"Yeah."

"All that fall. The fall of 1984. You continued to meet with Heather?"

"Yeah. Maybe not as often. Two or three times a week."

Charter mused, looking at Heather. "Always in the car?"

He nodded. "Always."

"Now," said Charter, "where was the baby while you were fooling around in your car? Did Heather leave the little baby home with her grandmother?"

Ashley shook his head. "No, we had her. She mostly slept."

"You had the baby in the car?" he said again. "I want to be clear about this. Heather took the baby along in the car when the two of you were having sex?"

He shrugged. "I guess she thought it was all right."

But the jury didn't. They glared, at Ashley, at Heather. Naomi's mouth was dry. She looked longingly at the full glass
beside Ashley, which he hadn't touched.

"Were you aware, Mr. Deacon, that Heather considered you
to be the father of her child?"

"I guess," Ashley said. "She sort of implied."

"Were you aware that she also implied this to others?"

He nodded. "Yeah. It kind of pissed me off, to tell you the
truth."

"Because you didn't think you were the father?"

"How the hell could I know?" he said, clearly, if briefly,
angry. "I mean, I don't know what all was going on with her.
It could have been mine, but it could have been somebody
else's."

Charter nodded sagely. "Would you say, by this time, your
affair was cooling down?"

"Well, I can't speak for anyone else," said Ashley, "but for
me, yeah."

Naomi wanted to touch Heather's back, which was near
enough if she reached, and trembling. She had never seen this
Ashley, and yet he was of a seamless part with the Ashley she
did know, the Ashley of great good humor and small good
turns. The Ashley of narrow, insinuating hips and generous
hands.

"Were you aware that many other people seemed to know
about the affair?"

Ashley, sublimely unperturbed, merely shrugged. "Small
minds, if they have nothing else to think about."

"I take it you were aware, but not particularly bothered,
then."

"Not particularly." He laughed. Then he said, "You know,
it was nobody's business but ours."

"And your wife's, perhaps?"

"Well, sure," Ashley said responsibly. "That's more or less
why I cut it off when I did. Because I could see my wife was
upset."

Naomi looked again at the jury. Her favorite alternate was
rolling her eyes. One of the other women, she was delighted
to note, had a look of utter incredulity on her face.

"Did Heather ever discuss with you any expectations she

might have about your support of her daughter Polly?" said Charter.

"No." Ashley's voice was firm. This point, Naomi thought, was somehow terribly important to him. "Never."

"She never said, 'As the father of this child, I expect you to . . .'" He waited for Ashley to fill in the blank, but Ashley seemed unable to do this. "'Contribute financially for her care? Spend time with her? Bring her gifts?'"

"Nothing like that," he said. "I told you, she could take care of herself."

"So she never requested that you be Polly's father?"

Judith stood. "Objection, your honor. I'd like Mr. Charter to clarify that he is speaking in terms of support and behavior. Mr. Deacon either is or is not the biological father of Heather's daughter Polly. One way or the other, it's a fact. He can't change his mind about it."

"Quite true," Hayes said. He looked at Charter expectantly.

Charter looked at Ashley. "She never said, 'Ashley, this is your child.' Did she?"

"Never," he said emphatically.

"All right," said Charter, evidently satisfied. He flipped a few sheets of his legal pad, then searched the yellow page with his fingertip.

"Let's talk about last January, Mr. Deacon. January 16. A Monday, I think."

"I remember." Ashley nodded. "We split up that day."

"You went to work as usual that day?"

"Sure. And after, Heather and I drove into the woods."

He let this sink in. "Was the baby with you that day?"

Ashley thought about it. "No. I guess she was home with Heather's grandmother."

"What happened in the woods?"

"There were people there. My wife was there. They were making a big fuss."

"What did you do?"

"Well, I couldn't drive out. My car was blocked. So we walked out."

"'We' being?" Charter nudged.

"Me and Heather. We walked out. We walked all the way back to the mill where she worked."

He nodded. "And what did you do when you got there?"

"Well," he said evenly, "we went inside."

"Oh," said Charter disingenuously. "Was it open?"

"No, no," said Ashley. "But I knew it wouldn't be hard to fix up the next day. So I broke the windowpane."

"Really!" Charter said. "Now, whose idea was that?"

Ashley shrugged. "I really can't remember. Might have been hers. She was pretty excited."

"Excited?" Charter said lecherously.

"Sexy excited," Ashley spelled it out. "Well, me, too. So we went upstairs. But after, I started to feel bad. About Sue. And I thought, This is just nuts. I've got Sue pissed off at me, and it isn't worth it. So I told Heather that was it."

"I see," Charter considered. "And how did she react to that?"

"Oh, fine. She just said good-bye. She didn't cry or anything, if that's what you mean."

She was crying now, Naomi observed. Little snorts of grief, tamped down, wetly stifled. It amazed her that they weren't all staring, but then Naomi had been watching only Ashley's face. Now she looked around and saw that, in fact, she and Ashley were nearly the only ones *not* looking at Heather. The jury gaped openly at her, their faces variously disapproving, and compassionate. Even Judith was murmuring something that sounded vaguely kind into Heather's ear. Heather, impervious, seemed to be reliving the moment of her abandonment with such uncontrollable force that Judge Hayes himself was leaning forward in his seat, first inquiring and then requiring a break for everyone. The jury was removed, some shaking their heads. When the door closed behind them, Charter leaped to his feet and condemned the defendant's "blatant grandstanding," her "cynical histrionics," but he could barely be heard over Heather's wailing. Naomi got up from her seat and went to Heather. She waited for someone to stop her, but no one did, so she put her arm around the girl and held her, hardening herself against the mucus-sweet smell of Heather's grief.

The break lasted ten minutes, during which Ashley excused himself to go to the bathroom and Charter, his face pink with anger, wrote notes in his tight-fisted hand. Heather, by tiny increments, seemed to bring herself under control. She rocked in small movements, her back slumped against her wooden chair. "I can't do this," she confided. Judith, angry, turned away.

"The worst is almost over, I think," Naomi lied. She was crouching next to Heather's chair. "Jesus, who knew he was such a bastard?"

"But he's not," she sobbed anew. "He isn't. I don't understand why this is happening."

To that, Naomi could say nothing. She gave Heather a last squeeze and went back to her seat. The jury returned. Then Ashley came back. His face had a sheen, though not of sweat. He looked cool, washed and blotted dry, his hands thrust deep into his jeans pockets. He passed them, rigorously impervious to their stares—Naomi's baleful, Heather's imploring—and returned to his seat. Charter, still red-faced in frustration, set off again without delay.

"So after you broke into the mill where Heather was employed, you went upstairs and had sex. Do I have that right?"

"Yeah," he said affably. "She was pretty wild that night. I remember that."

"Oh yes?" Charter said, discernibly eager. This, it struck Naomi, must be some kind of unanticipated morsel.

"Yes. I guess it kind of . . . well, the danger of it, right? Like, we ran away from all those people. I guess it turned her on."

Judith, cursing beneath her breath, quickly objected. "I wish the witness would stick to his own thoughts, rather than speculating on other people's."

Hayes leaned over to Ashley. "Mr. Deacon, kindly limit your testimony to what you experienced or observed, and refrain from making assumptions about what other people were thinking."

"Sure." Ashley said agreeably, as if the damage were not already done.

"There was something different in Heather's sexual *behavior* that night?" Charter immediately picking up the scent again and emphasizing the key word with a fairly unpleasant leer.

"She wanted me to do something different to her."

Heather, white, put down her head. She put it down on the table, turning one cheek to its surface. She looked alarmingly serene, as if she had been struck deaf and could not hear what he was saying about her. Ashley went on talking. In the jury box, fourteen faces reacted.

"And this was how Heather responded to being confronted by your wife and others in the woods?"

"She thought—"

"Your honor!" Judith slapped the table with her fist.

"Mr. Deacon, you could not possibly know what the defendant, or anyone else, was thinking."

"She *said* it. She said she thought I was going to leave my wife for her. I said 'no way.' I never said I was going to leave my wife. I wouldn't ever do that."

"So Heather would have been mistaken in that belief, then."

"Totally. It was just nuts."

"And after that night—after you left that night—where did you go?"

"Back home. I might have stopped off for a drink first. But I went home after."

"And did you speak with Heather after that night?" Charter said.

"Nope. Never. I don't know what she did, but I had no part of it." He paused, and looked at her for the first time since entering the courtroom. "I feel bad for her, though. I mean, I'm not a creep."

Naomi glared at him. Ashley looked back at Charter.

"Mr. Deacon, when did you become aware that Heather had again become pregnant?"

He pursed his lips. "Well, not till you told me," he said. "Would have been last fall, I guess."

"Miss Pratt did not contact you to tell you about the pregnancy?"

"Nope."

"But during Miss Pratt's first pregnancy, when she clearly considered you to be the father of her child, she did inform you, didn't she?"

"Sure." He shrugged. "I don't know. Maybe this time she thought it was somebody else's."

"I see," Charter said thoughtfully. He studied his legal pad for a moment, tapping the pencil in his right hand against the palm of his left. "Any ideas who that somebody might have been?"

Ashley looked up at the ceiling. "Well, she didn't tell me

who else she was seeing, so I really couldn't say."

"She didn't tell you she was seeing Christopher Flynn?"

Judith, her hands tied, moved her jaw in frustration.

"No."

"But as far as you're concerned, she might have been seeing Christopher Flynn, and indeed other men in addition to him."

"I don't know who all she was seeing," Ashley said tersely. "I told you, she didn't say, and I didn't ask. Most of the time I wasn't around her, you know."

Charter gave the jury a moment to give this observation weight.

"For the record, Mr. Deacon, where were you between September 19 and 20 of last year?"

Then he grinned, lit with paternal pride. "Well, down at Mary Hitchcock mostly. My wife went into labor on the afternoon of the eighteenth. I stayed in the room almost all the time. Her folks were there, too. And our son Benjamin was born the next afternoon at four. I just stayed at the hospital till she checked out the day after that."

Charter allowed Ashley to glow for a moment. Then he went still and solemn. "Mr. Deacon, did you have any idea what happened to Heather Pratt's infants?"

He had already begun to shake his head when Judith interrupted. "Objection, your honor. There's been no evidence to show that Heather's pregnancy produced two infants, rather than one. I don't appreciate Mr. Charter's attempts to introduce this notion."

"Nor do I," Hayes said dryly. "Mr. Charter, you are cautioned."

"And I apologize," the D.A. said smoothly. "Mr. Deacon, do you have any knowledge at all about what might have befallen the infant or infants to which Heather Pratt gave birth on or about September 19 to 20?"

"Absolutely not!" Ashley said fiercely, looking, for the first time, utterly affronted.

And on this note, Charter was finished.

They all took a break after that. Judith could barely rouse Heather, who gradually sat upright but was dazed and thick, anesthetized against pain by the force of her pain, like someone in new, cataclysmic grief. Naomi, watching her, thought for the first time that she might be ill—clinically, corporally ill—and wondered if she ought to say something to Judith. A doctor—not a psychiatrist, not some fertility specialist or forensic clinician, but a real doctor—ought to look at Heather, and do basic things like take her pulse and look into her mouth and ears. This wasn't normal. Nobody who stumbled through the day this way, this white and unsteady on her feet, was normal. She reached forward to touch Heather, and the girl remained inert, only her thin back making little, fluttering shudders. The jury went out, then filed back in.

Judith was itching for her crack at him. She leaped up and walked over, smiling with a warmth Naomi certainly distrusted. She was in her element already, thrilled, tensed for the starter's gun.

"Mr. Deacon," Judith said. "Ashley, after all. We've met before today, haven't we?"

"Yuh." Ashley nodded. "I put in some French doors for you."

"You did a great job." Judith grinned at the jury.

"Thanks," he said warily.

"Now, you've told the jury all about how you met your wife at the University of Vermont, and how you moved to Goddard after you got married and started up your business and had your two sons, Joseph and Benjamin. Is that right?"

"Sure."

"So you've been married for"—Judith looked down at her notes—"nearly six years, am I right?"

"Six years next June, right."

"Happy marriage, I take it?"

"Well, you know." He was catching on. "Ups and downs. Marriage can be hard."

Naomi smiled. Ashley Deacon: font of wisdom.

"I see. And how did you deal with the downs in your marriage, Ashley?"

He frowned at her suspiciously. "What do you mean, 'deal with'?"

"Well, did you, for example, seek the help of a marriage counselor? Did you try to sit down regularly with your wife to work out your problems?"

"I didn't say we had *problems*," Ashley said defensively. "I said it was ups and downs, like any marriage."

"Oh, sorry," Judith said amiably. "What do you think the downs were all about, then?"

"Just the normal stuff," he said, his voice tight. "Like, oh, I don't know, maybe she wanted to be living closer to her folks, that kind of thing."

"Really?" Judith seemed surprised. "That was the only topic of disagreement in your marriage?" She waited for him. He said nothing. Judith smirked at the jury. "I'd say you were pretty well off if that's the only thing you had to disagree about."

"It's a pretty good marriage," Ashley confirmed.

"Sure." She nodded. "So tell me, how many affairs have you had since your marriage?"

"How many . . . ?" he said in disbelief.

"Oh, okay," Judith said affably. "Let's just limit it to the period since you moved to Goddard. How many affairs in the last five years?"

Charter was looking grim, but he hadn't gotten up, Naomi noted. She smiled.

When Ashley saw he wasn't going to get any help, he scowled at Judith. "Couple, maybe."

"Maybe a couple?" she said brightly.

"Well, it depends on what's an affair." He sulked.

"Oh, you're right. We should define our terms. I mean, are we talking about only ongoing affairs? Like, when you have sex with the same person over a period of time? Or are we counting the one-night stands, too?"

He set his jaw. Charter made an objection, his irritation barely contained.

Judge Hayes called both attorneys up to his bench and Naomi watched their dumb argument of hisses and hands. When they turned back, Charter was enraged, Judith smug. She went back to her pose, her amiable perch near Ashley's elbow.

"So, what were we saying? Oh yes, whether or not to count the one-night stands, right?" She looked at him keenly. "You tell me how you want to do this, Ashley."

It was potent, Naomi thought. Like telling a kid he had to figure out his own punishment for an infraction, and Ashley knuckled under right away, though with the appropriately sour expression.

"I fooled around a little. It wasn't a big deal."

"You mean, I suppose, that it wasn't a big deal for *you*?"

"Well, it wasn't."

"And the women with whom you were fooling around?"

"They knew I was married," he said.

"Hm," Judith said noncommittally. "And how many women are we talking about here?"

"A few." His voice was tight.

"More than five?" He was silent. "More than ten?"

"I don't see what this has to do with *her*," Ashley said fiercely.

"More than twenty, Ashley?"

"*Not* twenty!" His voice was bitter. "Not *twenty*."

"Less than twenty," Judith went on, even and relentless.

"Of course, less than twenty!" He sounded ridiculous.

"But more than, say fifteen." She looked at him archly.

"I didn't say that. I didn't say fifteen. There weren't fifteen!"

"Come on, Ashley." Judith sighed. "Do I have to bring them in here?"

He glared at her, amazed. Naomi, who knew it was a bluff, could barely believe how still Judith's face was, almost serene in its confidence. The courtroom seemed to exhale collectively, and then Ashley shook his head.

"I honestly don't remember how many exactly," he said, blinking first. "There were some. Maybe . . . ten, twelve, or so. But they knew I was married," he insisted, as if this explained everything.

"And your wife? How did she feel about your sleeping with at least twelve other women since moving to Goddard five years ago?"

"I don't know," Ashley said unkindly. "You'll have to ask her."

Judith, wisely, gave the jury a moment to despise him.

"Would you agree that Goddard is a small town?"

Momentarily disarmed at the shift, he looked at her. "Well, sure."

"Would you agree that when a man moves into a small town with his wife and sleeps with at least twelve women in the space of five years, his neighbors are probably going to become aware of his activities?"

"It's possible, I guess," he conceded.

"So you're not surprised, Ashley, that your neighbors have been well aware of your many adulteries?"

"If you say so," he said resentfully.

"Did you discuss your adulterous affairs with your wife, Ashley?"

He gave Judith a bitter look. "I don't really see that that's any of your business."

Naomi looked instinctively at Charter. He was tense but still. Judge Hayes ordered Ashley to answer.

"Not really," he told her. Then, magnanimous: "I didn't want to upset her."

"That was thoughtful of you," Judith said sweetly. "To your knowledge, did your wife, Sue, find out about any of the twelve or more women you committed adultery with before your affair with Heather Pratt?"

He bristled at "affair," but said no. "I don't think so, anyway."

Judith looked perplexed. "You don't think so? You mean you don't know for sure? You never discussed this with your wife, even after the issues inherent in this trial were brought to light?" She half turned so that the jury could register her amazement, then turned back to Ashley. "She never confronted you with something she might have heard or seen, that made her think you'd been having sex with another woman?"

"No," he said stiffly.

"So as far as you're aware, Heather was the first of your girlfriends that Sue ever found out about."

"Yes," said Ashley.

"And how did you discover that Sue was aware of Heather?"

"Somebody told her," he said, his voice fierce, as if this person was responsible for everything. "Some *woman*. So when I came home that night, she was all worked up."

"All worked up," Judith mused. "And I take it you were honest in admitting the affair to your wife."

"She knew all about it, anyway."

"So there was no point in denying it?"

"Sure," he said.

"And was it shortly after this that your wife went to the sports center to confront Heather Pratt?"

"Next day, I'm pretty sure. But she was emotional. She was pregnant."

"Which one of them are you speaking of, Ashley? Who was pregnant?"

A titter from the back of the room. The women on the jury were smiling at their knees. The men, Naomi noted, lagged a step behind and looked merely confused.

"Both pregnant," Ashley said.

"Your wife and your girlfriend were having a confrontation in the sports center, and both of them were pregnant?"

He nodded tersely, once. "Yes."

"With your children."

"Well, I don't know that for a fact," he said, as if this were a point in his favor.

"You're not quite sure whose baby your wife was carrying?" Judith said, confused.

"I . . . no." He was furious. "My wife never fooled around!"

"Are you sure?" Judith sounded innocent.

Charter, delighted to have something to object to, shot to his feet. Over the low, ambient laughter, Hayes scolded Judith, but she didn't look particularly wounded.

"What you mean, then," she tried again, "is that you're not sure the baby *Heather* was carrying was your own."

"I don't know everything she was up to!" he shouted. "Hell, I only saw her an hour a day or so!" This disclaimer was something of a miscalculation. Charter, incensed, looked brutally at some anonymous point on the floor.

Judith nodded sagely, walked back to her table, and leaned casually back against it. The overture was over, and now the curtain went up. With her client's prostrate upper body only inches behind her on the defense table, but unacknowledged by any physical gesture, Judith began to ask about Heather. She moved swiftly, hitting her marks with a businesslike efficiency. At their first meeting, did Heather actually ask for a lift home, or did Ashley offer? He couldn't remember. How did they end up at the precise place in the woods where they parked and had sex? Well, Ashley knew the place. He had been there, sometimes. (Judith let this go, the suggestion of his other women, his army of afternoon engagements, lingering in the courtroom.) What, specifically, had Heather done to imply that she had been promiscuous in the past?

She'd said so, Ashley said, triumphant. She'd said she wasn't a virgin!

And might this not mean that she had had only a single lover before him?

He pouted, but he did the math. Yes.

"So what she might well have been saying was that, at the age of eighteen, she had had one sexual experience before her experience with you. Is that right?"

He supposed it could be right.

"Do you think a girl who has had one sexual experience by the age of eighteen is promiscuous?"

He considered, then shrugged. "I don't know."

"How many sexual experiences did you have by the time you were eighteen, Ashley?" Judith sounded genuinely curious. Ashley's outraged *It's different for a guy!* remained miraculously unspoken, but then he couldn't help boasting. "Maybe ten or twelve."

Another ten or twelve! American versus metric. Naomi grinned openly.

"So there you were in the back of your car, in a place back in the woods that you'd driven to because you knew the place from . . ." Judith shrugged, "*some other time.* And you're a twenty-six-year-old married man with . . . let me just do the math here, hang on a minute"—she screwed up her face to calculate—"uh, ten or twelve sexual partners before you were eighteen, then from eighteen to twenty-one we don't know, then another ten or twelve after you moved to Goddard with your wife, so that's at least twenty, plus your wife, twenty-one, plus Heather, of course, twenty-two, but if we go with the twelve, not the ten, it's . . . twenty-six? Could that be right?"

She looked at him, as if for an answer.

"If you say so," Ashley allowed.

"But I'm not saying so," she said innocently. "This is what *you're* saying."

"Then it's true." He folded his arms, tensing for whatever was next.

"And with you in the back of your car, in this spot in the woods, is eighteen-year-old Heather, whom you're giving a lift home to. And she's had one sexual partner. Maybe one sexual partner one time."

"Maybe more," he said harshly.

"But only one time that we can be sure of, I think you're saying." She waited for confirmation, and grudgingly, Ashley gave it.

"Tell me about the back of your car. Was it comfortable?"

"I put down the backseat, so there'd be room."

"Was it clean?"

"Clean?" he said, amazed, as if "clean" were a dirty word.

"Yeah, clean. You know, was it a nice place to have sex?"

"I had tools in the back. Ropes and stuff."

"You had sex on top of the ropes and tools?"

"She could have said no," he shot back. "I might have put down a towel or something. I know later *she* brought a towel to put down," Ashley said with some satisfaction, but the jury, Naomi was pleased to note, by now seemed rather less impressed with this fact.

"So you had sex in the back of your car, on top of the tools and ropes, with maybe a towel." She paused. "How was it?"

"Excuse me?" Ashley said, furious, so Judith asked again, and he shook his head and said it was just fine. "She knew how to move, all right," he added lasciviously.

"In your opinion." Judith nodded. "That is, based on your expertise."

Naomi, clasping and unclasping her hands, noted they were wet, and mashed her palms against the thighs of her pants.

"Now, when you testified earlier about your sexual relationship with Heather, I don't remember your mentioning which method of birth control you were using," Judith said, her voice studiously nonchalant.

He went dumb, struck motionless. Then he looked at her. "What do you mean, which method?"

"Is it a difficult question?" She frowned. "I'm sorry. I would have thought it was pretty straightforward." She leaned forward and said it again, enunciating carefully and with abundant sarcasm. "Which method of birth control were you using when you took Heather Pratt—who was eighteen, and clearly smack in the middle of her fertile years—into the woods, in your car, and had sex with her on top of the ropes and tools?"

"I don't know." He shook his head, furious. "How'm *I* supposed to know?"

"So I infer from this that you yourself were not using a condom."

What? Naomi thought gaily. *And decrease my pleasure*?

"Nope. Don't like them."

"Then you must have been under the impression that Heather was using birth control, I guess."

"It wasn't any of my business," he said stoically.

"Really?" Judith said. "Well, if you have sex with somebody without using birth control and they get pregnant, aren't you the father? I mean, isn't that how it works?"

"Maybe she was using something, I don't know."

"But you didn't ask."

He glared at her, steady and baleful. "I didn't ask."

"I see . . ." Judith nodded. "So there you are, having sex with an eighteen-year-old girl in the back of your car, without using birth control. Did you say, well, you know, if we're going to do this again, maybe we ought to get this birth-control thing sorted out? You know, just to make sure we don't have an unwanted pregnancy on our hands?"

"I didn't say that, no."

"Oh. But you did make plans to see Heather again, didn't you?"

"She didn't have a car," he said in explanation.

"No," Judith repeated in her patient teacher voice. "But then again, she did manage to get herself to and from work before she met you, didn't she?"

He shrugged. "I suppose."

"So it really wasn't about transporting Heather from work to home, was it? I mean, you were after something else, weren't you?"

"She wanted to." Ashley scowled.

"I don't doubt it," said Judith easily. "After all, she was deeply in love with you, wasn't she?"

To Naomi's surprise, Ashley didn't squabble over this point.

"She said so. Yeah."

"She said so frequently, didn't she? Right from the beginning."

"Yes," he said.

"And how did you answer her when she said she loved you, Ashley?"

"She knew I was married!" He was sounding weaker, more

petulant, and Judith let this linger for a moment before asking him how often he would take Heather to the woods. When he answered, the jury reacted with shaking heads.

"And you carried on this way—picking her up at work, making love in the back of your car, five days a week—for how long?"

He didn't know. He shrugged.

"More than a year and a half, is that right?"

"Must be," he said, sardonic.

"You tell her you loved her?"

"No!" He sounded scandalized.

"But you were affectionate. You were kind to her. You did her favors, like driving her around if she had an errand to do, even if it inconvenienced you that you were seen together with her in public."

"She didn't have a car," Ashley said again.

"You gave her gifts."

Now he looked uncomfortable. Briefly he glanced at Heather. "I might have. Nothing major, though."

"You gave her jewelry."

"It wasn't expensive," Ashley protested. Naomi felt her stomach tighten in distaste. Judith went to her table, opened her briefcase, and took out a small plastic evidence bag. She held it up: a puddle of gold glinted in one corner of the plastic.

"You recognize this?" Judith said. Ashley gave a brief nod.

"I gave her a necklace once. So what?"

"This the one? Are you sure?"

She made him take it in his hands, but he held the bag pinched between thumb and forefinger, and barely looked at it.

"What is it, Ashley?"

"I said. A necklace. It has a little *H* on a chain."

"*H* for Heather." It wasn't a question, and he did not feel compelled to respond. "That was a sweet idea for a gift. Do you think Heather appreciated it?"

"Who knows," Ashley said. "I don't know."

Judith entered the necklace into evidence. Then she went back to her table and lifted her legal pad, squinting at it a little.

"You testified that when Heather told you she was pregnant, in the winter of 1984, you 'had no way of knowing' whether the baby was yours. Is that correct?"

"Sure," Ashley said. "I didn't know."

She gave him a supremely dubious look. "Ashley, are you going to tell this jury that you entertained serious doubts that the baby was yours?"

"I didn't know," he said petulantly. "I'm not a doctor."

"No," she said carefully. "You were the man she was having sex with five times a week. You were the man she said was the father of her child. Either of these things alone would have been enough for you to at least consider the possibility, wouldn't you say?"

"I never said it wasn't possible," he pointed out.

"No. But you implied that some phantom lover had sneaked in and impregnated the girl you happened to be having frequent unprotected sex with."

"I just said I didn't *know*. I couldn't be *sure*."

"But didn't you *want* to know? I mean, one way or the other? Somebody says they're having your baby and you're not even interested in finding out?"

"Not really," he said, honestly enough.

"Did it occur to you to make any financial provision for Heather's baby?"

"She wasn't asking me for anything. And my wife was having a baby, too."

"Well, in that case, were you interested in establishing that you were *not* the father of Heather's baby? I mean, what if Heather decided to come back to you one day and demand money that should have gone to your rightful heir; that is, the child you were having with your wife, Sue? Surely you know that, if you were the father of Heather's baby, then Polly had a legal right to some financial support from you."

He shrugged. "I didn't really think about it, to tell you the truth."

"It really wasn't that important to you," Judith observed, "this child your girlfriend was pregnant with."

"She wasn't my girlfriend."

"Sorry. This child the woman you were having sex with five times a week was having. It wasn't very important to you."

"Well no," he affirmed. "I had other stuff on my mind. Like my own baby."

"Right." Judith smiled. "Little Joseph. Bouncing baby boy."

He grinned: proud father.

"Did you stop having sex with Heather when she became pregnant?"

He blushed briefly. Naomi couldn't imagine why. He said no.

"You continued to have sex with her? In the car?"

"She wanted to," he said.

"And you also wanted to, apparently," Judith observed. "Until what point in her pregnancy did you continue to have sex with Heather?" Ashley was silent. "Five months? Six months?"

"I don't know." He put up his hands. "She was pretty big the last time, I remember that."

"So pretty much all the way to the end, right?"

"Maybe," he said, offhand.

"And were you having sex with your wife at the same time?" Judith asked.

Ashley looked at her in horror. Charter objected loudly, and they went into a huddle at the sidebar again. Again, Naomi saw, Judith got what she wanted. She went back to her table and asked the question a second time.

"Sue didn't want to," he said tightly. "She said it hurt."

"So your wife didn't want to have sex during her pregnancy. But luckily for you, your g—Oh"—she grinned—"sorry again! But luckily *Heather* didn't seem to mind. So you got to keep having sex."

"Was that a question?" Ashley said dryly. Judith smiled, almost fondly.

"Now, when Heather's baby, Polly Elizabeth Pratt, was born the following summer, did it occur to you then to wonder whether you were her father?"

"She looked like Heather," he said.

"I'm sorry, is that an answer to my question?"

"She didn't look like me," he said again.

Judith shook her head. "In other words, no. You didn't wonder whether you were her father, even then, because she didn't look like you. Is that right?"

He shrugged. "Right."

"But even if the baby didn't look like you, in your opinion, the fact remained that your g—excuse me, the woman you were having sex with five times a week, had a new baby she said was yours. Did you *then* feel moved to make some kind of contribution to this child's care?"

"You mean money?" Ashley frowned.

"Well, money, support. Diaper changing. I don't know. Something?"

"I gave her my car," he said hotly.

"Yes, so you did. A curious baby gift."

"It wasn't a baby gift. It was for her, because I wouldn't be that free anymore to give her lifts."

"Or have sex with her."

"No," he agreed. "I was trying to break it off."

"But it didn't work that way. In fact," Judith said thoughtfully, "didn't you have sex with Heather on the very day you brought the car over to her house?"

He considered this. He looked away in disgust, and answered the question.

"So basically you weren't that committed to breaking it off, after all, were you?"

And on. The money he didn't give her, the toys he didn't buy, the doctor's appointments he didn't attend, the acknowledgement he didn't make, even as he proudly displayed his son Joseph to neighbors and acquaintances. Judith kept her disgust barely restrained. Ashley chaffed beneath her questions, but he never betrayed any sense that he had behaved at all badly. Polly might be his in the remotest sense, the logic seemed to go, but she was Heather's in actuality, and since nothing was asked of him, nothing was given. Judith got him to begrudge Heather's warmth as a mother, her love for Polly, her attentiveness to the baby's needs. She forced him to admit that even faced with the evidence of her fertility, he continued to have sex with her without using birth control. And finally, she hauled him through a narrative of that final night, their interrupted concord, in the backseat, atop the tools, in the winter forest. He didn't know how many people were out there, or who they were, most of them, because he had seen only Sue, and Sue's mother, who was barking that high, aggravating bark she made. There were flashlights, all aimed at him, and he was pissed, furious really. So yeah, he'd taken Heather's arm and they had gone away, the two of them, just to show them all that he wasn't going to knuckle under just because they said so and his wife bawled a little in front of strangers.

"You left your wife there," Judith said, her voice newly soft. "You took Heather and you left your wife and the others."

"Yup." He nodded, smug.

"How that must have hurt Sue, to see you walking off like that with Heather."

"Well, we're still married," he said in his own defense.

"You didn't mind hurting Sue, in other words."

He looked surprised at her obtuseness. "If she hadn't followed my car, she wouldn't have gotten hurt."

"And what about Heather, Ashley? How did you think Heather was going to interpret this, your having the choice to stay with your wife but choosing her instead?"

"I didn't *choose* her," he said scornfully.

"You don't think so? You don't think that's what it felt like to her? You took her arm and you walked away from your wife."

Charter objected. Ashley could not know what it felt like to Heather. Judith nodded. The question was as potent unanswered.

"So you left your wife in the woods and you went off with Heather. Whose idea was it to go to the mill?"

"I don't remember." He sulked. "Might have been mine."

"Whose idea was it to break in through the window?"

"I knew I could fix the window the next day."

Judith nodded. "I see. And do I understand correctly that you broke into the mill because you wanted sex?"

Again, that look of disapproval, for her coarseness.

"We had unfinished business. We both wanted it."

"I just want to make sure I understand," Judith said. "Heather never actually said, 'Let's go to the mill. Let's break into the mill. I want to have sex.' "

He shrugged. "She might have. I don't remember."

"You have no memory of her saying those things."

"I don't remember."

"And yet," Judith reflected, "those things happened. Is it possible that Heather communicated them to you telepathically?"

"What?" Ashley stared.

"Or is it possible that these were *your* decisions? That you did not consult Heather at all? Because, let's see, you were pissed, by your own account. And what better way to get back at your wife and all her busybody friends than to grab your girlfriend and go and have sex with her as soon as possible? And the mill was close, right? And it really didn't matter if you broke in, because you'd be the one to fix it, anyway. And when you get right down to it, this whole thing made you pretty horny, too, I guess."

"Hey," Ashley said, "just wait a minute."

"What, you weren't horny?"

"I didn't—"

"But after you were finished with Heather you knew you were going to go home and make it up with your wife some-how, right? So you looked down at this girl who adored you, who was lying there next to you, so completely happy because, after years of loving you, and bearing your child, and watching you go home to your wife, you had just chosen her, and taken her away, and made love to her. And you looked down at this girl and said, Well, so long, sweetie, this seems like a good time to break up. *Or words to that effect.* Right, Ashley?"

The room, was silent.

"Is that right?"

"I was a married man. I never said I would leave my wife."

"Well, I guess that makes you some kind of paragon, Ash-ley," Judith said cruelly.

He sulked, his arms crossed. The women on the jury were glaring at him.

"And she was pregnant. And you were the father of her second child."

"If you say so." He wouldn't look at her now.

"Because there was nobody else for Heather, Ashley, was there?"

"There might have been!"

"Because she adored you, and there was nobody else. And eight months later she gave birth to one baby, and you were its father."

That wasn't a question, Charter objected, and Hayes con-curred.

"And you never contacted her again," Judith said. "You never gave a damn about her. You just dropped her, isn't that right?"

"We broke up," he affirmed.

"Were you aware that Heather's grandmother died suddenly on the very day that you dropped her?"

"I heard that," he said.

"Did you call her to offer your condolences?"

He said no.

"Did it occur to you that Heather must be devastated, losing her only relative and the father of her child on the very same day?"

He scowled at her.

"Can you imagine how it must have felt for Heather to discover that she was again pregnant, so soon after this moment in her life?"

Ashley shrugged and examined his hands.

"You never gave her a second thought, did you, Ashley? You just went back to your wife and kissed and made up, and got her pregnant again, is that right? And it was all right with you because you were a married man, even if you didn't behave like one, and it was too bad for Heather if she made the mistake of thinking you cared. That about it?"

"Nope," he said, sarcastic, downright adolescent.

"Too bad for Heather. Too bad for Polly, who would never know her father. Too bad for the second child you'd already conceived with Heather, who would also never know her father. She knew you were married!"

"Hey," he shouted, "you can't just say I was their father. I don't know that!"

Judith sighed. She twisted on the desktop and opened one of her files, fishing out a form and holding it before her, peering at it. "Would it surprise you if I told you that a forensic serologist has concluded to—I'm quoting here—a 'high degree of certainty' that you are in fact the biological father of Polly Elizabeth Pratt?"

He took this in. "I guess not," he said grudgingly.

"You're not particularly surprised."

"I just said so."

"And would it surprise you if I told you that the same forensic serologist has concluded, to an equally high degree of certainty, that you are also the biological father of an unnamed infant girl, born last September, and in fact one of the babies at issue in this case?"

"You can get anyone to say anything," he said bitterly. "You just hire your own expert and pay them, isn't that how it works?"

Judith appeared taken aback. She fluttered the report in her hand. "Well, I wouldn't know. This report was actually made by the prosecution's expert." Wide-eyed, she let the jury note her surprise. She smiled.

"Ashley," she said after this moment had been milked for its worth, "let me ask you something. You knew Heather pretty well, obviously. By your own account, you saw her almost every day. Did she *ever* tell you that she was seeing another man?"

He shook his head. "She didn't *tell* me, no."

"Well, did you ever actually *see* her with another man?"

He hadn't *seen* her, either, he admitted.

"Or ever come across any concrete evidence that she had met with and had a physical relationship with another man?"

She would hardly leave *evidence*, he countered. But no.

"And you have no idea who this phantom Christopher Flynn is, do you, Ashley?"

"I said I never met him. I said that before."

Judith sighed, a mite theatrically. "You know perfectly well there's no such person as Christopher Flynn, don't you, Ashley?"

"I don't—"

"You know there was you and just you. A pregnancy that produced your daughter Polly. Then a second pregnancy that produced only one infant, your second daughter, who was born and died without a name. You know that, don't you, Ashley?"

"I don't know shit," he yelled, and then Charter was yelling, too, and Judith, with a deeply disingenuous smile, briefly thanked the witness and said she had no further use for him.

Chapter 33

Friends Can Quarrel

"GUESS I'M GOING TO NEED A NEW CARPEN-
ter," Judith said the next morning as Naomi approached. She
was waiting on one of the benches in front of the courthouse,
wrapped in her heavy coat, her briefcase pinched between her
calves.

"What, did he call or something?" Naomi said. She took a
seat and gave Judith one of the two takeout coffees she was
carrying. It didn't matter which one, they took it the same way.

"No, but Sue did. Around midnight. You won't believe what
she called me."

"What?" Naomi put down her cup, peeled off the plastic
cap, and carefully tore out a triangle. A triangle-shaped wedge
of steam hit the cool air when the cap went back on.

"A kike," Judith said smugly. "Can you believe it? I've
never known *anyone* who was actually called a kike." She
considered. "I'm not sure I even know exactly what it means."

Naomi shook her head and sipped, instantly scalding her
tongue. "Jesus, Judith. I'm really sorry."

"Don't be. My only problem was calming Joel down. He
wanted to call the papers. But I don't think it would actually
help." She peeled off the lid and blew at the black surface.
"For all I know, it might reflect badly on Heather if her lawyer
started whining about being called names. And frankly, those
eight or nine people in New Hampshire who can't figure out
on their own that somebody named Friedman is probably Jewish, why should I tell them?"

"But it's nasty. For you."

"Nah." She grinned. "Listen, it's rare in life you get to be
so totally on higher moral ground. Especially in my line of
work. This is just fine."

Naomi laughed. "Maybe she resented your implication that
her husband ought to keep his fly zipped a little more tightly."

"Maybe. *I* would."

"Maybe you were a little hard on her yesterday," Naomi said, testing the waters. She didn't actually believe that herself.

"I don't think so." Judith blew and sipped. "But if I was, it's because I had to be. In something like this, you just can't take prisoners. I needed to show that Ashley always went to Heather, you know? Never the other way around. He went to her when he wanted sex. He took her in his car. He chose the place in the woods. He went to her house. He bought her gifts. He called all the shots in the relationship. Sue's resentment was misplaced. I had to show that I would have been disgusted, too, if he'd been my husband."

"If he'd been your husband, he'd be an ex-husband."

"No shit." She grinned. *"Extend thy balls to another woman and I reserve the right to cut them off."*

"I was chopping onions, your honor, and I was crying, and I just couldn't see clearly! I had no idea he was resting them on the chopping block!"

"He fell on my knife, fourteen times!"

"But really, he looks fine without them."

"I never even knew he had 'em in the first place!"

Naomi was red-faced, sputtering glee. "Judith, you are *evil*."

"Yeah," she said happily. "That's why the boys all love me so . . ."

"Fuck the boys. *I* love you. I think you're swell," Naomi said.

Judith shook her head modestly.

"No, seriously. I thought you were brilliant with Martina yesterday. Did I tell you?"

"Sure." She nodded. "But don't let that stop you from saying it again."

So Naomi said it again, because Judith had indeed been brilliant. Martina Graves had testified about Heather's first months at the sports center: her own acts of friendship and neighborliness toward the new employee, then her gradual alarm at what was developing between Heather and Ashley, and her outright revulsion at the illegitimate pregnancy Heather flaunted. Christian values, Martina said, wringing her hands in her lap, rendered her incapable of continuing the friendship with Heather. She had been shocked to discover how vastly different a person her friend had turned out to be—profligate, prideful, wanton. Martina shook her hay-blond head. It was sad, she told the jury, but the fault was her own for not seeing sooner the true measure of Heather's character. She, like Sue Deacon before her, did not personally know Christopher Flynn, but Martina volunteered to the district attorney that she was praying for him nonetheless.

Charter, murmuring gratitude, then turned the witness over to Judith.

And so followed an hour's discourse on the essence of Christian values. Had Martina, Judith asked, ever offered counsel to her misguided young friend? No? What about support during her pregnancy? Solace during her bereavement? Succor during her imprisonment? Perhaps Martina would have preferred, under the circumstances, that Heather procure an abortion?

Judith downed the last of her coffee and crumpled the cup.

"I'm worried about Heather," Naomi said, understating the obvious. "She isn't strong."

"No," Judith agreed.

"I didn't think she was going to make it through Ashley's testimony," Naomi said, looking up at the prison wing of the courthouse. "I thought she was going to fall apart."

"She *did* fall apart," Judith said dryly.

"No, I mean . . . I thought she was going to start screaming, or have a fit or something."

"And that would have been worse than just moaning and groaning like a zombie? I don't think so. She made herself seem absolutely demented to the jury. I mean, here I am, building her up, *resilient girl abandoned by spineless bastard, mother of the year,* right? And instead of sitting there and attempting to look the part, she behaves like a wet noodle. I could use the support, you know. I mean, I'm only trying to save her life here."

"Well, of course," Naomi soothed. "I'm sure she knows that."

"Are you?" Judith said grimly. "You see, *I'm* not. I'm not sure she knows that at all. She just glowers at me any time I say anything bad about Ashley, that's all she cares about. You know, what is this about, anyway? I mean, what does she think we're all doing here? Does she think she did nothing to contribute to this mess?"

Naomi could not seem to say anything. Judith's voice never

rose above a whisper, but the whisper grew harsh and her face tight with aversion.

"You know, you ask any criminal defense attorney and they'll tell you: the worst thing isn't your generic evil guy—the one who wreaks havoc and then says he was somewhere else at the time. I mean, when that guy gets convicted he just shrugs, like, *Oh well, I gave it my best shot.* Nope! The worst thing is your basic sociopath. You know, it's not just that he's been falsely accused and he's innocent, but actually, *he's the victim here!* Can you believe it? It's all twisted around, it's a horrible perversion of justice that he should be in the defendant's seat, because the truth is that the real injustice has been done to *him!*"

"I don't—" Naomi began.

"Oh"—she held up her hand—"don't listen to me. I'm just tired. And she's pissing me off."

But Naomi's thoughts were coursing on ahead, even as the two women sat motionless and Naomi's coffee went stone cold between her palms. She was testing the notion, trying to dull it before having to speak it aloud, but it wouldn't dull. It was so obvious, and so totally impossible. She took a breath.

"You hate her."

Judith frowned at the broad gray wall of the courthouse. "Yes." Slowly, she nodded once. The wet breeze picked up and then dropped a stray tight curl. "I believe I do."

"But why?" Naomi wailed, unable to temper her voice. Judith looked at her sharply; then her face softened.

"I would have thought that was obvious, Naomi. I hate her because she killed her baby."

Naomi stared, numb and lost. She did not know how to look, or how to answer. Judith shrugged.

"She had a beautiful, healthy baby. And she killed it."

"But"—Naomi found her voice—"my God, Judith, there's no evidence for that at all!"

"Keep your voice down," Judith said. She put an oddly comforting hand on Naomi's arm. "Listen, Naomi. Heather hardly did anything *for* her baby, did she? Did she run up to the house? Or call the doctor? Or even slap it like they do in the movies? No. Which is amazing. I mean, everyone knows you're supposed to slap the kid, right? Isn't there some instinct that tells you you have to make sure the baby is all right? But not Heather. She never wanted that baby, so she just sat there and waited for it to be as dead as she wanted it to be." She paused and looked hard at Naomi. "Even if she didn't do anything *to* it. Even if there was no overt act to *harm* the baby . . . even if she didn't shoot it or . . . stab it. She *killed* it. She let it die. So yes. I hate her. You can feel what you like. You have some history with this person, but I don't. All I know about her is that she ran around with a married man and she killed her baby." She smiled softly, disconcertingly. "Please don't look so upset about it!"

"But you're defending her," Naomi said wonderingly. "I mean, if you think—"

"No. I'm defending a woman wrongly accused of stabbing her infant to death. I'm defending a woman who came to the attention of police solely because her fellow citizens condemned her moral character, and her sexuality, and her decision to have an illegitimate child, all of which I find reprehensible, as I've said before. I don't need to like Heather in order to defend her. Which, as it turns out, is no bad thing." She stopped and shifted on the bench. She was looking at Naomi, not unkindly, but with some amusement. "Actually, I doubt you like her much, either."

Naomi roused herself to object, but found herself strangely mute on the subject. She could only shake her head. "I just . . . It seems strange to me that you're so judgmental, that's all."

And Judith, to her surprise, laughed openly at this and shook her head. "Oh please! *Judgmental.* I can't stand this sanctimonious shit about being judgmental. I mean, come on—every single person is judgmental, especially the ones who whine about how it's wrong. We're just using our minds, that's all. Our *characters.* This is who we are, this is what we think. *It's our moral code.* Isn't that what separates us from the monkeys? You know? That ability to be judgmental?"

"But still," Naomi said, flailing a bit, still utterly thrown. Still *what*, she didn't quite know. "It isn't . . . I mean, it's not your place to judge Heather, no matter what you think of her privately."

Judith frowned, but affectionately. "Because somebody else is going to? Ultimately? Like, on the Day of Judgment when all sins are revealed? Goats to the left, sheep to the right? And we take our leave of Heather the murderess and go frolic in the land of milk and honey?" She shook her head. "Oh, Naomi, you of all people."

Naomi stared at her. "Did I say that?" It came out sounding not accusatory but stunned.

And Judith, to her further amazement, had covered her face with her hands. Naomi instinctively put an arm over Judith's shoulder and was instantly able to feel it shake, even through the buffer of their two heavy coats, but having moved her arm, was not able to move it again. She did not understand, in the first place, why she had abruptly assumed this posture, why it was called for, and above all what was happening to Judith. That their talk had turned the corner to this inexplicable barrier at all was surprising, but the suddenness of the turn left her lost. Now, the incongruity of their posture—two women in winter coats on a bench beside an ugly municipal building, one sobbing, the other sheltering the first with a useless arm—rendered Naomi inert. She had never felt so stupid, so ineffectual, so undecided about what to say next.

Then, as sharply as it had begun, it ended. Judith pulled herself together, and Naomi found her voice.

"Are you—"

"I'm fine." Judith put up her head. Her eyes, incredibly, held only the faintest aftermath of tears. "It gets me sometimes. This whole *mishegaas*. You'd think people wouldn't fuck up their lives like this, you know?"

"I know," said Naomi, who wasn't sure she did but thought it best to say so. She kissed her friend. "It's all right."

"You think so?"

"Of course," Naomi said heartily, glad that whatever had just passed between them appeared to have passed. "I'm sorry we quarreled," she said after a minute. "Did we quarrel?"

Judith looked surprised. "No. Not at all." Then she smiled. "I mean, I don't think we did."

"Friends can quarrel," Naomi said, offhand. "Not that we did."

"Sure." She looked at her watch. Ten minutes to court.

"Did you fix it so I could bring Polly to see her mom today?"

Judith nodded. "Yeah. They're expecting you around six."

"Good. That'll give me time to get up to Mrs. Horgan and back."

"Have you told Polly?"

Naomi bit her lip. "Well no. I don't think she'd get it, actually. So I didn't."

"Well, I'm sure you're right."

"It's the only thing I could think of yesterday," said Naomi. "I mean Heather was so . . ." She trailed off. She was not willing to open this subject again. "Anyway, I think it'll be good for them both. Get Heather back on track a bit, you know? Give her something to focus on."

"Hope so," Judith said briefly. She was looking past Naomi now, to the front steps of the courthouse with its little thicket of people and microphones. Naomi saw her concentrate, her lips pursed.

"What?" Naomi turned her head, too.

Judith was beginning to smile. "I spy . . ."

"What?"

"With my little eye . . . Well, well." She nodded. "So they actually made it."

Abruptly she grinned, and Naomi could only look blankly at her, struck speechless by the quicksilver of this transition.

"What?"

"Not a what. It's a who."

A who, Naomi thought, quickly turning to follow the line of Judith's gaze. Or indeed a what, for though two of the three people walking toward them were decidedly female, the figure at the forefront of their triangle was not immediately classifiable. It was tall, with slender hips and light hair close-shaved to a delicate skull. It wore a silver stud in one ear, a pair of corduroys the color of rust, and a dark green sweatshirt that said, bewilderingly, WAD. Or was it W.A.D.? Naomi peered. One of the women was carrying a knapsack over the crook of her elbow, unzipped and crammed with lavender paper.

"I'm Ella," said the one in front. A woman? Naomi frowned. She had a deep voice.

"Hello, Ella." Judith got up. Naomi got up, too.

"We spoke last night."

"So we did. I'm so pleased you could make it."

They shook hands all around. One of the others was called Simone. The third woman just said hi and ducked her head.

"We had a meeting last night," Ella said. She stood with her hands on her narrow hips. "I'm not the only one who'd seen the magazine. A bunch of us felt that we needed to get together and speak about it."

Judith nodded, reserved but open. "I'm glad."

"It was when we read that she'd been at Dartmouth that we more or less felt compelled to be here. You know?"

Naomi, who didn't, looked at Judith. Judith smiled and nodded.

"I mean, bad enough this should happen at all. Even worse that it should happen where we live ourselves. But the fact that she was a member of our own academic community—that's what sort of put us over the edge. So we started calling, and Simone set up a table at Thayer this morning with a sign-up sheet. We'll have a convoy here sometime around midday. After morning classes," she said, a touch apologetically.

Naomi, who was taking this in, looked in alarm at Judith. Judith wanted this?

But Judith seemed pleased. "And may I see the flyer?"

The as-yet-nameless woman handed Judith one of her lavender pages. WHY IS HEATHER PRATT ON TRIAL? Naomi read over her shoulder. BECAUSE A PATRIARCHAL JUSTICE SYSTEM WOULD RATHER FIND A WITCH TO BURN THAN EXAMINE ITS OWN CONSCIENCE.

"This is good," Judith said. She passed the flyer to Naomi. "How are you going to do this?"

"Loud and long," Simone said affably. "As loud we can and as long as it takes."

"Ah," Judith said. "Well, that might, in the end, be the less effective course."

Simone looked suddenly fierce, but Ella appeared to listen.

"The thing is, we all want the same thing here. We want to help Heather. Yes?"

A tentative nod from the nameless one. Ella still held her counsel.

"So we need you to make your points on her behalf without calling undue attention to other elements of your platform, regardless of how we ourselves are in solidarity with them. This is a very conservative community, as you know. This isn't Hanover."

The rolling of eyes. Hanover wasn't, evidently, Hanover either.

"I hope you're not expecting us to 'dress appropriately,' " Simone sneered.

"Not at all. By all means, be here and be yourselves. But you'll be doing Heather no good at all if you appear aggressive. Try not to give the impression that you feel bitterness toward the members of this community, or by extension the television or radio community. If you're asked to speak to the press, do it calmly, even though you're angry. You support Heather. You're here for Heather, because you think her treatment has been unfair, and you're ready to say why. But if you yell and scream, you'll alienate people who'd otherwise agree with you. Do you see?"

They looked uncomfortably at one another. "Thank you," Ella said finally. "We respect your opinion."

"And I yours," Judith said evenly. Naomi handed back the flyer. "I appreciate your being here, and I know Heather will, too."

"Tell her Dartmouth women support her!" the nameless one chirped, and Judith nodded and said she would. Then they turned in a single, formless group and went back to the courthouse to take up their assigned positions.

Chapter 34

There Is No Group Here

"DARTMOUTH WOMEN SUPPORT YOU," JUDITH said archly, as Heather was seated next to her.

"What?" said Heather. She looked, if possible, even more wan than the day before. The trial was acting as a kind of parasite, sucking her strength from within. There was, Naomi mused, some manner of race going on, to see whether it would finish its work before the proceedings were completed.

"Your sisters. Your fellow women of Dartmouth. They're turning out to support you in their covens. They're visualizing victory."

"I don't understand," Heather said fearfully. "I don't know anyone at Dartmouth. I only met a few people."

"Judith," Naomi whispered disapprovingly. "Come on."

Without turning around, Judith nodded consent. She went back to her notes for Ann Chase. She was looking forward to this. Heather, for her part, twisted around to give Naomi a querying look, and Naomi tried to hustle up an expression of warm encouragement.

"I'm bringing Polly tonight. It's all set."

Heather closed her eyes, briefly animated. Then that passed, too, and she turned around again.

Ann arrived, early and as bright as Naomi had ever seen her. She was dressed in something Naomi had never seen her wear—a magenta woolen dress with a lace collar—and she had had something done to her hair, Naomi thought: a kind of hardening rinse that lacquered it into place. She walked down the central aisle of the courtroom, passing the table where Judith and Heather sat, and somehow managing to convey her contempt for them without ever glancing in their direction. After being sworn in, a ritual she enacted with gravity and no small self-importance, she gave her name as Mrs. Whit Chase and took her seat. She did not seem to suffer on the witness stand, as Naomi had done. She spoke with confidence, if not perceivable glee.

Heather—the gist of her testimony went—was a slut.

Heather flaunted her affair, and then her pregnancy, and later her child.

Heather dressed provocatively. She even disrobed in public. In fact: on the deck of Tom and Whit's general store, Ann's own family business. This, as it happened, created such a horrendous situation that the police had to come to persuade her to cover herself.

That Heather had found herself in this situation was not remotely surprising. Heather had never shown the slightest regard for any but her own needs, wishes, and, above all, urges.

She had not personally met Christopher Flynn, Ann Chase concluded, but she had heard of him.

When Charter finished his direct examination, Ann looked smoothly at Judith without anxiety, even waiting calmly while Judith jotted notes.

Judith stood. She tugged the back of her jacket and stood at her place. "Hello," she said.

A wary nod.

"I'm Judith Friedman. We've met before, though I don't think we were formally introduced."

That day at the mill, Naomi thought. Clearly Judith hoped to unnerve Ann with the memory.

Ann pursed her lips.

"You stated your name"—Judith smiled—"as Mrs. Whit Chase." Her voice was warm. Alarmingly warm, Naomi thought, looking quickly at her. "Would it be all right if I called you Whit?"

"I . . ." Ann's composure drained immediately. "No. My *husband*. My husband's name is Whit."

"Oh, but you said . . ." Judith stumbled carefully. "I don't understand. Do you have a first name of your own?"

"Ann," said Ann Chase. "My name is Ann."

"Oh," Judith said. "I'm sorry. I was confused. Well, may I call you Ann?" Ann Chase clearly wished to say no, but instead she nodded.

"That's fine."

"Good. *Ann*. Now"—she made a show of shuffling her papers—"I've been listening carefully to your testimony, and I'm not sure I understand exactly why you're here today. Am I right in thinking that you have no direct knowledge that bears on the deaths of these two infants?"

It took her a moment to work through the syntax. Then she took umbrage. "You are not right. I know what I know."

"But what is that, Ann?" Judith said sweetly. "Your testimony has been wholly about what you considered to be Heather's sexual misbehavior. I never heard you even mention the two infants whose deaths are at issue in this trial. Am I wrong about that?"

"Well." She was thinking through her response. "It may be that my only *eyewitness* account was of her taking off her clothes and messing around with a married man, but *I* think that has something to do with the babies. If *you* don't . . ." She shrugged dramatically and rolled her eyes.

"Did Heather confide relevant information to you?" Judith pressed.

"Of course not," Ann said, offended.

"She never said, 'Ann, because we're friends or acquaintances, I want to unburden myself to you and tell you what is happening in my life'?"

"No." She shook her head to dislodge the disagreeable thought.

"Oh, but then you must have seen her do something to these babies, with your own eyes. And so you're here to tell us what you saw."

"Did I *say* that?" Ann sneered. "Did you *hear* me say that?"

"No, Ann," Judith said solemnly. "What I heard you say was that you did not like Heather. You did not approve of her choice of lover or her behavior with that lover. But you see, I can't for the life of me figure out what your opinion of Heather's personal life has to do with two dead babies. I'm just completely at a loss, and I need you to help me. That's all."

"Which part don't you understand?" Ann said cruelly. "The part about her running around with a married man and taking off her clothes in public or the part about her having babies out of wedlock and expecting that to be just super fine with everybody?"

"Ah," Judith said happily. "I'm glad you brought this up,

because I'd like to look more carefully at these things, if you don't mind."

"I don't mind," Ann said smugly, gearing up to vent again.

"I take it you disapproved of the fact that Heather and Ashley had a physical, sexual relationship."

"Certainly." She nodded. "It was disgusting."

"You must have been forced to witness many lewd acts, I suppose. For example, actual intercourse between Heather and Ashley?"

"Don't be ridiculous. They wouldn't do it in front of me!"

"No?" Judith said. "Well, perhaps you saw them fondle each other. Did you see that?"

"No." She was catching on, and naturally she didn't like it.

"Well, you must have seen them kiss, I suppose." She waited a beat. "You never even saw them kiss?"

Ann, tense, remained silent.

"What about hand-holding?"

Her timing, Naomi thought, was matchless.

"Did you ever see them speak to each other?"

Now Ann wasn't talking on principle. She sat, petulant, in her seat, her arms crossed. At this point Judith calmly asked Judge Hayes to request that the witness answer. To Ann's immense displeasure, he did so.

"I never *saw* those things," she spat. "All right?"

"Well, sure." Judith frowned. "But then how exactly did Ashley and Heather flaunt their sexual relationship in front of you? I mean, from what you describe, they sound as if they were pretty discreet about their activities."

"They would go off in the woods!" Ann shouted. "They didn't do it where anybody could see."

"Now how"—Judith smiled—"could you possibly know that?" She waited for the answer she knew wouldn't come. "Did you follow Ashley and Heather into the woods, Ann?"

"There was a group," she said, haughty but newly uncertain.

"I don't care about a group," Judith instructed sternly. She held out her hands, the palms up. "There is no *group* here. You've come forward voluntarily to lend the weight of your own testimony—your own evidence—to the serious charges against Heather. I'm interested in *you*."

"Fine." Ann jerked her head. Her red cheeks were flushed even deeper than usual. "That's fine."

"So you followed Ashley and Heather into the woods."

"There were—" She stopped herself and gave Judith a bitter look. "I did. Sure."

"Do you recall the date of this event?"

"Last January. I don't know the date."

"Could it have been January the sixteenth?"

She shrugged. "Could have been."

"And whose idea was it to drive out after Ashley and Heather?"

"Sue's idea," Ann said. "His *wife's*."

"Did you walk or did you drive your car?"

"I drove."

"Did you wait to see which way Ashley's car was going and then follow it?"

"I guess," she said tersely.

"And what was the route you followed?"

Ann frowned. "Along the Sabbathday River, past Nate's Landing. There was a logging road."

"Was it a long drive?" Judith voice was vaguely sympathetic.

"Not too long."

"And how far back in the woods?"

" 'Bout a quarter mile. Their car was parked."

"Was it light out, Ann?" Judith asked.

"No. It was dark."

"And were there lights on inside Ashley's car?"

"No." Then, unable to resist: "They didn't need any lights for what they were doing!"

Judith smiled at this unanticipated tidbit. "But how could you see what they were doing, Ann? By your own account it was dark out and dark inside the car."

"I had a flashlight!"

Judith looked studiously amazed. "You had a flashlight? You went up to this car, in the darkness, in the woods, and shone a flashlight in it?"

She was enraged. "You're making it sound worse than it was! You make out it was me doing something wrong. You don't care about what they were doing!" she yelled.

Naomi looked reflexively at the jury, as she did whenever there was some outburst. Her favorite juror, she was pleased to note, looked downright embarrassed.

"But that's just my point, Ann," Judith said kindly. "I *don't* care what they were doing. It's none of my business what those two consenting adults were doing in their car, in the woods after dark. What I don't understand is why *you* cared."

She waited for an answer, knowing there wouldn't be one.

"Is it possible that you got in your car on a winter's night and followed this young couple along a snowy, remote road into the woods, and then took out your flashlight and approached their car, because after eighteen months of what you considered a public affair, you wanted to see it with your own eyes?"

"That's absolutely revolting!" Ann said. "I resent that!"

"After all," Judith went on, impervious, "this wanton affair had been going on and on. You knew it had to be a sexual affair, because people said so, and because there had been a baby. Polly. But you'd never actually seen any action, had you?"

"I'm not going to answer that!" she yelped.

"So when you took your flashlight and approached their car, weren't you hoping you'd get to see an actual, carnal act? Something you considered obscene? Something you could tell your friends about? You were hoping to see some skin, weren't you, Ann?"

"I did see some skin!" Ann objected. "Like I said. This girl couldn't keep her clothes on. I told you—she got undressed on my own porch, for God's sake!"

"Ah yes." Judith switched gears. "The public nudity. This was"—she bent forward over the table to consult her notes— "October of 1984. A few months before you and your *group* followed Heather and Ashley into the woods, with your flashlights. Is that correct?"

She set her jaw. "The *date's* correct," Ann said stiffly, on her toes again.

"Now, when you described the incident a few minutes ago, for Mr. Charter, you said the porch of your store was full of customers—mostly tourists, by your account—and you suddenly saw Heather begin to strip. You said . . . you know," Judith considered, "I can't quite recall the exact words. Could we have them read back, your honor?"

The court reporter, a thin man with scurrying, arachnid fingers, found the place and read: "Answer: 'Next thing I saw, she had her shirt unbuttoned and her breasts hanging out. I asked her to button up her shirt, but she wouldn't.'

"Question: 'Did you remind Miss Pratt that she was on your property, and that you were requesting she button up her shirt?'

"Answer: 'Sure, I did. But she wouldn't do it. I suppose she didn't see anything wrong with it.' "

"Thanks," Judith told the court reporter. She turned back to Ann. "You used the word 'breasts.' Is that right?"

Ann looked at her as if she were a moron. "Sure, it's right."

"Breasts, plural. Two breasts."

"Well"—she was livid—"I saw one."

"*One* breast? Not *two* breasts?"

"What difference does it make!" Ann spat.

"Ann," Judith said, "you know perfectly well what difference it makes. You know, though you chose not to tell this jury, that Heather was not, in fact, stripping off her clothes in order to exhibit herself to the general populace, but was preparing to nurse her infant daughter, Polly."

"How do *I* know what she was doing?" Ann retorted.

"Well, might you have inferred that a woman with an infant in her arms, who is unbuttoning her blouse, is just possibly preparing to nurse her child?"

"Listen, I don't give a damn what she thought she was doing. She was taking off her clothes!"

"Really?" Judith asked. "Her pants? Her shoes? Or was she just unbuttoning her blouse?"

"Just the blouse, that I *saw*. Who knows where she might have stopped."

"Do you have children, Ann?" Judith said, her voice suddenly softer and more intimate.

Ann looked at her with intense dislike. "Four. They're grown now."

"Did you breast-feed your own children?"

"I don't see that's any of your business!" Ann objected. She looked to Charter for help.

"Well, it seems to me that if you had nursed your own children you might have recognized the gesture Heather was making. So I ask you again: Did you breast-feed your own children?"

"Certainly not. All mine got the bottle. They got formula."

Judith walked over to her for the first time. Ann watched her approach with something like wary repulsion. When she neared the witness box, she placed a friendly elbow on the railing.

"How do you feel about breast-feeding, Ann?"

She squared her shoulders. "It's fine. If you can't afford the formula, it's fine."

"So formula is better than breast-feeding?"

"It's cleaner. It's scientifically better."

"You know," Judith said kindly, "I think most mothers—and most doctors—felt that way during the time your children were young. Yet many women today who have the option to do either actually *prefer* to breast-feed their babies."

Another jerked shrug. "Why would someone do it if you could do what was cleaner? Only to make a display of yourself!"

"Someone might do it for the same reason you fed your own children with formula: because they believed it was the best thing for the baby. Are you aware, Ann, that doctors today feel that breast-feeding is, in fact, healthier for the baby than bottle-feeding? Perhaps Heather was following the best advice available to her, just as you followed the best advice available to you when you were a young mother."

"I hope you're not comparing me to her! I don't give a good goddamn what she does. I care where she does it."

"I'm well aware of that. After all, didn't you try to have Heather arrested for nursing her baby on your porch that day?"

"She was taking her clothes off!"

"She was nursing her baby, Ann. And it offended you so much that you called the police."

"Hey," Ann shouted. "I have a right to say what goes on on my own porch!"

"Without question," Judith said soothingly. "You could have gone over to Heather and suggested she move inside. You could have offered her a private room inside the shop where she could have fed her hungry child in warmth and quiet. Or you could have just told her the truth: that nursing in public made you uncomfortable and you'd be very grateful if she could find somewhere else to do it." Judith paused. "But for whatever reason, you felt unable to do those things. Instead, you called the police."

"I had a right to do it." Ann held her ground.

"And you encouraged Nelson Erroll, the sheriff who responded, to arrest Heather on a public-indecency charge, even though you were well aware that Heather was only attempting to feed her child."

"Like I said, I—"

"Had a right," Judith said fiercely. "Yes, I think we know about your right, Ann. I'd like to move on now."

She was so commanding, Naomi thought. She played it as if Ann were a fish on her line: a strong and pigheaded fish, but stupid. "You gave your place of employment as Tom and Whit's, the general store. Is that correct?"

"It's where I work," she confirmed. "With my husband. Have done for years."

"But you had a second line of work, didn't you? Until recently, that is."

"Only part-time," she said grudgingly.

"And what was that?" Judith asked. "This part-time work?"

"At Naomi's place," Ann told her. "The *collective*."

"Oh, you worked for Flourish. That's where Heather Pratt worked, isn't it?"

Ann gave her a dark look. "Last couple of years, she did."

"And did you do the same kind of work there as Heather Pratt?"

"No." She bristled at even this comparison. "I made rugs."

"Hooked rugs?"

"Yes." A quick, brutal glance at Naomi. "I was very good at it."

"I'm sure you were," Judith said disingenuously. "And how long did you work for Flourish, Ann?"

"From the beginning. Since before it was even a business."

"That would be about nine years?"

"I guess," she said.

"But you no longer work for Flourish."

"I said so," Ann said tightly. "I quit."

"*Did* you, now?" Judith said, delighted at this unexpected boon. "And why would you quit suddenly, after nine years?"

"Needed a change." She shrugged, evasive.

"Is that the truth, Ann?" Judith stood with her hands easy on her hips. She looked maternal, almost, a kind of 1950ssitcom maternal, with her features gentle and her voice full of loving authority. "Is that what really happened?" And Ann filled the role of the chastened child. Arms folded, she pouted in her seat. "Isn't it true that you were actually *fired* from the job you had held for nearly a decade? Isn't it true that you were asked to leave by Naomi Roth, because your tirades against your coworker Heather Pratt had become intolerable?"

"You'll have to ask *her*." Ann jerked her head at Naomi. "She's the *boss*, after all, for all her fancy talk about *communes*."

"Well," Judith seemed to consider, "we can do that. We can recall Naomi to the witness stand and ask her what drove her to fire one of her most accomplished rug-hookers and most faithful employees. I'm sure Naomi has her own take on the question. You know, employer and employee rarely see these things the same way . . ."

She went on. She dug and needled and punished and pretended to cajole. Naomi, who could not believe she was actually enjoying herself, sat stiffly on her hands, waiting for it to end but hoping it might last just a little longer as the successive Ann Chases were laid bare: a Peeping Tom with flashlight in hand, a pathological prude unable to countenance the sight of a woman's breast in a baby's mouth, a gossip, a snoop, a fellow worker who refused to be civil . . . It was a bloodbath.

Just before lunch, Ann Chase was asked again about Christopher Flynn.

"I said I didn't know him," she retorted, but feebly.

"No. You said you had not *met* him but that you had heard of him."

"Sure. Fine."

"So my question is, from whom did you hear of Christopher Flynn?"

"I don't know," said Anne wearily. "Everybody was talking about him. And Mr. Charter asked me if I knew the man."

"I see." Judith nodded. "And of all these people who were talking about Christopher Flynn, did *anyone* say that they had actually met him?"

She thought. She shrugged. "Nobody I can remember."

Judith walked back to her table, and her place. She might have looked finished, but in fact she had one more question.

"Ann," she said, "there's no such person as Christopher Flynn, is there?"

Charter frowned but stayed quiet. Ann Chase shook her head. One ragged breath escaped her throat. "I wouldn't know," she said.

Chapter 35

Witness for the Prosecution

HEATHER'S MIDWIFE WAS A SQUAT WOMAN with a single rope of black hair that she wore like an ornament across her breasts. She had not been subpoenaed, but Naomi felt sure that she had not precisely come willingly, either. Her first act, on being seated in the witness chair, was to smile consolingly at Heather. Her name was Randa Burns. Her affiliation was to Mary Hitchcock Hospital, in Hanover.

Heather, Randa Burns said, had been an extremely conscientious patient during her first pregnancy. She had attended her appointments faithfully, and eaten well, and generally demonstrated in every possible way that she was preparing for and looking ahead to motherhood. At Charter's prodding, she told the story of Heather's labor and delivery, and her account did not shy from detail: four centimeters by eight o'clock, five centimeters by ten, then the long hours spent at eight as the night dragged into darkness. Heather was strong, that was the point Charter seemed to be making. She did not ask for relief. She barely asked for diversion. And indeed, the birth was achieved with very little in the way of intervention, which— Randa Burns informed Mr. Charter—was certainly appropriate to her philosophy that labor was a most natural passage.

"In other words," Charter said, "you might just as easily have not been there at all."

"Well . . ." She considered. "I only helped her accomplish what she was quite capable of accomplishing herself."

"Alone."

"Well, it's always helpful to have others there. It's a fine thing to gather other women around the birthing woman. It can be very spiritual. And also, there is always the possibility that the mother or the baby could require some special assistance."

"You mean, there might be a need for medical intervention."

"For further support. And sometimes for the kind of support

generally available in a hospital environment, yes."

"The baby could die, for example."

"An extreme example. Also, the mother could experience difficulties."

Charter was not interested in the mother.

"When was the last time you heard from Heather, Miss Burns?"

Randa, a woman after Naomi's own heart, bristled at the "Miss."

"I made my last postnatal visit when Polly was two weeks old. She was doing beautifully. Nursing was well established, and the baby was growing. There was a good support system in place—Heather got wonderful assistance from her grandmother—and the household seemed to be in good shape."

"So your work was finished."

"Sure." Randa nodded. "She had things under control, and she was clearly elated by her daughter."

"Did she ask you any questions? You know, general advice? Things she might be worried about?"

Randa glanced at Heather. "She had no major concerns, no."

"What about minor concerns? Do you recall whether she asked you any questions at all?"

She shifted. "She only asked me one question, and it was entirely unremarkable under the circumstances. In fact," she said, openly irked, "most of the moms I've worked with asked me this question at one time or another."

"And what question is that?" Charter said, preemptively smug.

"When she could have sex again. After the birth."

"Really," Charter said. "*That's* what she wanted to know? Not what she ought to feed the baby? Or worries about the baby's health?"

Randa glared at him. "I think she was able to answer those questions on her own, Mr. Charter. Most mothers can."

"And all she wanted to know from you was when she could have sex again?"

A crisp nod. "As I said."

"All right." He emphatically flipped a page of his legal pad. "Now, at what point in her second pregnancy did Heather again place herself under your care?"

Momentarily thrown, Randa shook her head. "She didn't.

She didn't call to say she was pregnant again."

Charter mimed surprise. "Never? Despite the fact that her experience with you was so positive the first time around?"

"I didn't know she was pregnant again until"—another uncomfortable glance at Heather—"I was told. By you."

"In your opinion, Miss Burns, is it wise to go through a pregnancy without medical supervision?"

She appeared to consider her words. "It's far wiser to be supervised. Even women who have experienced a complication-free pregnancy could be at risk for complications in subsequent pregnancies. Of course, she might have felt that her first pregnancy had been sufficiently recent that she could recognize any symptom that might be abnormal and could contact me then. But no. It isn't wise. I certainly wouldn't encourage it."

"How would you characterize Heather's general health, Miss Burns?"

"Excellent, I'd say."

"And her general ability to bear children?"

"Well, in terms of fertility, she was obviously fertile. In terms of carrying a baby to term, she was clearly capable of that, too."

Charter nodded sagely. "So no outstanding difficulties, then?"

Randa said there weren't.

"In your opinion, could Heather have delivered an infant without assistance?"

The midwife looked uncomfortable. "It's really impossible to say. There are many, many cases in which women deliver unassisted. Most women, thankfully, don't have to. But certainly, it does happen."

"And would a strong woman like Heather, a woman who had already had one uncomplicated labor and delivery, stand a better chance of surviving such an ordeal than a first-time mom who might be panicky and not know what was happening?"

Randa Burns considered. "It would be an advantage in that situation, I suppose."

"So it's certainly possible."

She nodded grudgingly. "Yes."

"Could she have carried twins to term, Miss Burns?"

The midwife looked across to Heather. "I didn't see her during her pregnancy," she told Charter.

"I'm aware of that. That is not what I asked, however. Was there anything, any physical condition, that would have prevented her from either conceiving twins or carrying them to term?"

Randa sighed and shook her head. "I can't think of any," she said finally.

"Could she have delivered twins, alone and unassisted?"

"It would certainly add to the likelihood of an unfavorable outcome," the midwife said. She intended this, Naomi thought, as a jibe to Charter, but he did not seem to take it as such. Indeed, he shook his head with a kind of sage sobriety, looked meaningfully at the jury, and took his seat.

Judith, Naomi knew, did not consider the midwife the type of threat that Ann Chase represented, but Randa's very sympathy to the defense made it more difficult to score the kind of satisfying points Judith had won with Ann. She rose from her seat and smiled warmly at the witness. "Hi, Ms. Burns."

"Hello."

"Do you believe that, in ideal circumstances, women ought to be empowered to make their own decisions regarding their own health?"

"Absolutely," said Randa. "Women know their own needs and their own bodies far better than anyone else can be expected to."

"Do you consider pregnancy to be a kind of disease which must be medically supervised?"

"No!" she said forcefully. "Pregnancy is a normal physical and psychological passage in a woman's life. It is not a medical 'condition.' Western medicine insists on treating pregnancy and childbirth as a disease. I treat it as a different aspect of a woman's health."

"So you wouldn't *necessarily* feel that a pregnant woman who did not pursue medical supervision is showing depraved indifference to her health and her baby's health."

Randa considered. "I would not, no."

"Is it depraved indifference for a pregnant woman to engage in certain behaviors—such as smoking, or drinking alcohol, or taking drugs—which might harm herself or her baby?"

"No. Not depraved indifference. It's not wise, but I don't

think of it as criminal. If it were, the jails would be full of pregnant women."

"Is it depraved indifference for a pregnant woman to drive her car without a seat belt?"

"No." She smiled. She saw where this was going.

"What about skydiving?"

"Nope!"

"Race-car driving?"

"Not criminal."

"Is it depraved indifference for a pregnant woman not to seek medical supervision during pregnancy?"

"I wouldn't think so. No. As far as I'm concerned, it's kind of a dangerous question, too. Because, I mean, how many appointments would a woman have to miss before it *was* depraved indifference?"

Judith nodded. She walked around her desk and sat. Her way, Naomi knew by now, of signaling a change in direction.

"You testified that Heather established breast-feeding shortly after Polly's birth. To the best of your knowledge, did she continue to breast-feed her daughter?"

"I don't know exactly when she stopped. I remember discussing breast-feeding with her at some length. We discussed my own belief that breast-feeding can and should continue until either the child or the mother wishes to stop. In other words, there is no set age by which the child should stop nursing."

"A one-year-old child should still nurse?"

"Absolutely. If the child is still interested."

"Two years old? Three years old?"

"Why not? The notion of breast-feeding as only for very young infants owes everything to Western images of women and nothing to the physical abilities and needs of mother and child. In some cultures, children nurse until puberty."

The men on the jury reacted, Naomi saw, but the women were mostly nonplussed.

"Are you aware of the common belief that breast-feeding has a contraceptive effect? In other words, that so long as a woman is nursing she is protected from becoming pregnant?"

Randa nodded. "Certainly I'm aware of it. But it's not, unfortunately, true. There are plenty of unplanned children conceived while the mother is nursing. Breast-feeding may delay the recurrence of menstruation, and many people erroneously assume that pregnancy is not possible until menstruation recurs."

"When Heather asked you about resuming sexual activities after giving birth to Polly, did you warn her that she would require some type of birth control if she did not wish to get pregnant again?"

The midwife frowned. "I don't remember that coming up, to tell you the truth."

"So it's possible that Heather was having sex with the misconception that she was protected from pregnancy, when in fact she had no such protection."

Randa considered. With one hand, she fingered the end of her black braid. "Yes, maybe."

"Isn't the duration of a pregnancy usually measured from the first date of the woman's last period?"

"Yes, we use Nagle's Rule to determine due date and, by extension, the period of gestation. We take one year from the date of the first day of the woman's last menstrual period, then subtract three months, then add seven days. In other words, human gestation is, on average, 275 days from the first day of the woman's last period."

"But if Heather did not, in fact, recommence menstruating after the birth of her daughter Polly, wouldn't she find it rather difficult to gauge the onset of her second pregnancy?"

"Yes, she would," Randa said helpfully.

"Is it possible that Heather did not know she was pregnant in January of last year?"

The midwife nodded. "Sure."

"Is it possible she did not know she was pregnant in February of last year?"

"Yes. If she wasn't menstruating due to nursing her baby, then she might have been unaware for a long time."

"Could Heather have gone through the spring without knowing she was pregnant?"

More of a hesitation here. "Possibly. Less likely, though."

"Could she have been under the impression that she was pregnant but that the pregnancy was conceived later than January?"

Charter objected, of course. Randa Burns could not possibly

know what impression Heather was under, but the jury got the gist.

"In your opinion, without the anchor of a menstrual period to determine the onset of gestation, might a pregnant woman experience confusion about how pregnant she actually was?"

"Absolutely," Randa said helpfully. "In fact, I would *expect* confusion."

"Ms. Burns," Judith said, smiling, "you described Heather earlier as a conscientious expectant mother. Do you think that a conscientious mother would willfully take risks with her baby's life?"

She shook her head. "I never thought that of Heather, no."

"Do you think it's possible that Heather intended to place herself under your care again, but that she was under the mistaken impression that her pregnancy was not far along?"

Naomi looked instinctively at Charter, but he was offering no reaction except a composed, dubious expression.

"Yes. I think it *is* possible. I assume that, in fact."

Judith nodded sagely. "Are you aware that the support system you alluded to earlier in your testimony—Heather's grandmother, who helped her with the infant Polly—was no longer in place during her second pregnancy due to the grandmother's sudden death?"

Randa looked briefly stricken. "No. I didn't know that." She cast a brief, resentful glance at Charter. "I wasn't told that."

"Are you aware that this death occurred shortly after the conception of Heather's pregnancy?"

"No," she said angrily. "I think that changes things rather significantly."

"You do?" Judith sounded innocent. "In what way?"

"Well, it implies that Heather had her mind on other matters at the time of the conception. If she was occupied with the experience of grieving, she would have been paying even less attention than usual to the question of how fertile she was. If that was the case, then she might really have been unaware of when she became pregnant. She might have thought she had plenty of time to prepare for the birth." She shook her head. "It's so tragic."

"Thank you," Judith chirped. She sat down.

Charter, having gleaned that his witness was now openly hostile to him, opted not to redirect. Instead, the district attor-

ney swiftly moved on to his next witness, Nelson Erroll, who
now walked to the front of the room with a grim expression.
He looked tired, Naomi thought. The papery skin beneath his
eyes showed faintly blue, and his gold-and-silver hair had not
been recently brushed. She noticed these things, but she did
not linger on them, and if he saw her looking he did not look
back. This, it seemed to her, was a kind of agreement between
them. Not acknowledged, but an agreement nonetheless.

Nelson said his name. He said he was the senior ranking
police officer in Goddard township. He sat down.

"Officer Erroll," Charter began. He spoke from his seat.
"How did you become aware of the crimes in this case?"

Nelson cleared his throat. "Naomi Roth came to my office
on September 22. She brought the baby she had found in the
river."

"And would you describe what happened following this discovery." Charter nodded encouragement.

A call was placed to the district attorney's office in Peytonville, said Nelson, and to the medical examiner's office. Then
they waited for representatives of these offices to arrive. One
hour later, Dr. Ernst Petersen and Mr. Robert Charter arrived
in separate cars. They all went to view the site, with Naomi
Roth. Then Dr. Petersen took the baby's remains back to Peytonville, and Mr. Charter stayed to interview Ms. Roth.

"I interviewed Miss Roth, is that correct?"

"You did, yes."

"What happened then?"

"Well, over the next days we talked at length about how we
ought to proceed, and who in the area ought to be questioned.
We were also getting calls. Information. From people in the
town of Goddard and in Goddard Falls."

"Calls offering suggestions about whom you ought to question?"

"Yes," Nelson said.

"And whom did the people of Goddard and Goddard Falls
think you ought to question?"

He looked briefly at Naomi. "They said Heather Pratt."

"And others?" Charter pressed.

"Almost everyone said Heather. There were a few others,
though. We had a couple of calls about Appalachian Trail
through-hikers, and some about students in Hanover."

"What form did your investigation take, Officer Erroll?" Charter said.

He looked uncomfortable. "I did conduct interviews with a wide selection of townspeople, as well as some tourists and through-hikers. I was able to eliminate the hikers very quickly. I think a very pregnant hiker on difficult terrain would probably be noticed. I made some inquiries in Hanover as well. It was clear to me fairly early on that we were either dealing with somebody local or that the birth had occurred far away and, for whatever reason, this body had been deposited somewhere near Goddard. If that were the case, I felt it was very unlikely that I would be able to identify the baby's mother."

"And that was your object? To identify the mother?"

Nelson nodded. "Well, yes. That seemed like the right first step."

Charter stood up and walked around to the front of his table. The preliminaries were clearly over.

"Officer Nelson, at what point did your investigation focus on Heather Pratt?"

He looked down at his hands and seemed to sigh. "It began to focus almost at once. The name came up constantly. Those who had seen Heather over the preceding month had observed that she appeared to be pregnant. No one had definitive information, however."

"But it required looking into," Charter prompted, a little harshly.

"Yes. It bore looking into."

"At what point did you conduct an interview with Heather Pratt, Officer Erroll?"

"Well, we wanted to take our time. We were waiting for the medical examiner's findings, for one thing, and we wanted to be sure we had . . . that we were interested in talking to the right person. We conducted the interview on October 12. We invited Ms. Pratt to come talk to us at the police station, and she came at about five that evening."

Nelson was asked about the interview then. He described the room in which they had sat and counted the people present: himself, Heather Pratt, and District Attorney Charter. Later, another officer joined them to take Heather's statement.

"How long did the interview last?" Charter asked.

"Several hours all told. There were breaks, though. We weren't talking the whole time."

"Was Miss Pratt ever threatened or unduly pressured, Officer Erroll?" There was the briefest hesitation, Naomi thought, but perhaps only she would have noticed.

"No. Not at all."

"And did Miss Pratt have the option to call an attorney to be present during this interview?"

Again: so fleeting it barely registered. "She did. She chose not to call an attorney."

"Did Miss Pratt admit outright that she was responsible for the death of the Sabbathday River baby?"

"No," Nelson said. Heather had denied any connection to the baby. At first, indeed, she had denied a recent pregnancy outright. Eventually, after some discussion, she admitted her pregnancy, but suggested that she had miscarried her baby and flushed its remains down the toilet. Then she rescinded that information and claimed that she had had a full-term baby outside on the hill behind her house. Ultimately, she admitted stabbing her child with a sharp object and placing its body in the river. She signed a statement to that effect. She identified the sharp object as a fine blue metallic knitting needle that had earlier been collected from her house, in a search she had authorized by signing a release form.

Nelson was then asked to read the confession. He took the sheet from Charter's hand and seemed to read it briefly himself, frowning as he did.

" 'My name is Heather Ruth Pratt and I was born May 1, 1965. I live in the farmhouse on Sabbath Creek Road. This is the house left to me by my grandmother Mrs. Polly Bates Pratt. I am employed as a craftsman at Flourish, Incorporated, in Goddard. I had a sexual relationship with Ashley Deacon, who is a married man, from October of 1983 to January of this year, 1985. I am the mother of a daughter, Polly Pratt, born in August of 1984, now fourteen months old. In December of 1984, I became pregnant for the second time. I did not seek prenatal care for this child. I did not tell anyone I was pregnant. On the night of Tuesday, September 17, I went into labor in the middle of the night. I went outside into the back field behind my house. I had my baby alone and unassisted. I did not bring my baby into the house after it was born. I returned to my house without the baby. I went back to the field with a sharp object, a blue knitting needle, to make sure the baby was dead. I stabbed the baby once in the chest. Then I carried the baby's body across the field to the Sabbathday River. I laid it in. Like . . .' " Here Nelson raised his eyes, which for some reason found Naomi's. " 'Moses'. When Naomi Roth found that baby, I knew, deep down. I felt it was mine. I felt sorry. I am so sorry.' "

"The statement is signed?" Charter said, almost eagerly.

"Yes. This is Heather's signature." Nelson held it up.

Charter let this sit for a moment. Naomi, for her part, thought that the voice of Heather's statement was far more self-assured, far more emphatic, than anything she had ever heard out of the girl's mouth. That she herself was so sorrowfully evoked in the statement took her by surprise, and grieved her.

"Officer Erroll, were there other items of significance collected during the search of Heather Pratt's home?"

"Yes." Nelson nodded. "There were a number of towels with evident bloodstains. They had been left in a heap on the floor of an upstairs closet. Also bloodstained underwear."

"Are these the same towels?"

Charter produced them, bagged individually so their harsh brown stains would show to best advantage. Naomi found she could not look at them and averted her eyes.

"They appear to be, yes."

The towels were entered into evidence and passed to the horrified jurors.

"Any other items?"

"Yes. We retrieved an address book from Heather's bedroom."

"Why would an address book be of interest to your investigation, Officer Erroll?"

Your investigation. Naomi nearly laughed aloud.

"Well, we wanted to be able to speak with Heather's friends and associates. It was a way to confirm her statements or else to oppose them if she had not been truthful with us."

"Was this the address book?"

He brought it out. Another plastic bag with a thin booklet, dark green, with some kind of gold seal on the cover. Nelson took it between his hands and gazed down at it, almost sadly. This was indeed the address book, he said.

"And was the address book helpful in putting you in touch with Heather's friends and associates?"

Nelson shook his head. For an instant the remaining straw-colored hairs on his scalp caught the light. Then they let it go.

"No. There was only one name in the book, and it was not the name of someone we knew. There was no address."

"And that name, Officer Erroll?"

"Chris Flynn."

It went around the room like something electric. In this first tangible proof that the name existed, however, it was easy to overlook the fact that no actual person had been shown to be using it.

"What efforts were made to locate Mr. Flynn?" Charter asked, smiling broadly.

"Our efforts are ongoing. As yet, we have not found him."

"And what would be the purpose of finding him, Officer Erroll?"

"We would like to discuss with him the paternity of the Sabbathday River baby," Nelson said, and Naomi, for the briefest moment, wanted to laugh. A name in an address book? It was too crazy. But no one else was even smiling.

Charter moved closer to Nelson, marking another segue in his questioning. He propped a hand familiarly on the railing. "Officer Erroll, at what point did you realize that you were dealing with two murdered infants, not one?"

In front of Naomi, Judith straightened and loudly objected, "Your honor, we've had no proof as yet that either of these infants was murdered."

"Two dead infants?" Charter suggested sarcastically.

Judith sat, scowling.

"Well, about a week after Heather made her statement, Naomi Roth called me to come out to Heather's house. She had found a second baby in a little pond at the bottom of the hill behind the house. So we had two," he said lamely.

"And did you interview Heather Pratt about the second baby?"

"No. Her attorney would not permit a second interview." He paused. "I would very much like to have interviewed her again, but it just wasn't possible."

"You had questions you needed answered, didn't you?" Charter said with eminently false sympathy.

He nodded. "Many questions. Yes."

"Questions about the second baby?"

"Yes."

"Questions about other men in Heather Pratt's life?"

"Yes."

"But she was no longer cooperative, was she?"

"She did not agree to speak to us again."

"Officer Erroll, did you conduct your investigation in a responsible, professional, and thorough manner?"

He looked sad. "I tried to. I . . . There were others involved in the investigation. We worked together. We tried to do our best."

"Was the woman who eventually emerged as your suspect, Heather Pratt, treated with dignity and fairness?"

"She was," Nelson said.

"Was she forced in any way to make a confession, or identify the weapon she had used, or give a detailed statement to the police?"

He shook his head, but not very emphatically.

"I don't think so, no."

"Can you think of any reason why Heather Pratt should claim that she was forced to confess, and that she confessed falsely to this crime?"

"It happens very often that people recant their confessions," Nelson said. "But I can't think of a specific reason in this case."

"Thank you, Officer Nelson." And Charter was done.

Judith rose. Naomi, who lacked her habitual taste for revenge in this instance, did not quite relish the cross-examination to come. Nelson was drumming his fingers on the thighs of the brown corduroys he wore. He looked resigned, but not particularly strong. He looked as if he was not quite fortified, not quite committed to the cause.

"Do you often conduct your investigations by public opinion poll, Officer Erroll?"

Nelson, to his credit, took this without offense. "I've never conducted an investigation like this before. I was willing to take advice wherever I could get it."

"Including advice based on nothing more than suspicion?"

"Sometimes suspicion can be useful," Nelson observed. "People can certainly misplace suspicion, but often a person attracts suspicion because he does, in fact, warrant it."

"Did any of your callers possess actual, direct evidence that Heather Pratt was involved with this crime?"

"No one knew anything," Nelson said. "There was no direct evidence."

"And yet the consensus was that Heather Pratt was the guilty party."

"There were many calls about her," he said.

"She wasn't very well liked, was she?" said Judith. "I mean, by her neighbors."

Nelson nodded. "That's true."

"In fact, she was rather vehemently disliked, wasn't she?"

"True."

Judith gave the jury a sad look. "When these . . . *informants* called you to talk about Heather Pratt, did they only discuss her supposed pregnancy?"

"No. In fact, only one or two mentioned that they thought she might have been pregnant."

Judith looked surprised. She *was* surprised, Naomi thought. This was a windfall. "Only one or two? And the rest of them? What did they talk about?"

"Heather's . . ." He glanced at Naomi. "Her character, I guess you'd say. People knew about her affair with Ashley Deacon, and they knew who Polly's father was. I think they were pretty disgusted by the whole thing."

"I see," Judith said. "And so, this is how you came to focus your investigation on Heather? Because her neighbors were pretty disgusted by her affair with Ashley?"

He shrugged. "I guess you could put it that way."

"And is that, in your own opinion, enough reason to accuse a woman of murder?"

The question caught him off guard, but he didn't look angry. "No," he said carefully. "I don't think so."

"Then why did you accuse her, Officer Erroll?" Judith asked. "What was the evidence that convinced you Heather Pratt had given birth to the infant known as the Sabbathday River baby?"

He looked uncomfortably at Charter. Thus far, Naomi knew, Charter had had barely a walk-on role in the official story of the investigation. She wondered why Judith had chosen to let this falsehood alone, and if she ever planned to confront it.

"We had established from Ashley Deacon that the affair had ended the previous January. We had established that, in the opinion of some observers, Heather might have been pregnant in the late summer. These two things were enough to justify our interviewing Heather. Other information emerged from the interview."

Judith smiled. "Ah yes," she said, almost happily. "The *interview*. From the fact that you use the word 'interview' rather than the word 'interrogation,' I infer that this was a voluntary conversation, that you did not force Miss Pratt to come to the police station and speak with you."

"In no way was Heather forced," Nelson said, looking a little resentful for the first time.

"You gave her a call, asked her if she would come in and have a chat, and she came. Is that it?"

He shook his head. "No. We went out to her house. She came back to the station with us."

"Us?" Judith said. "How many officers makes an *'us'?"*

"I believe there were three cars. Six of us."

"Six officers? Three police cars? For a voluntary interview?" She sounded aghast.

"It *was* voluntary," Nelson said stiffly.

"And at what time of day was this invitation extended?"

"I believe it was late in the afternoon. About five."

"Was it dark out?" Judith asked.

Nelson nodded. "Getting there."

"And what was Heather doing when you arrived with three police cars and six officers to extend your invitation, Officer Erroll?"

He looked, for the briefest instant, at Heather. "Cooking dinner."

"In fact, you left her chicken roasting in the oven when you took her away, didn't you? I hope somebody remembered to turn the oven off," she said archly.

Nelson didn't answer, but his discomfort was eloquent.

"Let's talk a little bit more about this voluntary interview," said Judith. She was speaking without notes, her arms folded as she leaned back against her table. She was settling in. "It must have been after dark by the time this young woman and her fourteen-month-old daughter got to the police station in Goddard Falls with her six-police-officer escort. Did you place her in an interrogation room?"

"An interview room, yes."

"Was Polly just about falling asleep in Heather's lap?"

He knew what she was asking, and he didn't shy away from it. "She wasn't in Heather's lap. She was in another room. She was well cared for," he added.

"Well cared for?" Judith sounded amazed. "You take this baby out of her home, at night, and transport her in a strange car to a strange place, and then take her away from her mother, and you think that's well cared for?"

"A female police officer was with her. She was perfectly safe. And we needed to speak with Heather while she was not distracted."

"Don't you think the thought of her daughter in another room with a stranger must have been pretty distracting?"

He thought about it and answered honestly. "I don't know. Maybe."

"But that didn't bother you because you needed to have your voluntary talk with Heather."

"The interview was entirely proper."

"Yes, so you said earlier. You also said that Heather did not ask for an attorney. Was she made aware that it was her right to have an attorney present?"

Nelson considered. "I don't know for a fact that she knew that. Most people know that."

"But you don't know if Heather knew it."

"I don't know, no."

"And you didn't tell her, Officer Erroll, did you?"

"No."

"Because, as you're well aware, an attorney would almost certainly have ordered you to stop your . . . interview." Judith smiled.

"I was not under an obligation to tell Heather about her rights at this point. She was not under arrest."

"Oh?" Judith said, sounding surprised. "Could she have left if she'd wanted?"

"Sure." He nodded, but he didn't look at her.

"Just get up and leave? 'I don't feel like talking. See ya!' "

"She could have, if she'd wanted."

"But instead she elected to go with you and five other police officers in the middle of feeding her daughter dinner and then remain in the police station as the evening wore on and her daughter was kept with strangers in another room, talking about her sexual partners and her private experiences. She could have gotten up and left at any time, but she preferred to spend her evening this way, with you and District Attorney Charter?"

Nelson looked at the jury—but he did not like looking at the jury, either.

"I can't know what was going on in Heather's head, Ms. Friedman."

"Did Heather inquire about her daughter Polly, who was with a stranger while she herself was being interrogated?"

He reacted to the word, but he did not quarrel with her over it. "She might have. I don't really remember."

"You don't remember?"

"No."

"And she didn't ask for an attorney."

"I said she didn't."

Judith nodded. "Right. So you did. You said that Heather first denied her pregnancy, then admitted her pregnancy but said she had miscarried her baby, is that correct?"

Nelson said it was.

"And then she confessed that she had had a full-term baby which she stabbed and threw into the Sabbathday River?"

"Right." He ducked his head.

"Are you sure you're not leaving anything out? Are you sure you're not omitting any interim steps here? After all, this was a rather lengthy *interview*, wasn't it?"

"I don't think I'm leaving anything out," he said stiffly.

"No? What about the part where she consistently denied any connection to a stabbed baby in the Sabbathday River? What about the part where she said she had had a stillborn baby in the back field and placed its body in a pond, near the spot where it was born?"

"I don't remember that," Nelson said quickly. "That wasn't part of her statement."

"What about the part where she offered to show you where she had put the body of her own stillborn baby, and you refused to allow her to do so?"

"No," Nelson objected. "That didn't happen."

"What about the part where she was told that she would never be allowed to take her daughter home unless she confessed to a brutal crime she insisted had nothing to do with her?"

This was enough for Charter. He objected loudly and called Judith a bully, which, under circumstances, was only accurate. Hayes agreed, but Nelson was shaken. He was looking at no one now. His fingers, enmeshed, gripped together.

Judith took a moment, more to calm herself down than anything else. Then she adopted an air of sincere intellectual inquiry. "Officer Erroll, if Heather was going to the trouble of confessing to murder, why do you think she didn't add the detail that she had had two babies instead of one?"

He shook his head. "I wish I could answer that. It's one of the things I wasn't able to ask her in a second interview."

"I see." She appeared to ruminate. "Do you think it might have slipped her mind that she had had two babies instead of one?"

"I don't know. She might have been confused when it happened."

"But not too confused to murder them by separate methods and dispose of their bodies in separate places."

"Maybe she was confused then, too."

This comment, Naomi could not help but notice, earned Charter's silent displeasure.

"Officer Erroll"—Judith seemed to sigh—"did my client, Heather Pratt, maintain throughout her interrogation that she was entirely innocent of the death of the infant we refer to as the Sabbathday River baby?"

Nelson seemed to consider. His face grew slack, and he closed his eyes. "Not at the end, she didn't deny it."

"Did my client Heather Pratt confess to having a stillborn baby whose body she placed in a pond?"

"I don't remember," he said, with an air of defeat.

"Did she offer to show you the pond where her baby was hidden, an offer that was rejected?"

"I don't remember."

"Was my client told that her daughter would be taken away from her if she didn't admit stabbing a baby and putting it in the river?"

"I don't remember." He just wanted it to be over, Naomi thought.

"Did my client ask for an attorney to be present during this interrogation?"

"Interview," he muttered. He sighed. "I don't remember."

"Did she in fact ask for a lawyer at least *two times*?"

"I really don't remember."

"Officer Erroll, you seem to remember very little about an interrogation that is of the utmost importance to my client."

He looked at her with great sadness. Naomi, to her surprise, was suddenly aware that her eyes were wet.

"Officer Erroll, I have only one more question. Do you have any evidence at all, other than a name written in an address book that you found in Heather's house, that a man by the name of Christopher Flynn exists and is at all involved in this case?"

They waited. Nelson looked up at the ceiling, as if a better answer might be found there. But there was no other answer. "None," he said.

Chapter 36

"Dost Thou Know Thy Mother Now, Child?"

THE PROTESTERS HAD CLEARED OUT BY THE time Naomi made it back to the courthouse with Polly, leaving—like the aftermath of a small but lethally poised cyclone—a fluttering of lavender leaflets scattered about. She paused for a minute and stooped, with Polly at her hip, to take up one of the pieces of colored paper, thinking Heather might like to know what friends she had and doubting—for now she knew well enough to doubt—that Judith had made this gesture. A wet breeze hugging the ground swept past her and moved on, and Polly put her face against Naomi's jacket. "Hang on, sweetie-pod," Naomi said. She hiked up the baby and the diaper bag and her own purse, and walked around the building to the jail entrance.

At least Judith had set this up, and Naomi was only required to produce her driver's license before being shown into an interview room. The guard, a densely built man who walked in a shuffle, held the door for her. In his other hand he carried, bizarrely, roses: three of them, each white, each wrapped separately. They were for her, he said, meaning Heather. He left them on the table on Heather's side of the iron mesh. "A few came this morning, too," he told Naomi, rolling his eyes. "Girl's got a friggin' fan club in San Francisco."

Heather was not yet there. Naomi set Polly down on her lap and pulled off her parka. Beneath it the baby wore one of the Mexican overalls Naomi had ordered. Naomi gave her one of her board books, which Polly began to fan against her hand, making little chirping, birdlike sounds, the incomprehensible music of the as-yet-inarticulate. Naomi took off her own jacket. The room, so like the room in which she had talked with Heather months before, seemed less strange than the first had, and she wondered vaguely if she was not somehow getting used to all this, if it were not all becoming normal: her normal life and Heather's normal life and Polly's normal life.

If this was how it would be for all of them now: these strained meetings in queer rooms, with mesh between them. She had not said anything to Polly yet, but she took the little girl on her lap and said, with false brightness, "Mommy's coming soon. Your mommy."

Polly, her face blank, took hold of Naomi's sweater at the throat, curling her fingers over the fabric as if she were holding on to a subway strap. She had always been fond of this grip. The door on the other side of the grate creaked open.

For an instant, Naomi wondered if Heather might have forgotten that she was coming, and whom she was bringing. Heather's eyes, vague, came to rest on Polly as if she were only one piece of furniture in a crammed room, first gliding past her daughter to see what else might be here and then, by some process of elimination, returning. Naomi, unnerved, was still, but Polly sat riveted, her fingers stiff at Naomi's throat.

"Mommy," Naomi said, and was abruptly embarrassed that Heather should hear this voice of hers—this mommy voice, which she had, after all, appropriated from its rightful source. So she said it again, more sternly. "Polly, here is your mother."

Polly did not move. Heather felt for her chair and pulled it out. Behind her, the door was shut with a metallic click. She sat and looked down at the flowers.

"Who's sending you flowers?" Naomi said, thinking perhaps Heather ought to be distracted and trying to sound normal.

"Flowers?" Heather looked down at her own hands. The floral paper crinkled beneath her fingers. "I don't know. I got a white rose this morning. From San Francisco. I don't know anybody in San Francisco."

"Was there a note?" Naomi asked.

"Yeah. But no name. It just said I should keep my spirits up." She gazed mutely down at the three long cones of paper on the table. "How do they know who I am?" she said.

Naomi, feeling a little unreal, only said, "What a nice thing, to be sent flowers. Even if you don't know the person who sent them."

Heather looked up at her daughter. Her eyes seemed to focus slowly, as if adjusting to the light. There was a flicker of animation. "Polly," Heather said. "Hi, sweetheart."

Polly remained stiff and still.

"You remember Mommy?"

Naomi, to her distress, felt the little girl draw even closer.
Her hand gripped even tighter, the little nails scraping the skin
of Naomi's throat. "Polly"—her voice tried for warmth—"this
is Mommy. Your mommy."

"It's okay," Heather said sadly. "She doesn't have to. She
looks very well."

"She *is* well." Naomi tried to sound reassuring. But then she
felt bad, as if she were claiming that Polly was well with her,
better than she would be if she had remained with Heather. "I
mean," Naomi said, "she's growing, and she's been very
healthy. A little ear infection, I think I told you. But that
cleared up right away, and otherwise there haven't been any
problems. I'm taking her to the sports center once a week, for
swimming lessons. I go in the water, too, so it's perfectly safe,
and Polly really likes it."

"The sports center?" Heather said, and Naomi was instantly
horrified. That she had said this so unthinkingly was extraordinary.

"I'm sorry, I should have asked your permission."

"Is he there? At the sports center?"

Naomi stared at her, astonished. Abruptly she felt like throt-
tling Heather.

"I haven't seen him. No."

Though she *had* seen Sue, whose parent-toddler swim class
with her older son ended just before Polly and Naomi's began.
Sue was wont to look viciously at them as they waited at
poolside, but the two women had not spoken, and Naomi honestly had no idea what she would say if they ever did.

"You should see her," she told Heather, trying for equilib-
rium. "She just loves the water. She can put her face in and
kick. She's a natural swimmer."

"Good," Heather said. She was looking down at the flowers
again. She picked up one of the three and opened up the little
white envelope. Then she shook her head. " 'We just wanted
you to know that we are thinking of you and wishing you
well.' The Ann Arbor Women's Collective." She peered at
Naomi. "What is that?"

"Well," said Naomi, "I guess it's a women's group. Maybe
a commune, or an informal group. Or a political group. They
must have heard about what's happened to you, and they
wanted to express their support."

She shook her head. "But it has nothing to do with them."

"They disagree, obviously," Naomi said, seriously and deliberately, as if she were explaining something to a little child. "They apparently feel that this trial is important to women, and they are responding as women. And look at this!" She sounded, to her own ears, inappropriately bright. She extracted the lavender sheet from her back pocket and passed it to Heather. Heather read, frowning, "Women at Dartmouth."

"Yes. They were outside the courthouse, protesting."

For a long moment Heather only stared.

"I just want to go home," she said suddenly. "I want Polly, and I want to go home."

Polly, unaffected by her name, was heavy, stiff, and motionless.

"I'm sure that will happen," Naomi said, wondering if she was right to say so. "I think it's going well."

"I hate it!" Heather spoke sharply. "Oh, I hate this so much. I hate going in there. I hate to see him and hear him say those things about me. I love him so much!"

Naomi wasn't going to touch this. She frowned.

"How could he say he wanted to break up with me when Polly was born? How could he say I had another lover? I didn't! How could he say he didn't know he was Polly's father? I *told* him he was. How could he believe I was seeing another man. *What* other man? There was nobody else, he *knows* that!"

"I know," she tried to sound soothing. "I think the jury knows that, Heather."

"And that horrible Ann Chase, coming out after me in the woods, and calling the police as if I were doing something dirty when I was only feeding the baby. How could she hate me so much?"

Naomi, to her own surprise, felt relief that at least Heather had come to life. She nodded and clucked. "Ann's a sick person, that's all. She has nothing better to do than worry about you."

"But it's all so crazy," Heather moaned. "I *know* it is. I *know* I haven't done these things. But they all believe."

"No, that isn't true," Naomi said hastily. "I don't think many people really believe it. Only Charter. And maybe not even him. But he's dug himself in because of his own ignorance, and the only way he can get himself out is by making it seem as if he was right all along. He's using you to do that. It stinks, but it doesn't mean people really believe him, Heather."

"Ashley believes it," she said, her voice newly hushed. This, it came to Naomi, was the crux of her distress. "He thinks I had another man, and I had two babies and I killed them. But there was no other man."

Naomi couldn't bear this any longer. "Listen, Ashley is a complete bastard, Heather. I know you don't want to hear that."

"He's not!" And she was crying, freely. She didn't bother to try to stop, or even to wipe away the tears as they came. "He's not. He loved me."

"*Fine.*" She didn't want to talk about this. She gathered Polly a little closer. The little girl watched her mother weep, mesmerized and mute.

"I hate this," Heather sobbed. "I hate the way they talk about me, like I'm not there. When the midwife was talking about me, about how I had Polly, and the centimeters, and how I pushed her out, I hated that. And how I asked about having sex. It's so private. I never said they could talk about these things."

Naomi, who knew Charter had yet to call his physician and his psychiatrist, said nothing.

"I feel like I'm naked. Like my clothes have all come off and they're standing there to measure me and take pictures. All those people, they know those things about me."

"And Ashley," Naomi said harshly. "He didn't exactly respect your privacy."

This, to Naomi's abrupt shame, made Heather weep harder. "I can't do this," she sobbed. "I don't see how they can expect me to do this. I don't see why I have to be there."

"Because it's your right. It's your right to confront your accuser."

"My *right*," Heather said roughly. "Like my right to have a lawyer!"

"Yes." Naomi nodded, somewhat relieved at this apparent segue from pain to rage. "So we'll do this part right, at any rate."

She shook her head. "It won't matter. I won't get out of here. I'll never get out of here."

"*That* isn't true." Naomi tried to sound comforting. "Listen, Heather, I think Judith is winning. I mean, I can't vouch for it, but she's doing very well, and if you add that to the charges being so crazy, I think you really have a chance. And when you get up there and tell your own story, they'll see."

"I won't!" Heather shouted. "I mean, I can't. I can't talk about that."

"But you'll have to, Heather," she said, confident but not autocratic. Judith's only request had been that Naomi make Heather understand this. "People—I mean people on juries— say they don't hold it against a defendant who doesn't testify, but of course they do. They think, What is she hiding? She'd testify if she had nothing to hide. So you *have* to say what happened."

"I did nothing wrong," Heather shouted, her voice ragged.

"Of *course* you didn't. That's the *point*. But look," Naomi said, backing off, "just think about it, all right? Just give it some thought. And don't lose heart, okay?" She tried for a broad smile. "Like your friends in Ann Arbor and San Francisco keep telling you."

"I'm never going to get out of here!" she sobbed. Her tears ran down her face and her nose and clear into her mouth. "I'm never going to have Polly back."

The flash, mercury-fast, of hope: Polly hers, always. Naomi, shocked, pushed it away.

"Not true. Don't think that!"

"And even if I did," she wailed, "I can't live here anymore. They hate me here. Even if I won, where would I go?"

Naomi shook her head, but not because she disagreed. The problem of what would happen to Heather after was far afield. From where they all sat, there was not yet a glimmer of an after. And so she sat, watching Heather through the mesh, her head bent forward with its rough, hacked hair, her shoulders in a perpetual, arrhythmic shudder. The institutional uniform, a kind of army-navy house dress, puckered across her lap where she was thinning and thinning, withering back to the bone. And still Naomi could not quite—not quite, not completely—be moved, for which she did not forgive herself. She thought, without feeling herself reach back over the hours past, to the morning, the chilly park bench, and Judith, how she had wept with her morning coffee cold in her hands. How long ago that had been, she thought, and how much had happened since: the women of Dartmouth, Ann Chase and Randa Burns, Nelson Erroll and the stunning hilarity of that green address book with its single name. She thought how she had sat there so long ago, watching Judith weep, just as she was sitting here now, watching Heather, and how she did not understand why this was always her place, this comforting hand and tempered tone reaching out into the unknowable void of another human being.

Polly's fingers were sharp on her skin. Naomi, unthinkingly, plucked them away, and the little girl suddenly gave out a bleak cry of fear. Then, with her other hand, her other little-girl fist, she reached forward to the mesh, to her mother, and said, her voice piercing and clear, the word: Mama.

Heather, as if the air were choked from her throat, looked up and was silent.

"Mama," Polly said. But she was not smiling, and she did not sound happy. She pointed through the mesh, which was wide. She leaned forward, releasing Naomi's shirt. "Mama."

Heather's hand touched her own neck, between the clavicles. She was looking intently at her daughter. "Polly, sweetheart." She leaned forward until her face and chest were up against the wire. Naomi leaned forward, too, and put the baby up close. Polly put her hand through the wires and reached the place her mother was touching, pushing Heather's hand away. She stared at this triangle of white skin, and then, quite suddenly, started to wail.

"Polly," Naomi said. She started to pull her back, onto her own lap, but Polly cried louder. Heather closed her eyes.

"I'm sorry," said Naomi. "I don't understand."

"It's my necklace." Heather's voice was flat. "They took it away."

"What necklace?" said Naomi.

"The one Ashley gave me. I always wore it, and they made me take it off. Those people."

Meaning Charter, who had taken it away, and Judith, who had put it in a plastic bag for strangers to finger and examine. Now Naomi understood.

"She loved to play with it," Heather explained. "She held on to it. Oh, sweetie."

But Polly wouldn't look at her. She looked at her mother's neck, livid and dismayed.

"I can't," Heather said. She touched her own throat. "I wish I could." She smiled through her streaky face. "I don't think she recognizes me without it, you know."

"Oh, I'm sure she does," said Naomi, her voice unnaturally hearty.

Heather got to her feet. She picked up the three white roses and crushed the paper cones together. "You take them home," she said, pushing them through the mesh. The lavender flyer was left, facedown, on the table. "And take her away, Naomi. Please." Heather smiled weakly. "I know she's in good hands. But you were wrong about what you said, about how I was a good mother. I'm not a good mother at all, you know."

That isn't true, Naomi started to say, but she saw from Heather's face that she did not wish to be told otherwise. She watched Heather turn her back to them and knock for the guard. Polly turned away and gripped Naomi around the neck, her fist tight at Naomi's collar, as the door opened and her mother slipped away. For a minute Naomi stared after her, enervated, depressed, and relieved. Then she gathered up the white roses and her bags and her little girl, and went home.

Chapter 37

Horses and Zebras

THE PEYTON COUNTY MEDICAL EXAMINER HAD a shiny scalp, ringed by a fringe of white hair, and eyes visibly blue even across the ten feet between him and Naomi. His name was Petersen and his accent vaguely Southern, though he had a way of swallowing his own words that made it hard to tell for certain. When he was called the following morning, he walked easily to the front of the room, gave his name and title, and tried to make his tall, densely built body comfortable in the comfortless witness seat. He seemed very much at ease with Charter, which only made sense: their reputations, it occurred to Naomi, were symbiotic, and if one were to fail or err in some way, the other must suffer, too.

Charter began with the Sabbathday River baby. He still had Randa Burns's lingering evocation of a confused and tragic Heather to contend with, and his object was to replace this with the brutal imagery of two dead babies. It didn't take long. He passed photographs to the jury and waited helpfully until they were incapacitated by shock, one man green and three of the women weeping. No one was looking at Heather now.

Dead babies, after all, were incontrovertibly dead babies, and no one knew that better than Naomi. For the first time since the trial began, she did not have the option of resentment. She braced herself against what was to come.

The Sabbathday River baby, Petersen testified, was a full-term infant girl, weighing—at the time of examination—six pounds and eight ounces, with no evident deformities or defects. It was impossible to say how old the baby had been at the time of her death, but she had certainly breathed on her own. Her stomach was empty—no one had fed her—but there was the beginning of repair of the umbilical stump, which had evidently been cut with a sharp instrument. In her sternum, a single small puncture or stab wound was evident, round in shape and two inches deep. The wound appeared bleached,

Petersen said, with no blood and no surrounding redness. Naomi remembered, as he spoke, the moment she had turned the
baby over in the river, and the first jag of her thoughts on
seeing it: the bloodless laceration in the medieval painting,
Christ's immaculate suffering on the cross. Cause of death was
this puncture wound directly into the baby's heart.

"How did you go about determining the shape of the
weapon?" Charter said.

Petersen looked over at the jury and began his lesson. "You
can never take the shape of the wound at face value," he said.
"There are some layers of tissues beneath the skin that would
pull the wound apart, and others that would push it together
or distort it in some way. What we do," he informed them, "is
take the edges of the wound and tape them together. Scotch
tape works fine." He smiled, pleased to enlighten them with
this fascinating tidbit. "And when you've done that, you can
see the shape of the wound—whether, for example, it's a puncture or a slice, and whether it's a double-edged wound or a
single-edged wound. This baby's wound was a round puncture,
consistent with a very narrow spike."

"What kind of instruments would you associate with that
shape, Dr. Petersen?" Charter smiled obsequiously.

"Oh." Petersen thought, lifting his eyes to the ceiling. "I
suppose an awl, or an ice pick. Possibly a nail."

Charter went to the evidence table. The thin knitting needle
glittered blue beneath its plastic cover. He lifted it, held it up
to show the jury, and handed it to the medical examiner. "And
this?"

He frowned at it, though he must have seen it already, Naomi thought. "Yes. This would fit."

"In your opinion, this knitting needle could have caused the
fatal wound in the baby's chest?"

"Absolutely."

"All right." Charter nodded. "Were you able to determine a
time of death for this baby?"

The baby had been found on September 22, Petersen said.
At that time, it had been dead between two and three days.
Given that it was several hours old at the time of its death—
the early reactive changes of the umbilical stump attested to
that—this implied a birth date of September 19 or 20. More
exact dates were not possible.

"Fine," Charter said. "Now let's talk a little bit about the other baby."

More pictures. These were worse, Naomi thought, shuddering. Even more than the first, this was the image she still had to tear through in the mornings when she woke, this chalky mask of white from under the muddy water. Once, she dreamed that she had pulled it not from the pond but from a stone, hauling her weight against it as if the baby were Excalibur, the sword, resisting and then surrendering to her hand—her hand from that unremembered world above.

One of the jurors, a man, signaled the bailiff. A break was called, but only long enough for them to visit the bathroom. Heather, too, was taken away for a few minutes, led out in a soft stumble of movement. She looked pliable as paper, her line of sight imprecise. When she returned, murmuring swelled as she passed, was turned, and sat. Only Naomi, close enough to see, caught the small but constant tremble off the surface of her white skin. Hollowed out, a carapace where a person had been. Charter kept his seat, as did Petersen. Judith, who seemed happy for the extra time, wrote quickly on her pad.

When the jurors returned, Charter moved quickly to take advantage of their vulnerability. The baby found in Heather's pond was a full-term baby girl, weighing—at examination— seven pounds one ounce (though its long sojourn underwater, Petersen said, rendered this suspect as an accurate birth weight), with no apparent defects or deformities. Pockets of air were visible by X-ray both in the baby's lungs and in her intestines.

"And what is the significance of that, Dr. Petersen?"

"It implies that the baby breathed air. It implies that this was a live birth."

"The baby wasn't born dead, in other words?"

"Exactly. Though I do have to say that the conditions are far from ideal for a definitive forensic finding. That is my conclusion."

"Based on your years of experience, your conclusion is that the pond baby was born healthy and breathed?"

"Yes."

"And in what manner, based on your experience, was the umbilical cord severed?"

"It was not severed. It was, in fact, still attached to the remains of the placenta."

"So. The baby was born healthy. It breathed air. So far," he editorialized, "we have a live birth and a viable child. Now what, in your opinion, and based on your years of experience, caused this baby's death?"

Petersen frowned. "Once again, these forensic conditions are not ideal. But to the best of my ability to tell, I conclude that the baby died of asphyxia due to manual strangulation and obstruction of the external airway." He gave the jury an indulgent nod. "It was either strangled by choking around its neck or suffocated by covering its nose and mouth."

Charter let this sink in, then he let it lie for a moment. He studiously shuffled his papers. Judith, for her part, tapped her pen impatiently.

"How long had this baby been in the water, Dr. Petersen?"

The tall man shook his head. "It's just not possible to say. I've estimated a period of between four and five weeks. The water was cold, which retarded decomposition, but there were certainly bacteria present within the body. Between four and five weeks is the best I can do."

"I see." Charter nodded calmly. "Now, on what date did you take possession of the remains of the pond baby?"

Petersen looked down at the notes he held in his lap. "October 20."

"What would the calendar date between four and five weeks before October 20 have been, Doctor?"

"September 19 or 20," he said firmly. "Roughly my estimated birth date for the Sabbathday River baby."

"So it's entirely possible that these two little girls were born at the same time?"

Petersen nodded. The harsh fluorescent light glinted off his pink scalp. "Very much so."

"And died at roughly the same time?"

"In my opinion," he said, "yes."

"Dr. Petersen, I thank you." And indeed Charter bent forward in a half bow. He took his seat. Judith leaped up, so anxious she skipped the usual tug at the back of her jacket. She walked straight across the room and stood before him, drumming her yellow pad against her thigh. It was covered with scrawls, Naomi saw.

"Hello, Dr. Petersen," Judith said. "I'm Judith Friedman."

"Nice to meet you," he said.

"Dr. Petersen," she said, amiably enough, "are you asking us to believe that one young woman had a baby, cut its umbilical cord, and stabbed it to death with a knitting needle, then gave birth to a second baby, which she suffocated and threw into a pond with its umbilical cord unsevered and its placenta intact?"

"I am asking no such thing," Petersen shook his head. "I am merely reporting my findings, based on my experience."

Judith smiled. "Yes. Your years of experience, as I think you put it." She cocked her head. "Dr. Petersen, do you consider yourself a competent and professional medical examiner?"

He looked blankly at her for a moment, and then his face hardened. "I do," he said tightly. "I would be very offended if someone suggested otherwise."

"I can understand that," said Judith. But then she did it again. "Would you say that your methods are conscientious and thorough?"

"Without doubt," he said, now visibly angry. "If someone has said otherwise, I would like to know it."

She ignored this. "Dr. Petersen, when the body of the Sabbathday River baby was delivered to you, and you removed it to your office here in Peytonville, I take it you performed a physical examination as well as laboratory tests. Would that be correct?"

"Certainly." But he volunteered nothing else. He was going to make her work for it.

"What are some of the laboratory tests you performed, Dr. Petersen?" Judith said, bearing down.

"In addition to a thorough autopsy, I ordered basic tissue and blood typing."

She looked at him. Then let the moment stretch.

"And?" Judith said finally.

"And *what?*"

"And what other tests?"

"What other tests did you have in mind? The cause of death was quite obvious, I assure you."

Judith nodded. "And the cause of death, you stated earlier, was the single stab wound to the heart."

"Certainly," said Petersen smugly.

"And you felt comfortable with your assumption that the infant's cause of death was, in fact, the stab wound."

"I just said that," he said impatiently. "Look, there's a famous thing they tell you in medical school. When you hear hoofbeats in Central Park, think horses, not zebras. Here we had a newborn infant with a stab wound. This isn't a difficult equation."

"So you thought horses. You didn't think of doing, for example, a toxicology screening."

He looked at her as if she was crazy. "No. And I didn't think of testing to see whether the cause of death was cancer, either. Should I have done that?"

"You didn't feel it was important."

"Not unless there's evidence our newborn infant was a heroin addict, no." He gave a little laugh, and looked at the jury, but they weren't laughing.

Judith nodded. She went back to her table and found a pink form which she read provocatively before looking up. "Dr. Petersen, do you recall allowing the defense's own pathologist to examine Infant A in your office?"

"That's standard," Petersen commented.

"And do you recall releasing samples of the Sabbathday River infant's blood and tissue so that the defense in this case could order its own lab work?"

"That's also standard," he said tightly. "Certainly I recall."

"Do you recall signing this release form for the samples?" Judith asked, walking toward Petersen to hand him the pink sheet.

"Yes. This is my signature." He looked wary now, but he wasn't ready to concede anything.

"Do you see the sample identification number in the top right corner of the form?" She pointed helpfully.

"Yes."

"And here." She handed him another form. "From Peyton East Diagnostic Labs. The same diagnostic lab you use yourself, if I'm not mistaken. And here—the same identification number."

"Yes. This appears to be the same sample."

"As you can see, we too thought horses. We requested blood and tissue typing just as you did. But unlike you, we also wanted to rule out zebras. So we requested a toxicology screen. Would you read the results, Dr. Petersen?"

He was doing just that. He squinted at the page, then shook his head vigorously.

"No. It isn't right." But he didn't sound at all sure.

"What isn't right, Dr. Petersen?" Judith sounded innocent.

"This result. It's a positive result for opiates. It must be a mistake."

"You don't seem to be very confident in your own lab, Dr. Petersen."

He was furious now. He reddened and shook his head again. "No . . . this, it's just a human error. We're all human. It's a fluke. The test should be repeated, that's all."

To Naomi's surprise, Judith nodded in agreement. She went back to her table, opened her file, and extracted another pink sheet. "We thought so, too," she told him, her tone familiar and conspiratorial. "So here."

This time his sputter was gone. He only shook his head in wonder.

"What are opiates, Dr. Petersen?"

He was glaring at Charter, who looked—Naomi was delighted to see—absolutely stunned. But then, Naomi was, too.

"An opiate," the medical examiner said, "is a compound derived from the opium structure. It's a narcotic."

"Really?" Judith sounded interested. "Can you name some opiates for us?"

He could, and he did, grudgingly. Morphine. Codeine. Methadone. And heroin.

"Heroin," Judith said dramatically. *"Really.* Can you see on the diagnostic form which opiate was found in the Sabbathday River baby?"

He squinted. "Morphine." He shook his head. "They found morphine."

"Dr. Petersen, what do you think morphine was doing in the body of this baby?"

He gave her a look. "As you know, I could not possibly answer that question." Then he returned to the page in his hands. He was reading the form again. "I don't believe this." He shook his head. Charter, incensed at the unsolicited comment, looked furious. His scalp, beneath the ripple of gray hair, turned bright red.

"Is the drug easy to get?" Judith asked.

"It shouldn't be," he said, a faint edge of accusation in his voice.

"Would, for example, Heather Pratt have access to it?"

"No. I wouldn't think so."

"Who *would* have access to it, Dr. Petersen?" She stood with one lip thrust out, her arms folded confidently.

"Doctors. Nurses. Pharmacists, I suppose. Perhaps veterinarians. Home health workers. Someone taking care of terminally ill patients."

"But not a woman who does embroidery for a living?"

He shook his head. "No."

"How did the morphine get into the baby's body?" she asked.

"It could have been ingested," he said, but he wasn't really thinking clearly, because she jumped on him.

"Really? But didn't you say the baby's stomach was empty? Didn't you testify that it hadn't been fed?"

"Oh, that's right," he said lamely. "Yes, I said that."

"So how do you think the morphine got into the baby's body?"

"Injection. It would have to have been injected."

"With a needle," Judith commented.

"Well, that's usually how it's done."

She smiled at this. She went back to her table. From the large briefcase on the floor, she extracted a syringe with an attached needle. It was, Naomi thought, the biggest needle she had ever seen. Just looking at it made her think of the gamma globulin shots she and Daniel had endured before their graduation trip to India.

"Can you identify this, please?"

Petersen took it from her. "It's a large bore needle. Two millimeters or one-sixteenth of an inch in diameter and five inches long, I would estimate."

Judith showed it to the jurors. "And what would such a needle be used for?"

"Oh, many things. But getting meds into the heart quickly, or getting blood out is what comes to mind. Like epinephrine, to get the heart beating if it's stopped. In an emergency room, for example, you'd punch this right in. The needle has to be thick to get through the sternum."

"I see." She appeared to ruminate. "Now, a needle like this must make a visible hole in the skin."

Then he got it. He stared at it, then at her, and slowly he gave one elongated nod. "Yes. It would."

"Dr. Petersen"—Judith cocked her head—"is it possible that a large-bore needle like the one you just held was used to inject morphine into the heart of this newborn baby girl? Is that possible?" she said again, to remind him what the parameters of the question were.

He looked over at Charter. He was not pleased with Charter, Naomi saw.

"It is possible. Yes."

"All right. Let's talk about the second baby."

She was so crisp, Naomi thought with admiration. Judith walked back to her table, put down her notes, and picked up other notes. She never broke rhythm. It was a kind of dance.

"The pond baby. You testified, I believe, that there was air visible by X-ray in the baby's lungs, indicating a live birth. Is that correct?"

But he was still thrown. It took him a moment. "Yes. A live birth."

"And you also testified that the baby's body had been in the water for a period of approximately four to five weeks. Is that correct?"

"It is." Petersen nodded.

"Now, Dr. Petersen," Judith moved in, "would you agree that some decomposition would have taken place after four or five weeks in the water?"

He frowned. "Well, certainly."

"And this decomposition, would it necessarily be visible to the naked eye? For example, in the kind of photograph Mr. Charter showed us a few minutes ago?"

"Not always," Petersen said. "Decomposition may be more evident internally than externally. Bacteria in the gut, for example, are strong activators."

"In other words, the bacteria that's already inside the body begins work to decompose the body."

"Yes."

"I see," she considered. "Now, this bacteria, it produces gas in the process of decomposition, does it not?"

Again, he saw where she was headed, but the fight seemed to have gone out of him.

"It often does."

"And how would gas appear on an X-ray?"

The medical examiner looked at her dully. "Very like air, I would think."

" 'Very like air?' If gas appeared very like air, what criteria would you use to tell them apart?"

"It would not be possible to tell them apart."

"Oh? In that case, perhaps you do not mean to say 'very like air.' Perhaps what you mean to say is *identical* to air," she said firmly.

"All right. Identical. On X-ray."

"So it's possible, is it not, that what you identified as air on the pond baby's X-ray might actually have been gas produced by decomposing bacteria?"

He nodded grudgingly. "Yes, it's possible."

"Now, you did not testify to any ligature marks on the baby's neck, or other abrasions or signs of strangulation of the baby. Is that correct?"

"There were none," he agreed.

"So, without visible ligature marks or signs of strangulation, and without an ability to point to the X-ray and be certain that there are pockets of air in the baby's lungs and intestines, what other evidence do you have that this baby had in fact breathed after birth?"

He gave her a stony look. "My finding that the baby breathed after birth was based on my interpretation of the X-ray evidence."

"But you yourself stated that what you identified as air might conceivably be decompositional gases!" she said with theatrical confusion.

"My finding might have been in error," he conceded, though with bitterness.

"Your finding might have been in error," Judith repeated. "Like your finding on the Sabbathday River baby, in other words."

"Objection!" Charter exploded. "Mrs. Friedman has no call to insult the witness."

Judge Hayes concurred, and Judith was chastised.

"Dr. Petersen," she said when she resumed, "babies do

sometimes, tragically, die during or just before birth, do they not?"

"They do," he agreed.

"What are some causes of fetal death at these times?"

"Well, the placenta can detach prematurely from the wall of the uterus, inducing labor and cutting the blood supply to the infant. This kills the baby in utero. Or the placenta can be abnormally placed, blocking the birth canal. This is known as placenta previa. Or the umbilical cord might be knotted, rendering the fetus incapable of respiration. Or the umbilical cord might be looped around the baby's neck, strangling it."

"There are quite a few possibilities, aren't there, Doctor?"

"There are," he agreed, but he added hastily that an attentive physician or midwife could almost always prevent these tragedies. Charter, from his table, groaned audibly.

"Ah," Judith said sadly, "but as you know, Heather Pratt did not have an attentive physician or midwife. She gave birth unattended. Now, in your opinion, would an unattended birth give rise to a greater likelihood of these conditions?"

"The conditions themselves, no. But a bad outcome from one of these conditions, yes."

"A bad outcome being a stillbirth, yes?"

Petersen said yes.

"Then you *do* feel there is a greater likelihood that this baby died before birth or during birth, rather than after birth?"

"I didn't say that!" He was clinging to his dignity now. "I said it was *possible*."

"It's *possible* that this baby died during birth and was born dead, exactly as Heather Pratt has consistently claimed?"

"I am not familiar with Heather Pratt's claims."

"It's possible that this baby was born dead."

"It is," he said tersely.

"It's possible that this baby was not"—she walked back to her table and read from her notes his own words—"asphyxiated 'due to manual strangulation and obstruction of the external airway.' "

A look at Charter. A brief nod. "It is possible."

"In fact, you have no incontrovertible evidence at all that the death of this baby was due to any unnatural cause, do you?"

He thought about this for a long moment. Clearly, he was

searching for a way to disagree, but there wasn't one.

"No incontrovertible evidence, no."

"And yet you testified to the contrary," she said sharply. "Why is that?"

"The other scenario is also possible."

"That may be, but you did not present strangulation as one possible scenario. You claimed that it was the definitive scenario. Why did you do that?" She sounded caustically authoritative now, like a mother who'd caught her child in a lie.

"I might have been in error," he said again, and the skin of his scalp was sheened with sweat now.

"Yes," Judith commented. "So you said earlier. I'd like to ask you again, Dr. Petersen, whether you think of yourself as a thorough and professional medical examiner."

"I *am*." Though he sounded childish when he said it. "Of course I am."

"But you made assumptions, didn't you?" She walked briskly to Heather and placed a hand where it had probably never been before: on Heather's shoulder. "Because you didn't particularly care that this young woman's life is up for grabs here. Because it wasn't very important to you that an *error*, as you put it, might destroy her future and her daughter's future. So you thought of horses, and you left it to someone else to think of zebras. Isn't that right?"

Charter got up to object, though not before Petersen could make his final, ineffectual protest. "That is *not* right," the medical examiner said wearily. But by this point, everybody knew it was.

Chapter 38

Medical Oddities

"I'M A LITTLE WORRIED ABOUT YOU," NAOMI said. She and Judith were eating lobster rolls in one of the lesser-traveled corridors adjacent to the courtroom.

"And why is that?" Judith said kindly. "Because this is *treif*?"

"No. I have no concerns about your spiritual life. But you're sort of burning your bridges here, aren't you? I mean, not only in town, but in your work. I guess I was thinking about it, and it occurred to me, isn't that the guy you're going to have to cross-examine on every case you try? And isn't he going to hate you now?"

Judith took a sip of her iced tea and appeared to think about this. "You're right, but it's immaterial. They detest us anyway. They're in opposition to us on a fundamental level. If the jury acquits, the message is that the medical examiner either hasn't done his job by finding proof of guilt or hasn't managed to convince the jury of what he *has* found. So yeah. Of course they don't like us."

"But what about the people in Goddard? I mean, you've just moved here. Doesn't it worry you to start out this way? It's one thing for me, I kind of traipsed into town with a sign that said JEWISH COMMIE FEMINIST WANTS TO CHANGE YOUR WAY OF LIFE. But you just want to live in a gorgeous old house and have kids and commute to Peytonville, right?"

Judith shook her head. She chewed her sandwich thoughtfully. "You don't have to worry, Naomi. Though I appreciate it. I'm comfortable with my choices."

She wasn't quite sure she understood this. "But . . . you mean you were aware of what might happen and you chose to do it anyway?"

"Yes," said Judith. "I thought it was important. That's why I didn't care if it kind of queered me with some people. Those were probably going to be people I wouldn't like, anyway.

Because, to my mind, this is the most important case I've ever tried. It's probably the most important case I'm ever going to try."

Naomi looked at her in amazement. Judith, finishing her sandwich, crumpled the paper and set it aside.

"But how can you say that? You don't even *like* this case! And you don't like Heather."

"That's completely irrelevant. This case is about a great deal more than Heather, and you know it. It's important to me. I care very much about the outcome."

Ann Chase stalked past, returning from the women's room. She turned her head away from them at such a sharp angle Naomi wondered if she might lose her balance and fall. Beside Naomi, Judith took out her notes. The doctor who had examined Heather in jail was due to testify next.

"You're putting your politics ahead of personal inclinations," Naomi said. "I really respect that."

Judith looked up. Her face wore an expression of mild surprise. "Oh, I wouldn't be too impressed. What I'm doing here is not particularly admirable." Naomi began to disagree, but Judith shook her head briskly. "No. Let's not talk about it anymore. Besides, I need to ask your advice about Monday. Joel's already driving me crazy."

"What, he wants you to cover your hair or something?"

Judith smiled. "No. But he's afraid I'm not taking this seriously enough. He's afraid I'm going to 'entertain,' as he puts it, like this is a dinner party instead of a cultural lifeline all the way back to Mount Sinai. I'm going to botch the *haroseth*, or throw some pine needles on the table and call it bitter herbs."

"Well, don't look at me. I don't have a clue how to make *haroseth*. I told you, my grandfather used to spit at rabbis whenever he saw them in the street."

"This is going to be your first Seder?" Judith said. "Oh no."

"My second. Linda Grossberg had one, in sixth grade. Her mom got the matzo-ball soup at Zabar's, and the maid served it. I think we sang 'Dayenu,' but I can't remember the words."

"If you remember the title, you remember the words." Judith laughed. "You'll come at six?"

"Yes. With Polly, if that's okay."

"It's okay," Judith said. She hunched over her notes.

Naomi, watching her, sipped the end of her soda. It had been so long since she'd thought about any of this that she couldn't even remember what the *haroseth* was supposed to be for. Naomi's family, after all, had not been religious for generations. Their American story, so very unoriginal, had hit all the classic signposts in its eighty-year journey from immigrant to American, and from piety to smug disbelief. Early on, God had been revealed as the masses' morphine, a kind of colossal swindle visited upon people who would otherwise thrive, achieve, create. As for the vast migration from the laws of the Old Country to the rising red sun, this had been explained as a logical shift, and utterly in keeping with that Jewish habit of holding one's nose to the text. *Of course we're people of the Book, only the Book is by Marx and Lenin.*

It was not precisely the case that religious Judaism had been completely absent from her life. In college, there had been an annual attempt among her women friends to recast the Passover Seder into an expression of feminist ideology, and Naomi had once attended this curious event—with its cup of wine for Miriam on the table, and its orange sharing the Seder plate with the more familiar bitter herbs and eggs (not *specified*, the orange signified, but not expressly *forbidden*, either). The Haggadah had been clipped from *Ms.* magazine, Xeroxed into a gray blur, and annotated with references to female circumcision and foot binding. But it was still about God, and Naomi didn't believe it. Disbelieving it, she could not appreciate it, and after the first year she did not go back.

Even so, she had always considered herself a good Jew, given that, in her view, a good Jew was a person who did good things and happened to be Jewish. Besides, as far as she was concerned, their history of spectacular oppression, their very own wing in the cosmic museum of victimhood, meant that Jews should be allowed to claim solidarity with any other ethnic or cultural underdog, anytime, anywhere. That they had been enslaved, expelled, and butchered so relentlessly across countries and centuries gave them all sorts of special privileges, like the unique dispensation she currently enjoyed of not having to actually believe in God, so long as you did everything else right. Or, as her mother had once put it— meaning this to be funny—"We all know perfectly well what the God who doesn't exist expects of us."

So she was a Jew without a religion, but then religion was not relevant. The Nazis, Naomi grudgingly accepted, had understood this. After all, did Eichmann really care whether his cattle cars were full of atheists or dovening Hasids? And if it troubled Naomi that she used for Jewishness the precise requirements that the Nazis had, that they were even that much in agreement, she still could not help herself. Because it was true: Judaism was a tribe, not a faith. A genetic imprint, a specific river of DNA. Other religions might feature permeable borders, the ebb and flow of conversion or attrition—a person could join a church or become a Christian, but on the most essential level a person *was* Jewish. You could not become a Jew, in her view, any more than you could become Inuit or Aborigine; either your ancestor was waiting at the foot of Mt. Sinai for Moses to return or he wasn't. Also, you couldn't get out, even if you wanted to.

Naomi got up and wandered off down the corridor and outside for a breath of air. There were more women today, diffused over the steps and along the pavement—some students, but several older. One of the Boston affiliates had run a news segment the night before, at six and eleven, featuring Ella. As Ella had gleefully reported that morning, the telephone in her off-campus apartment had begun ringing before the broadcast even ended.

Today, they were organized. They had somehow procured a few seats inside the courtroom, and when Naomi turned to rise after Petersen's testimony, they could be seen glowering in the back row, dressed uniformly in white. They would be back in the afternoon, she knew, but she could not quite decide that this was a good thing for Heather, that these incensed women would win favor from the jurors, or indeed anyone else. But whether they did or not, they were indisputably here, and not banishable. Heather, Naomi knew, *belonged* to them in a way she did not belong to Naomi, or indeed even to Heather herself. She belonged to them in the pure way that symbols belong—deeply, intimately—the way Goodman and Chaney and Schwerner had belonged to Naomi, or Hannah Senesh had, or Harriet Tubman. For the first time, she wished that she *could* feel that way about Heather, that she could embrace the cause, if not the girl, with the passion of her past adherences. But she could not. The women of Dartmouth, the "friggin' fan club in San Francisco," were welcome to Heather-the-symbol. Naomi's far less glamorous job would be to pick up the pieces, wherever they were going to fall, when all of this was over.

Inside, she took her usual place behind Judith. Nelson, nodding to her as she passed, was seated on the aisle, his face strained. She was still angry and would not return his greeting, but she did manage a smile for Sarah Copley, who had turned up and was seated a row behind Naomi on her own side. For an instant it occurred to her to wonder whether this signified some change in allegiance on Sarah's part, as if the courtroom were divided like a church in a wedding—bride's side, groom's side—but Naomi quickly dismissed this thought. The courtroom, after all, was now jammed, and the few familiar participants of the trial's first days had been edged out by the avid faces of strangers, some clucking various disapprovals at the proceedings, some madly scribbling notes or sketching likenesses. A limitless nautilus had sprung up around them, Naomi thought, carrying their small local tragedy far out into the world of other people, wrapping up more and more of them into this laughable and pathetic drama. From that moment five months before when she had reached out to touch the lost baby in the Sabbathday River to this surreal permutation of justice, there had been only such a crazy circling, such an utter absence of lines logically straight. Perhaps the world would go on like this, Naomi thought. Perhaps this was how lives were actually lived, like great, swirling teacups in a child's amusement-park ride, one circle tearing around within a larger circle, but never actually making any progress. Perhaps it would all one day just stop, and she would climb out, dazed and dizzy, to see where she had got to. Then again, it might never stop.

Heather was brought in. Despite Naomi's pleading that she try to eat something for lunch, it was instantly apparent that Heather had not made much of an effort, if any at all. She stumbled a bit, and though her eyes passed over Naomi as she was led to her seat, they did not pause. Alarmed, Naomi reached forward for Judith, but Judith was already looking keenly at Heather. She pulled back the chair and the girl sat, half falling. Then she shrugged and went back to her writing.

The doctor arrived, a Peytonville obstetrician-gynecologist whom Charter had tapped to examine Heather. He was a bleak little man in a brown suit with an important-looking briefcase. From this he produced, by request, Heather's medical chart, a fan of blue X-rays that slapped together as he held them to the light, and volumes of notes, all of which, Naomi assumed, were intended to make him appear clinically disinterested and adept. They settled into dialogue, a genial tone belying the extraordinary content of their conversation, which was Heather.

All of Heather, Naomi thought, her jaw setting in disbelief. Everything that was private to Heather, revealed in pounds and centimeters, cycles and durations. The girl herself covered her face in her hands, as Naomi herself would have done. As any woman, she imagined, would have done, had she been stripped this way, not to mention spread, not to mention so intimately inspected. The doctor, flatly, disclosed the age at which Heather Pratt first menstruated, the perfect regularity of her twenty-eight-day cycle, the length and volume of her menstruation, her mid-cycle cramping indicative of ovulation. He revealed to one and all the width of her pelvis. He discussed in detail the shape and dimensions of Heather's uterus, its tip to the rear, its fibroid tumor the size of a silver dollar at its anterior end. He disclosed that her uterus, when he had performed a pelvic examination days after Heather's arrest, was 7.7 centimeters long, only slightly longer than the size of a normal uterus in a non-pregnant woman, which was 7.5 centimeters, but this was not surprising, given that the examination had taken place over three weeks postpartum.

Could she have had twins, was what Charter wanted to know.

Oh, certainly, the doctor said. No question.

Then they all had a lesson about twins.

Identical—or monozygotic—twins, the doctor lectured, were formed by the splitting of a fertilized egg. That was not the case here, clearly, as the two baby girls were not identical. Fraternal—or dizygotic—twins, on the other hand, were formed when two separate eggs were produced by the ovary, then fertilized by two different sperm, creating full siblings who were not genetically indistinguishable. A woman's natural production of multiple eggs—that is, production unassisted by fertility drugs—was due to higher levels of follicle-stimulating hormone and luteinizing hormone than are found in mothers who produce single babies. There may also be a genetic component determining a tendency in this direction. In other words, fraternal twins tend to run in families. The rate of dizygotic twins in North America was 7 to 11 per 1,000 births.

"I see," Charter said. He got up from his seat. Naomi tensed, sensing the absurdities to come. "Would you tell us, please, about the process known as superfecundation, Doctor?"

The man nodded, well rehearsed.

"Superfecundation, simply put, is the fertilization of two eggs by two fathers, producing dizygotic twins who are, in fact, only half siblings. This occurs when a woman has sexual intercourse with two men at short intervals within the same ovulatory period. One egg is fertilized by the first man, and a short time later, a second egg is fertilized by the second. They both implant in the uterus and grow normally."

"You mentioned a 'short interval' between these sexual contacts. How short?"

The doctor appeared to consider. "There has not been an overabundance of research in this field, so I can't answer the question with any certainty."

"Can you make an estimate, based on your expertise in this field?"

"I would say up to forty-eight hours. That is my estimate."

"Forty-eight hours!" Charter said, loudly surprised. "So if a woman had sex with one man and then with another two days later, she might plausibly produce twins by superfecundation?"

"If she had produced two eggs prior to the first contact, yes."

"She wouldn't have to, for example, jump out of one bed and run immediately to the other?" This attempt at levity, Naomi was sorry to see, won a smile from one of the men on the jury.

"No. Two days should be within a reasonable limit for potential superfecundation."

Each time he spoke the word it sounded more legitimate, it rolled more smoothly off his tongue, as if "superfecundation" were a commonplace term, often used, as familiar in the waiting room as in the laboratory. He made the phenomenon sound rather commonplace and unremarkable, so that when he was finished, one could not help but wonder why superfecundation did not, in fact, happen all the time. But perhaps that was Judith's job.

She got right down to this, standing at her table and giving him a very doubtful look.

"Could you tell us, Doctor, why—if superfecundation is so commonplace—it doesn't happen all the time?"

He shook his head. "I can't, really. I don't know the answer."

"Until this case was brought to your attention, had you ever, personally, cared for a patient who was, to the best of your knowledge, pregnant by two different men at once?"

"No," he said.

"Until this case was brought to your attention, had you ever *heard* of a woman who was pregnant by two different men at once?"

He nodded eagerly. "Yes, I had. There was something in the literature. I recall reading it, in medical school. There was a case in Europe where twins were born of different races. One white, one black. The mother was a prostitute."

Judith, to Naomi's surprise, smiled at this. "A recent case?"

"I believe not, no."

"Oh? Do you recall when this case occurred?"

"It was an old case. It was in a book of nineteenth-century medical oddities."

Judith grinned, savoring this. "Nineteenth-century medical oddities," she repeated. "And this was a required text in medical school?"

The man blushed visibly. "No, probably not. Most likely I just read it in my spare time."

"Ah. Leisure reading, in other words."

"Yes."

"To provide a break from the *legitimate* medicine you were studying."

Charter objected, of course. Judith withdrew the question.

"Are you aware of any more recent studies on superfecundation? Say, during this century? Controlled studies with published results?"

He wasn't, he said.

"Did you search for any such studies before coming to testify here today?"

"I made a search, yes," he said. "I couldn't find anything. That doesn't mean there isn't anything, but I wasn't able to find it. I grant you, it's not exactly in the mainstream of research."

"What about published case studies? Were there any cases of superfecundation written up in medical journals that you discovered?"

He shook his head. "No. But again, it's very possible they are out there. One day this will all be on computer, you know, and you'll be able to just look it up. But for now it's a matter of slogging through the literature, and there's a good deal of it out there."

"Still," Judith said unkindly, "nothing at all? You found not one reference to superfecundation? I mean, apart from *nineteenth-century medical oddities*?"

"I didn't."

Judith gave one of her deliberate, thoughtful nods. "So this was, to all intents and purposes, the first case of supposed twentieth-century superfecundation you had ever encountered."

"Well, yes." He nodded.

"Then I suppose it would be fair to say that you could not be considered an expert on superfecundation?"

"I never claimed to be an expert," he said hotly.

"You were asked earlier, I believe, for an estimate based on your expertise."

He looked uncomfortable. "That is an expression."

Judith grinned. "So you are *not*, strictly speaking, an expert."

"No."

"Are you an expert on multiple births in general?"

"I am not."

"What about on fertility?" Judith said.

"Most ob-gyn specialists are somewhat expert on fertility," he said, discernibly offended.

"Do you have many patients who are seeking treatment for infertility?" Judith said.

"I have many who come to me, yes," he said.

"And you treat them yourself," she prodded.

"Well, initially, yes. If they fail to become pregnant, I tend to refer them on."

"To an expert," said Judith with satisfaction.

"To an infertility specialist."

"By which you mean an obstetrician-gynecologist who is an expert on matters of fertility and infertility."

He saw where she was going. "Yes."

"So, by that token, I take it you do *not* consider yourself an expert in these matters."

"I do not consider myself a *specialist*. No."

"Doctor, at what point in your association with this case did you learn that police were investigating the deaths of not one but two infants?"

He frowned. He had a rather offensive habit, Naomi noticed, of pressing the side of his nose with his forefinger, as if trying to clear the other nostril. "I believe it was about one week after my initial examination of the patient."

"So you had already completed your examination of Heather and submitted your findings."

"Well, I hadn't submitted my findings. I had made notes, however."

"And did your initial findings, the ones based on the examination, include an opinion that Heather had recently given birth to more than one baby?"

"I am only saying that that is a possibility. I am not claiming it as fact."

Judith asked him to listen carefully to the question, which she repeated.

"No. My initial report included no mention of twins."

"So after you examined her, and after you had made your notes, but before you submitted your report to the prosecution in this case, you received a phone call from Mr. Charter. Is that right?"

He nodded. "That's right."

"And what was the content of this phone call?"

"That there was another baby. And could I please return and examine Heather a second time."

"To find evidence of a multiple birth, in other words."

"I was not instructed to find evidence, I can assure you."

"Perhaps not overtly, but that was the gist of it, wasn't it?"

"I don't understand your question," the doctor said flatly.

"Did you, in the course of your very thorough examination of my client, ever ask her about the circumstances of her pregnancy and her baby's birth?"

"Yes." He nodded. "She said that her labor had taken her

by surprise and that she had given birth to her baby unassisted."

"She did not mention that she had had two babies, rather than one?"

"No."

Judith smiled. "Doctor, did you see anything at all during either of your examinations of Heather that specifically suggested a multiple birth?"

"It is impossible to say. Her uterus was returning to normal size. If I had been able to examine her closer to the birth I would have had more to go on."

She sighed. "Doctor, once again you are failing to answer my question. Let me repeat it: Did you see anything that *specifically suggested* a multiple birth?"

His forefinger pressed his nostril. "No."

"And did you see anything that specifically *contradicted* the single birth Heather told you she had had?"

He sighed. "No."

She thanked him, though not very graciously, and sat down.

Charter rose and immediately put the doctor through his paces again. Superfecundation was possible. It was a recognized medical event, though rare. And there had been nothing, in his examinations of Heather, to rule out either it or twins in general.

But the jury, Naomi thought, was not convinced. And Judith's own witness, coming to testify next week, would put them over the edge. According to Judith, he had howled with laughter when informed that somebody was trying to prove superfecundation in a murder trial.

They were getting there. They were *almost* there—almost out of the woods, if these woods were all that Charter could muster. There couldn't be much left, Naomi thought. Judith expected only one prosecution witness to talk about blood groups, and a shrink, so barring surprises they were nearly finished with Charter and his fantasies. But how could there be any surprises? It was all crazy enough without them, and Charter was hardly going to produce his elusive Christopher Flynn now if he hadn't already. Shrinks could say anything— Judith's, undoubtedly, would place himself in total opposition to Charter's, that was the nature of psychological testimony— and the blood-group testimony supported a thesis that she had

already gone a long way toward discrediting. Naomi looked
at her watch. It was two o'clock. If they could press on now,
and if Charter didn't drag out the afternoon with these last
witnesses, then Judith might just possibly begin her case before
the day ended. This was important, Naomi knew. Judith had
said she wanted jurors to hear testimony for the defense before
the weekend break. When they thought of the trial—as of
course they would, despite Hayes's admonitions to the contrary—she wanted them to think of her witnesses, not his.

Charter, who did not share Judith's incentive for expedi-
ency, asked for a short break before calling his next witness,
a professor of hematology from the University of New Hampshire, but Hayes did not indulge him too far. "I'd like to move
things along, Mr. Charter. Unless you are unprepared to do
so."

"I am absolutely prepared," Charter announced.

"Good. Ten minutes, then."

Naomi moved up to Heather and tried to rouse her. The girl
was slumped in her seat, looking vaguely at the window.

"Come on, Heather. Hang in there."

"No." She sounded dull. "No. I can't do this."

"We're almost done."

Judith, tersely, glanced at Naomi.

"We're getting there," Naomi amended.

"They talk about me. Like I'm not here." She turned her
head to look at Naomi. "How can they talk about me like that?
How can they talk about . . . my period? My body? I don't
understand what it has to do with anything."

"It doesn't have anything to do with it. You just have to
hang on. Look," she said, pressing Heather's shoulder. She
wanted her to turn around, to see the women in the back row
in their white shirts. And Heather did turn. Simone raised a
white rose in salute.

"Who are they?" Heather said, uninterested.

"Women who support you."

She leaned forward and put her head on the table. "I wish
they'd go away," she said, her voice barely audible. "I wish
everyone would go away."

"Me too," Naomi said. "Come on, here's the judge." She
helped pull Heather back to a seated position, but the girl

swayed. The slightest wind, Naomi thought, and she might blow away.

They began again. Charter produced his professor of hematology, a young guy, rapidly shedding his blond hair, at least on the top of his head. For this he evidently compensated his vanity with an untrimmed beard and a rather pathetic skimp of a ponytail. He had brought a visual aid, a chart of phenotypes arrayed in an alphabet soup of A's, B's, and O's. We each have two copies of genotype, he explained as the jury began—visibly, and from the outset—to glaze over. One from each parent. Some types are dominant: A and B trump O, for example. Thus, if we receive an A from one parent and an O from the other, we have a blood type of A, but that recessive O hangs in there, waiting for a shot at the next generation, where it has a fifty-fifty chance of being passed on. Indeed, though the O genotype knuckles under to A or B, this does not prevent blood type O from being the most common phenotype among white Americans. Thus the prism of possible outcomes, the professor went on, rising from his chair to scribble equations on a large sheet of paper, angled for the jury: genotype to phenotype—which was "blood type" to the layman, he said, offhand, in case anybody was still following him. AO crossed with BO might produce AO, AB, BO, or OO, yielding, in that order, blood types A, AB, B, or O. And so on.

Heather's blood, said the professor, was type A, with a genotype AO. Ashley's, as it happened, was the uncommon AB, as was Polly's. The baby from Heather's pond was A, with a genotype AA. The baby from the Sabbathday River, however, was OO.

What this meant, in the English which Charter eventually extracted from his expert, was that Ashley might well be Polly's father, and was just as likely to have been the father of the baby in Heather's pond. He could not possibly, however, have been the father of the Sabbathday River baby, if Heather was its mother. Heather's second lover—the elusive Christopher Flynn, presumably—would have to have had blood type O. This (helpfully for Charter, Naomi thought) placed Mr. Flynn snugly within the majority of white American men.

There was a brief interchange about the reliability of the

testing, after which Charter got the witness to state his conclusions again. Then he sat down.

Judith moved quickly. "Dr. Leslie," she said, walking over
to the scramble of letters on the professor's work sheet, "can
I just review some aspects of your findings for a moment?"

Polly, she wanted it clear, was Ashley's child.

"Yes," the man said. "The blood types are consistent with
that."

And the pond baby. This infant was Ashley's, too?

"Certainly possible," he said. "AA is a potential outcome of
AA and AB."

"But the other baby, as I understand it, does not fit into the
family picture quite as easily."

"No," Professor Leslie said. "Mr. Deacon did not have an
O to contribute to the Sabbathday River baby's genotype. So
for the Sabbathday River baby to have been the child of this
mother, who did possess an O, an additional source of genotype would be required. Someone who also possessed an O."

"I see." She stepped up close to the chart and peered at it;
then she straightened, as if taken by some radical new thought.
She faced him. "Dr. Leslie, if you were to take away the notion
of the second father—the second source of an O, as you put
it—this chart really makes no sense, does it?"

He frowned. Perhaps, Naomi thought, Judith's choice of
term "makes no sense" offended him in some way, but after
a moment he shrugged. He had, after all, only been considering
the notion.

"No. The additional source is necessary."

"So, correct me if I'm wrong here—if you had to incorporate into your chart the information that this woman, the
mother of the pond baby, had not had sexual contact with any
other man but the father of the pond baby, what impact would
that have on your conclusions?"

Again the frown. He peered at his scribbles. Then he spoke.
"Well, if this woman had had sexual contact only with this
man, it would be impossible for her to have produced the OO-
genotype child."

Judith nodded. "I see. So, in other words, this baby here"—
she pointed to the Sabbathday River baby's genotype—"would
have to belong to an entirely different family, with other parents."

"Yes."

Judith paused. "Dr. Leslie," she said, "as a geneticist, do you have any opinion on superfecundation?"

He considered. "I don't think so, since I don't know what it is."

"Really? I thought superfecundation is an established medical event."

He shrugged. "I'm sorry. It's not a term I'm familiar with."

"Oh. Well, superfecundation is the conception of fraternal twins by different fathers."

He broke into a smile. He had, Naomi could not help but notice, a very sweet smile. "You're kidding. Really?"

"Really," Judith said, rolling her eyes for the jury's benefit. "I've never heard of it before."

"Dr. Leslie, when you analyzed the blood-type information in this case, were you aware that the prosecution contends that this baby"—she pointed to the Sabbathday River baby's genotype—"and this baby"—she pointed to the pond baby's genotype—"are fraternal twins, born to the same mother but fathered by different men?"

He was grinning widely now. He shook his head. "No, I didn't know. I was just asked to analyze the data. Wow." He looked over at Charter, then quickly stopped smiling. "I only analyzed the data. I don't have any other information."

She thanked him.

It was three o'clock.

Charter called his psychiatrist, a brittle woman with a flat, triangular face and a cap of tight gray curls who walked briskly to the witness chair, her little hips moving stiffly beneath a narrow tweed skirt.

Once she was sworn in, he began, in a loving, adulatory fashion, to recount her titles and degrees. (This, too, Naomi thought, was some kind of a stalling tactic, since Charter also evidently had his eye on the clock. But after the third honorary doctorate, Judith stipulated to the witness's expertise, and the district attorney had to move on.)

Her name was Roslyn Staple. She said that she had been asked to interview and examine the newly arrested Heather Pratt, and this she had done, in three sessions of one hour each, which had taken place in the Peytonville jail. The report of her findings, a document she held up helpfully, then placed in her lap, was bound in red covers. Heather, for her part, sat still in her seat, her hands folded before her on the tabletop as if she had been shut off or deactivated, but the psychiatrist did not look at her.

"What were your general impressions of Heather Pratt, Dr. Staple?" Charter said, folding his arms in anticipation of an essay-length answer.

Heather's emotional immaturity was the most striking element of her character, the psychiatrist went on. Under the circumstances, the defendant dwelt inappropriately on the topic of Ashley Deacon: her love for him, her sense of loss at no longer having access to him. She was also intensely narcissistic, showing no interest in others, apart from the aforementioned Ashley Deacon. She was withdrawn and noncommunicative. She refused to discuss one of the two infants—the pond baby—and showed a marked lack of interest in the other. She volunteered no information, asked no questions, and appeared generally to be without concern for either or both of the two infants who had died. From this it could be basically inferred that Heather possessed at least psychopathic tendencies, if not full-blown psychopathology.

"How would you characterize a psychopath, in layman's terms?"

As a person without conscience, the doctor said, and capable of violence. A person who would stop at nothing, including murder. "But I found, as I said, that the patient possessed psychopathic *tendencies*. I did not diagnose a full-blown psychopath. Rather, my diagnosis is of a personality disorder. To be specific, I concluded from my examination of Heather that she most closely resembles the profile of the Borderline Personality Disorder, although she does show some features of the Avoidant, Narcissistic, and Histrionic Personality Disorders. Her character and mood experience rapid shifts between grandiosity—the belief that she is better than everyone else, a "special" person—and feelings of worthlessness, with very little in the way of middle ground between the two extremes. This is normally a problem of arrested development. Borderline personalities seldom evolve to the point where they can have meaningful relationships, in lieu of which they might form alliances with unsuitable or unavailable people."

"Such as a married man?" Charter asked helpfully.

Such as a married man.

Instability of mood, she continued placidly, and relationships and self-image were marked by some of Heather's more notorious attributes: impulsiveness in self-damaging areas (such as sex and/or exhibitionism) and lack of long-term goals. There would also be, consistent with this disorder, a lack of control, such as Heather might have shown in her public fights with Sue Deacon in the sports center, or with Ann Chase on the porch at Tom and Whit's. Finally, the Borderline Personality's frantic efforts to avoid abandonment had significance as a motive for the murder of Heather's children. "She thought that killing them would bring her loved ones back," Dr. Staple said.

"Could you clarify that for us, Doctor?"

"Certainly. These were naturally stressful circumstances, but I do not believe Heather experienced a psychotic break. In other words, there were not, suddenly, voices or visions instructing her to murder the infants. What I do believe is that her psychopathic tendencies came into play, and she made a nonrational bargain to regain what she had lost—specifically, her relationship with her boyfriend—by sacrificing what she now had—the two babies. Heather had, after all, confronted death twice in the recent past: the death of her grandmother and the death of her relationship. Now here, in the face of these deaths, were two new lives. She did not want the lives, she wanted the deaths they had replaced. Her acts against the babies can be seen as a somewhat confused and certainly callous attempt to exchange what she had for what she wanted."

"But, at the same time, you are not calling this a mental illness."

"No. Her grip on reality was intact. She was not, for example, delusional. She did not attack her children because an aural or optical delusion instructed her to do so, as is sometimes the case in instances of postpartum psychosis."

It was possible, she went on, for a person under stress—an ordinary person whose defenses might successfully sustain her under normal circumstances—to lose her judgment under sufficient assault. "There can, in other words, be an eruption of neurotic and psychopathic symptoms which are normally latent."

"And that is what, in your expert opinion, occurred in this

case and caused the death of Heather Pratt's two babies?"

She inclined her head with confident gravity. "Yes. That is my diagnosis and my opinion."

Charter folded his arms and looked plaintively at the jury. "Dr. Staple, to most of us, the very notion of killing a child, let alone a newborn infant, is so reprehensible that we cannot even imagine it ever occurs. Have you worked with cases of infanticide previously?"

"I have. Several. And I have studied all the available literature on infanticide."

"So you are well qualified to determine if and how Heather Pratt might fit into the profile of an infanticide?"

"I would consider myself well qualified, yes," she said, her voice prim.

"And what, in your opinion, influences your decision to include Heather in this group?"

"Well, the diagnostic features I discussed a few moments ago, and in addition, the fact that, statistically, she does fit the profile of a mother who murders her infant child."

And what profile was that? Charter prompted.

In her still, flat tone, Dr. Staple informed the courtroom that fully 20 percent of babies killed during the first year of life are killed on the first day of life. Moreover, those infants killed on the first day of life are almost exclusively killed by their mothers.

This bleak statement Charter shrewdly gave a moment to sink in.

Methodology differed for women who kill and for men who kill, Staple noted. Mothers tend to be less violent—suffocation and drowning are the preponderant techniques. Fathers generally maim.

"So her suffocation of the pond baby in particular would be in keeping with the majority of mothers who kill their newborns?"

"Yes. She fits right into the profile."

"And the stab wound to the other baby?"

"Less familiar, but very conceivably the act of a psychopathic person."

Charter nodded, as if he were hearing this for the first time. "Dr. Staple, do you understand why Heather should have admitted having one baby but withheld the information that she had actually given birth to twins?"

"I think I can," Staple said, shifting in her seat. "It's possible that, having murdered one infant, she considered that her crime against the second might possibly be seen as 'not counting,' particularly since the second infant had not been discovered."

"In other words, she could get two murders for the price of one confession?"

And this, as luck would have it, was the very moment Heather Pratt passed out.

Chapter 39

Just Like the Sixties

IN THE END, IT WAS JUDITH WHO SEEMED TO suffer most. Judith, who checked her watch with increasing anxiety as the next hour slid by, as the doctor was called, as Heather slumped against the wall of the room they took her to, as the minutes passed and the chance of dispatching Charter's psychiatrist before the day was out grew more and more remote. Across the square her own witness languished in the diner, reading the newspaper (his meter running at the rate of one hundred dollars an hour) as he waited to be called. This man, an expert on false confessions, had driven up from Boston "just in case," at her request, and now he sat, eyeing the crush of press around the courthouse as they milled tensely about, knowing what was going on inside but unable to find anything to film or anyone to talk to who knew more than they.

Naomi waited in her seat in the courtroom, through the recess that was never officially called. She wished she had the authority to go back to where Heather was, but Judith had taken off without a backward glance, trailing her client's limp frame as the court officer scooped it and ran. Past her, through the milling, chattering crowd, came a doctor, flushed, with a proper medical bag, and as he passed her and rushed through the small door behind the bench, she thought, At least, at last, someone is going to look at Heather and see that she isn't all right, and try, honestly, to make her better. Someone with normal diagnostic tools and without an agenda will put a stethoscope to her chest and a finger to her radial, and ask her kindly where it hurts and whether anything can be done to relieve her suffering. In her seat across the room, Ann Chase reached into her bag and withdrew a lap-sized measure of monk's cloth, which she began, incredibly, to hook with some garishly bright acrylic fabric. A *fuck you*, Naomi knew, to herself. She shook her head and stared plaintively at the door.

In time, Judith returned, looking cross. She came and sat by Naomi and put her head close. "She's *fine*," she said preemptively.

"Oh, good."

"She fainted. What do you expect? She's been living on a cup of tea a day or something ridiculous like that. But when she came to, she started crying. She said she couldn't come back."

Naomi shook her head.

"If she knew what this is going to cost her she'd make an effort," Judith went on, her voice chilly. "Because this is it now. For the weekend. The last thing the jury got to see was this shrink calling her a manipulative psychopath, and then her fainting." She shook her head. "All my work. And of course Charter's just beside himself. He thinks I put her up to this so I could get a new trial later. He thinks this is how we try cases in New York, by manipulating the process."

Naomi clucked in sympathy, but Judith fumed on.

"So naturally there's no way we're going to get to my guy this afternoon. I called over to him at the diner. He's gone back already."

"Oh, I'm sorry."

She shrugged. "Well, if she wants to play Camille, that's what happens."

"But, Judith," Naomi said pleadingly, "you know she didn't do this on purpose. She just couldn't take any more. I mean, this girl's been drawn, quartered, dissected, and biopsied. There are people reading about her menstrual cycle over their morning coffee. I'd probably faint if it were me."

Judith looked sourly at the door, then exhaled in a rush.

"What did the doctor give her?"

"Valium. I could use some myself. She started screaming when I suggested we resume testimony."

Naomi, who hardly blamed her for that, kept her tongue.

"So that's it. Recess till Wednesday. No." She smiled for the first time since returning to the courtroom. "I don't think our Judge Hayes is taking Passover off. He's got a conference in New Haven. He warned us at the outset."

"Well, maybe it's for the best," Naomi thought aloud. "Give everybody a break. And you can concentrate on your *haroseth*."

"Breaks are only a good thing if you're screwing up," Judith said, ignoring the levity. "I really had some momentum going."

"You were doing great," Naomi confirmed.

"And Heather made her histrionic gesture right on cue! Shit, you call her a master manipulator, and presto! She manipulates."

"Come on," Naomi said. She helped Judith with her things. As they drew nearer the door, the din came up, of its own accord, a chatter and then a roar. "What are you going to tell them?" Naomi said.

"*Them.*" Judith looked tired. "Oh, fuck them." But Naomi saw that she was already thinking, turning it as best she could to Heather's advantage. They pushed out the door, walking into Charter's television backdrop. There was, as they took their first steps down the granite staircase, a collective gasp. Naomi looked at Sarah Copley, who was suddenly beside her.

"Can you believe he just said that?"

"What did he say?" Naomi said. She had to raise her voice.

"He said he was going to request that Heather have a pregnancy test. He said his office would want to be reassured that she wasn't pregnant, and that's why she fainted!"

From behind her, she heard Judith: "What a *shmuck!*"

"Do you have evidence that she's pregnant?" somebody shouted.

"Who's the father?"

"Has Ashley been to visit her in jail?"

They were swarming, like girls on a hockey field with their sticks flying and their heads down. It took a moment for somebody to identify Judith. One microphone was pressed into her face, then another, then a thornbush of electronics.

"Is your client pregnant?" a woman said. She was, Naomi thought, so perfectly, blankly, and unremarkably pretty that she must represent some major television market.

"Of course she isn't pregnant," Judith said with controlled rage. "The suggestion that she is pregnant is absurd, as Mr. Charter knows perfectly well. This is a blatant effort to gain in shock value what he is losing inside the courtroom, and I think it's appalling. My client has endured a week of having her character dissected by people who have never met her, and listening to the love of her life explain to the world that he only wanted her for sex, all because she had a stillborn baby and was too confused and bereft to notify what Mr. Charter considers the proper authorities. Frankly, I'm amazed Heather lasted as long as she did. I don't think I would have the strength of character to sit there while absolute strangers talk about me."

"Why did she faint if she isn't pregnant?" a man shouted. Judith gave him a look.

"She's barely eaten for a week. She misses her little girl, who she hasn't seen out of a jail cell in five months. Her heart is broken because of Ashley Deacon's testimony. She still loves him very much. All she wants is for this nightmare to be over so she can go back to her daughter and be the good mother that *everyone* in this trial, on *both* sides, has testified she is. I wish District Attorney Charter and Attorney General Warren would see that this has all been a terrible mistake, that they identified the wrong woman as the mother of the Sabbathday River baby, and that in the process they are ruining the life of an innocent girl. Once again I call on these two men to reconsider the charges against Heather. I hope they will have the bravery, and the decency, and the *honor* to do so."

There were more questions, but there were no more answers. Judith shook her head, reached up in a single, giveaway gesture to comb one curl behind her right ear, then took Naomi's elbow and pulled it after her down the steps. "You were . . . That was great," Naomi said, stumbling on in her wake. Judith, without turning her head, shrugged.

"C'mon, get me out of here."

They bucked a tide of white as women climbed the stairs. There were so many, Naomi thought. Even since lunchtime. Where had they all come from? Surely not Dartmouth—they were thick in the middle and gray, but also young, with cropped hair and long braids, in blue jeans and caftans and sweat suits. They looked like the followers of one of those color-coded swamis, and Ella led them up the steps, clutching her white microphone and a fistful of white blooms. Naomi, helpless, tugged Judith's hand, and they turned to watch.

She was in her element, Ella was. Flushed and alive, her brief hair almost architectural in its precision. Only her hands, chapped red in the March wind, gave away any frailty as she lifted the microphone and called to her the faithful. "We invite all women who are outraged by Heather Pratt's ordeal to come here to Peytonville and make their voices heard. Women who cannot travel to the trial have already begun to show their support for Heather by sending her a single white rose," and she lifted hers to the sky, "the same symbol of resistance against oppression that Sophie Scholl and her 'White Rose' comrades adopted in their courageous stand against the Third Reich. The woman on trial in this parody of justice happens to be Heather Pratt, but she could be any of us. Remember that, and be thankful it isn't you having *your* sexual history and *your* physical attributes discussed by these so-called experts." Ella adjusted her microphone, signaling a crescendo, and indeed, she jacked up her voice to a scream rendered downright painful by the further amplification of the loudspeaker: *"Women demand freedom for Heather Pratt, who has committed no crime! We demand the identification and interrogation of her male oppressors! We demand the restoration of her child! We demand that no other woman should ever be forced to endure what she has endured! We demand the end to this patriarchal repression of women's sexuality! We demand an end to this attempted annihilation of female power!"*

"Ain't it just like the sixties," Judith said in Naomi's ear in a strained, flat tone. Naomi thought for a moment that she must have meant this to be funny, but hadn't, after all, been able to muster the humor. Indeed, she held Naomi's elbow in a frantic grip, as if, without it, she might altogether sink from sight.

Chapter 40

Some Lives Won't Blend

IN HER FIRST MATERNAL SHORTCUT SHE HAD taken to giving Polly those freeze-dried noodle soups from Japan, where the ratio of noodle to actual soup is so utterly stacked that you don't really need a spoon at all. Just as well, Naomi thought, since she barely had energy to make the long trip into the next room. Polly adored the noodles. She sat delightedly making them wiggle through her fingers on the white plastic tray of her high chair and flinging them like rubber bands at the dining-room table, where Naomi, too, was attempting dinner.

But she had even less appetite than energy. It amazed her how swept away she felt, dragged on and under by the crowds of shouting women, the infamy of Charter and his experts, even the tug at her elbow as Judith forged her own indecipherable path through this madness. And to what possible future? The woman she herself had been, a woman living alone in a leaky little house, selling useless objects over the phone by day and then coming home at night vaguely bitter at something she could neither isolate nor name, that woman was gone. Just as she'd known it would happen on the first day, at that first moment on the riverbank. Gone, and only this suspension to replace it. Naomi's future was one week long, after all, and no longer. In only one week's time, the trial would end, and Polly must either return to her mother and whatever life Heather could provide or stay with Naomi in the ongoing tentativeness of their unnamed relationship. And when she thought of this, she was infused with rage. And when she knew it was rage, she understood how badly she needed a plan of her own.

She pulled Polly out of her high chair, the little girl dangling noodles. She was still hungry, so Naomi carried her to the kitchen and spooned her a few mouthfuls of yogurt right out of the cup; then she went to run a bath. Outside, it was inky dark: moonless and windless, the only sound the sucking of mud and the brook running its continuous loop of chatter. She peeled off Polly's clothes and removed her diaper, then helped her scramble in. She had a pink sand bucket and a shovel, which she used to consolidate the froth of her bubble bath, and this proved so distracting that Naomi was able to sneak a shampoo into the event—a rare occurrence. She was just combing through the detangler when she heard the car.

Instantly, Naomi went stiff with fear. No one was expected, of course. It was not possible that she had made some arrangement tonight and then forgotten. In fact, no one came over at all but Judith, and Naomi knew Judith would not come without calling, especially since she had been so exhausted only two hours earlier. Naomi's steep drive, moreover, was not the sort of place drivers chose to turn around in. There was no benevolent outcome she could conjure now, crouched by the bathtub, the comb suspended over Polly's bobbing head. This was a bad thing, like that thing from *Macbeth*, *Something wicked this way comes*, or the 4 a.m. phone call that cannot possibly be from somebody wanting to say hi, or the approaching stranger at the end of "The Monkey's Paw." She thought—inevitably—of Ann, rigged up with another posse of the righteous, ready to circle her sorry house with a line of fire. She thought of Sue Deacon, itching for another fight. Or any of the others—those authors of her hate mail, those breathy admirers on her answering machine, who might have decided it was time to meet, in person. The car sounds ground down the muddy drive.

Naomi scooped Polly up in a towel, grabbed her bucket of thinning bubbles, and set her on the kitchen floor. She picked up the phone and dialed the Goddard police, then, while it was ringing, withdrew the largest knife from her knife block and gripped it in a damp hand.

"Goddard police. Is this an emergency?"

"I don't know." Naomi's voice came out soft. "There's somebody at my house."

"Ma'am?"

The car door slapped shut. The squash of mud under heavy feet.

"Somebody's at my door," Naomi insisted. "Listen, will you just stay on the line for a minute? I'm—"

Then a knock.

"Who's at your door?" the voice on the other end of the line said.

"Hold on. Stay on the line. I'm going to see."

She put it down on the counter. Normal, normal. She held the knife behind her and walked toward the door. "Naomi?" a voice said, clear through Daniel's cheap pine.

She stopped in amazement.

"Can I speak to you, please?"

"Wait," she said. "Wait one minute."

Naomi went back to the telephone. "I'm sorry. It's a false alarm."

"Nobody there?" the voice said.

"That's right. Thank you for your time."

"Not at all." The man hung up. Naomi went to the door.

He was not wearing his uniform. He stood on the porch in corduroys, a big gray sweater with a raveled collar, and heavy boots.

"I just called you," Naomi said. She smiled a bit, since that struck her as funny.

"You called me?" Nelson said. "But why?"

"Because there was some unknown person coming down my drive. I got scared. So I called the police."

"And here I am. Who says we're slow on the uptake?" He gazed past her at Polly, on the floor. "Why is your car parked up at the road?"

"The mud. I'm scared of not being able to get it up the hill till summer. My ex-husband didn't exactly grade it properly."

"No," Nelson said. He frowned then. "When you talked to them just now, did you say it was me?"

"No. I said no one was here, after all."

He nodded, biting his lower lip. "That's good." He saw the knife she still held. "I don't think you're going to need that on me."

Naomi looked down. "No. Sorry."

"You really were scared."

"I've been getting calls. Judith has, too."

Nelson sighed. "Naomi, I need to speak with you. May I speak with you?"

And there it was: that flash of before. The chill blue of his eyes, and the withered places beneath them, that she had loved. The skin through his thin hair.

"Of course you can," Naomi said. She went back to get Polly, who held up her arms, shivering. "I need to get Polly ready for bed. You come, too."

He followed her. They went into Polly's little room, and he stood in the doorway watching her as she put on a new diaper and Polly's footed pajamas and finished combing her wet hair. She filled a spouted cup with water and placed it in a holder over the rim of the crib. Polly chose a book and Naomi read it to her, hearing as if from some distance the high, slightly disingenuous musicality of her voice as the little story—a small bird, ironically, in search of its mother—came around to its end. She did not want to sing Polly her lullaby, because she was embarrassed in front of Nelson, but Polly would not be left alone without it, so Naomi leaned close and crooned: *Now I'm glad to be a woman, glad to be alive, glad for the children to take my place, glad for the will to survive . . .*

Polly looked up at the doorway, her face blank but her eyes large and hard. Then she let Naomi cover her and watched them without protest as they left her to sleep.

"You're good at this," he said. His voice was quiet.

Naomi shrugged. "I don't know. She's pretty easy."

"The way you talk to her. You're good at it."

"Thanks."

"I always thought she was a strange child," Nelson said. They were in the kitchen. "A little strange. The way she stared."

"She's very contemplative. She takes things in, that's all."

"She makes me uncomfortable, to tell you the truth." He looked at Naomi, reddening a bit.

"Well, Nelson, you came into her house and took her mother away. What do you expect?"

His eyes widened. "You think she remembers that?"

"Remembers? Well"—Naomi put Polly's dish in the sink— "probably not the way we remember things. You know, not sequentially. But it must have been a big event for her."

"Yes," he agreed. He was frowning again. "God, I wish it hadn't happened. You couldn't guess how terrible . . ." He petered out.

"*Please* don't compare your suffering to Heather's. Or Polly's. Or mine, for that matter," Naomi said dismissively. "Just don't do that."

"I won't." He shook his head. "I won't." He seemed to be considering what he would say next. She decided to help him along.

"So why are you here, Nelson? What am I supposed to do, forgive you?"

He looked up at her, momentarily taken aback. "No, not at all. You're just supposed to listen to me. There are things I need to tell you." Nelson stopped. "You could give me something to drink."

She had a bottle of wine in her fridge, and two cans of Rolling Rock. She gave him one, and he thanked her. His hand, brushing hers, was hot against the cold metal. He opened the tab and sipped. He had never been a heavy drinker. She led him out to the living room and sat him down on the couch, brushing a few of Polly's toys off the Indian blanket that covered it. She wondered if Nelson ever thought of this couch.

"What things," Naomi said, "do you need to tell me?"

He closed his eyes. "Of course, I shouldn't be here."

"No?" Naomi said evenly.

"I shouldn't be talking to you. In talking to you I've already decided not to go on being a police officer. I want you to understand that."

Taken aback, Naomi stared. "Okay. But I don't want you to do anything that will make you lose your job."

"Doesn't matter." He shook his head briskly. "I couldn't do this anymore, anyway. Not now."

She held her own beer in both hands, nervously popping the metal tab in and out. "Okay, then."

"I went with Charter, back last fall. He was going downstate to meet with the attorney general. He wanted me there, so I went."

Naomi took a sip and waited.

"I was still kind of out of the loop. I didn't know what he was planning, really. I was just supposed to sit there and play the local sheriff. You know, the man on the scene. So it wasn't just like Charter came in and messed up a local investigation. I was supposed to make out that we never could have solved it on our own, if not for the D.A."

He laid his head back against the cushion, not looking at Naomi.

"You've got to understand, I didn't foresee any of this."

"Who could have?" Naomi said, trying for a comforting tone.

"So Warren says to Charter, Can we really win this case? He's been reading the reports, you see, and it seems farfetched to him, and he has a lot to lose if it all falls apart. He tells Charter he can go ahead, but only if he's sure this stuff about the two babies and the two fathers will hold up. He can see what they're going to make of this if it turns out Charter picked the wrong girl and the real person who stabbed the kid and killed it was just someone else completely. I mean, he can understand why Charter made the mistake, but he doesn't want to go forward with it if there's any doubt at all."

Naomi waited.

"So Charter says, The girl confessed to the stabbing. And he knew it was her, for both kids."

She sighed. "All right, Nelson. But you know, this isn't really news. I really could have imagined this exact scene, even without your telling me."

"No, there's more. So then Warren looks at Charter and asks him if there are any holes in the interrogation. Legal holes. Like, is it absolutely foolproof? Because if this thing is going to rest on the confession, it had better be perfect. And Charter says yes, it is."

"Naturally," Naomi said, shrugging.

"And then Warren looks at me and asks me the same thing."

She began to feel funny. It was the way he stopped here, where it made no sense for him to stop. He was waiting for her to prepare herself. Naomi looked at him. Nelson's eyes were closed, and she found herself watching the tiny pulses of motion beneath the lids, as if he were looking for the next words in that darkness.

"And what did you say?" Naomi asked.

"I said there was no problem with the interrogation or the confession." He considered his own hands. "That was a lie."

So, she thought. So.

"There was a problem with the interrogation. It wasn't clean."

"I see," she said softly.

"The confession wasn't clean."

"Okay."

They sat for a moment like this. Nelson took small sips of

his beer. His legs were crossed, the corduroy worn and shiny where they met. He looked, suddenly, flushed. She thought that she ought to say he should take his sweater off if he was hot, since she would have asked him to take his coat off by now if he'd come in wearing a coat, but that seemed awkward, so she said nothing. He was looking past her at the dining table, and beyond to the Eliot Porter poster on her wall, the same one everyone had, with the pink-tinged woods. Then he was looking at her.

"I'm sorry, Naomi."

She nodded, though she felt somewhat fraudulent accepting an apology that was more appropriately due Heather. "Why are you telling me this?" she asked.

"Because I'm going to do something about it. I'm going to do what I should have done last fall."

"You're calling Warren, then?" she said, her voice full of incredulous hope.

"I've already done it. This afternoon. When Heather collapsed like that, I felt like such a colossal piece of shit. And I never dreamed, all this stuff they said about her in court. That doctor talking about her, and the shrink saying she was a psychopath. And Ashley! Who gave it to just about every woman in town, pretending he was a family man! I knew I could have stopped this. And I'd lied, which I was miserable about. On the stand. So it's over for me, anyway. A police officer who commits perjury . . . Well." Unaccountably he smiled. "I mean, they do, of course. But a police officer who *admits* to committing perjury, that's the end of his life as a police officer, do you see?"

She looked at him, amazed and admiring. "I see. I'm sorry."

"My decision." His voice was thick, though he nodded when he said it. "I'll tell Judith to recall me. I'll say what actually took place."

Naomi swallowed. "You're really a decent man, Nelson."

"No. A decent man wouldn't have let it get this far. And that girl in jail all this time. And the little girl."

"It's all right. The important thing is, you're doing it now." She touched him. She touched the back of his head. He let his head sink back against her hand.

And there they sat for a moment, neither moving, both test-

ing the weight of this contact. Finally, he turned his head, still
in her palm.

"Naomi. Can I please stay a little longer?"

She kissed him. Her mouth remembered his mouth, her
tongue his tongue. She felt his hand against her face. *So he
does*, she thought vaguely. It wasn't only she who had
wanted . . .

"I wish," he said, though somewhat indistinctly. His fingers
were beneath her hair, lifting it. He seemed to pull it over his
own face, burying himself beneath it.

Now he took off his sweater, and he was hot, after all, she
saw, with dark spots under his arms that smelled sharp, though
clean, as if he had washed before coming here to sweat. She
wished she had done the same. She let herself imagine she had
bathed with Polly, the two of them as they sometimes did,
lapped in bubbles, but then thought how even more afraid she
might have been if she had been naked that way and the car
came down her drive, how vulnerable to cross the bathroom
floor dripping water and bubbles to the telephone, how she
would not want him to see her like that, barely wrapped in her
towel, because she was not beautiful. "I didn't know you were
coming" was what she managed to say at the end of this.

"You look wonderful," Nelson said, his weight across her.
"I love how you look. You smell wonderful."

The mechanics of first sex, she was thinking. That compulsion at the outset to just get it done. And the debate over
whether a finger's insertion made you a nonvirgin, and how
the clutch of a breast was supposed to give either party any
pleasure. Matthew Kaufman explaining why a French kiss was
not the same as an ordinary kiss in the spare room of his
father's weekend house in Pound Ridge. The terror of being
thought a prude *(What are you, hung up?)* or worse, a romantic, and the determined we're-way-past-that nocturnal mean-
derings in the college house she shared with three men and
two women. The shock of coming with another person in the
room; then, all too soon, the tedious politics of orgasm, and
Daniel, and their efficient, egalitarian fucking: one for you,
then one for me. And Ashley, whose excuse was that he loved
women and what was the matter with that? And now this.

"Can I?" Nelson said, but already he was. Her clothing unfurled, his face to her chest, and Naomi forgot herself in the

slip of his skin over her skin. How thin he was for the weight he made, and how pale he was not, though he was light in that pristine, Aryan way—hairless men *langlaufing* through the Nordic forests, surfer blonds, ice-pick blue in the irises, men who were not Jewish—*the unsnipped*, as her friend Shura had once called them. The purr of a zipper, his or hers? She really ought to be more on top of this, she thought, but then it was so sweet to lie here and be touched this way, so gently and with such focused intent. His mouth closed over her navel and she heard, as if from some great distance, the sounds she made.

"Wait." Naomi sat up. "Just wait."

"I'm sorry," he said quickly. "I should have—"

"No, it isn't that," she told him hurriedly. "I just, I don't want Polly . . ."

"Of course."

They both got up and walked away from their clothes. The light was on, four harsh bulbs. She brought him into her bedroom, where it was dark, and they fell over the bed, her mess of blankets. Nelson's big hand where her legs met, without delay, opened and touched her. Was she a nonvirgin? One finger, then two. She could barely remember what Daniel looked like suddenly, though she recalled the feline tautness of Ashley's long thigh, the pucker of his little ass. And of Nelson, who in his way had really loved her; this was the only memory she had taken away: the top of his rosy head, with its skein of silver-gold hair, bobbing in concentration as he stroked her and kissed her, reverent and courteous at once.

"Naomi," he said now, "I did miss you."

"Missed *this*," she said, and what she meant as a tease came out smacking of accusation.

"No, you. And this."

"But we're too different," she said, smiling. "At least that's what you—"

"Shh." He darted up to kiss her. Quite gently, he bit her lips. "Not now."

Naomi took his hand away. She didn't want his hand. She wanted to feel him push against her. She wanted to feel that again and see if she remembered how it felt.

"I didn't bring anything," he said suddenly. "I really didn't think about it. I would have. But I didn't think I would need—"

"I'm on the pill," Naomi said, without thinking. Then she was shocked at the words, though they came in her own voice. She had never been on the pill. She had always had a super-stitious notion that if she took a pill to keep from becoming pregnant it might work too well and she would never have children. Last summer she had used her diaphragm, but it had probably crumbled to dust by now, and anyway, she didn't know where it was.

"Oh. Fine," he said. He put his mouth to her breast. Her nipple rolled against his teeth. Had he done that last year? Did she forget that part?

Or this: Nelson's arm in the small of her back, lifting her up hard against him, or the glancing of hipbone against hip-bone, like somebody striking inefficiently a flint against a steel but somehow still managing to ignite sparks. She let her head fall back against the pillow. Let him lift me, is what she was thinking. Let him, since it feels good, and it felt good and she did not have to explain the right way to do it. Obviously I can't take care of myself. Naomi's arms flung up over her head, knuckles against the headboard. He said, "Oh, this is good. Oh, you are." Each word had its own breath. It took a long time to make sentences. He said other things. She wanted his mouth to be over hers when he came, and it was. And she closed her legs around him—thigh slick on thigh—as if to trap him forever in this happy place, with this sweetness between them. How long could it last before he moved, and got up and walked away?

"Naomi." A kiss for her ear: friendly, thick with affection. "I don't want to mess up your life."

"My unmessed-up life," she said ruefully, feeling him fall out of her: the little sadness after the little death.

"No, I mean . . . since last time it didn't work out."

"Well," Naomi sighed, "I'm not sure I know what it means anymore, to 'work out' with another person."

"No, I don't know, either."

He lay on his back beside her, one long leg bent so that the sole rested against her ankle.

"You didn't just . . ." He turned to her. "It wasn't because I went to Warren, is it? It wasn't a *reward*."

"No, of course not. Though I would give you a reward if I

could. I think it's great, what you did. But it's not why this happened. I'm glad you stayed."

"I should have come sooner."

Yes, she thought, though she didn't say it.

After a moment he got up to go into the bathroom. He turned the water on so she wouldn't hear him pee. Sweet, Naomi thought. Then the door opened. "Is this you?" Nelson said.

He was looking at the bathroom wall, over the toilet.

"Yes. My dad brought the dashikis home from Africa."

"Dashikis." He tested the word. He had evidently not heard it before. "Is that what they are?"

"Yes. Sort of African shirtdresses."

"This your brother? And your mom?"

"Yes," Naomi said. "In front of Grant's Tomb. That's in Manhattan."

"You were pretty," he observed. "What were you here, about eight?"

"Yes. Chubby."

"Plump," he corrected. "Pretty."

She thought she looked, in the photograph, about as untidy as she always felt. Now, rather belatedly, she wondered if she didn't always feel untidy because she saw this photograph every time she went into her bathroom.

"And that hair."

Which was frizzy-brown and down to her ass, caught at midpoint by an orange band.

"Ashkenazi deluxe," she said, more to herself.

He frowned, but didn't ask. Another new word.

"Where's your father?" Nelson said.

"Oh. He was seldom in the picture, if you know what I mean."

She saw him look at her through the open door. He didn't know.

"He took that photograph. That's why he isn't in it. But he ran off the next year, with one of his students."

Nelson nodded. "Sorry." He washed his hands, then flicked out the light and came back to bed. "They all still in Manhattan, your family?"

"My mom is," Naomi said. "My dad lives in California, near

San Francisco. My brother caught the tail end of the draft. He's been in Canada for the last decade."

He took this in. She waited for him to get angry, but he didn't. "What does he do up there?"

"Teaches school. He married a Canadian woman and had Canadian kids. They've been down to visit a couple of times." She shrugged. "We're not that close, really."

For a long minute Nelson looked at her, the arms still up over her head. Even in the half-dark she caught the warm tone of his skin. And she felt, rather than saw, the warmth in his looking.

"You are a very uncommon woman," he said seriously.

"In oh so many ways," she quipped, but he didn't smile.

"I mean that. I haven't met anyone else like you."

"Well, Judith," Naomi said. "Judith is like me."

"I haven't known Judith like this. And I don't intend to know her like this."

"All right, then. Assuming this is a compliment, I accept your compliment."

He didn't answer.

"Nelson? Did you change your mind about last year? Is that it?"

This will not hurt me, Naomi thought, chanting to herself. *Whatever he says will not hurt me.*

"Well, that's just it." He shook his sad head. "I didn't change my mind. I still feel what I felt then. But I also feel this. And there have been times when I just wanted to be here in this house, and of course I couldn't come here. Not only because of what I said to you when we stopped, but because of the babies, and Heather. I couldn't just come and talk to you, or do anything else."

"No." She nodded. "I see that."

"But I wanted to. I woke up in the night sometimes, and I *wanted*. Even though I knew we would always wind up struggling against each other. There are just some lives that won't blend. I said that, and I still think so. But I always thought of you with great . . ." He trailed off, unsure of what the next word ought to be.

"Yes. I know that." Naomi sat up next to him, her breasts

pendulous. He never took his eyes off her face. She thought, quite suddenly, of Mickey Schwerner and the mob, and how he really *had* understood just how they felt. "Nelson," she said, "whatever it is, I know that very well."

Chapter 41

The Chosen People

"NO WAIT," JUDITH SAID. "WAIT, YOU'VE GOT to hear this next bit."

"Okay," Naomi said, twisting her neck to pin the phone to her ear. She was trying to dress and watch Polly at the same time. Polly had, of late, developed an interest in steaming liquids.

"All right, so then it goes, 'Ironically, it is those movements and communities that view themselves as morally sanctioned who fail most strikingly to be moral. During the Crusades, for example, Christian soldiers paved a bloody road to Jerusalem, slaughtering men, women, and children as they traveled, all in defense of Christian values. And somewhat closer to home, in Salem, a society modeled on godliness behaved with savage paganism toward its weakest members: servant women, the old, and the friendless. The most distressing element of the Goddard Babies case is not that police authority was outrageously abused, or that a fiasco of Keystone Kops proportions was brought about, or even that an innocent woman has been wrongly accused of horrendous crimes, but that her neighbors have failed to register any complaint whatsoever about her treatment. Supporters from all over the Northeast have been flocking to Peytonville, where the trial is about to enter its second week, and thousands more have sent Pratt white roses, symbolizing resistance, but from her own acquaintances there has not been the smallest gesture of outreach. By distancing themselves from her, the upstanding citizens of Goddard, New Hampshire, apparently think they are showing us how much better than she they are. In fact, they are showing us precisely the opposite.' " Judith finished with a flourish of glee. "Isn't that—"

"Yes," said Naomi. "Of course it is. I hope Ann Chase read that."

"Joel was at Tom and Whit's yesterday. He said they were

sold out of the *Globe* by nine o'clock. Same at Stop & Shop. I'm so glad, Naomi. I mean, they don't care what we say, or those butch girls from Dartmouth. But you can bet they care that the *Globe* thinks they're savages."

"I would think so." Naomi sighed. She reached for her coffee, narrowly edging out Polly, and took the mug into the kitchen. The low heels of her shoes made an unaccustomed clack on the floorboards as she walked.

"I'm dressing up," she said. "I'm supposed to, right?"

"Well, a little. I want to make it special for Joel."

"Okay." She poured some Rice Krispies for Polly, pausing briefly to wonder if it was all right for an atheistic Jew to give leaven to a non-Jewish child before attending a Seder. Naomi sighed and added milk to the bowl.

"And my sister's here. Did I say?"

"No!" she said eagerly. Judith's sister, from the far, secret side of her life. "That's great. And her children?"

"Her daughter. Hannah is here. Her husband and Simon are in Providence."

"Oh," Naomi said awkwardly. "Well, good."

"And a friend from the city. Which is why I called you, actually. I mean, he reminded me. I forgot the horseradish, and I was wondering . . ."

"Oh sure. I think I have some, but I'll stop on the way if I don't."

"Thanks." Judith sounded distracted. "Now I have to go. I have a potentially serious gefilte-fish issue."

"Oh, that sounds bad." Naomi laughed. She said they would be there soon, hung up the phone, and went to the fridge. There, a dark back corner yielded one slender jar of horseradish, crusted at the rim but smelling reassuringly of horseradish inside. She gave Polly a few minutes longer to eat her cereal, wrapped her up in her coat, then ferried the baby and the fruit salad (her own contribution to the meal) up the driveway to her car.

It was a dark spring day, threatening rain. Polly, whom Naomi had buttoned into her best dress, sat in her car seat shaking a bottle of apple juice, sending the odd drop flying through the nipple. "Sweetie-pod," she said brightly, "do you know where we're going?"

Polly stuck the bottle in her mouth.

"We're going to a Passover Seder. At the Seder we celebrate the exodus of the Jews."

Polly stopped. She deliberately stopped sucking. "Juice?" she inquired.

Naomi burst out laughing. She drove into Judith's driveway, parking beside a blue van with Rhode Island plates. Judith's sister. The kitchen door opened as she was unsnapping the car seat.

"Hey," said Judith, leaning out. "You won't believe who just called."

Naomi straightened. "Charter. He's dropping the charges."

"No. But it's almost as good. Sarah Copley. She was so pissed about the editorial, she'll be there on Wednesday. With a squadron, she told me."

"A squadron of what?" Naomi said darkly.

" 'Heather's neighbors,' she said. Oh, this is great."

But Naomi wasn't sure whether she meant the squadron or the fruit salad, which Naomi handed her.

"What are these?" Judith peered, intrigued.

"Pomegranate seeds. In keeping with the Middle Eastern theme."

"Oh, fabulous. So isn't it great?"

Naomi tried to look happy for Judith's sake. "Good for Sarah. Of course, she might have done it last week. She might have done it six months ago."

"Better now than never," Judith said, leading Naomi up the stairs to the kitchen door. "Oh, this is David. Our guest."

David, standing in the doorway, was bearded and dark, a tall and thick man with hair that was bushy except, oddly, on the top of his head. He reached eagerly for Naomi's hand and shook it. The absence of something made her look down, and this was when she noted that the tip of his thumb was missing. "The famous Naomi Roth, I guess."

"The very famous," she confirmed, smiling. "So famous I didn't even know I was famous."

"Ah, but you are. Judith has been keeping me up to speed on the Goddard Babies case since last fall."

She looked at Judith, who was moving things around in the refrigerator to find room for the fruit salad.

"David's our expert," said Judith, offhand. "He's going to testify about superfecundation on Wednesday."

"And this is the little girl? The one whose mother is on trial?" David said.

"Yes. Polly. She's been with me for about five months."

"Wow. Hard on her. And you."

"No. I've enjoyed it."

"Well, it should be over soon," said David, looking rather longingly at the wine.

"I hope so."

"No, it's absurd. Superfecundation is far too fantastical to hang a case like this on. I told my colleagues at the lab and they all wanted to testify. They think I'm not going to be able to keep a straight face on the stand."

"You'd better," Judith said, from the stove. She was lifting a hard-boiled egg onto the Seder plate: one egg, one bunch of parsley, one roasted lamb shank, one small bowl of salt water, one little mound of something that looked like wet granola: haroseth.

The kitchen was bright and full, and she seemed elated in it, lifting the lids of pots and sheeting something in the oven with foil. Her husband, passing behind her to the sink, trailed an affectionate hand across her shoulders, and Naomi thought, without warning, of the morning on the park bench, those shoulders shaking with mysterious tears. "I think we're nearly there," Judith said, picking up the Seder plate. "David, would you put this on the table?"

He took it in his incomplete hand and carried it through Ashley Deacon's French doors, into the dining room beyond. "Hannah, sweetie." Naomi heard a woman's voice. "Hannah? Turn it off, it's time now."

"My niece," Judith said. And then, as a woman walked into the kitchen, she stated the obvious. "And my sister. This is Rachel."

"Naomi," Rachel said. She looked so like Judith, the tiniest variation on one genetic theme, and here again was that jolt of recognition, like in the supermarket that day when she had first seen Judith glowering at the iceberg lettuce and waxed orange tomatoes. Though her hair was cut to the nape of her neck and she seemed slighter, with narrower shoulders and hips, they were otherwise nearly interchangeable.

"You look exactly alike," Naomi said wonderingly, as if there might be something surprising in that.

"I know," Rachel said, her voice warm. "Tell me about it."

"I am *one inch taller*," said Judith with mock ferocity. "And she has an extra toe."

"Judith!" Her sister reached across the table to punch her. "Don't be disgusting."

"They say it's good luck," said Judith slyly.

Rachel turned to Naomi. "Don't pay any attention to her. And I'm perfectly willing to show you my feet."

"Not necessary." Naomi laughed. "That woman couldn't tell the truth if her life depended on it." She smiled at Rachel. "I'm really glad to meet you. I've heard so much about you."

But when she said that, she felt right away that it was wrong. Because she had heard so little, really, and what she had heard she did not, somehow, feel free to talk about. She hoped Rachel would not ask what Naomi had heard, but Rachel did not. Instead, she merely returned the conventional response.

"Me too. About you. I'm really happy Judith's found somebody up here who'll put up with her."

"Oh, I'm happy to put up with her," Naomi said. "She's the only one who gets my jokes."

"Let's start," Joel called from the dining room. "Are we ready?"

Judith said they were. She took off her apron. She was wearing a dress so modest and plain it seemed nearly prim, and her strand of white pearls. She looked beautiful. And serene. A matriarch-in-waiting. "Judith," Naomi said, "you look . . ."

"Thank you," said Judith. "Here." It was a plate of matzos, thin and irregularly shaped, covered by a linen napkin. "David brought them from the city."

"You have to go to Hester Street," he said amiably. "There's one little guy left. Every year, all the assimilated Jews troop down there to try to pay off their guilt."

"Is that what you are?" Naomi said, smiling. She took the plate in one hand and Polly's forearm in the other.

"No. I've unassimilated myself. But even so, I'm still guilty."

Joel, passing with his empty bottle of wine, laid an emphatic hand on David's shoulder. "David," he said, "please chill."

But he was grinning. They both were. She looked from one face to the other, bewildered. Then they went into the dining room, and as they stepped before her Naomi saw for the first time why she had imagined his hair to be so discordantly rough and smooth. He was actually wearing a black yarmulke.

She put the plate of matzos on the table and busied herself settling Polly in her high chair beside her. On Polly's other side, a little girl, Rachel's daughter, sat in her own seat, looking on with interest. The same black hair and rounded nose, but here the eyes were eerily green. She was not a pretty girl, but Naomi saw that she would be—like her mother and aunt—a striking woman. "Can I play with her?" Hannah said. "I like babies."

"Of course," said Naomi. "You must be Hannah."

"I'm Hannah. How old is she?"

About a year and a half, Naomi told her. The little girl's eyes widened. "Really?"

"Sweetie," Rachel said from across the table. The word was light, but there was within its tone an unmistakable note of warning. Involuntarily, Naomi looked at her.

"You have another child?" she heard herself say. That she had said what she was thinking, without censoring herself, surprised her. "I mean, I think Judith once mentioned a nephew."

"Yes," Rachel said. "Simon is just a bit older than Polly. He's home in Providence with my husband."

"Oh," said Naomi lamely.

"It was better not to bring him. Judith might have mentioned that he has a degenerative illness."

"She did. Yes." She didn't know what to say. "He must miss you," she finally uttered, loathing herself, but to her surprise, Rachel shook her head.

"No. He doesn't." Then she smiled at Naomi. It was not a happy smile, by any means. "But I miss him."

"Miss who?" Judith said. She was back in the dining room, handing each of them a slender book.

"Simon."

Naomi watched Judith's eyes.

"Yes. Shall we start?"

Abruptly Rachel laughed. "Judith, can you believe we're doing this? Mom would die if she could see us."

"Mom did die," said Judith. She took her seat. "David?"

"Thank you," said David.

They opened their books, Naomi from the front at first.

Then, when she saw her mistake, from the back.

She was surprised how quickly it returned. The washing of hands, the lifting and replacement of undrunk wine, the dipping of parsley in salt water. When the afikomen was hidden she had a sudden, giddy memory of tearing apart Linda Grossberg's Central Park West apartment looking for the matzo wrapped in a white embroidered cloth, and how she had found it, nestled improbably between the two volumes of the *OED*, and how Dr. Grossberg had ransomed it for a dollar. She remembered the hit of horseradish against the honey apple of the *haroseth*. She remembered the red drops of wine on the good white china: *the river of blood, the frogs, the lice, the wild beasts, the pestilence, the boils, the hail, the locusts, the darkness, the slaying of the firstborn.* Through it all, Polly sat quietly, sometimes shredding the stem of parsley Naomi had given her, but often staring at David, whose voice boomed with ceremony, his Hebrew guttural and hypnotic, his intercut English purposeful and choppy.

"Why is this night different from all other nights?" Hannah chirped, rehearsed and on cue.

Because it *reminded* us of other nights. Not only long ago, in Egypt, but black and torturous nights not nearly so distant. Because this was the night we told ourselves our own story, to make sure we never forgot it.

To Naomi, this was unexpectedly seductive. She thought of how, when Alex Haley had returned to Africa to find out about his slave ancestor, he'd had to sit through hours of tribal narrative before the small story of his own relative could be recounted. The story of the individual was inextricable from the story of the tribe. Our story, Naomi nodded, placing the dry, vaguely musty matzot on her tongue. The Exodus from Egypt, the sweep of Diaspora, the expulsion from Spain, the waves of emigration across the water, and the terrible sea that had closed over anyone left behind.

Then David recounted a part of the story she hadn't heard before. How the Jewish slaves toiled for hundreds of years in Egypt, and suffered terribly in bondage, and cried constantly to their God for deliverance, but were unheard, or at least unheeded. Why should He ignore them, His own chosen people? Then the angel Gabriel took a newborn child who had been maimed by the Egyptian overseers and carried it aloft to heaven, forcing God to look. God could not bear the sight of a mutilated Jewish child. Its wounds served to remind Him of His covenant with Abraham.

"He couldn't bear the sight of a mutilated Jewish child?" Naomi said aloud.

"That's what the Talmud says." David nodded.

"He's not very consistent," said Rachel. "There've been one or two since then."

"Well," said David, "God may have had other lessons to teach us at later times in our history."

"So cruel," Naomi said. "This God of ours."

"He never said He wasn't," Joel interjected. "He laid it all out for Moses, right off the bat. *I am a jealous God.* But He still chose us."

They went on. The glasses of wine. The bitter sandwich of matzo and maror. A tone-deaf rendition of "Dayenu," in which even Polly participated, beating her soggy parsley against the tray of her high chair. And, before the meal, one final blessing: "I believe with all my heart in the coming of the Messiah, and although he will be late, I will wait each and every day for his arrival."

Judith stood. She cleared away the used plates and collected the Haggadahs.

"It's funny the way it acknowledges that he's late," Rachel said to David. "I mean, it sort of has a castigating tone, doesn't it?"

"You think God feels castigated?" David smiled, taking a very unceremonial drink of wine.

"No, but maybe angry."

"Oh, He's been cursed before. We cursed Him from the moment He chose us as His people. And that's all right, because being angry with God won't hurt Him a bit."

Joel nodded his concurrence. "Besides, there are things God regards as far worse than our anger."

"What's worse?" Rachel said. She was cutting a matzo ball in Hannah's soup bowl.

"Worse than being cursed?" Joel said. "Being abandoned. By us." He smiled. Steam from the soup clouded his glasses. "We're all mad to assimilate in this country."

"Oh, I don't know that that's true," Rachel said. "Maybe the *Our Crowd* crowd, but not *shtetl* Jews."

David helped himself to the salt as it was passed around the table. "Is that so?" He smiled a little. "And what was Communism if not a mass abdication from Judaism? It was an old faith exchanged for a new faith. A faith of nonfaith."

"Hey," Naomi said, "it seemed like a good idea at the time. Besides, I never felt compelled to believe in a Creator. To me, nature and chance between them are sufficiently vast to explain just about everything."

"Nature and chance made you?" David said, frowning.

"Absolutely. Or, more precisely, they made the things that made me. The Big Bang, the double helix, the survival of the fittest, supernovas, the ascent of man . . . the world according to PBS. It works for me." She sighed. "Come on. You guys are scientists."

"Yes, Naomi." Joel's voice had an edge. "But I just don't see that it's enough to discount even the *possibility* of God. I mean, even for a questioning person like yourself?"

"Oh no," Naomi said, declining this appeal to her intellectual vanity. She tipped her soup bowl to fill her spoon. "I can do a little better than that. Understood, I'm not a philosopher."

"Understood," said Joel.

She paused, drank, and considered. "God, by definition, is omnipotent. Yes?"

"Yes," said David. "Limitless, omnipotent."

"God is perfectly good."

"Ah," David said noncommittally. "Go on."

"An omnipotent being can prevent evil. But there is evil *all the time*. So which is He not? Omnipotent or good? Or maybe He's both those things, but He doesn't actually exist."

"He never said He was good," Joel said passionately. "He wants *us* to be good."

"The suffering of children? Couldn't He prevent that, at least?" Naomi asked, raising her eyebrow. "I mean, the rest of us maybe. But not children."

David shook his head. "Maybe that's not the right question, Naomi. Maybe you are too inclined—well, understandably inclined—to look at the problem of human suffering in only one way: Why can't it be prevented? Maybe the right question is: What is the *purpose* of suffering?"

"I refuse to consider that," said Naomi. "No purpose can possibly justify suffering."

"No?" He smiled. "Doesn't suffering help us to appreciate good by showing us the contrast of the two?"

"Perhaps. But that's not enough."

"Aren't there virtues which are only possible against a backdrop of evil and suffering?"

Naomi frowned. "Such as?"

"Courage. You can't have courage without peril. You can't have forgiveness without the thing that has to be forgiven. These things require at least the risk of suffering to even exist."

She considered. "That's true. But I'd rather forgo some of these noble attributes and get rid of war and cruelty and disease at the same time."

"Wait a minute." Joel leaned forward. "God's ways are mysterious. We only see a fraction of the whole, you know. And on the basis of that, who are we to judge whether evil is necessary?"

"No, that doesn't wash." Naomi shook her head. "That's like saying, 'I reject your theory in favor of another theory which I can't think of.'" She reached down to retrieve Polly's fork. "Here, sweetie-pod." Then she broke off a piece of her matzo and gave it to the little girl.

"Racka," said Polly.

"Cracker. Yes."

"She really talks," Hannah said wonderingly.

"Yes. She has lots of words."

"It's amazing."

Naomi looked at her. She was staring at Polly.

"So you don't believe at all." David was intent.

"Afraid not," said Naomi. "Though I respect your belief."

"No, you don't," Joel observed, his voice tight. Naomi looked at Judith, who sat tensely, her eyes on her plate; then back at Joel, who waited for an answer.

"Well, I'd like to. Maybe that's the same thing."

"For the record," David broke in, "I don't think so. Wanting to believe isn't the same as believing. You can't get yourself to believe just through logic, or some kind of an act of will. Like learning a language or losing a few pounds."

"No, I suppose not." She smiled. "Otherwise everybody would be doing it."

"Not that people don't try," David said, sitting back in his chair. "I once had this born-again-Christian friend. She took me to a movie about the Rapture, at her church in Somerville. She was really after my soul." He grinned. "I thought it was my body, a little more in line with what *I* was after, but I flattered myself. So in the movie, the main character is this agnostic woman who wakes up one morning and half the people in the world are gone. Her folks, all her born-again friends, just gone. She waits days to hear from her husband, who's in the army overseas, and finally a letter comes. It's written the day before the Rapture, and it says, 'Darling, wonderful news. Today I accepted Jesus Christ as my personal savior!' "

"Good timing," Rachel observed.

"So then the armies of the Antichrist come and try to get this poor woman to accept Satan's mark. She has to accept it or be martyred as a Christian. And she wants *passionately* to believe, but she can't decide."

"And how did it end?" Judith said.

David shrugged, smiling. "It was one of those really nasty endings. The woman's being dragged to the guillotine, and the Antichrist folks are saying, 'Take the mark! Take the mark!' And then the movie just freezes, so you never know if she held firm and got to go to heaven or not." He sighed. "I remember when the lights came up, everybody in the whole place swung around in their seat and looked at me. I was such a challenge to them. Though whether because I was an atheist or a Jew, I'm not sure." He turned to Naomi, sober again. "You know what interests me, though? *Despite* your lack of belief, you do seem to consider yourself a Jew."

"One hundred percent," Naomi agreed. "Wanna make something of it?"

"But what does that mean to you?" said David. "Being a Jew without God?"

"Survival. My DNA is the beneficiary of countless generations of survival. I am absolutely humble before this fact. And grateful, please don't mistake that."

"Well!" He sounded triumphant. "Survival is not to be sneezed at. Survival is the theme of the Seder, after all."

"Oppression and survival, yes. Don't forget the oppression, though. I know I can't."

"I can't either," said David. "You know what's the subtext of every Seder since 1945? It's *Fuck you. We're still here.*"

Naomi grinned. David glanced at Hannah. "Sorry," he said to Rachel.

"That's okay. She's heard worse, haven't you, babe?"

"Yup," Hannah said.

David drank from his wineglass. "Well anyway, the Haggadah says, 'In every generation an enemy has risen to destroy us.' Pretty steep odds. There must be a reason for our having survived."

"Really?" Naomi said archly. "Why must there? Nature and chance saw to our survival, not to mention sheer will. That doesn't mean it has no meaning, or that we shouldn't attach great significance to it. But there was no *reason*. Because there is no God. It's a story we made for ourselves, to tell us how to live, and to preserve our tribe, and to sustain our self-image when we are persecuted and dispersed. And it worked beautifully. Whatever they did to us, we survived. And it has an *intrinsic* beauty, which I also respect. This"—she gestured at Judith's table, her good silver and crystal glasses—"is beautiful."

"Thank you," Judith said cautiously.

David leaned back as Judith removed his soup plate, but he never took his eyes off Naomi's face. "Interesting that you chose the pronouns 'we' and 'us.' "

"But that's just my point. Nothing brings out my Judaism like anti-Semitism." Naomi was cutting some of her chicken for Polly. There was a tzimmes of sweet potatoes, too, and noodle kugel laced with currants and apricots. Also Judith's transcendent (as it turned out) gefilte fish.

"Well, let me ask you something, Naomi. If an external force like anti-Semitism is required to keep Jews Jewish, is Judaism worth preserving at all?"

Naomi put down her fork. "I don't know. It's a good question."

"I think there are more pertinent questions," Rachel said. "I mean it's all very interesting to talk about faith as if this were just between the Jews and God, but there have been a few other players in our history. Like, I know you can see this coming, David, but if there is a God, where was He during the Holocaust?"

"He was there." David chewed his chicken. "He heard. It ended, didn't it?"

"It started," said Naomi darkly.

"He was there, but He doesn't control everything that we do. He made us and He gave us the choices. Man chooses between good and evil. Often, unfortunately, he chooses evil, and when he does, God suffers with the victims."

"Not good enough," said Rachel. "I mean, Christians, at least, have a reasonable response to this problem, but we don't. A Christian can say she knows she can handle sorrow, because she believes God won't give her something she *can't* handle, so she can draw strength from his belief in her. But what tools do we have to confront sorrow with? If we're punished, we must deserve it in some way. He even leaves it to us to figure out what we did wrong. Plus we don't get to burden God with our private prayers. Christians can talk about their personal relationship with Christ. He's their personal savior. But we're not encouraged to be intimate with the Master of the Universe. He's got bigger stuff on His mind, so He can't pay much attention to our little lives. We have to say the ancient words when we pray, and we're not allowed to improvise. Plus there's no promise of an afterlife, where we can look forward to seeing the people we love and mourn. All we have is this, and if our history is any indication, this is nobody's idea of a picnic. Sometimes I wish I could believe in the Christian God. He's so much friendlier."

"Oh, He is?" Joel said ironically. "I haven't noticed that the world's been a nicer place for the last two millennia. Besides, I've never understood how Christians can actually bring themselves to trust the God Jesus tells them to trust. Isn't this the same God we're talking about, after all? So if He abandoned the people of His original covenant, as they claim, what makes them think He'll honor His so-called new covenant with them?"

"Maybe they feel we blew it and they can do a better job," Rachel said.

"I think Joel's point is that you can believe in God but recognize that He does have limitations," David said, getting right back to what was, for him, the point. "It's not inconsistent to say that He hates suffering but can't eliminate it, at least not without taking away from us the gift of our own choices. And even if tragedy isn't God's will, overcoming it may be."

Naomi smiled and shook her head. "Is that the same as

saying that He takes credit for the good things that happen, but the bad things are our own fault."

"Not at all! It's saying that good can come from bad. From the Holocaust we got immeasurable suffering and sorrow. But we also got Israel. We got an opportunity for renewal."

"Great!" Naomi said maliciously. "Let's go dig up the mass graves and spread the news."

"I don't want renewal," Rachel said softly. "I want what I've lost. I don't want to hear about how my sadness will contribute to some future happiness."

"Rachel," her sister said.

"No, really. I hate it when doctors tell me how what they're learning from my child might save somebody else's child. I feel badly for the next mother. I do. But I still want my own child. How can I embrace a God who's determined this will happen to him? And it's all very well to say genetics determined it," she said, shaking her head, "but if there is a God, didn't He make genetics?"

"You're missing the point, Rachel." Joel spoke softly. "If you can think of God as a little bit like a doctor, this is all I'm saying. You know, we don't always understand what He is doing on our behalf. Our challenge is to believe that He knows what's best for us, and hang on to that belief, even when we don't see the whole picture."

Rachel was suddenly bitter. "So I'm being tested? That's great. He's obsessed with testing us, this God. And we never pass. It's rigged."

"Abraham passed," Joel said soothingly. "He had the hardest test of all, and he passed. That's why we can even sit here and have this discussion, thousands of years later." Polly put up her arms to Naomi. Naomi pulled her out of the high chair and settled the little girl on her lap. "One supreme act of faith, long ago. And surely the entire meaning of our history is that we were chosen because Abraham passed his test."

"*I'm* not so sure," Naomi said, her cheek to Polly's cool cheek. But nobody seemed to hear her.

"But this is just my point," said Rachel. "Here you have a God who, even though He's not going to let Abraham actually kill his child, is still more than willing to put them through unspeakable trauma. I mean, how's poor Isaac supposed to live a normal life after he's watched his father tie him up and raise a knife to slaughter him?"

"Let's get him on *Oprah* and ask him." David laughed.

"No, David. I mean it." Rachel shook her head. The tight curls bounced for an echoing minute. "What kind of God would put His most faithful servants through that just to prove what was already obvious. Just to reassure Himself?"

Joel sipped his wine. "Have you considered that God always knew Abraham would pass, and that the purpose of the test was for Abraham himself to see the extent of his own devotion?"

"That's an even more convincing argument for not having put him through it," Rachel said.

"And what about poor Sarah?" Naomi broke in. "Don't you think it was pretty presumptuous of Abraham to take Isaac off without even warning Sarah? Giving her a chance to prepare herself for the loss of her son? Or say good-bye?"

"Yes," Judith said. "I certainly do."

"But Judith"—Joel looked at her—"I think what you fail to see is that the story of Abraham is really a story of consolation. I think God means us to take comfort from this."

"Comfort." Judith shook her head.

"Yes. Comfort. This is the story that enables us to confront the worst things. The loss of a child, for example. When Jews were attacked in pogroms during the Middle Ages, they took their children's lives themselves to prevent their suffering at the hands of the attackers, and they invoked Abraham as they did so. They felt that if they could submit to God's will with Abraham's faith, then their tragedy was redeemed."

Judith looked at him, and neither spoke. Then, abruptly, she stood. She took her plate and his and went into the kitchen.

"Well, you know," Naomi said, with forced cheer, "maybe there's a certain twisted logic to that, but the fact remains that I don't particularly want to be involved with a God who would ask it of me. Frankly, I think we're in trouble when we have a God who's asking us to kill, for whatever reason."

Joel smiled at her. "Naomi, the notion of a father willing to sacrifice a son for the good of mankind is at the center of more than one religion, you know."

"Then what a terrible thing to base a religion on," Naomi said passionately. "Honestly, sometimes I'm embarrassed by the whole thing." She looked quickly at David. "I'm sorry. I shouldn't have said that."

Again that benevolent smile. "But it's all right. Talmud says that when the debate is in the service of heaven, both sides are sustained."

"But I don't even accept *that*," Naomi said. "I mean, how can this even be worthy of *debate*? The murder of a child can *never* be justified. Some positions are just indefensible."

Judith, returning to gather more plates, looked at her and shook her head. "But how can you say that, Naomi? Aren't you the one who said conditions always matter? You said that under oath, as I recall."

Rachel, too, turned to Naomi. "That's right. Aren't you defending a woman who's accused of murdering her child?"

"Yes," Naomi said. "But Heather is innocent. She's innocent of killing her own child, because that child was born dead. And she's utterly innocent of killing the baby in the river, because she has no connection to that baby at all."

"So then," Judith said, "you wouldn't defend the person who actually did kill that child in the river?"

"No. I don't think so." Naomi shifted Polly on her lap.

"No matter what the circumstances were?"

"What circumstances *could* there have been?" Naomi said caustically. "This was a newborn baby. I mean, Catholics might believe babies are born with some kind of sin already attached to them, but even they don't murder their infants for it."

Judith came back to the table and sat down.

"What?" Naomi looked at her.

Judith quickly shook her head. "I was just thinking. We don't know about that baby. And what we don't know might change our minds."

"No. However you look at it, it was wrong to stab that child. It can't be made all right."

"It was morphine," Judith said vaguely.

"No difference. And no difference between that and Abraham stabbing his kid with a knife. It's still murder, or attempted murder."

"But, Naomi"—Joel leaned forward—"Abraham *did* do the right thing. We know that, because we were chosen by God as a result of his choice."

Naomi thought for a moment. Even before she spoke, she
knew she was wrong to do this, but she couldn't stop herself.

"Chosen for what?" She looked squarely at Joel, even as his
look darkened in return. "See, I've always wondered about
this. Maybe Abraham didn't pass at all. Maybe he failed.
Maybe God wanted to see that Abraham's humanity *was*
greater than his faith. And God was enraged, because here
He'd made man in His own image, so it was a comment on
God, too. And was this barbarism really going to come out on
top of the love between father and son? Maybe Abraham was
supposed to get down on his knees and say, 'God, I love you,
but I can't do this. I'd rather kill myself if you'll only spare
my child.' But when that didn't happen, when Abraham just
went ahead without even hesitating and bound up his son and
raised his knife, maybe God said, 'Fine. If that's Abraham's
choice, then I'm going to single out his descendants for an
eternity of torments.' And so He did."

She looked at them in turn. No one seemed inclined to interrupt her, and she could not seem to interrupt herself.

"And so He started to punish us. He enslaved us for a couple
of centuries in Egypt. He gave us the Babylonian exile, and
the Diaspora. He gave us the Crusades and the Inquisition,
and the rap for Blood Libel, and pogroms. And then, just in
case there was any doubt left in our minds, He gave us the
Holocaust. You see, He wanted to make sure we understood
Him. He wanted us to look at each other when they turned on
the gas and think, *I guess we made a mistake. I guess we aren't
God's chosen people, after all.* But we're so stubborn. We
insist on not seeing the obvious. We're like little puppies who
keep cuddling up to the guy that's kicking us away. We just
don't get it, even when we look around now and the tormen-
tors are still out there, drinking rum on the verandah in Para-
guay, totally guilt-free. God doesn't care to punish them for
what they did to His so-called chosen people, because this *is*
what He chose us for. And all because Abraham was so willing
to kill."

In the silence, she could hear nothing now. Only, far down
the hill, the river's rumble. It began to be disturbing, this silence. "Well?" Naomi finally said.

"That," said David quietly, "is about the most cynical thing
I've ever heard."

Joel stood. His face, Naomi suddenly saw, was rigid white. Very deliberately he folded his napkin, placed it on the table, and left the room. She heard the kitchen door slam shut. She looked at Judith, but her eyes were fixed on some obscure point of the tablecloth. Belatedly, Naomi understood that she had done something unforgivable.

"Judith," Naomi said.

Judith shot to her feet. "No. I'll get the dessert." She walked into the kitchen.

This left Naomi and Rachel and David still at the table with the children. Only Polly seemed unaffected. She sat on Naomi's lap, calmly sipping her juice, as Hannah quietly excused herself and the adults remained in creaky silence. The truth was, Naomi couldn't seem to find the moment her talk had veered to this place, passing through whatever door had evidently closed behind her. Hadn't it all been, as David had said, debate for the sake of heaven? Wasn't it fair to try to prove or disprove God's existence by rational means? Isn't that what they had been doing? But on the other hand, there could be no debate if heaven was not theoretical to begin with. Someone had cheated, by actually believing. And yet it wasn't David who had glared at her with such fury and left the table. Naomi, unable to sit still any longer, lifted Polly to her hip and went into the kitchen. Judith was ladling fruit salad into little bowls. She didn't look up.

"Judith, I'm sorry," she said.

She looked tired. She gave Naomi a smile that was also tired.

"No, it's all right."

"I feel terrible. I had no idea I would offend Joel so much."

Judith shook her head. "No, you couldn't have known. Here, will you cut some of this onto the plates?" She passed Naomi the cake.

"I thought we were only talking," she went on, putting Polly down on the kitchen floor. "I didn't realize he believed so strongly. I mean, I knew he was thinking about these things, but I didn't know he'd actually reached the point where he believed."

Judith sighed. She looked at Naomi and then, quite unexpectedly, leaned forward and kissed her on the cheek. "But he doesn't. He wants to. He wants to very badly. But he doesn't

yet. What David said before? About getting yourself to believe
by an act of will? That's what Joel's trying to do. He's in a
war with himself, and neither side can get the upper hand. And
I can't do anything to help, even though I want to. Because
I'm with you. There's no God at all. Or if there is, He's a
complete shit and I don't want Him in my house."

Naomi watched her, smoothly contained, deftly scooping the
oranges and pomegranate seeds. "Joel will never speak to me
again," she said fearfully. "He won't, will he?"

"Oh, he will." Judith smiled. "He has a great capacity for
forgiveness."

She breathed in relief. "So I'll be forgiven?"

"Oh no, Naomi." Judith suddenly laughed. She picked up
two bowls of fruit and walked to the French doors. "Not you.
Himself. He'll forgive himself and you'll be friends again. You
wait and see."

Chapter 42

Daniel in the Lions' Den

THEY WENT ON, BUT IN STRAINED, SOMETIMES forced joviality. Joel did not reappear, though at some point he returned to the house and went up the back stairs. The sound of this was covered by David's suggestion that now was a good time to find the afikomen and Hannah's subsequent scurry around the living room. The linen-wrapped matzo, protruding between two Laura Nyro albums, was exchanged for David's crisp five-dollar bill. As soon as she could, Naomi claimed fatigue on Polly's part and took her home.

It was fully night now, and the rain had never quite materialized, which only meant that there was a superfluous fullness to the dark. In her headlights along Goddard Falls Road, an orange chipmunk with a racing stripe suddenly skittered across her path, its tail held straight up like a bumper car attached to nothing, then disappeared into the black field. Polly, who truly was tired now, dropped to sleep in the backseat, and Naomi envied her her oblivion. Oblivion, for herself, would not be easily achieved tonight. She pulled off the road at the top of her drive and got out; then, murmuring, she scooped the little girl against her shoulder, hitched up the diaper bag, and pulled out her flashlight. Then she shut the car door with her hip and started down.

Her circle of light bounced past trees, the deciduous ones bare even of buds, the pines boasting a powder puff of apple green at the fingertip of each dark, needled finger. The soggy mud sucked as she went down, sending the odd stone clattering before her, and she felt the motion of Polly's jaw, its mime of sucking, against her own cheek. She kept her eyes on the drive only a few feet before her and concentrated on where she was putting her feet. This was how she managed not to see the car, until she was nearly on top of it.

"Hey," a voice said, at nearly the same instant. The collation of unfamiliar car and familiar voice was paralyzing. Naomi stopped in her tracks. She threw up the beam of light in his face—her first instinct, she would later observe, to be as cruel as possible.

"Hey, get it out of my eyes, will you?"

But she wouldn't. She liked him like this: caught in the headlights, at her mercy. Daniel in the lions' den. This made her the lion, she supposed.

"What are you doing here?" said Naomi.

"You changed the locks. I couldn't get inside."

"I changed the locks?" She was incredulous. "Like, over a year ago. Why shouldn't I change the locks?"

"No reason," said Daniel mildly. "But you asked what I was doing here. I am here, on the porch, as you see, because you changed the locks. Otherwise I would have waited for you inside." He peered at her. "How come you walked down?"

"I don't trust the drive, Daniel. I never did in mud season, as you know." She stepped past him and got out her key. "I suppose you're coming in."

"Yes, I suppose. I've come a long way."

Naomi opened the door. She turned on the light and stepped in, wiping her muddy boots on the mat in the vain hope that he'd do the same.

"Is that mine?" said Daniel. She looked at him and he nodded toward Polly, who slept on.

For such a consequential question he looked remarkably unperturbed. Daniel's long face was pale but rather dull; his hands were casually stuck in the slack pockets of his blue parka.

"That," said Naomi stiffly, "was already six months old when you left town. It's Heather Pratt's daughter Polly. I've been taking care of her."

He nodded, off the hook and otherwise indifferent. "Fine, fine."

But this, too, enraged her. "If you'll excuse me, I need to put her to bed." She walked past him into Polly's room and, under a dim light, deftly changed her diaper and zipped her into her pajamas, all without waking her. Then she lifted Polly into her crib and covered her up with her great-grandmother's quilt.

Coming out of the room, she saw him there, his hands on his skinny hips, still in his parka. The sight of him in what was once this most familiar of places brought home to her quickly how much the house had been changed in his absence—the great room divided into a warren, the white porcelain gleam of the toilet through an open door. There were Polly's things now, too—abandoned stuffed animals and cairns of building blocks here and there. Also, down the brand-new stairs, the annex with its computer and television. He frowned at this.

"I see you put in a bathroom," Daniel observed, pursing his mouth. The black hair of his mustache, she suddenly noticed, was faintly gray.

"Yes. And an annex for my work. Business," she said gratuitously, "is going well."

"Business was always important to you, Naomi," her ex-husband commented. She half expected him to break into a wail, à la Jacob Marley: *Mankind was my business!* Instead, he went to the couch and sat, shrugging off his parka. "I'm glad to be inside."

Naomi stood looking at him. He wore a dirty flannel shirt beneath a dirty sweater—once discernibly blue, now dingy brown—and jeans. His unwiped boots were planted heavily on the light floorboards, shedding bits of mud around them. Had she passed him on a busy street she might have thought that he bore a slight resemblance to Daniel, something vague in the carriage, perhaps, but then it was a common enough look: gangly and hirsute, white-skinned, with a fading hairline and large knuckles. She had lived with him for thirteen years, and now she had no desire even to touch him.

"Want a beer?" Naomi said, more for something to say.

"No. I'll have tea, though. Do you have Lemon Zinger?"

Right where you left it, she thought. She went to put the kettle on.

"I've been here for a couple of hours," he called from the next room. "I knew you'd be back. I saw your purse through the window."

The thought of him looking through her window gave her a chill. "I was at a Passover Seder."

"A *what*? Here?"

"Yeah. A few more of the chosen moved into town after you left."

"Shit," he said. "I got out just in time."

Unexpectedly, Naomi found herself smiling at this. The kettle gave its banshee groan. She brought him his tea.

"Thank you," Daniel said, and as he took the mug she felt again that stab of the accustomed and had to shake herself to reinsert the missing year between Daniel's departure and Daniel's presence on her couch. "So, you look all right," he said, blowing on the liquid.

"If that's a compliment, thank you," said Naomi. She did not return it.

"You got the baby you wanted," he observed.

"She isn't mine. I told you."

"You got a boyfriend."

She looked where he was looking. To her surprise, she saw, crumpled at one end of the couch, Nelson Erroll's undershirt. Unnoticed by Nelson, evidently, and by herself, but not by Daniel. He had always seen the trees rather than the forest.

"No. Not really."

Daniel smirked and sipped. "And business is good."

"Yes. It really runs itself, at this point."

"Like any good collective," he said, a mite sarcastic.

"Yes." She was waiting. She wondered when he might get to the point. "You're still in Woodstock? I heard you went to live on Andy Greenbaum's place."

"Yeah." Daniel nodded. "But I was in the city last summer. I hooked up with somebody, and we moved back up to Woodstock together."

She was reluctant to tell him she knew this already, but she tried not to appear too curious, either. It was important to Naomi that he not think she cared, especially since she didn't.

"Her name's Katrina Frosch."

Naomi crossed her legs. "Didn't she used to live with a guy who used to be a Weatherman?"

"You heard that?" Daniel said with pathetic eagerness.

"Oh, somewhere. So what are you living on, anyway?"

Daniel looked at her steadily. He knew precisely what she was asking, and she knew precisely how he would answer. "The land, Naomi. We are living on the land."

"Well." She shrugged. "All right. So Katrina has a trust fund, I guess."

Anger swept over his face. "It's all you think about, isn't it? How things get paid for. We have a community in Woodstock. We help each other. Everybody gets along fine."

"Good," Naomi said. "You know, we really don't have to fight about this, Daniel. I mean, if we ever did need to, we certainly don't need to now."

He considered this, and backed off. "I'm glad you think so. I really am." He seemed to ponder his tea. "I want to sell the house, Naomi. Unless you're willing to buy me out, that is."

For a long minute she wasn't sure she had heard him properly. The words "sell" and "buy" seemed so unnatural in his voice that she wasn't entirely clear on what he meant by them. "Which house?" she finally said.

"This one. The one I built." He watched her calmly. "It's only fair, Naomi. I know you see that."

She gaped at him. "Wait a minute. Are we discussing property? As in private property?"

"I built it, Naomi. It's half mine. At *least* half," he said uncharitably.

"You might have said something earlier. I don't know if I would have made so many improvements to a house I considered half yours. I might have started over in a house that already *had* a bathroom."

He looked blankly at her. "It's fair, Naomi."

"What do you need the money for?" she demanded. "What could you possibly need to buy? I thought you all took care of each other down there in Woodstock."

"I'm going to be a father," Daniel said. "The baby is due this summer."

This, as he knew it would be, was stunning. Naomi sat, dimly wondering which of those responses offering themselves she ought to pick: disbelief, denial, bereavement, rage. Or self-loathing, because of the times he had said he did not want children, and how the meaning of that—that he did not want children with *her*—was now so palpably clear. Katrina Frosch was having the baby Daniel would not let her have. The baby scraped out of her years before, in Ithaca, while he waited out in the reception room, flipping through magazines. The baby they had fought over all their last summer and fall, until he stopped sleeping with her altogether, because, as he said, he didn't trust her. She had followed him here, she had lived in his miserable house without a bathroom down a muddy slope in the woods, and relinquished her friends and everything she

might have accomplished by now, and he didn't trust her not
to stick an embroidery needle through her diaphragm and get
herself pregnant with her husband's child. The baby Polly
could never be, because she was Heather's. And now, amid
the general loathing she felt for Daniel, there was an ice-clear
stab of loathing for Heather, too.

"Well," she finally said, "I see." All her energy was directed
toward not weeping. Not in front of him. "How unexpected."

"Not really," Daniel said proudly. "Katya and I made the
decision together. We wanted a child."

This was so wantonly cruel that she could only glare at him.

"You know what I mean, Daniel. What happened to your
stand on overpopulation? What happened to that line about
how it was narcissistic to replicate your DNA when there are
too many hungry and homeless children? You said having children was a bourgeois gesture in this country, like having a big
car, and you wouldn't do it. What happened to that?"

He shrugged. If he had insight into this, he was not moved
to share it.

"So you need money." She sounded, to her own ears, increasingly strident. "You yourself don't care about money, but
your child should have some."

"I don't have to justify this to you, Naomi. It's my life. My
life is no longer caught up in your life."

Another wound. *A blow upon the bruise.*

"Listen, there's no reason why we shouldn't do this in a
dignified and equitable manner."

"*Equitable*, Daniel?"

"There's no reason we should have to involve lawyers."

"What?"

"Though I've spoken to one of our neighbors in Woodstock,
who is an attorney. And he feels it would be best to have the
house appraised and take it from there. Certainly I have no
objection to your buying me out if we can reach a price we
both feel is fair."

She shook her head. "God, you're a bastard, Daniel."

"Of course you feel that way. It's normal," he reassured her
blandly.

She got to her feet, not entirely steady. "Well, while this
house is still mine, I'd like you to leave it, please."

He sighed, and stood. "All right. You know, I'm sorry

you're reacting like this, though I'm not really surprised. I thought, at least, you'd bring your business acumen to bear on the situation."

"My business acumen," she observed, shaking her head. "You detested my business acumen. You said my values were defective. You said my conduct was unbefitting a socialist."

"It was," Daniel said languidly. "And it is."

"You're too busy perfecting your own life to have an impact on anybody else's. Your mom and dad knocked themselves out to change the world, and you're just sitting there with the rest of the converted, preaching into thin air."

"Are you finished?" He half smiled.

"What have you done?" Naomi shouted. *"What have you done to make the world better? What have you done except talk?"*

Daniel shrugged on his parka. "I'm staying down in Hanover with Katya. If you want to reach me tomorrow, we're at the Chieftain Motel. If I don't hear from you, I'll have my neighbor write you a letter, and we can do all this by mail. You're looking well, Naomi."

"You said that already."

"Take care."

And he left. She stood where she had been standing, uncertain of where she would go when the potential for movement returned. On the floorboards in front of the couch bits of dried earth ringed the place where his feet had been. From outside there was the unmistakable sound of a car, slogging and spinning in muck, trying to make way. Then the tires caught and pulled him up—out of the mud and the stones, and away down the road.

Chapter 43

Human Error

JUDITH WAS WHITE. NAOMI SAT STILL IN HER
seat, mildly watching the mime of argument, the stray gestures
and overworking of jaws. They looked almost comical against
each other, Judith with her blanched skin and bobbing black
curls, and Charter red in the face with his colorless comb-over.
It amazed her how little she had come to care about all this,
even about Heather, who slumped a few feet before her, numb
with Valium and grief. This, she was beginning to understand,
would not end soon. They would always be here, the same
players in the same seats, watching the same mute drama. Only
outside, on the steps of the courthouse, would the participants
change. Today there were more—more Dartmouth students,
men included, more Boston matrons fired by the *Globe* editorial into a froth of righteous anger, and for the first time a
tentative cell of her own neighbors, each carrying a flimsy
placard that read GODDARD SUPPORTS HEATHER. This ought to
be remarkable, but Naomi was no longer in a mood to find
anything remarkable.

Nor was she surprised, any longer, to be still here in the
courtroom—though after Nelson's confession she had in-
dulged in a spasm of relief: surely it would end now. Surely
Warren, the attorney general and nobody's fool, would stop
the trial in its tracks and publicly haul Robert Charter down
to Concord and across the coals of his office portal before
summoning what dignity he could to drop all charges against
Heather. Judith did not concur, and of course she had turned
out to be right. No public announcement followed Nelson's
visit to Naomi, but Judith believed that Warren was watching
closely now, whether Charter knew it or not. He would not
compromise himself by drawing attention to Charter's exces-
ses, but he was watching closely.

In her lap, she held Ella's latest proclamation, a sheet of
lavender bearing what was by now the conventional wisdom

surrounding Heather's tragedy. Naomi, with nothing to do but watch Judith fight with Charter in the sidebar, read it again, straining for enlightenment:

WHO KILLED THE GODDARD BABIES?

1 man: Ashley Deacon, who refused to accept responsibility for his children.

2 men: Nelson Erroll and Robert Charter, who used intimidation to force a false confession.

A Town Full of Men: who condemned a woman for her sexuality.

A Society of Men: for whom a woman is always suspect.

Naomi sighed and crumpled the page. She knew why Judith was angry. She knew that David Keller was sitting outside in the courtroom hallway, waiting to testify, reading a copy of *The New York Times* and getting impatient, and that Charter, who had said his interrupted psychiatrist would be the final prosecution witness this morning, now wanted to put somebody else on the stand.

Hayes, evidently refreshed from his long weekend break, seemed to possess the patience neither of the two attorneys could summon. He sat placidly, his chin planted on his two fists, listening and nodding.

When he made his decision and sent them back to their seats, Judith turned with a bitter face. Naomi sighed. Evidently they were now going to hear from Charter's unanticipated witness, after all.

The door behind them opened, and a man named Bob Rena was called. Naomi did not know a Bob Rena and turned with mild curiosity. This was more curiosity than Heather herself seemed to muster. She continued to sit stodgily in her place, her white arms outstretched on the tabletop to maintain her balance, and barely shifted her gaze to look. Judith, as if in compensation for all the indifference, stared intently at this unanticipated personage, as if hoping to glean from his appearance some clue to who he was, or why he was here.

Bob Rena, for what it was worth, turned out to be a husky kid of twenty or so, with thick brown hair and a rather pleased expression. That he was a Dartmouth student was evident from his sweatshirt in green and white, which plainly announced Dartmouth Rugby, and the rest of his outfit (old corduroys and new Dock-Siders) did nothing to counter the impression. He walked deliberately up the aisle with a comfortable grin on his face, holding a small white paperback book in his hand as if it were a Bible. When he passed Heather he did not so much as look at her, so intent was he on getting to the witness seat and saying whatever it was that he had come to say.

He took the oath and sat down. Judith glared at him, her pen poised over her legal pad, waiting to learn who he was and why he was important enough to send the prosecution case into overtime.

"Mr. Rena," Charter said, "can you tell me why you contacted me last Friday afternoon?"

"Sure." The kid had a deep voice. "I saw something about this case in *The Manchester Union Leader*. I don't usually read the paper, but it was lying around the house and I saw her picture."

"Who do you mean by 'her'?" said Charter eagerly.

"Hers." Rena nodded in Heather's direction. "That girl. Heather. And I remembered her."

"You remembered meeting Heather Pratt?"

"Sure. It was a while ago, but I remembered. And I checked to make sure." He held up the white book. *Dartmouth Class of 1987*, it read in bright green letters. "Then I was sure, when I saw her picture."

"When did you meet Heather?" Charter moved to the front of his table.

"At Dartmouth. It was my sophomore fall. So two and a half years ago."

"That would be the fall of 1983, during Heather's first week at college. Before she dropped out."

Judith objected to the term, but was swiftly overruled.

"Did you meet Heather in one of your classes?" Charter said. "Or perhaps in the dining hall?"

Rena grinned. "I met her in my fraternity. Alpha Delta. In the basement."

"I see. You met Heather Pratt in your fraternity basement." Naomi sighed. Had it really come to this?

Bob Rena was now describing how Heather had looked at him, and what she had said, and how many plastic cups of beer he had filled for her from the keg before she'd gone upstairs with him. From the back of the courtroom, loud whispering signaled the disapproval of Heather's supporters.

"Did she seem hesitant about having sex on the first date?" Charter stressed the word "date," since it wasn't even that.

"Not at all. She was eager to have sex," Rena commented, pleased with himself.

"Did Heather say that she expected this encounter to lead to some kind of relationship?"

"Not at all. She got up and went home, all on her own. I got the impression she'd got exactly what she wanted from me, and that was it."

Heather the sexual predator, Naomi thought grimly. This was new.

"You're saying she was sophisticated sexually?"

"She was a natural," Bob Rena said. "Definitely."

Charter seemed to give this rather more consideration than it deserved. "Mr. Rena, do you happen to know a Christopher Flynn?"

He had obviously been asked this before, because he did not hesitate now.

"I don't know exactly, but I have known a few guys named Flynn, yeah."

"A few guys named Flynn," Charter intoned. "Could any of them have been at Dartmouth during the same time Heather was there?"

"Sure." He nodded. "I couldn't say for sure, but it's possible."

"Thank you, Mr. Rena. I appreciate your coming forward."

As if he had done something noble. This seemed to be Rena's interpretation, too, for he nodded with great solemnity. Then Judith got up.

"Mr. Rena, am I right in thinking that the only reason you are here is to inform this court that you had sex, on one occasion two and a half years ago, with the defendant in this case?"

"Well, if you put it *that* way." He grinned.

"Do you, in fact, have any information on anything that is actually at issue in this trial?"

He shrugged, nonplussed. "I thought I ought to come forward. *He* thought it was important." Rena nodded at Charter.

"Do you even know what this trial is about, Mr. Rena?"

He looked up at the ceiling. "Didn't she kill a kid or something?"

"Your honor!" Judith shouted, appalled.

Mr. Rena was given a brief instruction on the appropriate parameters of testimony. The jury was instructed to disregard what he had just said.

"No," Rena said next time around. "I'm not really clear on the details."

"You've testified that during her single sexual encounter with you, Heather was a 'natural.' Can you tell us what you mean by that?"

He nodded eagerly. "Sure. I mean she knew how to move like she'd been doing it for a long time. And she told me I was the first."

There was a sputter of shocked laughter from the back. Naomi looked at Charter, who evidently had not heard this part of Mr. Rena's braggadocio. Now the self-satisfied expression was waning on his face, and it was Judith who was smiling.

"So she was a virgin when you met."

"I was her first, yeah," he confirmed.

"And you slept with her once?"

"Yup."

"And this was September of 1983?"

"Yeah. Like I said."

"I see . . ." Judith nodded, letting the jury do the math. One lover, one time, before Ashley. So much for Heather's fabled promiscuity.

"Mr. Rena, you testified that you were not certain that you remembered Heather until you checked your book."

"Yeah. I thought so, because she looked familiar. But I was sure after I looked in the p—" He looked suddenly abashed. "In the face book," he amended, but not fast enough.

"I'm sorry. Were you about to call it something else?" Judith said, and Naomi was right there with her. There really was so very little new under the sun, she thought bleakly. The frat boys at Cornell had been just the same, circling the pretty girls in the directory and planning their strategies.

"It's just a name. It's not the real name."

"Well, I'm curious," Judith said. "Enlighten me, please."

"Some of the guys call it the pig book. It's not meant to be serious."

"Maybe not to you," she said archly. "May I see your pig book, please?"

He didn't want to hand it over, but he'd brought it with him nonetheless. It was duly passed to Judith, who flipped the pages, frowning.

"Now this is interesting," she said, walking over to the jury. "Here is Heather Pratt's name and photograph, right here. There's some other information, her home address and her dormitory address in North Massachusetts Hall. But her photograph has some notations in pencil, I see. It's been circled, and there is a check next to the picture." She looked innocently at Rena. "What does that mean, Mr. Rena?"

"I'm not the only guy who uses that book," he said, suddenly reticent.

"But you know what it means, don't you?"

"Well, sometimes it can mean somebody in the frat wants to meet the girl in the picture."

"Meet?" Judith said harshly. "Or screw?"

There were the expected objections. Even amid this mess, a bizarre pretense of decorum. But Judith was enjoying herself now.

"What does the check mark mean, Mr. Rena?"

He shrugged. He actually looked at his watch. He was told to answer the question, and so he did.

"So can we infer that you have had sex with every girl in this so-called pig book whose photo has been checked off?"

"I'm not the only one who uses that book," he complained. "Hey, I came here to do my civic duty!"

"*Really,*" Judith said dryly. "I would have thought you came here to boast of your many conquests. So why don't we do that?" She sat back against her table and started to read. "Laura Karris? She has three checks. What does that mean? Did you do her three times, or was she three times as good as somebody with one check?" She flipped pages. "Wow, you were busy in the G's, weren't you?"

"Your honor," Charter complained, "I really think Ms. Friedman has made her point by now."

Judith was reading and didn't look up.

"Mrs. Friedman," Hayes said, "do you think we can maybe move on?"

She still didn't look up. She was staring hard at the book in her hands, a look of rank disbelief on her face. Then, slowly, she began to shake her head.

"Mrs. Friedman?"

Judith roused herself. "What?"

"Can we move on, please?"

"Oh," said Judith. "Certainly." Briefly she leaned over and wrote something down on her legal pad. Then she closed the white book and walked across to the witness seat. "Here you are, Mr. Rena. Here is your pig book. And thank you for coming to do your civic duty today. I must say, you've added immeasurably to our understanding of the defendant. I know Mr. Charter thanks you, too."

Then, waltzing back to her seat, she pushed the folded page of her legal pad deep into her pocket and gave Naomi a rather baffling wink. Mr. Rena slunk out, to the guffaws of Ella and her gleeful band. Charter, glum in his seat, closed his eyes and breathed deeply. Then he rested the prosecution case, and Judith leaped to her feet, infused with momentum from her running start.

David came in then, looking professorial in a clean gray suit. His yarmulke, Naomi saw as he passed, had been removed for the occasion. He nodded shortly to Naomi, but he was studiously indifferent to Judith as he made his way to the front of the room. He had been advised, she decided, not to seem too familiar with the woman who would question him.

David had many degrees and was the author of many books. These, complete with their long, technical titles, were recounted in loving detail, until the room seemed to reverberate with the heady language of science. He was past chairman of the Department of Biology at N.Y.U. and held teaching positions at a variety of New York medical schools. He was also a consultant to two major fertility clinics and had already written extensively on genetic issues arising from the new in-vitro technology as it was beginning to be practiced. In all, he made a marked contrast to the Peytonville obstetrician-gynecologist who had told the jury all they knew thus far about superfecundation.

"Dr. Keller," Judith said, once his credentials had been, finally, exhausted, "can you tell us something about superfecundation?"

Now, abruptly, David grinned. "Superfecundation is the theoretical birth of twin children by different fathers. It's something of a medical fantasy. The idea has been around a long time, but frankly, even if it has ever occurred, its rate of occurrence must be so extraordinarily tiny that it simply has no statistical value." He looked at the jury and then translated from his own English. "To build a case for superfecundation would be overwhelmingly difficult. Frankly, it makes much more sense to look for another explanation when you have one mother and two seemingly different babies. You have to bear in mind that human beings carry the record of many generations of forebears in their DNA. Even full siblings, which fraternal twins naturally are, can possess widely disparate DNA. They might look utterly different from each other. One might possess genetic abnormalities and diseases while the other is normal. But I can assure you that there are many explanations I could consider before I was desperate enough to consider superfecundation."

Charter, predictably, objected to this. Judith did not even argue with him.

"But what about blood type, Dr. Keller? What if a baby's blood type indicated that, if it shared a mother with its supposed sibling, then there would have to have been a different father involved?"

"Again," David said, "I would look for an entirely different set of parents. It's bordering on the preposterous to claim superfecundation."

Judith looked at the jurors. "Dr. Keller, what was your reaction when you were informed that superfecundation was being suggested in a case of alleged double infanticide?"

He gave a short, involuntary bark of laughter. Then, recovering, he shook his head. "That somebody was off their rocker, to tell you the truth. This would be somewhat on a par with saying that Bigfoot came down out of the woods and clubbed your neighbor to death in his front yard, when it would be far less difficult to prove that the murderer was just a normal human being. To a biologist, it's simply that absurd."

Judith thanked him, and gave him to Charter.

"Dr. Keller. You're aware, are you not, that superfecundation is a recognized biological event."

David sighed, "I'm aware of no such thing. I can't recall the topic ever coming up in conversation with any other biologist I've ever known. Certainly there have been no major research papers or studies that I'm aware of. And I can assure you that obstetricians do not go around warning their patients not to engage in sex with more than one man for fear of giving birth to superfecundated twins."

"But it does exist in the medical literature, rare though it may be."

"I know of no instances with what I would consider proper documentation, no." David paused and seemed to consider. "That will change soon, however."

Naomi frowned at him. Charter, eager for any scrap, seemed to rouse himself a bit. "Oh yes? And why is that?"

"Well, because of in-vitro fertilization. With in-vitro fertilization, there will be far greater potential for superfecundation. Because of human error. But for twins conceived naturally, I think we may all quite comfortably consider it next to impossible and leave it at that."

Charter, in defeat, took this suggestion, and testimony ended for the morning.

Chapter 44

Confessions

SHE ATE HER LUNCH OUTSIDE, ALONE ON THE bench: a tuna-fish sandwich and a can of diet Coke. The tuna fish tasted like wet sawdust, glued but otherwise unmodified by white mayonnaise, and she ate it without relish. Judith had gone back to see Heather, though "see"—Naomi knew—was a euphemism for coerce. Between attorney and client there had been little communication and even less agreement, but over no other subject did the two become as intractable as that of Heather's testimony. Judith had never wavered in her insistence that Heather must take the stand. All roads led to this, she argued, and despite the lip service juries paid to the notion that a defendant would not be penalized for declining to give testimony, everyone expected that a truly innocent person could not be held back from taking the stand in her own defense. Everything Judith had worked toward, both in her cross-examination of prosecution witnesses and in the witnesses she was herself presenting, led to this: to Heather getting up there and saying, flatly and without dissembling, *The Sabbathday River baby was not mine* and *My own baby was born dead.* Heather absolutely refused. Neither would she give a reason. In all, she showed more forcefulness on this point than she had on her own behalf at any point since her arrest.

Judith had, of course, invited Naomi to attend this confrontation of wills (she continued to have an unrealistic appraisal of Naomi's influence on Heather), but Naomi had regretfully excused herself. Indeed, the confrontations of the days just past—with David and Joel, with Nelson, with Daniel—had left her little animation. Even the morning's reversals, the unexpected boon of Bob Rena and the more expected authority of David's expertise, had failed to lift her spirits. She sat now, drained and oddly bereft, gnawing her tasteless sandwich and looking out over the white tide of Heather's army.

Ella, in her element, led them on from the uppermost courthouse step, her strangely genderless form and beautifully angular head giving her a commanding height over the protesters. Sarah Copley's crowd, who had evidently not been informed of the dress code, were in their Sunday clothes, cacophonous in appearance but unified by their white placards. Naomi was mildly surprised to see many of her own employees present, including the Hodge sisters, who stood side by side, leaning slightly together—which was their way—sharing a single sign. And Mary Sully, whose sign belied the fact that she had never believed Heather to be anything but a murderer of babies. The mood had indeed turned, though the faces of the Goddard contingent were more grim than outraged, and Naomi wondered if what they actually felt was less love of Heather than that Heather was theirs, whatever she was. That she belonged finally to them and not to the wider world of *The Boston Globe* and *Ms.* magazine and the invisible senders of—by now— hundreds and hundreds of white roses.

The roses were no longer welcome in the jail block, so someone had taken it upon herself to pile them on the courthouse steps, and there they now sat—great piles of flowers, each wrapped in its own cone of green paper; each sporting a surrounding shawl of glassy green fern. They came from New Hampshire and Vermont, New York and California, and beyond, tumbling as from a cornucopia. The local flower shops had all long since been defoliated of roses, and *The Manchester Union Leader* reported in a sidebar to its trial coverage that truckloads of this suddenly sought-after bloom were en route from Boston and Hartford to Peytonville, where the two local florists anxiously awaited them.

All absurd. An outward spiraling of absurdity from a single, inexplicable event. Just half an hour earlier a cry of wild laughter had gone through the crowd when a vendor arrived and unpacked his wares: white sweatshirts boldly imprinted with the legend: I AM CHRIS FLYNN. The men, seemingly in unison, reached into their pockets, and suddenly there was an army of Chris Flynns, the phantom second lover, the state's laughingstock linchpin, the sadly absent proof of Heather's infamy. Naomi shook her head. She could not even any longer wish it to end, because she could not imagine what direction her life would take if it did. She drained her can of soda and sighed.

At her ear, a low voice spoke. "Oh, come on. It isn't *that* bad."

Naomi looked up. David was standing behind her.

"Thought you took off."

"I'm leaving now. I wanted to say good-bye." He stood hovering over her. She wondered, for an awkward moment, whether she ought to stand, too.

"Well, I enjoyed meeting you," Naomi said, shifting a bit in lieu of getting up. "And thank you for what you did for Heather."

"No, that was nothing. Poor kid. Whatever she did, it doesn't include having twin kids by different fathers." He looked off at the crowd in front of the courthouse. " 'Course, once those folks get their teeth in her, it'll be another story. I just hope she doesn't read too much of her own press."

"What do you mean?" Naomi said.

"You can't just elect a symbol and expect them to serve. I don't think the girl I saw in that courtroom wants what her fans want to give her."

"No, you're right," she agreed. "But that's a problem for tomorrow."

"Your problem," he said, with an understanding nod.

"Yes."

He smiled at her, and she—guilty again about having ruined the Seder—smiled awkwardly back. "Listen, Naomi," David said, "try not to think too badly of Joel for being a bit of a jerk. He takes these things very much to heart."

She wasn't sure what to say. "That's all right."

"He doesn't deal well with Rachel. With having Rachel around."

Now she was surprised. "But Rachel is lovely!"

"Oh yes, absolutely. He loves her very much. But he finds her sadness intolerable. And Judith's, of course. And he can't fix it. Well," David said, "that sounds absurd, but you understand."

Naomi nodded, though of course she didn't. "This is about Rachel's son."

"Yes. Simon. It's a very cruel thing, what he has. Because the baby looks completely normal at birth, and it does all the normal things for the first couple of months. It smiles on cue, and it grabs your finger. But then it stops smiling and it stops grabbing your finger. That's all gone. And there's your child. It's just an infant in a body that keeps growing for another couple of years before it dies. And you have to watch it die." He was looking past her, past the crowd and the courthouse steps, past the visible.

"Does it have a name, this disease?" she asked, and then remembered something Judith had once said, offhand: *You've never heard of it.*

"Sure. It's called Canavan's. It's part of a group of related diseases, all rare. All genetic, of course. This one's more or less confined to the Ashkenazi gene pool. Lucky us." He smiled ruefully. "Another gift of a loving God."

Your words, not mine, Naomi thought.

"Is it a brain disease?"

"Well, it affects the brain, but it's really a disease of the nervous system. These kids are lacking an enzyme which breaks down the fatty substances in the brain, and because the substances aren't broken down, they clog the neurons. It's like . . . you know how weeds can grow in a pond and choke it? You get stagnant water, then muck. It's like that. This stuff chokes the brain to death. When they autopsy Canavan's victims, the brains are like Swiss cheese."

Naomi, stung with pity for Rachel, shook her head slowly. "And there isn't a cure?"

"A *cure*?" He gave her one of those looks scientists save for laypeople. "There isn't even a treatment. There's barely a soul working on it, either, since it's so ridiculously rare. One day, when we get better at taking DNA apart, we might get lucky and find the gene, but the best we'll be able to do even then is test people to find carriers and try to dissuade them from having kids, since they've got a one in four chance of passing it on. Even that's not much in the way of progress." He sighed. "You know, it's eating at all of them. But in a way, it's actually hardest on Joel, because Joel has the least to do. Rachel needs to take care of Simon, and Judith needs to take care of Rachel."

"Poor . . ." Naomi began. But she couldn't pick among them.

"Yes, it's terrible. So forgive him. He's a guy whose instinct is to find the reasons for things, and this is a thing that can't be explained. Not really, even if they ever figure out the science. Sometimes I think he wants there to be a God because that would give him at least part of an explanation." He smiled at her. "But that's no reason to believe in God."

"Right," she agreed sadly.

"So now I must leave you." He straightened.

She stood, too, and kissed him lightly on the cheek, feeling the abrasion of his beard, and they parted.

When Naomi returned to the courtroom, she told Judith of the many Chris Flynns paying court on the steps outside, but instead of the laugh she expected, Judith merely groaned. "It's out of control."

"It's almost over," Naomi amended.

"Maybe, but I've still got a few miles to go before I sleep." Naomi nodded comfort. "Any luck with Heather?"

"It's like screaming at a wall. When you're done, it's still a wall. She says, 'I can't, I can't.' She doesn't understand that whatever I've gained goes out the window if she doesn't testify. They go back in the jury room and the first thing they think is, Well, if she really didn't do it, she would have gotten up and said so." She sighed. "I'll try again in the morning. It's got to be last thing before summations."

"All right." Naomi nodded encouragement, but it was false. The truth was that she no longer believed Heather could summon the poise to deliver her critical lines, to say with any authority at all that she was innocent, that she was not a murderer of infants. If they were to prevail, Naomi thought, it would be due to Judith alone and not to Heather, who could do little more for herself than offer her wounds for analysis. Naomi watched Judith write at her table, her dark head down, her hand frantic and fast. A few minutes later, when they got under way again, Judith called her own shrink, an expert in the phenomenon of false confessions. This was a cheerful, portly man named Theodore Harvey, who possessed a rolling Welsh accent and a ring of blond curls at about ear level, the rest of his head shiny, pink, and bare. Though something of a hired gun for defense attorneys, the man was nonetheless widely published, and in addition to four academic volumes comprising his work in the field he had produced a popular book of nonfiction called *Admitting a Lie*. This featured, on its bright red cover, an *As Seen on Donahue* sticker beside the author's name.

Why, Judith asked her witness, would someone confess to a crime they had not committed?

It was not a question of simple confession, Harvey explained. There tended to be a gradual progression from "I didn't do it" to "I don't remember doing it" to "I don't think I did it" to "I must have done it," each step achieved through the subtle power of modern interrogation tactics, an insidious feeding of information to the suspect, who is after all distressed and fearful. The phenomenon, he said, was somewhat akin to that of false memories, another by-product of forceful suggestion on a mind experiencing extreme stress.

"So the officers conducting such an interrogation would gradually introduce new information and incorporate it into their questioning?"

"Yes. They will subtly work in facts that only the perpetrator of the crime would know, so that when the subject of the interrogation responds in the affirmative to any part of the statement, it can be inferred that he or she is admitting to this specific information. They may also flatter the subject by implying that his help is needed to 'clear up' a problem, and invite him to create a kind of hypothetical crime scenario—'If you were going to do this crime, would you do it this way or that way?' And when this scenario fits the known facts about the crime, the subject receives the approval of the interrogator. 'That's exactly right! That's just how it was done!'"

"Dr. Harvey, would it be appropriate to suggest to the subject of an interrogation that the subject would be allowed to go home once he or she has 'helped' the police by giving the right answers in an interrogation?"

"Absolutely inappropriate," he said sternly. "Illegal, in my view."

"Would it be appropriate to imply that the subject's young child will not be returned to his or her custody if the right answers are not given."

"It would be entirely outrageous," he said heatedly. "But I'm afraid such a tactic is not uncommon."

"Would it be appropriate to restrain a subject from seeing her child, whom she can hear crying in another room?"

"Reprehensible, in my opinion."

"Dr. Harvey," Judith said, frowning, "were you able to examine the notes and tape recordings made during the Heather

Pratt interrogation conducted through the night of October 12, 1985?"

"I was not. In fact, I was informed that absolutely no notes and no recordings were made during the interrogation, and I consider this highly suspicious in itself."

"Suspicious?" Judith feigned confusion. "Why? Isn't that routine, not to make notes?"

"It is not routine. It is extremely unusual for there to be no documentation arising from a long interrogation, other than the resulting so-called confession."

"I see," she said, looking meaningfully at the jurors. "Tell me something, Dr. Harvey. Are we all equally prone to giving in under this pressure and confessing to crimes we didn't commit? Or are some people more prone than others to weaken under sophisticated interrogation techniques?"

"No, of course not," he said brusquely. "Some people have a stronger will than others. Some keep clearer heads. Then there are factors which can fluctuate, like recent trauma or mental illness. These can make us particularly susceptible at a given time."

"Recent trauma? Something like, for example, having given birth to a stillborn baby a few weeks earlier?"

"Well, I call that traumatic. I doubt very much that a mother whose baby had just been born dead would be thinking clearly at all, let alone about dead babies. Heather could easily have brought her own sadness and guilt about the baby she had lost to bear on this other dead infant. This, to me, is not really much of a stretch."

"So, in other words, her guilt or distress over her own baby might have made her susceptible to the suggestion that she had harmed another baby, a baby that—in reality—she had no connection to at all?"

He nodded in agreement. "Yes, this seems a very plausible scenario to me."

Judith smiled. "Doctor, is there any way to absolutely avoid the danger of giving false testimony?"

He grinned back at her. This was his punch line. "I tell people there are four magic words that eliminate all risk, and if they remember them, they will always be all right. The four words are *I want a lawyer*. That removes the problem entirely."

"Really?" Judith sounded innocent. "But what if they refuse to stop the interrogation?"

"Then," the doctor said disdainfully, "it's well and truly out of my field of expertise. In such a situation I would defer to a constitutional lawyer."

"It's unconstitutional," Judith said.

"To continue an interrogation after the subject has asked for a lawyer? Oh yeah."

"Thanks," Judith said. She gave him to Charter, who blustered up to the stand.

"Dr. Harvey, in all those titles of your books and whatnot, I didn't catch the name of the school where you got your medical degree."

Harvey looked bored. He had evidently heard this sort of thing before.

"I am a doctor by means of my doctorate. I received my Ph.D. from the University of Chicago. In psychology."

"*Psychology*," Charter repeated, the word drenched in scorn. "And you feel that this qualifies you to analyze police interrogation techniques?"

"Well," Harvey said blandly, "whether it does or not, I have made the analysis of police interrogation techniques my life's work. And in any case, I fail to see how a medical degree would make me any more qualified."

Charter tried to look disdainful. "In the course of your life's work, then, you must have given some consideration to the fact that the use of tape recording or notetaking during a police interview can have an inhibiting effect on the dialogue between subject and interviewer."

"I have considered that," Harvey concurred, "but I feel that tape recording, in particular, will become increasingly necessary to establish a clean interrogation. Certainly the lack of *any* documentation from this interrogation is suspicious to me."

"You are accusing Officer Nelson Erroll and myself of conducting a dirty interrogation," Charter said, his voice steely.

"I think it's very possible the interrogation was not fairly conducted, yes."

"You are accusing Officer Erroll and myself of feeding Heather Pratt information and then claiming she confessed."

"I think it's very possible." Harvey held his ground. It

seemed to Naomi that he, for one, was unlikely to crack under pressure.

"You are accusing us of withholding Heather's daughter from her and implying that her daughter would be taken from her if she did not give me the answers I was looking for?"

"Yes. Possibly."

Judith was smiling, and Naomi knew what she must be thinking—that Charter had to be losing control if he was asking these questions, if he was letting the jurors hear these ideas again, and from his own lips.

"You are accusing us of denying Heather Pratt the basic constitutional right of an attorney at her request?"

"If she asked for one and you didn't stop the interrogation, then yes, I am accusing you of that."

He turned from the witness in a rage, shaking his head in an exaggerated arc. "Are you aware, Dr. Harvey, that Officer Nelson Erroll, who—unlike you—was present during Heather Pratt's interview, has already testified to the fact that the interview was properly conducted? That no leading suggestions were made? And that Miss Pratt never asked for an attorney to be called?"

"I have not attended this trial, Mr. Charter. I am not aware of what has been said by other witnesses."

"But how do you respond when I say that this testimony has in fact taken place?" Charter raged. "How do you respond when I say that a police veteran of over ten years said under oath that the interview was entirely correct?"

Harvey shrugged. "Well, how *can* I respond. I mean, what *else* would the guy say? And if the confession is not corroborated by physical evidence, then it's going to be pretty important to your case, so Officer Erroll is hardly going to jeopardize it by admitting the interrogation was improper, is he?"

Livid, Charter glared at him. "It's easy to make accusations, isn't it?"

"It's neither easy nor hard," Harvey said blandly. "I've studied many interrogations. A small—though not tiny—percentage are suspect. This confession, in my opinion, is suspect. Look"—he leaned forward in his seat, his expression oddly sympathetic—"I am not—I repeat: not—suggesting that this has been done on purpose. That whoever conducted this in-

terrogation set out to force a confession. What I'm saying is
that there are mistakes being made in interrogations that are
contaminating them. And until interrogating officers learn
more about how they are manipulating capitulations, then confessions will continue to be contaminated."

"So we're ignorant!" Charter raged.

"Ignorant of this, yes. Training is certainly called for. It's a
simple thing to change, but until it is changed, innocent people
are going to continue to be convicted by well-meaning juries."

"No further questions," Charter huffed in disgust. He
stomped to his chair. Hayes was looking at his watch.

"Mrs. Friedman? You going to redirect?"

"No, your honor."

"How many witnesses do you have left?"

"Three, your honor," Judith said.

Still counting on Heather to see sense, Naomi thought. And
of course Nelson, who was ready whenever he was wanted.
But she didn't know who the third one was.

"There isn't much time left now. I'd rather start fresh tomorrow. Maybe we'll get lucky and fit them all in. Shall we
try that?"

"That's fine," Judith agreed. Naomi looked at her own watch
and saw, with a little lift, that she might actually be about to
get an afternoon off. It was Wednesday, too, the day of Polly's
swim class at the sports center, though it had been so long
since they'd attended that she wasn't even sure the session
was still on. As they stood for the judge to leave, she reached
down for her bag and whispered to Judith.

"I'm going to scram. I can make a toddler swim class in an
hour if I rush now."

"Good," Judith said. "Just don't miss tomorrow." Her voice
dropped. "Tomorrow's going to be lots of fun."

"Oh, I wouldn't," said Naomi, but she could not be quite
so elated at the prospect of Nelson sinking his own career,
though he had made his peace with that and they all knew
what an enormous difference it would make for Heather. She
rushed outside, gave Simone the briefest nod, and went to pick
Polly up at Mrs. Horgan's. Despite having to drive by the
house for their bathing suits and towels, Naomi still managed
to get to the sports center a comfortable ten minutes before
the class. She was glad she had made the effort. Polly, absent

for several weeks, was extravagantly fussed over by the instructor, a beefy girl much given to whistle-blowing, and Naomi was surprised to see that the other mothers in the group were suddenly warm to them, that she no longer had that sense of their restraining themselves from all but the most innocuous conversation. "Isn't she a love," one woman said, eyeing the compliant Polly as she forced her own squirming son to reach and pull fistfuls of water. They put the kids on their backs, dangling rubber ducks over their faces, and got them to blow bubbles in the cool water. Polly's face lit up as the instructor took hold of her feet and kicked them on the surface. A girl named Danielle announced, "I go poo!" with evident glee, and was whisked from the pool by her horrified mother. "What a darling bathing suit!" one of the moms cooed to Naomi during "The Grand Old Duke of York."

"I didn't pick it out," Naomi said. "Her mother did."

Actually, this wasn't true, and she wondered—not for the first time—how long she would continue to rehabilitate Heather in the eyes of her neighbors.

"Well, she has wonderful taste, doesn't she?" the woman said.

"Someone told me," another woman said, "that she makes all her daughter's clothes. I thought of asking her if she'd be willing to make some for *my* daughter."

"I don't know," said Naomi, fascinated. "I could ask her. Afterward."

"Oh, of course. Afterward. I wouldn't bother her now."

They all went back to the locker room together and changed their shivering children into warm clothes. They were talking about the child who would eat only white food, the child who howled when the television was turned off, the child who woke at three o'clock every night, screaming for formula. Naomi was asked her thoughts on the use of bribery in toilet training. She found that she had experiences to share, and opinions at the ready. She did not know the names of these women, but she knew the names of their children, and their children's ages and quirks. As she pulled on her coat, the woman who admired Heather's taste asked Naomi if she would like to set up a play date for their girls the following week. "Maybe Tuesday?"

"Yes," Naomi said, oddly elated. But then she remembered: next week. Next week Polly might be home with Heather, or

Heather might be in prison. Next week was to be the beginning of their new lives, and she couldn't make plans. "Can I let you know?" she faltered, and the woman wrote down her number and said good-bye.

Naomi carried Polly out into the lobby and went to return her towel at the desk, Heather's desk, she thought. There was a young man there now, dull-looking and blond, reading a paper. She tried to imagine that she was Sue Deacon, stepping up to the counter, her talons unfurled, but the boy only smiled vaguely. "Thanks," Naomi said.

"Yuh." He went back to his paper.

Up the hallway, a door opened and Stephen Trask stepped out. Naomi looked at him and smiled. He went white, stumbled, and stopped. Then he turned sharply and went back through the doorway.

Naomi stood for a moment, dazed and undecided. Then, flooded with acrimony, she set off after him, as the door snapped shut in her face. Without knocking, she opened it and flung it back. It smacked the wall, and Stephen looked up at her in surprise. This was how they remained for some moments.

Finally, Naomi arranged her thoughts. "Is this how it's going to be from now on, Stephen? I mean, what are we, in kindergarten? You going to run and hide whenever I'm around?"

He looked steadily at his desktop, his jaw fixed and still.

"Stephen, we used to be friends."

"Till I became a turncoat, is that it?" he said angrily.

"No." Yes, Naomi thought. "No, you did what you felt you had to do. For whatever reason," she couldn't stop herself from saying.

"But you don't respect my *whatever* reason," Stephen said. "Close the door."

Surprised, Naomi did. She hitched Polly up a bit.

"Basically, you don't have any idea why I testified against Heather, do you, Naomi?"

"Well"—she frowned—"I know you were disappointed in her. You thought she should have trusted you enough to tell you she was pregnant again." She glared suddenly at Stephen. "You always did have this paternal thing about her, didn't

you? You kept trying to fix her life, but she didn't want it
fixed."

He was looking at her intently.

"But I still don't understand why you turned against her. It
would have been nice if she'd known you believed in her. Not
even, you know, in her innocence. But *her*."

Stephen shook his head. "Naomi." His voice was tenuous,
breakable and low. "I'm . . . I didn't realize. All this time, I
thought you knew."

Then Naomi want cold. She gripped Polly. "Knew what?"

"I was sure Heather told you. I thought she must have told
you. I thought, who else would she tell?"

Like damp sheets on a cold night. Her hair was still wet
from the pool and she couldn't get warm.

"I thought it was why you were being such a bitch to me."

"I was a bitch to you?" Naomi said, amazed.

He shook his head. "Well, it can't be helped. I certainly did
what I could."

"Stephen, what the fuck are you talking about?"

He sat in his own seat and looked vaguely out the window:
dark sky meets dark ground. A New Hampshire evening in
mud time.

"I went to see her out at the farm, the day after Pick died.
Hell, I was probably the only condolence call she got. I didn't
know about the other thing. About Ashley. She told me when
I got there."

So *what?* Naomi almost said. But she said nothing.

"And of course she was upset. And don't worry, I know I
was an asshole to do what I did, but I can tell you it wasn't
forced. I can tell you that."

"You went to bed with her." She was astounded. "Jesus,
what a shit you are."

He looked stung, but he didn't deny it.

"You went to bed with her the day after her grandmother
died and her boyfriend dumped her."

"I'm not proud of it. But she reached out to me."

"For comfort, maybe. To be held, just possibly. But to be
fucked!"

"It's what she wanted," Stephen insisted. "She certainly
didn't protest."

"My God." She was shaking her head.

Stephen leaned forward, and his voice dropped even further. "So it was mine, Naomi. The other baby. One was Ashley's, but the other one was mine. And she wouldn't admit she was pregnant, even when I asked her straight out. Now, don't you think I had a right to know she was pregnant with my kid?"

"No," Naomi said cruelly. "And you don't know it was yours. There's no proof of any of this. That first baby had nothing to do with her."

"You still believe that?" He smiled sadly. "I wanted to believe that. I tried hard, but I know one of them was mine. And she killed them both. So she's a murderer. And if she goes to jail forever for what she did to those kids, then that's good enough for me. So what if she's got all those raving feminists thinking she's the second coming. To me, she's a murderer. And God knows, I don't think much of Ashley Deacon, but what Heather did to us both is past redemption. She can go to hell, in my view."

"Stephen." Naomi shook her head. Then she had another thought. "You didn't tell Charter."

"No. It wouldn't have changed anything."

"Of course it would have. It would have given him a much stronger case."

"It wouldn't bring the babies back, though. It wasn't worth it."

"You mean it wasn't worth Celia finding out."

He looked at her with new worry.

"Don't worry. I won't tell her. You never tell Charter and I never tell Celia. I think that's fair."

"I didn't mean for it to happen," he said. "I went out there as her friend. I just went to do the neighborly thing."

Naomi laughed darkly.

"She's the one. She put her arms around me. She kissed me."

"Please."

"I'd always done my best to think of Heather as a young person who needed guidance. But I couldn't after she kissed me."

"You're pathetic," Naomi said. "You're like those priests who molest children. You're just an ordinary man, after all. Just a bullshit sexual opportunist."

He got to his feet. "How dare you say that to me? I brought her to you. I *gave her to you!*"

"Good-bye, Stephen," Naomi said. She closed the door behind her and left him there.

Chapter 45

"I Am Christopher Flynn."

NOW SHE COULD NOT LOOK AT HEATHER. AS others were drawn around the girl, Naomi herself was repelled. Not that she believed it—that craziness of two men and two infants and two crimes. She could not believe something so irrational, something based as it was on how men both feared and were enthralled by female fertility and strength and mad power. But even not believing she now understood that Heather had never been the woman Naomi took her for—the one who had been used by Ashley for sex and by Charter for his bizarre version of perfect justice. She understood, for example, that Heather had indeed seduced Stephen when he went to her house the day after Pick's death, and that—even out of her pain as it had undoubtedly been—this was, at root, manipulative and cynical. It did not lessen at all the outrage she felt toward Stephen, but she did not question that Heather had initiated the encounter. She understood that Heather had not spoken of this to anyone, though it had obvious bearing on her trial and fate, and that therefore there might well be more that she hadn't told. For the first time, Heather's unwillingness to help herself struck Naomi as wantonly selfish, because after all, there were others involved now, whose lives and happiness had been knotted to hers—Polly, and Judith and Naomi, and even those crowds outside with their GODDARD SUPPORTS HEATHER placards and their I AM CHRIS FLYNN sweatshirts. And still she said nothing, blindly willing everyone else to carry on and make it all work out for the best. She would do nothing to help herself. Even testifying on her own behalf was too much to ask her for.

Heather arrived, red-faced, her eyes wet. As she sat, Naomi saw the shake of her shoulders and looked away. In front of her, the two women at the defense table leaned perceptibly apart, making no contact. Judith paused in her writing to say, so low that only Naomi could hear, "You're on third. I'm not going to discuss this anymore."

A soggy exhalation from Heather.

Charter took his seat. Nelson, Naomi noticed, was in the courtroom, but in civilian clothes. He sat behind Charter's table, looking calmly at the door through which Hayes was due to appear. She tried catching his gaze, but he did not want it caught, and she gave up. She had not heard from him since their night together.

The court was called to order. The jury entered, each assembling his or her serious expression, and they stood while the judge walked in his curious rocking gait to the bench. They knew it was nearing an end, if not a climax. The court reporter's hands began to move. Charter, too, was writing. Judith got to her feet. She stood in a posture of expectation, as if she were a schoolteacher waiting for the kids to shut up. Then she turned to Charter and half smiled.

"The defense would like to recall Nelson Erroll."

His head twisted around, his hand poised mid-scribble, lifting like a needle off a record. "What?"

"I'm here," Nelson said calmly. He rose and walked past Charter.

"Your honor," Charter complained, "Mr. Erroll has already been cross-examined by the defense."

"The defense has the right to continue the cross-examination if new evidence comes to light," Judith said firmly. Nelson, for his part, sat calmly in his chair, confident of the outcome.

"That's certainly true," said Hayes. "I take it you have some new evidence?"

"We do." Judith nodded, more gravely than eagerly.

"Let's hear it, then."

Charter braced his arms on the table. He stared at Nelson, his expression brutal.

"Officer Erroll," Judith said, moving up to him, "you testified earlier that when you went to bring Heather Pratt to the police station on October 12, 1985, she was being invited on a voluntary basis and she should not have inferred that she was actually under arrest. Is this still your opinion?"

"No," Nelson said. "I now feel that our arriving in the evening with six officers in three cars might have led her to believe that she was under arrest."

"But she was not read her rights?"

"No. Mr. Charter did not want to inform her of her rights because he did not want Heather to know that she had the option of calling an attorney."

The shock ran through the room. Charter was on his feet, stammering his rage, pointing but not looking at Nelson. Nelson was asked to confine himself to his own impressions.

Judith took this very calmly. "Were you asked not to read Heather her rights?"

"Yes. By District Attorney Charter."

She nodded. "You testified earlier that Heather could have elected not to accompany you to the police station and to refuse the interview. Is that true?"

"No. If she had tried to resist accompanying us, she would have been formally placed under arrest."

"So far, this was not precisely illegal, though, was it, Officer Erroll?"

"No. But it was not ethical. Heather's daughter was taken into another room, and Heather was not permitted to see her, though we could hear her crying. She asked to see Polly many times."

"And what was the response?"

"That she could not see her daughter until she cleared up the problem of the dead baby in the Sabbathday River."

"How did Heather respond to that?"

"She said she had no connection at all to that baby. Eventually she admitted that she had given birth to a stillborn baby whose body she had hidden. She offered to show us where the body was."

"Well," Judith said brightly, "that would have put an end to his nonsense about the baby in the Sabbathday River, wouldn't it?"

"Yes," said Nelson. "But District Attorney Charter refused to let Heather show us where the body was. He wanted her to confess to the death of the baby he knew about."

She nodded. Her arms were folded. She stood a few feet from him, half facing the jury box.

"Officer Erroll, how did Mr. Charter get Heather to confess to the death of the Sabbathday River baby?"

Nelson steadied himself. "He threatened her. He implied that she would lose custody of her daughter if she did not provide a confession."

Judith paused to let this sink in.

"How was this threat phrased?"

"He said Polly could not go home until this matter was cleared up, and she could only clear it up by confessing."

Judith looked pointedly at Charter, who fumed but was silent, reluctant perhaps to shut the barn door now that the horse was well and truly gone.

"Is this a common interrogation tactic, Officer Erroll?"

"I wouldn't know," he said tersely. "But I have never used it myself. I considered it disgusting. I'm ashamed of myself for not putting a stop to it." He was not looking at her now, or at anyone else. He could not seem to find the right place to look.

"So then Heather voluntarily confessed? She began to speak the words and phrases that you read out to us last week in this courtroom?"

"She did not," Nelson said tightly. "Those words were spoken by Mr. Charter. Heather just agreed to them. The only part I remember her saying came at the end. That she was sorry."

"And the knitting needle? How did she come to identify the knitting needle as the weapon with which she had supposedly killed her infant?"

"He put everything out on the table. Everything we collected at the house that fit what the forensic report said must have made the wound in the Sabbathday River baby. Then he just told her to pick one, and she did."

"I see." She looked disdainfully at Charter. "Officer Erroll, you testified last week that at no time during the interrogation did Heather ever ask to speak to an attorney. Is that, in fact, true?"

For the first time Nelson turned to Heather. His face held his regret. "No. She asked two times, at least."

Judith feigned amazement. "She asked to see a lawyer at least two times?"

"Yes. She was dissuaded from seeing a lawyer. Charter told her that if she hadn't done anything wrong, she didn't need a lawyer. He also said that this was an informal interview. That she wasn't under arrest. So it wasn't appropriate for her to have a lawyer."

"Officer Erroll, is it your understanding that when the subject of an interview requests a lawyer the interview must be suspended immediately?"

"That is my understanding. I have never acted otherwise." He eyed Charter. "Until this time."

"Do you feel that you were justified in ignoring Heather's request for a lawyer?"

He hesitated. "No. It was very wrong. I should have objected then, but I didn't. It's no excuse, but I didn't feel in control of the interview."

"Who was in control of the interview, Officer Erroll?"

"Mr. Charter conducted the interview. He denied Heather her right to a lawyer. His conduct was completely illegal, and I won't protect him."

Charter, fuming, kept his seat and scribbled on. Naomi wondered what he could possibly be writing.

"Officer Erroll, let's talk about the events that took place after Heather Pratt's interrogation. What was your reaction to the news that a second dead infant was found on Heather's property, precisely where she had informed you the body of her stillborn infant had been placed?"

"My reaction was an even stronger conviction that she had had nothing at all to do with the death of the Sabbathday River baby. That it was just an awful coincidence that the deaths had been concurrent, but that the two incidents weren't otherwise related."

"And yet you were the one who provided the theory of the second lover, by collecting an address book from Heather's house."

Nelson nodded. "Yes. It was after the forensic tests came back, and we knew there would have to have been a second father if this"—he could not resist a faint roll of the eyes—"*superfecundation* thing was true. I was told to go through Heather's house and find something to indicate a second man."

"I see." Judith smiled. "And what did you find?"

He shook his silver-gold head. "There was nothing. Only the address book, which was nothing. I shouldn't even have taken it out. It was only a man's name—what does that prove? I'm sure you could go through my house right now and pick up half a dozen women's names, but that doesn't mean I have a relationship with them. There must be a hundred reasons to write someone's name on a piece of paper."

"But even so, in Heather's house you could only find one name. Chris Flynn." She paused. "Tell me, Officer Erroll, do you believe that Heather Pratt had a relationship with Christopher Flynn?"

"I do not."

"Do you believe a Christopher Flynn exists and is relevant to this situation?"

"Exists?" He shrugged. "Probably. Somewhere. But not relevant, no."

Judith walked back to her table and sat. "Officer Erroll, what made you decide to return and correct your earlier testimony in this case?"

Nelson took a deep breath and closed his eyes. This was the important thing, the thing he had come to say. He looked at the jurors. "I believe that Heather Pratt is innocent of the charges against her. I believe that her own child was stillborn, and that she has absolutely no link to the Sabbathday River baby. There was no second lover and no superfecundation. I believe her interrogation was duplicitous and manipulative. Also unconstitutional. I'm sorry, Heather," Nelson said, looking directly at her. She straightened in her seat. For once, she did not cry or seem to lose her concentration. "I know it can't make up for the months you've been in jail, or the obscene way you've been treated in this trial."

Judith did not speak right away. Then, quietly, she said she was finished and took her seat. Naomi did not think Charter would respond, but before her eyes he blustered up to the witness seat and poked a finger in Nelson's face.

"Officer Erroll, have you not just admitted that you committed perjury in this courtroom?"

"I admit that," Nelson said sadly.

"You lied. You sat in that very chair and you lied."

"Yes."

"And yet now you wish us to believe that you are telling the truth. Before, you lied, but you're not lying now!"

Nelson sighed. He did not respond.

"How are we supposed to believe what you say, Officer Erroll?"

"You can believe what you want," Nelson said sadly. "My

conscience is clear now. I've admitted what I did wrong." He paused. "You said it yourself, Robert. If you hide guilt, it destroys you, but if you admit it, it makes you strong. Isn't that what you said?"

"There is nothing to admit!" Charter thundered. "And you are a perjurer!"

"Yes," Nelson agreed.

In the jury box, heads were shaking. How Naomi wanted it to be over.

"I will not cross-examine an admitted perjurer!"

"That is your option," Hayes snapped. "So sit down."

Charter looked at him in surprise. He sat. Nelson nodded at Judith, then walked out of the aisle. Heather, tall in her seat, turned to watch him leave.

"Mrs. Friedman, your next witness?"

Judith stood. She faced the back of the room. "The defense calls Chris Flynn."

There was a shriek of breath inhaled, the sudden, collective suck of air into shocked mouths and throats, leaving nothing behind. Even Charter was limp for a moment, but when he finally moved he moved quickly.

"This is . . ." He was up on his feet, waving his arms as if trying to flag a speeding car. "This is outrageous. We had no warning of this!"

"Of what?" Judith said mildly. "We were able to find the witness you told us you were looking for. So you should be happy."

"Mr. Charter," said the judge, "what is the nature of your objection?"

Naomi, stunned and exhilarated, began to grin. This, evidently, was what Judith meant by "lots of fun."

"I . . ." He could not seem to find words to contain his protest. That she had found the person whom he knew did not exist? That this person had materialized to *say* he did not exist? That in a world full of artificial Christopher Flynns there might, incredibly, be a real one?

Charter, unable to complete his sentence, sat down.

"Chris Flynn," the court reporter said through the open back door.

The occupant of each seat turned to look. Naomi, confronted with the impending entrance of the man, found that in his physical absence she had imagined him quite clearly as a tall and imposing person with blond hair and broad shoulders—an athlete—and it occurred to her that everyone must by now have an image of how he must look, based on nothing but a name. But there was no broad and tall man, only someone else, a latecomer looking for a seat, moving down the aisle. Naomi went back to staring at the door. The latecomer was nearly at the front of the room before she saw her mistake.

It was a young girl, twenty or so, and tiny. She wore a bizarre outfit comprising a white turtleneck imprinted with small green frogs under a mostly pink Fair Isle sweater, khaki pants, and penny loafers. Her blond hair was held back with a velvet-covered band, wedged over the top of her head and then pushed slightly forward, so the hair was mounded over itself, over air. A gold ring on a gold chain bounced against her flat chest. She looked about her somewhat fearfully and gave Judith a downright terrified nod when she got to the front of the room. Judith pointed at the witness chair.

"Please state your name for the record," the court officer said.

"My name is Christina Flynn." Her voice was high and little.

Again, Charter leaped to his feet. "Your honor, I don't appreciate these theatrics. I don't know what Ms. Friedman hopes to prove by this, but a Christina is not a Christopher."

Hayes looked at Judith, but he was way ahead of Charter.

"Neither is a Chris necessarily a Christopher," said Judith. "The word in the address book was Chris, not Christopher."

"So it was," Hayes said. "You may proceed, Mrs. Friedman."

Charter sank to his chair.

"Christina, what is your occupation?" Judith moved close to her. The girl looked as if she needed the support.

"I'm a junior at Dartmouth College. I'm majoring in English."

"When did you enter Dartmouth?"

"The fall of 1983." She kept her eyes glued to Judith's face. "I grew up in Virginia, but I wanted to go to school in the Northeast. My father went to Dartmouth."

Judith nodded. "When you arrived on the campus for your freshman year, were you assigned to a dormitory?"

"Yes." Christina Flynn blushed. "My father wanted me to

be in an all-female dormitory. I was in North Massachusetts Hall. Fourth floor. There were two other girls in my room."

"How many girls were in North Massachusetts Hall, Christina?"

She thought. "About fifty. Maybe a few less."

"And of those, how many would have been freshman girls like you?"

"Maybe twenty. Upper-class women sometimes move off campus or into sorority houses."

"I see." Judith smiled. "Do you remember meeting a freshman woman named Heather Pratt at the beginning of the fall term? She would have just moved into North Massachusetts Hall, like you."

Christina Flynn shook her head vigorously. "No. I mean, possibly I did meet her. They had parties for the new girls in the common room. But I don't remember meeting her. I've tried, but I don't remember."

"Okay," said Judith. "Christina, do you remember buying a new address book for yourself when you arrived at college for your freshman year?"

She bit her lip. "I really don't remember. I know you asked me before, but I don't remember. I might have."

Judith went to the evidence table. Under Charter's apathetic gaze, she found the address book in its plastic bag. "An address book like this?"

Christina took it. Naomi saw recognition fall over her face. "Oh . . . I think I did. I remember buying this at the Dartmouth bookstore!"

Judith turned it over in Christina's hands. "This thing on the cover? What is it?"

"It's the college crest. It says *Vox Clamantis in Deserto*. It means 'A voice crying out in the wilderness.' "

"Did you write your name inside, Christina?"

"I don't know. Maybe."

Slipping the address book from its plastic bag, Judith opened its green cover. She showed it to the girl. "Did you write this?"

Now Christina blushed again, even more fiercely. Naomi thought she looked as if she might cry.

"Yes. That's my writing."

"But it's not exactly your name, is it, Christina?"

"No," she said, ducking her head. "I thought . . . This is embarrassing."

"It's all right," said Judith. "It's important."

"I thought, when I went to college, I might try not to be so . . . In high school I was shy. And I'd never really been away from home before. And my family. And everybody I knew always called me Christina. Except my father. He calls me Tina. And I thought maybe now that I was in a place where nobody knew me, I could start with a new name. But I didn't, really. I mean, I'm still Christina and everybody still calls me Christina." She looked at Judith. "I don't really remember any of this. I mean, it was two and a half years ago. I don't remember losing my address book."

"But, looking at it, you do recognize that this was once yours," Judith said gently.

"Yes," Christina said. "It was mine."

"You are the Chris Flynn whose name is written in this address book."

She sighed. She would never be that Chris Flynn now, Naomi knew. "Yes," the girl said.

Judith faced the jury. "Christina, how did you first learn about the case on trial in this courtroom?"

She took hold of the ring around her neck and fiddled with it nervously. "I think one of my sorority sisters mentioned it. She was my roommate freshman year, in North Mass. She asked if I remembered this girl Heather who dropped out during freshman week. I didn't remember. She didn't remember her, either," Christina said, a little defensively. "And the rest of it, I mean, what the trial was about, I didn't know that part till you called me yesterday. I didn't know till yesterday."

"So as far as you were concerned, this girl Heather and the crime for which she was on trial had absolutely nothing to do with you?"

She looked at Judith in intense alarm. "No! It has nothing to do with me! I don't know anything about it!"

"And how did you learn that Heather Pratt was alleged to have had a child with a person named Chris Flynn, an allegation that arose entirely from an address book you had once lost?"

Now she did cry, quite suddenly, with one hand pressed to her nose, her cheeks flushed deeply red. Beneath her fingers,

her skin had a sheen of running tears. "Please!" She wept. "I
don't know anything about this! I don't know her! I don't even
recognize her—is that her?" She pointed at Heather, who now,
for the first time, had turned to Charter with a look of unmistakable triumph. "I don't remember her at all if that's her.
Please"—she choked—"can I leave now? I don't know
anything about dead babies!"

Judith looked at Hayes. "I'm finished," she said mildly.

Charter was asked if he had questions, and he rose and
swayed for a moment, eyeing the by now sobbing girl in the
frog-covered turtleneck: Chris Flynn. He lifted one finger, as
if to point it in accusation, but there was too much laughter,
and the sound of the laughter first competed with and then
muted the tears of Christina Flynn. In the jury box they were
not successful in silencing the laughter, and in the spectator
seats they were not trying. Even Heather laughed. Naomi,
watching the sad little girl in the witness seat, did not laugh.
Charter had no questions. Christina Flynn walked away, wiping at her face with the back of her small hand.

"Your next witness, Mrs. Friedman?" said Judge Hayes.

Judith stood. She was going to call Heather now, Naomi
knew—call her and make her recite her lines of denial: *My
baby was stillborn, I don't know anything about the other
baby*—but Judith wasn't talking. She stood transfixed, buoyed
by the laughter, suppressed and unsuppressed. She looked at
the jury box, letting her eye run over the men and women,
their rhythmic shoulders and red, merry faces and shaking
heads. Then at Charter, who was still and sagging in his chair.
Then at Heather, who looked back at her, pleading and waiting. And finally at Hayes again.

"The defense rests," she said.

ON GOOD FRIDAY MORNING, GILMAN WARREN, THE
Attorney General of New Hampshire, made his first and only
appearance at the trial of *NH v. Pratt*, sitting not near Charter
but rather noncommittally in the back of the room to watch
the final arguments. The jury was out for thirty minutes.
Twenty-five of them, Naomi later learned, were spent waiting
for the right form to fill out.

They made their way outside in a kind of rugby scrum
around Heather, half-pressing, half-lifting her ahead through

the people, Naomi and Judith on either side, Ella and her squadron of triumphant women running interference before. The cheer that rose to meet them interrupted Attorney General Warren's speech to the cameras, and he turned them a grim face.

"Will you be remounting an investigation into the death of the Sabbathday River baby?" somebody shouted over the din.

Charter, leaning out in front, spoke with bitter restraint. "We had the right person on trial," he said, glaring at Heather.

"Mr. Warren? Is that your statement?"

The attorney general spoke into a brush of microphones.

"I think we're all glad to put this sad case behind us," he said, his voice oddly still. "We will not try any part of it again. And that *is* my statement. Thank you." Then, leaving Charter motionless in his wake and cast adrift, Warren moved away down the steps.

Naomi, watching him leave, thought at first that he must be truly, personally, bereft, so utterly was the sound of weeping enmeshed and in sync with his descent, and this is why nearly a minute had passed before she understood that it was actually Judith who wept, and not loudly at all but in a free way, and close by. She turned to Judith and saw that she had covered her face, like that day on the bench, but Naomi felt as helpless now as then. "Oh, Judith," she said, and in reaching for her she took her hand off Heather's wrist. The crowd came up around them, pushing at Heather, surging in a wave of white. Naomi felt herself take an involuntary step away. Then, this time by choice, a second step. The bodies of strangers pushed her in a different direction. Someone thrust a mass of roses into Heather's arms.

Part 5
Pharaoh's Daughter

Your mother shows me a photograph of you got up in lace.
White crêpe-de-chine. White bonnet. White mittens.
Once, on a street in Moscow, a woman pushed snow in my
*   face*
when it seemed I might have been frostbitten.

> —Paul Muldoon, "White"
> In Memory of Thaddeus
> Wills (June 19–20, 1996)

Chapter 46

The Pond

ON A HOT JULY AFTERNOON, NAOMI DROVE down Sabbath Creek Road in her station wagon to return the last of Polly's things. There were two socks, mismatched, the plastic pail from the bathtub, and a collection of small books found beneath her bed when she was rolling up the rug. None of these items—she was the first to admit—was precisely crucial, and the socks, for that matter, were probably outgrown, but Naomi needed to see Polly before she left. And, she supposed, she needed to see Heather, too.

By now, people seemed to understand that Naomi was leaving, though how this understanding had come about she wasn't sure, since she had not told anyone except Judith of her plans. It was not only time to go, she thought, but past time. For years she had groped, in her inefficient manner, for the catalyst of her own transformation and departure, a thing so bad, Naomi reasoned, that she would tear herself away in order to run from it. It had not been Daniel's leaving. It had not been her failure with Nelson. It had not, in the end, even been Heather. Finally, it had not been a thing to run *from* at all, but a thing she was compelled to run *to*. Not, in other words, the babies she had pulled from the water, but her own baby, the one inside and growing.

Sometimes over these past months she had wondered what she would miss when she was gone from this place, and was surprised to find, when she imagined her life in the city, that it was not the people who lingered—not Nelson, who was beautiful to her, and not even Judith, the only friend she had made in a decade here—but the look of the mountains, the blackish-green and sharp edges of the Whites, so raw and rough. It struck her only now that there was a specific smell to the air here which she had failed to discern, and failed to appreciate as it deserved. It struck her that pavement would never duplicate the bounce beneath the sole of the shoe that old mud and pine needles made, and to her own surprise, she mourned this.

But she was going, anyway. The idea, formed in her the night of the verdict when she had handed Polly back to her mother, had grown over the next days, mutter to drone to din, until she found herself rushing to make arrangements, catching up to her own yearning. In a week's time, now, the A-frame would be on the market and she would be back on the West Side. She wasn't the only one, either. Ashley was already gone—back to Burlington with his wife and kids, to be anonymous in his indiscriminate love of women. Charter was gone—he had slunk back to Peytonville and was not missed. And Nelson was gone. His farmhouse was locked and empty. Naomi had no idea where he was.

She had not been to Heather's house since the day she had found the second baby, ten months earlier, and coming down the long drive she was surprised to see that the house gleamed, newly white with paint, its trim dark blue. Someone, in addition, had moved the grass beside and behind the house, so that the back field had a graceful slope to it, and there was a lush summer garden by the back porch, with peas climbing a tepee of strings. There, bent over in an undershirt, a woman with short dark hair worked with her hands in the dirt. Not Heather, Naomi thought. A big yellow dog, lolling on the sun-warmed stone doorstep, lumbered over when the car stopped and thrust its wet nose against the window.

"Amiga!"

The woman came to the car, a spade in one hand. The other reached for the dog's collar.

"Amiga, down!"

Naomi rolled down her window. "It's Simone, isn't it?"

"Oh. Naomi, right?"

"I was looking for Heather," said Naomi. "I didn't know you were living here."

"Since the end of spring term. We've been helping Heather get some things in order."

"The house looks great," Naomi said. "Did you do that?"

"Mostly Ella," Simone said. "She's good with tools. I planted the garden."

"That's very good of you." Naomi looked around. "Is Heather here?"

She nodded. Naomi got out of her car and took Polly's things. They found Heather on the back porch steps, watching Polly play in a sandbox that looked new. Heather was still too thin, but her hair was growing back and someone had given her a fairly flattering haircut. She looked up in surprise when Naomi rounded the house.

"I didn't hear you!" she said.

"Yes. I'm afraid your Amiga's not much of a watchdog."

"She's Ella's dog, really. She sleeps under Ella's bed." Heather didn't get up. Naomi knelt by Polly.

"Hello, sweetie-pod." She didn't want to say any more. She didn't want to cry. Polly looked at her briefly and went back to work, filling and upending a bucket.

"Polly, say hello," her mother said.

"No, it's all right," said Naomi. "I just brought some things I found." She put them on the back step. "She used to love this book about fingers and toes."

"Thank you," Heather said.

Naomi sat beside her. "I didn't realize Ella and Simone were living here."

"Oh, I couldn't have gotten myself together without them," Heather said quietly. "They really helped me. And the others. There was a bunch of women who came up from Boston and helped me fix the roof. They brought things for Polly, too. Simone planted the garden. I haven't had a garden since Pick died. It's wonderful."

Naomi smiled. "How long are they staying?"

"Oh well, Simone's going to France this fall on a language program, but Ella's going to stay. And another student, a friend of hers who has a little boy. We'll take turns looking after the children and going down to Hanover."

She turned to Heather. "Hanover?"

"Mm," she said, with a shrug. "I didn't tell you, I guess. They took me back. At Dartmouth. It actually wasn't a big deal at all. They had me down under 'leave of absence,' and you can keep that up for like ten years before they unenroll you. So I enter the freshman class in September."

Naomi stared at her. "Heather, that's wonderful. That's just the best news."

"Well, I guess. I guess it's the right thing to do. Ella says I have to start with myself. She says the best way to avoid being a victim is to cultivate power." She looked at Naomi. "Do you think that's true?"

"I think every woman has to protect her own interests, and her children's interests."

Heather nodded, but she looked glum. Polly, spotting the bath bucket, came to collect it from the step, and took it back to the sandbox.

"I'm moving away," said Naomi. "I'm going back to New York."

"I heard that." Heather didn't look at her. "I guess I won't see you again."

"Oh, I'll still be involved with Flourish, though Sarah Copley will run things for the time being. I'll probably set up some kind of outlet in New York, to sell things down there. So I'll be up and down."

"Ashley moved away, too," said Heather in a small voice.

"I heard that."

"Back to Burlington. I think nobody would hire him here. I think people were really mean to him."

Naomi said nothing.

"It wasn't his fault. I feel so badly about that, that he had to move. I should have been the one who moved."

Naomi, who did not see the logic of this, kept still.

"After all, he didn't do anything wrong."

"Neither did you, Heather," Naomi said wearily.

Heather nodded quickly. She had heard this before. Suddenly she got to her feet.

"Come with me. I want to show you something."

What? Naomi thought. She stood. They left Polly in her sand and walked downhill. "What?" Naomi said. Then, looking ahead, she saw where Heather was taking her. She did not want to go there. "I know this," she said. "I was here."

"No. I want to."

She walked on, and Naomi followed. Surely there was some rule of etiquette that precluded showing visitors the site of your baby's stillbirth. Naomi moved in dread. "Heather? You don't have to."

"Look," said Heather. She had turned and was staring uphill, a look of amazement on her face. "Look how far from the house it is! I came all the way out here, in the middle of the night. Maybe I was remembering the night Polly was born. I walked then, too. Up and down the hill. I remember, I had Pick following me around, and the midwife. I guess it took my mind off the pain."

"Well," Naomi said, "I guess that makes sense. You did what you'd done the last time you were in labor."

"But I wasn't in labor. It didn't feel like labor. Nothing felt the same as it had the first time, because everything was different. Pick was gone, and Ashley was gone. And from the time they left, there was this thing in their place." She waved her hands over her abdomen, quickly, as if she were shaking her fingers. "I didn't want it. It's just like that woman said. That psychiatrist. I didn't want it. I wanted to trade. I wanted the other things back—the things I had before I had this . . ." Heather stopped in frustration. She could not even name the thing she had so despised. "I didn't really believe I could trade, but I wanted it so much." She looked at Naomi. "And nobody knew about it. I didn't tell Ashley. I didn't tell anyone. I thought if anyone knew, they'd make me keep it, and I didn't want to keep it. I hated it."

"Don't, Heather," Naomi said.

"Don't what?" Heather said sharply. "It's all done now. It must have died from my hating it all those months, because when it came out, it was still. And it didn't make a sound, either. I just pushed it out on the ground. It didn't even hurt very much, if you want to know the truth. I'm telling you, it was already dead. I'd already killed it."

"Okay." Naomi nodded. She desperately wanted to leave. "It was stillborn. You couldn't help that."

"But that's what I'm *telling* you!" she shouted. "I didn't *want* to help it. I *wanted* it to be dead."

"Fine," Naomi said, feeling sick.

"It was right there." Heather pointed. Her face was dull. "Right there. By that rock. And I remember thinking, It's dead just like I thought, because I didn't hear anything. And I put my hand over its face, just to make sure there was nothing there. I held my hand there till I was sure. There was nothing there. It wasn't breathing."

Naomi, who wasn't breathing either, stared at the ground.

"But I'm not sure I hurt it," Heather said suddenly. She stared at Naomi. "Didn't that doctor say he couldn't prove it had been alive?"

Naomi, numb, nodded. "He said that."

"So. All right, then." She looked down. A few feet past them, the little pond gave its dull reflection of the afternoon sun. Naomi could not look at it.

"I don't think I hurt it," Heather said suddenly. "I'm not sure, but I don't think so." She shook her head. "I only wanted to be sure."

Naomi took a step back. "I have to leave."

"When you found that other baby, I thought . . . no, I knew it couldn't. I didn't stab my baby like that other person. My baby wasn't breathing. I made sure it wasn't breathing before I put it in the water."

Naomi turned and ran, away up the hill, her breath wet and rough in her ears. She could not leave fast enough. Behind her, Heather was kneeling by the water, reaching out to break the surface with a fingertip.

Chapter 47

The River

SHE HAD TO SPEAK TO JUDITH, BUT JUDITH WAS missing. Naomi called her between bouts of packing and trips to the dump, between bouts of packing and sessions over the mill computer with Sarah. She phoned Judith from Tom and Whit's, or the mill, or the gas station, spilling pockets full of change onto the top of the pay phone just as she'd done years before, when she'd first moved to Goddard and had no home and no phone of her own. Judith was not answering. Finally, fighting the beginnings of paranoia, she took to driving by Sabbathday Ridge. The cars were gone. Judith wasn't answering because she wasn't there.

Naomi had an appointment in the city for the following Monday, a meeting with a woman who knew one of her Cornell friends and had a storefront on Sixty-eighth, near Broadway. The notion of sitting down to discuss Manhattan real estate was at once so thrilling and so bizarre that she could not think of it without shaking her head, but as the day drew close and with it her own departure, Naomi shrank in dread. She had to see Judith, and Judith wasn't there.

When she was through packing, it surprised her to see how little she was actually bringing with her, and most of that was in the form of Flourish overstocks and other things having to do with the business. The furniture she had bought with Daniel (or which he had fashioned in his imprecise way) stayed where it was—the real estate agent said its presence might make the A-frame marginally easier to sell—and what remained were books she would never read again, clothes inappropriate to the Upper West Side, and a stereo system moaning for replacement, all of which she hauled to the Salvation Army in Peytonville. There was only, in the end, a photograph of Polly taken on the first day of toddler swim class, her bright face wide with delight in the water, in Naomi's arms, and this, Naomi now understood, was the strongest link she had forged in Goddard—to a child who no longer even recognized her. And to Judith, of course. But Judith wasn't there.

The day before the day she planned to leave was a Friday, wet with July heat. Naomi drove again to Sabbathday Ridge, sour and pessimistic, thinking to leave, at least, a note wedged under the kitchen door, but as she swung her car around the turn she saw Judith's car, and Judith herself, unloading bags of groceries from the trunk. Judith straightened and gave Naomi a weary wave, and Naomi was so surprised to see her that her heart raced. Judith wore, despite the heat, a black sweater, a black skirt. "You're here!" said Naomi delightedly. "I was going to leave a note."

"I've been in Providence," Judith said. "My nephew died."

Half out of her car, Naomi froze.

"I just got back an hour ago. I'm sorry." She looked at Naomi. "Were you trying to reach me?"

"Yes," Naomi said. "Oh, Judith. How awful."

"It isn't, really." Judith reached for a grocery bag. "I mean, it is. But we've been preparing for this for a long time."

"But Rachel." She took another bag and followed Judith inside.

"Rachel is surprisingly all right. It's Hannah who's a mess. She understood 'dying,' but 'dead' is different." Judith set down her bag on the counter. "It's so hot." She looked around the kitchen. "Let's go down to the river. Maybe it's cooler there. We can put our feet in, anyway."

"All right."

Judith poured them tall glasses of seltzer, and they walked out back and down the slope. The river was sluggish in the heat, but far cooler than the air. Naomi took off her sandals and moved her toes in the current. "That feels good," Judith said. She sighed. "I didn't think it would get this hot in New Hampshire. I remember last year, I was so surprised by the heat. I told Joel I thought we'd need air conditioners. But then the fall came, and I forgot all about it until now." She smiled suddenly. "Like labor, I guess. They say you forget how bad it is, till the next time."

Naomi frowned. "I didn't know you were here last summer. I thought you came in the fall."

"Well"—she shrugged—"I was here. I wasn't going out

much." She drank her seltzer, then pressed the glass against her forehead. "So. You're off, then."

"Tomorrow. Yes."

"End of an era," said Judith. There was an edge to her voice. "What will you do when you get there?"

Naomi looked off downriver. There was a straight view from here, down a good half mile to where the river curved out of sight. Just beyond was the site of the "Sabbathday incident," that streak through the night woods when she caught Daniel howling in fear to the God he denied. And past that place, the Drumlins, the sharp rocks under the surface. And past that place, the eddy where she had found a doll facedown in the water, which had turned out not to be a doll at all. For some reason, she had not realized till now how close Judith's house was to the place.

"Naomi?" Judith kicked her feet under the surface, making the water swirl.

"Oh, I don't know. I thought maybe I could do what I did here. Maybe there are old ladies in Brooklyn making quilts and things. I can start a collective to sell the results."

Judith sighed. "Come on, Naomi."

Taken aback, she frowned. "What?"

"It's time now. This isn't for you."

"What are you talking about? It worked the first time."

"But that's my point," Judith said. "It worked, but not by itself. You *made* it work. First of all, you took a bunch of women who'd never earned a wage and you gave them an income. That's one thing. But you did something else, even harder. You not only found a niche in the marketplace, you found a whole *marketplace* where there wasn't one before. People can't be taught what you know. Don't denigrate your talents."

"Oh, there's no talent." Naomi shook her head. "I just followed the protocol. This is what they told us to do at VISTA. I mean, it wasn't an original idea."

"Jesus." Judith shook her head. "How can you be so obtuse about yourself? There is no VISTA anymore. All that's finished. We tried, we gave it our best shot, and now it's time for the next thing. You're not part of a trend, Naomi. What you did showed initiative!"

"No," Naomi said fervently. "I did what I was supposed to do."

"Listen to me, Naomi." Judith leaned forward. "I admire you. You have enormous capabilities. But you are laboring under a serious misperception. You seem to feel that you're a civil rights worker. But you're an entrepreneur."

"Oh," Naomi said, horrified. "I'm *not*."

"Jesus Christ, Naomi! I saw you fire a woman because she didn't agree with you!" Judith rolled her eyes. "Be glad for what you can do, but be clear about what it is."

"No." Naomi shook her head. "You're wrong."

"Fine," Judith said harshly. A first breath of estrangement rose between them. Naomi remembered why she had come.

"I saw Heather," she told Judith. "I went to say good-bye. Judith"—Naomi's voice began to shake—"you were right. You were right that she killed her baby."

Nonchalant, Judith sighed. "I tried to tell you that."

"She put her hand over the baby's mouth. She said so. She said she hated the baby."

"I don't need to think about Heather anymore, thanks."

"Don't you care?" Naomi said wildly. "Shouldn't you do something?"

"Shouldn't I *do* something?" shouted Judith. "I already *did* something! I got her off. I got the attorney general to say on television that he'd never try any part of the case again. I think I've done enough."

"But she really killed her baby!" said Naomi.

Judith put up her hands.

"Don't you care about the babies?" Naomi said hotly.

Judith glared at her. "I care. I care far more than Heather did, I can tell you that. I care that a healthy child was suffocated and buried underwater. And the other one. Of course I care." A single tear appeared in one eye; then symmetrically, a tear in the other eye.

"I don't expect you to understand this, Naomi, but I'm going to try to explain it anyway. When my nephew was born, he was the most beautiful baby I'd ever seen. He laughed and smiled. He reached out to us. I don't know if you've spent any time around infants, but there's this sense, the first couple of months, that the person inside is just waking up and noticing the world. It's like they climb up out of a hole in the ground and see the world, and Simon did. He saw the world. But then he started to go back down into the ground. He didn't want to, but he had to. It took three months to crawl up to the world and then two and a half years to crawl all the way back down into the ground. And we had to watch. Every inch, we watched him go back into the ground." She wiped at her face. "He's in the ground now."

Naomi, perplexed but disinclined to interrupt, moved her feet in the water and watched her friend cry.

"I wouldn't do that," Judith said suddenly. "Do you understand?"

Naomi frowned.

"If I had a child, and the child had what Simon had, I wouldn't do what my sister had to do. I wouldn't watch it die like that. *Do you understand?*"

"But you can't know," Naomi said. "I mean, you can't tell in advance, can you?"

Judith looked out across the river, her face streaked. "You can, actually. There's something you can test for, in the blood. Even the blood from the umbilical cord. There's an elevated level of a certain hormone, and you can tell. If you happened to be looking. If you had a reason to look. Like, a relative who had it. You could tell. You just need a lab, and you need to know what to look for." She looked back at Naomi. "It's so pathetically rare. No one would think to look for it unless they had a reason. Not at birth. Not in an autopsy. Do you see?"

Naomi, who began to, stared back.

"I need to make this clear to you, Naomi. A baby who has this disease is already dead. There isn't any cure. They can't do a damn thing, not even to slow it down. There's nothing but watching your baby go back into the ground. I wouldn't do that! Rachel didn't have a choice. Simon was nearly four months when they found out, so she didn't have a choice. But I wouldn't!"

"All right," Naomi said, but she didn't know what she was saying.

"I wouldn't watch a child of mine die the way Simon did. Not in that long, horrible way. Joel wouldn't, and I wouldn't."

Numb, Naomi watched her own hand move. It placed her glass on the level surface of a boulder. Then she looked at

Judith. "So if they're going to die they'd better do it and decrease the surplus population, is that what you're telling me?
I mean, is that it?"

Judith was staring at her, white-faced and speechless. A long
moment passed before she found her words. "No. That is not
it. We're talking," Judith said, her voice ragged with grief,
"about a loved child. We're talking about a mourned child.
Please"—she wept—"at least tell me you understand that."

Why that, Naomi thought dully, when I understand nothing
else?

"You hate me, don't you?" Judith said.

And Naomi was bereft to find that she did not. In fact, there
was nothing inside her at all, only a numb place where the
hate ought to have been, and the horror. And while she was
aware, vaguely, that she was supposed to tell someone, that
justice required her to tell, to report what she knew to whatever
"authorities" remained, Naomi also knew that she would never
do that. As surely Judith must have known.

"You do hate me," Judith said. "I see that. But you don't
understand."

So Naomi nodded, because her ignorance, at least, was
something they could agree on. But Judith doesn't *look* like a
murderer, she was thinking, though if there was the smallest
solace in that, it passed quickly enough, because maybe this
was what a murderer looked like, after all. Her friend: who
was so strong, whose eyes were so wild with sadness. A murderer.

"I hate what you did," she said aloud, thinking this might
represent some kind of middle ground, but she found, to her
great dismay, that she could not bring herself to hate even that.
And how terrible a person she must be, not to hate even that!

"What I did"—Judith moved her feet in the water—"I did
to spare us all. Her suffering. Because she would have suffered. Later on, I mean. And as it was, she didn't. It was fast,
Naomi. Joel made sure." She shook her head, as if to dislodge
the memory. "That's all I cared about, really. For Joel it was
a little bit more complicated, of course."

Naomi, cautious, waited. She kept her eyes on Judith's ghost
feet, white underwater, as they made the current swirl into a
circle.

"For Joel it would have been a question of faith, do you

see? Of saying, to *God*"—she spat the word—"that he accepted this. God did it, but Joel accepted it. Like, he said, when Abraham did what God asked him to do. Or when Miriam put Moses in the river, she was telling God she trusted Him to do the right thing. Even if the right thing was to send him over a waterfall, then it was all right. She would accept it. We had to be the same way, he said." She shook her head. "He actually believes that, you know."

Naomi, who by now did know, nodded in silence.

"I mean, he has to. He'll do anything for a little hope. A little hope is so fucking narcotic." She laughed, darkly, her eyes were wide and flowing like the river's surface. "Maybe he thought there was going to be some Pharaoh's daughter out there for us, to save her. But we got you instead."

I'm sorry, Naomi nearly said. For not being a Pharaoh's daughter. For not letting that poor cold baby float away in the first place. *Because I was wrong about everything*. From the very first moment to this moment, from the eddy in mid-river to this one by the riverbank, at Judith's feet, Naomi had done everything wrong.

"Did you get the hope at least?" she said, thinking aloud.

Judith surprised her by shrugging. "Well, I guess so. I'm pregnant," she said, and the extra word, the word she didn't say, hung for a moment on the stagnant air between them, then was lifted by a small, stray breeze and taken off down the Sabbathday. Naomi, watching it go, thought how alike they were, in the end, Judith and Heather, though they each would have shunned the comparison. How Heather had given back her baby in wild hope for what she had lost, and Judith for what she had not had in the first place. Perhaps it would work better for Judith than it had for Heather, Naomi thought, though she herself would not wait to see if it did. She would not know what happened to the baby Judith carried, since she would not know Judith after today. Grieving for a dozen things at once, she got unsteadily to her feet and reached down for her sandals. She did not look at her friend. "I have to go."

"You're going now? Right now?" Judith spoke harshly, her face streaky and tight. "Right this second?"

And that was when it occurred to Naomi that she *could* go. And yes, right this second. She could leave right away, after all—not tomorrow, as she'd planned, but now. Since she had already packed what little she was saving, her vital places filled with vital things, and there was nothing to keep her. She could get in her car and floor the gas, and drive and drive until she would have to close her eyes to see the people she had left behind. But only see—because they had passed by now beyond her reach, even if she were still inclined to reach for them.

Author's Note

Canavan disease is a rare neurodegenerative disorder caused by a deficiency in an enzyme called aspartoacyclase, which in turn causes progressive spongy degeneration of the brain. In the most common form of the disease, onset occurs in the first few months of life and death by three or four years of age. The enzyme was identified in the mid-1980s, but prenatal diagnosis by amniocentesis was extremely difficult and unreliable due to very low enzyme expression in amniotic fluid cells. In 1994 the gene for aspartoacyclase was mapped to the short arm of chromosome number 17. The most common mutation was identified at nucleotide 854, with suggested carrier frequencies ranging from 1 in 36 to 1 in 59 in the Ashkenazi Jewish population (similar to the frequency of the Tay-Sachs gene), though the disease also occurs in other ethnic groups. Since 1994, DNA testing has allowed parents to undergo carrier testing and accurate prenatal diagnosis to determine if they are carrying an affected fetus. There is no cure for Canavan disease and the only available treatments are supportive and palliative.

DNA testing for the purpose of establishing parentage or kinship was not available until 1990.

Acknowledgments

During the writing of this novel I relied on the kindness of friends. Linda M. Bonnell, Pharm D. and Leslie Vought, M.S., C.G.C., gave me invaluable and enthusiastic assistance with serology and Canavan's disease. Peggy O'Brien lent me her snowbound house for two critical weeks. Deborah Michel provided her customary close readings and one-woman cheering section. Five years ago, Sally Kahler Phillips told me that I really ought to write a novel about that strange Irish case. This turned out to be a good idea, and one for which I am appropriately grateful.

I thank Dr. Vivian Fromberg for her guidance through the *Diagnostic and Statistical Manual*. Dr. Eleanor Nicolai McQuillen, M.D., M.S.A., my consultant in forensic medicine, solved every problem I presented her with and several she didn't know I had.

I am beholden to the Virginia Center for the Creative Arts for a fellowship during the winter of 1997.

The "Sabbathday Affair" on pp. 25–28 owes its genesis to "The Pemi Affair" by Kirk Siegel, which appeared in the Summer 1993 issue of *The Dartmouth Alumni Magazine*. I appreciate his forbearance in allowing his true misadventure to inspire my fictional one.

I am so grateful to Pam Bernstein, Donna Downing, Arabella Stein, Judy Klein, and Jonathan Galassi for believing in this novel and its author.

*In memory of two children who died during the
writing of this book:*
Olivia Kuenne, *aged five years*
Thaddeus Wills, *aged twenty minutes*

*No room has ever been as silent as the room
Where hundreds of violins are hung in unison.*
—Michael Longley, "Terezín"

The *New York Times* Bestselling Author of *Practical Magic*

ALICE HOFFMAN

"takes seemingly ordinary lives and lets us see and feel extraordinary things." —Amy Tan

- ❑ ANGEL LANDING   0-425-13952-2/$7.50
- ❑ AT RISK   0-425-11738-3/$7.50
- ❑ HERE ON EARTH   0-425-16969-3/$7.99
- ❑ PRACTICAL MAGIC   0-425-16846-8/$5.99
- ❑ PROPERTY OF   0-425-13903-4/$7.50
- ❑ SECOND NATURE   0-425-14681-2/$6.50
- ❑ TURTLE MOON   0-425-13699-X/$7.50
- ❑ WHITE HORSES   0-425-13980-8/$7.50